If all the world were...

For everyone who misses someone - JC

To dearest Sunday,
and thank you, Zoë - AC

First published in 2018 by Lincoln Children's Books, an imprint of The Quarto Group,
The Old Brewery, 6 Blundell Street, London N7 9BH, United Kingdom.
T (0)20 7700 6700 F (0)20 7700 8066 www.QuartoKnows.com

A catalogue record for this book is available from the British Library.

ISBN 978-1-78603-059-7

Illustrated digitally
Designed by Zoë Tucker
Edited by Kate Davies
Published by Katie Cotton
Commissioned by Rachel Williams
Production by Catherine Cragg

Manufactured in Dongguan, China TL012018
9 8 7 6 5 4 3 2 1

If all the world were...

Joseph Coelho
& Allison Colpoys

Frances Lincoln
First Editions

It's spring.

I take long walks with my grandad.
I hold his giant hand.
He says, "You're too old to hold hands."

We explore,

hand in hand,

the budding springtime.

If all the world were springtime,
I would replant my grandad's birthdays
so that he would never get old.

It’s summer.

Grandad buys me a racing track.
It’s second-hand with missing bits.
We fix what we can together.

We use our hands to
zoom the cars up and down,

up and down,

up, **up, up**
and fire them off
into deep space.

If all the world were deep space,
I'd orbit my grandad like the moon
and our laughs would be shooting stars.

It's autumn.

My grandad makes me a notebook
with handmade paper
of brown-and-orange leaves
that rustle when I turn the page,
bound with ruby Indian-leather string.

Grandad gives me a pencil
with a rainbow nib.

"Write and draw,

write and draw all
your dreams."

If all the world were dreams,
I would mix my bright Grandad feelings
and paint them over sad places.

It's winter.

My grandad tells me tales from when he was a boy,
of Indian sweets and homemade toys.

There are ships,

snakes

and tigers in his stories.

If all the world were stories,
I could make my grandad better
just by listening, listening, listening
to every tale he has to tell.

But some tales are silent.

I help Mum and Dad clean out Grandad's room.

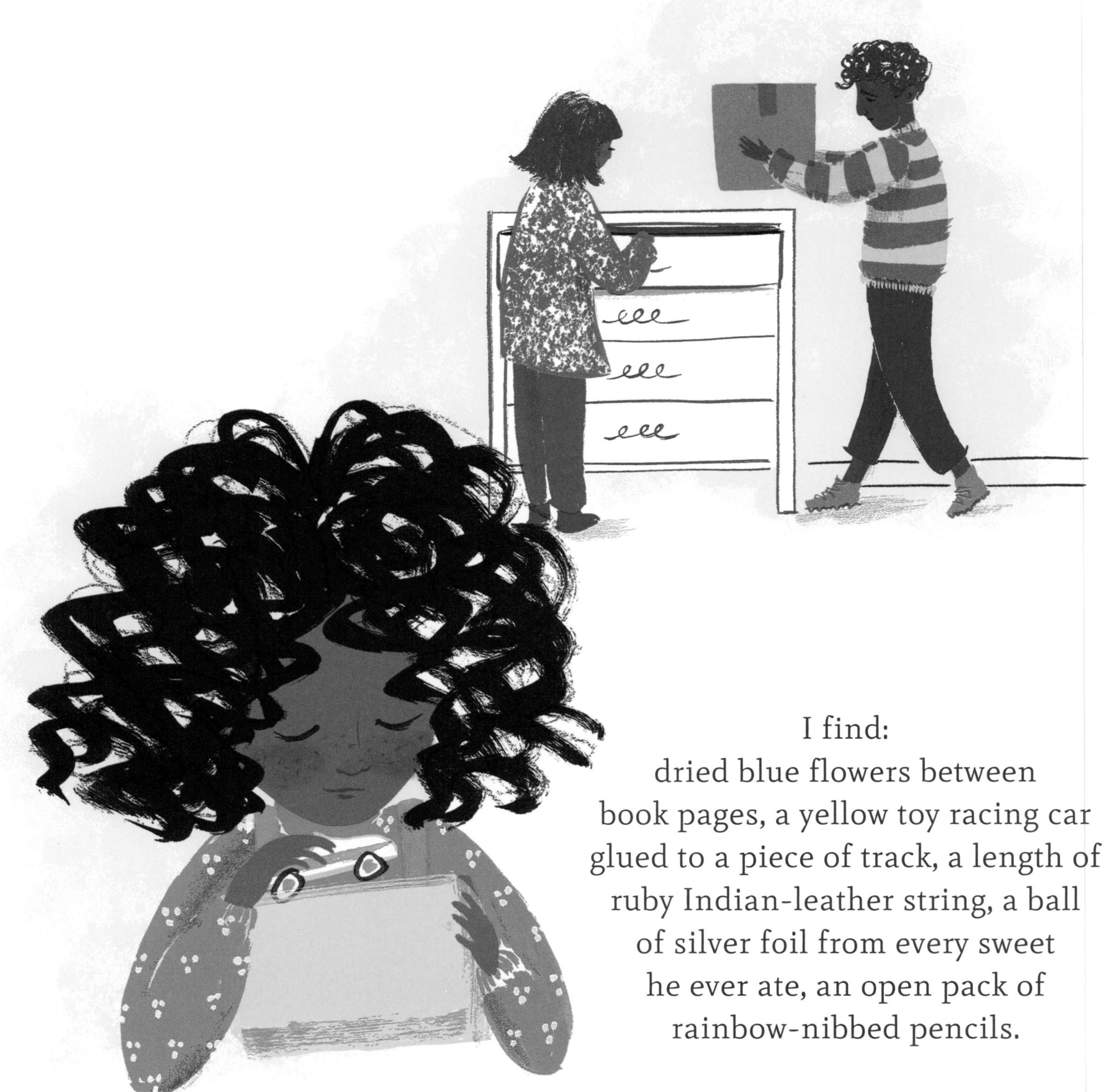

I find:
dried blue flowers between book pages, a yellow toy racing car glued to a piece of track, a length of ruby Indian-leather string, a ball of silver foil from every sweet he ever ate, an open pack of rainbow-nibbed pencils.

A kaleidoscope of memories.

If all the world were memories,
the past would be rooms I could visit
and in each room would be my grandad.

On Grandad's chair is a new notebook,
newly made with spring-petal paper,
newly bound with a length of Indian string.

My name is written on the front.
It's new and empty
and was made by my grandad.

So I write
and draw

and write and draw

and write
all my Grandad
memories inside.

I write and draw
lots of different worlds,

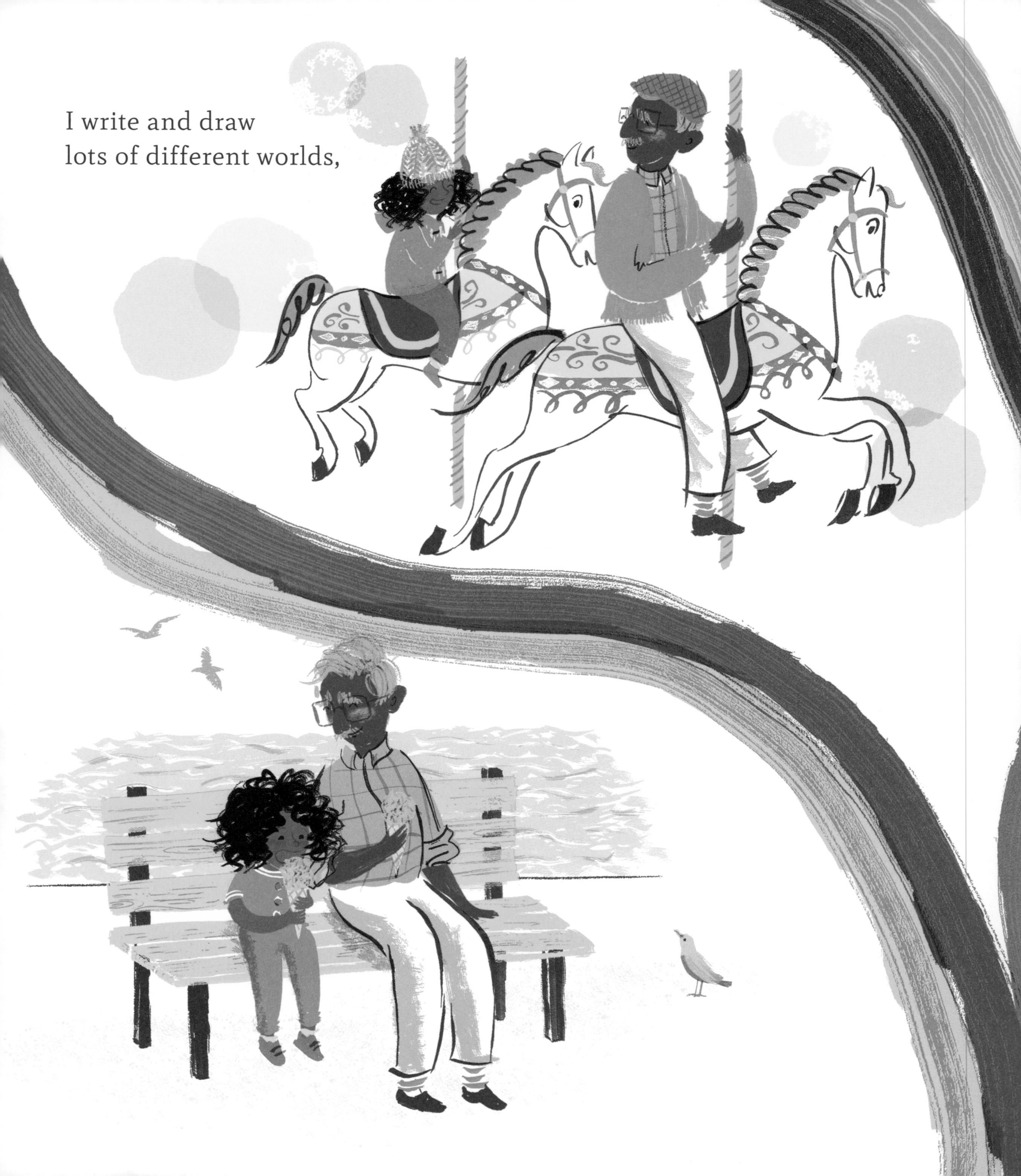

and all of them
have my grandad,

smiling
and laughing,
laughing,
laughing.

He says,
"You're too old to hold hands."

But still I hold his giant hand.
And we explore, hand in hand.

Reader's Digest

GUIDE TO NEW ZEALAND

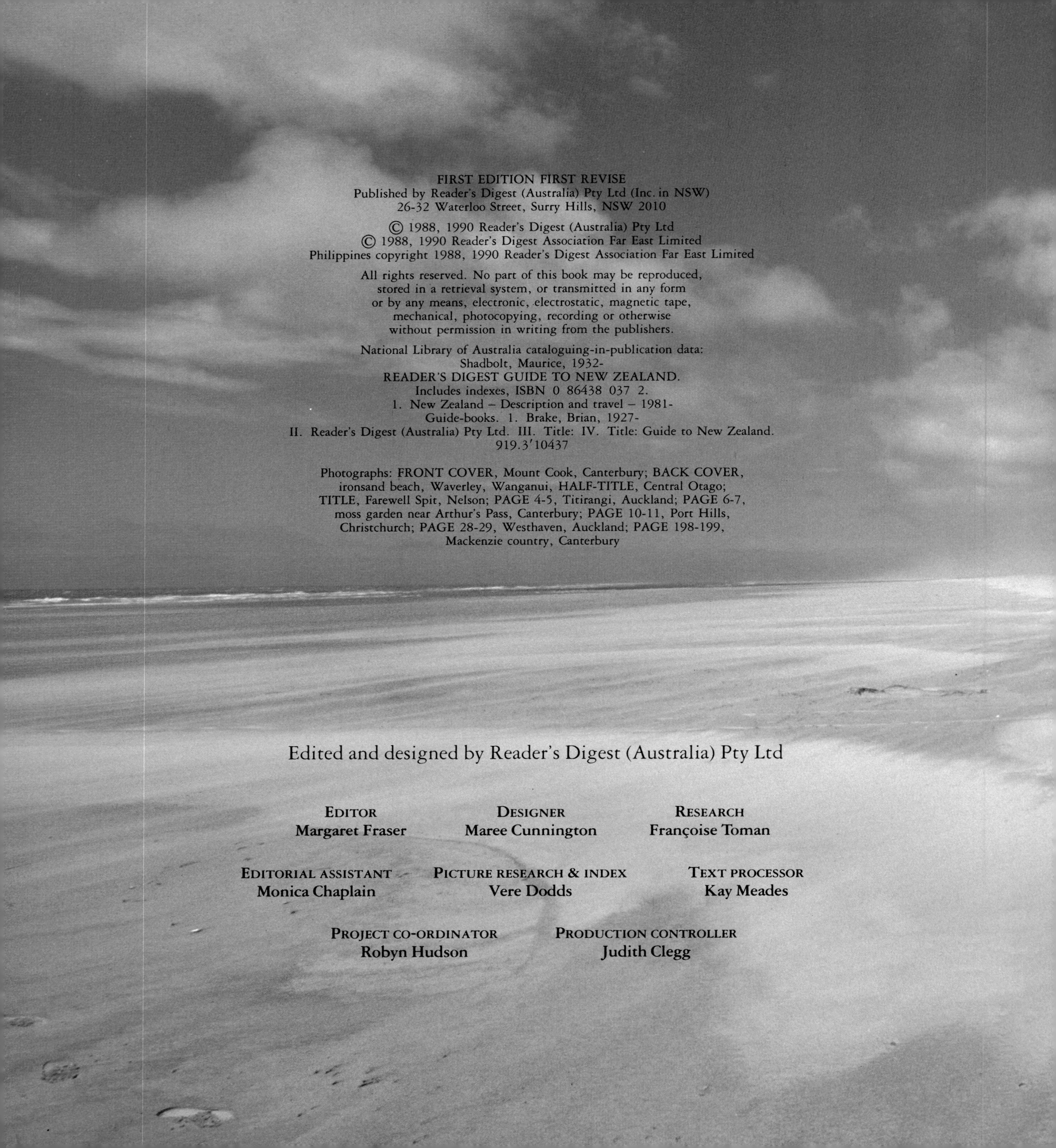

FIRST EDITION FIRST REVISE
Published by Reader's Digest (Australia) Pty Ltd (Inc. in NSW)
26-32 Waterloo Street, Surry Hills, NSW 2010

National Library of Australia cataloguing-in-publication data:
Shadbolt, Maurice, 1932-
READER'S DIGEST GUIDE TO NEW ZEALAND.
Includes indexes, ISBN 0 86438 037 2.
1. New Zealand – Description and travel – 1981-
Guide-books. 1. Brake, Brian, 1927-
II. Reader's Digest (Australia) Pty Ltd. III. Title: IV. Title: Guide to New Zealand.
919.3′10437

Photographs: FRONT COVER, Mount Cook, Canterbury; BACK COVER, ironsand beach, Waverley, Wanganui, HALF-TITLE, Central Otago; TITLE, Farewell Spit, Nelson; PAGE 4-5, Titirangi, Auckland; PAGE 6-7, moss garden near Arthur's Pass, Canterbury; PAGE 10-11, Port Hills, Christchurch; PAGE 28-29, Westhaven, Auckland; PAGE 198-199, Mackenzie country, Canterbury

Edited and designed by Reader's Digest (Australia) Pty Ltd

EDITOR
Margaret Fraser

DESIGNER
Maree Cunnington

RESEARCH
Françoise Toman

EDITORIAL ASSISTANT
Monica Chaplain

PICTURE RESEARCH & INDEX
Vere Dodds

TEXT PROCESSOR
Kay Meades

PROJECT CO-ORDINATOR
Robyn Hudson

PRODUCTION CONTROLLER
Judith Clegg

Reader's Digest

GUIDE TO NEW ZEALAND

Text by Maurice Shadbolt
Photography by Brian Brake

READER'S DIGEST
SYDNEY

CONTENTS

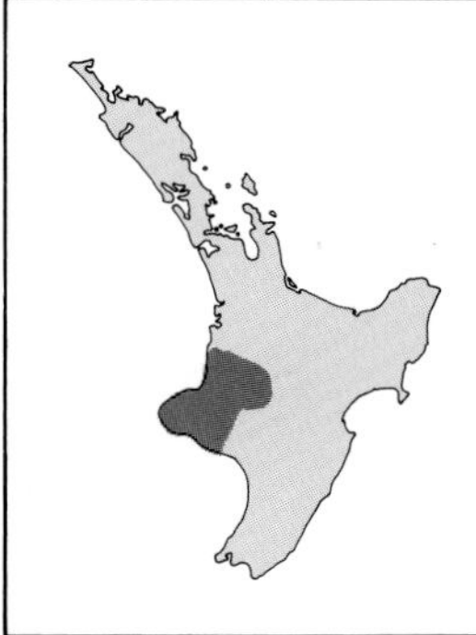

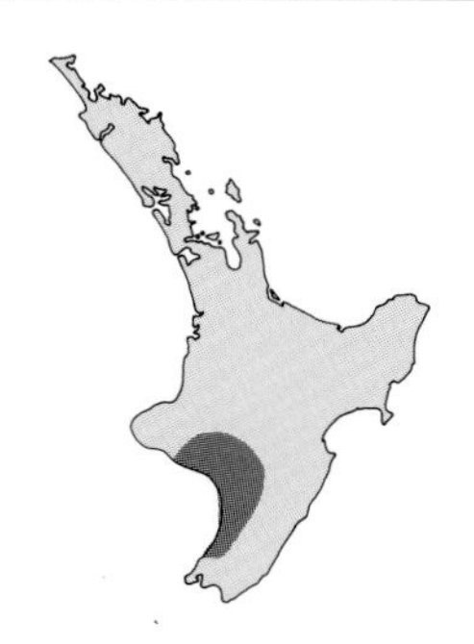

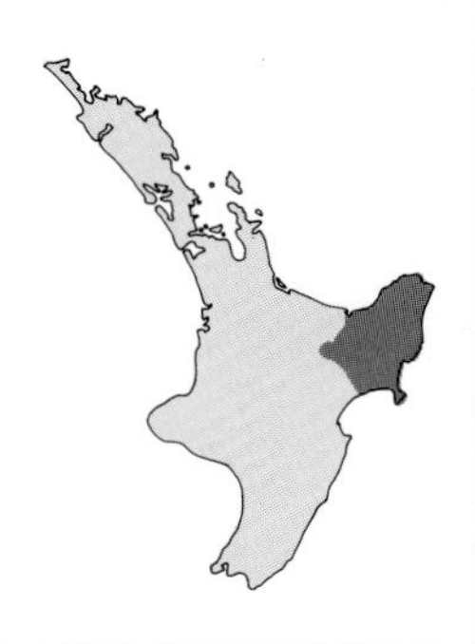

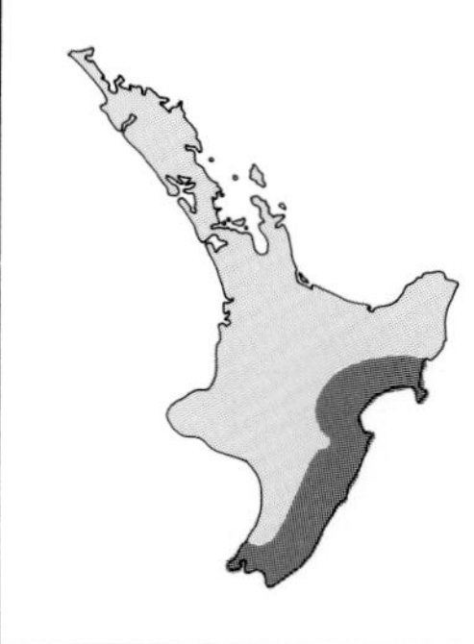

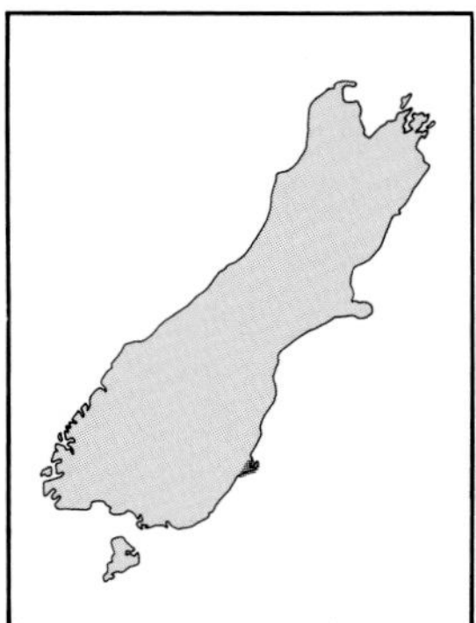

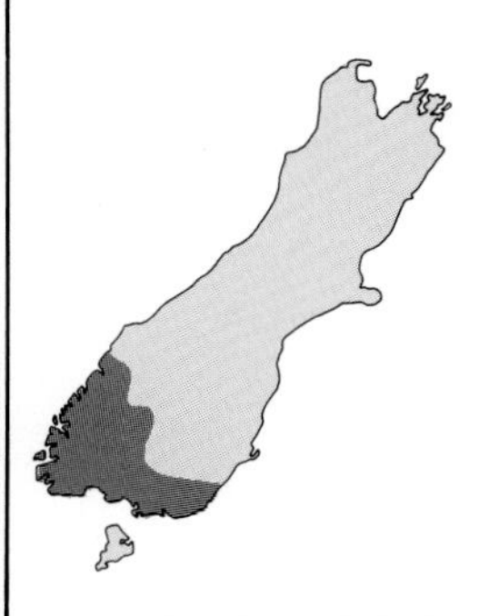

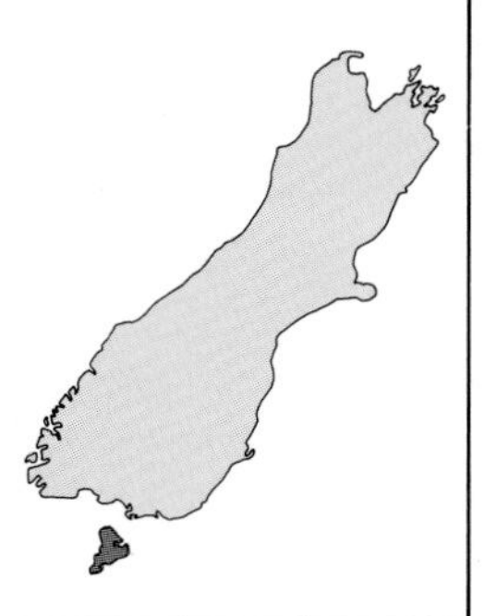

THE STORY OF A LAND
FIVE MILLION YEARS YOUNG

JOHNNY-COME-LATELY LAND

Newly formed, marooned in oceanic solitude

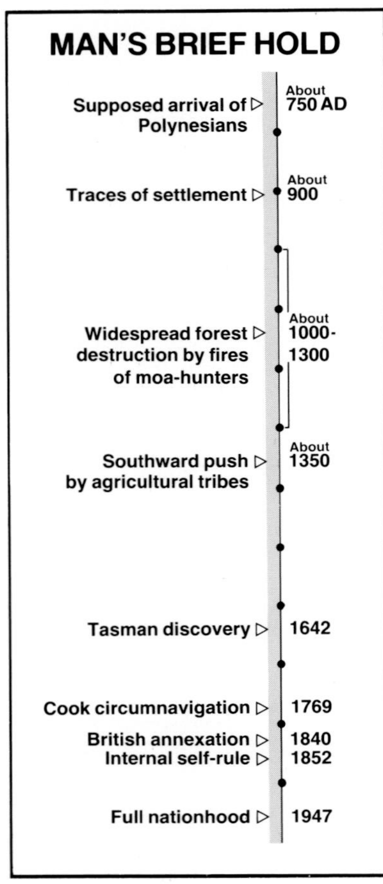

New Zealand as we know it is a geological infant. It rose out of the sea in something like its current shape only about five million years ago. Land was forced up by a buckling of the earth's crust that started about twenty million years before, and continues today. All the while, weathering has added its own shaping influences.

Over millions of years, cycles of upthrust and wearing-down had produced many lands, which came and went, different in shape and form from the New Zealand we know today. Nor did they appear in the same part of the ocean New Zealand now occupies: New Zealand's basement rocks were laid down at an edge of the ancient supercontinent that scientists have called Gondwanaland.

Material eroded from the far older lands of Australia and Antarctica collected in a submarine trough and formed sedimentary rocks. When squeezed by movements in the earth's crust, they pushed out of the ocean as new lands.

New Zealand's oldest ancestral land is in the South Island region where pliable sedimentary rocks were thrust up in rippling folds. Later, made hard and brittle by submarine pressure and heat, they became the broken, tilted mountain blocks characteristic of more recent versions of the country. Meanwhile, near the end of the disintegration of Gondwanaland, the New Zealand area rafted away from its neighbours. Considering the fluctuations of land and sea levels that followed, it is remarkable that any of its ancient inheritance of plants and animals survived.

Ocean-going boats that brought early Polynesians were probably catamarans with fore and aft sails of woven palm leaves. Voyagers occupied a raised deck lashed across twin dugout hulls, in which food could be stored. Hokule'a, *a modern re-creation, was sailed from Hawaii to Tahiti and back in 1976. It was built on design principles that Maori and Hawaiians still had in common, despite a thousand years of separation*

UPS AND DOWNS OF ANCESTRAL NEW ZEALAND

25-present day Southern Alps and North Island block mountains raised; uplift continues

Island remnants preserved plants and some animals

NZ region isolated 70 m.y.a.

140-95 Block mountains in south, folds in north

Gondwanaland break-up started 165 m.y.a.

360-310 Fold mountains arose in South Island region

0 | 100 million years ago | 200 | 300 | 400 | 500

The giant flightless moa, Dinornis maximus, *was built like an ostrich and may have stood more than three metres tall – though no one knows if it held its neck erect. Easily hunted because it came out of the forests to graze, this lordly creature was probably totally extinct by the seventeenth century. Catlins, at the most southerly tip of the South Island, was possibly its final home. Other species ranged down to turkey-sized 'bush' moas, which survived for at least a century longer. Bones of more than twenty moa species have been found*

Much of Australia already 3000 million years old

Oldest NZ rocks laid down 600-700 million years ago

600

700

Few New Zealanders live far from sight and sound of the sea. The ocean has determined the nature of their country – and the events of their history. In faraway lands, civilisations grew, changed and sometimes faded, but the Pacific's vast expanses protected these mountainous islands from human contact until about the eighth century AD.

Distance from the great continents, from their markets and cultures, meant that New Zealand's twenty-seven million hectares were the earth's last major area of useful land still uninhabited when the first Polynesians arrived. Even the oldest hint of human tenancy found here postdates the dramas of the great early civilisations in Egypt, Greece and Rome. The shores and rivers of this restless land were still shifting with earthquake, its mountains often boiling over in eruption, as it cooled on creation's wheel. If estimated human time upon this planet were condensed to twenty-four hours, then Polynesians arrived here barely a minute ago and Europeans merely a few seconds.

When the Polynesian voyagers settled here, they lost all contact with their far off tropical homelands and evolved one of the Pacific's most piquant cultures. Late-arriving Europeans measured distance from ancestral lands by miles and kilometres rather than mythology. New Zealand is eight thousand kilometres from Asia, seven thousand kilometres from South America and nineteen thousand kilometres from Europe where most had come from. Australia, the nearest landmass apart from Antarctica, is sixteen hundred kilometres away.

Brief though New Zealand's history is, most of the land is firmly in human hands. New Zealand has been primarily an agricultural country, and although much of the land was populated by the gold-rushes, minerals have played a small role in its prosperity. Elsewhere in the world such prosperity, achieved in remoteness, might have come from exploitation of the people, as well as of the country's natural resources. Not so here. This is not to say New Zealand's story lacks incidents of cruelty or injustice, but rather that the familiar elements of European colonisation are missing. The Maori people were not extinguished and were never enslaved. European immigrants were free, ever ready to fight or strike for their rights. A feature of New Zealand's early history was the belated charity shown by missionaries and enlightened liberals towards the aboriginal inhabitants of the Pacific world. Another was egalitarianism, seeded in the rough and tumble of the goldfields, which soon shaped the new country's social legislation.

Development has often been ruthless – expressed by the crack of axe, the rasp of saw, the blast of fire. Taller native trees were harvested for timber. Then fire razed lesser growth and grass seed scattered in the cooling ash. In the wake of this nineteenth-century devastation came twentieth-century efficiency. New Zealand farmers have had to be low-cost, highly mechanised producers to counter the effects of their distance from world markets. They can ship their goods round the world and still undersell all competitors, no small triumph.

Both past ruthlessness and present efficiency can be seen in the rural landscapes. Gaunt uplands may still be littered with charred stumps, streaked with erosion or freckled with regrouping forest. Lush pastoral lowlands have been coaxed out of swamp, then fertilised and nursed to provide grazing for sleek herds and fat flocks.

And yet great tracts of barely touched wilderness still exist, mostly set aside in national parks. They distinguish the country and grain the character of even the city dweller. Much of the country's long and fretted coast is uninhabited; there are rugged heartlands that never hear a human footfall from one decade to the next.

The greater part of New Zealand's livelihood may come from the land, but most of the population is urban. Towns and cities contain something like eighty per cent of the country's three and a third million people. More than half the population live in four cities. In cities too, the traveller can detect past battles with the land in reshuffled shorelines, trampled native contours and suburbs bulldozered into the hills. Small towns, still wearing a frontier heart on their sleeves, are often little more than wooden encampments grown hastily along the highways and railways of the hinterlands.

Rarely have towns and cities grown gently, other than in remoter reaches of the South Island where communities have been left high and dry by economics and history. There was little time for dignity and less for planning in a century and a half of fast growth and obstinate endeavour. In the past two decades, the conservation movement has had many triumphs saving forest and bird, but it has had few in the human environment. Cities and towns continue to grow haphazardly and often destructively. In downtown Auckland and Wellington in particular, buildings are often levelled just as they reach their prime, when time and history have lent grace and distinction. Yet here and there throughout the country are communities that respect the past. Dunedin and small towns like Akaroa, Naseby, Reefton, Coromandel, Russell and Thames have retained the colour of their nineteenth-century origins.

ON A RESTLESS RIM OF THE PACIFIC

New Zealand is a remnant of a vanished supercontinent called Gondwanaland, which once also consisted of Australia, Antarctica, India, Africa and South America. The country was formed during five hundred and fifty million years as the plates of the earth's crust collided and shifted, heaving again and again from the ocean floor. Eighty million years ago, New Zealand finally parted company from the last of its sister territories, Australia and Antarctica. Flowering plants had evolved, but mammals were yet to appear. At first, New Zealand was an archipelago repeatedly attacked and subdivided by the sea. A major uplift created the North and South Islands more or less in their present shapes as recently as five million years ago. With the continuing activity of earthquakes, the uplift continues and the Southern Alps imperceptibly inch higher.

Geologically, New Zealand has little in common with its nearest neighbour, the aged, long-stable island-continent of Australia. New Zealand's rocks are relatively young. The oldest began as oceanic sediment and contain the fossils of extinct sea creatures that flourished five hundred and fifty million years ago. Fierce volcanic activity formed many rocks and continues to shape the land. The country is part of the 'circum-Pacific mobile belt', the name given to the structurally restless rim of the Pacific shakily connecting lands as far as Chile and Japan.

Most of the land's present shape was sculpted throughout the Tertiary era and into the Quaternary, from fifty million to half a million years ago. Early sedimentary rock compressed and folded, the strata faulted and fractured, making the country more or less a concourse of earth blocks. Volcanic outpouring was often occurring at the same time as the faulting.

North and South Islands were parted by a tear fault. The much younger North Island contains no metamorphic or plutonic rocks (ancient formations sunk deep in the earth's crust, transformed and raised again as schist or gneiss, or as coarsely crystalline granite). By contrast, half the South Island is made up of metamorphic and plutonic rocks laid bare by uplift and erosion. Its sedimentary rocks can be over four hundred million years old, more than twice the age of the oldest sedimentary rocks in the North Island.

New Zealand's soils are young too. In many places they are only a generation away from parent materials, such as weathered sandstone – greywacke – alluvium, volcanic ash or windblown sand. Mineral deficiencies, notably of cobalt, have

WHEN THE EARTH MOVES

Quakes change the face of the land

New Zealand straddles a zone where mobile plates of the earth's crust collide. Along deep faults where the basement rock has cracked, enormous blocks are pressed in opposed directions. When there is a yielding at some point, the pent-up energy is released in a jolting wave that travels through the earth in all directions.

Earthquakes are commonplace in New Zealand, though to call these 'the Shaky Isles' is scarcely fair. Major quakes are not nearly as frequent as they are in Japan or in many other countries on the Pacific rim. On average, only one a year reaches Richter magnitude 6, one a decade 7, and one a century 8. The Richter scale, indicating the extent of to-and-fro surface motion above the centre of a quake, is logarithmic – magnitude 7 is ten times greater than 6.

Relatively few lives have been lost through earthquakes, and precautionary building methods considerably reduce property damage. Quakes have their greatest impact on the land itself, bringing down hillsides and gorge faces, diverting rivers and, in extreme cases, altering the level of wide areas.

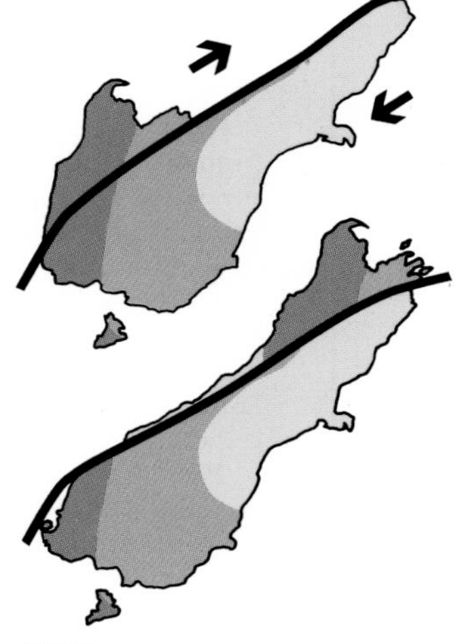

Above: *Earthquakes, infrequent but heavy, occur along the Alpine Fault, where basement rock fractured more than a hundred million years ago, slowly tearing away the South Island. Forces pushing crustal blocks in opposite directions have caused almost five hundred kilometres of horizontal displacement. Uplift to the east of the fault – creating the Southern Alps – still continues, although much of the gain in height during the past twenty-five million years has been lost to weathering. More recent extensions of the fault run from Marlborough through Wellington to the Bay of Plenty. The strongest earthquake since European colonisation – thought to have been of Richter magnitude 8 – gave Wellington its Basin Reserve cricket ground* (**left**). *It was once a low-lying swamp intended to become a shipping basin linked to the harbour by a channel. The channel route became Kent and Cambridge Terraces, now forming a spacious boulevard*

Before the disastrous Hawke's Bay earthquake of 1931, Napier Boat Harbour (**right**) *led to a lagoon that curled round to the foot of Bluff Hill. This was Port Ahuriri, a spacious inner harbour for ships drawing up to five metres. Almost four thousand hectares of new land arose with the quake and the rest of the lagoon was left uselessly shallow. Maruia Falls* (**below**) *would be a bare rock shelf but for the Murchison earthquake of 1929 which changed the course of the Maruia River. Measured at Richter 7.8, the quake also caused eighty square kilometres of land to rise almost half a metre. It was felt everywhere in the country*

had to be remedied before these soils could become productive. Where forests of native species like kauri, totara, rimu, kamahi and beeches have been cleared to enable farming, soils have become leached and acid, requiring replacement of their natural nutrients with chemical fertilisers.

Some ten million hectares of forest, more than a third of the country's total area, have been felled or fired. By the end of the nineteenth century, half a million hectares were being cleared every year. Land has been ploughed, drained, irrigated and cropped. Alien grasses and grazing animals have been introduced. To rectify past plundering of the soils, hundreds of thousands of tonnes of fertiliser are dumped every year from low-flying aircraft. This technique, pioneered in New Zealand, has enriched and won back much steep and pastorally marginal upland, but the change to the soils most difficult to control has been, and is, erosion. In recent decades, the price has been paid for the pioneers' ruthless deforestation, as bald hills sag and slip away into rivers and the sea. Vast plantations of exotic pines have been planted to hold the hills together and have become an increasingly valuable resource in themselves, in places displacing agricultural land. In the very texture of the rocks and soils, the traveller can see New Zealand's youth.

A MARITIME, MOODY BUT MOSTLY MILD CLIMATE

Lying between thirty-three and fifty-three degrees south, the sixteen-hundred-kilometre length of New Zealand falls entirely within the temperate zone, just south of the subtropical high pressure belt. For the most part, New Zealand's climate is maritime, mild and equable with abundant sunshine, high rainfall and few extremes of heat and cold. As might be expected in a country rich in mountain ranges, there is much regional variation. There is no marked dry season, though drought can scorch the countryside, especially on the eastern seaboard of the South Isiand. Weather is dictated by anticyclones moving east across the country and by low-pressure troughs between them, which bring strong westerly winds and unsettled conditions. Cook and Foveaux Straits, two breaks in the north-south mountain chain, act as funnels, creating most of New Zealand's gales. The mountains also steer beating dry, hot nor'westers upon inland Canterbury and Otago.

Settled weather can never be counted on, at any time of the year. Summer and winter are relative terms, especially in the northern North Island, where introduced willows lose their leaves for only a few weeks of the year. Most New Zealanders may have seen snow from afar upon mountains, but have never seen it fall. Many sea-bathe for more than six months of the year. The amiable climate is best demonstrated by the long grass-growing season and the practice of agriculture in the open all year-round.

February, March and early April are the most attractive months for travellers, although an erratic summer can begin in October in many places. Only in central Otago and on the east coast of the South Island, shielded by the Southern Alps, temperature variations approach those of continental climates. In Canterbury, when a cold and wet southerly sweeps in behind the hot nor'wester, temperatures may drop fifteen degrees Celsius in hours. At its most temperamental, New Zealand can offer the traveller all four seasons in one day. This long and lean land is fated to fickle weather.

If distance and isolation have spurred human ingenuity, nature has been no less inventive. Over eighty per cent of the country's native flowering plants are peculiar to here and so are all twenty species of conifers, which include kauri and rimu, although some have relatives in South-East Asia, South America and Australia. Some trees and palms, such as the nikau, are a reminder of New Zealand's Gondwanaland connections when it lay in subtropical regions, but its eighty million year-old isolation has provided New Zealand with a remarkably unique pattern of wildlife.

No one would call New Zealand's vegetation colourful, despite the yellow bells of kowhai, the rich reds of pohutukawa and rata flower, or the white and waxy cascades of native clematis. Rather it is dour and evergreen, shy in tint and feeble in scent. Ferns grow prolifically, and from filmy mites to soaring sixteen-metre monsters, they provide the distinctive character of the New Zealand forest. Even in summer, the sun reaches thinly into its deepest green vaults. This was a world for plants and birds only, a wayward corridor of creation, where nature was content to weave elaborate conceits . Mammals, like humans, were strangers here.

Bats are the only native mammals: one species has no close relative elsewhere, the other is probably a late arrival from Australia. Other land vertebrates are frogs, lizards and the tuatara. Three species of native frog are the world's only survivors of a primitive form which bypasses the tadpole stage of growth. The lizard-like tuatara, the world's most ancient reptile, is often called a living fossil. Its pedigree can be traced back beyond the age of dinosaurs. Rats and dogs exterminated it on the mainland and it now survives only on offshore islands.

Birds are New Zealand's most colourful native inhabitants. Most of the country's remarkable range of flightless birds appears to have developed in the absence of competition from mammals. The kiwi and the elephantine and now-extinct moa may have been flightless when they arrived here; other species, like the kakapo or native parrot, certainly gave up flying here. Birds blown or flown from far lands developed in isolation. Overseas ancestors of birds such as the native wood pigeon or kereru, tui, bellbird, takahe, weka and kakapo are not easy to determine, so distinctive have these birds become.

The first major change in the ecology was made by Polynesians. They burned off vast tracts of forest, hunted birds to extinction (although it has been argued that the moa, for example, may already have been a doomed species) and introduced two destructive mammals, the rat and the dog. They also introduced food plants like the kumara, the taro and the yam. Europeans brought the birds and deciduous trees of the northern hemisphere; and browsing animals, not just cattle and sheep, but deer, opossum, goat and rabbit to prey on vulnerable vegetation, often reducing it to crumbling desert. All four were hunted as pests, although farming of deer and goat is now a profitable business. In time, the land may learn to harbour alien creatures comfortably; in the twentieth century, its wounds are still visible.

Most of the story of human existence in New Zealand is misty with mythology. Archaeologists have parted the mists here and there; they have persuaded the land to yield not only bones, shells, tools and weapons, but also traces of old fires, all of which help tell how people once lived here and how long ago.

It is reasonably certain that there was no human occupation until 700 at the earliest. By 1000, there were settlements in a number of places. By 1250, there might even have been as many as twenty thousand people in occupation. Who were they, where did they come from and why?

They were Polynesian, a voyaging people who began pushing out of Asia and through Pacific archipelagos perhaps two or three thousand years before the birth of Christ. Persecution or deprivation possibly set them travelling in the first place, through the Malay archipelago, then round New Guinea and south among the scattered islands of the eastern Pacific. These voyaging feats need no stressing. While Europeans were still paddling about lake-like seas such as the Baltic and Mediterranean, seldom losing sight of land, Polynesians were colonising virtually every scrap of habitable land across the Pacific Ocean. How they travelled so far without the conventional tools of navigation has been long and sometimes ferociously debated. Some would say chance finds played a large role. But the odds against chance settlement of Hawaii to the north, New Zealand to the south, let alone tiny Easter Island far to the east, are extraordinary. It can only be explained by systematic exploration. As one tiny island after another became overcrowded, the boldest of Polynesian sailors set forth to find fresh land as their forbears had done. Island groups such as Tahiti, Rarotonga and the Marquesas would seem to have been populated from a base in Samoa. And it was almost certainly from that eastern quarter of Polynesia that New Zealand was ultimately located and settled.

By far the greatest landmass the searching voyagers were ever to claim, New Zealand represents ninety per cent of Polynesia's land area. The first encounter may well have been by accident – a party of Tahitian or Rarotongan fishermen blown far into cool southern seas may have seen land miraculously crowding the horizon. If fishermen, they would have established no durable settlement, since women

ALONG A LONELY PATH

Isolation fosters unique forms of wildlife

Aeons of oceanic isolation and near-submergence left New Zealand deprived of many animal families. But those that survived from antiquity, or managed to reach here more recently, were treated to an extraordinary variety of climates and habitats. They evolved to fill every vacant niche, often producing species found nowhere else.

Birds made the most striking adaptations, taking advantage of a lack of land-based mammals and predatory reptiles. Not needing to fly, some groups lost the ability. Amply fed, they gained unusual size. Along with the moas there were giant swans and water hens. But when humans made a belated appearance, bringing rats, dogs, spears and firebrands, many unique forms of life were to face extinction.

Now the dominant animals of New Zealand are introduced species. Farm livestock in scores of millions trample deforested land. Feral mammals, whose ancestors were brought as hunting targets or out of misguided sentimentality, have largely become pests. But remoter bushland districts, some fascinating examples of older fauna can still be found.

did not go on fishing trips. It is possible that such a chance expedition might have successfully found its way home two and a half, or even five thousand kilometres to the north-east and reported its astounding discovery. And that this voyage led to other, deliberate migratory voyages. This account, or something like it, is what some Maori legends argue. They tell of a voyager named Kupe who was tugged by a mighty octopus into cool seas and found the great uninhabited land he named *Aotearoa*, most commonly translated as 'land of the long white cloud' or, 'long bright world'. Kupe's discovery, it is said, led to Polynesian voyages a few generations later. He is supposed to have returned to his homeland with the pronouncement: 'I preferred the warm breast to the cold one'. Even so, his descendants, perhaps after a defeat in war, or as a result of religious persecution, or perhaps because they were plain hungry, seem willing to have risked their lives to embrace that cold breast.

According to Maori folklore, creation began when the primary gods Rangi (the Sky Father) and Papa (the Earth Mother) were parted by their divine offspring (among them tall Tane, god of the forest and turbulent Tangaroa, god of the sea). Mortal beings grew in the gap. One of these, Maui, a folk-hero through much of Polynesia, who brought fire to earth and snared the sun, is also credited with the making of New Zealand. An impressive fisherman, his prize catch was the North Island, *Te Ika-a-Maui*, 'the fish of Maui', his canoe was the South Island *Te Waka-a-Maui*, and his anchorstone was Stewart Island, *Te Puka-o-te-waka-a-Maui*. Versions vary; there are also alternative names for the South Island and Stewart Island, *Te Wahi Pounamu*, 'the place of greenstone' and *Rakiura*, 'glowing sky', but the North Island is always called Maui's fish.

Tales continue with the adventures of mortals who imposed themselves on the temperate land. The most popular and abiding version of events (still accepted uncritically by most New Zealanders, who were taught it at school) is that a number of canoes set out to settle New Zealand some time about 1350. These canoes, such as *Tainui*, *Te Arawa*, *Takitimu*, *Mataatua*, *Aotea*, from whose hardy crews Maori tribes claim descent, have commonly been referred to as the 'Great Fleet'. There is little if any substance to that story. It can be identified as an early twentieth-century European concoction about as reliable as the tale of extermination of the Moriori people by the Maori after arriving in New Zealand. In fact, the Moriori lived in the Chatham Islands. They were killed mostly, or assimilated, by Taranaki Maori in the nineteenth century and never settled on the mainland.

Even if two or three canoes had set out from tropical Polynesia at the same time, it is unlikely that they could have remained together for long. Even so, canoe traditions need not be entirely discounted. Northland tribes, probably the largest in pre-European New Zealand, have traditions suggesting random arrivals over a long period, a century or longer. Further, recent research argues that some of the famous voyages celebrated in Maori folklore were migratory journeys from one part of New Zealand to another, as population grew and tribes warred.

The greatest sceptic on the subject of Polynesian voyaging is the historian Andrew Sharp. He asserted that New Zealand could have been populated by one canoeload of accidental arrivals twelve hundred years ago. He sees the rest of the story as a colourful fabrication on the part of European scholars confused by oral sources.

Archaeologists are faced with the problem of explaining New Zealand's two distinct Polynesian cultures. In the first period, known as Moa Hunter, but mostly referred to as Archaic Maori, settlement was relatively simple and apparently nomadic. In the second period, large hilltop fortifications, or pa, weapons of close combat, complex agricultural methods with a system of food storage pits, and cannibalism were just some of the striking features of the society encountered by the first Europeans. This is the period known as Classic Maori, a remarkable stone-age culture that was still flourishing in the eighteenth century.

Did Classic Maori evolve from the first, or was it imposed gradually by a later wave of Polynesian arrivals? Evidence suggests that there were two groups of arrivals (possibly in the eighth century, then again in the twelfth or thirteenth) with clear cultural and social differences. However, if this hypothesis is accepted, the mystery of New Zealand's prehistory deepens. How could one or two boatloads of lost voyagers – a couple of hundred people at most – work so vast a social

A flightless swamp hen, the takahe (**opposite page, far left**) *disappeared at the end of last century. Then in 1948 about two hundred pairs were found west of Lake Te Anau. New Zealand's only dangerously venomous animal is the katipo spider* (**opposite page, left above**). *It is virtually identical to the redback of Australia and the American black widow and is most common on the west coast of the North Island. Of more than eight hundred bat species in the world, only New Zealand has one that can run on all fours* (**opposite page, above**). *The short-tailed bat folds its wings away so snugly that its forelimbs are freed for use as legs. It also has an extra hook, unique among bats, on each of its needle-sharp claws. The nocturnal kiwi* (**opposite page, below**) *is seldom seen but surprisingly common. It shares with the extinct moas the most ancient lineage of New Zealand birds. A busy hunter of garden pests, the hedgehog* (**this page, left below**) *is one of very few introduced wild animals to have brought benefits. How the tuatara survived* (**this page, left**) *is one of the great riddles of zoology. It is not a lizard but the last member of a separate order of reptiles, the* rhynocephalia *or beak-headed creatures which thrived about two hundred million years ago. Most fearsome-looking of the insects encountered in the bush – and in suburban gardens – is the tree weta* (**this page, below**) *which can reach five centimetres in length. In fact it is a placid vegetarian, inoffensive unless handled. Then its jaws can pierce the skin and its hind-leg spines may inflict scratches*

KINGDOM OF THE TREES

Forests preserve a primordial heritage

Evergreen forests are the natural rulers of New Zealand. Before the coming of man they clothed virtually all of the country, from coastal margins to mountainsides more than twelve hundred metres up. No mammals grazed and browsed and trampled their understoreys. They yielded – temporarily – only to encroachments by the sea or by glaciers, or to destruction and burial in volcanic eruptions.

Our trees and other seed plants are highly evolved and diversified, about eighty-five per cent of them occurring nowhere else. But the lineage of the main forest families can be traced, through pollen fossils, to the most ancient supercontinental beginnings – in the case of the kauri, for example, perhaps two hundred million years ago. Kahikatea goes back in a direct line of ancestry for one hundred and ten million years or more. The other podocarps and the beeches can claim an antiquity almost as great.

*Beside almost any forest or swamp the rounded tufts of cabbage trees (***far left above***) give a characteristic look to the countryside. The most common local species,* Cordyline australis, *can reach twenty metres. Its pith, called* ti, *was an important Maori food. Flax (***far left below***) was the chief spur to early interest in New Zealand. While not related to the European flax used to make linen, Maori women worked it to produce fabrics almost as fine. Flax products were New Zealand's first manufactured exports. Silver fern (***centre top***), New Zealand's national emblem, grows luxuriantly in and around damp forests. Of ten species, eight are found in no other country. Spring blossoms cascading from drooping branches make the kowhai (***centre***) one of New Zealand's most beautiful trees and a leading attraction for native birds such as tuis. A totara forest (***centre bottom***) – totaras in Maori lore symbolised strength and virtue. Their red timber, easily worked and durable, was favoured for war canoes, meeting-houses and food stores. Europeans also used it widely for bridges, wharf and house piles. The straight-trunked trees of the evergreen beech (***left***) grow densely, reaching thirty metres and allowing little room for undergrowth. The New Zealand Christmas Tree (***below***), flowers profusely in December. It possibly shares a remote ancestry with Australia's eucalypts*

change over the country and over a population totalling somewhere between ten and fifty thousand? Superior skills and tools, even when combined with aggression, provide only a partial answer. And perplexing evidence that the two cultures persisted alongside each other into the seventeenth century has been found in the Auckland region. Those who argue that the second culture evolved from the first see a clue in climatic change in the thirteenth and fourteenth centuries. In colder temperatures, areas suitable for cultivating kumara, the staple of Maori diet, shrank; remaining areas had to be protected from raids by hungry tribes. So fortifications proliferated and war, for *mana* (status) or *utu* (vengeance), became an end in itself.

There was a season for fishing, a season for harvest and a season for fighting. One of the prizes of battle was the acquisition of slaves to perform the victors' menial tasks. Archaeology does not show much about the role of slaves, but they seem to have been crucial. The need to replenish stocks may well have been an uncelebrated motive for war. Oral tradition is quiet on the subject: few care to claim slaves as ancestors.

Clearly though, New Zealand's early culture of hunters and fishermen was finally buried by the weight and warfare of the Classic and agriculturally based Maori. In the centuries before European arrival, the land, particularly on the North Island, developed into a complex of tribal territories, sometimes changing hands, but always bloodily defended.

Pre-European Maori life has been much romanticised, first as a Never-Never land by sentimental Europeans and more recently as an innocent Disneyland by Maori radicals. Examination of human remains suggests that old New Zealand was far from being a Pacific idyll. Life was as brief, anguished and brutal as that of stone-age men anywhere. The few who lived beyond thirty were prematurely aged, frail and plagued by all the common illnesses. Worse, they were always in fear of violent death. Their struggle for existence and short lives shaped their vivid art. On the face of it New Zealand should have been a paradise, but the human race has always managed to foul its own nest and find excuses to slay or enslave.

In the Archaic Maori period, settlement concentrated about river mouths and estuaries of the South Island. Rivers and the sea teemed with fish, and inland the fleshy moa was plentiful. As moa numbers decreased, the warmer northern half of the North Island became, by the Classic Maori period, the most desirable and densely populated terrain. Defeated tribes made their way south, some eventually to be harassed to extinction.

Estimates of the total population by the eighteenth century range from one hundred thousand to a quarter-million. Exhausted voyagers, wind-borne from warm islands and cast up on a challengingly cool shore, had become by far the most numerous and powerful of the scattered Polynesians. The contours of their new land seeped through chants and genealogies, tributaries to a swelling river of mythology, much as the whorls of the ponga fern spiralled through their carving. And perhaps it was the land's starkness which had another effect: where other Polynesians sang of love, the Maori sang of war.

The Maori, living in an isolated culture with little memory of its Polynesian origins, had no identity save that of the tribe and no notion of being part of a race or nation. The word Maori, which means normal, was a self-description invented in reaction to the arrival of the first European explorers, who were alien, distinctly not normal. This lack of racial identity, and innocence of the outside world, were largely responsible for the outcome when European colonists began to encroach on Maori land in the nineteenth century. Tribal wars and faction fighting within tribes meant that the Maori never put up a united resistance. Even in the late twentieth century, they seldom speak as one.

From these prehistoric beginnings comes New Zealand's recorded history. Today, its prehistory, preserved in cave paintings of faded grace, in the eloquent shapes of once trenched and palisaded hills, in the cryptic poetry of place names, in myths, legends and carvings which weave earth and air, fire and water, sun and moon into resonant harmonies, lends an often melancholy charm to the wild landscapes and a dignity to remote mountains and lonely waters. The stone age is never more than two centuries away and often it seems much closer.

RECORDED HISTORY BEGINS WITH EUROPEAN ARRIVALS

European voyagers began harvesting Pacific islands in the sixteenth century and took three hundred years to locate them all. It is not known who were first to discover the long land of Aotearoa. Claims have been made both for French and Spaniards and conceivably some lost vessel could have made early contact but was later wrecked in a Pacific storm. However, it is certain that a Dutchman, Abel Tasman, sailing in search of a great southern continent, found himself off the western shore of a strange land at the end of 1642. He clashed bloodily with Maoris during his only attempt to land and then sailed away from a country which, with its giant warriors, seemed to breathe death. Yet his voyage was to leave a new name, Nieuw Zeeland, on maps and a shaky line that might have been a continent's edge. Some imaginative map-makers invented an eastern coast extending almost to South America.

James Cook, the boldest of the eighteenth-century navigators, demolished what botanist Joseph Banks called 'the aerial fabrick called Continent'. Nearly one hundred and thirty years after Tasman's aborted visit, Cook and the Frenchman de Surville rediscovered New Zealand almost simultaneously in 1769, each without the other knowing it. But it was Cook who circumnavigated the land and outlined a new, but much shrunken shape on maps of the Pacific.

A third explorer who came looking for Tasman's mystery coastline was Marion du Fresne, who died in the Bay of Islands in 1772. Although well-intentioned, he was slain, possibly because he unwittingly offended Maori custom.

In savage reprisal, his crew stained the pale sands of the Bay of Islands red with the blood of scores of Maori and burned their villages. It was a portent of conflicts to come.

Cook's maps and reports inspired European settlement. Footholds were won first on the land's extremities – Northland and Coromandel peninsulas and on the broken bulge of Murihiku (Southland–Fiordland). From the seventeen-nineties onwards, timber and seals, flax and whales drew adventurers and speculators. European settlements soon developed mixed blood. This was the earthy, colourful 'Old New Zealand' of Pacific notoriety, now a staple of popular fiction – a world of grog shops and wild carousals, of escaped convicts from Sydney and ships' deserters, of bewildered missionaries and vagabonds of all kinds, but most of all, of that distinctive Pacific character, the 'Pakeha-Maori', the European living as a Maori tribesman, sometimes to the extent of acquiring face tattoos.

Friction between Maori and European was frequent but seldom lethal. Even when it was, both usually profited. When, for example, most of the crew from the timber-seeking ship *Boyd* were massacred in Northland's Whangaroa Harbour in 1809, British ships were back within a decade trading with the tribe responsible.

The most devastating European introduction was the musket. Maoris living closest to European settlement soon used them to settle old scores and the fragile balance of power between tribes was destroyed. Possibly thousands perished, although it has been argued that the unreliable musket may have made Maori warfare safer than traditional hand-to-hand combat. Undoubtedly, possession of muskets encouraged ruthless figures like Hongi Hika in the north and Te Rauparaha in the south to stalk the country leaving smoking villages and scorched flesh in their wake.

Shattered tribes were often further weakened by unknown diseases, such as measles or influenza, from which they had no immunity. The effect was permanent. It has been estimated that but for the musket wars and European disease, the present Maori population would be nearer three million than three hundred thousand, allowing for an annual increase rate of two-and-a-half per cent, although actual increase has often been greater. At any rate, by the time Europeans had begun to arrive in mounting number, Maori grip on many parts of New Zealand was enfeebled or lost.

Still soured by its American experience, Britain was reluctant to encumber itself further with colonies. Pressure to take New Zealand came from two quarters: from missionaries and humanitarians anxious to see its native people protected from corruption and predators; also from 'colonial reformers', notably those associated with Edward Gibbon Wakefield's New Zealand Company, which planned to demonstrate how a new British society should be founded. There was no place for notions of human equality.

Wakefield's scheme also made little or no provision for Maori people. Wakefield himself has been characterised as an 'intellectual confidence man'. In spite of a racy career, including three years in prison, he won distinguished sponsors such as the Duke of Wellington, for his idea of systematic colonisation. In 1839 land was purchased hastily from Maori for New Zealand Company settlements at Wellington (named for Wakefield's patron), Taranaki and Nelson.

Obliged to act, Britain dispatched a naval officer, Captain William Hobson, to annex and govern New Zealand. In 1840, a number of tribal chiefs signed or placed their marks on a document known as the Treaty of Waitangi, which

WHARE WHAKAIRO

Meeting-houses embody tribal pride

Maori architecture reached its zenith in the construction of meeting-houses, *whare whakairo*. No other Polynesian culture has produced such elaborate or exacting buildings. More than mere places of assembly where decisions are made, guests entertained and the dead lain in state, they are expressions of tribal dignity and visible proof of pride in ancestry.

Often a *whare whakairo* is named after a heroic ancestor, and becomes his embodiment. The ridgepole is his spine, the rafters are his ribs, the bargeboards at front his welcoming arms. To enter is to be taken to his bosom – not to idolise him, but to gain inspiration from the carved records of his feats and other glories of tribal history.

Traditional *whare whakairo* had thatched roofs of reeds, sunken earth floors, and only one door and window. For health and safety, those built this century are better ventilated and exploit many modern materials. But the skills demanded of carvers, weavers and decorators remain largely undiminished.

guaranteed their lands and rights in return for British sovereignty. Some tribes abstained, but many who signed had no clear notion of what sovereignty meant. Hobson and the humanitarians who backed him meant well, but for arriving British colonists the treaty was never to mean much. New Zealand's parliament never ratified it, even after independence.

Today, the treaty is still contentious. Conservative Maoris earnestly continue to plead for ratification nearly one hundred and fifty years later, while others denounce the treaty as a pious fraud, or argue that their land has been governed by an illegal regime since 1840. In 1974, in response to Maori wishes to highlight the treaty's significance, February 6 was declared New Zealand's national day. Then in 1986, the Government, sensitive to the criticisms, temporarily discontinued the established official celebration of the treaty's signing. Nevertheless, the treaty *was* remarkable, certainly in an age when Europeans felt they had the God-given right to rule the earth for their own ends. For the first time in the story of European colonisation, a native people had been approached as equals. And although land-hungry settlers were soon to breach the letter of the treaty, much of its spirit has survived. When Maori seek rectification of past injustice, especially over land and fishing rights, it is the Treaty of Waitangi they quote. It remains the first and last court of appeal to the conscience of fellow New Zealanders.

A TURBULENT GROWTH TO NATIONHOOD

There was steady growth in the European population between 1840 and 1860. Hobson chose the mostly abandoned isthmus of Auckland as the new site for the capital of the colony in 1840. (It would be moved to Wellington in 1865.) Further New Zealand Company settlements were founded at Christchurch and Dunedin. In the South Island, newcomers spread across the land with relative ease. The small Maori population, made even smaller by war and disease, was now willing to part with land cheaply. (As little as three hundred gold sovereigns bought the thinly inhabited west coast of the South Island.)

In the one notable armed clash between Maori and colonists, over a land grab, twenty-two colonists were left dead. To the indignation of the settlers, British authorities judged the Maori response justified. Not a shred of South Island land was taken by conquest.

In the North Island, where tribes remained large and powerful, friction lasted longer. First it was over the apparent inconsistencies of British authority – Hone Heke's 'war in the north' in the eighteen-forties – and then over disputed land sales. Yet it was a golden time for many North Island tribesmen. Under missionary influence they made immense agricultural progress on their traditional lands. The new European settlements made good markets for Maori produce; indeed, they depended on Maori farmers for survival. Some fifty Maori-owned vessels kept Auckland fed. Maori produce even travelled to Australia and to California. Fertile Maori soil was coloured with ripening grain and wheat mills flourished through the Waikato. Landless colonists, cooped up in Auckland, looked on with ill-hidden lust for Maori lands.

A belated sense of racial identity, at least among the central North Island tribes, who were the most menaced by European encroachment, led to the crowning of a Maori king in the Waikato as

New Zealand's greatest Maori carver, Pine Taiapa, worked on the reconstructed whare whakairo *at Takitimu, Wairoa* (**opposite page, far left and above**)*, opened in 1938. Politician and Maori leader, Sir Apirana Ngata, was reponsible for the general design, architecture and supervision of the tukutuku work. The meeting-house was named after the sacred canoe which brought the ancestors of Ngati Kahungunu to New Zealand. According to Maori lore, Takitimu became the mountain range in Southland. The building is steel-framed but, by tradition, the roof is lined with kakaho reeds. An exceptionally large meeting-house can be seen in Ruatahuna* (**opposite page, below**). Te Whai a te Motu *means 'flight across the island' and celebrates Maori hero Te Kooti's successful evasion of government forces late last century. Today it is the main meeting-house of the Tuhoe tribe of the Urewera. The largest building on the Turangawaeawe marae in the Waikato is over two thousand square metre Kimiora* (**this page, above far left**) *opened in 1974. It contains a concert hall seating over a thousand, two dining rooms, a conference room, coffee lounge, shop and a great deal more. Projecting from its roof is* Mamuhau, *the bird of knowledge, sacred to the Tainui tribes. Rongopai* (**this page, below far left**) *is an example of Maori art in transition. Built by young people of the Whanau a Kai section of Te Antanga-a-Mahaki tribe of Gisborne, it is painted not carved and the style shows strong European influence. Local personalities and dignitaries are represented in some of the panels* (**left below**) *and sacred ancestors are sometimes depicted in modern style, even to having blue eyes.* Rautahi (**left above**)*, the marae at Kawerau, means 'many in one'*

a counter-balance to Queen Victoria. European hostility mounted. At its most extreme, there were calls for extermination of the Maori. Ranks tightened and when the first explosion came, over Taranaki land, local tribesmen found allies in their Waikato ex-enemies.

Although it was a popular nineteenth-century view, it is absurd to represent the conflicts of the early eighteen-sixties and the largely guerilla warfare that followed, as a struggle between civilisation and savagery. If literacy, for example, is a measure of civilisation, then missionary-educated and Bible-quoting Maoris who boldly confronted illiterate soldiers and settlers had civilisation on their side. Neither literacy nor heroism could have contained the disciplined, gunboat-backed British invasion of the Waikato. The Maori inability to remain long united was a more serious drawback than their lack of artillery. The Northland Ngapuhi had pursued and ended their own quarrel with British authority more than fifteen years earlier and, in any case, were unenthusiastic about allying themselves with their long-standing enemies in the Waikato. Other North Island tribes remained neutral or saw more advantage in joining forces with the tribe that was not to be beaten – the British. The final act was a Maori civil war. During the Hauhau and Te Kooti rebellions in the late eighteen-sixties, colonial troops were often spectators while Maori warriors like Ropata and Kemp repaid old tribal scores and heaped up rebel dead on Queen Victoria's behalf. Gone was the chivalry which had distinguished earlier fighting. Increasing desperation threw up charismatic rebels such as Titokowaru and Te Kooti, who struck ferociously at missionaries and colonists, but even more so at Maori indifferent to their leadership. Massacre was answered with massacre, fire fought with fire. In the end, the so-called 'loyalist' Maoris, tribal to the end, prevailed. The Queen's writ ran the length of New Zealand, with one exception. A central North Island enclave, still called the King Country, existed for two or three decades as an exclusive Maori preserve, a refuge for dissident tribesmen and their leaders.

Ruthless land confiscation followed the rout of Maori rebels. Maori land was also purchased, but not always honourably. Tribesmen were obliged to camp outside courthouses for weeks. They were wooed with liquor while land titles were settled and politicians talked with seeming compassion of smoothing the pillow of the 'dying Polynesian race'. One way and another, the way was made clear for large-scale pastoral farming to begin and for roads, railways, towns and cities to be built. The passive resistance movement led by the remarkable Te Whiti on confiscated land in Taranaki was more of a Maori 'last stand' than any pitched battle. Peacefully dissident Maoris were ringed with firepower, Te Whiti was arrested and his movement suppressed in 1881. Colonists' command of the North Island became complete in 1883, when the feared Te Kooti, still at large in the King Country, was pardoned so that the railway could be pushed into the region.

The South Island, through this period, saw spectacular advance. Pastoralists launched their flocks across plains and plateaus, past lakes and rivers, up to the peaks of the Southern Alps. Then came the gold strikes of inland Otago and the West Coast, leading to the stampeded growth of Dunedin. History was gentler in the South Island, even allowing for the drama of the gold rushes. That gentleness survives in South Island life and landscape today. It is a land of extremes, an island with the characteristics of a continent. Sunny communities sit on intensively cropped coastal plains; lonely mountain homesteads rise on stark and stony landscapes; glaciers beat a path to the sea; silent fiords twist among forests and mountains. Christchurch and Dunedin, reminiscent of English and Scottish towns, both have a durable air, as if they have already survived for centuries, while much of the North Island remains in untidy flux. In noting the differences between New Zealand's north and south, the traveller underlines and postscripts history.

From the eighteen-nineties, New Zealand's story is less one of land conquest than the shaping of a distinctive Pacific community. Despite Edward Gibbon Wakefield's dream of recreating a stratified English society with a few tactful modifications, a strong sense of social justice existed from the beginning of organised settlement. In 1840 at Wellington, for example,

A PLACE TO LIVE

Individuality has been slow to emerge

Thanks to a generally plentiful supply of land and to the prevalence of timber in housing construction, many New Zealand houses convey a mood of lightness and freedom.

But flair in design is a rarity. Styles have been imported one after another – not from 'Home' so much as from Britain's other colonies and later from California and even the Mediterranean. Most builders have been speculative devoid of inspiration.

Some pleasing examples of deliberate eccentricity emerged in the nineteen-seventies, outwardly expressing new ideas for the disposal of internal space. In the balmy north especially, houses were increasingly adapted to outdoor leisure pursuits. But perhaps the only dwellings with a claim to be peculiar to this country are some whose oddness was forced on them by the steepness of their sites. And if a 'typical' Kiwi home exists, by sheer weight of numbers it must come from among the limited variations of state housing design.

tradesmen struck for an eight-hour day. That happened in what should have been the showpiece of Wakefield's settlements, and it would be echoed in others. Unplanned Auckland had never been much other than egalitarian. Goldfields in the south and gumfields in the north confirmed the democratic frontier spirit. Towards the end of the century, it found political expression in the long-lived Liberal administration of John Ballance and then of Richard John Seddon, 'King Dick'. After a sickening dip into economic depression in the eighteen-eighties, when the country became all but bankrupt, social misery was widespread. Increased state intervention was seen as the remedy for the country's mounting ills. New Zealand soon led the world in social legislation; its example was studied in many countries. To some, it seemed to be perilously Utopian; to others, notably a then obscure Russian revolutionary named Lenin, it seemed merely to be attempting to buy off revolution with reform. New Zealand's social legislation was more the work of pragmatists than of ideologists, a straightforward response to human need and the problems of a newly settled country. New Zealand had taken leave of Wakefield and launched into the twentieth century as an embryonic welfare state, the world's first.

The Labour administration of 1935-49 fell heir to the Liberal tradition. It reinforced and expanded the earlier legislation in the middle of world depression and then world war. Succeeding conservative administrations, which have tended to prevail since 1949, have been loath to tinker and have added their own innovations. Some soon considered the state too powerful and oppressive. Checks and balances include the office of ombudsman as mediator of disputes between citizen and state. It was a Labour administration, paradoxically, which began the retreat from state intervention in the nineteen-eighties. New Zealand society is still finding shape.

*The Colonial House at Pipiriki (**far left**), now a museum, is a typical example of colonial architecture which borrowed the idea of the verandah from the brick and stone buildings of India. Cost led to the use of attic bedrooms with their dormer windows rather than entire second floors. Before and immediately after World War II, the building industry was booming. Around Wellington and Auckland areas of private ownership (**centre**) were augmented by thousands of state houses. They merged pleasantly enough but social problems arose when later state housing developments were isolated in outlying districts without adequate community amenities. By 1903, tiny sections at the foot of a steep bank flanking Tinakori Road, Wellington were too precious to waste (**left**). Brewery workers' homes were built five storeys high but only one room wide – and only one room deep on the upper floors. Rear access was by precipitous external steps. The houses had ironclad sides to stop fires spreading. Roger Walker's designs raised eyebrows in the 1970s and were often the butt of mockery but they proved successful (**left above**). Occupants chose their own uses for a multiplicity of spaces and levels. Viewed from outside, the houses look different from every angle. When timber was scarce, early houses were made of rammed earth or cob, such as this cottage at Lovells Flat in Otago (**above**). Cob was clay mixed with straw, either formed into bricks or packed between forms. It provided some insulation against severe South Island winters*

ARTS OF THE MAORI

Motifs bring echoes of an Asian homeland

Spiral patterns in Maori carving, painting and tattooing support the belief that Polynesians came into the Pacific from South-East Asia. Similar designs are found on Chinese bronze from around 500 BC. Some elements of Maori artistry seem to have even older roots. Stylised heads are carved in the fashion of animal masks that were introduced to China by invading nomads. The tongue-poking motif can be traced to western Asia, before 1000 BC.

As such influences spread, techniques varied according to available materials. In New Zealand, above all, they flowered in the working of abundant and durable timber. The swirling symbolism took on exclusively Maori meanings, relating to tribal history and mythology. But side by side with this adaptation of prehistoric culture – a manly pursuit – Maori women developed a contradictory tradition of straight-line design in the ornamentation of clothing, mats and the linings of buildings. It was based on the skills that they had acquired in weaving and dyeing flax fibres, and is our one truly home-grown art form.

*This skilfully carved canoe prow (**above**) from Tolaga Bay shows the spiral patterns so favoured by Maori craftsmen, perhaps inspired by the spiral fronds of ferns. The figure on the gateway, or* waharoa, *to Pukeroa Pa in Rotorua (**right**) shows the artistic licence taken with the human form. No attempt was made to capture a likeness, although great care was taken in reproducing characteristic tattoo patterns. Kaitai lintel (**below**), one of the most famous of Maori carvings*

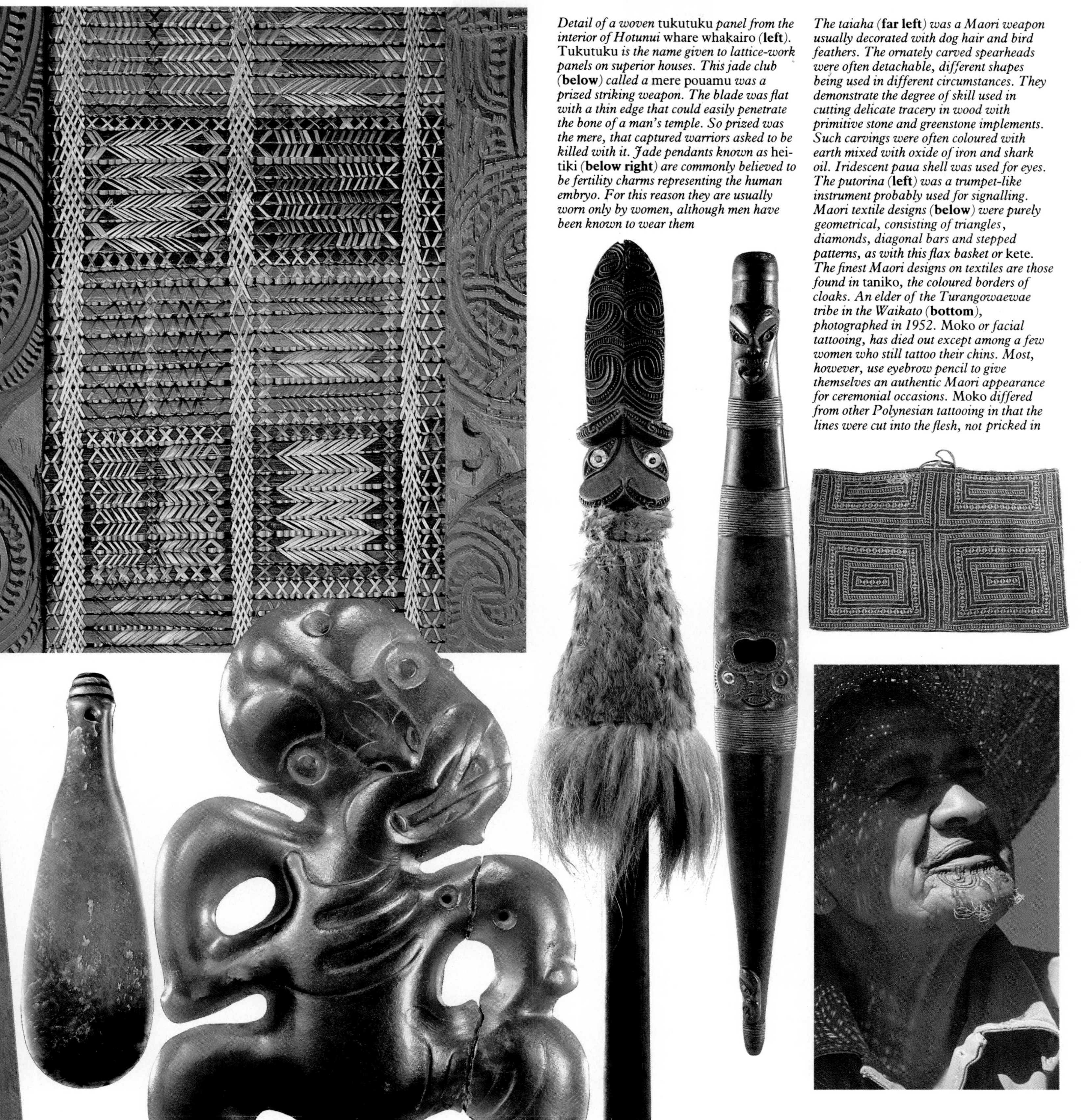

Detail of a woven tukutuku *panel from the interior of Hotunui* whare whakairo *(**left**).* Tukutuku *is the name given to lattice-work panels on superior houses. This jade club (**below**) called a* mere pouamu *was a prized striking weapon. The blade was flat with a thin edge that could easily penetrate the bone of a man's temple. So prized was the mere, that captured warriors asked to be killed with it. Jade pendants known as* hei-tiki *(**below right**) are commonly believed to be fertility charms representing the human embryo. For this reason they are usually worn only by women, although men have been known to wear them*

*The taiaha (**far left**) was a Maori weapon usually decorated with dog hair and bird feathers. The ornately carved spearheads were often detachable, different shapes being used in different circumstances. They demonstrate the degree of skill used in cutting delicate tracery in wood with primitive stone and greenstone implements. Such carvings were often coloured with earth mixed with oxide of iron and shark oil. Iridescent paua shell was used for eyes. The putorina (**left**) was a trumpet-like instrument probably used for signalling. Maori textile designs (**below**) were purely geometrical, consisting of triangles, diamonds, diagonal bars and stepped patterns, as with this flax basket or* kete. *The finest Maori designs on textiles are those found in* taniko, *the coloured borders of cloaks. An elder of the Turangowaewae tribe in the Waikato (**bottom**), photographed in 1952.* Moko *or facial tattooing, has died out except among a few women who still tattoo their chins. Most, however, use eyebrow pencil to give themselves an authentic Maori appearance for ceremonial occasions.* Moko *differed from other Polynesian tattooing in that the lines were cut into the flesh, not pricked in*

PALETTE AND BRUSH

A changing view through painters' eyes

Most early artists in New Zealand painted simply to produce factual records of a fresh country. Maoris seem never to have attempted any such imagery. Professionals were rare among European visitors and colonists, but art tuition was part of any good British or Continental education. Surveyors and military officers in particular were often highly skilled. Nevertheless they struggled to capture unfamiliar, sharply etched landforms.

English tastes in water-colouring prevailed as the colonies became established, and with later Victorian gentility came glimmerings of romanticism. Impressionist views of the landscape gained little ground until the nineteen-thirties, generations after their European vogue. Since the Second World War, many artists have combed the country in search of scenes to use as expressionist vehicles for interpreting their own inner feelings. The leader of this movement, the late Colin McCahon (1919-1987), established the foremost international reputation of any New Zealand painter.

Augustus Earle painted Hokianga harbour in 1827 (**far left top**). *His paintings are the most important record of Northland and its people in the pre-colonial period. James Nairn's scene of Wellington harbour, 1902,* (**far left bottom**) *shows his mastery of light on disturbed water and is rated among the best impressionist works done in this country. Robin White's 1974 encapsulation of the small township of Mangaweka* (**centre**) *strikes a chord with every traveller on Highway 1 or on the North Island trunk railway. She sees her country with startling simplicity and clarity – and a gentle hint of humour. Michael Smither's view of Mount Egmont* (**top**) *borders on surrealism while John Weeks's treatment of limestone rocks in a King Country gorge* (**left**) *blends cubism with realistic landforms. Four times premier, William Fox, captured in watercolour tranquil Akaroa as it was in 1850* (**above**). *Fox was a dauntless high-country explorer who painted or sketched wherever he went*

Its imperfections, like its considerable successes, at least are its own. New Zealand has had to travel a lonely road, without precedents and without easy borrowing. Since the nineteen-sixties the right to dissent from conventional wisdom on moral, racial and international issues has been more and more vigorously exercised. In the nineteen-eighties it is possible to claim some maturity for the society.

A NATIONAL AND CULTURAL IDENTITY EMERGES

The country's colonial status ended in 1907, and the last legislative link with Britain was severed in 1947. It is a member of the British Commonwealth of Nations, with Britain's Queen as symbolic head represented by governors-general. Since the nineteen-sixties, all have been New Zealanders, and in 1985 the first governor-general of Maori blood was appointed. Britain's closer links with continental Europe in the nineteen-seventies hastened New Zealand's development as an independent nation. New markets have had to be found and new friends made. As the country has taken on international style, pride in nationhood has become more apparent. Satellite communication, television, and the jet plane especially, have shrunk distances and ended the isolation which determined the human character of New Zealand for more than a thousand years. London is only twenty-four hours away, New York much less.

It was said that New Zealand's sense of national identity was born in agony on Turkey's Gallipoli peninsula in the First World War. In that poorly led, murderous British campaign nearly three thousand New Zealand lives were lost and many were left maimed. The claim is true in a negative way. For the first time, New Zealanders knew they were not Britons, and that they were distinct even from the Australians they fought alongside. Who they were was another matter; they had little cultural tradition to fall back upon.

The new national sense did not usefully survive the First World War in which remote New Zealand lost more combatants in proportion to population than any European power involved. Even so, the country continued to identify itself with the British Empire. In 1939, when the Second World War broke out, New Zealand's Prime Minister announced that where Britain stood, New Zealand stood, not a view which would win much applause now. It is a measure of New Zealand's independence that in the nineteen-eighties it was ready to risk the displeasure of the United States and Britain, even of Australia, in international matters. In turn, it found French terrorists sinking an anti-nuclear protest vessel in Auckland's peaceful harbour. If that event reverberates, it is because New Zealand has discovered itself suddenly alone in the world.

It is not warriors, or politicians who give a country its real spirit, but its artists. The makings of a national tradition in the arts were first apparent in the nineteen-thirties, mainly in the work of poets who began shedding genteel English tradition and to speak as themselves. In the work of such as A.R.D. Fairburn, Robin Hyde and Allen Curnow, New Zealand was for the first time seen not as a lost limb of Britain, but as a nation in its own right. Novelists and storytellers, painters and musicians, dramatists and film-makers have pitched camp in the territory won by the pathfinding poets.

Perhaps the most potent, and certainly the most perplexing trail-blazer of all was the poet and social iconoclast James K. Baxter who finally identified with the Maori race and the spirit of *aroha*, love, and was buried as a Maori tribesman.

Historians and essayists such as Keith Sinclair, E.H. McCormick and M.H. Holcroft have been writers of prophetic inclination. They and their successors have laboured to give their countrymen a sense of the past and a feeling for their land. Cultural growth may have been slow, and initially furtive, but no one now can be deaf to New Zealand's native accent. In recent years, the feats of artists have rivalled that of sportsmen and women. This is true too of craftspeople. Workers with clay, wood, bone, stone and fibre now have a reputation reaching far beyond New Zealand.

New Zealand artists, working within European forms, always have the example of the Maori before them. The Maori, entirely possessed by the new land, its experiences and materials, transformed migrant arts and crafts almost beyond recognition and gave the Polynesian Pacific its most vivid culture. That culture's capacity to adapt and survive is perhaps best seen in the work of Maori writers and painters who speak to their fellow New Zealanders in an accent new. They may write in English or paint in an international style, but the spirit is their own.

Although Maori separatists became media personalities in the nineteen-eighties, seeming to advocate something akin to South African apartheid, their battle was lost more than one hundred and fifty years ago, when the first marriage between a Maori and a European was celebrated in the Bay of Islands. Widespread intermarriage since, means that by far the majority of people who identify themselves as Maori are of mixed blood, inheriting both the country's cultures. And there are tens of thousands of New Zealanders of mixed ancestry who do not claim one race or the other. In addition, there are now something like one hundred thousand Polynesians of Samoan, Cook Island or Tongan descent to be taken into account. Migration from the tropics has already transformed many urban and suburban areas. Statistics suggest that the representative New Zealander of the twenty-first century will be part European and part Polynesian. That is already true of at least half a million New Zealanders, or one in six, a proportion fast increasing.

Today the traveller through New Zealand will find a land of sometimes enigmatic signposts, pointing to both the past and the future. A guidebook may suggest where those signposts are to be found, but it is up to the traveller to read them. Travel is nothing if not expansion of the mind, an adventure of the spirit. This book is meant for all travellers, armchair or active, who wish to make New Zealand such an adventure.

NORTH ISLAND

Northland

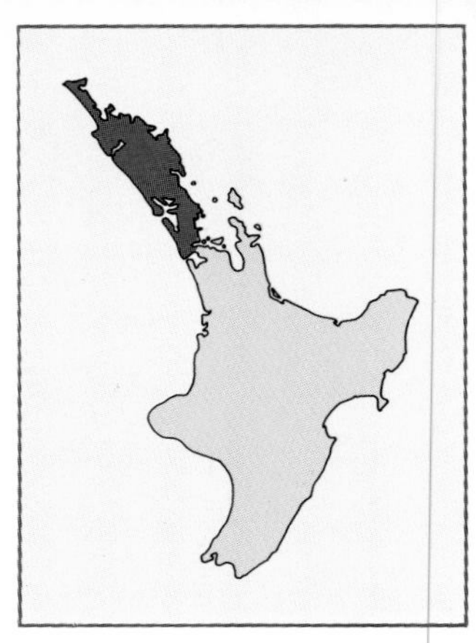

Nowhere in New Zealand is land entangled more vividly with sea than round the long, lumpy and sunny Northland peninsula. Nor is there a region where landscape and architecture speak more potently of New Zealand's history and prehistory. The land's human beginnings have left plain print here. More than a thousand years ago, Polynesian voyagers made homes in its many harbours before dispersing deeper into the country they called Aotearoa. At the beginning of the nineteenth century, white whalers, sailors, timber traders and missionaries created tiny bases which became New Zealand's first European settlements.

The terrain is rugged, with no plains and many heights that are hills by New Zealand measure, mountains by most other. Eruption and earthquake ceased here long ago. Northland seldom feels more than a faint shiver from subterranean shifts farther south. The region's often labyrinthine coast was formed by rising oceans after the end of the last ice age, ten thousand years ago. One valley after another was flooded. On the west coast they left huge, shallow harbours and intricately tentacled estuaries; on the east, deeper harbours and a swarm of islands. Wind and tide have created the landscape. The prevailing westerly bends vegetation, whips sand inland to make miniature deserts, and piles shoals across the mouth of harbours open to its bluster.

Because it is tempered by the sea (it is impossible to be more than a couple of dozen kilometres from salt water), the climate is mellow, mostly frostless, certainly snowless. Winter rain can be frequent and tropically lashing; summers often bring drought. Sometimes in late summer, cyclones from equatorial seas bang down the coast. Though something short of winterless, as Northland's more enthusiastic publicists claim, warmth is a reasonable expectation for nine mostly subtropical months of the year.

The natural vegetation is distinctive. When human beings first reached it, Northland was greened by some of the tallest forest known on earth. This was the kingdom of the muscular kauri, a tree with no rival in bulk, and is surpassed only by California's sequoias in its lusty surge to the sun. Extinct forests have created uncanny and silent graveyards, known as

CRADLE OF THE NATION

gumland. Along the coastline, mangroves teem in tidal waters, their marine roots trapping silt and algae, and making breeding grounds for fish. The prolific pohutukawa, its roots tenaciously gripping rock clefts and cracks, cliff-hangs fantastically where no other vegetation climbs.

Folklore holds that this region was the part of New Zealand that the pioneering Polynesian navigator Kupe knew best. It was on the east coast of Northland that he is said to have first set foot, and the west coast that he farewelled before voyaging back to his native islands to break the news of a large and uninhabited land to the south.

Archaeology appears to argue that it was here, somewhere around 800, that tropical Polynesians first adapted to amiably temperate shores before pushing south, as population grew, to claim cooler coast and heartland. The moa was fast hunted to extinction, but forest and sea remained rich in fleshy bird and fat fish. No part of New Zealand was more densely populated in the Classical Maori period – that is, between the fourteenth and eighteenth centuries. Evidence of long and intensive occupation can be seen in the abandoned and now lonely heights sculpted, sometimes over centuries, for pa, or fortified settlements. Below these sites were gardens in which the kumara, brought here in the great voyaging canoes, was harvested. It was said that the early ripening of the kumara gave Northland tribes a tactical advantage over southerners.

EUROPEANS BRING CHRISTIANITY

In December 1769, James Cook dropped anchor in the Bay of Islands. Nothing was ever the same again, though it was another fifty years before European dwellings began to dot Northland in number. The kauri first drew adventurous Europeans. As boat-building timber it had no peer. Maori tribesmen were not slow to make the most of their asset. They began tree-felling and rafting logs downriver to cater to the demand. Kauri masts and spars were soon sailing the world, and by the eighteen-twenties, Northland even had a shipyard of sorts. Flax was bought from toiling Maori tribes too. Whalers came to the Bay of Islands for rest and recreation, and Maoris began to crew British and American vessels. (In Herman Melville's *Moby Dick*, Queequeg is plainly a Maori mariner.)

On Christmas Day 1814, the Reverend Samuel Marsden, visiting from Sydney, preached the first Christian sermon in New Zealand in the Bay of Islands. He left behind missionaries to fly the flag of faith among pagan Maoris. The endeavour was to take most of two decades. It was not until 1830 that Northland tribes could be considered possessed of Christianity. By then, they were also, alas, possessed of the musket. That weapon offered a final solution to unsettled intertribal scores. Northland's Ngapuhi tribe raged south in a storm of gunpowder smoke to decimate tribes half the length of the North Island. The ensuing massacres have not been forgotten or forgiven. Southern Maoris still grieve for slain ancestors.

European settlements were not initially an attractive sight, especially not their rum-trading and generally mercenary inhabitants, often from the convict settlements of Sydney and Hobart. The voyaging naturalist Charles Darwin, visiting the Bay of Islands in the *Beagle* in 1835, said it was populated by 'the very refuse of society', although he was impressed by Maori progress under missionary tutelage farther inland at Waimate North.

It was to prevent the exploitation of the Maori by unscrupulous traders and land-sharks that missionaries pressed a reluctant Britain to take New Zealand as a colony. So it was that on February 6, 1840, at Waitangi, a covenant enabling New Zealand to shelter under Queen Victoria's wing was entered into between Maori and Briton. Okiato, across the water from Waitangi, was briefly New Zealand's capital before the Auckland isthmus was considered more suitable, its Maori population having been cleared by Ngapuhi muskets.

When political power and European population moved south, Northland went into sharp decline economically. One direct consequence was the first extensive clash between Maori and European, fuelled by the rebel chief Hone Heke's felling and refelling of the British flagpole above Russell in 1844 and 1845. British regular soldiers took tremendous losses until they embraced the advice and manpower of loyalist chiefs, thus establishing a precedent for the more savage wars of the eighteen-sixties, in which Northland tribes would have no part, but in which Maori would conquer Maori on behalf of *Kuini Wikitoria*.

For the rest of the nineteenth century the wealth to be won from war on the kauri tree determined Northland's human character and its fate. Men with axe and saw skirmished deeper into Northland's forests. Milling made town after town. An armada of vessels carried the timber not just the length of New Zealand, but round the world. Many Northland harbours are still littered with the ballast dumped by skippers before taking the coveted kauri aboard.

It was not just the living tree which showed a profit. Kauri gum, the fossilised residue of long dead trees, was used in the manufacture of varnish and linoleum. In the eighteen-nineties it was one of New Zealand's major exports, outshining even gold. Those bleak gumlands, where ancient kauri had exhausted the soil, were attacked by bands of roving diggers, many of them migrants or refugees from the then Austrian, now Yugoslav, province of Dalmatia. Many of the men who lived rough and lonely lives in this *Land of the Lost*, as novelist William Satchell styled it, gathered enough wealth to establish farms, orchards and vineyards. When the kauri forest and gum deposits shrank to remnants, Northland drifted into the backwaters for half a century. Until well into this century the region was mostly roadless, scantily populated and easily forgotten.

Agriculture, fisheries and horticulture have since worked change, hastened in more recent years by industry and energy projects in and about the swiftly grown city of Whangarei. But it is tourism, centred in the Bay of Islands and fast spreading elsewhere, which now most indelibly colours the region. The revival of Northland owes much to New Zealand's discovery of itself as a distinctive Pacific nation. New Zealanders come here not just to rejoice in the physical pleasures of a diverse and sea-girt region, but also to discover a sense of their country's beginnings.

For the most part Northland's story is virtually New Zealand's. It was here that New Zealand began in every way. Yet it is made of more than history, more than mere landscape; it is a place that has enriched the human spirit and been enriched in return. No region of New Zealand has been made more precious by writers and artists defining and celebrating the country that is and the country that was. The lives lived here for ten centuries sigh from headland, harbour and hill.

The long, white stretch of Baylys Beach near Dargaville offers excellent swimming and fishing all year round. The all too scarce and protected toheroa is to be found here.

'THE DESART COAST'

New Zealand's far north from Kaitaia to Cape Reinga was known by the Maori as Muriwhenua, or Land's End

The last, lonely limb of New Zealand is a place of sandscape rather than landscape. Almost everywhere it is confined and coloured by the glittering residue of the sea's long and see-sawing argument with land. This extremity of Northland became a cluster of islands as the ice age ended and the oceans rose. Then sand, carried up the west coast by inshore currents, filled in the archipelago, joining island after island to the mainland by a long and slowly widening spit of sand. The dunes grew taller, the waterways shrivelled, and vegetation took grip and turned sand to soil. New Zealand's distinctive far north region was born.

James Cook, tacking round this coast in 1769, called it 'The Desart Coast' on his charts; it nowhere much took his fancy. That description certainly still could be applied to Ninety Mile Beach (its length is closer to ninety kilometres than ninety miles), monumentally empty, its spellbinding surf beating into the misty distance as far as human eye can see. Poet Barry Mitcalfe called it 'this good-for-nothing, going-nowhere laze of a long beach at the edge of the world'. Behind its bulky dunes, though, the land is now green with productive farms, darkened with recently planted pine forest destined to be even more profitable than dairy herds.

A narrow road threads up the centre, passing the last tiny settlements of New Zealand – the last pub, the last store, the last petrol pump – and then swoops through bleak gumland with scanty patches of forest, before rewarding the traveller with the breathtaking sight of sea-bitten Cape Reinga, a lighthouse on its rump, pushing into the hiss and roar of the vast Pacific. New Zealand is suddenly behind: that is the world out there.

Left: *Sharp rock formations provide a stark contrast to rippling sand dunes at Ahipara, at the southern end of Ninety Mile Beach* **Above:** *Gathering tuatua on Ninety Mile Beach* **Right:** *Cape Reinga stands at the meeting point of two great seas: the Tasman and the Pacific Ocean*

In the old days, Maori tribesmen of the north looked on the sweep of Ninety Mile Beach with its mists of spray and muttering winds as a highway that held their world together, literally and spiritually. It was a warpath when warriors were pursuing their vocation; it was a peace path when talk of truce and trade was desirable. Above all, it was the route travelled after death by all Maoris before looking their last on New Zealand and returning to the lost but never forgotten Polynesian homeland and spirit world of Hawaiki. On the hill of Haumu, just short of Cape Reinga, the spirits rested and knotted wild grasses, in order to point the direction for those who would follow. 'The rope of night binds us', they mourned. On the hill of Maringi-noa, a little farther on, they shed tears of farewell for Aotearoa and those who still dwelled there.

Finally, after fording a creek called Waioterata, beyond which there was no return, a Polynesian parallel to the waters of Lethe in Greek legend, they leapt from the limbs of a gnarled pohutukawa tree, which, so tradition says, grows immortally from a rock cleft at the tip of Cape Reinga. Doors of kelp, surging in the ocean below, opened to receive them into the underworld. They took, if they cared to, a last gulp of earthly air on distant Three Kings Islands, which on a clear day can be seen on the Pacific horizon.

On Ninety Mile Beach the passing shades could be heard, it was said, as a faint puff of ocean breeze; sometimes, such as after a great battle, they sounded like a giant flutter of birds above. That mighty flutter can be heard still, in March. It is the time of year when the kuaka, the bird best known as the godwit, gathers after a summer spent in the harbours and estuaries of northern New Zealand and begins its marvellous migratory journey to its breeding grounds in Siberia and Alaska. Those who have witnessed the departure have found it unforgettable. 'An incalculable feathered multitude', said one nineteenth century chronicler. 'Higher and higher the host rose until it was just a stain in the sky.'

Because of its long isolation from the mainland, the far north holds plants and shrubs rare or unknown in the rest of the country. Here is the home of the large and elusive native land snail *Placostylus ambagiosus*, which long ago abandoned the sea and survives here in tiny colonies.

GIFT OF THE GODS

More reluctant to quit its marine habitat is the deliciously sweet bivalve mollusc called the toheroa. Growing deep in the sand on Ninety Mile Beach, it fattens on brackish water from dunes backing the beach. Maori legend says the toheroa came into being as a gift of compassionate gods. It was bestowed on a famished war party trudging home along the beach. The gods, alas, have since been intermittent with their favours. Since Europeans began keeping tally, this shy king of clams, coveted by the world's gourmets and rejoiced in by British royalty, has mysteriously come and gone from the beach, seeming to vanish completely several times during the past century. When it returns, it is found, not in juvenile thousands, but in mature millions.

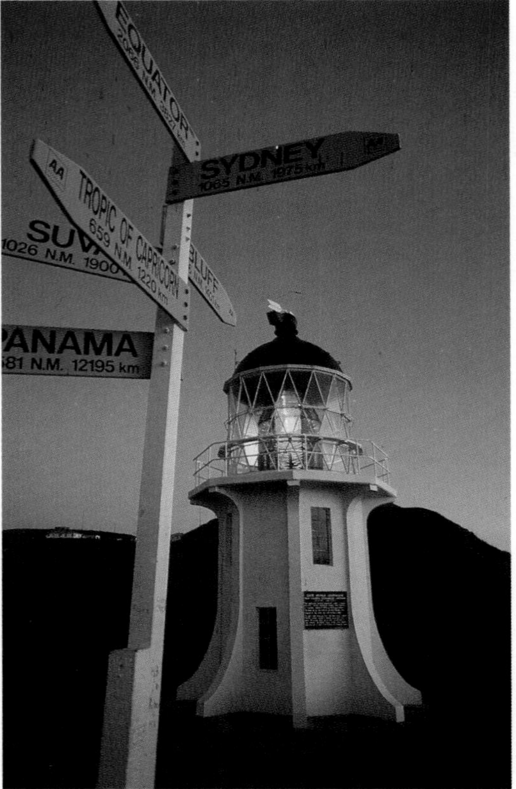

Cape Reinga's lighthouse guides passing craft, as it has done since 1941. The signpost in the foreground reminds visitors of its extreme distance from world centres

The astonishing Wagener Museum at Houhora Heads houses one of the world's most remarkable collections of Victoriana, including the piano, clocks and glass lamps seen here. The museum also has an extensive collection of Maori artefacts

Gathering of the relatively few toheroa persisting on Ninety Mile Beach has been forbidden for most of the past two decades. The hope is that their kinsmen, presumably hugging deep water, may be tempted to return. Visitors had best resign themselves to feasting on the toheroa's tasty commoner cousin, the tuatua, which prospers around the low tide mark the length of Ninety Mile Beach.

Whereas the far north's western coast is mostly sand and surf, with occasional rocky headlands, the east coast is distinguished by the harbours of Parengarenga, Houhora and Rangaunu fingering far into the land, greened densely with mangroves in their upper reaches and rich in fish and birdlife. The population from Kaitaia north is mostly Maori, with a dash of Dalmatian blood here and there. A few hundred now live where thousands of tribesmen once thronged the fortified hills, certainly more than enough to persuade the seventeenth-century Dutch voyager Abel Tasman to sail towards safer seas. He left a name – Cape Maria Van Diemen – in honour of the wife of the governor of Batavia; and another, on the twelfth day of Christmas, on the Three Kings Islands.

European settlers began to arrive during the first half of the nineteenth century. They were adventurers, ship deserters and missionaries, one of whom tried unsuccessfully to cut down the sacred pohutukawa tree on Cape Reinga, but finally saw wisdom in leaving well alone.

PIONEER HARDSHIP AND ISOLATION

In contrast to the rest of Northland, there was no extensive kauri forest here to bring millers, but there was kauri gum in plenty under the scrub and hard blue clay. Settlements based on gum-digging grew at places like Houhora, Te Kao, Awanui and Ahipara. Contact with the outside world was slight, and by sea. A little gum is still dug here and a dealer is still functioning. Farmers can make it a summer pursuit when drought dries off their dairy herds early. On a tall plateau behind Ahipara, at the south end of Ninety Mile Beach, an impressive stretch of typical gumland is under the care of the NZ Historic Places Trust. A walk through this scrappily vegetated terrain, scoured out in places by sluicing and pitted with the holes dug by the Dalmatians who sweated and toiled to get at the gum, gives the visitor a powerful glimpse of pioneering hardship and isolation which survived well into the twentieth century. The walk also provides a magnificent vista of Ninety Mile Beach and the entire peninsula curving towards tropical seas.

Campers and trampers roam the region in summer. Much of the northern end is now a state-managed farm park for the public, with coves and salty hideaways each can call his or her own. The region swallows numbers, and even at the height of summer, human beings merely dot its spaces. Farming and forestry, roads and a town or two have brought change, but nothing dramatic. The sunny far north of New Zealand is still much as the sands of the sea made it, as precious and remarkable a region as it was in the mythology of the Maori. Despite the influx of holidaymakers, it is destined to stay that way.

HISTORY'S BAY

If New Zealanders are possessed of the notion of an earthly paradise, it has to be the Bay of Islands, where their history began

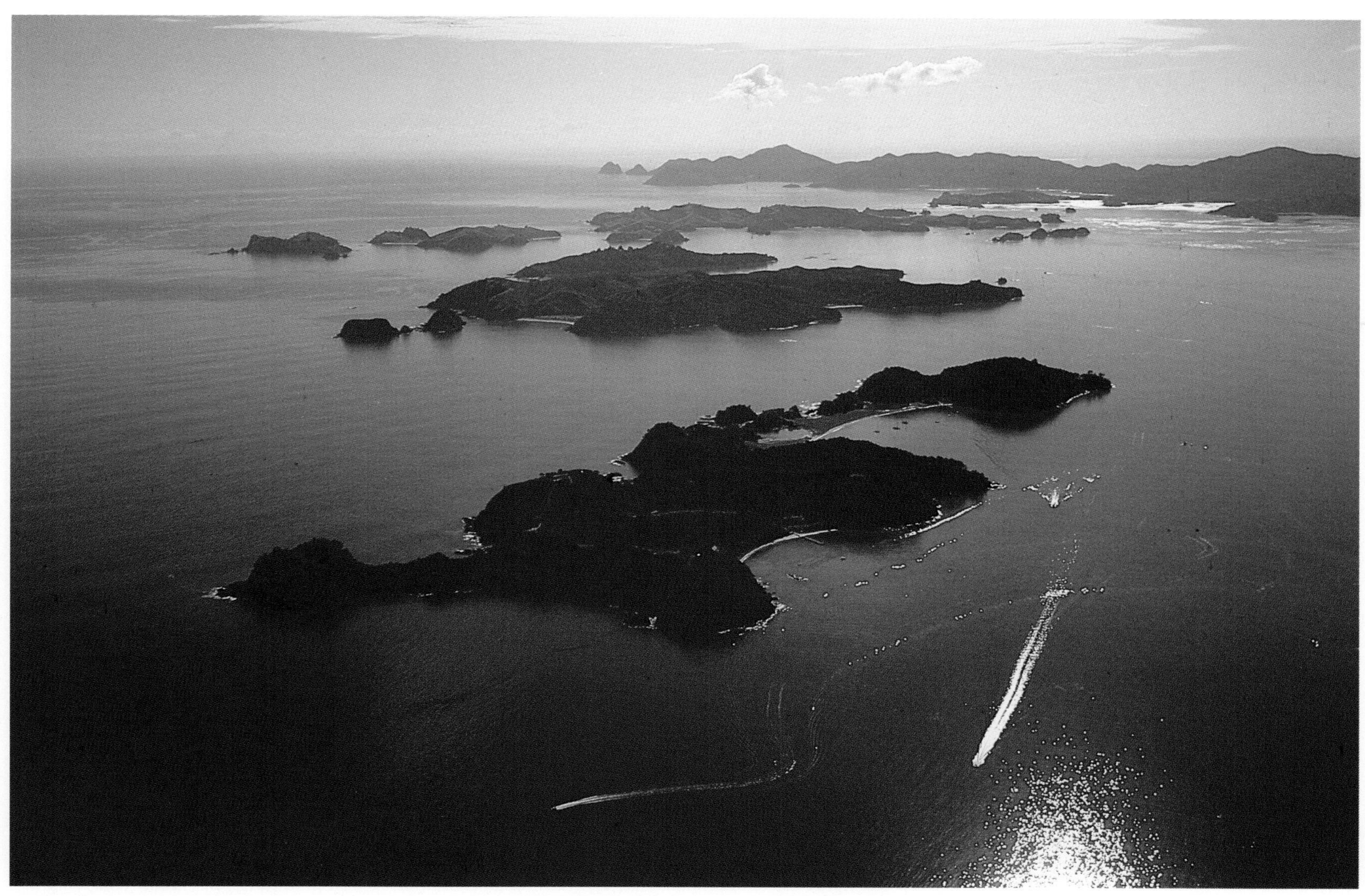

Whispering of history, the Bay of Islands' dramatic coves and beaches draw thousands of seaborne visitors annually

On this tide-washed stage, the first act of a nation-making drama was played. Nature provided a magnificent arena, humanity a cast of thousands. Nature's design work remains vivid; the human presence is less apparent. Today many New Zealanders dream of retiring to beachcomb lazily somewhere along its bright shores. Most will do no more than visit and go home to dream again.

Consider nature's handiwork first. Strictly speaking, the vista is that of a drowned river system. Half-scuttled hills stud the vast bay – islands and islets now, nearly one hundred and fifty of them, some just rocky stumps, others sizeable enough to farm. Fish teem in a region rich in reefs for feeding and mangroved estuaries for breeding. Above pale beaches and oyster-clad rocks, pohutukawa trees hug and shade cliffs and slopes. English artist Augustus Earle, as vivid with the pen as with the brush, said it best in 1827: 'The Bay of Islands is surrounded by lofty and picturesque hills, and is secured from all winds. It is full of lovely coves and a safe anchorage is to be found nearly all over it; added to this a number of navigable rivers are for ever emptying themselves into the Bay, which is spotted with innumerable romantic islands . . .'

POLYNESIAN AND EUROPEAN INTRUDERS

Humans, when they came, made the most of the harbour's hundred safe havens. Polynesian voyagers settled virtually every bay, fortified almost every promontory. They planted kumara, taro and yam, tubers brought from the tropics. The sea lavishly provided a wealth of native, fleshy foods.

James Cook, when he sailed into the bay in 1769, was the first European to marvel. He named it and pronounced it blessed with 'every kinds of refreshments', a verdict still more than fair two centuries later. (By far the best way to become intimate with the Bay of Islands is as in Cook's time, under the silence of sail, with the faint creak of ropes, as islands and headlands parade past the voyager.) Maori canoes poured out to meet him. When tension mounted, Cook demonstrated his firearms, but took no life. He thought the bay Maori superior in physique to those he had observed elsewhere in New Zealand. He flogged sailors who plundered their gardens and he made friends.

The next European voyagers were not so lucky, nor were the local Maoris. An explorer influenced by the French philosophical concept of the noble savage, Marion du Fresne arrived in the bay in 1772, three years after Cook. Du Fresne expressed the gentlest intentions towards native inhabitants. 'As I do good to them', he said, 'assuredly they will do me no evil'. But good intentions went awry, possibly through misunderstanding and violation of Maori custom. A large party of Frenchmen, including du Fresne, were surprised and slain when ashore. In savage reprisal the surviving French slew scores of Maoris – many or most of whom had not taken part in the initial massacre – and left blazing villages.

This bloodied French expedition supposedly claimed New Zealand for France. A bottle said to have been secreted on Moturua Island, with a pronouncement to that effect, has never been recovered, though many have dug. The Bay of Islands thus took its bow in the theatre of European history. In France the fate of du Fresne at the hands of the noble savage reverberated in the debates that preceded the French Revolution.

GOD AND THE DEVIL

For the next thirty years European sails were seldom seen in the bay. It was not until the beginning of the nineteenth century that it became an established watering place, especially for whaling vessels. An untidy community grew at Kororareka (now Russell) on the southern side of the bay. This was 'the Beach', where weary voyagers found their land-legs while sinking liquor with the locals. To many observers it looked very like hell.

News of heaven came with Samuel Marsden's 1814 Christmas Day sermon, at Rangihoua, on the north side of the bay. Notorious in Sydney as a churchman who thought flogging sped convict souls to God, Marsden showed a gentler side to Maoris. But New Zealand had the last word in the case of the missionary Thomas Kendall, who saw that pagan belief must be understood before Christianity could be made acceptable.

He was soon in isolation, and physical and spiritual torment, succumbing to 'the apparent sublimity of the pagan'. He finished up bedding with a Maori woman, and – to put it mildly – doing nothing to impede the Maoris' acquisition of firearms. His agonised fall from grace was the first and perhaps still most spectacular drama of the cultural clash in New Zealand. The Bay of Islands rarely lacked histrionics.

God and the devil contested the bay. The missionaries based at Paihia glared across the water at the sinful settlement of Kororareka. Compromise was impossible. A third element entered the picture when Britain appointed a resident administrator in the eighteen-thirties. James Busby, 'a man o'war without guns', took up residence at Waitangi with both Paihia and Kororareka in view, but powerless to do much more than mediate. Certainly he could do nothing to curb European excesses as more and more colonists arrived looking for land, most of them not anxious about legal niceties but concerned only to acquire as much land as possible.

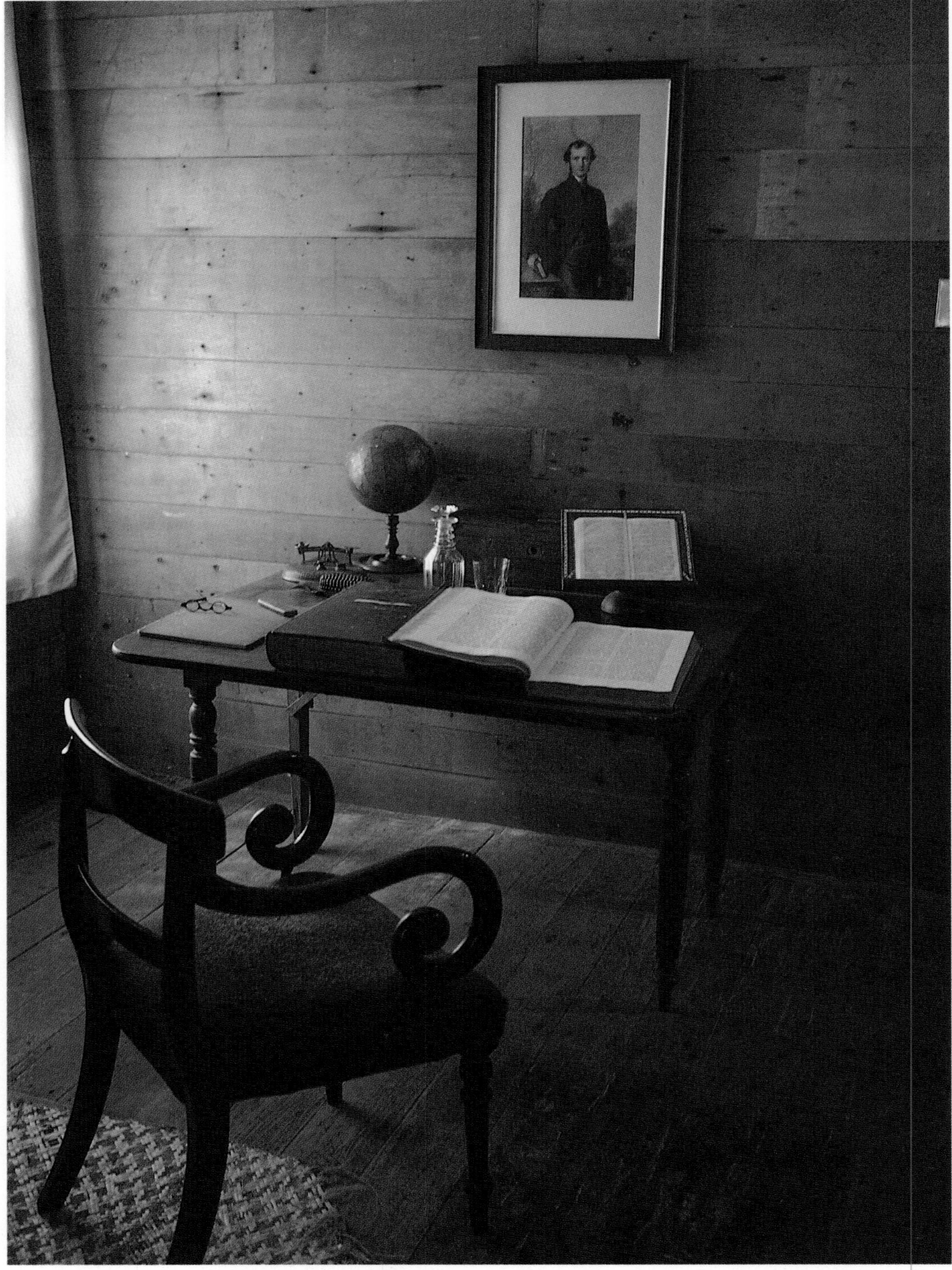

The enchanting Regency interior of the Mission House (1832) at Waimate North has been carefully restored and furnished. Part of the original timber structure is seen in the study

When Britain was finally persuaded of New Zealand's potential as a jewel in the imperial crown, it was on the lawn before Busby's residence that Maori and European met to debate and then sign the Treaty of Waitangi on February 6, 1840. Those who appended their signatures – or their marks – to the document could never have dreamed that it would still be in contention nearly one hundred and fifty years later; that in the nineteen-seventies and eighties, battles between Maori protesters and policemen would sour the annual celebration of the treaty's signing. At the time it must have seemed so simple – the Maori were being placed on par with Europeans.

Nothing was that simple from the start. When New Zealand's governor, Captain William Hobson, took the seat of authority to Auckland in the south, trade suffered and European population dwindled. Worse, loss of Maori sovereignty meant customs duties were levied and discouraged calling vessels. And ironically, in view of New Zealand's later history, Maoris protested that the new government was preventing the sale of their land to Europeans.

Above left: *A wooden headstone outside Christ Church in Russell remembers seamen from HMS* Hazard *who died in the defence of Kororareka* **Above:** *Meticulously reconstructed, Rewa's village at Kerikeri shows how pre-European Maori lived* **Left:** *The magnificent meeting-house at Waitangi is uniquely carved in tribal styles to celebrate Maori spiritual and cultural revival in the twentieth century. It was carved under the direction of the master Pine Taiapa*

Poverty and resentment of British government steadily increased and, in 1844, the headstrong and disillusioned chief Hone Heke, the first to sign the Treaty of Waitangi, hit at the most evident symbol of authority, the flagpole from which the Union Jack fluttered above Kororareka. He felled it again and again in 1845, before sacking and burning the settlement by way of emphasis, leaving British defenders dead. (Churches and mission houses were excluded from Heke's fury.)

The Bay of Islands was in armed uproar for a year. At first British troops employing conventional infantry tactics against the Maori were gunned down. They had to relearn their trade from loyal Maoris. A somewhat fortuitous success, the storming of the rebel fortress at Ruapekapeka on the sabbath while warriors were at prayer, brought the rebellion to an end. The peace of the Bay of Islands was never again disturbed in the nineteenth century.

For the remainder of that century, and for much of the twentieth, the Bay of Islands sat on the sideline as New Zealand shook itself into shape. Its early dramas were forgotten, its fine old buildings mouldered. When it made news again, it was because Zane Grey, the celebrated novelist of America's Wild West, established its reputation as perhaps the finest big-game fishing ground in the world. In the nineteen-twenties he based wanderers upon the Pacific found themselves blessed with 'every kind of refreshments' in the green embrace of the Bay of Islands.

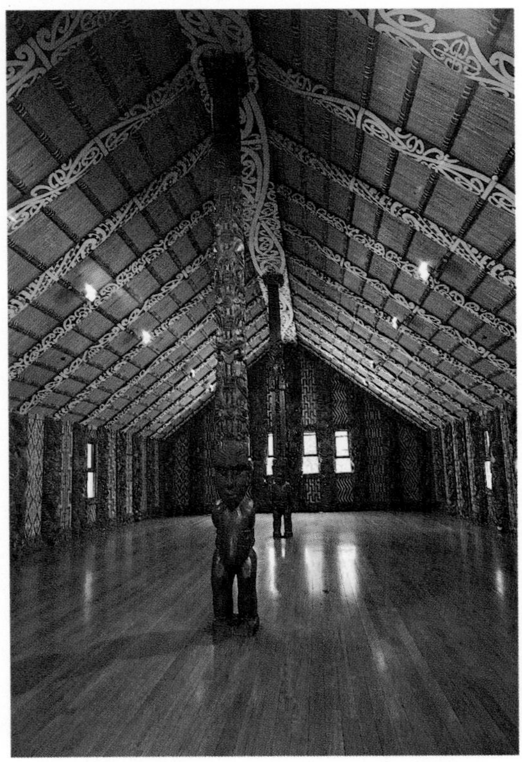

formidable size. The bay's fortunes revived, as adventurous sportsmen from many countries journeyed here to partake of the primitive life and pit themselves against the sea's largest creatures. The Bay of Islands, and notably the sleepy township of Russell, became the provider, as it had been for whalers of an earlier era.

History – at least the romance of it – has done the rest. With the demise of the British Empire, and the birth of a native nationalism, the Bay of Islands was seen afresh. Not before time, and often in the nick of time, New Zealand raced to preserve and restore its pioneer heritage. Buildings such as Christ Church and Pompallier House at Russell, the Treaty House at Waitangi, the Kemp House and Stone Store at Kerikeri, and the Mission House at Waimate North have been saved and refurbished. They now annually provide tens of thousands of New Zealanders with a vivid glimpse of their beginnings. Tourist development has conspicuously disfigured only one community in the bay, that of Paihia. Elsewhere, conservationists have seen that it is circumscribed. More and more New Zealanders have settled here precisely because of its whisper of history, isolation and serenity. Writers, painters and craftsmen, especially from North America, have made a modest Cornwall of the region since the nineteen-sixties.

Yet it is still the natural world that most bewitches the visitor. Those dreaming islands and dramatic headlands, those coves and beaches, are still much as they were when brown and white wanderers upon the Pacific found themselves blessed with 'every kind of refreshments' in the green embrace of the Bay of Islands.

HAUNTED HOKIANGA

This fiord-like arm of the Tasman Sea, sometimes called a river by locals, straggles more than halfway across Northland

Hokianga Harbour lives in the shadow of the Bay of Islands. There are no trendy boutiques here, few motels, and tourists are seldom conspicuous. It was not always so sleepy. In the first half of the nineteenth century it was often the first port of call for sailing vessels, being hundreds of nautical miles nearer Sydney and Hobart than the Bay of Islands. Visitors made their way overland to the east coast of Northland rather than endure further voyaging. Its pioneer beginnings were, if anything, even more boisterous than those of the Bay of Islands. Thanks to Frederick Maning, it is also the birthplace of New Zealand literature. His lusty book *Old New Zealand*, a tale of 'the good old times' on the Hokianga, and likely more fiction than fact, has seldom been out of print in more than a century.

Tall surf buckets over perilous shoals at the harbour entrance. The roaring water was styled by the Maori *kaiwaka*, or canoe-eater, and it proved to have a large appetite for European vessels too. The south side of the harbour is mostly steep and green, patched with farmland now, and a few rags and tatters of its old forest cover. It is the north side that steals the breath. Golden sand dunes, which have been heaped up to one hundred and seventy metres high by vigorous westerlies, stride magnificently inland. No New Zealand harbour has a more striking entrance. Farther up the harbour the rising tide hisses through mighty forests of mangrove and fills wide rivers.

The long verandas of the Mangungu Mission House near Horeke look out onto Hokianga Harbour. The building was moved to Onehunga, Auckland, when the Hokianga declined in importance, but it was transported home again in 1972

So intricate a tapestry has to be storied. The Maori attributed the making of the Hokianga to the most potent creature in their mythology, the *taniwha*. Although its imaginative origin probably sprang from dolphin or whale, in character it was often distinctly dragonish. But it was a friendly and vastly pregnant *taniwha* that led the first human beings to the then tiny haven of the Hokianga. The humans found little cause to linger there. The *taniwha* took itself to a sea cave and proceeded to give birth to a dozen juvenile monsters. They chafed in their cave and then began shovelling their way out with their noses, digging channel after channel through which the sea might ride, until finally the Hokianga found its present irregular form.

Tradition also says it was on rocks on the north side of the harbour entrance that the Polynesian voyager Kupe finished exploring New Zealand, a thousand years before Cook ducked fleetingly past and missed the entrance altogether. It is from Kupe the harbour takes its name – in full *Hokianga-nui-a-Kupe*, 'the departing place of Kupe'. He is said to have raised a kumara crop at nearby Pakanae to provision for the long journey home to the tropics.

The Hokianga still breeds legend. In 1956 a dolphin, seen by Maoris as a descendant of the founding *taniwha*, swam into the harbour and befriended the human race. It was named Opo after the small Hokianga village of Opononi, where it first made itself evident offshore. It was a thing of one fickle summer, but drew thousands of entranced visitors by taking children on its back, tossing rubber balls and beer bottles in the air. In a curious replay of events in the Roman town of Hippo, nearly two thousand years earlier, Opo appears to have perished by human hand. (In Hippo too, hordes of humans descended on the town and ended its quiet character. The dolphin was put to death.)

The restored dining room of Clendon House at Rawene displays some of the Clendon family's original treasures

It was the Hokianga's wealth of kauri forest that first drew Europeans. One durable Hokianga story has it that kauri spars from the region served on British naval vessels in the Battle of Trafalgar in 1805. Maoris floated vast rafts of logs downriver to vessels waiting to ship the precious timber round the world. In the late eighteen-twenties, up-harbour at Horeke, a shipyard was functioning. And there were soon many mills.

Shops on stilts over water – here seen at Rawene – distinguish Northland's older communities

The harbour also drew less commercially minded adventurers, notably the talented artist Augustus Earle, who has left us with vivid pictures, in words and in paint, of the Hokianga he saw in 1827 and which for the most part can still be seen today. After meditating on the spectacular entrance to the harbour, one side light, the other dark, he recorded, 'Floating gradually into a beautiful river, we soon lost sight of the sea, and were sailing up a spacious sheet of water which became considerably wider after entering it; while majestic hills rose on each side, covered with verdure to their very summits... We beheld various headlands stretching into the water, and gradually contracting its width, till they became fainter and fainter in the distance, and all was lost in the azure of the horizon.' Ashore, he was shocked by the Maori custom of cannibalism, but awed by the natural world, especially by 'wood so thick that the light of heaven could not penetrate the trees.

Above: *Clendon House, Rawene's most famous house, was built in about 1868 by James Clendon, onetime US consul and man of considerable authority in New Zealand at the time* **Right:** *A lone church is situated in isolated farming country near Motukaraka*

The forest had a short time left. Ruthless felling and milling would soon expose most of the Hokianga's rugged contours to heaven's light. The first Europeans were not an especially appealing collection. According to Frederick Maning, they lived in a 'savage-and-a-half state, being greater savages by far than the natives themselves'. They certainly feuded and fought as much as their Maori neighbours. But the harbour's most freakish colonist was a Frenchman who aristocratically meant to put New Zealand to rights. Baron de Thierry (1793–1864), celebrated compassionately in Robin Hyde's novel *Check to Your King*, claimed sixteen thousand Hokianga hectares bought for thirty-six axe heads and proclaimed himself 'Sovereign Chief of New Zealand' to the laughter of most in the land. His antipodean domain failed him and he died impoverished in Auckland. He was the first in a long line of Hokianga eccentrics. Missionaries established themselves up-harbour, particularly in the waterside village of Horeke where, at the Mangungu Wesleyan Mission House, many local chiefs would fix their names and marks to the Treaty of Waitangi in 1840.

END OF A SLOW DECLINE

Trade in kauri timber and then kauri gum made small and durable communities such as Kohukohu, Rawene and Horeke along the upper Hokianga in the nineteenth century. Colonial homesteads and wooden churches still grace the harbourside. Elsewhere history seems to have been little more than a passing dream. Maori hilltop fortresses are crumbled and quiet. European communities have foundered to a few relics among the ferns. Farms have been abandoned to scrub and forest. Jetties once busy with shipping have rotted to stumps on which oysters congregate. Mullet swarm up the tidal estuaries where canoe-borne Maoris once battled and timber barques glided.

Yet all is not lost. Since the nineteen-seventies young people, many of them craft workers, have been resettling the region in search of a quiet life in a picturesque environment far from the cities. Land and large kauri homes go cheap, fish are free and the climate mild. In places new arrivals now outnumber the oldtimers. Locals new and old love the Hokianga the way it is – hauntingly coloured by its pioneer past, gently paced and friendly. Who would have it otherwise?

The visitor might echo the adventurer Edward Markham. 'There is', he recorded in 1834, 'something so beautiful in the rivers in this Country. A Stillness, fine sky overhead!no Noise! now and then a Fish will leap or a King fisher dart down . . .' The serenity remains, the fish still leap and kingfishers still dart down.

Looking toward the entrance of Hokianga Harbour. This long and luminous arm of the sea was once a highway for trader, timberman and missionary

THE KINGDOM OF THE KAURI

Follow Northland's western shore south from the Hokianga or north from Dargaville and climb into the high, cool realm of the kauri

California's sequoia surpasses it in height and age, but never in magnificence. For bulk and timber content the kauri has no peer. It soars up to fifty-five metres tall, its girth can be sixteen metres, its age two thousand years.

The nine thousand hectare Waipoua Kauri Forest, along with the neighbouring five hundred hectare Trounson Kauri Park, contains the most extensive stand of mature trees left in Northland. Although it is a mere remnant of the hundreds of thousands of hectares that once clothed the region, it is awesome for all that. This is a vivid sample of the forest which sustained and sheltered New Zealanders for four generations and enriched the country far more than gold; the forest that fleets of vessels sought and from which fleets of vessels were built; the forest on which fortunes were founded and from which entire communities were fashioned. For a time kauri timber was New Zealand's major export and kauri gum not far behind. Much of the country's early history is inextricable from the melancholy fate of the kauri.

About half Northland's kauri forest was gone by 1885 and three-quarters by 1900. A few years into the twentieth century, when it was first seen that exploitation of the kauri might make it extinct, the government saved this stretch of forest from ruthless millers, intending that the timber still be harvested but with greater discrimination. Public protest and petition in the nineteen-forties ensured that logging here ceased altogether. It was the first great triumph of the conservation movement in New Zealand, which has since managed to halt milling of the kauri virtually everywhere. The NZ Forest Service developed a policy not only of protecting mature trees but of encouraging regeneration. Kauri are now planted rather than plundered. Kauri forest, for the first time in two centuries, is extending.

The Waipoua Forest has become a sanctuary and shrine to the tree; it has never lacked reverence. First were the Maori, who venerated the kauri for its size, sang of its beauty, and felled and hollowed it out for canoes. Among the early Europeans impressed by its stature was Charles Darwin, not greatly excited by New Zealand flora, still less by its human beings, whose heart went out to these 'noble trees' which 'stood up like gigantic columns of wood'. The kauri has become as much a symbol of New Zealand as the kiwi or silver fern.

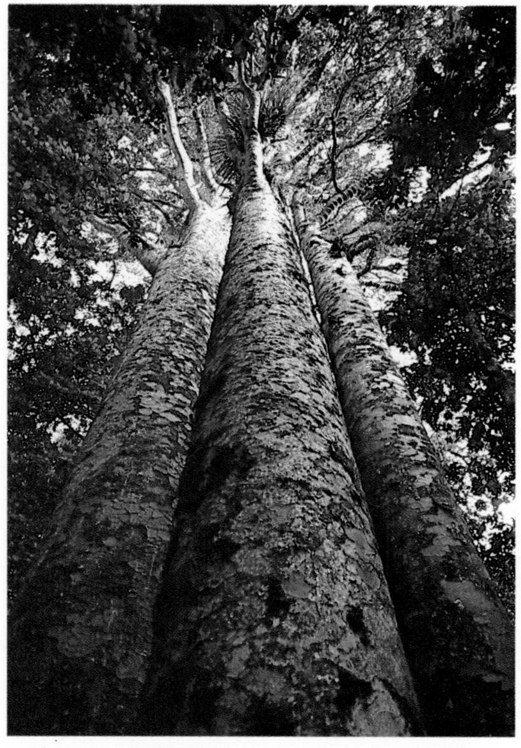

Left: *The great clump of kauri known as the Four Sisters is an intriguing attraction in the Waipoua Kauri Forest*

Below left: *Lush vegetation surrounds dense stands of kauri at the edge of a stream deep in Waipoua Kauri Forest*

Above: *Intricate patterns in kauri reflect a constantly changing evolutionary process that spans millions of years*

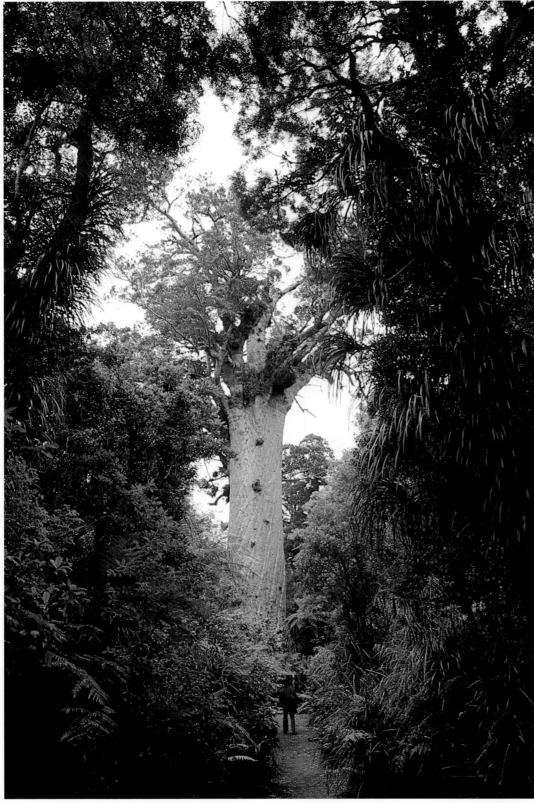

Above: *New Zealand's most famed kauri tree, enormous twelve-hundred-year old* Tane Mahuta, *'god of the forest', is near the road which threads through Waipoua Kauri Forest*

Right: *Younger kauri, soaring far above visitors to Trounson Kauri Park, form fascinating groves; a cathedral-like hush prevails in the forest*

Above: *About a third of Waipoua Kauri Forest bears mature kauri; young, rich ferny vegetation covers the rest*

It is the kauri's brawn and potency that bewitches most. To encounter the Waipoua's more accessible giants like the Yakas tree, or *Te Matua Ngahere*, 'father of the forest', is rather like finding the pocked, silver-grey face of a cliff suddenly in your path. It takes time to comprehend that this is living texture, not dead rock.

As for the celebrated *Tane Mahuta*, 'god of the forest', you need to beat a slow retreat to consider its miraculous substance. The physique of the kauri is phenomenal. As it climbs skyward and sunward, rising from the forest's olive-green canopy, its trunk does not taper off, as those of other trees do. On the contrary, its girth can be greater at the point where the first limbs emerge, and that point can be twenty metres from the ground. And these are *not* the greatest kauri known. Larger were logged in the nineteenth and early twentieth centuries, measured and photographed. Even now, there are tales of colossal trees hidden in difficult terrain and dense foliage. (The Yakas tree, after being a rumour for years, was only recently rediscovered by an old Yugoslav bushman. He claimed to know of an even greater tree, but it has yet to be found.)

The kauri belongs to the araucaria family, which includes the Norfolk Island pine and the monkey puzzle of the Andes. It has some less impressive cousins in Malaysia, the Philippines, Australia and Fiji. Its leaves are thick and leather-like, its timber is straight-grained, silky, honey-coloured and tough. The tree exudes a resin which, bled cruelly from living trees, or dug from ground where ancient forest had expired, had a commercial value rivalling that of the timber.

CATHEDRAL-LIKE CALM

Though most travellers treat the Waipoua Forest as a wayside stop, content with a quick glimpse of *Tane Mahuta* just off the roadside, a visit is best not rushed. The forest deserves at least a full day or, better still, two. Clearly marked tracks take the tramper among groves of mature kauri, small forests in a mosaic of many, even more magical than individual monsters. Miscellanous vegetation parts suddenly to disclose graceful galleries of stone-coloured trunks and evergreen arches of foliage. There is more the sense of some lost city than of constantly regenerating forest.

A kauri grove permits little competition. In its shade other growth is feeble and slight. A deep carpet of shed bark and fallen leaf whispers underfoot. Sunlight finds its way through a green mist, and even the birds seem hushed. The calm of a great cathedral prevails, a place of worship. And why not? Such a grove argues that we make our peace with wild places, make a pledge to preserve them for as long as our planet lasts. In the Waipoua Forest we have.

Detailed texture etched into the bark of an aged kauri tree presents shapes that resemble an ancient tribal pattern

MIDDLE NORTHLAND'S WORLD

Most of Northland's population lives here, inland round the harbourside city of Whangarei and the riverside town of Dargaville

Timber village church at Te Kopuru, near Dargaville

This region is often neglected by the visitor with the spaces of the Bay of Islands and the even lonelier far north most in mind. Middle Northland's history may be less spectacular, its charms are not. North and south of Whangarei is a coastline as magical as any in settled New Zealand, with bright coves and beaches, and a fleet of islands anchored offshore. To the west, a vast sweep of surf-beaten sand backs Dargaville. The town is joined by the wide northern Wairoa River to the Kaipara Harbour, New Zealand's largest, and by far the most elaborate of Northland's drowned river systems.

Though James Cook found the fishing excellent outside the fantastically shaped heads of Whangarei Harbour he was not tempted into it. In 1769, he named Bream Head and nearby islands, the Hen and Chickens and Poor Knights, and sailed on. It was not until 1839 that a European settler, William Carruth, established himself in the harbour's upper reaches among friendly tribesmen. By 1845 three or four dozen Europeans had settled there, but in that year Hone Heke's war against British authority promised to spill south from the Bay of Islands. Europeans fled to Auckland, leaving their homes and possessions to be pillaged. Over the next ten years, they warily re-established themselves, and their numbers were augmented by arrivals from Nova Scotia at neighbouring Waipu.

Whangarei grew slowly. A shipbuilding yard was opened in the eighteen-sixties, beginning a robust tradition of marine design and craftsmanship. More than a century later, Whangarei's boatbuilders would become best known for a remarkable replica of Captain Bligh's *Bounty*, used in a film of the mutiny story.

Yachts anchored at Whangarei Harbour, a base for sailing and big-game fishing. The harbour is dominated by Mount Manaia, which has several curiously shaped, jagged peaks

Like most of Northland, Whangarei suffered for much of a century from isolation. The often boisterous sea was the only highway to large centres of population farther south. Travellers endured a sometimes week-long journey on schooners, cutters and steamers crowded with cattle. The railway did not reach the town until the nineteen-twenties and there was no reliable road to Auckland until the nineteen-thirties. Meanwhile, the district won a modest prosperity from farming, horticulture, coal-mining, kauri-milling and gum-digging. The town grew on reclaimed mangrove swamp. Until the beginning of this century, dinghies and timber scows lifted on high tides into what is now the commercial heart of the city.

In the second half of the century, things changed dramatically. The population almost tripled from fifteen thousand in 1951 to forty-one thousand in 1985, with another eighteen thousand just outside the urban area. Whangarei became the country's fastest growing city. A nondescript and rather neglected town leapt into urban sprawl. Much of the population increase is due to industry – the city now has close to four hundred factories. Major enterprises are glass-making, engineering, boat-building, fisheries, cement-making, and most noticeably, oil refining at Marsden Point.

Left: *Rocks deposited on the shore at Mangawhai Heads bear a curious cell-like pattern, the result of erosion over time*
Below: *The Clapham Clock Museum in Whangarei is known for its vast collection of five hundred antique clocks*

Brightly coloured paintwork gives character to the timber decoration on a simple house at Te Kopuru, near Dargaville

Still developing, with raw suburban edges, Whangarei may make no claim to being the fairest city of them all. What it can claim with confidence is a dramatic landscape and a ravishing seascape to rival any other city's. There is the harbour itself under the striking peaks of Mount Manaia, which Maori legend says are five feuding human beings turned to stone. North and south are long, sandy ocean beaches. The big-game fishing base in Tutukaka is half an hour from Whangarei city and only minutes from some of New Zealand's most bewitching waters.

Poor Knights Islands are wildlife sanctuaries and landing on them is forbidden. But the sea around ripples with surprises. The islands are remnants of once vast lava domes corroded and perforated by the sea. They survive as rock faces intricately and deeply carved with arches, caves and tunnels. One tunnel travels four hundred metres inland. Inside the caves are meadows of multi-hued sponges and shoals of bright fish. A subtropical current is two degrees Centigrade warmer than coastal waters and tropical fish have become established in this congenial environment. The theory is that the islands function as a gate through which New Zealand's marine animal life is enriched by fresh species.

THE WIDE AND WINDING WAIROA

On the other side of Northland, the Dargaville district is dominated by the great northern Wairoa River which feeds Kaipara Harbour. Although the Wairoa is not the largest river in New Zealand, it is the most impressive in its winding width, and is celebrated in Jane Mander's novel *The Story of a New Zealand River*. When the Ngati Whatua tribe, whose territory this was, first welcomed missionary and trader, the harbour and river banks were smothered in kauri forest. For the next eighty years the kauri determined the character of the district. Kauri-built colonial homes and hotels still colour the community. But vessels loading timber, five or six abreast on the riverside, have long gone. Yugoslav influence has been strong here since gum-digging days. Much gumland and swamp that were once near lifeless have been turned into productive pasture. Only the river, riding down to the Kaipara, and the surf that beats up the sands at its back door remain the same.

PLACES OF INTEREST

AHIPARA
Small, mainly Maori community at south end of **NINETY MILE BEACH** set under dramatic hills. In recent years it has become a modest resort, still rich in atmosphere, with the beach sweeping into misty distance. Gumland nearby has been made a historic reserve with walking tracks through the bleak plateau that once sustained several hundred people. At Shipwreck Bay, where the beach terminates in sea-lashed rocks, the wreck of the vessel *Favourite*, which foundered here in 1870, is visible at low tide.

Thirteen kilometres round the rocks, on a risky road, is one of the country's most isolated and ramshackle communities, Tauroa Point, where Maoris harvest the seaweed agar six months of the year. Processed agar is used as a food additive and for laboratory cultures.

Beachcombing, fishing, swimming in mild surf and taking tuatua are the special delights of Ahipara, not to speak of rejoicing in one of New Zealand's greatest vistas. There is access to the beach for motorists wishing to brave it.

CAPE REINGA
Sacred (*tapu*) to the Maori, this was where the spirits of the dead departed on the subterranean journey to the Polynesian homeland of Hawaiki. The pohutukawa tree where they leapt from New Zealand is plainly visible. Cape Reinga is not the most northern point of New Zealand (the nearby Surville Cliffs extend 4.8 kilometres further), but near enough. Swimming and camping are possible at nearby Tapotupotu Beach and Spirits Bay. There are tracks for those who wish to adventure afoot through this fascinating and sandy surf-beaten region.

The lighthouse has functioned reliably since 1941. Uninhabited Three Kings Islands can often be seen in the distance. Dutch explorer Abel Tasman passed this way in early 1643, terrified by Maoris seen on the hilltops. Rather remarkably, the next Europeans to come this way – the Frenchman de Surville and Englishman Cook simultaneously 126 years later – all but met each other in the waters off Cape Reinga. Storm and high seas kept them apart.

Early light as the sun rises over sweeping Ninety Mile Beach

BAY OF ISLANDS
One of New Zealand's most popular tourist regions, with its bush-covered islands, transparent waters and pale beaches, the Bay of Islands provides for most recreational needs. But it also provides for those New Zealanders who need to feel their history. Most of the bay's historic buildings are open to the public – at **RUSSELL**, **WAITANGI**, **WAIMATE NORTH** and **KERIKERI**.

Visitors' centres at Russell and Waitangi provide an abundance of information and assistance. They also offer fascinating audio-visual shows depicting main events and prominent characters in the region's lively past. Waterborne excursions round the bay and its storied islands leave from **PAIHIA** and Russell.

DARGAVILLE
Founded as a trading post by Australian Joseph Dargaville in 1872, it grew with trade in kauri timber and gum to become a rural town of 5000 people, pleasantly placed with water-lapped lawn and bandstand beside the northern Wairoa River. Many sturdy Victorian buildings survive here, and at former mill towns like Te Kopuru near by. The museum at Harding Park offers a splendid view of the town and its environs as well as fascinating exhibits within, much of strong nautical flavour. Paddle-steamer and steamer across the **KAIPARA** to the railhead at Helensville once linked the town with the rest of New Zealand, and the waterfront was busy with shipping. (For the flavour of the Kaipara region, read Jane Mander's *The Story of a New Zealand River*.) Let locals tell you of a mysterious Spanish wreck yet to be discovered near by.

Thirteen kilometres from the town centre is the sweeping sand and surf of Baylys Beach. A 67 kilometre drive to Pouto on the north head of the Kaipara Harbour, and then a two-hour walk, take the visitor to the historic kauri-timbered lighthouse (more than a century old, and the last in New Zealand to be built of wood), which once guided mariners into the treacherous harbour. It was taken out of service in 1952 and is now the precious property of the NZ Historic Places Trust.

Dargaville is a base from which to leap into the **WAIPOUA KAURI FOREST**. Those reluctant to take the forest road may enjoy the impressive Trounson Kauri Park nearer at hand. Pines on the shores of the Kaiiwi Lakes in the Taharoa Domain just off that route create a surprising and pleasing Scandinavian flavour. The lakes offer swimming, sailing, trout fishing, water-skiing, camping grounds and vivid tramps to the west coast. Two-day 'Kauri Coaster' tours from Dargaville take in the entire region from the Kaipara heads to the Waipoua.

DOUBTLESS BAY
Named by James Cook as he sailed past, deciding it 'doubtless' a bay. A pohutukawa-patched region of silvery beaches and waterside hamlets – **MANGONUI**, Coopers Beach, Cable Bay, Taipa – nestles under the sheltering limb of the lovely Karikari Peninsula. Mangonui, one-time timber port, and longest established of the townships, has mellow colonial charm.

The Karikari Peninsula is rich in lonely seascapes and ripe, alas, for development. The pure waters of the bay delight skin-divers. The French explorer de Surville was the first European to enter the bay, in 1769, only days after Cook had sped past. He and his scurvy-ridden men, anxious for nourishment, fell out with the Maoris and kidnapped a local chief. Both de Surville and the chief perished as the voyage resumed. Three anchors he abandoned were recovered in 1974 and 1982. One of them is displayed in the nearby **KAITAIA** museum.

HOKIANGA HARBOUR
A long and luminous arm of the sea nursing more legend, history and visual delight than most places in New Zealand. The neglected and largely depopulated region has never been at pains to advertise itself, nor to open itself up especially. Most of its historic buildings are still in private hands, but two that are not, (see **HOREKE** and **RAWENE**) must not be missed. At the harbour mouth are the resort villages of **OPONONI** and **OMAPERE** with gentle foreshores. Round the corner of South Head is an ocean beach. Farther up-harbour, among tidal estuaries and mangroves, are picturesque Rawene, Horeke and **KOHUKOHU**. South Head Reserve Lookout (along Signal Station Road, above Omapere) offers a stunning vista of the harbour and its northern head, also of the seething bar which claimed wreck after wreck. Fishing is good, sunsets superb. Don't look for night life; dawdle and dream.
See page 40.

HOREKE
One of New Zealand's first European settlements, tucked among mangrove forest and the ebb and flow of the **HOKIANGA**'s tides, Horeke is well off highways and now little more than a pub, a few shops strangely stilted over the sea, and some sturdy old dwellings. Yet New Zealand's first shipyard functioned here in the 1820s; missionaries were busy too. The low offshore island of Ruapapaka was the setting of New Zealand's first judicial execution, in 1838, of a Maori who murdered a European. A little upriver from Horeke, at Rangiahua, Frenchman Baron de Thierry, in one of the Hokianga's more bizarre episodes, proclaimed himself 'Sovereign Chief of New Zealand' in 1837. (A plaque on Highway 1, beside the access road into Horeke, marks the site where his monarchical ambition foundered.) Don't let the rough road deter a visit.

The two highlights of Horeke are the splendidly restored and furnished Methodist Mission House at nearby Mangungu (under the care of the NZ Historic Places Trust, open 10–4.30 school and public holidays; 12–5 the rest of the year) and the richly atmospheric oak-shaded graveyard close by, where some of the first European residents in New Zealand are buried. On the foreshore is the rock to which recently converted Maori Christians tied their canoes. The mission house was the setting for the second major signing of the Treaty of Waitangi. When the Hokianga declined in importance, the building was shipped off to Auckland's Manukau Harbour, but was brought home again in 1972. The pleasant waterside Horeke pub, though largely modernised, has a claim on history that reaches beyond satisfying pioneer thirsts – part of the building goes back to the early 19th century.

HOUHORA
The last substantial settlement, certainly the last pub, on the dry road north to **CAPE REINGA**. The publican was king of this once gum-digging community on the shore of Houhora Harbour, dominated by Mt Camel (so curiously named by Cook). Now there is a new pub next to the old.

At Houhora Heads just south is the rather astonishing Wagener Museum, surely one of the most remarkable collections of Victoriana in the world, with much of local interest too (open 9–5 daily, except Christmas Day and Good Friday). With luck and good timing the

FALLEN MAN OF GOD

Pre-colonial New Zealand's most haunting and enigmatic figure casts his tragic shadow over the Bay of Islands

An oil painting by James Barry depicts Kendall in London, with Maori chiefs

Thomas Kendall was born in England's Lincolnshire in 1778, and began adult life as a draper and grocer. At the age of twenty-seven he was gripped by evangelical religious fervour, became a schoolmaster and finally offered himself to the Church Missionary Society.

He arrived in New South Wales in 1813 and in 1814, with another lay missionary, sailed to the Bay of Islands to explore the potential of that increasingly unkempt South Sea shore as a base for Christ. Later that year, on a second visit with Samuel Marsden, he was witness to the first Christian sermon preached in New Zealand.

Kendall established New Zealand's first school in 1816. He was astute enough to see that knowledge of Maori language, customs and beliefs was needed if these warlike people were to be persuaded of Christian virtue. However, commonsense was also a fatal flaw: he succumbed to the subject of his study. 'All their notions are metaphysical', he wrote, 'and I have been so poisoned with the apparent sublimity of their ideas that I have almost completely turned from a Christian to a heathen'.

Kendall not only fell out with fellow mission workers. He was also increasingly a slave to his loneliness and its temptations. He traded in muskets, drank immoderately with visiting whalers and finally took a Maori woman as a second wife. In 1820, he shepherded the powerful Ngapuhi chief Hongi Hika to London, a visit that permitted him to compile the first Maori language grammar and vocabulary. More ominously, it also enabled Hongi to turn gifts from George IV into weaponry.

By 1823 Kendall's luck had gone and he was suspended by the Church Missionary Society. In 1825, after living for a time among friendly Maoris, Kendall sailed for Valparaiso and a new life. He was back in New South Wales in 1827, trading in timber rather than souls. In 1832 he was drowned when his vessel foundered.

Kendall was long a murky and misunderstood figure in New Zealand history. His scholarship, though fumbling, enabled much Maori traditional belief to be saved before it shrivelled. Later generations would see wisdom and virtue in the man.

visitor may also see bullock teams working. Beside the museum, the rugged Subritzky Homestead, built in the 1850s, plastered with powdered seashell, is now open to the public. Mt Camel, just across the water, is the site of one of the earliest Polynesian settlements in New Zealand. Long-isolated, Houhora Harbour once had a reputation as a smugglers' base.

KAIKOHE

This market town of 4000 people serves the farmers of Northland, in a region of distinctively shaped hills which were fortified by the powerful Ngapuhi tribe. They were the first Maoris to take up arms against the British, under the leadership of Hone Heke in 1845. At nearby Ohaeawai, 9 kilometres outside the town, Heke left 41 British dead and 73 wounded in his most devastating triumph. A charming little Maori church, built as a peacemaking tribute to the dead of both races, stands gracefully on the old site of the battle.

On the road to Ohaeawai there are the Ngawha hot springs (6 kilometres from Kaikohe) to soothe the traveller's aches. Large and shallow Lake Omapere, a feature of the Kaikohe region, is also fed by hot springs on its south-west shore. The lake was a source of freshwater fish for the Maoris, who occupied the surrounding hills as early as the 11th century. A battlesite (signposted) on its western shore is where Heke's warriors first dented British bayonets. Kaikohe town itself has an interesting and growing pioneer village in Recreation Road. It includes the old Kaikohe prison, an 1862 courthouse, an old bush railway and a restored kauri mill.

KAIPARA HARBOUR

With more than 3000 kilometres of shoreline, it is New Zealand's largest harbour, and perhaps the least seen. For one thing, seeing it is difficult – it cannot be glimpsed by the traveller on Highway 1, and even from a by-road running between Helensville and Wellsford its bulk is only partially apparent. Its tides feel into the farmlands of middle and lower Northland. Once, and for most of a century, it was one of New Zealand's busiest waterways. Skippers chanced its dangerously shoaling entrance to take on kauri timber and gum. Today a few pleasing townships and villages survive serenely where timber towns boomed. Two such, ideal for picnickers and campers, are Pahi and Tinopai on the north-eastern side. Pahi can be found off Highway 12, at Paparoa; Tinopai via MATAKOHE a little farther along the highway. But there is still only one way to comprehend the Kaipara, and that is to get out on the water of this vast harbour and see its winding and mangrove-tangled shores float past in the same way that thousands of timber-seeking seafarers once did.

KAITAIA

The far north's dominant town, its 5000 people are often a mellow mix of Maori and Yugoslav. Outside the town a sign greets the traveller in three languages: Maori, Serbo-Croat and English. Grown on kauri gum-digging ($40 million-worth of gum was dug in the region), sustained in the 20th century by the growth of farming, easy-going and mostly summery Kaitaia is now also distinctly flavoured by mounting tourist interest in the far north. It is the base for minibus excursions along NINETY MILE BEACH to CAPE REINGA and for excursions to the AHIPARA gumfields and coastline. The town's Far North Regional Museum in South Road is superb.

In traditional New Zealand small-town mould, Kaitaia was founded by missionaries in 1834. Access to Ninety Mile Beach is only a few kilometres either from Waipapakauri or Ahipara. North is the Aupouri Forest, where newly planted pines hold some of the 29 000 hectares of drifting sand that invades the far north. Omahuta Forest Sanctuary (38 kilometres south-east of Kaitaia, access road off Highway 1) has some of the most impressive kauri left standing.

KAWAKAWA

Upriver market town (population 1600) for the BAY OF ISLANDS. Motorists share the road with trains in the main street. Near by is RUAPEKAPEKA pa, Hone Heke's fortress in the 1840s war. Just south are the fascinating limestone formations of the Waiomio Caves (conducted tours daily).

KERIKERI

A greenly secluded jewel in the crown of the BAY OF ISLANDS, upriver Kerikeri is New Zealand's best known citrus-growing centre, but also prospers with kiwifruit and other tropical species on rich black volcanic soil. With a population of 1700, it is a leafy retreat for the artistic, eccentric and retired. It is Northland's most culturally sophisticated centre.

The Kerikeri Basin has two of New Zealand's architectural treasures. Kemp House, the country's oldest wooden dwelling, missionary-built of pit-sawn kauri in 1821, has been splendidly refurbished by the NZ Historic Places Trust (open daily to the public except Christmas Day, Good Friday, 10.30–12.30, 1.30–4.30). An oil lamp in the window once guided mariners up the estuary. Today an electric lamp still does so. The neighbouring old Stone Store (1833), originally a mission store, then an ammunition magazine during Hone Heke's war, is the country's oldest stone structure. Today it is a small general grocery with upstairs museum.

Across the water is Rewa's Village, a meticulous reconstruction of a pre-European Maori village (open daily). Craft workers colour Kerikeri's community. Travel past New Zealand's oldest road towards WAIMATE NORTH Mission House.

KOHUKOHU

Tiny upriver HOKIANGA village with a history as old as European New Zealand. A bawdy timber town from the 1830s, with a population of 2000 at the turn of the century, it now musters less than 200. The once busy commercial seafront area (largely built on the compacted sawdust that also clogged Hokianga waterways) has twice been devastated by fire, and is now a few sad remnants, but a rich colonial atmosphere still prevails in the residential area behind it. There has been more loving restoration of Victorian kauri homes here than anywhere else in Northland, largely by craft workers and alternative lifestylers who began taking over the village in the 1970s and now outnumber the original locals.

A stone bridge crossing a creek in the school grounds is said to be the country's oldest. New Zealand's first Catholic mass was celebrated near by in 1838; a memorial 8 kilometres north on Totara Point marks the site. To the west is the superb 24 kilometre ocean beach of Mitimiti. An hourly car ferry links Kohukohu with **RAWENE** on the south side of the Hokianga.

MANGONUI

Principal settlement of **DOUBTLESS BAY**, originally a whalers' base and timber port. Sometimes vessels still crowd offshore. Pioneer atmosphere is retained with its old kauri homes climbing steep slopes, and its seaside buildings. A sea-lab and aquarium is open daily.

MATAKOHE

A hamlet 46 kilometres south of **DARGAVILLE**, near the shore of **KAIPARA HARBOUR**. The Otamatea Kauri and Pioneer Museum is quite the most extraordinary and vivid specialist museum in New Zealand – devoted almost entirely to the kauri tree. All the romance of pioneer Northland parades past in magnificent displays. It is best visited before or after a trip through **WAIPOUA KAURI FOREST**. Matakohe was the birthplace of the country's first native-born prime minister, Gordon Coates, and a memorial church opposite the museum records the fact. He is buried nearby.

NINETY MILE BEACH

Its mesmerising sweep – nearer 90 kilometres – is best comprehended from the air or from the gumland plateau behind **AHIPARA** at the south end of the beach. Although the world land-speed record was made here by Australian Norman 'Wizard' Smith in 1932, a motorist may find its entire length dull and certainly corrosive driving (a bus tour from **KAITAIA** or the **BAY OF ISLANDS** is a safer bet). A surfcasting contest every January offers thousands of dollars in prizes and draws thousands of people too. Any other day in the year, the visitor may feel the whole beach is his or her own. Toheroa, the shellfish for which the beach is famed, can seldom be taken now; instead, try the tuatua.

OMAPERE

Village on south side of entrance to **HOKIANGA HARBOUR**. Omapere has a superb outlook up-harbour, across the wild sand bar that has taken its toll of shipping since sailors first ventured here, and over the immense sand dunes that have swallowed the north side of the Hokianga entrance. There is good swimming, fishing, and a fascinating walkway from the end of Signal Station Road. The remains of Hokianga pilot station can be seen. A blowhole on the open sea is impressive at high tide. Omapere and neighbouring **OPONONI** are the only resorts on the Hokianga.

OPONONI

This gentle **HOKIANGA** village had a season in the world's headlines in 1955–56 when a wild dolphin, named Opo after the village, befriended the human race here for an all-too-short summer (see page 41). In a scene suggestive of some biblical miracle, hundreds stampeded into the sea when Opo appeared. A sculpture by Russell Clark outside the Opononi pub recalls the event. Anthony Alpers' *Book of Dolphins* tells the tale. Opo's grave is near by.

Behind the pub one of the Hokianga's grandest surviving dwellings may be glimpsed (no public access), the homestead of pioneer John Webster (1870) and once the centre of social life on the harbour. The cannon outside were retrieved from a wreck on the Hokianga bar. The sea wall is built of ballast dumped from timber ships to carry kauri to convict Sydney.

Tours of the harbour leave from Opononi wharf. Author Frederick Maning's fortress-like homestead (*c.* 1865), with the first Maori land court alongside, can be seen on the point at Onoke (it is in private hands). At nearby Pakanae, on the road up-harbour, stands a memorial to Polynesian navigator Kupe featuring what is said to be his anchorstone. The conical hill opposite, Whiria, figures prominently in views of the Hokianga painted by the visiting English artist Augustus Earle in 1827. On the summit of this one-time fortress is a memorial to a 16th-century chief, Rahiri, who united the Ngapuhi tribe from here to the Bay of Islands.

PAIHIA

With a population of 2100, it is the principal **BAY OF ISLANDS** resort centre. Indiscriminate 20th-century development now swamps its 19th-century associations. Yet it was here that beleaguered missionaries built New Zealand's first church in 1823. The church of St Paul's (1926) is fourth on the site, built as a memorial to honour pioneer preachers Henry Williams and his brother William. It was in Paihia that possibly one of the country's first mixed marriages, between a blacksmith and a Maori girl, was celebrated in 1830. In 1835 New Zealand's first successful printing press functioned here, later to publish the Treaty of Waitangi.

Bay of Islands cruises and big-game fishing trips leave from the busy Paihia wharf. There are also bus tours to the far north and **CAPE REINGA**.

Along the sunny, sandy foreshore, plaques mark historic events. Moored by **WAITANGI** bridge, the three-masted, fully rigged barque *Tui* houses the Museum of Shipwrecks; many relics of New Zealand's shipwrecks are on display. Over the bridge is the Waitangi Treaty House.

PAKARAKA

Near Ohaeawai, close to the junction of Highways 1 and 10 and some 12 kilometres from the soothing Ngawha hot springs, this small town is the site of two of Northland's most distinguished buildings. The Retreat (1850) was the handsome home of the distinguished missionary Henry Williams (1782–1867) after his retirement in disgrace. Across the road is the exquisite little Holy Trinity Church (1851), built by Williams and his sons. In the oak-shaded churchyard Williams, his wife and other members of his family are buried. Williams's disgrace was due to supposedly dishonest land dealings with the Maoris. He was exonerated in 1939, more than 70 years after his death.

PUHOI

Pioneered by bold Bohemians in the 1860s, this tiny community less than an hour's drive from urban Auckland, just off the route north on Highway 1, can be considered the beginning of Northland. Descendants of the early colonists who braved wild ocean, winding river and dense forest to establish themselves here (from a region of Europe far from the sea) now prosper the length of New Zealand, but enough remain to give the valley distinct character. A little of the old language is still spoken. A Bohemian band can often be heard in the pub on Saturdays. A wayside shrine – rare in New Zealand – greets the visitor at the entrance to the village. The Church of St Peter and St Paul dates from 1881 and expresses the devout character of the then isolated colonists. (The New Zealand expression 'up the boo-ay', meaning lost in the wilderness, supposedly derives from 'up at Puhoi'.) There is also a museum, but Puhoi's *pièce de résistance* is its amiable old pub; festooned with photographs and pioneer relics. (It was once known as 'the German hotel'.) Aucklanders, particularly on sunny summer days, travel more than 50 kilometres north to savour its atmosphere.

RAWENE

Perhaps Northland's most picturesquely placed village. The churches and dwellings of its 350 people cluster on a lean shoulder of land in upper **HOKIANGA HARBOUR** and many of its shops are perched on stilts over the water. Its older buildings are testimony to the community's colourful and robust past.

Rawene was almost New Zealand's first planned settlement (in the 1820s) but prospective settlers fled at first sight of Maori tribesmen in a feuding mood. Later it was a timber town of substance, with a large and long-lasting mill that prospered from the kauri-gum trade. In 1898 the town was evacuated when a large armed clash between Maori and European seemed to be shaping, sparked by the imposition of a tax on dogs, which nearby Maoris refused to pay. It was a far from comic affair, despite its seemingly trivial cause. Maoris saw the tax as a last straw in a decade of grief, with lands lost and their

FATHER OF NEW ZEALAND'S LITERATURE

Hokianga's most celebrated citizen lived at Onoke Point for forty years. His homestead still stands there

Literature had an odd beginning in New Zealand, which was, and is, a land with no Homer or Chaucer. Translations of Maori oral tales, the country's nearest equivalent, were published in 1854 by Sir George Grey. But a native literature of New Zealand as such began in the eighteen-thirties with the unlikely Frederick Maning, an adventurer, trader and sawmiller in the early, lawless days of Northland's Hokianga.

As he lay dying in London, Frederick Maning, the witty chronicler of life along the Hokianga Harbour, asked that his body be returned to the land he loved

Dublin-born in 1811, Maning arrived on the Hokianga via Hobart. He found the Northland location to his liking, married a Maori woman by whom he had four children, and settled on Onoke Point.

In the eighteen-sixties, when New Zealand society was more sedate and the wild heyday of the Hokianga already a faint memory, Maning composed and published two manuscripts of unusual power, wit and distinction under the pseudonym 'A Pakeha-Maori'. *Old New Zealand*, subtitled 'A Tale of the Good Old Times'; and *War in the North*, an extraordinary feat of mimicry, in which the tale of Hone Heke's war against colonial authorities during the eighteen-forties is convincingly narrated in the words of a Maori.

Both books may be seen as more fiction than fact; the liveliness of Maning's imagination is always apparent. Alas for New Zealand, Maning did not pursue the literary life. He destroyed later manuscripts as his relationships with the Maori race, and particularly with his half-Maori children, turned sour. In 1865 he was appointed Judge of the Maori Land Court. He died in 1883 while seeking a reprieve from cancer in London, and his body was taken home to New Zealand. On his gravestone are his last words: 'Let me be buried in the faraway land I loved so well.'

Down a path from the Treaty House is a large carved canoe, capable of carrying 150 paddlers and passengers. It was built from three large kauri trees for the 1940 centenary celebration, and is used on ceremonial occasions.

An excellent visitors' centre offers an audio-visual show. A walkway from the Treaty House takes visitors through to the Haruru Falls, much admired and painted by early travellers. There is also a boardwalk through mangrove forest where marine life swarms and magnificent specimens of mangroves can be seen (on the frost-free shore of Northland they can grow to 9 metres). The Waitangi Resort Hotel provides a Maori feast and historical pageant on Sunday evenings (October to March).

WARKWORTH

Sleek country town, 69 kilometres north of Auckland, set on the winding Mahurangi River, with pleasure-craft moored in the town centre. Settled before 1830 by timber men, today its population of 2000 services local rural and resort industries. There is access from here to the lovely shores of the Mahurangi Peninsula with its offshore islands and islets, to the attractive coast of Leigh and to historic Kawau Island by regular ferry from Sandspit (see page 63).

Parry Kauri Park and the Warkworth Museum are just south of the town. The park has a huge 800-year-old tree, and the museum displays interesting relics of the timber and kauri-gum trade. The town is best known for its satellite-earth station, 5 kilometres south. It has a public observation gallery.

WHANGAREI

Northland's one city, and undisputed capital of the thinly populated region, has a population of more than 40 000. Its urban character has lately been accelerated by the building of an oil refinery and oil-fired power station at nearby Marsden Point on large and convoluted Whangarei Harbour.

Satellite-earth station near Warkworth

The attractions of Whangarei's natural environment are many, but the sea-flavoured city itself holds some pleasing surprises. Not least of these is the remarkable Clapham Clock Museum (weekdays 10–4; weekends and holidays 10.15–3), where 500 clocks of three centuries click, tick, ding and sing the hours away.

The Northland Regional Museum, 8 kilometres along Highway 14 to DARGAVILLE, incorporating the Clarke homestead (1885), has a growing collection of colonial buildings that have been shifted here and restored. There are working exhibits in the 25 hectare park and demonstrations of bullock teams at work are regular. Contact information office in Forum North building.

Especially notable are the Oruaiti Chapel (1861) and the odd hexagonal tower where Northland novelist Jane Mander (1877–1949) wrote, among other things, *The Story of a New Zealand River*. A fine view of Whangarei and its harbour can be seen from the war memorial on 241 metre Parahaki. Along the road to Ngunguru are Mair Park, with bush walks and picnic area; the A.H. Reed Memorial Park, with stands of kauri; and the impressive Whangarei Falls. Two drives from the city are especially appealing. One is out to the harbour head past the strange rock outcrops of Manaia and to the beach at Pataua. The other is north to Tutukaka (where sightseeing and diving trips may be taken out to the Poor Knights Islands), and to beautiful bays and coves farther up the coast.

WHANGAROA HARBOUR

The wandering entrance to this far northern harbour, hardly visible from the small settlement on its eastern shore, makes it one of New Zealand's most spectacular. Its fiord-like character comes from jagged volcanic pinnacles soaring from the waterside and, in particular, the curious domes of St Peter and St Paul at its head. History has added its own drama. In 1809 the convict vessel *Boyd*, here to take on kauri spars, was razed to the waterline. More than 60 people were slaughtered and at least some apparently served up in a cannibal feast. The massacre stemmed from the ill-treatment of Maori seamen during the vessel's voyage from Sydney. It was widely publicised through the Pacific and beyond. For a few years many mariners had second thoughts about closing with the New Zealand coast. Certainly all gave Whangaroa a wide berth. Today it is a base for big-game fishing. A two-hour cruise from Whangaroa township takes visitors over the water where the remains of the *Boyd* rest, and on to the dramatic harbour entrance. There are also harbourside walkways. Remnants of much-plundered kauri forest can be seen in the 8000 hectare Puketi Forest which straddles the Northland peninsula between Whangaroa and the HOKIANGA. Information on walking tracks can be obtained at forest headquarters.

THE PIOUS PIONEER

He led hundreds of fellow Scotsmen a fantastic dance round the globe and finally delivered them into a promised land – at Waipu

Reverend Norman McLeod, centre, with members of his congregation at Waipu

Early Northland was coloured by many colonisers larger than life-size. By far the most ferocious and God-fearing was that ruthless autocrat, the Reverend Norman McLeod.

Born in 1780 of farmer-fishing stock in Sutherlandshire, he studied for the ministry, but found himself at odds with the established Church of Scotland. For a time he went back to fishing, but never ceased teaching and preaching. He denounced the Church as a harlot, men of the ministry as flabby and loose-living. Moral purity was his message. He was especially damning of women as crinolined and beribboned tempters and corrupters of the sons of Adam. Soon McLeod had a church of his own and a following.

It was the time of clearances in the Scottish Highlands. Small farmers were fleeing starvation by emigrating to Canada and other countries. Rather than war with the Church further, McLeod chose pastures new, perhaps free of vice, in Nova Scotia. He sailed there in 1817 with his wife, two sons and a few parishioners. The first stop was Pictou, a rough and ready boom town, which seemed a suburb of Sodom. His fiery sermons, denouncing the fallen condition of its inhabitants, nonetheless drew crowds.

In 1819 McLeod sailed on, in a vessel he built and named *The Ark*, and founded his own community at Saint Ann's on Cape Breton. For over thirty years he ruled as magistrate, preacher and bullying baron, while his parishioners worked his farm. There was no mercy in the man. A boy accused of theft had his ear cut off on McLeod's command.

When dissidence grew and his community divided, McLeod – though now more than seventy years old – thought it time to try again. In 1851, with his wife, six sons, two daughters and a hundred and forty loyal followers, he sailed for South Australia. He lost three sons to typhoid and others of his flock to gold fever. Finally he decided to move across the Tasman to New Zealand.

In September 1854 McLeod's people took up coastal land at Waipu, south of Whangarei. A sturdy and devout community grew fast, supplemented by arrivals in five ships from Nova Scotia. Even old enemies sold up and followed their fierce Moses. Soon nearly nine hundred settlers were cutting into Northland forests, building homes, establishing farms.

Patriarch McLeod preached four times on Sunday, twice in Gaelic, twice in English, and never ceased patrolling his domain to keep the devil at bay. One Waipu tale says that when a girl became pregnant out of wedlock she was, on McLeod's order, locked up in her room and never seen again –nor was the child.

McLeod died in 1866, twelve years after founding the Waipu settlement. His followers fought to carry his coffin. No minister was thought worthy of taking his place in the pulpit, which remained empty for years. One story says it was dismembered and the pieces shared among his flock.

Today descendants of McLeod's successful Waipu settlers number tens of thousands, the length and breadth of the country.

Auckland

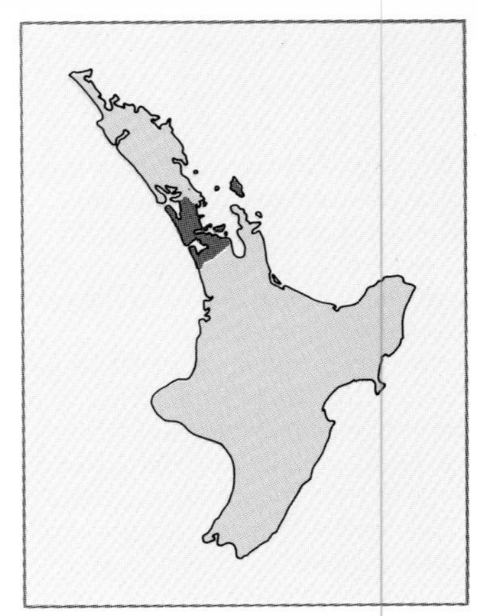

The Maori named the isthmus of New Zealand's largest city, washed by the tides of two harbours, *Tamaki-makau-rau*, 'the place of a hundred lovers'. Today it has a million suitors – nearly one third of the country's population. Close to that number disport themselves spaciously across Auckland's urban expanses. A modest enough population by international standards, but in dimension the city outdistances many of the European capitals. A metropolis? Well, yes, an Aucklander would say. Well, no, a sour outsider might argue, citing an untidy collection of suburbs with no centre, no soul. Auckland's problem is that it began as a protest against planners. Though politicians and civic leaders have tried to harness it, the place has been on a runaway course for most of its one hundred and fifty years.

Unlike New Zealand's other main cities, Auckland stumbled into existence. When New Zealand began as a British colony in 1840, Captain William Hobson governed the country from the Bay of Islands. A more central and spacious capital was needed, and the Auckland isthmus was chosen. Always warred over, the isthmus between Waitemata and Manukau Harbours had lately been depopulated by the muskets of Northland's Ngapuhi tribe. The surviving Ngati Whatua parted with what is now central Auckland in return for blankets, trousers, tomahawks, pipes and tobacco.

When Hobson arrived to take up residence he found a shipload of colonists making camp on the Auckland shore. In flight from the New Zealand Company's elegant planners in Wellington, these refugees wanted no part of Edward Gibbon Wakefield's little Britain of the South Seas. Forelock-tugging was not in their scheme of things. So Auckland began, at first no more than a few huts and tents under the Union Jack on a scrubby, muddy foreshore.

Today no one is quite sure where Auckland begins and ends – it seems to be about eighty kilometres long, and between one and ten wide. And it still grabs green land north and south. It lies about thirty-six degrees south of the equator with 'a sort of shipboard weather', as poet C.K. Stead has described it, an amiable if moist climate of no extremes. On the west coast its limits are largely defined by the vast and shallow Manukau Harbour; on the east coast by the deep Waitemata. Beyond the Waitemata's one hundred and twelve square kilometres is the Hauraki Gulf, with a wealth of islands.

The human explosion mirrors that of nature. Auckland began with a bang and may end with one. For fifty thousand years before humans arrived, more than fifty volcanoes hammered out its landscape, averaging one eruption every thousand years, and made a shaky bridge between the subtropical north and the temperate south of the North Island. When the earth finished heaving, water lapped among cooling limbs of lava, lacing the isthmus with creeks. Mangrove and fern greened their banks. The last and largest of the volcanoes, Rangitoto, the serene and symmetrical island which shelters the entrance to Waitemata Harbour, erupted only seven hundred and fifty years ago, after the first Polynesians had begun to settle near by. Geologists say the volcanic story is still unfinished. Aucklanders listen with no more than mild interest.

Maori defending this fertile and coveted region found a practical use for Auckland's volcanic cones. Tens of thousands of labourers with primitive tools and buckets levelled off the untidy cones and patiently built them up again as elaborate fortresses to command the isthmus. Three centuries of constant restyling and reshaping made them seemingly impregnable, so that they became almost as artificial a creation as Egypt's pyramids – and are surely one of the world's least known wonders, ranking with the Great Wall of China or Stonehenge as marvels of human enterprise. Today only tourists, lovers, joggers and kite-flying children populate these abandoned bastions.

HARD-WON PROSPERITY

Besieged in Classic Maori times, the isthmus was beleaguered in the nineteenth century too. In the eighteen-sixties, its citizens made ready for a long siege by Waikato Maoris contesting British sovereignty. Every fit male Aucklander between fifteen and sixty-three was pressed into military service. Refugee colonists streamed back into town from disputed lands to the south. And British troops marched off to battle.

Peace brought no joy. Without military custom Auckland was impoverished. As a final humiliation, Wellington was thought a more convenient site for the capital of the colony. Aucklanders were slow to recover. Prosperity came first with gold strikes on the nearby Coromandel Peninsula, then with the kauri timber and gum trade, and finally and durably with the expansion of agriculture, speeded by the founding of the frozen-meat trade with Britain in the eighteen-eighties. New road and rail links made Auckland the port for a large hinterland.

By 1900 Auckland had five hundred gas lamps, sixty thousand people, and a rough and ready society of democratic temper. The Auckland working man was notoriously difficult: if dissatisfied with his lot, he was likely to head off for cheap land, or go north to the gumfields.

After the Depression of the nineteen-thirties had demonstrated New Zealand's vulnerability, and the Second World War its need for self-sufficiency, industry grew. There was no looking back; Auckland left all other New Zealand cities behind. By 1964, with the Waitemata bridged at last and new suburbs appearing, Auckland was home to half a million people. In twenty years there were more than another three hundred thousand. The millionth Aucklander is due around 1990. For a country so dependent on agriculture, a city of such substance seems incongruous; small wonder that southerners see Auckland as making New Zealand top-heavy.

POLYNESIA'S NEW PARADISE

Aucklanders, meanwhile, get on with making the best of it. This poses no great problem in a city of a thousand bays and beaches, one which sings of the Pacific in everyday life. After the Second World War, small trading vessels, which chugged into port with copra, bananas, cacao and citrus from the tropical Pacific, began bringing people too. Since then the jet plane has taken over the task and Auckland is now home to tens of thousands of migrant Pacific Islanders.

Auckland has the greatest concentration of Polynesians in the Pacific, from Samoa, the Cook Islands and Tonga as well as from rural regions of New Zealand. Wellington may be the capital of New Zealand, but Auckland is the capital of Polynesia. Some twenty Polynesian languages and dialects are spoken. Garments such as the lava-lava and muu-muu colour staid colonial streets. The Polynesian population, including Maoris, approaches one hundred and fifty thousand. Auckland has become the paradise towards which the so-called people of paradise most aspire.

The city's character has been flavoured by the appearance of *marae* – meeting places and carved meeting-houses – by markets Polynesian in colour and commotion, by Samoan cricketers in teams of a hundred or more swarming over inner-city parklands. A bronze sculpture of a Maori chief, a tribute to the original people of the isthmus, presides over the foot of Queen Street.

PLACE OF A MILLION LOVERS

Up to 1950, most outsiders saw the city as a stolid and dull Anglo-Saxon outpost, in spite of Rudyard Kipling's flattering description, 'Last, loneliest, loveliest, exquisite, apart . . .' New Zealand writers, especially from the south, have been less kind. The impish Denis Glover wrote, 'Auckland in its indolence and conceit is far worse than any other part of New Zealand. Untypical, even when they speak English, Aucklanders honestly consider they *are* New Zealand.' D'Arcy Cresswell, a wandering pedlar of poems, announced that Aucklanders were 'grasping in business, destructive and wanton in Nature, dishonest in dealing and dissolute with their lives, but delightful to know, lavish and open with strangers, loving indulgence and pleasure, and more acclimatized than New Zealanders elsewhere, with whom they have little in common . . .'

Auckland writers, of course, see their city differently. Poet Allen Curnow, long acclimatised to the landscape, sees 'Latin skies upon Chinese lagoons' and a 'tousled, sunny-mouthed, sandy-legged coast'. When leisure-loving Aucklanders are not sailing, they are probably fishing. Auckland claims the greatest number of pleasure-craft per head of any world city. There is one to every four households. In summer it seems half the population is seaborne.

Culturally the city has grown lively too. There are professional theatres, and dealer galleries and craft shops at every turn. Auckland's distinctive culture is its own, not a nineteenth century colonial transplant shallowly rooted in native soil. It has grown with the city from inner need and matures with it. And the Polynesian influx already makes its cultural life more piquant. It is a city that has never been much given to airs and graces, never much inclined to be other than it is. No one could ever identify the Auckland isthmus as a lost limb of Mother England. It is very much a Pacific original.

What of its sprawl, though, the despair of tidy planners? The fact is that Aucklanders see no virtue in living like bees in a large urban hive. High-density housing has not been their inheritance, nor do they see it as a legacy for their children. They demand space and sea and sun. 'Auckland', predicted one awed American town planner, 'will become one of the great new cities of the world by the environmental and recreational standards of our time. And I am betting on it.' Aucklanders wouldn't hesitate to have a flutter too.

AMP

Next to Victoria Park Market, the Leopard was first established in 1857, only seventeen years after the colony was founded. Now gracefully restored and rebuilt in places, it serves Leopard Lager, a popular New Zealand beer

Queen Street is still the city's busiest thoroughfare. Auckland's central business district has developed along Queen Street, dictating the changing face of the city

Auckland's modern cityscape is seen through a Japanese designed contemporary steel sculpture that acts as a shade over a public rest area at Queen Elizabeth Square

OF MARKETS AND MONEY

From the city's centre to its outermost suburbs, Auckland is a mosaic of many markets with character

Markets made cities; cities make markets. Auckland's first market, near the foot of Queen Street, was Maori. Tribesmen arriving in canoes, and later in sailing vessels, sold meat, fish and vegetables to famished British colonists who were beginning to settle the Waitemata shore.

Queen Street, once a swampy canyon hosting a murky creek, is now typical of the big-city golden mile. Its skyline changes shape from year to year as fast dollars flow into further speculation. Here, and in arcades wandering off it as well as in neighbouring small streets, are most of the high fashion boutiques, galleries, craft and souvenir shops one might expect of any modern city. Two interestingly restored arcades dating from early this century are Queens Arcade with forty-nine shops and the Edwardian Strand Arcade, Queen Street's oldest.

Above: *Victoria Park Market, housed in the shell of the city's old rubbish destructor, is an example of successful urban renewal* **Right:** *Avondale market specialises in Pacific Island food for its predominantly Polynesian neighbourhood*

Just off Queen Street, at 22 Customs Street, is the Customhouse. Built in the eighteen-eighties and saved from developers in the nineteen-eighties, this is the best surviving example of the monumental Victorian architecture that once distinguished Auckland's commercial heart. Inside, the building has been remodelled to accommodate craft and fashion shops, a tavern, a restaurant and a cinema-cum-theatre. Adjoining the Customhouse is the busy Albert Street Market, open on weekends with art and craft stalls.

Karangahape Road, running along a ridge above the central city, is where Auckland shows its Pacific face; and mostly a brown one. This street services the tens of thousands of Maoris and Islanders who have taken up inner-city residence since Polynesian migration into Auckland became a stampede after the Second World War. This street was never especially fashionable, and until

Above: *The monumental Victorian building that was once the Customhouse now plays host to craft shops, restaurants and a theatre* **Below:** *The up-beat atmosphere of Parnell Village is reflected in its trendy boutiques and cafés*

lately, down-at-heel. Restaurateurs have moved in, but its shops remain traditional. Its north-western end is distinctly dedicated to the flesh, with massage parlours and strip clubs. Beyond the gaudy blaze of neon at the junction of Karangahape and Ponsonby roads, the lively Ponsonby Fair Market fills with inner-city bargain hunters on Sunday mornings.

Ponsonby Road is third in this pecking order. On the seaward side of the road young professionals have moved in and renovated the colonial buildings of a once decadent district. The landward side remains traditionally working class, now with many Polynesians. Ponsonby Road, however, caters to both groups. Up-market delicatessens, restaurants, boutiques and furniture stores share commercial space with butchers and bakers; antique shops with tried and true second-hand dealers. There is a strong emphasis on interior design business, and there is also almost the last of Auckland's traditional grill shops: Ivan's, which is popular with taxi-drivers on late shifts. The road is an intriguing medley of trend and tradition.

CONSERVATION AND CANNIBALISATION

Downhill, between Ponsonby Road and Queen Street, Victoria Park Market in Freemans Bay is one of Auckland's most spectacular and certainly most original pieces of urban renovation. The city's one-time rubbish destructor, built in 1901 and closed in 1972, has been vividly transformed. Stables for the hundred horses that once collected inner-city rubbish have now become specialty shops. The names of the horses are perpetuated in the names of the carts that trade in the mall. There is nothing especially precious about the restoration; nor are the merchants hard on the pocket. There are three craft markets, three restaurants, and fish, meat, and fresh vegetables. And there is entertainment at weekends.

Across the city and up-market again, is Parnell Village, situated in Auckland's first suburb. Here, the maverick and conservation-minded property developer Les Harvey, honoured for his services to Auckland, saved several splendid city dwellings from destruction. He also haunted demolition yards and harvested remains of buildings gutted by wreckers. Magically, he patched them together, giving new life to much precious Victoriana. The result is a marvellously elegant colonial Disneyland owing as much to cannibalisation as conservation. Lanes, stairways and boardwalks lead the visitor through a maze of boutiques, design stores, furniture shops, craft galleries, restaurants and cafés.

Most colourful of all the city's markets however, are those that have grown in Polynesian-settled suburbs like Otara in the south, and Avondale to the west. Otara's ebullient flea market spills over space beside the Otara Town Centre on Saturday morning, Avondale's market over enclosures at Avondale racecourse on Sunday morning. The emphasis is on food, especially Maori and Pacific Island – kumara, taro, puha and pawpaw, fish and fowl – but hunters of bric-a-brac and antiques can find bargains too. Here the wheel of history seems to have come full circle. These markets have all the clamour the city's first Maori market had one hundred and fifty years ago.

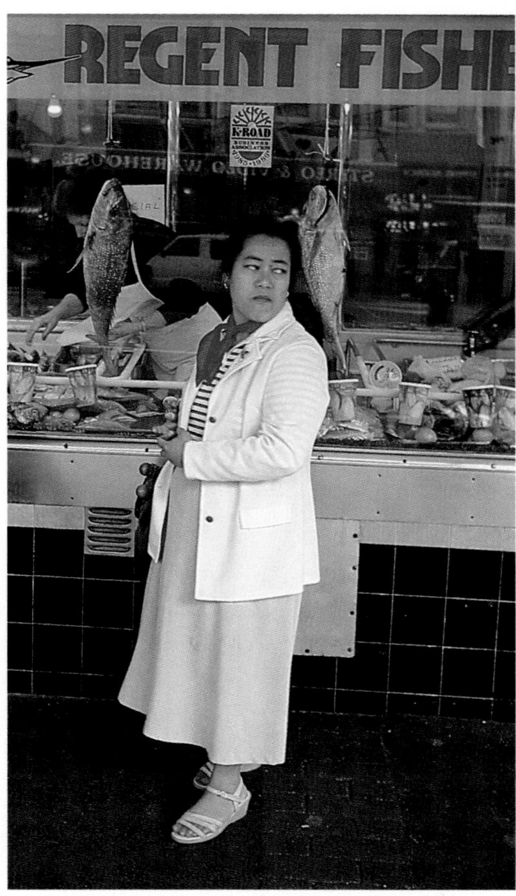

Traditional rather than fashionable, the fish and fruit shops of Karangahape Road are popular with Auckland's large inner-city Polynesian population. Restaurateurs are now moving into the street

THE SELWYN CHURCHES

Auckland boasts some of the finest examples of these wooden churches which are a lyrical expression of New Zealand's colonial past

The city has seldom managed to grow with much grace – its face still changes inelegantly. In the meantime many of its finest Victorian buildings have been demolished while approaching their prime. If the city has a still centre, it is to be found in the so-called Selwyn churches.

Selwyn was not their architect: the name merely acknowledges the distinctive ecclesiastical architecture – it has been called a *tour de force* – which evolved during George Augustus Selwyn's quarter-century as Anglican Bishop of New Zealand from 1842 to 1868. Selwyn was more a man of action than a theologian. He made epic tramps through most of New Zealand during the course of his ministry. He was more a mentor than an architectural thinker. His first inclination was for Norman churches; he also favoured stone rather than wood. But when talent was disposed to adapt to local circumstances, and make free use of New Zealand materials, Selwyn let talent have its head. That talent was to take a gracefully Gothic turn; its most admirable legacies are of New Zealand timber.

The man who determined the Selwyn style was Frederick Thatcher (1814-90), an architect, later a cleric also, and Superintendent of Public Works during the eighteen-forties. His designs can be seen elsewhere in New Zealand, notably St Paul's in Wellington, the Gables hospital and St Mary's in New Plymouth.

Thatcher's first major undertaking for Selwyn was St John's College Chapel in Meadowbank, finished in 1847. The 'temporary' chapel (Selwyn remained wedded to the notion of stone) is still in use one hundred and forty years later. It has all the distinguishing features of the Selwyn style – low eaves, steep pitched shingle roofs, small narrow windows with diamond-shaped panes and timber tops stepped to echo the pointed stone arches of early English churches.

MIRACLE IN WOOD

St John's College chapel was the seedbed for Frederick Thatcher's gentle genius. Eight churches and chapels for Auckland were framed in the college workshops by European and Maori craftsmen and then transported to their sites; All Saints Church (1847) in Howick was one of these. Churches elsewhere followed Thatcher's forms. Selwyn was later to have his way with stone: the

Top: *Handsome Selwyn Court, built in 1863, is one of the country's most compelling examples of colonial architecture*

Above: *All Saints Church (1847) at Howick was planned and framed elsewhere and then transported to its present site*

Above: *Detail of the timber decoration in All Saints Church at Howick shows a combination of European and local styles*

Melanesian Mission building (1859) in Mission Bay, and St James (1857) at Mangere are two examples. The irony is that the 'Selwyn style', commonly meaning that of wooden churches, is named for a man who persisted in believing timber second best.

As for Frederick Thatcher, who formed that style, his most familiar memorial may be found at Parnell's Judges Bay. The tiny and exquisite St Stephen's Chapel (1856) is on an enchanting harbourside site where one of Selwyn's stone churches had collapsed. Thatcher again worked a small miracle in wood, in the shape of a Greek cross composed of five squares measuring three metres in each direction. Otherwise, it has all the distinguishing features of Thatcher's work: steep roof pitch, vertical boarding, lancet windows with lattice panels, rose window over the doorway and belfry over the crossing. There is no lovelier church in New Zealand (unless it is Thatcher's own All Saints at Howick). In the churchyard are the graves of prominent Auckland colonists.

Also in Parnell is the equally handsome Selwyn Court (1863), the last and precious flower of the Selwyn style in Auckland. Its delicate geometry within, its striking appearance without – it appears to be almost all roof when seen from the courtyard – make it one of New Zealand's most compelling pieces of colonial architecture. The steepled octagonal tower at the north-east end of the library is a local landmark. Although modifications have been made over the years, the building is still unmistakably Thatcher's, the man who gave New Zealand timber a tongue; and left an inspired idiom.

Above left: *The tiny St Stephen's Chapel (1856) and its charming harbourside site* **Left:** *Thatcher's initial commission for Bishop Selwyn, St John's College chapel in Meadowbank* **Below:** *The interior of the chapel*

THE FLOATING ISLANDS

Seen from a city height, these peaceful islands and islets drift in a bright haze on the horizon and melt greenly together

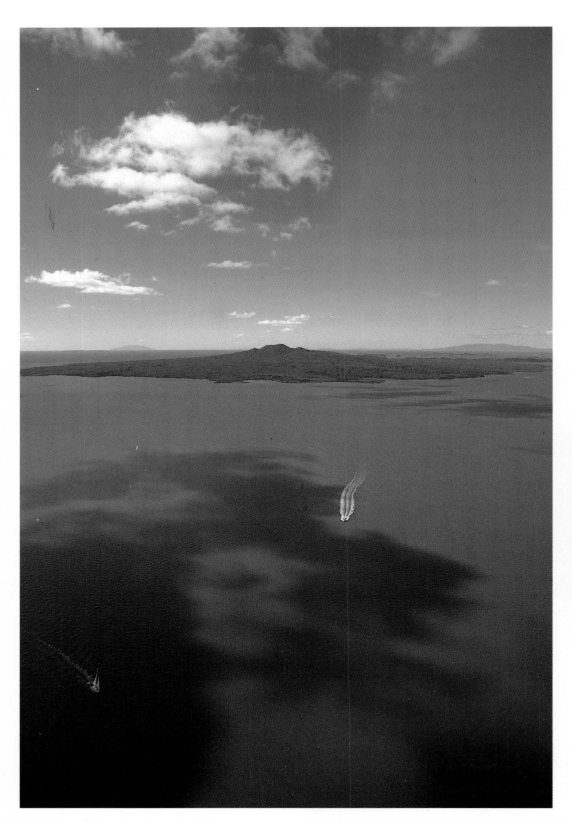

Head out towards the islands of the Hauraki Gulf Maritime Park in a launch or hovercraft, and pathways of sparkling water open between. Island after island begins to air its idiosyncrasies. Each has its own story to tell. The Maori called them *motu whakatere*, 'the floating islands'.

The youngest of the islands, Rangitoto is also the most striking. It lifts above the city skyline and shelters the sealane into Waitemata Harbour. Almost all other islands in the gulf are remnants of land never completely swallowed up by the Pacific when the last ice age ended.

Rangitoto thundered up from the seabed seven hundred and fifty years ago, and Polynesians dwelling near by were still feeling its blast in the seventeenth and eighteenth centuries. Rangitoto is the last and largest of the volcanoes that shaped the Auckland region – two hundred and sixty metres high and five kilometres in diameter. Composed entirely of lava and cinders, the island has no soil worth the name and no water. On sunny days, the surface temperature there can leap to seventy degrees Celsius. As new land, it has been fascinating to botanists, one of whom ungrammatically termed it 'the most unique island in the world'. Over two hundred native plant species, including forty ferns and twenty orchids, miraculously find sustenance in the fissured and fragmented moonscape.

Left: *Rangitoto, the flat volcanic island of lava and cinders, forms a striking centrepiece in the Hauraki Gulf*
Above: *Small waves break gently onto the shores of Kawau, one of the most settled yet still tranquil islands*

Launches carry day-trippers across to the island to tramp, browse, picnic and bathe. The four-kilometre climb to the summit offers impressive views of city and gulf. (Roads on the island were built by convict labour.)

Near by is another, older volcano, Browns Island, its lava flows now drowned by the risen sea. Its grassy and sheep-grazed slopes are marked by the walls and trenches of Maori fortification.

Above: *Once a mining centre because of its copper and manganese deposits, the now peaceful island of Kawau offers excellent scenery and many easy walks. Remnants of bygone mining days, such as the chimney above, can still be seen*

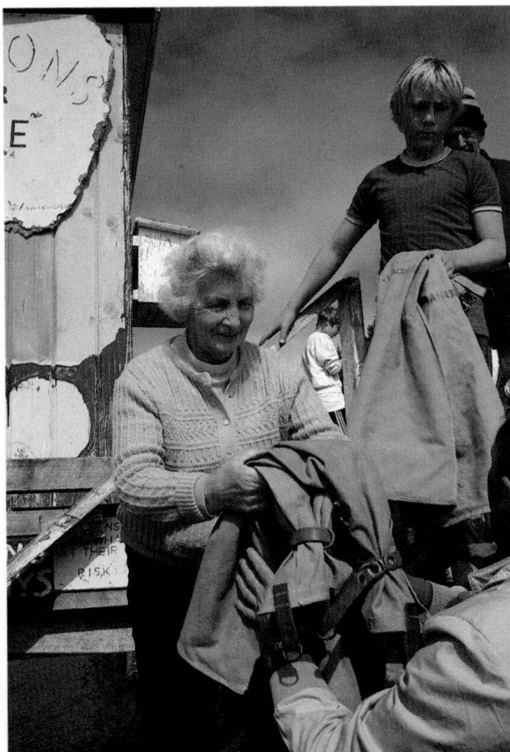

Inquisitive locals and tourists from far afield take the half-hour ferry trip to Kawau. Ferries and launches run regularly from Sandspit near Warkworth and there is an extra service during summer to transport holiday visitors

Ex-governor Sir George Grey's magnificent house has been completely restored and is open to tourists and locals

The so-called 'Father of Auckland', John Logan Campbell, purchased the island from Maoris (it was then known as Motukorea) in 1840. He drove a party of pigs ashore, feasted on oysters and with his partner William Brown became the first European settler in the Auckland region. There is no public ferry service to the island.

The rolling grassland of fifteen hundred hectare Motutapu is connected by causeway to Rangitoto. Enriched by the ash of Rangitoto's eruptions, the fertile island is now farmed as part of the Hauraki Gulf Maritime Park and is open to the public. It was settled intensively by both Archaic and Classic Maori, and their footprints have been found in the volcanic debris. Four hundred archaeological sites have been recorded. Fortifications built to protect Auckland in the Second World War share the island with the remains of old Maori forts.

Motutapu was a popular site for Victorian picnickers who were ferried over in their hundreds for the day. 'No distinguished visitor that comes to Auckland but makes a trip to Motutapu', recorded the *New Zealand Graphic*. The island was grazed by deer from England's Windsor Park, ostrich, emu and even a buffalo. Today's visitors don't have to fight through a throng of people. Ferries provide a service during summer, and there is a camping ground, also a youth camp serving Auckland schools.

Another of the gulf's popular islands, Motuihe, covers just one hundred and eighty hectares. It too was densely settled by the Maori but also holds some colourful European history. Count Felix von Luckner, the buccaneering German sea raider, was confined on the island after his capture in the First World War. In 1917 he made a dramatic escape by commandeering a timber scow and hundreds of Auckland yachtsmen gave pursuit. He was finally recaptured in the Kermadec Islands nine hundred and sixty kilometres north. Motuihe was a long-time quarantine station for Auckland, and holds graves of many victims of the 1918 influenza epidemic. It was also used as a naval training base. Today it is farmed as part of the Hauraki Gulf Maritime Park. The olive grove on the island was planted by John Logan Campbell, Auckland's first European settler. Ferries run regularly in summer.

Among the swarm of islands within the gulf, most of them accessible only to sailors, two especially stand out – Little Barrier and Tiritiri Matangi. Both are wildlife preserves. It is necessary to seek permission to land on forested Little Barrier, one of the world's most important bird sanctuaries and where endangered species like the kokako and kakapo have been successfully colonised. This is the only place where the stitchbird, for example, survives.

Tiritiri Matangi, on the other hand, is an interesting experiment in conservation as an 'open sanctuary'. Here the public can view rare animal species in the wild. The island was once farmed, but it is now being allowed to revert to native forest with plantings to speed regeneration and provide food for birds transplanted from Little Barrier and elsewhere.

KAWAU, A COLONIAL PARADISE

The three most settled islands are Kawau to the north, Waiheke at the centre and Great Barrier at the perimeter. Kawau, reverberant with early colonial history, is where Governor Sir George Grey made his own miniature Eden. It was a retreat and, for a considerable period, his home. The two-thousand-and-twenty-hectare island was uninhabited when he purchased it for three thousand five hundred pounds in 1862. The local tribe had been decimated by marauding Ngapuhi earlier in the century. Copper and manganese deposits had brought Europeans here as early as 1838, and at one stage there were two hundred people involved in mining and smelting ore. Remnants of their labours, including a twenty-one-metre-high chimney, can still be seen today.

In 1862 the mine was closed. Grey took over the mine manager's house, remodelling and extending it, and lavishing a large part of his personal fortune on the estate. He introduced Brazilian palms, Indian rhododendrons, Australian gums, Mediterranean olives and English oaks, as well as zebras, monkeys, antelopes, emus, deer, pheasants, peacocks, rosellas, kookaburras and wallabies. Up to seventeen gardeners worked on the estate.

The result was ecological disaster, but also an island of faery flavour. Visiting British historian James Froude thought it as 'pretty as Adam's garden before the Fall'. A generous host, the antipodean Prospero seldom turned visitors away. He let boating parties wander in awe through his magnificent house and grounds. 'They do no harm,' he observed, 'and goodness gracious, they might just learn something.'

Fall the paradise did finally, when Grey sold up and departed in 1888. His mansion became an increasingly down-at-heel boarding house, and then a licensed hotel. Most of the fauna he introduced failed to survive. In 1967 the Hauraki Gulf Maritime Park became the owner. The hotel was closed and in the nineteen-seventies the building and grounds were elegantly restored to their original splendour.

CASUALLY SUBURBAN WAIHEKE

Waiheke, eighteen kilometres across the water from the city, is the best known of the gulf's islands and the largest of those inshore, twenty-five kilometres long and twenty kilometres across at its widest. Fast sea transport has made it virtually a dormitory suburb of Auckland. Its population, now about five thousand, doubled between the nineteen-seventies and eighties. Land sales have soared and builders are busy.

In 1827 the French navigator Dumont d'Urville pronounced it 'admirably fitted for settlement'; his words have at last been heeded. Much of the island has been farmed for more than a century; settlement, mainly by retired people and refugees from city living, some artists and writers, has been most dense on the slender city end of the island, which is served by ferries. The casual, restful atmosphere of the island has survived the commuter invasion. It is circled by delightful beaches, the most accessible at Oneroa and at Onetangi, which has the island's one hotel. At Stony Batter are a network of tunnels and the remains of an immense gun emplacement, which guarded the gulf in the Second World War. The two small islands next to Waiheke are the resort island of Pakatoa, served from Auckland by ferry, and Rotoroa Island, a treatment centre for alcoholics administered by the Salvation Army (landing is forbidden).

Seen from the air, the grassy Motutapu Island, open to the public, is connected to Rangitoto by a causeway

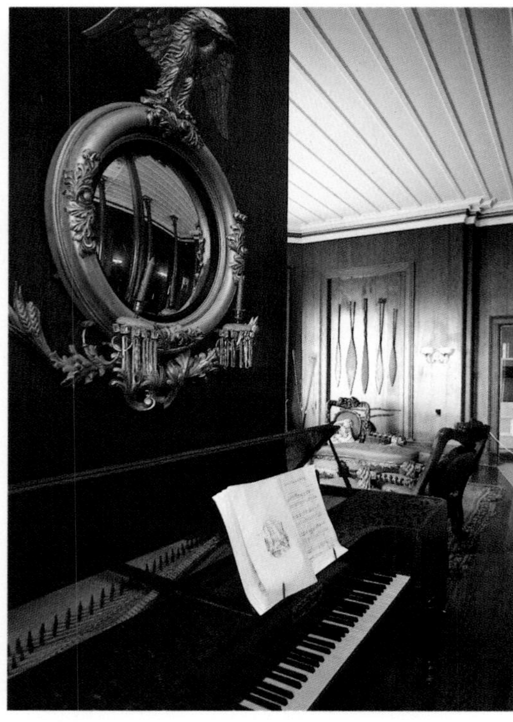

Above: *Sir George Grey would be delighted to see the rooms in his house so well restored with original artefacts*
Below: *Rangitoto, the largest volcano in the Auckland region, shelters the sealane leading into Waitemata Harbour*

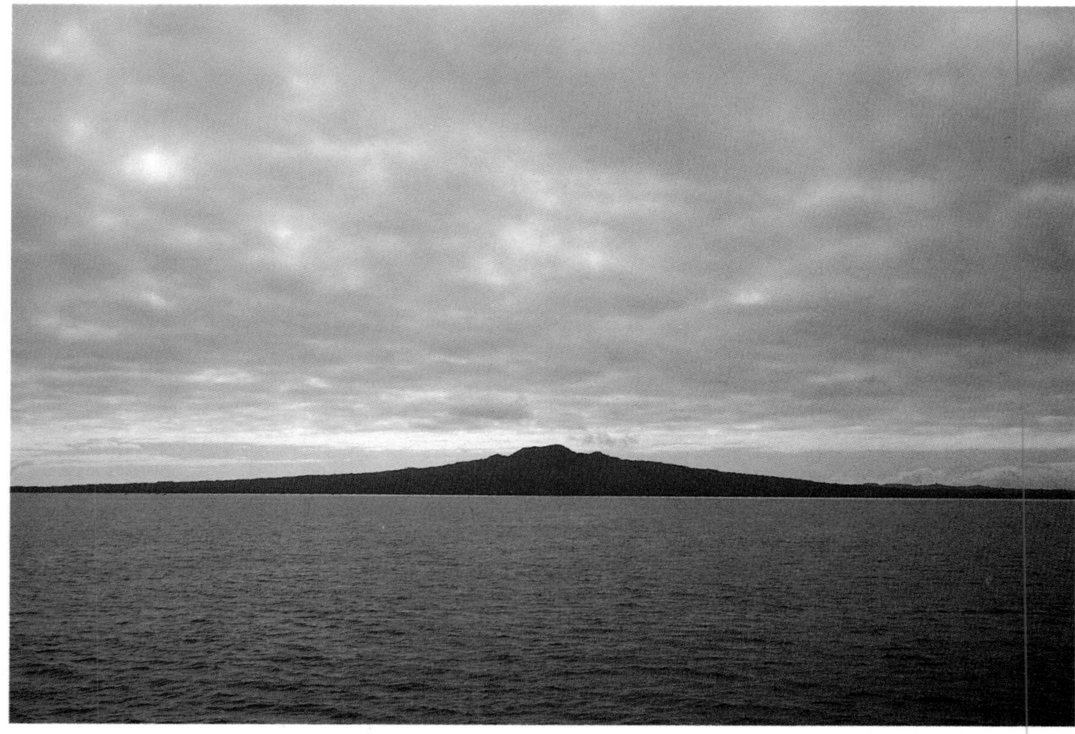

Rugged Great Barrier's two hundred and eighty-five square kilometres make it the country's fourth island and the largest off the North Island coast. Although Auckland is only one hundred kilometres across the sea, the island's eight hundred permanent residents dwell in one of the country's most isolated communities. Great Barrier is a remnant of the Coromandel Peninsula; it was severed from the mainland ten thousand years ago.

Tall stands of kauri timber once distinguished Great Barrier but they were all plundered before the end of the eighteenth century. This was the beginning of a period of ruthless exploitation of the island's few resources. After the timber men came miners, then kauri gum-diggers, and finally aspirant farmers using fire to clear the island. From the early nineteenth century until as recently as the nineteen-sixies, whalers struck at the herds of humpbacks spouting offshore. These whales have been known to beach themselves here by the hundred.

In the second half of this century the NZ Forest Service began restoration of the island's natural cover. They planted approximately seven thousand hectares of kauri with a mix of other native trees. Much of the area is now a forest park and there are one hundred kilometres of tracks. The often ravishing and pohutukawa-clad coast, where beachcombers and fishermen wander now, has been the stage for several of New Zealand's more spectacular sea dramas, notably the wreck of the *Wairarapa* in 1894, when one hundred and twenty-one people perished. With tourist accommodation readily available, and frequent air services from Auckland, Great Barrier may now be less lost to the world, but an outsider is unlikely to notice much change in the island's pace of life. Here, as elsewhere in the Hauraki Gulf, the Pacific still means peace.

LOOKING WESTWARD

Beyond the Manukau Harbour, the Waitakere Ranges and the west coast provide the city-dweller with an escape to wilderness

The east of Auckland, past the Waitemata Harbour, offers a vista of islands and blue Pacific. Look westward, and the eye falls first on the huge and shallow Manukau Harbour, with its stormy sand bar and vigorous tides tapping on the city's back door, then on the ferny summits of the Waitakere Ranges, a bulwark against the tempests of the Tasman Sea. Beyond are cliffs and roaring surf. The contrast is striking. On the one hand New Zealand mild, the other, New Zealand wild. Maori acknowledged the difference. For them the east was feminine, the west masculine. Many Aucklanders try to keep the yin and yang of their environment in balance: their homes are in the tranquil east, their weekend cottages in the turbulent west.

Much of Auckland's west is made of Manukau waters and mud flats. Unlike the Waitemata, pleasure-boats are few and far between; only the launches and powerboats of dedicated fishermen speeding along channels to the Manukau Heads. Canoe-travelling Maori appreciated the three hundred and ninety square kilometre harbour's rich supplies of food. So did the birds after which the harbour is named (*manukau* means 'the place of wading birds').

The harbour was first a great bay into which the ancestral Waikato River flowed, until sand and volcanic eruption forced it into a new route to the Tasman. The Manukau was left to its own devices. The Maori have a different story: Manukau is said to cover the fruitful land of Paorae, a lost Atlantis. It was a warm, sandy plain extending beyond the mouth of the harbour to the open sea. Kumara and taro grew in abundance and its lagoons were rich with eels and wild duck.

Fossilised kauri stumps in mud flats towards the head of the harbour seem to confirm this tale of a drowned land. Certainly offshore remnants of sandy land were still visible in the nineteenth century. Today the shifting sand banks of the Manukau entrance are all that survive of the enchanted land of Paorae.

By the time missionary Samuel Marsden, the first known white man to wonder at the vast harbour, had seen some of its four hundred kilometres of shore in 1820, the land had long gone. He noted fine timber and a safe harbour. He was at least right about the timber, which brought Sydney traders and land speculators in the eighteen-thirties.

At the western foot of the Waitakere Ranges, Piha beach is frequented during summer by surfers and swimmers

Above: *Credit for the European discovery of Manukau Harbour goes to missionary Samuel Marsden. Once busy with sailing ships and canoes, it now see only light traffic*

At one time the harbour had a short-lived settlement on indifferent land at Cornwallis. It was intended to put the present site of Auckland in the shade but it soon collapsed and famished settlers took refuge on the Waitemata shore.

The harbour proved far from safe. On 7 February, 1863, its shoaling entrance took one hundred and eighty-nine lives when HMS *Orpheus* bringing in men to fight the Waikato War foundered. This war ended much of the Manukau's Maori character. British troops, suspicious that tribesmen along the harbour might join the Waikato rebels, scoured estuaries for canoes which might bear war parties and burned and sank the vessels. (The only one spared, *Te Toki-a-Tapiri*, is in the Auckland War Memorial Museum.)

Today the harbour's shipping traffic is mainly that of small vessels working the New Zealand coast, and fishing trawlers. They moor in the port of Onehunga. Despite a lighthouse and modern aids, the sand bar still tests seamanship. The northern shore, from Titirangi to the harbour mouth, is still well wooded, with seaside homes nesting in pohutukawa and tree-fern. Even the site of ill-fated Cornwallis is now within commuter territory. Wounds left by the timber-seekers have begun to heal; young kauri grow tall. Between Titirangi and the head of the harbour, Auckland's Polynesian population wanders over sand and rocks at low tides on weekends to gather mussels and oysters and crabs, pipi and paua and cockles. They bring back to the shore something of the colour and tribal life of pre-European times.

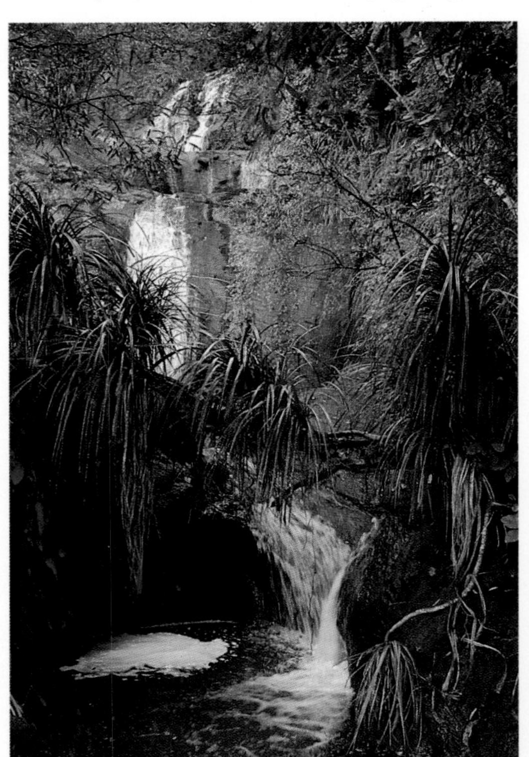

Fairy Falls' cascading water twists and tumbles over forest terraces, ending in a torrent that dumps onto the forest floor

At Piha beach, high tides beat rough surf and dangerous currents into the ironsand, on rocks and into the land

Huge, shallow Manukau Harbour appears serene but its shifting sand banks and fast tides have taken lives. Wistful Maori legend tells of a long-lost Eden beneath its waters, a land rich with nature's bounties

At Whatipu, where kauri once slid from forest tramways onto waiting vessels, the tides funnel in and out from the open sea. Here the Manukau meets with the west coast proper. To the north are Karekare, Piha, Anawhata, Te Henga (Bethells) and Muriwai beaches where surf beats up black ironsand between the sea-bitten shoulders of the Waitakere Ranges.

The Waitakeres not only muffle the biting westerly winds bound for Auckland, they provide the city with a green playground only half an hour's drive from the hot central city. A Scenic Drive, built to provide employment during the Depression, winds between Titirangi and Swanson along ridges and beneath the summits of the range. Walking tracks lead off to kauri groves, waterfalls and down to west coast beaches.

Plunder of the kauri was at its most ferocious here during the late nineteenth century. Observing the destruction, the German scientist Ferdinand von Hochstetter said, 'With the last of the Maoris the last of the Kauris will also disappear'. After watching a woodman 'triumphing over a huge monster', English novelist Anthony Trollope lamented that, 'Very soon there will not be a kauri tree left to cut down'.

They could easily have been right. But by the twentieth century, New Zealanders had a conscience about their environment. Today some six thousand five hundred hectares of the Waitakeres are protected in the Auckland Centennial Memorial Park. The most inaccessible kauri survived and young trees regenerate through the ranges. On their eastern side, slopes and valleys are softened by orchards and vineyards planted largely by descendants of Dalmatian kauri gum-diggers. It is the most concentrated wine-making region in northern New Zealand.

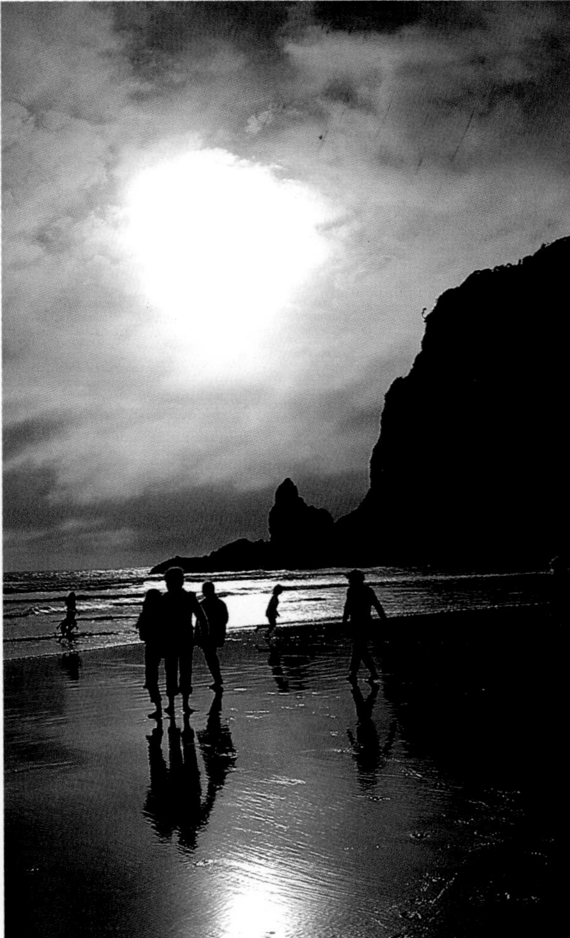

The black ironsand of Piha beach on the west coast

Nothing softens the western side;the boom of surf sounds up bush-bearded valleys. According to legend, the *Turehu*, a shy and wilderness-loving fairy people once lived here high in trees and mist. With a little patience and imagination, they can still be heard whispering. And to the south of Piha, on the ocean, an enormous marauding *taniwha*, or water monster, took huge toll of humans from an underwater cave and blowhole plainly visible at low tide. Fatalities on this coast suggest that he still does.

The few Maoris found dwelling here by the first Europeans have long gone. Today only a few terraces and pits, remnants of fortified villages, tell their story. Rusting and rotting relics of foresters' camps are also fading away.

The city has reached out in the form of weekend cottages and permanent residences, most of them at Piha and Karekare. Surfers glide in on tall waves. Families picnic under giant pohutukawa. Rock fishermen spin their lines beyond the breakers. Trampers in boots and backpacks head into the hills. Maoris leaping from rock to rock, sometimes lost beyond the spray, gather mussels from the rocks much as their ancestors did. Fortunate is the city still with wilderness close to its heart; fortunate the soul of the city-dweller partaking of it too.

PLACES OF INTEREST

VANTAGE POINTS

AUCKLAND DOMAIN
Crowned by the **AUCKLAND WAR MEMORIAL MUSEUM**, this verdant spread of inner-city parkland and sportsfield offers a striking vista of metropolis, harbour and gulf from the museum steps. Set aside by New Zealand's governor, William Hobson in 1841 when Auckland was founded, it is the city's oldest park. In Victorian times military bands serenaded Sunday strollers here.

It contains the site of the former Maori village of Pukekaora, where a memorial palisade now stands. The remarkable Waikato leader, Princess Te Puea (see page 84), planted a totara there in memory of her distinguished ancestor Te Wherowhero, who as King Potatau I became the first Maori monarch in 1858. The spring, where Californian rainbow trout were first acclimatised to New Zealand in the 1880s, provided early Auckland's water supply.

The tea kiosk and nearby band rotunda are survivors from the 1913 Auckland Exhibition, when the aspiring city paraded its wares. Behind them, the handsome and lush Winter Gardens – formed by two large glassed-over wings linked by a graceful courtyard studded with statues – are also a legacy.

BASTION POINT
Overlooking the approaches to Waitemata Harbour, the Rangitoto Channel and the nearer islands of the Hauraki Gulf, Bastion Point is a fort built not by Maori, but by Europeans in anticipation of a Russian invasion in the 1880s and later a Japanese invasion in the 1940s, neither of which came to pass.

In the 1970s however, this green space above Tamaki Drive became the most embattled piece of land since the New Zealand wars of the 19th century. Maoris squatted here for more than a year to protest against the sale of traditional and now Crown Reserve land for the building of luxury homes. Finally in 1978, in an operation involving hundreds of police, army vehicles and helicopters – a scene queerly echoing events at Parihaka in Taranaki in the 1880s when colonial militia closed on the peaceful Maori community of Te Whiti (see page 140), the shanty town was encircled, demolished and scores of arrests made. The land is now largely Maori again.

In 1940 the body of Michael Joseph Savage, the prime minister who led the country out of the Depression and into war during the 1930s, was buried in the vault of old Fort Bastion at the tip of the point, amid scenes of grief never seen before or since in New Zealand for a politician. A pleasant park has been established round the memorial.

MOUNT EDEN
Maungawhau to the Maori, this extinct volcano and former fortress 196 metres above sea level offers panoramic views from the Hauraki Gulf to the Waitakere Ranges and far Manukau Heads, and of the city's suburban tapestry. A steep but safe road takes visitors to the summit. Like most of the volcanoes on the Auckland isthmus, Mt Eden was shaped over centuries by vast Maori fortifications. Storage pits and terraces are still evident. The site accommodated up to 3000 people in times of war. Tradition says that occupation was ended by summer drought, which meant the fortress defenders during a siege were waterless, weakened and massacred. Certainly Mt Eden was no longer in business as a fortress when the first Europeans arrived. Other volcano-forts such as Mt Albert and Mt Wellington can be seen in the distance.

ONE TREE HILL (MAUNGAKIEKIE)
Another extinct volcano, vantage point and fortress. Rising 183 metres above sea level, Auckland's most distinctive landmark is known to the Maori as *Maungakiekie*, 'mountain of the kiekie plant'. Maori defence systems extended over 2.5 or more square kilometres, sheltering perhaps 4000 people, making it the greatest prehistoric fortress known to humankind. Outside the palisades the land was extensively cultivated. The summit was called *Te Totara-i-ahua*, after a lone totara tree which crowned it, to commemorate the birth of a notable Maori chief. Soon after European arrival, the tree was felled by an axe-happy colonist. Pioneer John Logan Campbell planted another tree there by way of apology to the *tangata whenua*, 'the people of the land'. A 21 metre obelisk also stands here, Campbell's tribute to the Maori. Campbell was buried on the hill top, now part of the 120 hectare Cornwall Park, his green, sheep-grazed gift to the city. The road pushes to the summit, cutting through contours moulded over centuries by the Maori.

THE GOVERNOR WHO CREATED AUCKLAND

William Hobson was a brilliant sailor, but the founder of Auckland was plagued by administrative and financial problems, and died before London could recall him

The Treaty House at Waitangi where Maori chiefs signed away their land

Lieutenant-Governor William Hobson (1793-1842) became the second governor of the colony in 1841, after the largely forgotten Sir George Gipps. Hobson is now remembered mainly for his proclamation of British sovereignty at Kororareka in 1840, for organising the Treaty of Waitangi and for his decision to purchase land on the Waitemata to build and develop the town of Auckland, which in 1841 was to become the new capital.

An enigmatic and solitary figure, Hobson died a broken leader. His portrait reveals an earnest man with pointed features and a detectable air of uncertainty, in curious contrast to his record as a brilliant sailor. He served throughout the Napoleonic Wars from the Mediterranean to the West Indies – at one stage for an uninterrupted thirteen years. He also fought pirates off the coast of Cuba where he contracted yellow fever, which later undermined his health.

In the eighteen-thirties he was posted to Australia on survey duties, where he became involved in the early planning of Melbourne. He was then selected to go to New Zealand as lieutenant-governor under Gipps (the then Governor of New South Wales) to negotiate the transfer of sovereignty of that colony to the British crown.

Hobson named his new capital after Lord Auckland who, as First Lord of the British Admiralty, had saved him from the retired list and was obviously owed a favour. Unfortunately this act brought no further luck. Hobson's brief period of governorship in Auckland was notable only for the impossible position in which he found himself. Given no soldiers to back his authority, he relied on the cooperation of Maori tribes, many of whom had not signed the Treaty of Waitangi. He was constantly needled by the New Zealand Company and by Wellington and Nelson settlers in their desire for land. But the crux of his problem was financial: there was simply not enough money in the coffers to run the colony.

Taking matters into his own hands, Hobson began to issue unauthorised Treasury bills. There is little doubt that his death in September 1842 saved him from his many enemies and a day of reckoning. It is almost certain he would have been recalled ignominiously to England.

MUSEUMS AND GALLERIES

AUCKLAND CITY ART GALLERY
New Zealand's premier gallery, in the South Pacific second only to Australia's National Gallery of Victoria for its collection of European Old Masters. For most visitors the gallery's highlight is its powerful range of New Zealand works, which includes the world's finest collection of the internationally renowned expatriate Frances Hodgkins (1869-1947); also the remarkable and distinctly non-expatriate Colin McCahon (1919-87), now more and more commonly seen as the greatest painter to emerge from Australia or New Zealand. McCahon worked in the gallery for a time and made gifts of much of his visionary work. Friends of the gallery also made many fortunate purchases before McCahon prices escalated beyond the reach of most New Zealand galleries.

The gallery's collection includes a sample of the first European painting done in New Zealand, in the 18th century by William Hodges on Cook's second voyage. It had a hand, along with the local scenery, in inspiring McCahon's luminous waterfall paintings two centuries later. Colonial artists are comprehensively represented here too, particularly Van der Velden (1837-1913), an associate of Van Gogh, with his dramatic paintings of New Zealand's mountain wilderness.

The gallery is housed in one of Auckland's most distinguished early French Renaissance-style buildings (1888). Most of the city's major dealer galleries, showing contemporary work, can be found within short walking distance (locations from the Auckland Public Relations Office).

AUCKLAND CENTRAL PUBLIC LIBRARY
Opposite the **ART GALLERY**, on Lorne Street, the library holds many rare manuscripts, some from the 10th and 11th centuries; and books printed by Caxton soon after the advent of printing. There is also a Shakespeare first folio of 1623, and the largest collection of Alexandre Dumas' manuscripts outside France. Of more local interest is a parade of material relating to Maori genealogy, mythology and legend.

The library's greatest benefactor was the 19th-century politician Sir George Grey, twice governor of New Zealand, who made it his business to preserve the spirit of Maori culture in print by publishing the first collection of Maori legends, even as he conspired to suffocate that culture in the flesh. His statue can be seen in nearby Albert Park.

AUCKLAND MUSEUM OF TRANSPORT AND TECHNOLOGY
From modest beginnings in the 1960s this museum, located outside the central city on the lakeside at Western Springs, has become one of the country's most beguiling and by far the liveliest. Its central point is one of New Zealand's best preserved industrial monuments – the old Auckland pumphouse (1876) which fed the water of Western Springs out to the city for decades. (Nowadays Auckland's water comes from dams in the Waitakere and Hunua Ranges.) Aside from vast displays of material relating to New Zealand's technology, the museum holds a splendid pioneer village composed of buildings rescued from wreckers as Auckland expanded. There are also locomotives and a blacksmith. A tramway links the museum with **AUCKLAND ZOOLOGICAL PARK**.

A 12 hectare area adjoining the museum has been developed as an airfield of World War II vintage – the Keith Park Memorial Airfield. [Sir] Keith Park was the Aucklander who commanded British Spitfires in the Battle of Britain. The display of aircraft would be the envy of more richly endowed museums. A prize exhibit is the freakish aircraft built by New Zealand farmer Richard Pearse (1877-1953) at the beginning of the century. Debate surrounds the date of his flight, but Pearse may well have beaten the Wright brothers to be the first man to rise in a heavier-than-air craft. His second aircraft, similar to the modern vertical take-off aeroplane, is also exhibited, as is a motorcycle of his design.

Aerial view of Auckland with the Harbour Bridge and suburbs beyond

AUCKLAND WAR MEMORIAL MUSEUM
A huge, squat classical building overlooking the city and harbour, the museum was developed in the 1920s to commemorate the country's 18,000 World War I casualties. It now encompasses the dead of both world wars, with the names of Aucklanders listed in a gallery inside the building. An exterior frieze details the most significant engagements fought by New Zealanders in both wars. (For full effect, walk right round the building.)

The museum houses one of the most comprehensive Polynesian displays in the world, with natural emphasis on the New Zealand Maori. In recent years the Maori Court, with its carved meeting-house Hotunui (1878), has functioned as a marae for formal occasions. Among other items of distinction there is the magnificent 25 metre war canoe, *Te Toki-a-Tapiri* built in 1836, and a British prize of war in the 1860s, and the strangely un-Maori but certainly Polynesian Kaitaia lintel, carved up to 1000 years ago, before Maori carving had evolved its own distinct character; and a mighty carved gateway and food storehouse from the Rotorua region. In the Maori Court a number of portraits of 19th century Maoris by the celebrated painter Charles Goldie (1870-1947) can be seen.

Elsewhere, there is a reconstruction of the great moa, the most startling bird ever known and by far the largest fowl ever to have been eaten; and an imaginatively reconstructed Victorian Auckland street. At the rear entrance of the museum, up two floors, is the handsomely endowed but little known Auckland Institute and Museum reference library, one of the country's largest and most useful collections (open to the public).

AVIATION'S UNSOLVED MYSTERY

Inside the Museum of Transport and Technology at Western Springs lies the strange creation of a forgotten genius of the skies who was perhaps the first to fly

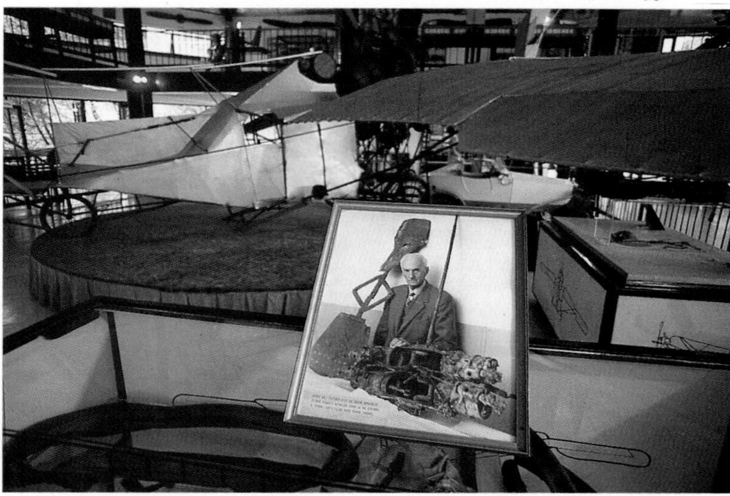
At the Western Springs museum Pearse's flying machine is raised up on a stage

The flying machine on display was designed and built by Richard William Pearse (1877-1953), the man who will probably remain the great unsolved mystery of early aviation. The tantalising question now seems doomed to haunt the history of flying: was Pearse, in fact, the first man to achieve controlled, sustained, engine-powered, heavier-than-air flight?

This achievement is almost certainly the secure honour of the Wright brothers following their famous flight at Kittyhawk, North Carolina, in December 1903, although it is conceivable that Pearse may have beaten the Wrights into the air one year and nine months earlier at Waitohi.

Pearse was a visionary and a recluse, with a mind both obsessive and secretive. He was an unsuccessful farmer and a poor businessman, with no sense of promotion for his ideas and ventures. All his time, money and energy were devoted to the invention of home-made aeroplanes, motorbicycles and agricultural machinery.

It was never claimed by Pearse himself that he was the first man to make a successful powered flight, for he considered the Wright brothers' effort to be a more controlled display than his own experience of careering through the air and into the gorse bushes by the Waitohi main road. Pearse saw his own attempts to fly as experimental. He considered that his real achievement had been to develop, years ahead of his time, features such as landing-gear, new engine design and wing control mechanism.

One of Pearse's brilliant inventions anticipated developments in aircraft design. As far back as the nineteen-thirties he was working on a 'utility' or 'convertiplane' not dissimilar to the modern vertical take-off and horizontal flight aeroplane. This revolutionary machine can be seen at Western Springs.

HISTORIC HOUSES

ACACIA COTTAGE
Auckland's oldest dwelling, but no longer *in situ*, this modest cottage was the first Auckland home of the city's founding father, John Logan Campbell and his partner William Brown in 1841. The cottage once stood near Shortland Street, close to the sea in what is now downtown Auckland. It is now located opposite the tearooms in Cornwall Park on the road to **ONE TREE HILL**. The cottage and park are open daily.

ALBERTON
This house was the family home of colonist Allan Kerr Taylor who arrived in New Zealand in 1849 and found wealth in farming, the timber trade and gold. A family home until 1972, it has since been restored and redecorated in the care of the NZ Historic Places Trust. Its farmland setting was whittled away by financial need. Now surrounded by 20th century suburban dwellings, it allows a glimpse of Auckland's grander rural beginnings (100 Mt Albert Road; open daily 10.30–12, 1.30–4, except Christmas Day and Good Friday).

EWELME COTTAGE
This simple kauri cottage was built in 1863-64 as the family home of Archdeacon Vicesimus Lush (1817-82), first vicar of beautiful All Saints Church at **HOWICK**, an earnest and often witty chronicler of his times. It is largely

unchanged inside and out since his descendants left in 1968 – the family's books, furniture, portraits, silver and chinaware are displayed. Now the property of the NZ Historic Places Trust (14 Ayr Street, Parnell; open daily 10.30–12, 1–4.30 except Christmas Day and Good Friday).

HIGHWIC

Closer to the city than **ALBERTON**, Highwic provides another glimpse of Auckland's past: the setting of a merchant's more urban life. Like Taylor a leader in colonial society, Alfred Buckland dabbled in banking, land and shipping. He owned a stock and station agency, fathered 21 children in two marriages, and added to the building (bought in 1862) as his personal fortunes waxed. It is considered the best New Zealand example of a grand house in Early English Gothic style. Its spacious ballroom was once a centre of the city's social life. A family home until 1978, it is now in the care of the Auckland City Council and the NZ Historic Places Trust, and refurnished in the style to which it was once accustomed. Highwic is situated at 40 Gillies Avenue, Epsom (open daily 10.30–12, 1–4.30, except Christmas Day and Good Friday).

HULME COURT

Still in private hands (it may be viewed from the street), this stone-built 1843 dwelling with a distinct Regency air is the oldest house left standing on its original site in Auckland (in Parnell Road). Its 19th century occupants included a colony governor, two prime ministers and Bishop Selwyn. It was supposedly convict-built for a racy and politically powerful lawyer, Frederick Whitaker, who rose to become premier.

KINDER HOUSE

A modest, two-storey stone dwelling, pleasingly simple in line. Built in 1856, it was for many years the home of John Kinder (1819-1903), churchman, school headmaster, and also distinguished painter and photographer who left a vivid record of Auckland's early life. Inside is a display of his photographs and paintings. Creeper that once threatened to strangle the building has been subdued to reveal the elegant windows and wall texture. There is a Victorian garden and tearooms. Now the property of the Auckland City Council (2 Ayr Street, Parnell; open daily 10–4.30).

JOHN LOGAN CAMPBELL

A pioneer who, even in his own lifetime, was called the 'Father of Auckland'; he lived in Acacia Cottage, which is now in Cornwall Park

John Campbell's restored cottage now sits among the gardens of Cornwall Park

Acacia Cottage, once the harbour-side home of John Logan Campbell, is Auckland's oldest wooden building. Campbell (1817-1912) first lived in the cottage, then in O'Connell Street, with his partner William Brown, who eventually made sufficient money to retire to his native England.

From the city's foundation, Auckland's social and political life had been dominated by men of enterprise and commerce. Of all its triumphant business personalities, Campbell was destined to remain its leading citizen (though he once took a ten-year 'holiday' abroad) and to stand head and shoulders in vision above his contemporaries.

Born in Edinburgh, Campbell trained as a doctor but abandoned the medical profession in favour of the attractions of commerce. After a brief stay in Australia he arrived at Coromandel at the age of twenty-two. There he joined up with Brown and the two set off for the Waitemata where they had heard Governor Hobson was about to found the new capital of the colony. Campbell later recorded their adventures in the pioneer classic, *Poenamo – Sketches of the Early Days of New Zealand.*

Campbell and Brown had hoped to purchase land which they would subdivide and then sell to the settlers they knew would follow Hobson to Auckland, but the Waitemata Maoris refused to deal with them, except to sell them Motukorea (Browns Island). Disenchanted with their real estate prospects, they decided to become merchants and crossed to Commercial Bay (now Shortland Street) where they set up in business.

As other enterprises foundered in the hectic commercial ups and downs of those early years, Campbell became determined to be a success in Auckland. To him, money was never an end in itself. He cherished a dream of performing great works with the wealth he accumulated. The opening for one of his most generous benefactions came with the visit of the Duke and Duchess of Cornwall to New Zealand in 1901. To mark the occasion, Campbell presented the whole area he named Cornwall Park to 'the people of New Zealand'.

Campbell is buried near the summit of One Tree Hill. Beside his grave stands his huge obelisk to the Maori people, one of the proudest features of the Auckland skyline.

HISTORIC BUILDINGS

BANK OF NEW ZEALAND FACADE

In Queen Street conservation has largely been a lost cause, as this curiosity testifies. The bank has gone; only the facade remains, backed by a modern building. Said to be the finest classical facade (1865) in New Zealand, it was designed in honey-brown Tasmanian sandstone in Greek Revival style by the celebrated Melbourne architect Leonard Terry, amid protest from local architects who resented the commission from the bank, then only four years old, going to an outsider. Time has proved the locals wrong; it has defied the wreckers.

Auckland University's fretted Gothic tower stands above the city's skyline

CHIEF POST OFFICE AND ENVIRONS

This bulky offshoot of the English Baroque style was built between 1910 and 1912 at the foot of Queen Street, now overlooking Queen Elizabeth II Square and the Maori warrior chief sculpted by Molly Macalister. A short distance away is a distinctive Auckland building of the same vintage, the Auckland Ferry Building (1912), from which ferries crossed the Waitemata to North Shore communities until completion of the harbour bridge in 1959. Only a few vessels still use it, among them the surviving service to Devonport. In the 1980s the building was spared demolition and was handsomely restored. At the farther end of Auckland's golden mile, the Auckland Town Hall (1908) is a third building testifying to the city's boom era.

CHURCHES

Except for the **SELWYN CHURCHES**, most of Auckland's major churches are second or third generation on their sites, their original wooden structures bowing out to stone. Nothing remains of the original St Patrick's Cathedral the foundation stone of which was laid in 1846. The present unexciting St Patrick's was built in 1907. Anglican St Matthew's in Hobson Street, designed by the architect of Truro Cathedral in Cornwall, dates from 1905. Built of Oamaru stone, it is one of the best examples of the English Gothic style in New Zealand. St Andrew's Presbyterian Church in Symonds Street is a fine example of colonial classical form. It has a nave dating from 1847, and the tower and portico date from 1882.

CIVIC THEATRE

Not far from the Town Hall, this is one of the few surviving movie palaces of the many that arose in towns of the Western world during the 1920s and 1930s and spared capital punishment so far. It is Art Deco without; pure thousand-and-one nights fantasy within. Stars twinkle above the main auditorium. If Clark Gable, Rudolph Valentino, Jean Harlow and Lilian Gish have a heaven, then here it is: nostalgic moviegoers have been known to weep.

CUSTOMHOUSE

This monumental building, spared demolition during the 1970s, is no longer a warren of bureaucracy but now contains a market, restaurant and a tavern (among other things). Designed by Thomas Mahoney in the then fashionable French Renaissance style, it delighted Aucklanders when it was opened in 1888 and delighted them as much in the 1980s when its future was assured.

MOUNT EDEN PRISON

The **SUPREME COURT** (now the High Court) delivered its clientele to this building. Few cities have a functioning medieval fortress in their midst, yet understandably the Mount Eden Prison

Preserved from structural alteration, Renall Street's early bungalows now rate among the inner-city's most expensive real estate

has never been Auckland's particular pride and the centenary of this impressive 1882 bluestone building passed uncelebrated. It was designed by the acting colonial architect Pierre Finch Martineau, who was evidently inspired by a Maltese castle. It is always possible that posterity may find a happier function for it.

NORTHERN CLUB

Opposite the gate of **OLD GOVERNMENT HOUSE**, in an area rich in architectural interest, this creeper-covered Italianate three-storey building of 1870 vintage sometimes housed the overflow (and their entourage) of Government House guests. Novelist Anthony Trollope stayed here, as did the British historian J.A. Froude, who called it 'a staring unbeautiful building, but internally of ascertained excellence'. It was designed by architect J.A. Wrigley, whose reputation was later blemished when a large building he designed in Queen Street collapsed.

OLD GOVERNMENT HOUSE

In Waterloo Quadrant, this is now the senior common room of Auckland University. Its pleasant grounds are open to the public. It was built in 1856 by the distinguished architect William Mason, using wood to imitate stone in late Georgian style.

Governor Gore Browne was the first occupant, followed by Governor George Grey. After Auckland's demise as capital the imposing building was used as the summer residence of Wellington-based governors for a century. It was also an Auckland roof for visiting royalty, not least Queen Elizabeth II when she first visited New Zealand in 1953.

RENALL STREET

This Ponsonby street (near Three Lamps shopping centre) provides a refreshing counterbalance to grand homes and public buildings. Preserved for their colonial character, its tightly packed 19th century cottages (still occupied privately) convey some sense of how life was lived, in a network of narrow streets, by working men and women of early Auckland. The stuccoed brick building, Forresters Hall, was used for social functions and political meetings. Those working men and women of the past might well marvel at their impoverished street now being thought fashionable; real estate in this inner-city vicinity is among Auckland's most expensive. A short walk reveals much elegant renovation. Ponsonby Post Office (1912) has been styled by one architectural authority as 'grossly ill-proportioned, indefensible as a piece of architecture, yet oddly lovable, like a mongrel pleading its good character'. It derives from the Edwardian fashion for English Baroque and still serves the population of Ponsonby.

ST MARY'S CHURCH, PARNELL

Considered one of the finest wooden churches in the English-speaking world, St Mary's was built between 1886 and 1898 by the Christchurch architect Benjamin Mountfort, who died before its completion. Modest in stance and spacious in interior, it sings with light, grace and surprise. It has served Anglican Auckland as cathedral for most of the 20th century. Said one architectural authority: 'If good architects go to heaven, this building must have played its part in putting him [Mountfort] there'. The building was uprooted from its original site by ecclesiastical authorities in 1982, moved across the road and deposited beside the new Holy Trinity Cathedral.

SELWYN CHURCHES

By far the most distinctive buildings in Auckland (see page 60), these churches were meant to be within easy walking distance for the perambulating Bishop Selwyn and his fellow churchmen. They are now in densely built-up areas. Those in proximity to the central city include the delicate St Stephen's Chapel (1856) in Judges Bay, Parnell, and Selwyn Court (1863), also in Parnell. Farther out, there is St John's College in Meadowbank (202 St John's Road), with its exquisite 'Selwyn' chapel (1847) and the college dining hall (1849). At **HOWICK** is All Saints (1847), the sole survivor of eight churches prefabricated and shipped from the St John's site. Perhaps this is the most beautiful church of all.

SUPREME COURT

A minute's walk from **OLD GOVERNMENT HOUSE** along Waterloo Quadrant. The foundation stone of this magnificent Tudor-Gothic colonial structure was laid in 1865 with ceremony surpassing any Auckland had known. A military band, 200 distinguished citizens in a flag-bedecked pavilion, a lavish banquet and all of 34 speeches marked the occasion. The court opened for business in 1868 with bitter complaints about baffling acoustics, a leaky roof and odours from the water closets.

However, derisive predictions of a fast collapse of the building were not fulfilled. Designed by Edward Rumsey, a pupil of the famed George Gilbert Scott in England, it survives as one of the city's largest architectural pleasures with its red brick walls, buff facings and window mullions. Especially fascinating are the carved gargoyles and portrait heads that encrust the building – Queen Victoria, Sir George Grey and the first Maori monarch Te Wherowhero among others – the work of a visiting German engraver Anton Teutenberg.

SYNAGOGUE AND ENVIRONS

Opposite **OLD GOVERNMENT HOUSE**, Auckland's first synagogue was built in 1884 to a rather eastern design by Edward Bartley. As a bank it now makes a splendid temple to Mammon. Beside it along Princes Street is an impressive group of five merchants' houses in wood or plastered brick, with bay windows and hipped roofs dating from the expansive and speculative colonial period of the 1870s and 1880s. The group is but a vestige of many once in this vicinity before the expanding Auckland University ploughed much of the city's past under. All (including the synagogue) are now preserved by the Auckland City Council for historic interest.

The fretted Gothic tower of Auckland University (1926) which stands out above the central city, and the colourful flowerbeds of Albert Park, are of much more recent vintage. Within the university grounds is a wall of the old Albert Barracks (1847) which housed imperial troops when Auckland seemed under siege in the 1860s.

ENVIRONS

HELENSVILLE

Only 50 kilometres to the north-west of Auckland is a town of 1400 slow to shake off its frontier associations. Comprising a cluster of kauri homes on sunny slopes near the bank of the mangrove-edged Kaipara River, the town has a history intimately linked with the great harbour of the same name that the river feeds. Helensville was once the railhead for Northland. Goods and passengers were ferried by steamer across Kaipara Harbour (see page 49) to Dargaville and other places north. The town also milled much of the kauri felled about the harbour; it arrived in great rafts.

Today the traffic on the river is mostly that of amateur and professional fishermen motoring out to the rich grounds of the Kaipara. The town is best known for the hot springs at neighbouring Parakai where complexes of pools and other diversions are popular with Aucklanders especially in cooler months (all open daily until 10). The town has a museum celebrating past glories in a large old kauri house dating from 1910 (behind the War Memorial Hall; open Sunday afternoon, otherwise by arrangement). Adjoining it is Helensville's old courthouse (1864). The drive north from Helensville to Wellsford via Kaukapakapa takes in striking vistas of river and harbour. In the other direction via Parakai it is possible to drive towards the south head of the Kaipara.

HENDERSON–KUMEU

After the heyday of kauri gum-digging, Dalmatian migrants settled in valleys and on sunny slopes footing the Waitakere Ranges to the city's north-west. They founded prolific orchards and vineyards on obstinate Auckland clay. It was natural to drift towards the growing city where their produce might find a market.

That this district has remained the most concentrated wine-making area in New Zealand, with a distinct Mediterranean colour is less due to climate and soil than that accident of history. (Not that all of the vineyards are Dalmatian.)

Most vineyards are only too hospitable towards visitors. To follow the wine trail and sample distinguished vintages is both a peril and a pleasure (maps available from Auckland Public Relations Office or from most vineyards). An organised excursion is available, otherwise take a non-drinking driver. At Oratia, just off West Coast Road, there is the John Waititi marae, with a finely carved meeting-house by John Taiapa, typical of urban marae that have risen to serve Auckland's Maori population over past decades. Near by is the Oratia folk museum in a pioneer cottage (open weekends).

HOWICK

Now a suburb of Auckland, seaside Howick was once one of a chain of so-called Fencible settlements. Fencibles were retired British soldiers who signed on as armed settlers for seven years. They received a free passage to New Zealand, and a cottage with a small landholding, theirs on completion of service.

All Saints Anglican Church, completed in 1847, is perhaps the loveliest of all **SELWYN CHURCHES**. It was designed for the Fencibles' spiritual needs, and its lychgate is a memorial to them. Its small graveyard is just as eloquent about Howick's beginnings: in one grave, having died within weeks of each other, lie the three children of the church's first vicar, and early colonial chronicler, Vicesimus Lush. There are also the graves of two brothers killed by Maoris in 1863, when the woes of the Waikato washed this far. (The settlement was never attacked.)

Just down Selwyn Road towards the sea, is Shamrock Cottage (1847), which followed fast on the church as wet canteen serving spirituous need. It now functions as a restaurant.

For a sense of Fencible days and ways, the energetic Howick Historical Society has relocated several Fencible cottages in the Howick Colonial Village, just outside the suburb proper, in Lloyd Elsmore Park, Pakuranga. Perhaps the most rewarding of its kind in New Zealand, it has an overwhelming flavour of the period. See Howick's first vicarage (1848), the former general store (1847), Howick courthouse (1848), Ararimu Valley School (1876), Pakuranga Methodist Church (1852), an early settler's sod cottage of the 1840s, and the Bell homestead (1851) (now a restaurant).

From Howick there is access to several beaches – Bucklands, Eastern, Howick itself and adjoining Cockle Bay. At Musick Point, north of Bucklands Beach, there is a conspicuous Art Deco building (1942) built as a memorial to the American aviator Captain Edwin Musick, who piloted the first Pan American flying boat to Auckland from San Francisco in 1937, inaugurating New Zealand's air link with North America. It is now used as a radio station.

NORTH SHORE

This region of attractive beaches is backed by the homes of the Auckland affluent, with vistas of Rangitoto Island. Much of the area retains a casual early-century quality in architecture and atmosphere, with waterfront pubs and restaurants. Devonport, left out on a limb when the harbour was bridged in 1959, is one of the city's oldest suburbs and has changed little since vehicular ferries left for ever (passenger ferries still run).

To the north, Takapuna is one of Auckland's most popular and populous beaches. The place has a racy, raffish air with its restaurants and sunburned citizens. At its northern end (a walkway runs along the shore) there are pretty coves all the way to Milford. Thereafter, bay after bay and beach after beach continue on to the Auckland Regional Authority reserve at Long Bay.

ONEHUNGA

This Fencible community (see **HOWICK**) of the 1840s was established at the same time as Howick on the upper reach of the Manukau Harbour, which was then lively with Maori canoes ferrying produce to Auckland from the Waikato.

Today Onehunga still functions as Auckland's back-door port, serving mostly coastal traffic and fishing trawlers. In Jellicoe Park there is a surviving brick and kauri blockhouse (1860), characteristic of those built to protect the approaches to Auckland as tension grew between the British authorities and the Waikato Maori. Cruciform in shape, the sturdy building had its loopholes bricked up when it served as council chamber for the Onehunga Borough. Next to the blockhouse is a replica of a Fencible cottage, now holding a private museum (open weekend afternoons).

OREWA–WAIWERA–WHANGAPARAOA

Between 40 and 48 kilometres from the city, now within commuter orbit as development and motorways have pushed north from the Harbour Bridge, this outlying east coast resort and retirement region looks more and more suburban. Nevertheless the charm of its pohutukawa-clothed coastline remains largely intact, somewhat reinforced by two large and graceful reserves. Whangaparaoa Peninsula, which has become densely settled in past decades, is frilled with coves and sand. At its tip is 376 hectare Shakespear Regional Park, a working farm park where the pukeko (the New Zealand swamp hen) flourishes in large numbers. There is one of the best peninsula beaches here.

A HUMBLE LITERARY LANDMARK

A spartan dwelling in Takapuna's busy Esmonde Road has been preserved as a memorial to one of New Zealand's most distinguished writers

This tiny house was lived in by Frank Sargeson (1903-82), an accomplished short-story writer and novelist who spent his whole writing life in New Zealand. Surely the first fibrolite shrine to literature in the world, the house is the only place where the public can witness the creative and domestic environment of a writer.

Frank Sargeson's study displays how he lived and worked during his life time

The sign in the front garden announces that Sargeson 'lived at this address from 1931 until his death. Here he wrote all his best-known short stories and novels, grew vegetables, and entertained friends and fellow-writers. Here a truly New Zealand literature had its beginnings'.

In spite of the opposition of some Takapuna residents who felt that the 'shack' should be pulled down, the Frank Sargeson Trust tidied up the section and restored the interior of the house to show how the writer lived from day to day, and the austere conditions under which he wrote. The writers' organisation PEN helps maintain the property.

The Trust also supports a Frank Sargeson Writing Courses Program (write to PO Box 77, Albany), and it provides a nine-month Sargeson Literary Fellowship, with accommodation in premises near Albert Park. Esmonde Road is now too noisy with traffic from the bridge for the old house to be suitable for most writers to work in. The late twentieth century has caught up with and isolated this extraordinary literary landmark in a way that seems appropriately fictional.

The key to the Sargeson house can be obtained on application to the Takapuna Public Library.

With a population of 6000, motels and fashionable shops, Orewa is the natural centre of the area. Its long vivid beach is one of Auckland's best, with grassy seaside picnic areas, though much untidy development blocks access. At Silverdale (5 kilometres south) there is a pioneer village, with buildings dating from the 1860s and 1870s. To the north is Waiwera, with a thermal pool complex between wooded headlands in a handsome cove. Here Maori once scooped therapeutic hot baths for themselves in the sands. In the 19th century Aucklanders made it a spa, and steamers ferried day-trippers up the coast.

Less than a kilometre farther on is Wenderholm Regional Reserve, one of Auckland's gems. The former British prime minister Anthony Eden tried to find peace here (when the 134 hectare property was in private hands) after the debacle of his Suez adventure in 1956. The homestead (*c.* 1850) was also a base for visiting royalty. Over the hill is the Bohemian-founded community of **PUHOI** (see page 50) with its colonial pub. Farther on is Warkworth (see page 53) and the pleasures of the upper Hauraki Gulf, the Mahurangi Peninsula and Kawau Island (see page 63).

TAMAKI DRIVE

Along the southern shore of the Waitemata Harbour from the central city, this drive passes some of Auckland's plusher seaside suburbs and most pleasing beaches. Near Orakei wharf is one of the world's great marinelands, fulfilled dream of the diver Kelly Tarlton, who recovered relics from wrecks round the coast and died shortly after completing this masterly celebration of the underwater world. At Orakei there is a multi-cultural Maori marae overlooking the harbour, with a 900 square metre meeting-house built by local Maoris and Europeans (open Monday to Friday 9–4).

Off the drive is **BASTION POINT**, resting place of one-time prime minister Michael Joseph Savage. The adjoining land was battled over in the 1970s by police and Maori protesters. On the foreshore of elegant Mission Bay there is the durable Melanesian Mission House (1859), the most significant stone structure of the Selwyn era in Auckland, built originally as a college for Pacific Islanders. In the 1920s it was one of New Zealand's first flying schools. It was later turned into a museum dedicated to the missionary era. Since it was taken over by the NZ Historic Places Trust it has been refurbished as a tearoom and decorated with reminders of the building's past.

Out to sea is distinctive Bean Rock lighthouse, like a house on stilts, which for decades guided mariners entering the Waitemata. The lighthouse is now also refurbished as an historic place. Farther on is StHeliers Beach and Ladies Bay. The vistas of harbour and gulf are splendid; at weekends the offshore waters shimmer with sail.

WAHARAU REGIONAL PARK

South Auckland, as well as west, has its forest. This 169 hectare park, 38 kilometres south of Clevedon, on the coastal Orere-Kaiaua road beside the wide Firth of Thames, gives access to the Hunua Ranges, which were once rich in kauri like the Waitakeres and also in Maori legend. There are walking tracks, picnic areas and campsites. The coastline is especially pleasing.

This shore was densely settled in pre-European times, and two Maori burial sites demand the visitor's respect. On the shore is a traditional Maori stopover still used by Waikato Maori making their way north or south. Kauri felled here was used to build the gold-rush town of Thames across the water. Many European farms failed and the land is now reverting to forest. The park is slowly being enlarged to provide access to even more of the Hunua Ranges.

WAITAKERE SCENIC DRIVE

Some two or three dozen kilometres of sightseeing road built by Depression labourers in the 1930s weave through 6400 parkland hectares of forest and fern in the western hills of Auckland (see page 67). At one extremity it begins in the leafy Auckland suburb of Titirangi, 25 minutes from the inner city, its houses attractively set in native greenery above the Manukau Harbour. At the other it dips into the wine-growing district of Swanson and **HENDERSON**. Between are vistas of both Manukau and Waitemata Harbours, and of the distant city. Graceful groves of the native nikau palm and tall tree-ferns lean over the route. Though most of the magnificent kauri in the Waitakeres were plundered before conservation became a cause, some mature survivors are signposted.

Six kilometres from Titirangi there is an information centre with maps of the trails and nature walks that intersect the region. Roads and walking tracks lead off to the **WEST COAST**. The Fairy Falls are at the end of a one-hour walk. Water twists and tumbles from terrace to terrace down to the forest floor – an inspiration for the celebrated paintings of Colin McCahon.

Just off the scenic drive, down Mountain Road, former accommodation houses can be seen. A recently built lodge on the drive itself accommodates today's visitors. At the far end of the drive a detour can be taken down the road towards Te Henga (Bethells) through the Waitakere Golf Course to the especially handsome Cascades and Kauri Park picnic area with its walking tracks, waterfall and kauri glade.

WEST COAST
Beyond the Waitakere Ranges are the surf-beaten beaches of Auckland's west coast. The most celebrated and accessible is Piha, seldom without scores of wet-suited surfers teetering on tall waves in any season of the year. The one-time Maori citadel of Lion Rock lends character to the long beach. At the south end the blowhole was in legend the residence of an especially ferocious *taniwha* (or water monster) which fed on the fishermen of the Manukau Harbour. While the south of the beach can become crowded with surfers and their retinues, the north offers quiet picnic areas and shady pohutukawa. There is also the chance for the daring to pluck mussels from the rocks between breakers. A track up the Piha Valley, beyond Glen Esk Road, takes visitors to the Kitekite Falls.

Karekare (the turn-off just short of Piha) is a less generous but also less frequented stretch of sand at the end of a twisting road. The pohutukawa glade at the south end is especially pleasant, with a walking track to the Karekare Falls. Also at the south end are relics of the railway that once took Waitakere timber to ships at the Manukau Heads. Both Piha and Karekare are patrolled beaches on weekends and holidays, with a rescue helicopter often in attendance. The undertow can be treacherous.

Isolated Anawhata, reached by a turn-off before Piha, is free from crowds and from cars thanks to the steep track leading to the shore. There are plenty of walks here too. As everywhere on the west coast, the surf can be hazardous and the holes and rips fatal. North of these beaches is Te Henga (Bethells), a long, exposed, desert-like strip of sand dune and surf between bulky headlands. There is lake swimming among the dunes here for those not inclined to dare the surf. Farther north still, beyond the Waitakeres, long Muriwai Beach (accessible from the route to **HELENSVILLE**) is another popular with surfers, and more so with the lovers of that great New Zealand delicacy, the toheroa, although seasons for its harvesting have been rare.

For alternative west-coast vistas there is the route from Titirangi via Huia, along the northern shore of the Manukau Harbour, to wild Whatipu at the Manukau Heads. The Manukau's waters are mild in temperature and temperament. There are beaches, picnic areas, walking tracks and spectacular lookouts along the route. Cornwallis Peninsula, the site of a failed pioneer settlement, offers the largest beach area. Huia has a splendid roadside lookout on the Manukau Harbour and the seething sandbar at its mouth, which in 1863 engulfed HMS *Orpheus* and 189 lives in New Zealand's largest shipping disaster. Huia itself has a small and informative museum, open at weekends. On the farther side is Mt Donald Maclean, the summit, accessible by road and track, with even more extensive views.

Beyond Huia the road is rough with walking tracks winding on to Whatipu. Here fishermen flock along the natural wharf where timber ships were once moored and smugglers plied their trade. Huge caves rear dim under the cliffs. Vast stretches of sand are punctuated by only a few clumps of rock and remainders of the railway which ran along the coast to drop timber into the once busy port. There are no facilities other than a fishing lodge with a small shop. Otherwise there is everything money cannot buy. *Waitakere Walks*, a booklet published by Wilson and Horton, is useful for visitors.

ENTERTAINMENTS

AUCKLAND ZOOLOGICAL PARK
New Zealand's largest and liveliest, its wildlife is scattered in attractive grounds adjoining Western Springs and the **AUCKLAND MUSEUM OF TRANSPORT AND TECHNOLOGY**, to which it is linked by a vintage Auckland tram. There are picnic places, tearooms, and even a nocturnal kiwi house (Motions Road, off Great North Road; open daily).

FOOTROT FLATS LEISURE PARK
Named after (and celebrating) New Zealand's most popular cartoon strip, this is an entertainment park with a boating lake, bumper boats, a drivers' town and mini-golf (Te Atatu, off North-Western Motorway; open Fridays, weekends and holidays, 10–9).

GLENBROOK VINTAGE RAILWAY
A delightful excursion back to the age of steam. Located in South Auckland, the railway is signposted at Glenbrook on the approach to Waiuku (see page 87) (functions Sundays and most public holidays, 11–4).

HERITAGE PARK
Heritage Park is designed to encapsulate the New Zealand experience in one 12 hectare location. There is a resident Maori cultural group, also agricultural and horticultural displays, and glimpses of New Zealand history. A Maori carver can be seen at work (the staff of the park is 75 per cent Maori) and there are women craftworkers and even a garden with traditional Maori herbal remedies. Timberworld demonstrates the forgotten trade of kauri gum-digging, as well as celebrating the great tree itself. An underwater grotto allows viewing of giant rainbow trout. The largest free-flight aviary in Australia or New Zealand holds native birds. There are audio-visual shows, and a licensed restaurant features New Zealand delicacies. Maori food from a *hangi*, or earth oven, is prepared regularly. (Harrison Road, Mount Wellington open daily 9.30–6 summer; 9.30–5, winter).

KELLY TARLTON'S UNDERWATER WORLD
The dream of the intrepid New Zealand diver Kelly Tarlton was to share his experience of the ocean with those tied to *terra firma*. This magnificent and ingeniously devised marineland was the result. Tarlton died soon after it opened, and it will remain his memorial. A moving walkway takes the visitor through transparent tunnels in a giant tank where creatures of the sea glide past. The experience is designed to duplicate that of diving and it does so dramatically (**TAMAKI DRIVE**, near Orakei wharf; open daily 9–9).

LION SAFARI PARK
On the now familiar overseas model, a park designed to permit creatures to be seen in the wild during a slow drive. There is a playground and a picnic area (Red Hills Road, Massey, off the North-Western Motorway; open daily).

RAINBOWS END
A lively adventure park with an array of breathtaking rides (Manukau City, open daily 10–10).

THEATRE
Auckland has two active professional theatres, the Mercury and the Theatre Corporate, both situated in the inner city. The two venues of the Mercury Theatre provide classics, contemporary drama, musicals and operas. Theatre Corporate is best known for its elegant interpretations of the classics, and more adventurous modern drama. Visiting groups are usually seen at His Majesty's.

WAITEMATA'S SPARKLING WATERS

Auckland's eastern harbour, Waitemata, provides a one hundred and eighty square kilometre playground for the city's pleasure-boat-crazy population

A typical summer's day at the races on Waitemata Harbour, where hundreds of sailing and speed boats jostle for water

Waitemata is the name the Maori tribes along the seashore gave to at least part of the eastern harbour of Auckland. The translation of the Maori name implies 'sparkling waters' – an interpretation that no one would dispute on a sunny day.

The Waitemata is the city's largest playground where its citizens swim, paddle, sail, fish, dive, row, water-ski or just cruise. On Auckland's Anniversary Day holiday (the Monday nearest 29 January) the harbour is the setting for what is claimed to be the world's largest single-day yachting regatta. A thousand boats ranging from two to thirty metres compete in a kaleidoscope of multi-coloured sails.

At a conservative guess there are between seventy and eighty thousand boats, powered by engine or sails, that go out on the harbour and that estimate does not include the swarms of dinghies and canoes. This means there is at least one boat to every four households in Auckland, probably the most pleasure-boat-crazy shore-city in the world.

A flotilla of islands, some maintained as reserves and others populated to almost suburban levels, give the horizon of the Waitemata a beauty and drama that few other harbours in the world can match. Its hundreds of sandy beaches begin at the city coastline and continue far to the east, and to the north across the Harbour Bridge. Or, they can be reached by launch, ferry or private boat. Swimming is safe, and sunbathing is a popular pastime.

It should always be remembered that Governor Hobson chose the Waitemata as his new capital (which it remained for only twenty-five years) not for its beauty but for its attractions as an administrative centre. Businessmen quickly realised its commercial potential. To this day it remains the site of New Zealand's main naval base at Devonport; and its port facilities are a vital link with the rest of the world. A spectacular daily entertainment is provided by ships of bizarre shapes, sizes and colours, which dock in the heart of the city.

South Auckland – Waikato

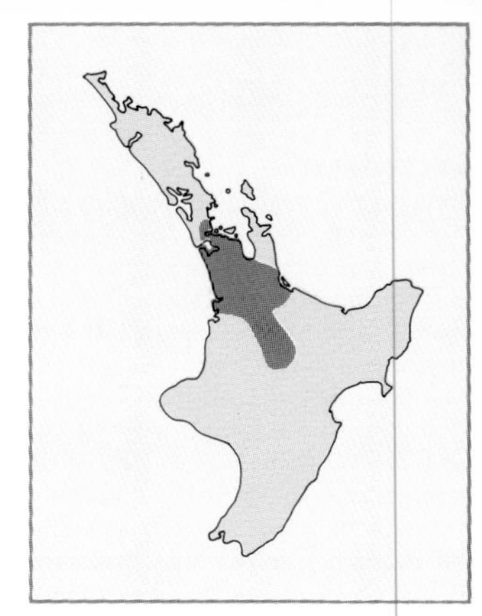

To journey south from Auckland into the green Waikato basin is to travel a highway created by war. The busy Great South Road between Auckland and Hamilton, following the curves of New Zealand's greatest river, began as a military road built to assert British authority and to challenge the Maori. Horse-drawn gun carriages and munition wagons used the riverside road after it had been levelled by the boots of tramping infantry. From fortified hills Maori defenders of the region looked down on the invading British regiments backed by menacing gunboats. The Waikato was the setting for the largest and most formal war between Maori and Europeans in the nineteenth century.

Today fast roads slice through battle sites and scenes of slaughter are grazed by sleek dairy herds. The land defended bitterly by the Maori now displays the richest of pastoral panoramas. There are nearly three dairy cows for each of its two hundred and thirty thousand people, as well as beef cattle, sheep, thoroughbred horses, deer and goats. Hardly a hint of old conflicts remains.

At the centre of the region is New Zealand's greatest inland city. Hamilton has a distinct and affluent urban identity; it is no satellite of Auckland, though little more than a hundred kilometres south. As long ago as 1940 the essayist Oliver Duff observed, 'The South Islander entering Hamilton wonders where all those shops and offices come from, who built them, who visits them, and what right the Waikato has to be so flagrantly prosperous . . . As long as its cows calve and its bulls gender money will flow into its pocket and petrol fumes will rise like incense from its main street'. The South Islander – indeed any outsider – still has cause for wonder. Hamilton's prosperity has never been any less flagrant in the half-century since, although that prosperity has seldom translated into civic and cultural landmarks. Unkind outsiders call Hamilton a cowshed culture. Hamilton and all the Waikato turn the other cheek. The city's most celebrated citizen, especially in the Rugby season, is not the mayor but the mascot of its brawny footballers, Mooloo, a larger than life-size model of a dairy cow. When the gladiators of the Waikato down Canterbury or Auckland – or better still, an international team – cow-bells clamour.

The Waikato has little high-lying land of significance. Mountain, river and sea form its boundaries. To the east lie the Coromandel and Kaimai Range; to the north is the Waikato River mouth and the Manukau Harbour; to the west is the surf of the Tasman's shore beneath rugged Pirongia Mountain; and to the south the slow Puniu River flows, with the hills of the King Country beyond. The region's soil consists largely of debris left by the Waikato's waters as it flowed first into the Firth of Thames on New Zealand's east coast leaving the Hauraki-Piako Plains behind, and then swerved west into its present course. These alluvial lowlands have been laboriously ditched, drained and dyked against floods. They are now New Zealand's most valuable and productive land.

Moa-hunting Polynesians were the first people to make themselves familiar with the region. In pursuit of the giant bird they burned off forest cover, but left little other evidence of their life here. According to the tradition of the Classic Maori, the entire Waikato region was populated by the occupants of one migratory canoe, the *Tainui*. Recent research suggests that the *Tainui* may not have been a canoe from the tropics, but rather from the north of New Zealand, and that its occupants were people on the move south because of overcrowding or war. Folklore says they did not find the region altogether empty. The Waikato's western shore was occupied by a people (presumably descendants of the original moa hunters) named Kahu-pungapunga, who dyed their garments yellow. They were dispossessed and driven inland, eventually to be extinguished on the tall rock of Pohaturoa near Atiamuri, above the Waikato River.

Certainly the Tainui tribes – including the Ngati Raukawa, the Ngati Paoa, the Ngati Toa and the Ngati Haua – were among the strongest and (as Europeans were later to find) the proudest tribes in all-Maori Aotearoa. The Waikato was the most densely populated inland region in the Classic Maori era. It also seems to have been the most rumbustious. Despite ancestral affinity the tribesmen of the Waikato tore themselves apart with petty vendettas that became wars. The last great traditional battle, just north of Te Awamutu in about 1807, involved an estimated nine thousand warriors. Fifteen years later invasion by Northland's Ngapuhi armed with muskets meant the end of traditional Maori warfare. Possibly as many as ten thousand Waikato people were killed or enslaved.

The result was that the Waikato tribes welcomed European traders. They could barter flax and other produce for muskets. With these they not only repelled further Ngapuhi incursions (in 1832), but invaded parts of Northland in reprisal. Though there was a trading post at the mouth of the Waikato River by 1830, and soon another at Raglan, Europeans were not fast to move far inland. The difficulties, once the river highway was left behind, were immense. 'We tramped on in the rain and wet brushwood and swamp', records one early traveller. 'Now and then the mosquitoes' hum announced that the insects were waiting for their prey . . . [There were] fern wastes and steep tree bridges wet and slippery over foaming torrents.'

BRIEF GOLDEN AGE

Missionaries were the first to establish themselves deep in 'the wild Wykatto', as it was soon known. By 1835 the Reverend John Morgan had set up a mission station at Mangapouri, at the confluence of the Puniu and Waipa Rivers near Te Awamutu. At this time warfare in the Waikato was ferocious. Rather than present a united front to outsiders, Waikato tribes were feuding lethally among themselves again. The more war-wearied were ready to hear the Christian message from Morgan and to consider the crafts of peace. Not that transformation was quick. Mrs Morgan, while getting the family breakfast, once witnessed slaves being slain for a cannibal oven.

Morgan, meanwhile, taught the Maori how to use a plough (drawn by men until horses arrived) and the sturdy virtues of sowing wheat, rather than the seeds of war. Fruit trees, then entire orchards, began to blossom throughout the Waikato basin. Vegetable plots multiplied. Soon there were thousands of hectares of rolling wheatfields and close to twenty Maori mills grinding out flour. Morgan was firmly of the view that stomachs filled with bread would end appetite for war and it seemed he was right.

In 1840 the Treaty of Waitangi was signed in the north, and then borne about the country for further signatures. Many Waikato tribes held aloof from the document; they also retained possession of their lands. European colonists remained few in their region, which had entered upon a sadly brief golden age. From 1840 to 1860 Christian Waikato dedicated itself to agriculture. Huge quantities of food were sold to the settlement of Auckland and exported to Australia. One chief declared, 'We have abandoned our old ways. The rule now is kindness to the orphan; peace, and agricultural pursuits'. 'There were no quarrels', one old woman later sighed in an interview with the historian James Cowan. 'We lived happily in the midst of abundance'.

SERENE TAPESTRY OF LUSH PASTURES

That abundance was observed with envy by land-hungry colonists cooped up in Auckland. The prospering Waikato Maori set themselves against land sales. Having progressed so far and fast agriculturally, they didn't need the money, as other Maori tribes might. Alarmed by the European influx into New Zealand, Waikato leaders saw the need to take the survival of the Maori race into their own hands. British institutions, notably the monarchy, could not be relied on for protection. The result was the *kotahitanga*, or tribal unity movement, which in 1858 elected a Maori king – the elderly Te Wherowhero. On his death in 1860 he was succeeded by his son, the younger and vigorous King Tawhiao. The British view was that this dissidence could not be countenanced; there was room for only one monarch, Queen Victoria.

TRIUMPH IN THE MIDST OF DEFEAT

Recent scholarship tends to argue that colonists were looking for an excuse for war and a lightning land grab and now had a convincing pretext. A land dispute at Waitara in Taranaki heralded the Waikato conflict. Waikato tribesmen travelled south to help out in the fight. In 1863 Governor George Grey decided it was time to impose his will on the recalcitrant Waikato. Despite Maori warnings he pushed a military road south from Auckland to the bank of the Waikato River where it moves west to the Tasman (near present-day Mercer). This was no bluff; Grey knew the act must mean war. As fighting developed there were up to eighteen thousand soldiers – with artillery and gunboats – against perhaps only twelve hundred part-time warriors, armed with tomahawks, antique muskets, and fowling pieces.

After sortie and skirmish, Maori and British met in formal battle at Rangiriri, where a Maori fortress stood on a slender bridge of land between the river and Lake Waikare. Shells crashed into the fortress and gunboats hit at it from the river. Thirty-eight British lives were lost in ineffectual attempts to storm the Maori stronghold, and it was not until their gunpowder was gone that the Maoris conceded. Thereafter the British campaign was mostly downhill. They took the headquarters of the Maori king at Ngaruawahia without a fight and discreetly they managed to avoid the Maoris entrenched at Paterangi, near Pirongia.

The army was dedicated to ending Waikato's golden age. Villages were razed and rebel crops destroyed. At the undefended village of Rangiaowhia – until now a model of Maori

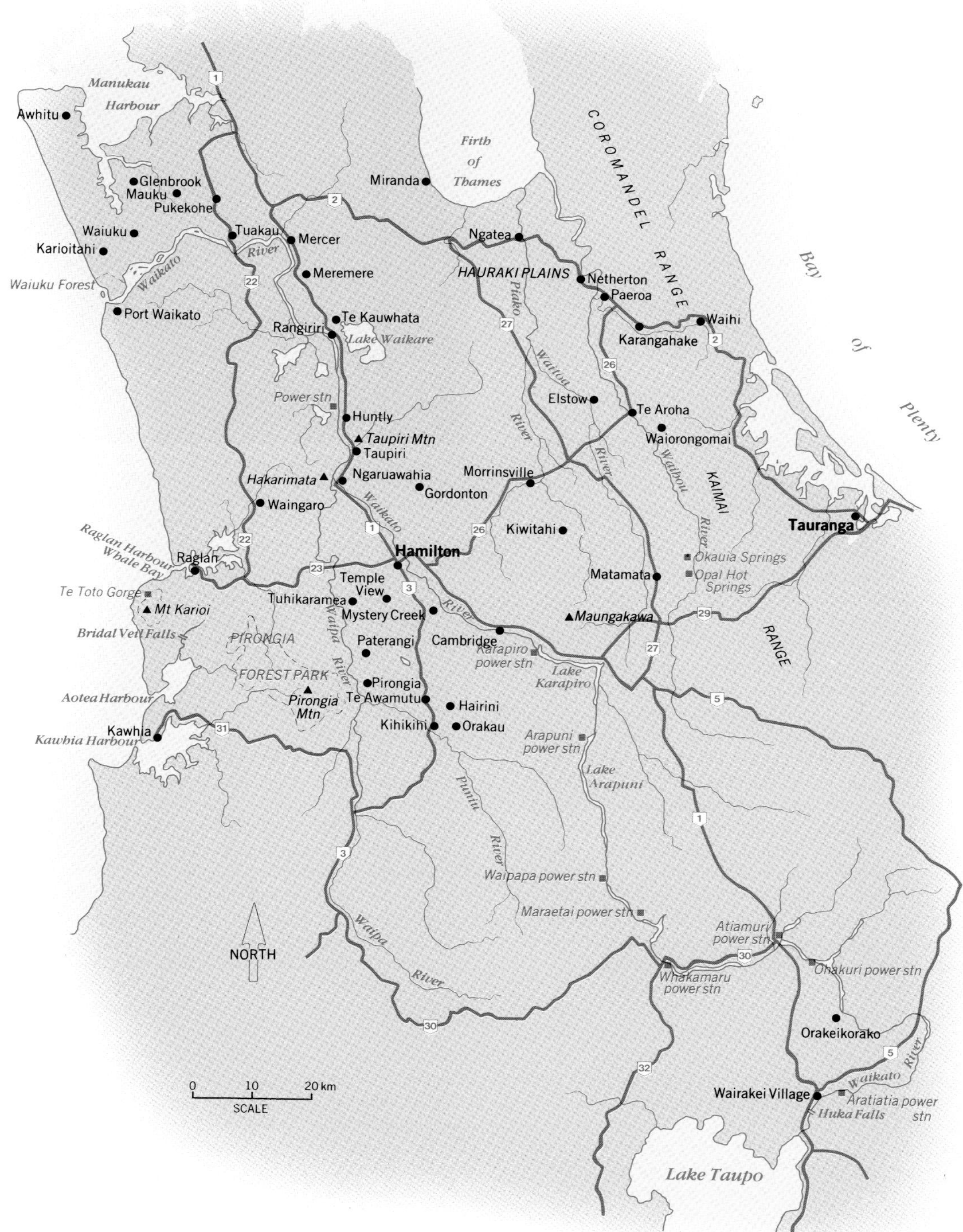

agricultural enterprise – women and children left behind by warrior husbands and fathers were killed along with a number of elderly men courageous enough to fight. It was the first major atrocity of the war, and the later Hauhau insurgents would use it to justify their own merciless campaign against colonists. By that time the cause of the Waikato Maori was lost.

Yet there was one more act to be played. Joined by zealous Tuhoe tribesmen from the mountainous Urewera, the rebel chief Rewi Maniapoto wearily decided to dig out a fortress at Orakau among peach trees and wheatfields to the west of Te Awamutu and there wait upon Britain's wrath. The ensuing siege has been romantically celebrated as 'Rewi's last stand'. It was less than that, and more. The fight seems to have been against Rewi's better judgment, but his *mana* would have been diminished had he not hospitably offered a battle to the Tuhoe.

For three days, in the most awesome pitched battle of the Waikato War, three hundred Maoris, soon starving and thirsty, held out against two thousand troops and a rain of shot and shell. When offered surrender, they answered, 'We shall fight you for ever and ever'. When mercy was offered to women and children within the fort, the reply came that women and children would fight and die too. And most did die. Their courage melted even hardened martial hearts. On the third day a hundred or more weak survivors charged out in a phalanx through British lines. Though many were shot down in the pursuit that followed, many others, including Rewi himself, escaped through swamp and forest and across the Puniu River into territory thereafter known as the King Country, a sanctuary for Maori dissidents. In that sense Orakau can be seen as a Maori triumph – Maori spirit there helped persuade the British to press no further. But the Waikato was no longer a Maori domain. In the ruthless confiscations that ensued, the colonial government took land as far south as Kihikihi.

So began the European history of the region. Maori land was surveyed, subdivided and distributed among the colony's militia: fifty acres (twenty hectares) for soldiers and up to four hundred (one hundred and sixty hectares) for officers. Many were drifters and misfits recruited in Australia on that mercenary basis. Until peace was assured, they were expected to win a living from the land. They were little more effective as farmers than they had been as soldiers. Worse still, their holdings were often under water.

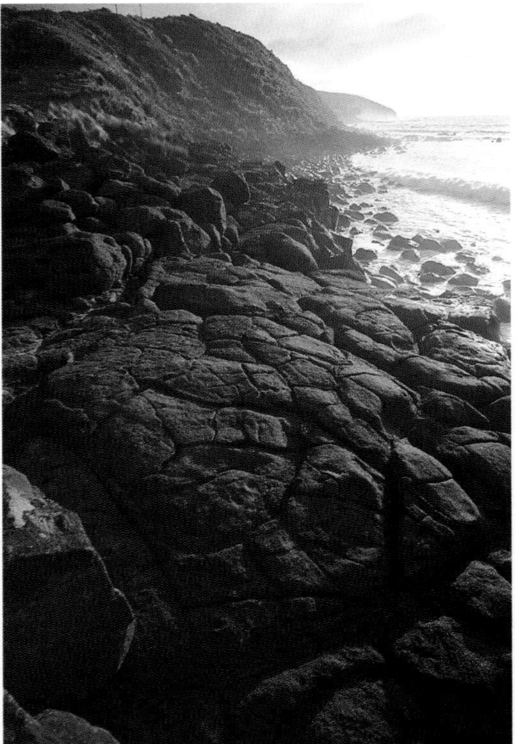

Though viewed best at low tide, the mysteriously patterned Tattooed Rocks near Raglan have never really been explained by Maori folklore. The shapes incised into the rocks bear curious resemblance to the traditional body tattooes worn by Maori warriors preparing for battle

The government soon reneged on promises of financial support. Few militiamen had capital to develop their land, and their debts mounted. The clearing of fern and draining of swamp took further toll and, sick of slaving waist-high in mud, many reached for the bottle. Most of these soldier-settlers finally fled the field, lucky if they could sell off their allotments to land speculators for ten shillings (one dollar) an acre. Gold strikes on the Coromandel Peninsula offered more wholesome prospects. Storekeepers shut their doors and garrison towns like Te Awamutu, Cambridge and Hamilton all but died.

More colonists moved into the region, taking up the land militiamen had bitterly abandoned, this time with a little more capital and a little more rural experience. They struggled too, as the colony itself reeled from depression. Even large landholders – like Josiah Firth on his twenty-two thousand hectare estate at Matamata – came to grief. Settlers of lesser substance survived by flax dressing and gum-digging. Yet scrub was cleared, swamps were drained and once bleak hills and once dank plains took on a green glow. Dairying, in place of sheep-raising, began to spread through the region, its appeal immediate to smallholders who needed quick returns. Directly to the south of Auckland, especially on volcanic soil round Pukekohe, market gardening was favoured.

After 1908 drainage of the sodden Hauraki Plains opened up a large new dairying district. Following the First World War production increased with effective use of fertilisers, better roads and better breeding techniques. Taranaki was outstripped as New Zealand's principal dairying region. About half New Zealand's population of dairy cows are now located in the South Auckland–Waikato area. But rural diversification, especially into deer farming and horticulture, has been pursued since the nineteen-seventies. Giant fields of corn now flutter where tides of grass once washed to the roadside; kiwifruit plots and vineyards hug sunny slopes.

Hamilton, always the Waikato's first town, became its first city in 1945, when the population exceeded twenty thousand. It had taken eighty years, but in the next forty, with the growth of industry, it increased five-fold to more than a hundred thousand, finally edging out Dunedin as New Zealand's fourth city in 1986. Industry has changed the South Auckland region too, with the growth of the Glenbrook iron and steel plant near Waiuku on the south side of the Manukau Harbour. The demand for energy has reshaped the landscape, and great hydro-electric dams and lakes have grown along the Waikato River. The coal of the lower Waikato basin, an energy source since the days when it fired the boilers of British gunboats, remains precious. Large coal-burning power stations have risen at Meremere and Huntly; more coalfields are opening, and older fields are being reworked.

Nevertheless, Mooloo still reigns supreme. The Waikato, with Taranaki, is home to one of the most native species of New Zealand fauna: the 'cow cocky'. Dour in feature and casual in dress, terse in wit and aggressive in stance, he is best observed on market days and at agricultural shows. He has made the Waikato what it is, and New Zealand too, and isn't slow to say so.

In no other part of New Zealand have human beings imposed themselves more durably and more comprehensively than in the peaceful Waikato region. Of the land of the moa hunter and Tainui tribes, of the swampy wilderness the soldier-settler knew, just scraps of scrub and shreds of forest remain. Most of the Waikato is a serene tapestry of shelter belt, farmhouse, prosperous small town and dairy factory. The voices of the past are faint. Best to listen to the river. The wide Waikato, weaving between willowy banks and rushing out to the Tasman, knew it all.

Sharp tree shapes silhouetted against a dusky early-morning sky are mirrored in the Waikato River near Rangiriri, where Maori defence systems defeated Europeans in one of the most crucial and hard-fought battles of the eighteen-sixties

THE MISSISSIPPI OF THE MAORI

Long a revered accomplice to survival for tribes who lived along its banks, New Zealand's greatest river is still a precious resource

In 1859, the Austrian geologist and explorer Ferdinand von Hochstetter declared, 'It is only with the Danube or the Rhine that I can compare the mighty river we have just entered'. After sailing farther up the wide Waikato, Hochstetter had to summon up a third great river of the world to convey his awe. He styled it 'the Mississippi of the Maori'.

The longest river in New Zealand – four hundred and twenty-five kilometres from headwaters to sea – the Waikato flows out of the ruggedly volcanic heart of the North Island and drops three hundred and thirty-three metres in its journey. For the Maori it was a precious highway and an even more precious reservoir of food. The hills overlooking the river made superb sites for fortified villages. Other villages sat along the banks where the kumara flourished in silt and sand deposited by the river. The water swarmed with small fishing and hunting canoes and large canoes constructed for war.

Generations of Maoris knew the Waikato as a capricious and venerated accomplice in survival; generations were buried within sight and sound of the river. *Waikato* means 'flowing water', but the name of the river in full was *Waikato-taniwha-rau*, 'the flowing water of a hundred water monsters'. This was another way of saying that the river ruled Maori lives. Water monsters may not literally have menaced every bend and backwater of the great river, but there was certainly a powerful chief who had best not be challenged.

Sand barges dredge sand and shingle from the Waikato River not far from Mercer **Below:** *Colourful river canoes and war canoes are brought out, and traditional Maori dress worn for the Ngaruawahia Regatta, held annually in March*

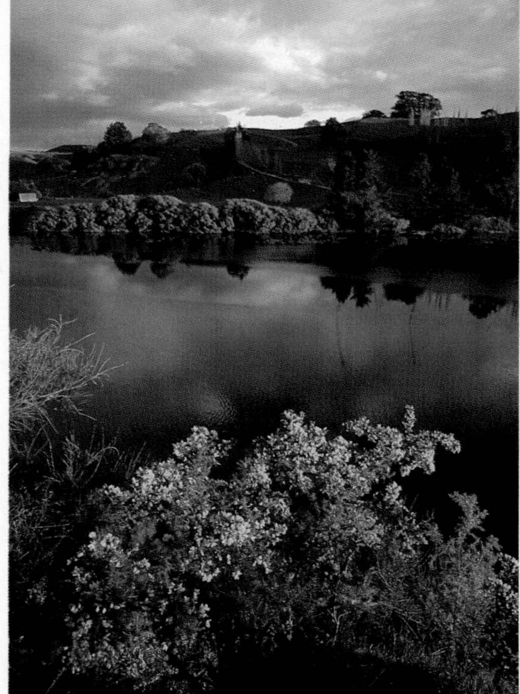

Sweeping past rich farmlands, the Waikato River pauses at Lake Karapiro, the twenty-four kilometre artificial lake

Up to the twentieth century, the Waikato roamed where it willed. The New Zealand painter Charles Blomfield, observing it in the eighteen-seventies, recorded that in flood it presented 'a most beautiful appearance . . . tops of cabbage trees, flax and ferns just showed above the water, with here and there the roof of a Maori whare.

Below: *The country's largest power station, at Huntly, on the west bank of the Waikato River, generates half as much more electricity than all of the river's eight hydro stations*

Behind this, bush and trees of all kinds, through the branches of which you might row a boat, in many instances for three or four miles. In some places the river appeared ten miles wide'.

It was Maori belief that mist on a sacred mountain could disclose visions of the future. In the early eighteen-sixties Maoris dwelling by the river are said to have gazed with astonishment as the sun's early rays played through the mist on the *tapu* summit of Maungaroa. They saw battles, a steamboat and European towns. Soon after, the battles began. Not one steamer but three sailed up the Waikato, with gunboats spitting shells among Maori warriors. More vessels followed and armed colonists disembarked. The towns came when conquest was complete. The Mississippi of the Maori was soon as British as the Thames.

After the cruel confiscations that followed the war, Maoris returning from sanctuary in the King Country had to buy back ancestral riverside lands if they had the money, and make their way in the white man's world while the river rolled past. A century and a quarter later the Waikato remains precious. Without the energy it provides, New Zealand's cities would dim and industry would falter. The torrent has been tamed, its currents channelled, yet the river still dominates.

The Waikato begins its long surge to the sea as a dribble of melting ice and snow on the slopes of steamy Mount Ruapehu, high on the Volcanic Plateau. It meanders through the Rangipo Desert, and grows into the body of water that most New Zealanders know best as the Tongariro, but which Maori still call the Waikato. Pushing through a forest of mountain beech, it feeds the inland sea of Lake Taupo at its southern end and leaves the lake again at its northern end.

From Lake Taupo the Waikato hurtles down the Huka Falls and races – hydro-electric needs permitting – through the Aratiatia Rapids. Here steam rises above its banks. The land is noisy with geysers. Submarine thermal springs warm the river; hot streams feed it. Dark pine forests grown on pumice wastes rise tall on the hills. For the next one hundred and fifty kilometres seven great hydro-electric power stations trap the river's bulk in valley after valley – the first of them, Arapuni, built in 1929; the remainder since the Second World War. Farther downstream, the last of these giants is Karapiro, where the river has been raised as high as thirty metres to create a lake twenty-four kilometres long.

Top: *A beautiful rainbow in stormy sky creates a dramatic backdrop to cattle grazing rich pastures just near Matamata*
Above: *Wild seas swirl about the rugged west coast where the great Waikato River finally empties into the Tasman Sea*

From Karapiro into the Waikato region proper, the river's journey is gentle. For the remainder of its course it has expanded in time of flood to form lakes and swamps. Little forest now darkens the hills above. The countryside is pastoral with cows grazing to the water's edge. The river passes the pleasant town of Cambridge, pushes through the heart of Hamilton and joins the Waipa River at Ngaruawahia. Here the Waikato is again distinctly Maori. It glides past the complex of carved buildings that constitutes the headquarters of the forty thousand Maoris of the Waikato, and the official residence of their monarchs. On festive occasions, and especially during the Ngaruawahia Regatta in March, the river once again swarms with colourful Maori canoes.

From here, the Waikato has only ninety kilometres to travel and forty metres to fall. Just north of Ngaruawahia, two hundred and eighty-seven metre Taupiri Mountain (sacred to the tribesmen of the Waikato) rises starkly at the

Above: *Early morning at Elkayel Stables near Cambridge. The area is famed for its fine stud properties*

waterside. Once a strongly fortified pa, it is where the mighty chief Te Putu (ancestor of the present Maori queen) ruled and was slain. For the past one hundred and thirty years Maori monarchs have been interred on its steep slopes, along with many of their Waikato subjects.

At Ruakura Animal Research Station, east of Hamilton, cattle and sheep management techniques are studied

Broader now, the river rolls across the rich coalfields of Huntly and past the tall chimney-stacks of the coal-fired Huntly power station. Dykes have been constructed here to narrow the path of the river. Until the nineteen-fifties the area between Huntly and Mercer was often badly flooded – sometimes becoming one large lake.

Near Rangiriri and Meremere the waters pass battlesites of the eighteen-sixties. At Meremere, Waikato warriors checked the British advance on their lands for three months. At Rangiriri they

Below: *Its smooth waters and perfect conditions have made Lake Karapiro, on the Waikato River, a headquarters for New Zealand rowing. Teams compete regularly in regattas*

demonstrated their capacity to die for those lands – and to leave an imposing list of British dead. At Mercer, where road and then railway once dropped travellers for the upriver journey, the ever-swelling river swings through swamp and wetland towards the Tasman. Between 1840 and the early eighteen-sixties, in the golden age of the newly Christian Waikato, produce from the fertile Maori hinterlands was ferried this far downriver. It was then portaged across to the Manukau Harbour and on to Onehunga for sale in Auckland's markets.

At Tuakau the Waikato washes under its last bridge and begins to taste of the Tasman's tides as it eddies past marshy islands greened with willows. The great journey – from 'the very core of the land' in Hochstetter's words – is all but done. Finally it forms a delta a kilometre wide, fluttering with duck, shag, pied stilt, heron, mallard, pukeko and swan. Flounder, mullet and (in spring) whitebait flourish, as do fishermen. The mountain and desert that gave birth to the river are half the land behind. The great hydro-electric dams are lost. As it finds its way between black dunes of ironsand and into the sea, the Waikato is again much as it was when the first humans adventuring here found a mighty river worthy of their wonder.

Left: *Near the centre of Hamilton a brightly painted facade gives new life to an old building* **Below:** *The symbol of Hamilton during the Rugby season is without a doubt Mooloo, the mascot of the city's football team. When the team scores a victory, cow-bells ring out in unison across the region*

The wild and windswept coast near Raglan has tramping tracks leading round headlands and up Mount Karioi

An orchard in full bloom on the Cambridge–Hamilton road

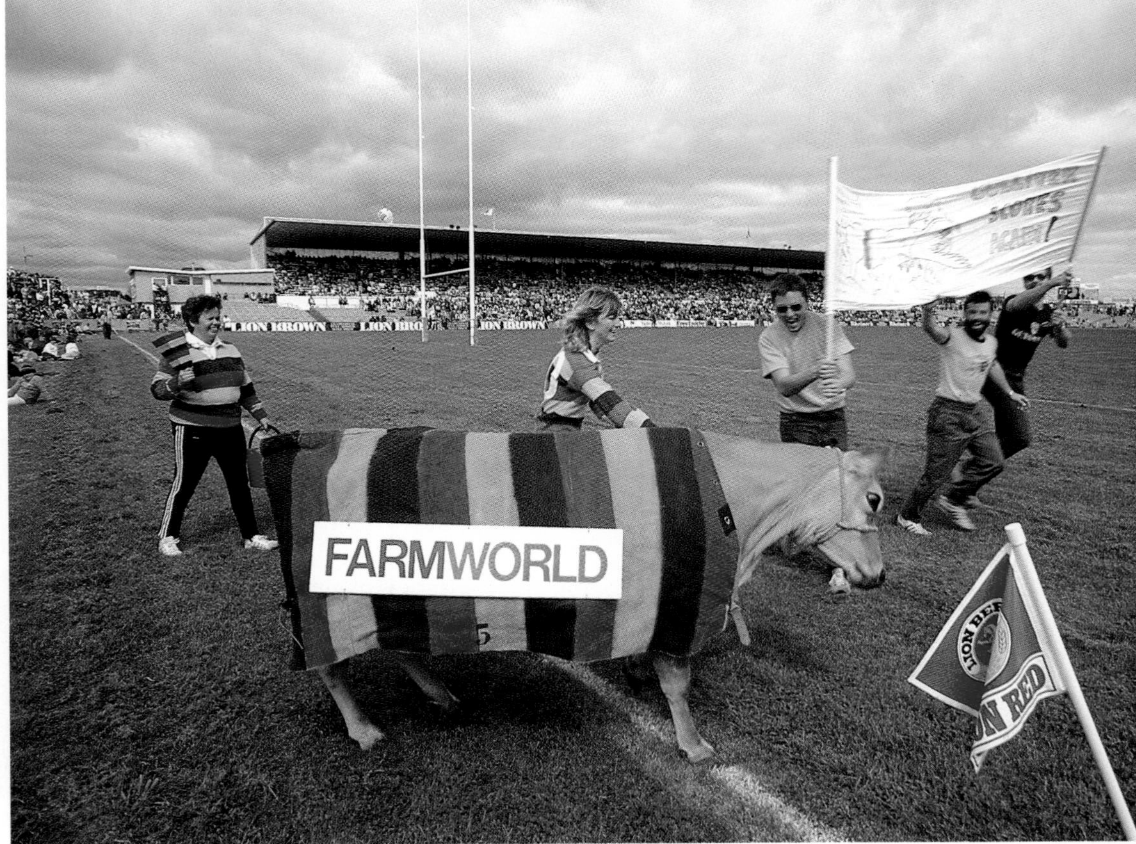

PLACES OF INTEREST

CAMBRIDGE
Home to 10 000 people, 24 kilometres from **HAMILTON**, Cambridge is the most elegant of the Waikato's towns, with its tree-shaded streets, village green, clock tower, band rotundas, pioneer hotels, antique shops and tall-spired Anglican church. It began as an outlying British garrison during the wars of the 1860s – it was the farthest point upstream that gunboats could travel.

The town is not named after the English university town, as is often assumed, but was so called by the garrison's commanders in honour of their commander-in-chief, the Duke of Cambridge. St Peter's private school, established in 1936, is set above the river to the west of the town. Modelled on an English public school, it is known nationally for a summer music school housed here in January.

St Andrew's Anglican Church at Cambridge

Cambridge has a number of distinctive buildings, including St Andrew's Anglican Church (1881), with its impressive timberwork, and the Cambridge Primary School (1879) in Duke Street, with its fine four-gable kauri facade.

At the heart of the town there is a bird sanctuary, at Te Koutu Lake and Domain (with picnic areas). The lush Cambridge countryside is known for its thoroughbred studs where some of New Zealand's most famous racehorses have been bred. The Maungakawa Scenic Reserve (8 kilometres north-east on Maungakawa Road) has pleasant walking tracks and impressive river views. Lake Karapiro (8 kilometres south-east) extends 24 kilometres behind one of New Zealand's largest hydro-electric dams. It has been the setting for both Commonwealth and world rowing championships and offers all forms of water sport.

HAMILTON
New Zealand's fourth largest city and the country's largest inland city, with a population of over 105 000. Like **CAMBRIDGE** it began as a British garrison on a defensive position beside the Waikato River, but unlike Cambridge it lost its gentle frontier quality in headlong 20th-century growth. The town was named after a naval captain who perished fighting at Tauranga in 1864, the year of the town's founding. An interesting relic of that era is what remains of the British boat *Rangiriri*, raised from the riverbed in 1982 and now preserved.

Though struggling for survival in its early years, Hamilton now embodies the prosperity of the Waikato region (see page 74). Its large new university, opened in 1964, has gone far to confirm the city's growing eminence and to colour its character. East of the city, the Ruakura Soil and Plant Research Station and Ruakura Animal Research Station are dedicated to the efficiency of New Zealand farming. (For visits, contact Hamilton Public Relations Office.) There is also the Clydesdale Agricultural and National Dairy Museum, at Mystery Creek (16 kilometres south; open daily 9–5, except Christmas Day), with displays that bring rural pioneering to life. There are also stables and a blacksmith's shop.

The city's Mormon Temple at Temple View (7 kilometres south-west on Tuhikaramea Road) is a centre for South Pacific members of the faith, with an information office serving visitors. Victoria Street, Hamilton's main street, runs parallel with the great Waikato River. Parkland and fine homes among lush growth grace the riverside. Among many interesting exhibits, the Waikato Art Museum has a splendid example of the great Maori canoes that once rode the river – *Te Winika*, built in the 1830s. At 339 River Road are the earthworks of Miropiko Pa, an old Maori fortress.

Hamilton's notable 19th-century buildings include the Bank of New Zealand (1878) at the corner of Hood and Victoria streets, an excellent example of Victorian classical style; Beale Cottage (1872) at the corner of Beale and Grey Streets, built for a surgeon serving with the 4th Waikato Militia Regiment; the striking stone building at 7 Hood Street (1878); Hockin House in Selwyn Street (1893), now the home of the Waikato Historical Society and furnished to period (open Sunday 2–4, from October to June); and Lake House (1873) in Lake Crescent, a splendid example of a Victorian colonial home. Two schools – Waikato Diocesan School for Girls and Southwell School – have grown around grand 19th-century homesteads. Another distinguished specimen is Woodlands, at Gordonton, built in the 1870s as a farm manager's residence. The Waikato Historical Society can arrange visits to some of Hamilton's historic buildings, but most are in private hands and/or closed to the public. One exception is the splendid old Hamilton Hotel, which survived a fire in the 1920s and has been remodelled as an arts complex.

Other attractions include scenic river cruises and a paddleboat restaurant. Although at the heart of the North Island, Hamilton is less than an hour's drive from **RAGLAN** Harbour on the west coast, and not much farther from the Bay of Plenty on the east.

HUNTLY
Grown on coal, fed by coal and still commanded by coal, this lower Waikato town of 8000 is slenderly strung along the riverside. It was named after the Scottish home of the then tiny township's first postmaster. The town is now also distinguished by the 150 metre tall chimneys (coloured orange to deter low-flying aircraft) of the immense coal-fired power station, which has given the town new life and made the vast coal deposits of the district more precious. The station, fed by a 2 kilometre long conveyor system from an underground mine, is capable of producing more electricity than all eight Waikato dams. The Huntly Mining and Cultural Museum, in a restored mine manager's residence in Harlock Place (open daily 10–4), records the history of mining and brick-making here in interesting displays.

At Waahi Marae, near the power station, is the striking Te Tumu ancestral tree, a carved block of totara that records the *whakapapa* (genealogy) of the Tainui tribes who settled the Waikato region. Waahi Marae is the principal marae of the Ngati Mahuta tribe and home to the King movement's paramount family. Just south of the town is sacred **TAUPIRI** Mountain, burial place of Maori kings.

KIHIKIHI
Four kilometres south of **TE AWAMUTU**, this satellite township of 1500 people began as a British garrison on the Puniu River, the border with the King Country, now bridged, and crossed in a flash by the modern motorist. The village was also famed for having the last pub between here and Taranaki's Urenui, for the King Country Maori wished to keep their region temperate.

Commanding the main street is a memorial to Rewi Maniapoto, the hero of the battle of Orakau (see page 76), who took up residence here in a house provided by the colonial government when peace was made in the 1880s. Four kilometres along the road east to Arapuni is the site of the battle with a plaque indicating the disposition of Maoris and Britons during three bitter days of fighting in 1864.

MATAMATA
This eastern Waikato town of 5500, set in lush pastures warmed by thermal springs, is near the Volcanic Plateau and stands on a fast alternative route to and from Auckland. It is noted for sleek cows and fleet racehorses. Matamata is coloured by the memories of two famous 19th-century New Zealanders, the Maori Wiremu Tamihana (1802-66) and the European Josiah Clifton Firth (1826-97), whose lives were linked.

Once a well-known drinking spot the old Hamilton Hotel has been successfully converted into an arts centre, with a gallery, a restaurant and an attractive riverside theatre

Tamihana refused to countenance the Treaty of Waitangi in 1840. Later, in the 1850s, he determined the course of the Waikato King movement and saw to the election of Te Wherowhero as first Maori monarch. Kingmaker yet peacemaker, a truly tragic figure in New Zealand history, he took up arms only when British artillery began to roar upon Maori militants. For the last two years of his life Tamihana pleaded in vain with the colonial government for the return of confiscated Waikato land. Yet he saw the speculative Josiah Firth as a friend and leased him ancestral acres (Firth finished up owning 22 000 hectares outright). When Tamihana died, Firth erected a memorial cairn on the site where he expired. Firth transformed the district, clearing snags from the Waihou River to ship produce to Auckland, and pushing a road through to the military garrison of **CAMBRIDGE**. He also met unarmed at Tamihana's memorial cairn with the murderous Maori rebel Te Kooti when the latter was terrorising the central North Island. Firth counselled peace, though to no effect. His huge estate was broken up in the late 19th century, and Matamata was founded in 1905.

Firth's most durable legacy is the eccentric tower (1881) that was designed to keep watch for Maori incursion, but which was built nearly two decades after Waikato warfare had in fact ceased (3 kilometres from Matamata along the road to Okauia Springs). This reserve also features Firth's homestead (rebuilt after a fire in 1902), a country schoolhouse (1882), a church (1912), a post office, many pioneer artefacts, and Tamihana's memorial cairn. (The Firth Tower Historical Reserve is open daily except Christmas Day.)

Not far is Stanley Landing (on the Waihou River), which once served Firth as a port and is now a pleasing site for picnics. Six kilometres outside Matamata are the Opal Hot Springs with private and public mineral pools. Farther east the Kaimai Range between Matamata and Tauranga offers superb views.

MERCER

This riverside township once sat on the southern limit of the Great South Road. A 19th-century connection was made here with river steamers to convey soldiers, settlers, speculators and traders into the Waikato. Here too the modern southbound motorist meets the wide river and begins to travel beside it.

Mercer takes its name from a British artillery captain who died in the battle of **RANGIRIRI**, just upriver. At the township's centre is an iron turret from the British gunboat *Pioneer*, which now forms a base for a memorial to the district's dead of World War I. Four kilometres south is the large Meremere coal-fired power station. On the hill above it are the remains of a large Maori redoubt (access south of the power station along Meremere Lane), where a thousand Waikato Maori checked British advance into the region for two months in 1863.

MIRANDA

Warmed by thermal waters, this township on the western side of the Firth of Thames is on a route neglected by travellers but abundant in charm and sea views. Named after a British naval vessel that bombarded Maoris entrenched here in the Waikato War, Miranda has a large thermal pool complex and picnic area (closed Tuesday, except during school holidays).

MORRINSVILLE

Market town of the eastern Waikato with 5500 people. Established on once waterlogged land at the edge of the even soggier Hauraki Plains, it was named after Thomas Morrin, an abentee Auckland landowner who became bankrupt. Local legend has it that the eccentric bend in Thames Street was so surveyed to keep the street above the encroaching swamp. The name of the town's first pub (1873) seems to say something about early conditions too: The Jolly Cripple. Until the region was drained, Morrinsville almost sank.

Since the beginning of the century, dairy farming has determined Morrinsville's quintessentially Waikato character. The Pioneer Cottage Museum in Lorne Street, in a restored settler's dwelling of the early 1870s, has a large Maori war canoe (open Sunday 1.30–4 and otherwise on request). Mt Kuranui (156 metres), just out of town along Kuranui Road, offers a green panorama. The district has one of the world's highest densities of dairy cattle per hectare, as well as the world's first wholly automated dairy factory.

NGARUAWAHIA

At the confluence of the Waikato and Waipa Rivers, Ngaruawahia is the historic headquarters of the Maori King movement and surely the spiritual heart of the Waikato; it has certainly been the soul of Maori renaissance in the region. With a population of 5000, and only 19 kilometres north of **HAMILTON**, it is now almost a suburb of that city.

Sitting on two major canoe routes into the North Island interior, Ngaruawahia was always a place of importance to the Maori. It was even more important after 1858, when the first Maori king, Potatau I (formerly Te Wherowhero) was proclaimed here in defiance of British authority. The village was abandoned in 1863 when the King Maori saw British gunboats in action downriver at **RANGIRIRI** and **MERCER**. Within a year the land of Ngaruawahia Maori was being carved up for European settlement, and for the next 70 years it was markedly a white man's domain. In the 1880s King Tawhiao came out of exile from the King Country and announced that Ngaruawahia would always be his *turangawaewae*, his 'place to rest his feet'. For Maoris who returned, however, there was only poor land, or none at all.

The most remarkable Maori woman of the 20th century, Princess Te Puea Herangi (1884-1952) was determined that Maori identity should survive, starting at Ngaruawahia. She raised money so that ancestral riverside land could be rather humiliatingly bought back from Europeans. In 1921 she and 170 followers settled on a scrubby riverbank. Te Puea lived to see the building of the complex of Maori buildings (known as Turangawaewae Marae) that dominates Ngaruawahia.

The marae includes Turongo House (1938), with its elaborately carved and distinctive pentagonal tower, the official residence of the present Maori monarch, Te Arikinui Dame Te Atairangikaahu, DBE; the meeting-house Mahinaarangi (1929) with a carving showing the *Tainui* canoe; and the imposing Kimiora Cultural Complex (1974), with an especially impressive mural by the well-known modern Maori artist Para Matchitt. Access is limited to festive days, or to advertised weekends. Otherwise only roadside and riverside glimpses are possible.

In March, on the closest Saturday to St Patrick's Day, the Ngaruawahia Regatta

THE DUKE OF MATAMATA

A rare combination of visionary and scientific innovator, Matamata landowner Josiah Firth was one of the Waikato's most extraordinary characters

Firth's Tower and complex of restored buildings near Matamata are open to visitors

Also known as 'Hohaia','The Lion of the North' or 'Duke of Matamata', Josiah Clifton Firth (1826-97) made his first thorough visit to the area near Matamata in 1859, but it was not until the Waikato War had come to an end in 1864 that he made his move to acquire vast tracts of land.

Firth built upon his long friendship with Wiremu Tamihana, the influential chief of the Ngati Haua, to negotiate the lease of an immense area popularly believed to be equivalent to the size of a dukedom. Following the death of Tamihana, Firth purchased the twenty-two thousand hectares of his 'dukedom' for just twelve thousand pounds.

In addition to an intuitive commercial sharpness, Firth possessed skills and ambitions far in advance of his time. He was instrumental in the development of agriculture in the Waikato region. He advocated rotation cropping, swamp drainage and the mechanisation of agriculture. At its prime, his land boasted eight reaper-binders, two threshers, ten mechanical rakes and thirteen mowers – a huge assortment of machinery in those labour-intensive days. He also had windmills built to raise water from low-lying lands and he ensured that roads were planned and built, and telephones installed.

Firth's enthusiasm was unique. Ironically, however, he was defeated by the very virtues he had practised to his advantage: vision and daring. The depression of the eighteen-eighties brought increased risks to his capital ventures, and he lost money firstly on a mining project and then on a dairy factory. He failed in an attempt to bring a railway to the area so that he could subdivide land at high prices; and his refrigeration scheme was too far in advance of the technological constraints of the time. For a while, he retreated to Auckland.

Eventually, Firth's ambitions were fulfilled through the actions of a less flamboyant character named John McCaw. Though McCaw did not own land himself, he worked through banks and mercantile agencies to subdivide the Matamata area into its present rich farmlands. However, it was Firth who led the way by the scope of his imagination and ambition, his technical foresight and his willingness to take risks.

brings out river canoes and war canoes in one of the most colourful events in the New Zealand calendar. Off the main road, near the junction of rivers, is the former building of the Maori Parliament (1920), now used for other purposes. Near by is a monument to the first Maori monarch and a gun turret from the vessel *Pioneer*, which helped to wrest the Waikato from Maori hands in the 1860s.

North of Ngaruawahia is **TAUPIRI** Mountain, the final resting place of Maori monarchs. To the west are the Waingaro Hot Springs, a large thermal pool complex with picnic areas and a camping ground. Off the Waingaro Road is the Hakarimata walkway, one of the most rewarding in the Waikato. It follows the forested range behind Ngaruawahia and takes in wide views of the region.

PAEROA

This eastern Waikato town, with one foot in the pastoral Hauraki Plains and the other in the wild Coromandel Peninsula, now has 3700 people. It grew as a river port serving nearby goldfields. Prosperity came more reliably with the draining and settlement of the Hauraki Plains. It is now best known for a national drink, Lemon and Paeroa, made from the town's mineral waters and once used by miners

The giant model of a Lemon and Paeroa drink bottle, a famous Paeroa product, reminds visitors of its national importance

as a cure-all for post-alcoholic woes. The drink is now manufactured elsewhere.

Paeroa's bulky old wooden pubs testify to robust pioneer thirsts. The dramatic landscapes that fuelled those thirsts can be seen on the drive through the old goldmining district between Paeroa and Waihi via the craggy Karangahake Gorge. At Waihi there is a museum and mining camp. An especially interesting goldfield walkway, created in part on the old rail route to the Bay of Plenty, includes a tunnel with glow-worms and passes mining remains. Part of the now abandoned line is used for holiday excursions for Waihi visitors and steam-train enthusiasts (see also page 98).

Paeroa has not been a port since the 1930s. It has an interesting Historical Maritime Park at the old shipping depot on the Waihou River (four kilometres outside town on the road to Auckland; open weekends and holidays). There are a number of restored vessels, including the paddle-steamer *Kopu*, and the old packet *Settler*. The museum building was once a goldminers' post office at Waitekauri.

A reconstructed early Paeroa street may be seen at Paeroa's own museum in the library building in Belmont Road (open 11–3 Monday, Wednesday and Friday, and daily during holidays). At nearby Netherton (9 kilometres) a museum features the famed gemstones of the Coromandel Peninsula. At 13 River Road, Ngatea (23 kilometres), a supermarket sells raw and processed gemstones for jewellery.

PIRONGIA

In the lee of Pirongia Mountain, this small community of 600 was known as Alexandra in the soldier-settler frontier era and seemed destined to be the Waikato's chief town. Nearby **TE AWAMUTU** and the city of **HAMILTON** have since left it with only faint memories of its former importance.

Just outside the township is the best preserved British redoubt in the Waikato, built by the Armed Constabulary in 1869; the buildings have gone but the earthworks are impressive. (Look for the signpost 100 metres south of the Alexandra hotel.) North of the town are the older Maori earthworks at Matakitaki where the tribes of the Waikato felt the murderous sting of firearms for the first time, at the hands of Northland's Ngapuhi. A memorial (on the northern outlet from the township) records the death of hundreds, perhaps thousands, of Maoris. Pirongia's most venerable buildings are the public library (1864) and the Pirongia Playcentre (1873), both originally schools.

PIRONGIA FOREST PARK

For the Maori, the many-peaked mountain called Pirongia was sacred. It was wedded to **TAUPIRI** Mountain on the Waikato River, and was also the home of *patupaiarehe*, or fairy people, who are said to have been the first gentle Polynesian inhabitants of New Zealand, swept up onto forested summits like Pirongia by tides of later, more warlike migrants. After the Waikato War, it was part of the uneasy frontier with the King Country. Any European surveyor pressing too far on its slopes was slain.

The 959 metre extinct volcano – a two-million-year-old basalt mountain with a base 17 kilometres across – shadows the western horizon of the central Waikato, collecting mist and wild weather from the Tasman Sea. It is the centrepiece of the 17 000 hectare Pirongia Forest Park (which includes 756 metre Mt Karioi, another volcano). The vegetation – in a botanic transition zone – is distinctive. Trees of New Zealand's north mingle with those of the south. Giant, mossy bluffs soar above treetops; native birds, with lean pickings elsewhere in the grassy Waikato, flourish in broadleaf forest. There are walking tracks, sweeping views, picnic areas, huts and camping sites (information available from park headquarters in **PIRONGIA** township).

PORT WAIKATO

A haphazardly grown resort settlement sitting on the southern shore of the Waikato Heads. Traders and missionaries set up shop here in the 1820s and 1830s. In 1832 it was the site of the last battle for supremacy between Waikato tribes and Northland's Ngapuhi, involving thousands of warriors. It was a busy base and dockyard for British forces in the 1860s during the Waikato War. The fishing is splendid; so is the vista of the Waikato River bursting through black sands to the sea.

PRINCESS OF THE PEOPLE

At Ngaruawahia, the Turangawaewae Marae forms a permanent memorial to Princess Te Puea Herangi, the first Maori woman to become a national leader

The carved gate to Turangawaewae Marae, built in honour of Princess Te Puea

Born in the Waikato, at Whatiwhatihoe, Princess Te Puea (1884-1952) grew up at a time when many tribes were dispirited by land losses, internal quarrels and the spread of European diseases to which they had no natural resistance. Her mother was the eldest daughter of Tawhiao, the second Maori king, and this made Te Puea *kahui ariki*, one of the king's closest relatives.

When her mother died Te Puea was only fourteen,and she soon gained a reputation for stubbornness and recklessness. From an early age she immersed herself in Maori knowledge and legends. Later, when she gained prominence, she used this store of information to powerful effect as a speaker at Maori gatherings.

Mahuta Te Wherowhero, the third Maori king, provided great support for Te Puea. He gave her a deep sense of mission, which was even further developed by her close association with the fourth king, Te Rata.

While her critics accused her of being arrogant, Te Puea felt it necessary to summon all her mental and emotional strength to rally the spirit of the Maori people and revive their cultural pride. She believed that if they were to compete in New Zealand's changing society, they would have to plan day-to-day practical methods to achieve this ambition.

In 1920 Te Puea acquired four hectares of land at Ngaruawahia. She established a small power-base encouraging social progress and cultural renewal,despite opposition from local *Pakeha* who felt she would lower standards in the area. In 1929, she presided over the opening of the great carved meeting-house, Mahinaarangi.

In later life this remarkable Maori princess widened her interests to include efforts for women's organisations and work among children. She encouraged the development of Maori lands, often labouring on farms to set an example. She is also remembered for her revival of old crafts such as carving, rebuilding marae, and canoe construction.

One of the best-known and most admired Maori leaders of this century, Te Puea combined her ambition and vision with an understanding of practical realities. She was a supporter of the King movement, and became the first modern Maori woman to transcend the definitions of tribe to become a national leader.

TWENTIETH CENTURY ENGINEERING TRIUMPH

Just south of Cambridge at Karapiro is one of the eight hydro-electric sites that harness New Zealand's most valuable natural power resource, the mighty Waikato River

Visitors can watch the opening of the spillway gates at Karapiro Dam

From Highway 1, near Karapiro, visitors can view teams of rowers scudding across the waters of a twenty-four kilometre artificial lake. Although Karapiro is the headquarters of New Zealand rowing – one of the country's most successful international sports – its primary function is to generate hydro-electric power for the North Island.

The sites for this remarkable system of hydro-engineering are strategically placed along the Waikato River on its journey from the centre of the North Island to the Tasman Sea.

Aratiatia was built in 1964. The natural fall of the awesome Aratiatia Rapids supplies generators with eighty-four megawatts of power without the need of a true dam. The spillway gates at the top are closed to allow the rapids to reappear at 10–11.30 and 2.30–4 daily. The power station is easily approached by a short drive from Wairakei Village.

The station at *Ohakuri* generates one hundred and twelve megawatts of power. Constructed in 1962 it shows how the need for power has taken precedence over the environment. Three-quarters of the famous Orakeikorako thermal area was flooded by the thirteen square kilometre artificial lake created by the station's dam.

Just two square kilometres in size, the tiny artificial lake at *Atiamuri* produces eighty-one megawatts of power. It was built in 1958.

The *Whakamaru* station, completed in 1956, produces one hundred megawatts of power from a narrow, eight kilometre long lake.

The powerful dam at *Maraetai* was completed in 1952 as part of a double scheme. There are two powerhouses capable of producing three hundred and sixty megawatts. The five square kilometre lake, surrounded by a nature reserve, is popular for boating and fishing.

Although the dam at *Waipapa*, built in 1961, provides the smallest hydro-electric output – only fifty-one megawatts – it has created the most beautiful of engineered lakes.

Arapuni station produces one hundred and fifty-six megawatts. It was built in 1929 and its power capacity has since been increased twice.

The scheme at *Karapiro* (1947) produces ninety megawatts, and completes the complex system that exploits the waters of the Waikato River for the hydro-electric power.

PUKEKOHE

This multi-racial capital of one of New Zealand's major market gardening areas is 51 kilometres south of Auckland. Its 14 000 people are a mix of Chinese, Indian, Maori and European. Here fertile volcanic soil provides much of the country with potatoes, onions and many other vegetables. The principal industry is food processing. Pukekohe also provides the nation with thrills on its motor racing circuit.

Settled early by Europeans on land purchased from local Maoris, the district also saw the early clashes of the struggle for the Waikato in the 1860s. The most vivid reminder of those days is the bullet-scarred Pukekohe East Presbyterian Church (1862), 5 kilometres out of town. Local Scottish and Cornish settlers made it a stockaded garrison and in September 1863 fought off 200 Maori warriors until reinforcements arrived. St Bride's Anglican Church (1859), on Findlay Road at nearby Mauku, was likewise stockaded and loopholed, but never menaced. The Pioneer Memorial Cottage (*c.* 1859) in Roulston Park (open weekends and holidays, otherwise by arrangement) was also a garrison.

Fourteen kilometres in the direction of Tuakau are the now cemetery-surrounded earthworks of the Alexandra Redoubt, on a bluff 90 metres above the Waikato River. The redoubt was one of the riverside garrisons established by the British to consolidate their grip on the lower Waikato and protect river traffic. The memorial at its centre records the names of soldiers killed in the vicinity. From the earthworks there are impressive glimpses of the river below.

RAGLAN

The Waikato's oldest town, Raglan was European-settled from the 1830s and named in the 1850s by patriotic colonists after Lord Raglan, commander of British forces in the Crimean War. It is now a gentle palm-shaded seaside town of 1500 people, set on a splendid harbour under hills given symmetry by ancient Maori settlement. The extinct volcano of Mt Karioi (756 metres) looms over the town. A resort frequented by the people of **HAMILTON** and the central Waikato, Raglan is also much favoured as a weekend retreat by pop musicians, who make evenings at the grand old Harbour View Hotel (1890) lively.

Raglan's former golf course was a source of conflict in the 1970s. During World War II, patriotic Maori owners lent the land to the New Zealand government for an airstrip that was never built. Although some of the land was sacred to local Maori, it was made into a golf course. After decades of agitation, the deeds to the land were handed back to Raglan Maori in 1983.

A drive to Whale Bay (10 kilometres) has superb views of the west coast towards the Waikato's mouth. Just off this route are the mysterious and unique Tattooed Rocks. Never satisfactorily explained by surviving Maori lore, they are incised with patterns resembling the body tattoos of Maori warriors. The rocks probably had ritual and religious significance.

On the coastal road south of Whale Bay is the Te Toto Gorge Scenic Reserve, providing rugged scenery and intimacy with Mt Karioi, part of **PIRONGIA FOREST PARK** (a two-hour track leads to the summit). On the road south to the King Country's Kawhia there are the spectacular Bridal Veil Falls in a 218 hectare bush reserve. Good bathing at Ocean Beach; safe harbour swimming.

RANGIRIRI

Once a coaching halt between Auckland and **HAMILTON**, Rangiriri is now little more than a pub and a store. It was the setting for the most decisive battle of the Waikato War, when the British unleashed artillery and gunboats on rebel Maoris strongly entrenched between the Waikato River and Lake Waikare. Nevertheless nearly 40 British lives were lost and 93 men wounded in futile attempts to storm the Maori fortress. The issue was decided less by Maori casualties than by lack of Maori gunpowder. The British command rather unchivalrously declined a rebel request for more. Even less chivalrously they occupied the fortress while Maoris were under the impression that a truce was to be discussed. The site of the central Maori redoubt, with much of the surviving earthworks, may be visited just to the west of Highway 1.

To the east 400 metres are other earthworks known as Te Wheoro's Redoubt, which was occupied by Maoris as allies of the British during the unease of the late 1860s, when it was thought that Poverty Bay's marauding Te Kooti might reach this far north. Opposite the pub, British casualties of the battle are buried in a small but vivid cemetery. Maori dead were eventually transferred to tribal burial sites.

It can be said that Rangiriri (which means 'angry sky') is the birthplace of the Waikato as it discloses itself to today's traveller. Just to the north, off the main highway, Te Kauwhata (population 900) enjoys a national reputation for its wines. A government viticultural research station began functioning here at the beginning of the century, and more recently vineyards were established by one of the country's largest winemakers (visits to both are possible).

TAUPIRI

Village under the commanding 287 metre Taupiri Mountain which rises from the riverside between Huntly and Ngaruawahia. The mountain, once a mighty fortress overlooking the lower Waikato, is sacred ground to the Waikato Maori. Maori monarchs are buried here. At the end of the 19th century, Maori bones were brought back to Taupiri Mountain from battlefield

At Mystery Creek between Hamilton and Cambridge, farmers and agricultural workers display their produce at a special exhibition

graves and far places of exile to be reunited with the remains of their ancestors. In 1975 the New Zealand government finally returned the confiscated mountain to Maori hands. The village below grew as a soldier-settler community in the 1860s, sustained by the milling of timber and flax on former Maori land.

TE AROHA

This tidy east Waikato town, with a population of 3600, takes its name from the 952 metre peak that backs it and which, like **PIRONGIA** Mountain, was home to the fairy people of Maori folklore. The mountain in turn derives its name from a Maori chief's love of his native landscape (*Te Aroha* means 'the love'). Lost in the New Zealand interior, he climbed the peak and glimpsed his beloved home village. He jumped for joy, and when he landed the thermal springs flowed from the side of the mountain. In 1880 the New Zealand government settled yeoman farmers from England's Lincolnshire on 20 000 hectares here. The same year, a Maori prospector discovered gold on the mountain. Later, a larger and longer-lived field was found at nearby Waiorongomai. (More recently the mountain has been mined for lead and zinc.) But it was the real or imagined curative qualities of its thermal springs, along with the Victorian and Edwardian custom of 'taking the waters', that gave the town most character, and in the late 19th century and early 20th century it became a fashionable spa.

The spa atmosphere survives vividly in the mountainside Te Aroha Domain – now declared a historic precinct by the NZ Historic Places Trust – with its marvellously elegant old buildings, trees and lawns. It isn't all history; the spa still functions (open daily for bathing 10–9).

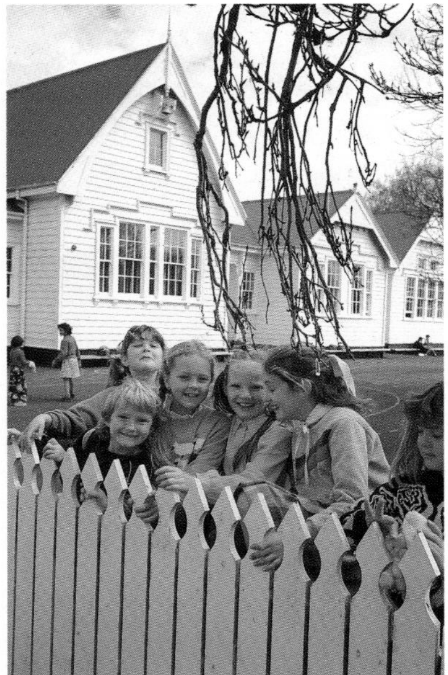

In Duke Street, Cambridge, the town's primary school, constructed in 1879, has an impressive four-gable kauri facade

There is also what is claimed to be the world's only hot soda water geyser, which plays every 30 to 40 minutes from a depth of about 60 metres. Mineral waters of the Vichy kind may be sampled at fountains, and tea may be taken in the splendid old kiosk (1908).

The large old Cadman bathhouse (1898) has been stripped and converted into a museum (open weekend 1–3, and daily in summer holidays). One or two accommodation houses of Te Aroha's heyday survive, as does the refurbished Grand Hotel, now a tavern. The climb to the top of the mountain is rewarding, with views of the Hauraki Plains, Hauraki Gulf, Coromandel Peninsula and Bay of Plenty from the summit. There is also a bus providing regular excursions up the private road to the top. The NZ Forest Service reopened the old goldmining trails here and in the Waiorongomai Valley, where 2000 miners once toiled. Five kilometres towards Elstow is the Bellevue Wildlife Park; arrangements can be made to visit.

TE AWAMUTU

Wealthy town of 8000 people set in rich dairyland 30 kilometres south of **HAMILTON** and a few kilometres north of the King Country. It grew on the site of a struggling village in the second half of the 19th century. Missionary John Morgan, who made the town a base for his civilising mission between 1841 and 1863 (see page 74), may be considered its founding father. But the prospering Maori agricultural communities were demolished by British guns at nearby Rangiaowhia (Hairini) and at Orakau. Morgan, who took the side of authority and had begun to function as an informer, fled to become chaplain to British troops. Many of his Maori parishioners likewise decamped, forced by hostilities over the Puniu River into exile among the untamed hills of the King Country.

Few of the soldier-settlers who took up confiscated land here lasted long. When imperial regiments departed, the bustling garrison became all but a ghost town. The arrival of the railway (1880), the end of tension on the King Country frontier (1881) and the founding of the North Island's first cooperative dairy factory (1882) ended the region's isolation.

Today Te Awamutu's treasure for the traveller is St John's Anglican Church (1854), set among the evocative headstones of a colonial graveyard. Maori Christians raised money (and provided pit-sawn timber) for its construction. After the battles of 1864, however, it became a prize of war for British Anglicans. Its simple and symmetrical interior and splendid stained glass windows make it one of New Zealand's most interesting churches; more so because it holds a memorial tablet possibly unique in warfare. Placed there by the soldiers of Her Majesty's 65th Foot Regiment in memory of Maori foes who fell defending their lands near by, it bears the inscription 'I say unto you love your enemies'. Outside, there is an equally remarkable memorial from the colonial government to 'the Maori heroes' who fell at Hairini and Orakau.

At nearby Rangiaowhia (now called Hairini), St Paul's (1856) is another fine church of the Morgan era in close to original condition. It also has beautiful stained glass windows (which Ferdinand von Hochstetter marvelled at in 1859 as 'mellow tints into my wondering eyes'). Warriors of the Maori king once marched to services here but, like St John's, it was later a prize of war. Little else survives of the Maori community that once prospered at Te Awamutu with flour mills, store, courthouse and racecourse. The battlefield of Orakau is to the south.

Te Awamutu's celebrated rose gardens, with 2500 bushes of 80 varieties (blooming from November to May), present a more peaceful perspective on the Waikato to more than 50 000 visitors a year (access by way of Gorst Avenue or Arawata Street). The Te Awamutu and District Museum (Civic Centre, Tuesday to Friday 11–4; weekends 2–4) has a rich collection, including war mementoes. Its prize exhibit is the Polynesian carving Uenuku, a sacred relic with no counterpart elsewhere. It is said to have travelled here with the *Tainui* canoe. The town's first public school (1879) now houses the Te Awamutu Little Theatre. The Waikato Railway Museum (Racecourse Rd, open occasionally Sunday) is dedicated to the days of steam. The hill overlooking Te Awamutu, Kakepuku, was strongly fortified in the pre-European period.

MAORI SKILLS OF WAR

At Meremere and Rangiriri, Highway 1 cuts straight through two pa sites of great significance in the Waikato War of 1863-64

Sketch of the Maori pa at Rangiriri, showing the unique defence system that held off Europeans during the eighteen-sixties

These fortifications were of such revolutionary design they held up the advance of a well-equipped British Army which outnumbered the Maori opposition by a ratio of four to one. Eventually the ratio increased to ten to one as the war petered out with no decisive victory to either side.

Although the remains of the pa sites can be seen, it is difficult to trace the features of the engineering novelties developed by Maori to adapt the old principles of fort construction to the demands of warfare employing muskets and cannon. The main innovations were: a bunker system built inside the pa to provide deep shelter from artillery bombardment; carefully positioning of firing lines to enfilade oncoming troops so that Maori musket defences were able to repulse heavy assault; erection of light defences to make the fortification appear weak, luring attackers into traps where they offered easier targets; outerworks, of scrub and other light materials, which looked flimsy but managed to hold up an advance to provide defenders with extra volleys.

Engineers of pa such as those at Meremere and Rangiriri developed a system of defence against artillery bombardments and infantry charges similar to those later used in the stalemates of the terrible trench warfare of the First World War.

It is strange that this brilliant means of defence against the superior numbers and firepower of the British army in the Waikato was not widely recognised for being such a novel advance in military tactics. That their adaptations of the skills of war were more than half a century ahead of their time is a tribute to Maori generals and their organisation of slender resources.

Above: *On the bank of the Waikato River, at Ngaruawahia, a solitary rotunda stands in peaceful parkland*

WAIUKU

With a population of 4800, this South Auckland town is on a mangroved estuary of the southern Manukau Harbour, 65 kilometres south of Auckland. It sits on the old Maori trade route between the Waikato and Auckland, where goods were portaged from river to harbour, and then on to the Auckland port of Onehunga. There were European settlers here before the Waikato War, but most fled when hostilities began. They returned to fell forests, drain swamps and establish a prosperous farming community, leaving a number of colonial cottages and farmsteads.

In the second half of the 20th century technology was devised for extracting ore from the ironsand dunes. The Glenbrook Steel Mill, 7 kilometres east of the town, is now expanding production to 750 000 tonnes of raw steel annually and employs 1500 people (guided tours Tuesday and Thursday). The sand is piped in slurry form from a mine site on the north head of the Waikato River, 13 kilometres south, where deposits of an estimated 150 million tonnes go down 100 metres. The mine site is within the exceptionally pleasant Waiuku Forest, 1500 hectares of pineland, with picnic spots above the Waikato River.

At Glenbrook there is also a functioning steam train and railway (Access Road, Sunday and public holidays 10–4). Waiuku has a museum (open Sunday and public holidays 1.30–4.30; also by arrangement) that documents the present thriving district. Near by is Hartmann House, a restored pioneer cottage, now a craft centre (open 10–4 Thursday to Sunday). Moored close is the veteran scow *Jane Gifford*, which is being restored to sail the waters of the southern Manukau again. At the town centre a monument marks the portage that made Waiuku a trading post. To the west of the town is the fine surf beach of Karioitahi (7 kilometres). At Awhitu the Auckland Regional Authority has a working farm park with water and wildlife views, barbecue areas, good bathing and the pioneer Brooks homestead (1860s). By way of Awhitu there is a fine drive along the rugged southern shore of the Manukau Harbour, with the green summits of the Waitakere Ranges looming across the water. Beyond the road's end is the Manukau signal station which beckons voyagers through the shoaling Manukau mouth.

Coromandel – Bay of Plenty

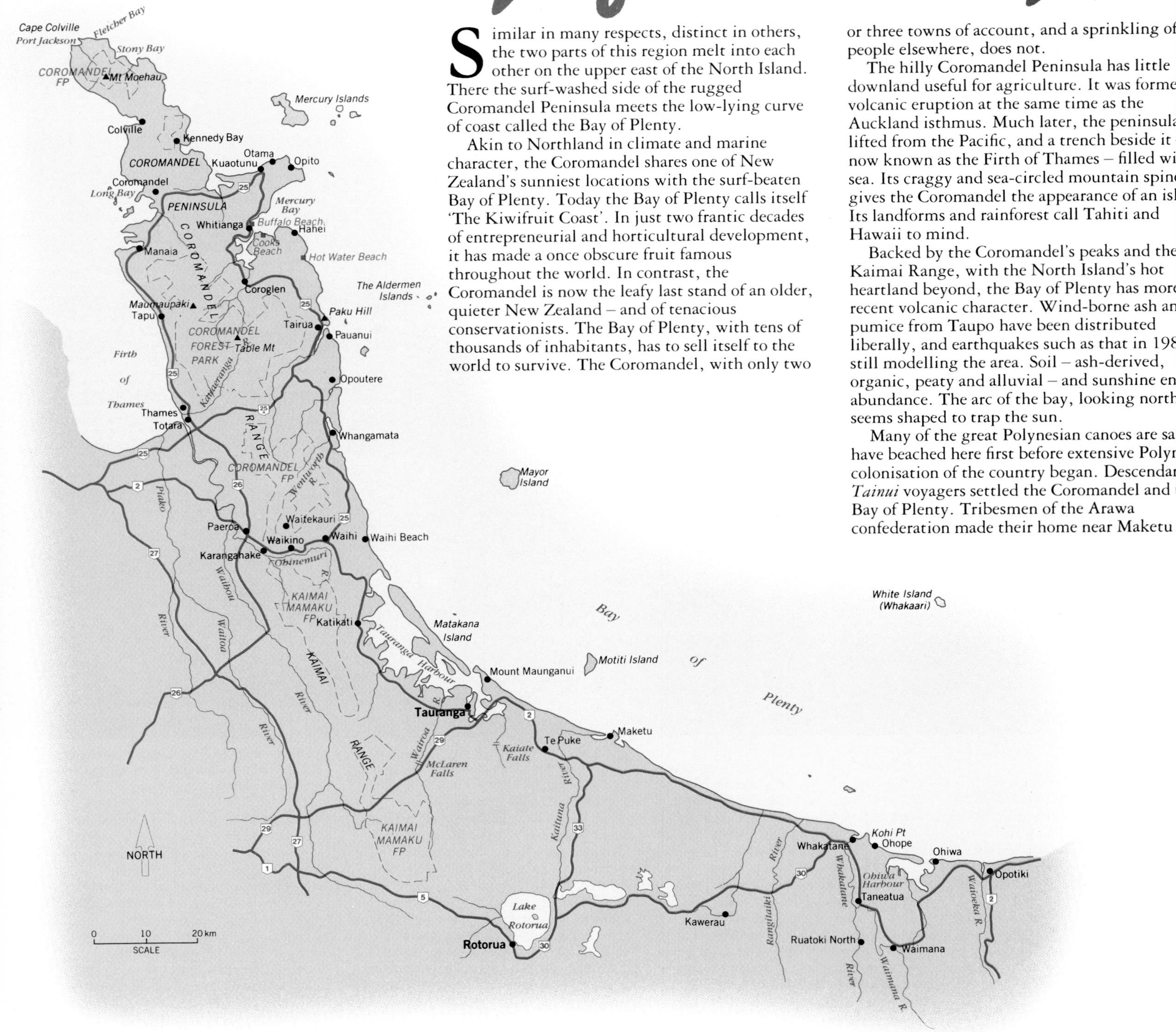

Similar in many respects, distinct in others, the two parts of this region melt into each other on the upper east of the North Island. There the surf-washed side of the rugged Coromandel Peninsula meets the low-lying curve of coast called the Bay of Plenty.

Akin to Northland in climate and marine character, the Coromandel shares one of New Zealand's sunniest locations with the surf-beaten Bay of Plenty. Today the Bay of Plenty calls itself 'The Kiwifruit Coast'. In just two frantic decades of entrepreneurial and horticultural development, it has made a once obscure fruit famous throughout the world. In contrast, the Coromandel is now the leafy last stand of an older, quieter New Zealand – and of tenacious conservationists. The Bay of Plenty, with tens of thousands of inhabitants, has to sell itself to the world to survive. The Coromandel, with only two or three towns of account, and a sprinkling of people elsewhere, does not.

The hilly Coromandel Peninsula has little downland useful for agriculture. It was formed by volcanic eruption at the same time as the Auckland isthmus. Much later, the peninsula lifted from the Pacific, and a trench beside it – now known as the Firth of Thames – filled with sea. Its craggy and sea-circled mountain spine gives the Coromandel the appearance of an island. Its landforms and rainforest call Tahiti and Hawaii to mind.

Backed by the Coromandel's peaks and the Kaimai Range, with the North Island's hot heartland beyond, the Bay of Plenty has more recent volcanic character. Wind-borne ash and pumice from Taupo have been distributed liberally, and earthquakes such as that in 1987 are still modelling the area. Soil – ash-derived, organic, peaty and alluvial – and sunshine ensure abundance. The arc of the bay, looking north, seems shaped to trap the sun.

Many of the great Polynesian canoes are said to have beached here first before extensive Polynesian colonisation of the country began. Descendants of *Tainui* voyagers settled the Coromandel and upper Bay of Plenty. Tribesmen of the Arawa confederation made their home near Maketu and

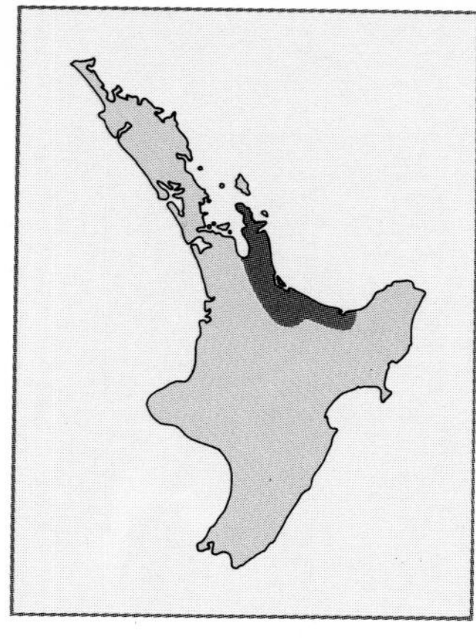

A PROMISE FULFILLED

inland, after the *Te Arawa* came to rest there. People descended from the *Mataatua* populated the coast from Whakatane up to Cape Runaway.

But it was James Cook who bestowed a lasting name on the coast in 1769. His first stop, where he had been greeted with hostility and no sustenance, was scornfully dismissed as Poverty Bay. Here, he was able to barter with tribesmen who canoed out to the *Endeavour* with fresh food. The great bay was plainly a place of plenty. He observed landscape 'pretty clear of wood . . . full of plantations and villages.'

Cook left more playful names on the bay's islands – Mayor, and the Aldermen, because,'thick or squat or lank and tall', they seemed to resemble respectable citizens of London. The pale and smoky island-volcano the Maori called Whakaari, he named White 'because as such it always appeared to us.'

It was the eastern side of the Coromandel that Cook found most congenial. It also seemed a safe place to observe the transit of Mercury, and establish his exact longitude. After a ritual show of truculence, the Maori were at pains to be friendly. Cook's famished sailors feasted on oysters, fish and wildfowl. In return they presented their hosts with potatoes, the first to be planted in New Zealand. It was the first extended intercourse between Maori and Europeans.

Cook formally claimed New Zealand for Britain and, having located himself precisely, marked the name Mercury Bay on his maps. Then he skirted the peninsula and sailed down its western shore along the firth he called Thames.

Cook's visit precipitated the arrival of more Europeans. In 1794 the first timber-seeking British ship, the *Fancy*, sailed up the Firth of Thames. Commanded by Captain Dell, the ship took aboard more than two hundred spars for the British navy. Entire subtribes of Maori were soon employed to fell, trim and drag kauri trees from the dense forests of the Coromandel. During the nineteenth century, approximately one hundred and fifty-two million cubic metres of kauri were taken from the Whitianga district alone. The present township of Coromandel took its name from the timber trade, after the arrival of HMS *Coromandel* in 1820.

As the forests of the peninsula were levelled by European axes, so were the Maori by European muskets – but in the hands of Northland's Ngapuhi tribe. It was the same along the Bay of Plenty shore. The missionary Samuel Marsden had made a reconnaissance of the Bay of Plenty, but the intertribal holocaust of the eighteen-twenties and early thirties deterred both missionary and trading ventures.

A bold Dane, Philip Tapsell, set himself up at Maketu in 1830 and began bartering for flax. Others risked visits to Tauranga and both places became centres of a flourishing flax industry.

Missionaries followed the traders. The site of the present city of Tauranga, with its fine harbour, seemed suitable for Anglican missionaries, but the first attempt to establish a Christian base in 1834 foundered within two years as tribal wars raged again. Undaunted, the Reverend Alfred Brown arrived in 1838, and Catholic missionaries in 1841. Timber towns had grown on the Coromandel, but there was no serious European settlement of the Bay of Plenty until after the Maori-European conflicts of the eighteen-sixties.

War came to the Bay of Plenty almost as an afterthought. People of the Ngai Te Rangi tribe of Tauranga had allied themselves with supporters of the Maori King in the Waikato, supplying the inland rebels. After British regulars had broken the back of the Kingite army at Rangiriri and Orakau, they marched east to teach the Tauranga rebels a lesson. At Gate Pa, near Tauranga Harbour, the British again learned that an infantry attack on an ingenious Maori defence system, even after long artillery bombardment, was an exercise in suicide. At the end of April, 1864, thirty-one lay dead and eighty wounded; their storming party was gutted and the fortress was still intact. But the battle was to be remembered most for chivalry and compassion. At night, a Maori heroine named Heni Te Kirikaramu crept outside the rebel defence line to tend mortally wounded British.

Soon afterwards, however, in the savage and far less chivalrous battle of Te Ranga, the Ngai Te Rangi were surprised while establishing another fortress, and one hundred and twenty of their warriors were left dead or dying. That ended formal hostilities, but not horror. The Hauhau rebellion came here in 1865, when the missionary Carl Volkner was beheaded at Opotiki. In 1869 Te Kooti, conducting a pitiless guerilla campaign from the forest sanctuary of the Urewera, descended on Whakatane, killed both Maoris and Europeans, and left the settlement in flames.

The Coromandel knew no battle, but after the heady riches of the timber trade, from which both races profited, there was a loss of trust rather than loss of blood. Maori suspicion of settlers delayed the exploitation of the peninsula's most spectacular resource – not timber, but gold.

In 1852 two brothers, Charles and Frederick Ring, located gold just north of the present township of Coromandel. A short rush ensued, but the fields were difficult to work as most of the gold was embedded in quartz. Discouraged by growing difficulties with Maori landowners, and attracted by discoveries in the south, most diggers left when war broke out in the Waikato.

In 1867, after the war, gold was uncovered in electrifying quantity at Thames. There was a stampede from Auckland and the bleak Waikato farmlands. New finds followed in the ranges behind the township of Coromandel, not far from the Ring brothers' initial discovery. In the eighteen-eighties another rich field was established at Kuaotunu, on the eastern side of the peninsula. But here only large companies had the resources to exploit the reefs. Later discoveries south at Waihi, Waikino, and Karangahake were the most durable.

KIWIFRUIT BRINGS FORTUNE

Military settlements established on confiscated land at Tauranga, Whakatane, and Opotiki were the Bay of Plenty's lasting legacy of the eighteen-sixties' conflicts. Soldiers received half a hectare in the townships, and up to eighty hectares outside, according to rank. At first the communities failed to prosper; some settlers drifted off to the Coromandel goldfields or sold to speculators.

In the eighteen-seventies the Ulsterman George Vesey Stewart failed in his attempt to establish a community of gentleman farmers and cap-doffing labourers at Katikati. Stewart and fellow Ulstermen had more success on fertile land at Te Puke. They prospered from the sale of horticultural produce to miners – a pointer to the Bay of Plenty's real role.

The Bay of Plenty was slow to develop. Its European population grew from thirteen hundred in 1874 to only four thousand by 1901. It seemed that the dairy cow might, as in the Waikato, be the district's salvation. But in 1910 the first citrus orchard was planted near Tauranga. By the middle of the century, horticulture was taking over from agriculture along the coastal belt. Tauranga and Te Puke were patchworked with orchards, and close to fifty per cent of New Zealand's citrus crop came from the region. Tauranga turned on an Orange Festival in August. But that was just the beginning; the Bay of Plenty had a second rendezvous with prosperity.

Gently arching, a flowering pohutukawa tree shades the coast road that winds round the Coromandel coastline. Still the domain of serious travellers and seekers of solitude, this arresting stretch of coast is covered in wild bushland, remote valleys and tiny bays interspersed with sleepy towns

The kiwifruit comes from the Yangtze Valley of China. Known as the Chinese gooseberry, the hairy, egg-shaped fruit was introduced to New Zealand early this century; it was a smaller and nuttier fruit than it is now, but it has been hybridised to produce a larger and sweeter version. At first it was no more than mildly popular with the New Zealand public. Vines burgeoned in many North Island gardens and home orchards to the point of being a nuisance.

In 1963, with only about seventy-five hectares in commercial production, experimental shipments were shyly sent abroad. The fruit was soon as familiar in Boston or Berlin, Tokyo or Tel Aviv, as in Tauranga. By the mid-eighties there were more than fifteen thousand hectares of kiwifruit in New Zealand, mostly in the Bay of Plenty region. Production had risen to one hundred thousand tonnes annually. New Zealand, particularly the Bay of Plenty, was earning millions of dollars exporting the fruit.

Above: *Mount Maunganui overlooks a fine ocean beach from the end of a long narrow peninsula* **Below:** *Ships bringing eager gold-seekers have long disappeared but the township of Coromandel retains its lively colonial character*

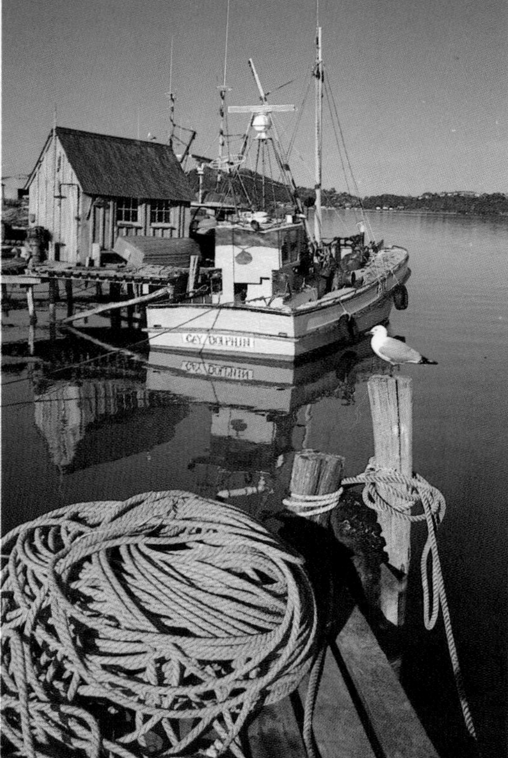

Because vines are slow to yield, the establishment of a large commercial enterprise is costly. Small producers began to give way to companies with vast capital. That has not prevented hundreds of entrepreneurial New Zealanders investing in kiwifruit, in the form of wine too. Te Puke's Kiwifruit Festival in May far outdoes Tauranga's Orange Festival.

Where the kiwifruit has not worked change, *Pinus radiata* has. Tauranga's hinterland and the great pine forests of the Volcanic Plateau have turned a slow seaside town into New Zealand's fastest growing city. The annual tonnage of timber it ships out makes it New Zealand's largest export port.

Yet the coast retains its native character. Surfers ride its rolling waves; long beaches welcome sun-lovers in summer. Big-game launches ride out to deep water; dinghies putter across fish-filled harbours; and lagoons glimmer with the lights of spear-fishermen in the evenings.

As for Coromandel, its great natural resources – gold and kauri timber and gum – seemed largely to have been ransacked by the beginning of the century. Communities dwindled and disappeared. Today, time has greened the scars, and the kauri slowly regenerate in the Coromandel Forest Park. The entire peninsula, with its natural history and human relics, its faded boom-time buildings and its pohutukawa-encrusted bays, is best seen as a park, and is certainly used as one by the population of the upper North Island.

Above: *The Elms mission house has changed little since it was built by Archdeacon Alfred Brown in 1847. It was the headquarters for the Te Papa mission station. In 1867 most of the land was transferred to the Crown. Brown later bought the house and lived there until his death in 1884*

THE LEGACY OF GOLD

Dominated by gold for decades, Coromandel's towns reflect the former importance of the mining industry on the peninsula

The discovery of the Coromandel's riches was well-timed. In 1867, after warfare in the Waikato, the upper North Island – especially Auckland – was deep in depression. Soldier-settlers who had failed to make the swampy Waikato region prosper, were trudging wearily back to town. Many settlers sailed off to South Island or to the Australian goldfields. The traces of gold found on the Coromandel by the Ring brothers in 1852 had largely been forgotten.

The old Martha Mine pumphouse (1904) stands above Waihi near the site of one of the richest gold strikes in history

The news of a strike at Thames, at the foot of the peninsula, was 'like a lifebuoy to a drowning man', said the early colonial artist Charles Blomfield, one of many ambitious young Aucklanders who set off for the Coromandel. He recalled: 'The first reports were so extravagant that few believed them; but when solid bars were exhibited in a jeweller's shop in Queen Street, citizens took the fever . . .' It was said that Shotover miners had taken out twenty-seven thousand pounds worth of gold just by scratching the clay off their claim. Thames soon had nearly twenty thousand people, almost double Auckland's population. It was estimated that there were some seven hundred productive mines in the vicinity of the town; many more were quarried.

Watching his congregation dwindle and depart for the Coromandel, one Auckland clergyman asked them to return sufficiently wealthy to pay off the church debt. Another, more practical, saw no hope of his stipend ever being paid, and set out for Thames himself. The name of that young vicar was Vicesimus Lush. He was bewildered by the rowdy grog-shops, the creaking watermills, the smoky chimneys, and the thud of hundreds of ponderous batteries that left the earth trembling. The mines posed perils, some 'like very deep dangerous exposed wells, others driven into the side of the hill, looking from their number like the entrances to a huge rabbit warren.' Lush found a miner digging beside his church, endangering its foundations, but uncovering a reef with impressive glitter. Soon half the public road was pegged out in claims. Finally, Lush himself took shares in a mine.

Above: *Thames is one of the few towns of gold-rush days that still thrives. Its colonial buildings remain intact*
Below: *The Thames School of Mines displays a fascinating collection of relics of the district's goldmining days*

Left: *In the eighteen-sixties and seventies Thames was the centre of the goldmining industry; its prosperity was reflected in the buildings and homesteads erected at the time*

Above: *In Thames, wooden buildings retain the flavour of the frenetic gold rush that swept over the region. The town once had a population of twenty thousand; although now reduced to six thousand, Thames is still a thriving centre*
Below: *Miners who came to Thames in search of gold lived in simple weatherboard cottages*

Charles Blomfield's first glimpse of fortunes in the making was a man on horseback with a butcher's basket. He was not delivering meat to miners, but over five hundred ounces of gold to the bank. But that was as near as Blomfield and most miners ever came to wealth. They found only mud and mosquitoes, floods and fleas. A Welsh workmate of Blomfield's became insane as a result of his disappointment. Blomfield himself found his talents lay more with paints and brushes than pick and shovel.

Gold-bearing quartz reefs, unlike alluvial fields, required more than muscle and a spirit of adventure. There was a need for heavy industry, for miners on a payroll, and for company capital to push tunnels farther through the already honeycombed hills. This made mining towns like Thames and Waihi very different from the waxing and waning goldfield communities of the south. Here, shanty towns disappeared, and industrial conglomerates moved in. Thames and Waihi became New Zealand's first true industrial towns.

Battery stampers banged at the quartz day and night, while foundries flashed and roared. Merchants and mine managers erected substantial buildings; publicans too. At one point Thames had between eighty and ninety pubs; only a few have survived and only one as a pub.

The Martha Mine at Waihi reached peak production as late as 1909, and continued working until the nineteen fifties – one of the world's richest mines. Most gold left New Zealand as ingots sent to British bank vaults, or dividends sent to large British shareholders.

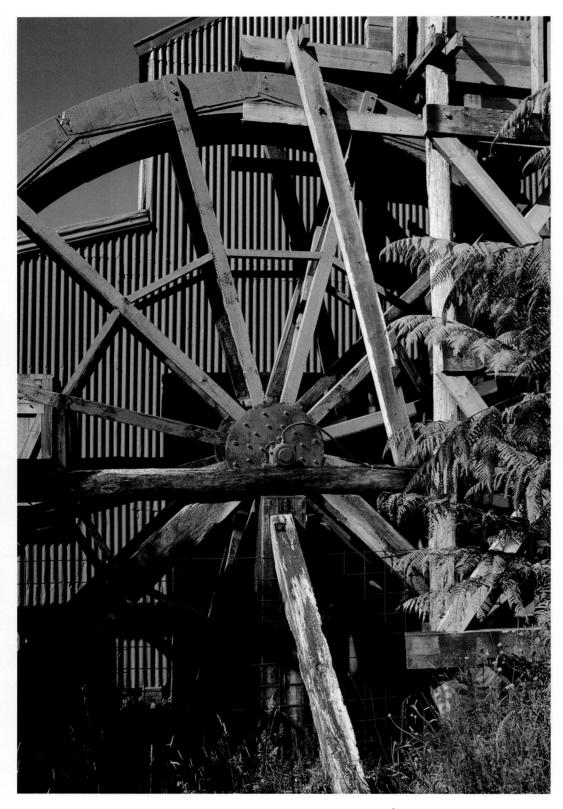

In 1912 Waihi became the setting for the most vicious of New Zealand's early labour struggles between miners and mine-owners, which came to a head with company-employed lynch mobs, gunfire and the killing of a strike leader. The grief of the Waihi strike reverberated the length of New Zealand, and heralded the beginnings of the New Zealand Labour Party. In the hills, the traces left by gold-seekers have grown fewer. Tunnels erode and collapse; tracks sink under fern and regenerating forest. Here and there machinery rusts, and old huts rot. In the townships magnificent Victorian buildings testify to the Coromandel's hour of glory in the long history of humanity's hunt for gold.

Waihi and Thames have survived despite the closing of mines and loss of employment. They have developed their own industries, and they also serve prosperous rural areas.

Above: *The massive panning dishes outside the historic Technical School in Waihi indicate the type of equipment miners used* **Left:** *Extracting gold from quartz required considerable energy. At Coromandel's Government Battery (1897) a waterwheel powered the extraction process*

One local historian said memorably of Thames, after the gold-rush fever had subsided: 'It lay sleeping, waiting the magic kiss of a golden prince. It awoke to the warm breath of a cow licking its face.' That was largely true of Waihi too. The town of Coromandel, nearer the heart of the forested peninsula, with no hinterland to serve, simply shrank to a gentle fishing-farming community of a thousand. It is distinguished most by its craftspeople, who often live in splendidly restored dwellings. All three areas are cornucopias of elegant colonial architecture, redolent of the colour and activity of the late nineteenth century.

There is still gold in the Coromandel – estimated to be worth more than fifteen billion US dollars at present world prices. At Waihi, the old Martha Hill is being reopened. A claim with a potential output of six hundred and fifty million dollars in gold, at nearby Waitekauri, was waiting on government approval for exploitation. It may all happen again. In the south, where large-scale mining persisted until relatively recent decades, it appears certain to resume. Meanwhile the peace of the ferny and sea-lapped peninsula seems worth more than all the world's bullion.

PLACES OF INTEREST

COLVILLE

Once a kauri-millers' camp, Colville is now home to communes and the last settlement (and last stop for fuel and food) on the spectacular coastal road north to the extremity of the Coromandel Peninsula. North and south huge pohutukawa command the coast, while 892-metre Mt Moehau reaches for the sky. The shadowy blue mountain was used as a Maori burial site, and retains its sacred character. There is an all-day climbing track to the summit, and spellbinding views of the peninsula and the Hauraki Gulf.

In the vicinity of Moehau, the rare native frog, *Leiopelma archeyi*, may be glimpsed. One of the earth's oldest creatures, it bypasses the tadpole stage in frog growth, and hatches from an egg. The Department of Lands and Survey has bought up private farmland here to create the Cape Colville Farm Park. Seaside campsites have been established, and there is a spectacular walkway between Stony Bay and Fletcher Bay. Accommodation is bring-your-own, and cuisine is catch-it-yourself, with oysters for entrée.

COROGLEN

Rural community on the east side of Coromandel Peninsula. It was once called Gumtown, after the commodity that established it. More than 100 000 tonnes of kauri gum are estimated to have been exported from the district. Near by is Hot Water Beach, where warm springs are accessible at low tide. Hahei beach also has pohutukawa, distinctive pink sand and a giant Moreton Bay fig.

COROMANDEL

With a permanent population not much in excess of 1000, this tranquil township is set on an island-studded coast beside a harbour once busy with ships taking on kauri timber and depositing gold-seekers. Its name is derived from the British naval vessel HMS *Coromandel*, which took aboard spars in 1820. A lively colonial character remains, though typical inhabitants are no longer miners and millers, but fishermen, oyster-farmers, potters and other craft workers. The gold drama which played here well into the 20th century, and may yet have a third act, is still scene-set in the town's architecture, from simple and often lovingly preserved miners' cottages to substantial public buildings. Just north of the township, a plaque on a bridge marks where gold traces were first discovered by the Ring brothers in 1852.

The grandest reminder of the town's heyday is the courthouse, now the council chambers. Built in the late 1860s, with wings added in 1873, it is a distinctive blend of colonial and classic styles. The Assay House, another elegant 19th-century building, stands at the centre of the commercial area. Across the way is the Golconda Tavern, still in business.

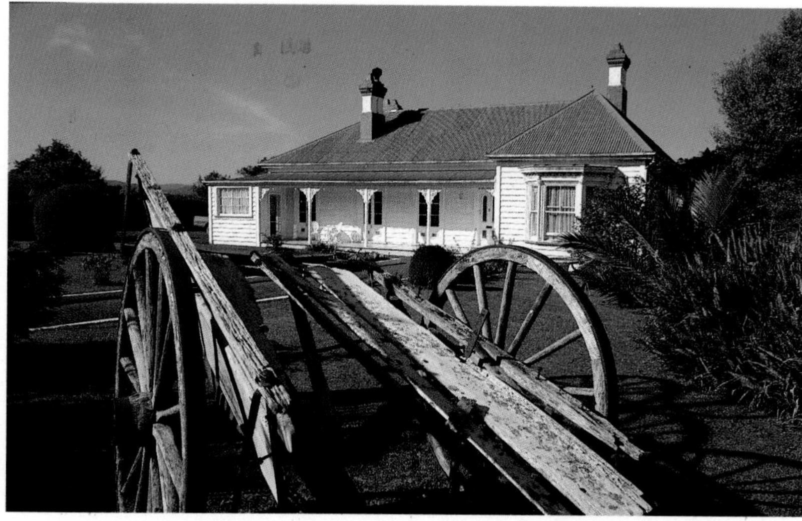

The manager of Kapanga Gold Mine at Coromandel in the 1880s lived in a comfortably spacious wooden house, as befitted his social standing

Opposite Coromandel's cottage hospital is the gracious residence of the manager of the English-owned Kapanga Mine, built in the 1880s. The small former School of Mines is now a fascinating museum displaying peninsula gemstones, photographs and gold-rush relics (open 10–12, 2–4 in summer). The restored Government Battery, with its giant waterwheel, built in 1897 to house a five-stamper quartz-crushing battery, is also open to summer visitors.

Long Bay is the nearest beach to the historic town, but there are many others also in close proximity. The drive north from Coromandel through COLVILLE to Port Jackson is distinguished by giant pohutukawa and lonely coves. Here as elsewhere on the peninsula, hunting gemstones is an exciting pastime. The winding road up and over Tokatea Hill to Kennedy Bay passes mine tunnels just off the road. At Kennedy Bay, which takes its name from an early trader murdered by a ship's crew, the peninsula shows its Pacific face: bright sand and blue sea, surrounded by forested ranges, and the Mercury Islands offshore. Briefly a goldfield in the 1860s, Kennedy Bay has been a largely Maori community.

COROMANDEL FOREST PARK

Including small neighbouring reserves, the park's 73 000 hectares of wilderness extend to the farthest tip of the peninsula. Formed too late to spare much of the original magnificent kauri forest, it nevertheless contains hundreds of mature trees never logged because of their isolation in the peninsula's interior. Manaia Sanctuary alone has 400 trees, including the 47-metre tall *Tane Nui*, the sixth largest kauri in the country. There are 8000 hectares of young kauri ('rickers'). For the most part, the native vegetation of the park is characteristic of Northland rainforest – with rata, tawa, rewarewa, rimu, matai and miro – but on the heights there is a dash of the growth characteristic of New Zealand's cooler south, including alpine plants and beech.

Reminders of goldmining and the timber industry also give the park character: miners' tracks, abandoned mineshafts, remains of bush tramways and logging dams. Striking volcanic landforms include the 836 metre Table Mountain, and the 819 metre Maumaupaki (Camels Back).

Steep roads – such as the one between TAPU and COROGLEN – carry the traveller into the Coromandel's heartland. Foot tracks offer further adventure. At the forest headquarters information office (Kauaeranga Valley road, near THAMES), details of campsites, walking tracks and a summer program of walks and talks can be obtained. In valleys and ravines of the park, gemstones like jasper, agate, amethyst, carnelian and chalcedony are abundant. Depart from tracks carefully as mine shafts may be hidden in scrub.

KARANGAHAKE GORGE

Dramatic gorge between WAIHI and Paeroa once filled with busy goldtowns.

KATIKATI

This northern Bay of Plenty town of 2000 has quickly developed to cash in on the kiwifruit boom. Fruit-packing sheds have risen on the roadside, and shelter-fences enclosing kiwi vines stand where dairy herds once grazed. Founded as a European town by George Vesey Stewart and fellow Ulstermen in 1875, it has only recently attained the prosperity they envisaged.

One of New Zealand's most notable literary families, the Mulgans (Alan Mulgan, 1881–1962, and his son John, 1911–45) began here. Alan Mulgan wrote movingly of his return to his ancestral land in his autobiography *The Making of a New Zealander*. The Sapphire Hot Springs are 6 kilometres outside town (open daily). Just along the road to TAURANGA are the Katikati Bird Gardens, overlooking Matakana Island.

KUAOTUNU

On the eastern side of the Coromandel, overlooked by a striking Maori pa site, this small community, composed mostly of holiday homes, was the site of one of the last large gold strikes on the peninsula in the 1880s, made by Maori prospector Charles Kawhine. He took ten ounces of gold from his first tonne of quartz. Hundreds of diggers soon arrived, and the scars they left persist to this day. The remains of the Try Fluke Mine – which worked until 1902, employed 50 men, and produced 30 000 ounces of gold – can be seen on the road to WHITIANGA.

Nearly 100 000 ounces were extracted in this area. Remnants of that harvest, and some alluvial gold, can still be fossicked. The once considerable town had hotels, boarding houses, a butcher, a baker, a bootmaker, a dressmaker and a draper; not to speak of a racecourse and a brass band. Notorious Black Jack Road, now more modestly thrilling, starts here and crawls along the steep Kuaotunu Peninsula, rewarding the traveller with delightful Otama and Opito beaches.

MAKETU

Twice over the birthplace of the Bay of Plenty, this coastal village with a population of 1000, sits at the mouth of the Kaituna River. According to tradition, the *Te Arawa* canoe beached here after its long voyage from the tropical Pacific. The voyagers and their descendants populated the bay, and the Volcanic Plateau too, creating settlements as far south as Taupo. A roadside cairn marks the resting place of the canoe. The eminence of Maketu in Maori lore is reflected by two fine Maori meeting-houses just outside the township, where carvings tell the story of the canoe people. The landscape around is now patterned with kiwifruit vines.

Missionary Carl Volkner's blood still stains the pulpit in his church at Opotiki

THE COROMANDEL'S FROGS

In the dense bush of the Coromandel Range live communities of two of New Zealand's three species of native frog

Leiopelma archeyi, *like the other indigenous frogs, is protected by law*

Casual visitors are unlikely to discover these tiny, rare frogs. Research teams have uncovered few, and it seems they were unknown to the Maori.

A native frog, *Leiopelma hochstetteri*, was first discovered in 1852 under a rock in a Coromandel stream. It has been sighted from just north of Auckland to the middle of the North Island, and possibly it exists elsewhere. Another species, *L. archeyi*, found only in the high bush country of the Coromandel, was discovered to exist as recently as 1942. The third species, *L. hamiltoni*, lives only on Stephens Island and Maud Island in Cook Strait.

All three frogs are very small, between thirty and forty millimetres long, and they are difficult to locate, for they do not need to live near ponds or streams as do the two common Australian varieties, which have colonised here so successfully (the green tree frog and the brown tree, or whistling frog with which *L. archeyi* is sometimes confused). They have tail-wagging muscles, but no tails. They have no vocal sacs (they can squeak but not croak), and no ear drums or Eustachian tubes. They have large eyes which reflect at night. The frogs have no tadpole stage – they develop from an egg inside a capsule and emerge as a miniature adult.

Because it would have been impossible for frogs to have reached New Zealand by sea, these creatures provide us with a useful biological clock. Their existence indicates that New Zealand probably separated from a larger land mass during the reptile age, perhaps one hundred and twenty million years ago.

Maketu was also the first European foothold in the Bay of Plenty. Danish flax trader Philip Tapsell braved intertribal Maori warfare to establish a base. Also at pains to repopulate the region after the slaughter, he married three times, and left many Maoris bearing the name Tapsell (including a cabinet minister).

The small St Thomas' Church (1868) is set on the site of the original mission overlooking the town. Above the church are the remains of Pukemaire Redoubt, built when Maketu was menaced in the 1860s. In the church graveyard stands a government memorial to the Arawa chief Pekanui Tohiteururangi, who died leading fellow tribesmen against Maori rebels. (Most Arawa people took the side of the colonial government during the war.) Maketu was named by the Arawa people after a plantation in Hawaiki.

MAYOR ISLAND

This extinct volcano was named by James Cook, together with the neighbouring Aldermen Islands. Once a highly fortified Maori bastion, it is now a base for big-game fishermen and skin-divers. Mainland vegetation has colonised the once molten slopes, and native birds flourish. The pohutukawa-clad island rises 355 metres at its highest point and has two lakes below sea level, one green, the other black. The fiery volcano once forged obsidian – valued for its cutting qualities – which was more precious than gold to the pre-European Maori as a vital trade commodity. Mayor Island obsidian has been found on Maori settlement sites throughout New Zealand. During the big-game season (December to May) the island is at its busiest and the sea bristles with launches in pursuit of marlin, kingfish, mako and thresher. Excursions to Mayor Island are possible from TAURANGA, MOUNT MAUNGANUI and WHANGAMATA.

MOUNT MAUNGANUI

A popular holiday resort, its permanent population of 13 000 triples in summer. *Maunganui* means 'big mountain'. The 232 metre high former Maori fortress, at the end of a long, narrow peninsula at the mouth of Tauranga Harbour, overlooks one of New Zealand's most magnificent ocean beaches. The many amusements and facilities of the town include the Leisure Island complex (open daily, from October to Easter) and a natural hot saltwater pool (open daily 8–10) in the domain. There are fishing trips, excursions to MAYOR ISLAND and scenic flights out to the active volcano of White Island. A new bridge now links Mount Maunganui to near neighbour Tauranga, making the two communities even more indistinguishable. A slow-paced seaside community until recent decades, Mount Maunganui has grown quickly with the timber trade. The port now services the 500 vessels that annually pass the sculpture of Tangaroa, Maori god of the sea, at the harbour entrance. Although the harbourside has changed to accommodate the timber industry, the ocean frontage of 'The Mount', as it is popularly known, remains unblemished.

OPOTIKI

The Bay of Plenty's gateway to the dramatic East Coast region (see page 156). This marine town is at the junction of two major routes: one passes through the wild and often misty Waioeka Gorge to Gisborne, and the other borders stunning seascapes up to Cape Runaway and on to Gisborne. With close to 3500 people, the town is set beside a once important pioneer harbour.

The pretty little Church of St Stephen the Martyr (1864) was established by Lutheran missionary Reverend Carl Volkner (1819–65). It was here that he was murdered by Hauhau rebels, who justly suspected him of informing on his Maori flock. His execution was also said to be a reprisal for British atrocities at Rangiaohia and elsewhere in the Waikato a year earlier. He was hanged, beheaded, and his eyes gouged out and eaten by the fiery Hauhau leader Kereopa (later to be hanged himself). His blood was collected in the church communion chalice and sipped ceremonially by those who slew him. After serving for a time as the centre of a British redoubt, the church was reconsecrated and renamed in 1875. The pulpit is still stained with the missionary's blood and the desecrated chalice and Volkner's Bible are on display. His remains are now enshrined within the church walls. The original grave headstone is at the rear of the building. The east window depicts the martyrdom of St Stephen and, by implication, of Volkner.

More than most Bay of Plenty communities, Opotiki suffered from skirmishes of the Hauhau uprising and then of the guerilla Te Kooti. After his pardon in 1883, the latter eventually settled with a grant of government land at nearby Ohiwa, where he perished in 1893. A memorial records his demise, but the exact location of his grave, on one of Ohiwa Harbour's islands, is now lost.

Hikutaia Plant Domain (7 kilometres outside town, just over the Waioeka Bridge) is noted for its splendid 5 hectares of native vegetation. A giant puriri, *Taketakerau*, is possibly the oldest in the country and was once used as a burial tree by Maoris.

PAUANUI

Upmarket seaside resort, on a long, low, pine-covered spit of sand to the south of TAIRUA Harbour. Homeowners often fly their own planes in from Auckland for weekends. There are tennis courts, a golf course and many other amenities.

TAIRUA

Community of 900 on Coromandel's eastern coast under twin-peaked 179 metre Paku Hill, once a Maori fortress. In the heyday of kauri-felling, the harbour was sometimes solid with rafts of logs. Kauri gum travelled out by the tonne too. More than 50 000 ounces of gold were taken from 15 mines in the hills behind the township. The resort offers rockclimbing, surfing and safe harbour swimming. Reefs and islands make it popular with divers. The Shell Museum contains 2500 species. Across the water is the Coromandel's newest community, the expensive resort of PAUANUI.

An original collection of books, paintings and ephemera is housed at The Elms, Tauranga

TAPU

Between THAMES and COROMANDEL, on the western side of the peninsula, Tapu is a small cluster of holiday homes, with a store and hotel, set under steep ranges. Once it had ten hotels to serve 2000 thirsty miners, some of whom are buried in the township's tiny seaside cemetery. The goldfield here was mostly alluvial, and miners were spared the backbreak of

Modern Tauranga displays wit and style, as in this ingenious trompe l'oeil *street mural*

extracting the metal from quartz. *Tapu* means 'sacred'; the township takes its name from a sign local Maoris placed on their burial ground to keep miners away. A goldpan and patience may still reward the fossicker here, at least with some gemstones.

The road to **COROGLEN** takes the traveller into the heart of the Coromandel's spectacular heights with 819-metre Maumaupaki (Camels Back) commanding the eye. At Rapaura Falls Park (7 kilometres) a beautifully landscaped valley (open October–April) makes a pleasant picnic halt. The celebrated 'square' kauri – (26 kilometres from Tapu) is reached after a short signposted walk from the road.

TAURANGA

The city's name means 'resting place' or 'safe anchorage'. It is the best natural harbour between Auckland and Wellington. For the Maori it was a haven; for the Europeans a port. Close to the Volcanic Plateau's great pine forests and its associated industries, the harbour is still the city's most important resource. The city has grown swiftly, its population doubling in two decades to 43 000 (55 000 including **MOUNT MAUNGANUI**).

In 1769 James Cook marvelled at the many forts visible along this coast. By 1835, Anglican missionaries had established themselves on Te Papa Peninsula, close to the heart of modern Tauranga, but fierce intertribal Maori conflict ended the missionary effort in 1836. The Reverend Alfred Brown began again in 1838, but it took seven years of peacemaking before his base was secure. Catholic missionaries arrived in 1841, making Tauranga New Zealand's oldest Roman Catholic parish.

Maori suspicion of white settlers mounted and the local Ngai Te Rangi began to align themselves with the Maori King movement in the Waikato. Brown's flock dwindled again, and in 1863, when the Waikato War began, European settlers and most at the mission station fled to Auckland. Brown returned but his mission station was now a military camp and he himself was thought to be a military spy, which indeed he was. In late April 1864, on the night before the lethal battle of Gate Pa, he entertained thirteen British officers. He was soon conducting burial services for all but one of his dinner guests. It was nearly another decade before Tauranga had sufficient serenity for European settlers to establish themselves again. It was yet another 50 years before Tauranga's hinterland was recognised for its horticultural potential.

Today Tauranga's beginnings can be seen in the rooms and grounds of The Elms (1847), Brown's mission house, (still occupied by his relatives). The library in the grounds (1839), where Brown composed his sermons, still contains his books and documents. The original chapel was demolished in 1920, and replaced in 1964 with a replica that is still used for services.

The elegant grounds – though now separated by industrial reclamation from the mission's natural constituency, Tauranga Harbour – are open to the public daily; there are guided tours of the house Monday to Saturday at 2.

Along Cliff Road, the earthworks and surviving cannon of Monmouth Redoubt can be seen. British troops established themselves here before their fatal clash with Ngai Te Rangi rebels. At nearby Otemataha Pa cemetery, headstones tell of the gallantry of Maori and British antagonists. The site of the celebrated battle of Gate Pa is in Cameron Road, 5 kilometres from the city centre, where the lovely little Anglican church of St George's (1899) now stands as a memorial. Inside, the church's font commemorates the compassion of the Maori woman Heni Te Kirikaramu, who carried water to British wounded. The approach to the church has been landscaped symbolically. Water flows from a rock pool surrounded by indigenous plants into a second pool surrounded by European plants. A plan of the engagement can be viewed in the church foyer.

The Bay of Plenty's subsequent history is displayed in Tauranga Historic Village (17th Avenue West). More than 6 hectares of pioneer dwellings and colonial settings include a goldmining camp with a working battery, and a pre-European Maori village. It is particularly colourful at weekends, when many exhibits are working (open daily 10–4, except Good Friday and Christmas Day).

Today's Tauranga holds many attractions for the tourist. There are excursions to **MAYOR** and Motiti islands, fishing trips (for big game and small) and scenic flights inland to the thermal region or over the sea to volcanically active White Island. At **MOUNT MAUNGANUI**'s magnificent ocean beach, and at nearby **MAKETU** and **KATIKATI** there is surfing and warm-water swimming. White-water rafting on the Wairoa River, picnic and freshwater swimming places at McLaren Falls Park and Kaiate Falls, and bushwalking in the Kaimai Mamaku Forest Park add to the variety of choices. Information can be obtained from the public relations office in The Strand, where some of the city's early buildings have survived the rapid growth of the late 20th century. At the end of the Strand is the large kauri-carved Maori canoe *Te Awanui* (1973) carved by Tuti Tukaokao.

TE PUKE

Named humbly 'the hill' by the Maori, this fertile site in the Bay of Plenty now calls itself the 'Kiwifruit Capital of the World' – with some justification. Pioneered by Ulstermen in the 19th century, and a market-gardening centre since, it now has nearly 6000 busy inhabitants. The population has doubled in two decades. Kiwifruit Country, an educational and recreational centre, offers guided tours through an extensive kiwifruit and horticultural theme park. Another project is Longridge Park.

CONFRONTATION AT WAIHI

Walking through the streets of Waihi, it is difficult to imagine this peaceful town as the scene of the country's first violent clash between capital and labour

Generations of miners quenched their thirst at the rambling Rob Roy Hotel in Waihi

The Waihi Strike of 1912 had its origins in a complex web of inter-union rivalry, economic and political confrontation and the developing but still immature power of the labour movement. An additional factor was contributed by a grievance generated in the gold mines. The Waihi Mining Company required a huge capital investment for its quartz-crushing and gold-extracting processes. This capital came from abroad, and the profits were returned there.

In 1908, the Waihi Miners and Workers Union, to which all local mine workers had belonged, affiliated with the Federation of Labour. Through the efforts of Bob Semple, an organiser of the Federation, the workers won better conditions.

However, in 1911 the Union voted to cancel its registration and a group of engine drivers decided to break away and form their own union. The miners threatened to strike unless the company dismissed the engine drivers. It refused and the strike began.

The Union called on the Federation of Labour for support. It too split into factions. National support evaporated but the strike went on. There was persecution and violence in the town from both sides. Tension further increased in July when the conservative Massey government came to power and sent in more police.

After five months of bitterness and brutality, the miners' hall at Waikino was raided by strikebreakers. They wrecked the building and beat up some of the strikers. Next evening the hall at Waihi was stormed, shots were fired and a miner was clubbed to death. The strike leaders were given two days to leave town.

The scars of this struggle took almost half a century to heal and it was almost a death blow to the Federation of Labour. Labour leaders such as Bob Semple and Paddy Webb, who later became cabinet ministers, were to transform the strike into a potent labour myth, although they had learned the practical lesson that if they were to achieve power, they needed unity, popular appeal for their policies and the broad support of the whole country. Today's Federation of Labour has approximately four hundred and fifty thousand members

THAMES

Unlike most towns of gold-rush days, this community beside the Firth of Thames is still thriving. When gold-seekers stormed into the Coromandel in the late 1860s, Thames had a population of 20 000 – close to double that of Auckland. However, a century of slow decline has left no impression of a ghost town. Few of its colonial facades are faded and the town has never emptied. More than 6000 people are reliably employed in this market town.

Arhitecture – apart from the largely undistinguished main street – tells the story of New Zealand's first true industrial town, from the graceful homes of mine managers to the simple cottages and villas of miners. There is a claim that Thames had 111 hotels, but the likely figure is around 80. The Brian Boru, in the main street, is the most prominent of the survivors. Built in the 1860s, it was burned down at the beginning of the 20th century, and rebuilt in 1905. Two other notable hotels are the Cornwall Arms Hotel (now a club) and the Junction Hotel. The magnificently rambling Lady Bowen (1850s), by the waterside, was damaged by fire in the 1980s, but has been restored. Near by is the Thames School of Mines (1886). It is now a museum in the care of the NZ Historic Places Trust. Displays include an assay room and furnace, laboratory, a large working model of a mine and battery, lecture rooms and mineral exhibits (open Monday to Saturday, 2–4). The Thames Museum houses photographs of goldfields days and other pioneer relics (open Wednesday, Friday and Saturday, 1–4). To the north of the town is a working goldmine and battery that functions for visitors throughout the December–January holiday period. There are walking tracks to some of the more interesting of the town's 2000 claims. Ask at the Thames Information Office, which may also provide information on back-street buildings of note. (The information office for the **COROMANDEL FOREST PARK** is on the Kauaeranga Valley road in the hills behind Thames.)

Extensive views of Thames can be seen from the World War I memorial (signposted north of the town) or from Totara Pa cemetery, once the site of a Maori fortress overwhelmed by Northland's Ngapuhi in the 19th century (3 kilometres south). Nearby Totara vineyard has some distinguished wines. The seaside road to **COROMANDEL**, is overhung with giant pohutukawa, and passes coves, bays, wooded valleys and rocks white with oysters.

WAIHI

Like **THAMES**, Waihi is a substantial community (3600) that has survived the ups and downs of gold-digging. Inland Waihi is set in a mountain-shadowed valley where the wild Coromandel Range slumps into the tame coastal terrain of the Bay of Plenty. The old and new facades of the town's rather wild-west main street tell of the community's mixed fortunes.

Martha Hill, above the town, was the site of one of the richest gold strikes in history. The original mine functioned from the 1880s to the 1950s, and in the 1990s it is being exploited again. At the beginning of the century, when the Martha Mine was at its peak, Waihi had 6000 people. Their cottages and villas remain evidence of that vigorous era, as does the rambling 19th-century Rob Roy Hotel in the main street, where generations of miners killed their thirst and the cathedral-like ruin of the old Martha pumphouse (1904) standing sentinel above the town. After a long and violent miners' strike in 1912 when a strike leader was slain, victory went to British mine-owners and hundreds were driven from the town. The event was a proving ground for founders of the New Zealand Labour Party.

After the mine closed, electronics manufacturing sustained the town from the 50s to the 80s. Meanwhile Waihi draws strength from a substantial rural area, and is also increasingly popular with retired people. Waihi Beach, one of the Bay of Plenty's most spectacular, is only 11 kilometres away and **TAURANGA** Harbour a little farther.

The wealthy heyday of Waihi and the surrounding area is recalled in the Waihi Arts Centre and Museum, with a fascinating scale model of the Martha Mine, the galleries of which extended far under the town (open daily 10.30–4, except Wednesday and Saturday; 1.30–4 Sunday; winter hours vary). The Waikino Pioneer Museum (9–4 Sunday to Friday), just outside Waihi, has a splendid collection of pioneer machinery.

The area between Waihi and Paeroa (see page 84) – via Waikino and the Karangahake Gorge – can be seen as one vast open-air museum. Across the river at Waikino, there are the remains of the Victoria Battery. The road through the gorge, twisting between the Coromandel and the Kaimai Ranges, and following the course of the once poisonously polluted Ohinemuri River, passes the sites of goldmining towns and townships that have disappeared with few traces. Of the once throbbing town of Karangahake only a remnant survives, with the old schoolhouse (1889) conspicuous above the river. There is a picnic area by the river. Remains of the Crown, Talisman and Woodstock quartz-crushing plants are near by, and patient panning can still disclose alluvial gold.

A FORTUNE IN KIWIFRUIT

Along the roadsides of the Bay of Plenty, poles and wires and windbreaks proclaim the fastest-growing horticultural bonanza in New Zealand history

Flourishing kiwifruit vines at Te Puke sustain the prosperity of the area

The volcanic soils and the warm, moist, almost subtropical climate of the region provide an ideal environment for nurturing kiwifruit, with its confusing flavour that is a mix of bananas, watermelons, strawberries and oranges. Each year, thousands of tonnes of this brown, furry fruit are flown all over the world.

Vines were first planted in the Bay of Plenty area in 1925. Prolific growth encouraged use of a hard-pruning technique developed by the local Bayliss brothers. They also were first to invest in the new hybrid fruit bred by Hayward Wright in Auckland. (It is now the dominant strain.)

When it was first brought to New Zealand from its native China in 1906, the fruit of the wild vine *Actinidia chinensis* was known as the Chinese gooseberry, though it is not a gooseberry. This name proved a handicap during the first attempts to sell the fruit abroad. Gooseberries had been generally unpopular and thought of as bitter. Strained American-Chinese relations in the nineteen-fifties dampened any cultural appeal the fruit might have had. In a brilliant stroke of marketing, a new name, kiwifruit, was invented, and the export markets responded eagerly.

Sales are helped by the advantage the crop has over most other fruit. If picked just before it becomes ripe, kiwifruit can be chilled and stored for up to six months, then taken out and ripened for a few days before it is displayed in the shops.

The continuing success of the Bay of Plenty's investment in this remarkable export industry depends on the reaction to a spin-off. Hundreds of thousands of kiwifruit plants, including the Hayward variety, have been sold abroad. Will the United States, Italy, France, Australia or Japan soon prove as productive as the rich belt of vines from Tauranga to Opotiki?

At the Bird Garden and Gold Museum above the river and town at Karangahake, visitors can hire prospectors' kits and try panning for gold

The church at Tauranga Historic Village has been created using sections of old buildings, including part of a hotel. The village itself captures the style of Victorian colonial life

One or two hundred metres on towards Paeroa, across a bridge, begins a historic walkway that follows the bed of the now disused railway between Paeroa and Waihi. It takes in a tunnel where glow-worms light the way. Between Waikino and Waihi the railway line is now maintained by the Goldfields Steam Train Society, which runs regular weekend and some weekday excursions in summer, and occasional outings the rest of the year. Both terminals of the 6.5 kilometre line are being developed as tourist attractions and visitors' centres, with a museum at the Waihi end. At Karangahake (which means 'meeting of the hunchbacks', derived from the close-pressing hills) Bird Garden and Gold Museum, visitors can hire prospectors' kits and try panning.

Waihi's many attractions include the spectacular Waterlily Gardens (8 kilometres out of town in Pukekauri Road), where some 60 varieties of lilies grow among lakes, waterfalls, flowerbeds and lawns. There is also a picnic area, a camping ground and tearooms (open October to April).

A short drive on from the gardens finds the east entrance to Kaimai Mamaku Forest Park, where walking tracks pass rusted machinery and other relics of sawmilling days. At Bulltown Road the Waihi Hydroponic Gardens exhibit ideas for the future nourishment of the world, (open 9–5 summer; 10–3 winter). The Waihi Museum of Technology has 30 vintage tractors, more than 5000 antique items, and it provides gig rides (open 9–3 Saturday, Main Waihi Beach Road).

WHAKATANE

The Bay of Plenty's second urban centre, with 17 000 people. Its paradise-like setting beside a lagoon and close to one of New Zealand's most splendid surf beaches was the home, it is said, of an early Polynesian navigator named Toi. Generations later the *Mataatua* canoe beached here and left its present name. When the men rushed ashore to rejoice in the new land, the women were left in the canoe which began to drift away to sea. Women were forbidden to use paddles, lest they breach *tapu*, but a bold girl named Wairaka announced that she was unafraid to take the male role. Other women followed her example and took up paddles and the canoe was saved. Today Wairaka's boldness is commemorated not only in the town's name, which means 'to act the man', but also in the sculpture of Wairaka herself at the mouth of the Whakatane River.

Elsewhere too, the town is rich in Maori lore. A commanding rock arch, Pohaturoa, at the town centre was once the site of sacred ceremonies performed by tribal *tohunga* (priests). A model of the *Mataatua* canoe now stands beside it. Another natural feature in the town centre, also enshrined in tradition, is the Wairere waterfall behind the Commercial Hotel in Mataatua Street. The short drive to the mouth of the Whakatane River passes the Wairaka Marae, and a plaque marking the landing place of the *Mataatua* canoe. There is also The Cave of Muriwai, once the hermit retreat of a woman who played Delphic oracle to Whakatane tribesmen.

Whakatane has one of New Zealand's most energetic historical societies and the local museum in Boon Street (open daily 10–4) reflects its industry. The Whakatane Board Mills, which pioneered exploitation of North Island exotic timber resources, has been the town's largest employer, although threatened with closure in 1986. Over the hill from Whakatane proper is long, pohutukawa-backed Ohope, densely settled and popular with sun-lovers and surfers. Its special attractions include the Kohi Point Walkway. The road along Ohope beach leads on to the gentler marine environment of Ohiwa Harbour, where the pardoned Te Kooti lived out his last years. Near Whakatane is access to his former stronghold, the Urewera, now the Urewera National Park (see page 168). A park ranger at Taneatua has information on tracks through the Waimana and Ruatoki areas, and shooting permits for prospective hunters. The Waimana valley was once a stronghold of the latter-day prophet and passive resister Rua Kenana (see page 168).

Whakatane is a base for big-game fishermen. Scenic flights and helicopter excursions to volcanic White Island, and jet-boat trips up the wooded Rangitaiki River are also possible. The Whakatane Public Relations Office in Commerce Street has full details. The lakeland drive between Whakatane and Rotorua, via Hongis Track (see page 114), with warm pools on the way, is one of the North Island's most spectacular, with uninterrupted views for much of the way.

WHANGAMATA

This settlement on the eastern side of the Coromandel Peninsula is named after the MAYOR ISLAND obsidian that Maori once gathered on its shore line (*Whangamata* means 'harbour of obsidian'). Today it is a prospering resort town of 1800 people, offering visitors safe harbour swimming, splendid surf and seaside activities. It is the nearest harbour to Mayor Island, and a departure point for deep-sea fishermen. Just north is Opoutere beach, one of the Coromandel's least-exploited jewels. Inland, especially on walks up the Parakawai and Wentworth valleys, there are reminders of Coromandel's colourful kauri-milling and goldmining past.

WHITIANGA

The major eastern Coromandel resort with a permanent population of 2000 that increases up to tenfold during the summer, Whitianga lies in Mercury Bay, where James Cook had his first significant interchange with Maori. He also observed the transit of Mercury and claimed the country formally on behalf of George III of England. The community is divided by an estuary and boat harbour – with a ferry for pedestrians only.

Running north from the town is 4 kilometre Buffalo Beach, named after HMS *Buffalo*, a British convict ship from Sydney carrying kauri spars and wrecked offshore in 1840. Relics have sometimes washed ashore and remaining timbers of the vessel have been exposed at extreme low tides. To the south, beyond the boat harbour (a 40 kilometre drive, but five minutes by ferry) is the memorial to Cook, above Shakespeare Cliffs. The lovely 3 kilometre Cooks Beach, the eastern end of which he used for his observations, also commemorates his visit. In the 19th century, millions of metres of timber and thousands of tonnes of gum were shipped from the plundered Whitianga area. Today most exploitation is of the offshore waters, keeping the local fishing fleet and processing plants busy. A major base for big-game fishermen, and rendezvous for divers, Whitianga is a comfortable location from which visitors can explore the Coromandel.

STEAMING WHITE ISLAND

On a sunny day the smudged plume of White Island, New Zealand's most consistently active volcano, may be seen curling into the sky above the Bay of Plenty

Today a colony of gannets and pohutukawa trees are the island's only living inhabitants

Just over fifty kilometres offshore from Whakatane, White Island was named by Cook, who first saw its white steam in 1769. Its highest point, Mount Gisborne, is a modest three hundred and twenty-one metres above sea level. The crater floor of the volcano is mostly just above the high tide mark.

Jets of steam, mixed with a rich dose of hydrochloric acid and sulphur dioxide, issue from its vents. In recent times, billowing clouds of ash and a lava flow also have poured out, forming one of the most spectacular sights of the region.

The island is privately owned and permission must be obtained to disembark. Visitors should be careful as the volcano's gases can be unpleasant and even dangerous – and there is always the possibility of another eruption. Since 1885, several attempts to mine the sulphur which lies in vast deposits about the volcano have failed. A violent eruption occurred in September 1914, killing eleven men who were living on the island and working the deposits. It is believed that a landslide blocked the vents and became a huge pool of boiling mud. The pressure of steam and water then forced out the mud across the crater floor, burying the huts and entombing the men. The eight to ten metres of hot crust that covered the victims proved impossible to dig through. The only living creature found by the rescue party was one of the worker's cats.

Volcanic Plateau

New Zealand's youth is most evident in the heart of the North Island. From fizzing Rotorua in the north to the flickering volcanoes in the south, the old fires of the earth still burn; here man dwells in a landscape subject to the whim of his planet's hot core.

Only a century ago a seemingly serene mountain split apart and unleashed fireballs and sulphurous mud on the surrounding landscape, obliterating communities and darkening the sky over much of the country. And in the melancholy desert south of the plateau a convulsive volcanic lahar has more recently taken one hundred and fifty-one lives.

Yet man has always managed to coexist with the menace inherent in this region, even turning the idiosyncrasies of the plateau to his advantage. The peace of this once seething region still does much to beguile. Only patches of its past rampages remain. Cooled craters are now lakes, and forests drape land uplifted by eruptions. Fat trout fill the rivers, skiers flit down volcanic slopes, and everywhere the plateau bubbles with warm pools that ease the aches of the flesh.

Much of the Volcanic Plateau, built up by the convulsions of the past, is more than five hundred metres above sea level. Volcanic mounds and peaks are to be found throughout the region, mainly low and extinct to the north, high and active south. At 2797 metres, Ruapehu is the North Island's highest point. The greywacke undermass of the land has been deeply buried by ignimbrite, a powdery ash from eruptions, compressed and consolidated by time and movement into hard sheets of acid rock. In places it has warped and fractured and been exposed by rivers – notably the Waikato – cutting deep gorges. But for the most part layers of pumice ash from recent eruptions have buried the ignimbrite. The region is distinguished most by its diversity: sharp gorges and flat basins, volcanic mass and tussock highland, tall bluffs overlooking calm lakes. East and west its boundaries are emphatically defined by bulky and heavily bushed mountain ranges.

For the Maori, so awesome a region required explanation. They had one in a fabulous Polynesian forefather named Ngatoro-i-rangi. A *tohunga*, or high priest, who arrived here in the canoe *Te Arawa* with his slave Ngauruhoe. It is said that he determined immediately to explore the cool new land surrendered by the ocean. This magician stamped his foot on the ground in each dry valley, producing springs and lakes. When he came to the inland sea of Lake Taupo, he found it empty of fish. He made an incantation, shook his cloak over the waters, and suddenly the lake teemed with creatures. Finally, in order to claim and name the land, he climbed Mount Tongariro with Ngauruhoe.

Blizzards lashed the two as they toiled towards the peak. So preoccupied was Ngatoro-i-rangi with the marvels around – for Polynesians knew nothing of ice and snow – that he failed to notice the loyal Ngauruhoe slowly perishing of the cold. Beginning to succumb himself, Ngatoro-i-rangi called upon his sisters in the far-off Polynesian homeland of Hawaiki to bring him fire. They sent their sacred flame racing under the Great Sea of Kiwa; it surfaced in the Bay of Plenty where the very water caught fire and became the still-smoking place called White Island. The flame then struck through the centre of the North Island, bursting out here and there and scattering sparks to create the hot springs and geysers of Rotorua, Waiotapu, Orakeikorako and Wairakei, among many other places, before it flashed around beleaguered Ngatoro-i-rangi. The cold mountains burst into huge eruption, warming and reviving the old *tohunga*. But it was too late for Ngauruhoe; the slave lay dead in the melting snow. To this day the peak is known by the name of Ngauruhoe.

But Ngatoro-i-rangi's epic expedition was far from finished. Returning towards the resting place of the canoe *Te Arawa* in the Bay of Plenty, and setting up shrines to confirm his claim to the land, he was confronted on the summit of Mount Tarawera by one of New Zealand's original inhabitants, an evil man-eating creature named Tama-o-hoi. A trial of potency followed, and Ngatoro-i-rangi stamped on the earth creating a great chasm. He forced Tama-o-hoi within, finally covering the creature over. It is said that Tama-o-hoi remained captive there until he was free to force his way out again, thereby bringing about the most devastating eruption ever seen in these islands.

As for the volcanoes, their summits were *tapu*; early European explorers were warned away. It was Maori veneration of the mountains and fear of their falling into unsympathetic hands that prompted chief Te Heuheu Tukino IV of the Ngati Tuwharetoa tribe to make them a gift to the New Zealand government in 1887 for the country's first national park. They would now, Te Heuheu said, be 'a sacred place of the Crown and a gift forever from me and my people'.

Until the nineteenth century the descendants of Ngatoro-i-rangi remained safe within the region where he had set his shrines. When the explosion came, it was not from within the earth but from the massed muskets of the marauding Northland Ngapuhi chief Hongi Hika in 1823. Hongi slaughtered his way down the Bay of Plenty and inland. Arawa tribesmen sought safety on the island fortress of Mokoia, in Lake Rotorua, but Hongi's reaction was swift and terrible. He had his sweating legions drag their canoes forty kilometres inland from lake to lake, and over rugged and forested terrain. Finally they launched them on Lake Rotorua and almost annihilated the Arawa tribesmen on Mokoia. Nor was that the end of Arawa grief. The Arawa who had survived Hongi's raids were slain by the chief Te Waharoa, from the eastern Waikato. This devastation goes far to explain why the Arawa later saw fit to ally themselves with the British in the wars of the eighteen-sixties.

In the eighteen-thirties, the first Europeans made their way into the region. The Danish trader Philip Tapsell, from Maketu in the Bay of Plenty, came in pursuit of dressed flax while the English missionary Thomas Chapman pursued Maori souls. Tapsell, like all traders of that time, found muskets the most desirable item of exchange, whereas Chapman saw hundreds of his potential converts sliced up for cannibal ovens as war raged, subsided, and raged yet again. ('God Almighty grant that I may ever be preserved from witnessing such sights again,' he wrote in despair. 'About fifty bodies, horrid to say, have been eaten here this morning.')

A more dispassionate chronicler was the New Zealand Company naturalist Ernst Dieffenbach, the first scientist to appraise the North Island's volcanic region, in 1841. He marvelled at the way the Maori of Rotorua lived on so thin a crust of earth: at Ohinemutu he found a community 'intersected by crevices from which steam issued, by boiling springs, and by mud volcanoes. It requires great care even for a native to wind his way through this intricate and dangerous labyrinth. Accidents are common . . . the ground sometimes suddenly gives way where shortly before it appeared to be perfectly firm.'

When battle began between Maori and colonists in the eighteen-sixties, most inhabitants of the plateau – with warring regions on each flank – either sided with colonists or remained neutral. In 1869 however, the remarkably ferocious Poverty Bay rebel Te Kooti left his forest

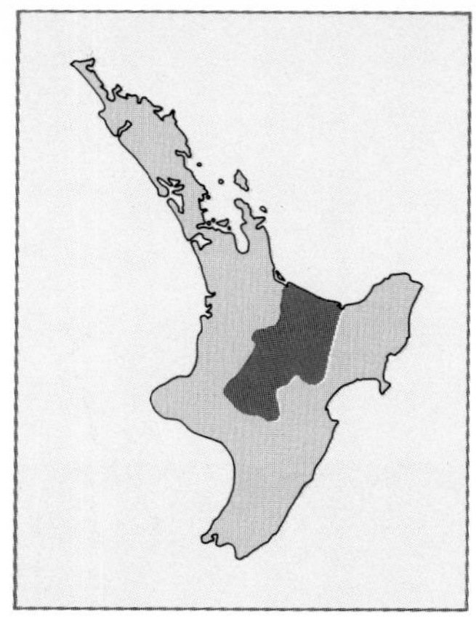

IN THE THROES OF EVOLUTION

sanctuary in the Urewera mountains and led his guerilla force through the Taupo district. Though his slaughter of fellow Maoris won few allies, he briefly found support and sympathy among Tuwharetoa tribesmen to the south of the lake.

Emboldened, he threw up earthworks for a fortress in the desert between Lake Taupo and the three great volcanoes and there determined to repel pursuing columns of colonial militia and Maori allies. Perhaps despair as much as arrogance prompted his stand in so barren a place: the result was the same. His army was crushed, and Tuwharetoa sympathy for his cause cooled. Te Kooti, making yet another magical escape, left legend behind on New Zealand's loneliest and most haunted battlefield.

When peace returned to the North Island, the rumbling region was soon on tourist itineraries: the geysers, boiling mud, warm pools and above all the glowing silica formations of the Volcanic Plateau were seen as one of the earth's more picturesque wonders.

DISASTER AND DEBRIS

The place seemed far less quaint on a June morning in 1886 when Mount Tarawera, a few kilometres from Rotorua, roared open. Whole villages near by were buried, and scores of lives were extinguished as the North Island sky grew bright and with day, dark with fine debris. The Pink and White Terraces, already famed worldwide for their colour and majesty, were shattered and submerged. The fragility of human lease on this region could not have been more powerfully demonstrated.

The twentieth century was to bring an equally savage reminder when on Christmas Eve 1953 Mount Ruapehu released its crater lake and a wall of mud, rock and ice stormed down a narrow riverbed destroying bridges, and killing one hundred and fifty-one railway passengers. This is one region of New Zealand which human energy and ingenuity can never really tame.

All the same, man has worked some gentle marvels here. Vegetation was often not more than a skimpy cover of manuka scrub and ferns. Today, especially to the north, there are vistas of prosperous farms and pine forests. While the patchy fertility of the pumice soil defeated many early pastoralists, fertilisers, particularly superphosphate laced with the missing trace element cobalt, have since made good soil deficiencies. Trim farms and communities now green the once sombre terrain.

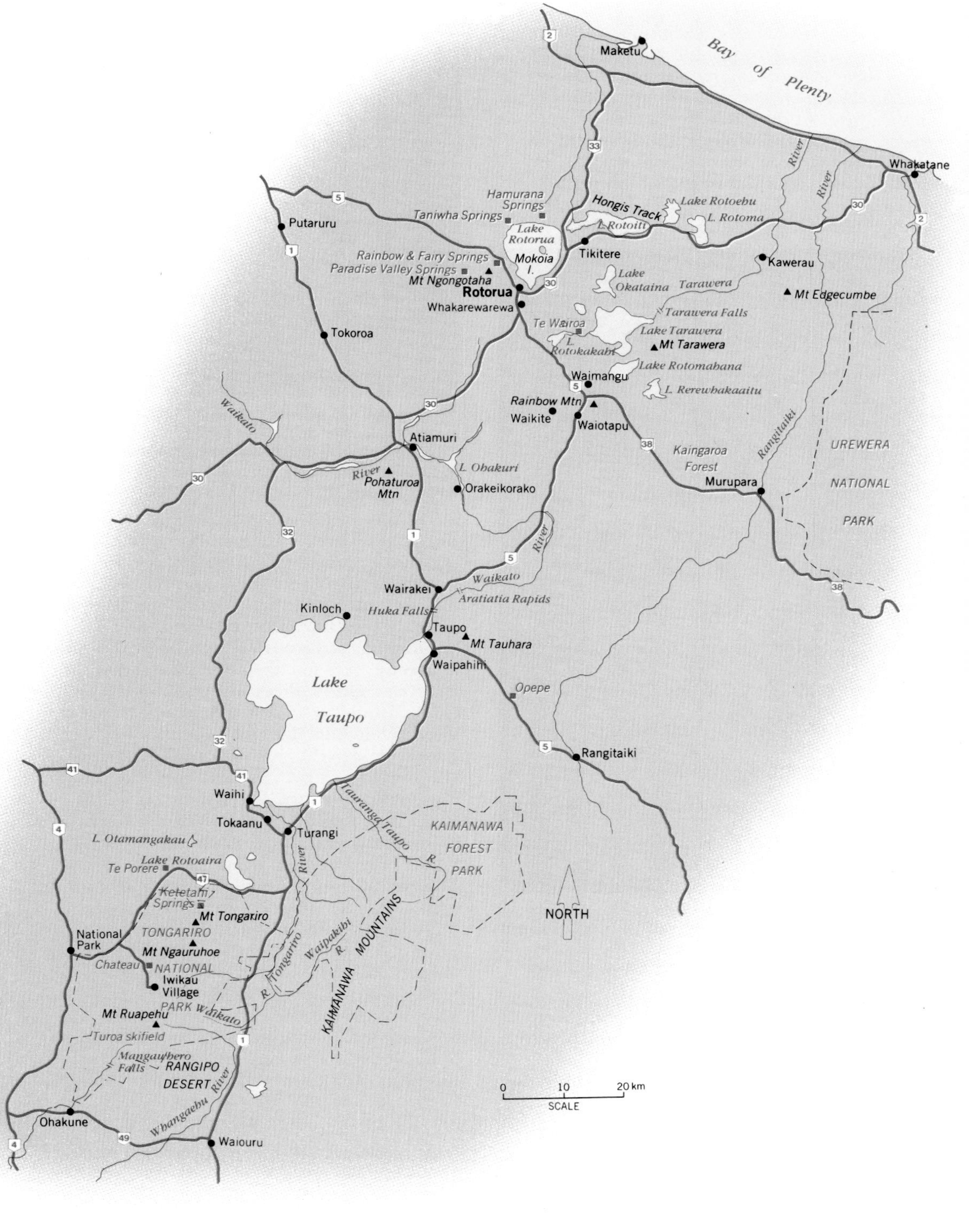

But the greatest change came with the planting of the first exotic pines in the region in 1898 and the discovery that *Pinus radiata* here grew twice as fast as in its native northern hemisphere. Planting continued apace in the twentieth century, and today there are four hundred thousand hectares of trees in the region, the greatest forestation project in the world. As the forests developed so did towns, first for the few tending and thinning the trees, then for the hundreds of mill workers, and finally for the thousands employed in timber-based industries. The huge forests sit at the heart of the region's economic life.

Two Maori women posing in the marae in Kawerau. The marae, called Rautahi meaning 'many in one', houses carved panels that can be seen in the background. These represent all the races in the area, as well as Maori tradition as a whole

Hydro-electric development, especially along the upper Waikato, created other communities, as well as an impressive line of dams and generating stations. In the late nineteen-fifties the hot earth itself was persuaded to surrender pent up energy in the geothermal field at Wairakei. In the nineteen-sixties hydro-electric builders and dammers exploited more of the plateau down to the southern shore of Lake Taupo and into the bleak desert beyond.

Although they now use modern tools and equipment, the carvers and weavers at the New Zealand Maori Arts and Crafts Institute at Whakarewarewa keep the traditional crafts alive. The Institute was established in 1963

The tiny anglers' resort of Turangi became – and has remained, despite the departure of construction workers – a considerable town. Rotorua, for decades a sleepy tourist town, was the first centre in the region to register change. After the war its population tripled, then quadrupled, to thirty-two thousand by the nineteen-sixties and fifty-three thousand by the nineteen-eighties. Proportionately, Taupo was not far behind. A modest lakeside settlement of seven hundred and fifty inhabitants in 1945, it grew tenfold in the next two decades and doubled again in the next two, to pass fifteen thousand in the nineteen-eighties. In the summer holiday season, like Rotorua, it hosts tens of thousands more inhabitants. At the sharp end of New Zealand's last frontier, the timber town of Tokoroa has grown in three decades from a village of three hundred to a city of twenty thousand.

Tourism has had a large hand in the region's growth. Yet by international standards it seldom seems crowded. The vistas of the Volcanic Plateau remain dramatic – with its lakes and legends, its rumbles from the earth's core, its steaming hillsides, smoky mountains and strange deserts. Wily old Ngatoro-i-rangi might still, for the most part, call it his own; the sacred fire his sisters lit may smoulder for millenniums yet.

Right: *Solemn and stately, a vast Maori carving stands at Whakarewarewa, south of Rotorua city. Above the main thermal reserve at 'Whaka', as it is known to locals, is a pre-European palisaded village with a model pa and carvings*

RUMBLING ROTORUA

The Rotorua area, with its spectacular thermal cauldrons, is famed for its bubbling mud and boisterous geysers

For something like one hundred and fifty thousands years Rotorua has been rumbling with subterranean energy. Only in the past one thousand years has man been intimate with the forces at work here; and only in the past one hundred has he fenced them off, so far as the tumult permits, to turn a profit. New Zealand's first tourist town, Rotorua lies in one of the world's most active volcanic zones. It is a city literally on the boil, with a powerful smell of hydrogen sulphide. The great Irish playwright and wit George Bernard Shaw visited in 1934.

Above: *The celebrated Pohutu Geyser in Whakarewarewa Thermal Area plays to a height of an impressive thirty metres*
Right: *Waimangu's Cathedral Rocks, always shrouded in steam, were created by the eruption of Tarawera in 1886*

After gazing pensively into an inferno, the devout atheist pronounced himself lucky to have looked hell in the face and lived to tell the tale. 'Damnable,' he judged. 'I should willingly have paid ten pounds not to see it.'

Satanic some of Rotorua's sights may be, but for more than a century people have enthusiastically paid for the privilege of box seats in this untidy theatre of the thermal where steam issues from gratings in the street and craters hiss open suddenly in backyards or parks.

Below: *The hot white-rimmed pools of Orakeikorako were once used as mirrors by Maori women when dressing. When translated, the name means 'the place of adorning'*

Right: *At Waiotapu, murky pools of boiling mud belch and hiss. In dry weather they become mini-volcanoes, ejecting mud missiles from crusty craters* **Below:** *The silica terraces and hot pools of the Artist's Palette at Waiotapu form a fascinating and colourful, constantly changing spectacle*

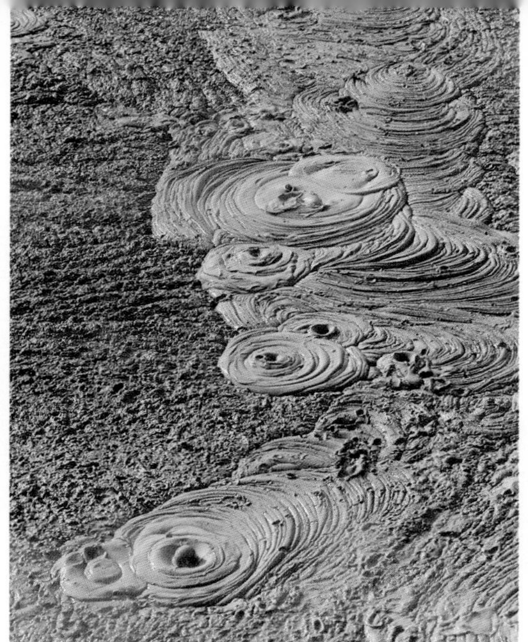

Yet Rotorua's story is human too. Maori life constitutes a great part of its panorama. Humans have lived here with the hot earth for centuries. The city has a greater proportion of Maori than any other of a similar size: one in four of the fifty-three thousand. Elsewhere in New Zealand the Maori population has migrated to the city. Here the city has migrated to the Maori. For close to a million visitors every year, the Maori concerts, arts and crafts, and living traditions, are a highlight. It has been that way since Queen Victoria's son Prince Alfred, the Duke of Edinburgh, arrived in Rotorua in 1870 to be greeted by Maori feasting and dancing. He took to the waters, rode horseback to the thermal areas and confirmed the future of the place. Guest houses and hotels were built and the Victorian fashion for 'taking the waters' ensured there was no off-season. Cars soon replaced horses, but most itineraries remained the same. Many came to settle in the town for its medicinal waters.

The one rift in Rotorua's rushed growth was the Tarawera eruption of 1886: not only were one hundred and fifty-three lives lost but also the Volcanic Plateau's premier attraction, the glittering Pink and White Terraces which colonial painters had already made famous. Predictably, the site of the eruption – and the mini-Pompeii of Te Wairoa village that was excavated from the rubble – became a tourist attraction too. The eruption also opened up a spellbinding new thermal area in the Waimangu Valley.

The best known and most accessible of the district's thermal hot spots lies a kilometre or two south of the town, in and around the Maori village of Whakarewarewa. In a zone only a kilometre long, and half that wide, some five hundred hot springs simmer and spit. Three impressive geysers – the best known, Pohutu, spraying up to thirty metres – work regularly. Hot mud – actually rock broken down by acid gases – mutters everywhere. The crust of the earth here could hardly be thinner; under foot the ground vibrates as the geysers roar. But perhaps the most astonishing sight at Whakarewarewa is that of human beings living intimately with land in upheaval, their homes set in the steam; even their dead, in one of the world's oddest graveyards, are laid to rest among hissing fissures.

More astonishingly, the place was populated by Maori who lost their homes and loved ancestral landscape when Tarawera blew apart in 1886. Tribal cousins offered them Whakarewarewa by way of consolation. Already veterans of the tourist business, having guided, watered and fed visitors to the Pink and White Terraces until their destruction, these singed survivors soon made the most of Whakarewarewa too, turning out as guides and entertainers. For a century they and their descendants made Whakarewarewa the most profitable patch of Maori land in New Zealand. At lakeside Ohinemutu village, a few minutes' walk north from the town centre, another Maori community lives among fumaroles and sometimes ferociously explosive pools.

Within easy reach of Rotorua there are several distinctive thermal pockets. Tikitere, named Hells Gate by a nineteenth-century visitor, is perhaps the most sulphurous. It seldom seems more than a minute away from convulsive eruption. Waiotapu, a half-hour drive south, is remarkable for its colourful silica formations. Here one can glimpse the hues which made the vanished Pink and White Terraces legend. Most haunting is the Waimangu Valley, its boiling lake and steaming craters within rents in the land left by Tarawera's eruption a century ago.

Elsewhere, old upheavals have left craters transformed over centuries into a mosaic of serene and shimmering lakes with ferny shores. Without a single geyser, the Rotorua region would still have immense appeal, which is just as well, for the city's largest nightmare is a decrease in thermal activity. As tourist numbers rise, more and more hot water is drawn from bores for spa pools and heating. Already there has been a noticeable effect on Whakarewarewa's display. The warning is plain: Sulphur City, as Rotorua now likes to call itself, risks consuming the goose that lays its aromatic egg. Meanwhile Hades, the longest-running show in the land, still draws full houses.

Above: *A pre-European Maori storehouse, with rare stone carvings on either side, was excavated at Te Wairoa in 1936*

Below: *A warm thermal pool glows in vivid blue, part of the unusual Artist's Palette thermal area in the Waiotapu reserve*

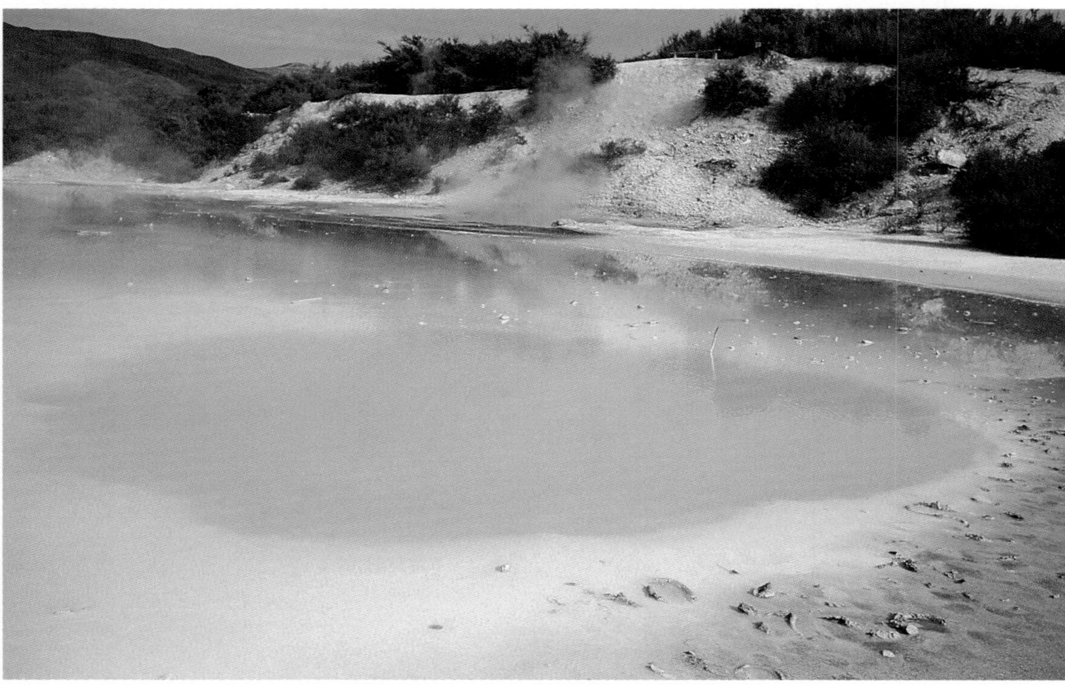

Above: *Rotorua's therapeutic Polynesian Pools are one of the most popular bathing spots for locals and tourists alike*

TAUPO'S TIDELESS SEA

On a summer's day, yachts gliding across blue waters can make Lake Taupo appear the most tranquil place in New Zealand

Serene appearances deceive. This vast lake – its six hundred and six square kilometres make it more a tideless sea – is the legacy of almost unimaginable violence. Taupo is more than a lake. It is a volcano with no top – or a volcano that blew its top again and again in one of the most devastating eruptions ever detected in our planet's past. There had been earlier eruptions here three hundred and thirty, and twenty thousand years ago, but the last, in about AD 135 sent sheets of red hot rock and debris soaring faster than the speed of sound more than two thousand metres high over the summits of rival volcanoes to the south. It bombed and buried forests and left much of the North Island a dusty desert. Airborne ash rained down darkly as far north as present-day Auckland, and south as far as present-day Wellington. Rivers changed course.

The statistics are staggering. Enough material was emitted from this giant crater to bury all of New Zealand to a depth of forty-five metres, although most fell within the volcanic region itself. It was a far greater eruption than that of the Mediterranean's Santorini, or Indonesia's Krakatoa. But in AD 135, New Zealand had no inhabitants to witness or suffer Taupo's last lake-making explosion. The story of that event was written not in human hand, but in the rock and pumice of the Volcanic Plateau.

The Maori had two names for Taupo: *Taupo Moana* or 'Sea of Taupo' acknowledged its dimensions; *Taupo-hau-rau*, or 'Taupo of the Hundred Winds' acknowledged its unpredictable nature. The waters, one minute peaceful and next vicious, are subject to sudden whims of weather passing over the high heart of the North Island. Polynesians whose ancestors had chanced voyages of two thousand nautical miles or more to reach New Zealand seemed to find the lake far more fearful than the open Pacific. 'Worse than the sea,' they warned one early European explorer. They would not paddle directly across it; they cautiously and laboriously followed the shore, from bay to bay, and even then only after lengthy meditation. This was not only due to the risk of change in the weather; they believed a *taniwha*, or water monster, dwelled deep in the lake, and sometimes surfaced to create commotion, overturn vessels and destroy humans. It is likely the story originated not only in Taupo's sensitivity to wind change, but also in residual volcanic shifts.

Lake Taupo is at the very heart of North Island; it is a peaceful place today, but it has had a violent past

Above left: *Lake Taupo's six hundred and six square kilometres make it the largest lake in all of New Zealand* **Left:** *Billowing clouds of steam in Wairakei Valley are part of a geothermal power scheme* **Above:** *Many of Lake Taupo's surrounding slopes are covered with pine forest*

Europeans who have been caught in an abrupt and rather mystifying Taupo storm far from shore are less inclined to laugh at legend. One nineteenth-century missionary who mocked the lake seemed to bring tragedy to the tribesmen he was trying to convert. In the end, he moved elsewhere. The tale of the *taniwha* dies hard. As late as the nineteen-eighties the lake was plumbed for an antipodean version of the Loch Ness monster by a team of credulous Australians, even though no prehistoric creature could be living in its depths, since the lake as we know it now is less than two thousand years old.

The Taupo environment is still volcanically active. To the south of the lake above Waihi village the cliffs steam and hot streams flow into the lake. More than fifty people perished here when honeycombed cliffs collapsed in 1846. There was another landslide with only one fatality in 1910. At nearby Tokaanu the atmosphere is sulphurous with thermal activity, and small geysers and steaming fissures spit on the Taupo golf course. Thermal waters warm homes, hotels and motels to the north of the lake, and the thermal field at Wairakei is harnessed for electricity by a geothermal power station.

Rogue geysers near by are not uncommon. Yet chance of a second sky-blackening cataclysm in any one resident's lifetime seems remote, however much vulcanologists may mutter. The shores of the lake were densely settled in pre-European times; in recent decades they have been again.

The Maori who dwelled here must have felt compensated by the thermally warmed lakeshore during the sometimes bitter winters of the area. There were plenty of small native fish, the kokopu and inanga, and freshwater crayfish, the koura. Freshwater mussels, the kakahi, provided another nourishing food source. There were no eels, for eels need the sea to spawn, but there were duck, and pigeon to be trapped in patches of forest that had survived volcanic devastation. There was a little horticulture where rivers and streams had built up deposits of fertile silt in areas above the inhospitable pumice.

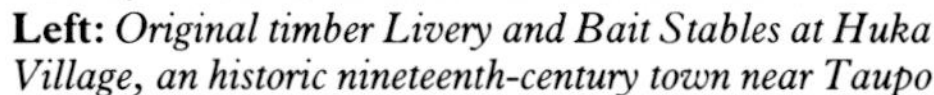

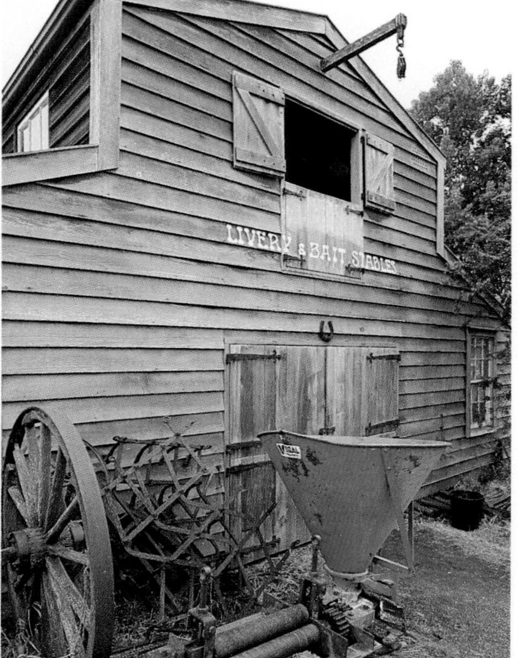

Left: *Original timber Livery and Bait Stables at Huka Village, an historic nineteenth-century town near Taupo*

Nineteenth-century Europeans apparently found no great incentive to settle the Taupo district. After all, it sat in a landscape one early missionary called 'desolate beyond description. Thousands and thousands of acres without Tree or Shrub. . . of the great and terrible wilderness spoken of in Scripture.' But missionaries had souls to save; and soon soldiers had rebels to subdue.

The town of Taupo began as an Armed Constabulary outpost during Te Kooti's long and bloody campaign against the colonists in the late eighteen-sixties. Not far from the east shore of the lake at Opepe, nine patrolling troopers were slain. At Te Porere to the south, Te Kooti's force was finally tamed and the rebel leader reduced to the existence of a fugitive. The fort remained until 1883. When back from patrol, saddlesore men dug out baths on the banks of a hot stream where they could relax and lose their aches. The Armed Constabulary (or A.C.) Baths – now considerably developed and modernised – remain one of the town's special pleasures.

Above: *The once impoverished volcanic lands about Lake Taupo have been greened with cobalt-enriched fertiliser; thousands of sheep and cattle now graze the hills around*

In the late nineteenth century the town was not much more than a dusty stopover for travellers in the North Island interior. There was hotel accommodation and spa bathing, but little more. Taupo was not a developing or prospering rural region: it had few farmers to serve. Yet one of the first Europeans to visit the district, the naturalist Ernst Dieffenbach, glimpsed its potential as early as 1841. Bewitched by 'the scenery of Taupo lake, the whole character of the landscape, the freshness and peculiarity of the vegetation, the white smoke rising around' he saw a beauty 'well calculated to attract visitors from all parts of the world'.

Two things have largely conspired to bring Dieffenbach's vision to pass: trout and trustworthy roads. Brown and then Californian rainbow trout were introduced to the lake towards the end of the nineteenth century. With little competition and an abundance of food the fish grew to phenomenal size. The trout of Taupo, a story in themselves (see page 112), became legend among the world's anglers. Getting to them, however, was another matter. The main trunk railway between Auckland and Wellington ducked the Taupo district. Storms of dust from the pumice roads suffocated travellers in summer; and deep and sandy mud bogged coaches and cars in winter. Today the road journey to Taupo is comfortable and far less desolate. Farms, forests and timber towns are strung along the route.

New Zealand's postwar affluence has confirmed the district's resort character. Summer homes rise thick on the lakeshore, and settlement after settlement has grown. Luxury motels and hotels have opened their doors, not only to the world's anglers, but also to lovers of water sports and to skiers on Ruapehu's slopes to the south in winter. The shore of Taupo, halfway between Auckland and Wellington on Highway 1, with warm pools and soft beds for the weary, still makes a logical stopover for the traveller through the North Island interior. For all the change, visitors first glimpsing the lake can still share the astonishment and delight felt by the famished and footsore explorers of the nineteenth century when, after days spent travelling through desolate wilderness, they found streamers of steam and a great inland sea brimming to the farthest horizon.

ICE AND FIRE

The area to the south of the volcanic plateau has always been 'a place of wild and chaotic grandeur' watched over by a trio of mighty volcanoes

Few places on this planet are starker than that built over the past half million years by eruption after eruption and volcano after volcano at the centre of the North Island. Three volcanoes – Tongariro, Ngauruhoe and Ruapehu – are the living descendants of dozens which once populated the North Island interior. Most are extinct now, some merely slumber, and the surviving trio announce that creation is still in business and New Zealand's profile still unfinished. Meanwhile, their tremors are monitored electronically; their flutters photographed through stop-motion cameras; alarm systems are primed. Such technology may not be able to provide protection, but can warn of a fresh and potentially lethal commotion.

Seldom are there fewer than hundreds, often thousands, of human beings in the immediate vicinity. New Zealanders have made the mountains a playground and the snowy winter slopes of Mount Ruapehu provide the North Island's most popular skifields. Snow-fed rivers offer anglers brown and rainbow trout. Tracks winding up and among the mountains give striking glimpses of the earth's beginnings: of moonscape vistas and alpine massif. The three volcanoes are contained within the seventy-eight thousand hectare Tongariro National Park, New Zealand's first, and one of the world's most bewitching areas.

HIDDEN AND CAPRICIOUS FORCES

Volcanoes have always taxed the imagination; they speak of hidden and capricious forces beyond comprehension except in mythological terms. The Romans had Vulcan, their god of fire, pumping flame from a forge beneath peaks such as Etna and Vesuvius. The Maori had Ruaumoko, god of earthquake and of volcanic fire. The youngest child of Rangi (sky-father) and Papa (earth-mother), Ruaumoko was still at his mother's breast when these primary gods were forced apart by older and rebellious offspring. Ever loyal to his mother, Ruaumoko considered human beings to be trespassers on his mother's flesh and he sent earthquakes and eruptions to shake them off like fleas. The towering cones of Tongariro National Park are testimony to his past tantrums; and so is the strange and sterile wilderness around, the blasted landscape that envelops visitors approaching the mountains.

Here and there the terrain is as sandy as the Sahara, patched with tussock and stunted scrub, and often littered with the limbs of long dead trees. Much of it is a chilly one thousand metres or more above sea level. The wetter western side – with up to two thousand millimetres of rain annually – supports some belts of subalpine forest (where not left sterile by eruption). The eastern side is bare. Wild summer winds dry it fast.

Maori travellers through this dead and dreaded land were at pains not to speak to each other and shielded their eyes with wreaths of green leaves as they tramped it, never looking up towards the mountains lest they risk the wrath of Ruaumoko and other vengeful gods. Murky clouds might suddenly appear, and snow too, or cutting winds. Tradition told of parties of people swallowed up and never seen again.

Mount Ngauruhoe seen from Desert Road

Nor did Europeans when they first walked here find the landscape any more inviting. 'A most desolate and weird-looking spot,' lamented missionary-explorer William Colenso when he shivered across it in 1847. 'A fit place for Macbeth's witches!'

Today the traveller through the central North Island cannot avoid it: Highway 1 cuts through on the Desert Road between Turangi and Waiouru. Even if wreaths of green leaves are no longer necessary, the atmosphere of menace is still palpable, more so with the mountains beyond.

Ngauruhoe conforms to the conventional expectations of a volcano. It has a classically conical peak, seldom without a distinct plume of steam and gas. Ash often discolours the snow that covers it for much of the winter. A quickly grown two thousand five hundred years old, it has always been active, according to human memory. Large eruptions of lava occurred in 1870, 1949 and 1954, each lasting for months. In 1974 and 1975 columns of ash-laden gas lifted from two to nine kilometres above the cone; the cloud climbed as high as twelve kilometres and ash fell finely for kilometres around. Avalanches of hot debris endangered walkers on the mountain slopes. Unpredictable Ngauruhoe will erupt again.

Tongariro is much less single-minded, much older, and of marvellous complexity, with a maze of cones and craters. It is a volcanic massif built by many eruptions over hundreds of thousands of years, but most decisively within the past twenty thousand. Born during the ice ages, many of

A trio of volcanic mountains – Tongariro (in foreground under cloud); Ngauruhoe (middle distance); and Ruapehu

Cloud lightly veils the multi-cratered summit of Mount Tongariro, a volcanic massif built up by many eruptions

Tongariro's cones have been shaped and softened by great sheets of glacier. Recent eruptions have not been spectacular, though Maori tradition tells of much activity. There were small eruptions of ash in 1855, 1927 and 1928.

It is the most various, vivid and hospitable of the three volcanoes, with its colourful crater lakes and warm springs, and fields of red, black and grey scoria. The waters of Ketetahi Springs, a popular destination, had healing powers, according to the Maori who reserved this patch of mountain when they made a gift of the three volcanoes to the Crown in 1887.

Ruapehu is always snow-covered, always breathtaking, a bulky giant bestriding the horizon of the central North Island. From a distance it appears a picture of peace but it simmers as much as its neighbours, and sometimes more. A sulphurous seventeen hectare lake steams on its summit; beneath it Ruaumoko remains at work.

Mount Ruapehu's sulphurous crater lake simmers menacingly on top of the highest mountain peak in the North Island

Like Tongariro, the mountain is an accumulation of hundreds of thousands of years of eruption. From time to time it still gives cause for panic. In 1945 the lake disappeared after lava burst from its centre and an eruption dumped ash up to ninety kilometres away. The lake rose again, and brimmed higher than ever in 1953, with sudden and terrible consequences. The water found a way out through weakened ash in an ice cave and thundered down the mountainside, carrying boulders and blocks of ice before it in a wall of destruction called a lahar. It grabbed up bridges on its route down the Whangaehu River and left one hundred and fifty-one passengers on a passing train dead. Eruptions remain frequent; the nineteen-sixties and seventies saw many, the largest in 1975.

In June 1969 during the night a lahar whipped down on to a popular skifield carrying away a refreshment kiosk. A few hours earlier or later it might have carried away up to two thousand skiers. Yet that has never deterred lovers of winter sport dicing with one of the world's most industrious volcanoes, risking a thrill undreamed of by skiers elsewhere in the world, that of careering downhill ahead of a lava flow or lahar. On a crisp winter day there are up to ten thousand people skiing. As the snow retreats, small parties of trampers and sightseers begin winding along the walkways, guests in the realm of Ruaumoko.

TALL STORY TROUT

Elsewhere in the world tall stories commemorate freshwater monsters that got away; here the tales are of finned giants that did not

The North Island's Volcanic Plateau has been called the world's greatest trout factory. Figures are hard to come by and poachers' catches cannot be tallied, but it seems that somewhere between fifty and one hundred thousand brown and rainbow trout annually fail to elude anglers in this region. Anglers from all over the world rejoice in the rivers and lakes of the steamy plateau. For them, a chance to fence with New Zealand's robust sporting fish crowns a lifetime of dedication to their skills. Many of the more affluent return year after year.

Above: *A proud group display their booty after a successful expedition. The large brown and rainbow trout caught in the region weigh in at an average of two kilos, often more*
Below: *At Rainbow and Fairy Springs trout and wildlife park, rainbow and brown trout can be seen in sparkling pools*

New Zealanders are less excitable about landing the big ones. In most countries, trout fishing is equated with wealth and privilege, but here it is Everyman's right, on payment of a modest licence fee. Furthermore, to keep matters sporting, unlike anywhere else in the world, there is no commercialisation of trout: no trout farms, no buying and selling of the fish. The only way to treat yourself to a trout dinner here is to catch your own fish. Any suggestion of change in the *status quo* can and has cost a government votes. New Zealand's trout fishing lobby, as potent as any in the country, talks with religious fervour of keeping commerce clear of their sport. Sport? Vocation. It was the Babylonian belief that the gods did not deduct from man's allotted span the hours spent fishing. From the first day they can toddle to a river, tens of thousands of New Zealanders test the gods to the limit.

Colonists in the late nineteenth century began to pine for fishing and hunting. They introduced deer, game birds and freshwater fish, but the fish were to prove the most sensational migrant. Lake-dwelling brown trout ova from Britain were first introduced to the region. In the late eighteen-nineties, steelhead – sea-running rainbow trout – from California were introduced to the lakes (most importantly Taupo) and they travelled up rivers and streams to spawn. With no competition, and with small native fish to feed on, they ate their way into the record books.

A state-operated trout hatchery at Turangi breeds rainbow trout which are then released into nearby rivers and lakes

Fishermen feasted too. There are tales of anglers landing a half-tonne of trout a day. Rainbow trout weighing ten kilos were not uncommon. The largest rainbow weighed and recorded from Lake Taupo is 12.4 kilos; the largest brown taken in the region, from Lake Rotorua, is 17.7 kilos. In the days when world travel was still an adventure, anglers rose to the lure of New Zealand's legendary giants, packed their rods and flies and set out for the far South Pacific. Fishing lodges began opening; the rainbow meant a pot of gold.

By the time of the First World War, the first fine rapture seemed to be over and there was to be no pot of gold after all. It was not that there were fewer trout; they simply shrank. The food supply was depleted and there were too many of them. To combat the problem it was decided to net trout at river mouths and, for the first and only time in New Zealand, sell them commercially. The experiment succeeded and by the nineteen-twenties, Taupo's trout were bigger and better than ever. The average fish landed was around five kilos. When it seemed the cycle of diminished food supply and smaller trout might be repeated at Taupo, smelt were introduced from Rotorua lakes as a fresh food source.

Since then, the population has stabilised. The average trout weighs in at between two and three kilos – still a spectacular weight by international measure – and it is estimated that there are more traditional 'four pound trout' caught on the Volcanic Plateau (proportionate to the anglers hauling them in) than anywhere else in the world.

In the nineteen-eighties the plateau's trout were bigger than they had been for two decades. Indeed, the lusty and pure-bred character of New Zealand's rainbow trout is such that they have been reintroduced into the Californian rivers whence their ancestors came a century ago.

Right: *Fishermen from all over the world travel to Taupo to battle with the region's famous pure strain of rainbow trout*

PLACES OF INTEREST

ATIAMURI

A small township 40 kilometres north of TAUPO, once a dusty coaching stop (the Waikato River was bridged here) and now presiding over one of the eight great hydro-electric dams and lakes built on the Waikato. Set in a giant pine forest, Atiamuri is overlooked by the queerly shaped Pohaturoa Mountain, where the first Polynesian settlers in the central North Island were annihilated.

The area around the rock is now a reserve, with picnic places. The road through to the King Country (Highway 30) from here is supremely scenic, with rocky cliffs, pine forests, riverside reserves, and the Waikato fattening into yet another hydro lake. Farther is Pureora Forest Park (see page 127).

KAWERAU

Between ROTORUA and the Bay of Plenty's Whakatane, this town of 9500 was built in 1953 to serve the Tasman Pulp and Paper Company's large plant. Towns like Kawerau and TOKOROA came into being as the harvest of logs grew from the Volcanic Plateau's hundreds of thousands of hectares of man-grown pine forest. The plant engulfs and processes two million cubic metres of logs annually. (Tours of the mill are possible, other than on weekends and public holidays; 1.30 at the main gate.)

Conspicuous above the town is 821 metre Mt Edgecumbe, venerated by local Maori, and dedicated to their dead. The climber is rewarded not only with vistas but also with a reviving swim in this old volcano's crater lake. The Tarawera Falls, 22 kilometres out of town, at the end of Fentons Mill Road and a short bush walkway, are a striking spectacle. Here, the Tarawera River, after a subterranean journey from Lake Tarawera, leaps from tunnels and lashes rocks 60 metres below.

The local marae, Rautahi, meaning 'many in one' embraces all the races in Kawerau. Its carved panels pay tribute not just to Maori tradition, but also to the cultures of others. Between here and Rotorua, the road (Highway 30) travels through superb lakeland, taking in leafy and lovely Hongis Track, the route along which the Northland chief Hongi Hika portaged his canoes in his lethal campaign against the Arawa people of the Volcanic Plateau in 1823.

MURUPARA

In the lee of the immense 140 000 hectare Kaingaroa pine forest, on the approach to the Urewera National Park, this timber town of 3000 provides KAWERAU with logs to produce pulp and paper. About 8 kilometres west of the town, just off Highway 38 are a number of intriguing old Polynesian canoe drawings in a rock shelter. Permission to enter the forest must be obtained from the forestry headquarters in town. There is also an information office for Urewera National Park (see page 168).

OHAKUNE

Just to the south of TONGARIRO NATIONAL PARK, this former milling and mainly market-gardening centre on rich volcanic soil was once known as the home of the humble carrot. Indeed, it even promoted itself as the Carrot Capital of New Zealand. But with the opening of new skifields near by on Ruapehu's slopes, the homely town of 1500 has changed to become the North Island's prominent mountain town. In all seasons there is a splendid 17 kilometre drive up the Ohakune Mountain Road and through the vivid forest of the national park to the Mangawhero Falls and Turoa skifield. Ask for information from the national park ranger at the start of the road; the ranger can also tell you about the Mangawhero Forest Walk and the Waitonga Falls Walk. In the town proper there is an information office.

ORAKEIKORAKO

One of the Volcanic Plateau's most bewitching thermal attractions, Orakeikorako is especially celebrated for the glitter and glow of its silica formations. The name means 'the place of adorning'. Maori women, it is said, used a pool in what is now known as Aladdin's Cave as a mirror to preen and adorn themselves. The spectacular Golden Fleece Terrace, a 38 metre long, 5 metre tall rampart of silica encrustation is the area's major claim to fame and suggests why the lost Pink and White Terraces are so long remembered. Colour-filled Aladdin's Cave, born of volcanic uproar, was originally named Ruatapu, or 'sacred cave'. The thermal area is open daily and must be reached by jet boat across Lake Ohakuri. It is accessible from either Highway 1 (Tirau–Taupo) or Highway 5 (Rotorua–Taupo). Watch for signposts.

PUTARURU

Yet another of the Volcanic Plateau's sudden timber towns, with a population of 4300. Just south of the town on Highway 1 is a particularly comprehensive and fascinating specialist museum devoted to the timber industry and those who created it (open Sunday to Friday 10–4). There is also a pleasing little tearoom and picnic area for travellers.

ROTORUA

Love it or loathe it: no city in New Zealand is more dedicated to the tourist dollar. It's a steamy Kiwi Las Vegas, minus casinos, but with a convincing whiff of brimstone in the middle of one of the planet's liveliest fields of thermal activity. Visitors should forget the tinseltown architecture and turn to nature's handiwork. Within quick reach of the lakeside city are most of the Volcanic Plateau's more bizarre sights: Whakarewarewa (see page 106); Tikitere, or Hells Gate; and WAIMANGU THERMAL VALLEY, WAIOTAPU, and ORAKEIKORAKO to the south.

Te Wairoa village, 14 kilometres out of town was excavated from under tonnes of mud and ash after the 1886 eruption. A testimony to the potentially terrifying subterranean forces at work here, it sits near Lake Tarawera, with the once deadly volcano looming beyond. For less provocative views of the plateau and sight of the huge trout of the region, try Rainbow and Fairy Springs, Paradise Valley Springs or Taniwha Springs outside the city, or Hamurana Springs around Lake Rotorua (all open daily).

In the city, one oasis of visual pleasure is the Government Gardens where steam winds gently around trim lawns and bright flowerbeds. Sleepy early-century Rotorua still resides there in the form of the one-time Government Bathhouse (1907), now known as Tudor Towers, a marvellously rambling building with Elizabethan pretensions meant to give Rotorua something of the elegance of Europe's fashionable spa towns. It now holds a museum with restored bathhouse mud baths in the basement, an art gallery also paying attention to the rich history of the region, and a restaurant. The gallery and museum are open 10–4 weekdays and public holidays; 1–4.30 weekends.

Amid the gardens and steam vents of 25 hectare Kuirau Park just to the west of the urban area is the Rotorua Settlers Museum (open 9–5 weekends); and around the lake at Holdens Bay there is the Te Amorangi Trust Museum (1–4 Sundays and public holidays) with an especially impressive collection of horse-drawn agricultural machinery and a miniature steam railway. A cable car up Mt Ngongotaha provides panoramas of contemporary Rotorua. Scenic flights can take in the entire Volcanic Plateau, from the steaming mountains of the south to explosive White Island (see page 99).

Rotorua has long had a reputation for the best (and most genuine) Maori arts and crafts. Purchases may be made at the Maori Arts and Crafts Institute adjoining the thermal area at Whakarewarewa, where for much of the year women weavers and Maori carvers, pupils and instructors, can be seen at work. The past is always alive at Ohinemutu village where the visitor walks without need of guides among dwellings set on steaming lakeside. This was the main Maori settlement in the area, and where Rotorua began as a tourist town in the 19th century. Maori still use the thermal pools for cooking, washing and bathing. Here, and elsewhere in the city Maori entertainment groups are a feature and hangi food can be enjoyed.

St Faith's Anglican Church (1910), shaped in Rotorua Tudor, is rich in Maori carving and decoration. A sand-blasted window depicts a Maori Christ who appears to walk on the waters of Lake Rotorua seen through the window. Outside, queer concrete graves set on the thin earth – among steam, subsidences and craters – hold some of the distinguished dead of the district, among them Captain Gilbert Mair (1843–1923), who led the Arawa tribesmen in battles first with Hauhau insurgents, then with Te Kooti's rebels in the late 1860s, and was made an Arawa chieftain. Near by in a Maori-carved shelter is the bust of Queen Victoria. This was presented to the Arawa tribesmen by Prince Alfred, Duke of Edinburgh, in 1870 to mark the aid and comfort they provided soldiers of the Queen in the wars of the 1860s. The carved meeting-house Tamatekapua, which commands the village centre, dates back to 1878, and has been remodelled since. Some of the carving inside is by Maori craftsmen working with stone tools.

Tank artillery at the Queen Elizabeth II Memorial Army Museum, Waiouru

The curative virtues of Rotorua's waters are still sworn by. Most motels and hotels have their own hot pools and the largest complex in the city is Polynesian Pools, adjacent to the Government Gardens. This establishment draws waters from three famed springs, the Rachel, the Priest and the Radium. Each is said to have a particular therapeutic value, especially for sufferers of rheumatism and arthritis. The tired sightseer soaking here certainly finds them magically restorative. In summer there is also freshwater swimming in lakes in the Rotorua area such as Rotoiti (celebrated for its trout), Okataina and Tarawera. The drive towards Whakatane is especially pleasing. About 30 kilometres north-east the road travels through the lovely woodland known as Hongis Track, between Lakes Rotoiti and Rotoehu.

As a tourist centre, Rotorua now has many sideshows. Unique among them, particularly for strangers to New Zealand, is the Agrodome at the north of the town, where the sheep industry is turned into lively entertainment. It was founded by the famed Bowen brothers, once the world's fastest shearers and the men who made shearing a national sport.

TAUPO

One of the more conspicuous results of New Zealand's 20th century affluence, the town of Taupo – now with 15 000 people – has grown in the past four decades largely as a resort, a place of retirement, and a home from home for fanatic fisher folk. Most motels and many homes in the town can boast magnificent views of the rippling 606 square kilometre Lake Taupo, often with the snow-whitened summits of the three volcanoes, Ruapehu, Tongariro and Ngauruhoe in the background. Like ROTORUA, the town is warmed by thermal waters. Just to the north of the town at WAIRAKEI is the most thunderous field of thermal activity on the Volcanic Plateau, this one of man's making for the production of electricity.

Gentler and less garish than the city to the north, Taupo takes in tens of thousands of holidaymakers at the height of summer, yet much of the lakeshore remains uncrowded. Launch excursions and scenic flights make the visitor more intimate with the terrain around.

Taupo began as a military outpost in the 1860s, and its beginnings may be glimpsed at the heart of the modern town. Above the boat harbour are the remains of the redoubt that stood here, some earthworks and a small pumice-walled hut used as an ammunition magazine (1874). Near by stands the old Taupo courthouse (1881), and the Taupo district museum which displays some of the titanic trout caught here. Otherwise the 19th century is hardly to be glimpsed, though Historic Huka Village 4 kilometres north of the town has an assemblage of pioneer artefacts.

The Armed Constabulary who used Taupo as a base for their patrols into territory menaced by rebel leader Te Kooti were also the first Europeans to exploit the thermal virtues of the region; the baths they established (now known as the A.C. Baths) to take the sting from saddlesore buttocks and frozen feet have been used and appreciated for more than a century since. (Along Spa Road: open daily 8–9.) Another complex as refreshing and reviving is the De Brett Thermal Pools half a kilometre along the Taupo–Napier road, set in a steamy valley behind the especially splendid pioneer pub formerly known and famed as The Terraces (now prosaically De Brett). The pools are open daily 7.30–9.30.

A climb up Mt Tauhara offers splendid vistas. As trout turned Taupo into a rather glitzy and cosmopolitan lakeside resort with many motels, hotels and restaurants, the district's dangerous frontier days at the heart of 'the great and terrible wilderness spoken of in Scripture' have become folklore. A few material remains still command the traveller's attention. At Opepe, 17 kilometres along the Taupo–Napier road and a short walk through woodland, is a lonely cluster of nine graves. These are of the troopers patrolling the Volcanic Plateau in 1869 who were ambushed by Te Kooti's irregulars. Opepe was once a military post of 300, a town bigger than Taupo.

Nineteen kilometres farther along the Taupo–Napier road is the site of the famed Rangitaiki pub, which grew around Opepe's former martial messroom when it was moved here in 1887. In its heyday it actually advertised 'bad beer, dirty glasses, crook change and incivility'. Tradition tells that the legendary 1960s gaol-escaper George Wilder drank here with impunity for months, while police hunted him elsewhere. A modern tavern now serves nostalgic travellers.

In and around the town the once bleak and dusty environment has been softened and coloured by laboriously enriched and lovingly tended gardens – especially at 35 hectare Waipahihi Botanical Reserve at the end of Shepherd Road, where rare alpine plants flourish and rhododendrons and azaleas garland the paths. To the west of the lake, and now included in launch excursions, a huge Maori head carved into a cliff looms above the water. This was the work of young Maori of the 1980s wishing to leave a mark of their ancestors on the landscape beside the increasingly European lake. Although they succeeded, it has, like everything else on the Volcanic Plateau, become another tourist attraction. Even honey has been made one. The Honey Centre on the road to Kinloch celebrates the bee as if its nectar were a local invention. There are flavours of bewildering combination, and everything you ever needed to know about the product and its maker.

A drive around the lake is rewarding, though it is a long trip of 150 kilometres. Following the Waikato along its journey from Taupo, there are the Huka Falls, Wairakei geothermal field, Aratiatia Rapids and ORAKEIKORAKO.

FISHING FANTASTIC

New Zealand lakes and rivers provide some of the best trout fishing in the world, especially those of the Volcanic Plateau

Legendary among the world's anglers, the plateau's trout are fished all year

It is claimed that New Zealand waters provide a better fish-per-angler catch than anywhere else and that a higher proportion are heavy fish, weighing over two kilos. The two main species trout are the rainbow – a powerful fighting fish introduced from North America – and the brown trout, its European relative.

The Volcanic Plateau boasts some of the country's finest sport. *Lake Taupo* is one of the most popular fishing grounds on the plateau. It can be fished all year round. Trolling from boats is the favourite method on the lake itself, using surface lures or streamer flies in the summer months. During winter when trout tend to move to deeper waters, weighted lures on leaded lines are used.

But it is the stream and river mouth fishing that have made Taupo world-famous. There is excellent upstream fishing in the Tauranga Taupo and the Tongariro Rivers. Most of the better areas are restricted to fly fishing only. The east side of Lake Taupo – and the best streams – is easily reached from Highway 1. (It is a good idea to avoid the January holiday period.)

The finest trout fishing river in the North Island is the *Tongariro*. Rainbows can be caught in its middle and upper waters and browns farther down. April through to December is the best time, as the river becomes a spawning ground during summer.

Lake Rotoaira and *Lake Otamangakau* are approached from the Turangi–National Park road. A special licence, available from the Trust Board headquarters at the lakeside, is necessary for fishing Rotoaira. Otamangakau is fished mainly from the lake's edge.

Within thirty kilometres of Rotorua are the *Rotorua lakes*: Tarawera, Okataina, Rotoiti, Rotoma, Rotoehu, Rerewhakaaitu, Rotomahana, Okareka, Tikitapu, Rotokakahi and Rotorua itself. All lakes fish well, though a boat is sometimes necessary.

Fishing licences must always be carried. Government Tourist Bureau at Rotorua and other main centres, or fishing tackle shops, can provide details. They may also help with information and advice concerning boat hire for trolling, and professional fishing guides for beginners. A twenty metre right-of-access applies along most waters, but this does not include the right to cross private land (for which permission must always be sought). Gates should always be left opened or shut, depending on how they were found.

TE PORERE

Just outside the boundary of TONGARIRO NATIONAL PARK, and a short walk off the TURANGI – National Park road, Te Porere stands in bleak, tussocky and patchily forested pumiceland overlooked by mighty Tongariro. This is New Zealand's queerest and loneliest battlesite, by far the most evocative, and the last more or less traditional Maori fortress ever constructed. The final pitched battle of the wars of the 1860s was fought here, between Te Kooti Rikirangi, the Israelite rebel of Poverty Bay, and colonial militia with their Maori allies. Harried from the forested Urewera country, and seeking to impress potential Maori recruits to his cause, Te Kooti was pushed to making a defiant stand in this exposed terrain. His rapidly dug fortress grew at the end of a long ridge with clear views of the ground across which his pursuers must move. But

THE PLATEAU'S NATIVE SANCTUARIES

Vast, diverse and beautiful, the volcanic plateau's state forest parks are sanctuaries for the area's wildlife

Whakarewarewa Forest Park has easily accessible tracks for all trampers

Whakarewarewa Forest Park, on the southern outskirts of Rotorua city is one of the most popular attractions of the Volcanic Plateau region, yet its size (thirty-eight hundred hectares) means that it is never overcrowded. Its forest walks, tracks, picnic sites, trail-bike and pony-riding areas can all be easily reached by car.

The park also has commercial use. It is carefully and selectively logged, and it houses a sawmill, a timber industry training centre and a forest research institute. Over forty species of birds live in the forest, as well as introduced animals such as sambur, red deer and wallabies. The forest contains magnificent examples of North American exotics, including the coast redwood and the Douglas fir. There are also some attractive stands of larch which turn brilliant emerald in spring and golden-orange in autumn.

Just outside Rotorua on the edge of the park is the Redwood Memorial Grove dedicated to the men of the New Zealand Forest Service who died in the two world wars. Giant coastal redwoods soar over fifty metres above many species of native shrubs and ferns. The park can be reached by Highway 5 or Tarawera Road.

South-east of Lake Taupo and east of the Tongariro National Park is the *Kaimanawa Forest Park*. Access to the park from the west is via Highway 1, and from the north via Taharua and Clements Roads, off Highway 5.

This park, larger than Whakarewarewa, comprises seventy-six thousand hectares, including the Kaimanawa Mountains. A fine reserve for trampers and hunters, the park also provides roadside picnic areas. There is camping and pony-trekking in the Waipakihi Valley. At the end of some roads (such as Clements) there are picnicking and swimming areas. The many rivers provide good fishing.

The park is renowned for its beech forests. There are mountain beech on the heights, podocarp beech to the north-west, and red and silver beech to the north and east. All three species are found in the Waipakihi and Ngaruroro valleys. Wildlife includes kiwis and paradise ducks, as well as red deer, the elusive sika deer, rabbits, pigs and wild horses.

Adequate clothing, including waterproofs and boots, is recommended for walks, as the climate is changeable and can quite suddenly become wet and cold.

on October 4, 1869, his skirmishers were shot down, his parapets stormed, and the deep trenches filled with dying warriors became gutters of blood. Te Kooti escaped and survived another two or three years of pursuit, then lived in exile before his pardon in the 1880s. The vivid fortress, now tended by the NZ Historic Places Trust is also the grave of scores of men and women who gave the reckless Te Kooti their loyalty to the last.

TOKAANU

Set amid thermal activity on the southern shore of Lake TAUPO, this village of a few score people has a national reputation among fishermen quite at odds with its diminutive nature. In 1869, Te Kooti, during his last days of martial bravado, made it a base while he wooed Maoris in the Volcanic Plateau and farther west into joining the rebellion under his flag. Later it was an Armed Constabulary outpost.

The village is near the trout-rich delta of the Tongariro River. There is a small and most active thermal park beside public and private thermal pools (open daily 10–9) where chilled and cheated anglers warm away their woes. St Paul's Anglican Church, flavoured with Maori *tukutuku* and *kowhaiwhai* (wall panels and rafter patterns), is a memorial to the missionary Thomas Grace and his wife Agnes, the first Europeans to settle at this extremity of the lake.

TOKOROA

With a population close to 20 000, Tokoroa is the Volcanic Plateau's fastest grown timber town. In the 1950s it was hardly more than a store, a post office and a cluster of houses. Just south, visible from Highway 1 amid plumes of steam, is the vast Kinleith Pulp and Paper Mill which employs 4500 locals. (Tours of the mill 10.30 Monday to Friday.)

TONGARIRO NATIONAL PARK

New Zealand's first national park, a Maori gift to the New Zealand government to preserve its sacred character. About as far from the sea as the traveller can be in New Zealand, the park's 78 651 dramatic hectares of blasted terrain has three active volcanoes, Ngauruhoe (2291 metres), Tongariro (1968 metres) and Ruapehu (2797 metres) as centrepieces. This great volcanic upland has a lonely and continental character, albeit with an ominous tinge. Botanist-explorer J.C. Bidwill was the first European to investigate the region, in defiance of Maori *tapu* on its peaks, in 1839. This was the first ascent of a volcano – indeed, of any mountain – in New Zealand. After gazing into Ngauruhoe, he reported 'the most terrible abyss I have ever looked into or imagined'. A strange roar, perhaps preliminary to an eruption, sent him scurrying down the mountain again, and Ruapehu was not climbed until 1879.

Volcanic activity here is now monitored carefully. Tens of thousands of skiers use Ruapehu's slopes in winter, and its popularity as a summer resort is growing. The two main approaches are from the Chateau (from the north) or OHAKUNE Mountain Road (from the south). There are park rangers and information offices at both approaches. Comfortable walkways – long and short – and huts available for overnight stays thread the park.

The walkways offer unrivalled glimpses of our planet in the making. Volcanic activity here possibly started two million years ago, and became concentrated 20 000 years ago. By that measure Ngauruhoe is only 2500 years old and still capable of tantrums. In the 1950s it spouted lava 300 metres in the air.

Quite the most strikingly situated hotel in New Zealand, the government-owned Chateau is more than 1100 metres above sea level, a lonely oasis on stark tussock terrain under bulky Ruapehu. Built in the 1920s when the potential of the park as a playground became apparent, it remains magnificently palatial. The road winds on up Ruapehu to the ski lodges of Iwikau Village at more than 1600 metres. Behind the Chateau is the park headquarters providing excellent models and an audio-visual show. In summer there are guided walks and lectures. The half-day tramp to Ketetahi Springs on Tongariro is outstanding – with the bonus of a swim in a warm pool.

Altogether the park offers some of New Zealand's most intriguing browsing and walking. Everywhere the country's geologic past is evident. Alpine forests and deserts host some 500 species of plants. The strange and haunting Rangipo Desert to the east is the landscape through which John Mulgan's hero Johnson laboured as a fugitive in the classic New Zealand novel *Man Alone*.

TURANGI

Now with fewer than 4000 people, this town on Lake Taupo's southern shore once had about twice that number, including hundreds of Italian tunnellers during the 1960s and 1970s when it was the base for the construction of the vast Tongariro hydro-electric power scheme. Although it remains a service centre for that scheme, Turangi has resumed its serene existence as a recreational town accommodating trout fishermen all year and skiers in winter.

The Tongariro River feeds into Lake Taupo here. It is possibly the most famed stretch of trout-fishing water in the world. There is a Silly Pool (for idiot anglers?) and others are named after successful fishermen or for their natural features. The Breakfast Pool was once convenient for Turangi residents who wished a rainbow trout on the table to start their day.

The Tongariro Fish Hatchery (visits possible in working hours) on Highway 1 just south of the town rears rainbow trout fingerlings to replenish stocks elsewhere in New Zealand. It also exports them around the world, even to their native California where the original rainbow

St Paul's Anglican Church at Tokaanu is a memorial to Thomas Grace and his wife Agnes

have interbred and lost their purity and fighting mettle. Turangi adjoins **TONGARIRO NATIONAL PARK**, and is a base for excursions in that area.

On the way to the Chateau are two items of considerable historic interest. On the shore of Lake Rotoaira there is a recently excavated and partly reconstructed Maori village (about 1840). Farther, is Te Kooti's lonely fortress at **TE PORERE**. To the east of Turangi there is the large aboriginal wilderness of Kaimanawa Forest Park, with tramping and hunting (permits available for hunting at Forest Service in Taupo) and overnight huts.

WAIHI VILLAGE

A picture-postcard Maori hamlet, this is the informal headquarters of the Ngati Tuwharetoa, under steamy cliffs and beside peaceful waters on the southern shore of Lake Taupo. It has been rebuilt twice after lethal landslides from the honeycombed hills above. Its most distinctive landmark is the graceful Catholic Church of St Werenfried (1889), decorated in Maori style inside, with stained-glass windows portraying Christ and the Virgin Mary as Maori. Next to it, the meeting-house Tapeka, (1959) contains carving from earlier meeting-houses on the site. Also of interest is the Te Heuheu Mausoleum, where the mighty Tuwharetoa chief Te Heuheu Tukino II who perished in the 1846 landslide is interred with other members of his family. Beside the village, Waihi Falls leap 90 metres into Lake Taupo.

WAIMANGU THERMAL VALLEY

Most arresting of the many thermal sights in **ROTORUA**'s vicinity, this valley was born of the violence of Mt Tarawera's eruption. Part of a 19-kilometre fissure that snaked from the volcano as it took life and landscape on June 10, 1886, the valley derives its name – *waimangu* means 'black water' – from a rogue now extinct muddy-coloured geyser, the largest ever known. It once played to 500 metres.

Among the Volcanic Plateau's spectacles there is nothing more sinister than the Waimangu Cauldron, one of the world's largest boiling lakes with close to 5 hectares of simmering water. The incongruously named Cathedral Rocks lurk reddish and murky among the steam beyond. Reserve the valley as the finale of any Rotorua itinerary, otherwise all else will be anti-climactic.

The valley also holds memorable silica terraces (Warbrick Terrace) and a smaller cauldron, Ruaumoko's Throat, named for the tantrum-throwing Maori god of earthquakes and eruption. It is possible to walk through the valley unguided, after payment of an admission fee at the coffee shop. The full guided round tour, including a launch cruise across Lake Rotomahana (created by the Tarawera eruption), passing steaming cliffs and the site of the lost and lamented Pink and White Terraces, is highly recommended. It climaxes with a crossing of Lake Tarawera and a visit to the excavated Maori-European village of Te Wairoa which was buried by Tarawera's lava in 1886. (The tour runs daily and is day-long. There is also a half- day excursion.)

WAIOTAPU

Mid-way between **TAUPO** and **ROTORUA** on Highway 5, this is a multi-coloured patch of thermal energy, pitted with craters. There is a rich hectare of silica terraces and a man-made geyser, the Lady Knox, which is shamelessly soaped daily to encourage its performance (10.15). Close to the reserve, on the loop road, are large pools of boiling mud, which in dry weather become mud volcanoes, scattering their murk and building small cones. The 3000-hectare Waiotapu Forest, established by prison labourers as early as 1901, has warm streams and waterfalls, but bathers must treat them with caution and keep their heads above water, as a rare but commonly fatal form of amoebic meningitis is possible if water is inhaled through the nose. Nearby Rainbow Mountain, so named for its colours, and often misted by steam, is prosaically capped with a fire lookout which is manned in summer. There is a picnic area and a road leads to the top. Ten kilometres to the west, there is warm-water bathing at the Waikite Thermal Baths (10–10 daily).

WAIOURU

More than 800 metres above sea level in chilly terrain, as inhospitable a place as almost any in New Zealand, is home for more than 3000 people, most of them linked to New Zealand's largest army training establishment. The unpopulated tussock terrain around can be pulverized with impunity for artillery practice. Its remoteness makes it admirable for manoeuvres and mock battles.

The treat for the traveller in this strange martial oasis is the fortress-like Queen Elizabeth II Army Memorial Museum, set behind a moat. Marvellously comprehensive, the museum covers all the campaigns New Zealanders have ever fought. There are life-size dioramas, an audio-visual show and video recordings. A recent extension to the museum is dedicated to the ferocious Gallipoli campaign of 1915. Of note is a large-scale model of the rugged Turkish landscape where New Zealand troops battled to the summit of Chunuk Bair on August 8 of that year. On video, old survivors tell movingly of their trials (open daily 9–4.30, except Christmas Day). Allow an hour or two. The museum has a bookshop and a very pleasant and scenic coffee shop – with views of Ruapehu beyond the windows. Army efficiency has made this the best and most appetising pit-stop for motorists between Wellington and Auckland. To the north is the Desert Road, 60 kilometres between here and **TURANGI**, with the bleak Rangipo Desert to the west.

WAIRAKEI

Ten kilometres north of **TAUPO** on Highway 1, with spouts of steam and powerfully rumbling bores, Wairakei presents a compelling vista of thermal uproar harnessed for human ends. The Wairakei geothermal power station is the second largest in the world (the other is in Italy). But the technology developed to meet local needs has been unique. Wairakei expertise has been used around the world since it began functioning successfully in 1958. There is an information office on the site open daily 9–12, 1–4. North of the field is the detour to what remains of the Wairakei Thermal Valley. Though its vigour has been tapped, the silica still glows brightly. South of the township are the haunting Craters of the Moon (signposted), where visitors can wander through a valley pitted with the evidence of past and present thermal violence.

Just over 2 kilometres south of Wairakei is a turn-off to the Huka Falls where the Waikato River explodes through a 15 metre wide chasm shaped by thermal upheaval. Nowhere else along its 425 kilometre journey is the thrust of New Zealand's greatest river so apparent. Also near Wairakei (5 kilometres east), is another residual glory of the river, the Aratiatia Rapids, now seen only on timetable. The Aratiatia power station releases the Waikato at 10–11.30 and 2.30–4 daily. When the power station was built, defacing the most dramatic reach of the river, there was strong public protest and this strange compromise is the result.

TARAWERA'S GHOST CANOE

The long stark mass of Mount Tarawera, rising to the south-east of Rotorua, forms a dramatic backdrop to New Zealand's most famous ghost story

Lake Tarawera, where a phantom canoe presaged the eruption of Mount Tarawera

On May 31, 1886, a party of tourists crossed Lake Tarawera, at the foot of the mountain. Their destination was the glittering Pink and White Terraces, more than four hectares of almost perfect silica steps forming one of the natural wonders of the world.

The lake was quiet as the tourists crossed, until a large war canoe, paddled by about a dozen warriors, appeared about two kilometres in the distance. The tourists watched the canoe skim across the lake and one of them, Josiah Martin, actually made a drawing of the craft.

Sophia, the Maori guide, was evasive and embarrassed when asked for more details of the strange canoe. Some crew members mumbled *atua*, 'spirit', and word soon spread that the party had observed *waka-wairua*, the 'phantom canoe'. Its appearance was sure to spell disaster, and Tuhuto, a *tohunga* said to be one hundred and ten years old, confirmed that there would be a catastrophe.

Ten days later Tarawera – a mountain of apparently cold stone – suddenly erupted. The whole of the south-west corner of the mountain was blown away by an explosion. A one kilometre long crack in the earth swallowed nearby Lake Rotomahana (one hundred and fifteen hectares) and the Pink and White Terraces. Millions of cubic metres of ash fell on an area of over sixteen thousand square kilometres. The settlements at Te Wairoa, Te Ariki and Moura vanished. More than one hundred and fifty people perished.

Just seven years after the disaster, water began to well up again and Lake Rotomahana was recreated twenty times its previous size. The Pink and White Terraces lie one hundred and fifty metres below its surface.

Since that fateful day in 1886, the phantom canoe has not been sighted. Visitors wishing to search for it may take the Lynmore turnoff from Highway 30 to Lake Tarawera.

King Country

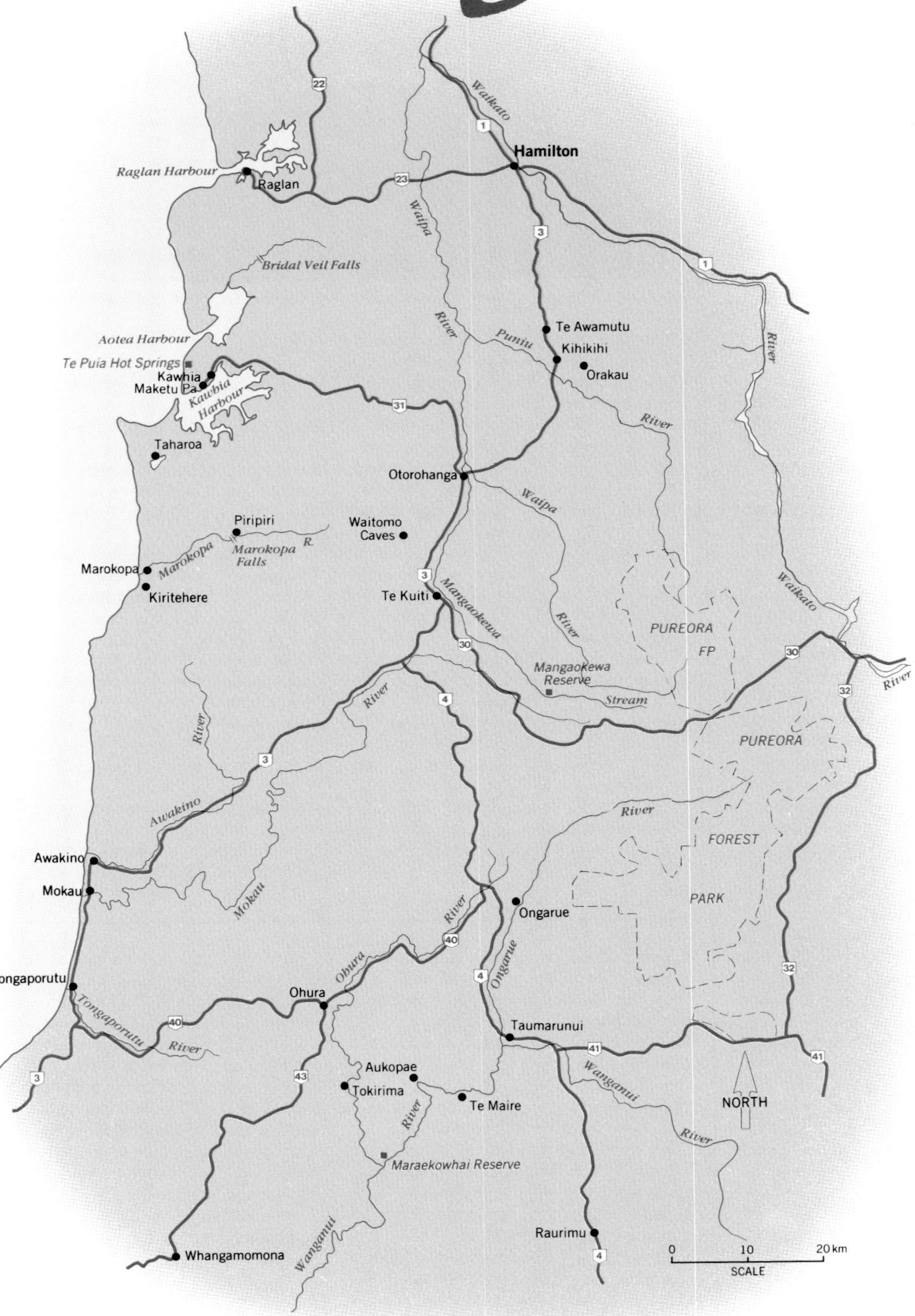

The King Country was a creation of war. Its boundaries were determined by battle, its name by a defiant people. For much of the nineteenth century, this misty heartland was largely a mystery to Europeans. For the Maori too, the rugged region inspired great awe. Driven by British firepower from the Waikato in the eighteen-sixties, the Maori King's followers crossed the Puniu River, south of Kihikihi. British troops, bruised by Maori resistance, gave no pursuit, and land was confiscated as far as the north bank of the river.

Beyond was the land styled by the Maori *Rohe Potae*, 'the brim of the hat'. Tradition says that the Maori King, Tawhiao, threw his hat down on a large map of the North Island and said, 'There I shall rule.' Under that hat, all those who had given offence to the Queen of England could find protection, and Tawhiao's word would be law.

Conflict and confiscation also decided the coastal boundary to the south. To the west, the land was bounded by the Tasman; and to the east by the forest and tussockland next to Lake Taupo. The territory became known as the King Country: the stronghold of the Maori King and his fierce fighting men. A century after they finally laid down their arms, this peaceful patchwork of pasture, forest and coast still bears the name.

INHOSPITABLE LAND

South of the Puniu River, the terrain leaves the Waikato physically as well as spiritually. The hills become more imposing, with abrupt limestone crags and canyons. Herds of dairy cows dwindle and flocks of sheep begin to fleck the hills. Though axe and fire have tamed it, the landscape still presents a challenge. It is not a naturally fertile region. Timber has been felled and coal has been mined. Small towns have flourished briefly, and foundered as mills and mines closed. To the south, soil erosion and a few sad fragments of rural occupation tell of frustration and defeat.

When human beings arrived here, the region was virtually covered with forest, except where volcanic eruption had singed its eastern edge. We know little of the people who once hunted the moa in these valleys. Presumably they travelled from coastal settlements, camped, slaughtered and returned home. The later Polynesians, or Classic Maori, either displaced or absorbed them. We know much more about the latecomers, recorded in oral tradition. Like the Waikato, the

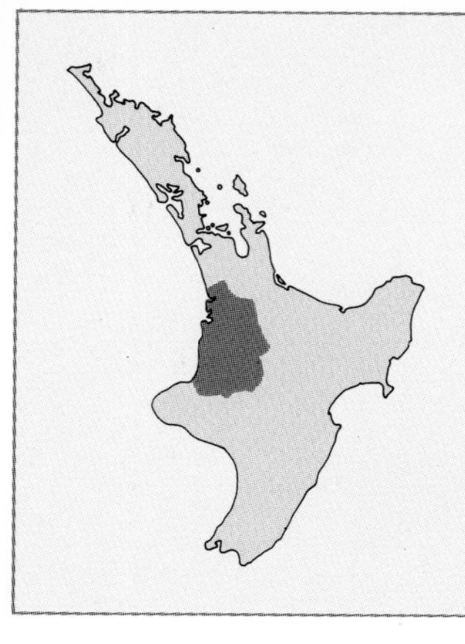

REFUGE FOR A MONARCH

northern and central King Country was settled by the voyagers of the *Tainui* canoe and their descendants. The *Tainui* travelled down the west coast of the North Island as far as the Mokau River. What is said to be its anchor stone may be seen there. Then the canoe turned back to drop settlers off at Kawhia, where it was finally buried on a site now sacred to the Waikato and King Country Maori. The descendants of those pioneers spread along the coast and pushed inland up river routes to form the large, powerful and never-defeated Ngati Maniapoto tribe. The southern King Country near the Mokau River was also populated by arrivals in the *Tokomaru*.

The King Country's waters teemed with fish, but in the Classic Maori era the region was famed for its birds especially the fat wood pigeon. After the *Tainui* reached Kawhia, a priest and oracle named Rakataura is said to have buried sacred objects (*mauri*) in the hills. These objects had been brought from the Polynesian homeland of Hawaiki and would ensure that the birds did not flee. On the other hand, the strange water-whittled land shapes, the caves and the underground rivers of the inland limestone territory struck fear into the Maori. For them these places were populated by *taniwha*, or water monsters, fairies and demons. One malign spirit, Tara Pikau, was said to entice visitors, especially women, into his dark domain. A red eel in a river served as a warning that beyond was Tara Pikau's territory. Ngati Maniapoto women never travelled alone in his forests.

CHRISTIANITY BRINGS PEACE

The first Europeans to arrive in the King Country were traders at Kawhia and Mokau in the nineteenth century. They brought muskets needed by the Ngati Maniapoto if they were to defend themselves against the northern Ngapuhi tribe, or battle with cousins of *Tainui* ancestry. The elusive chief Te Rauparaha was driven south by the Ngati Maniapoto. He then turned muskets on the lower North Island Maoris, and most of the Maoris in the South Island, leaving village after village smoking and lifeless.

Preferred items of exchange for muskets were dried heads, finely tattooed. Such heads were provided in number, and often to order. The heads of doomed captives could fetch thirty guineas each in London.

John Whiteley, the first missionary to reach the King Country coast, reported in 1834 that he found the local Maoris 'prepared for the Lord'. They were certainly desperate for peace and had already built a chapel in which he could preach. By the end of the decade more and more Maoris of the coast were becoming Christian. Slaves were freed, and peace prevailed. Missionaries established themselves up the region's rivers. As in the Waikato, agriculture proved the better part of Christianity in the northern King Country. Wheatfields were sown, flour mills built and food was shipped to Auckland and Australia from the port of Kawhia.

The Ngati Maniapoto, and especially their leader Rewi Maniapoto (*c.* 1815-94), were the most militant of the Maori King's supporters in the events precipitating the war of the eighteen-sixties, and in the ensuing battles. Rewi and his men marched south to join Taranaki Maoris in their first battles with colonists. Rewi himself wanted to raid Auckland and drive the colonists into the sea. Had he done so New Zealand's history might have been different, but the diminutive warrior did no more than enshrine himself in military history at the battle of Orakau (see page 76) before withdrawing across the Puniu River into his native King Country. He and his men escaped not just with their lives, but also with their land. Although they were the most determined rebels, the Ngati Maniapoto suffered no land confiscation. Paradoxically, it was their sometimes less militant Waikato brothers who lost all they held dear.

The King Country became a closed shop to colonists. Rewi did his best to preserve peace there. When Poverty Bay's ravaging Te Kooti asked for King Tawhiao's help in 1869, Rewi counselled the king against an alliance, presumably to keep the King Country from colonial intrusion. With a price of one thousand pounds on his head, in 1872 Te Kooti was finally granted sanctuary at Te Kuiti, where he lived safely among the Ngati Maniapoto until he was granted a formal pardon a decade later.

Meanwhile, the impressive Rewi met often with colonial politicians, and when he visited Auckland in 1879 he was given a hero's welcome. In the eighteen-eighties, after King Tawhiao laid down his weapons, a rift developed between Rewi and his monarch. Rewi favoured leasing and selling land to white settlers and allowing the railway to be extended into the King Country. King Tawhiao did not. It was Rewi, the local man of *mana*, who prevailed. The region's isolation ended when the first train steamed into the King Country with land buyers aboard.

From the beginning of the twentieth century, and especially after the completion of the Auckland-Wellington rail link in 1908, the region was one with the rest of New Zealand, its challenging Maori character gone. It was a place of muddy pioneer pastoralists, and even muddier trading posts such as Otorohanga, Te Kuiti and Taumarunui which fast became towns. The railway stations were crowded with land-sharks offering bushcovered – and sometimes inaccessible – blocks of Maori land to innocent arrivals. In New Zealand's last great land rush, the influx of people desperate for land taxed the towns, and accommodation had to be improvised. Outside the towns and townships trees were toppled for timber and mills began to whine. Elsewhere, fire stormed across the hills and pastures were sown. Dairy factories opened and saleyards began to function.

By the First World War the King Country, no longer a mysterious backwater, was in business. Just one distinction remained. A government understanding with Maoris meant that no liquor could be sold in the region. This regulation stayed in force until the nineteen-fifties, a bonanza for bootleggers and sly-groggers, but a nightmare for police. Hangover followed pioneer intoxication. The land's fertility was fast exhausted, and Maori leases were sometimes too complicated. Dairy farms bringing meagre returns were too small to support sheep. The world Depression of the nineteen-thirties was a last nail in many coffins. Bitter families walked off their farms. For those who survived the bleak years, prosperity came with better breeding stock, the sowing of clover and an improving world market. Here, as in other rugged regions of New Zealand, the spreading of fertiliser from aircraft over hill country after the Second World War consolidated that prosperity.

Today, most of the King Country's woes are of the past. Its towns are modest, the fascinations of its landscape are many. Much of it is still unfarmable ravines and mountains densely covered with forest. The coast remains wild too: one of the loneliest, least celebrated and yet most magnificent seascapes in New Zealand. For today's visitor, the crowning glory of the King Country is in the wonders that water, wind and time have worked upon the limestone at its heart – the sculpted battlements, towers and caverns that may yet outlive the work of human architects.

Golden light on Kawhia Harbour at sunset.

LAND OF LIMESTONE

At the heart of the King Country, the gleaming underground galleries of the Waitomo Caves lie under a bizarre limestone landscape

Limestone was formed on the sea floor. Over millions of years the shells and skeletons of sea creatures were broken down to fine sediment by the surge of water, finally to be compacted under pressure and cemented solid. Over these deposits, other sedimentary rocks, such as mudstone and sandstone, formed. When New Zealand began to lift from the sea more than ten million years ago, limestone rose up under its overlay. In the Waitomo district, as in much of the central King Country, the mudstone and sandstone were eroded to leave vast limestone crags and formations exposed.

Local Maoris were afraid to explore the Waitomo caves. The giant eel they fished from rivers flowing out of the caves suggested that even more awesome creatures lurked within

Typical limestone landscape known as karst country to geologists seems to ramble haphazardly. It is distinguished by tall cliffs and canyons, by queerly contorted crags, by deep well-like holes the Maori called *tomo*, by rivers disappearing and reappearing, and – particularly in this region – by labyrinthine caves. Perhaps one hundred kilometres of caves have been explored in the King Country. The longest, Gardners Gut near Waitomo Caves, has more than eleven kilometres of passages. There are hundreds of kilometres of cave still unexplored.

Above: *Weather-beaten outcrops of Waitomo's limestone reef stand sentinel to a still largely uncharted series of caves*

Brittle and easily powdered by the elements, limestone is most vulnerable to the carbon dioxide in water. Karst country, with its rugged nature and absence of surface water, is usually covered with dense forest. Rotting vegetation in those forests eats away at the limestone beneath. Then rainwater seeps downwards, working into cracks, widening fissures and finally carving vast underground channels. Charged with lime in solution, the water drips from cave roofs, leaving deposits that slowly solidify as stalactites. On the cave floor, stalagmites, formed by the same dripping water, grow upwards towards them, eventually forming limestone pillars. Continual seepage from the land above brings more encrustation. The spellbinding formations of the Waitomo Caves have been as long as one hundred thousand years in the making, and they are still being formed to this day.

Left: *Massive limestone rocks and crags in the hills of the Waitomo district* **Right:** *A carved ancestral figure in Te Tokanganui-a-Noho meeting-house, at Te Kuiti*

For thousands of years, the one witness to the work in nature's underworld studio has been the New Zealand glow-worm (*Arachnocampa luminosa*). Dangling fine and sticky threads to net prey, these grubs shimmer by the thousand from the ceiling in the Waitomo Cave's Glow-Worm Grotto. Unlike the European glow-worm, (which is a species of beetle), the New Zealand glow-worm is the larva of a luminous gnat, and grows up to five centimetres in length.

According to oral tradition, the Maori camped in the cave entrances and used them as refuges in time of war. The caves were not used as permanent dwellings. A superstitious dread of water monsters, whose voices could be heard in the subterranean waterfalls, deterred explorers. The Maori used dry caves to deposit their dead.

A few white adventurers made their way into the King Country before it was closed off to Europeans in the eighteen-sixties. They were impressed by the beauty of the few caves they saw, even more by the discovery of the bones and skulls of extinct moa. The local Maori, no longer able to feast on the living creature, ground the skulls to powder for use in tattooing.

Waitomo Cave's magic casts a spell on visitors. Inside its underground chambers of limestone, galaxies of glow-worms glimmer next to new and old stalagmites and stalactites

It was not until the eighteen-eighties, when surveyors entered the region to expedite the sale and leasing of Maori land, that the number and extent of the caves were realised. Towards the end of the decade came the most sensational discovery. A surveyor's assistant and farmer named Fred Mace floated up an underground river on a flax raft with a Maori friend, with candles providing weak light. They eventually found themselves drifting under shining arches into places that resembled medieval banqueting chambers and cathedrals. They were exploring what is now known as the Waitomo Cave.

Before the decade was finished, a secret official expedition was mapping, photographing and reporting on this 'domain of beauty [in] forbidding darkness'. Waitomo Maoris had already begun to guide visitors through, for the modest payment of one candle per head. By the end of 1890 sightseers numbered in the hundreds. Following the loss of New Zealand's most renowned nineteenth-century tourist attraction, the Pink and White Terraces near Rotorua, in the Tarawera eruption of 1886 (see page 106), a substitute was needed. Alert to potential profits, the New Zealand government finally dispossessed the Maori owners of the Waitomo Cave, who took three years to win meagre compensation.

Coach after coach of tourists soon jogged along rugged roads to view the spectacular caves of the region. A boarding house that had sprung up on a stark limestone promontory above the entrance to the Waitomo Cave became a grand hotel. The advantage of its position was confirmed when a part-Maori farmer disclosed that near by there was another impressive cave, the Ruakuri, on his property. This too was taken over by the government, in 1906. A third cave was discovered in 1910 when a pig-chasing Maori followed his quarry down a great hole. Striking a match, he saw a cave rivalling and perhaps surpassing the other two in magnificence. It was formally opened in 1911 and named Aranui (great path) after its discoverer, Ruruku Aranui.

Between 1910 and 1955 the caves became the most lucrative tourist attraction in New Zealand. Electricity was run into them and underground walkways were improved. Roads were upgraded and accommodation became still more lavish. Conservation problems came as the government chased tourist money. The warmth generated by electric lights and the press of human beings precipitated the growth of alien algae and moss in the anciently cool caves, menacing their beauty. This has been countered by limiting the number of people allowed in the caves at one time; and by cleaning out intrusive growth.

Although it is possible to visit all three caves in one day, there are rewards for visitors who take their time. There are many good tramping tracks and the winding road from Waitomo Caves down to the Marokopa coast is worth taking slowly. The region has a wealth of reserves to explore. With strong shoes, a reliable torch, and caution, the novice can explore caves alone and discover galaxies of glow-worms.

The marvels are not all of the underworld. Collapsed cave systems have created limestone gorges, bluffs, arches, tunnels, bridges and spectacular tumbling torrents. Everywhere, the King Country's perforated land of limestone shows creation at its most capricious.

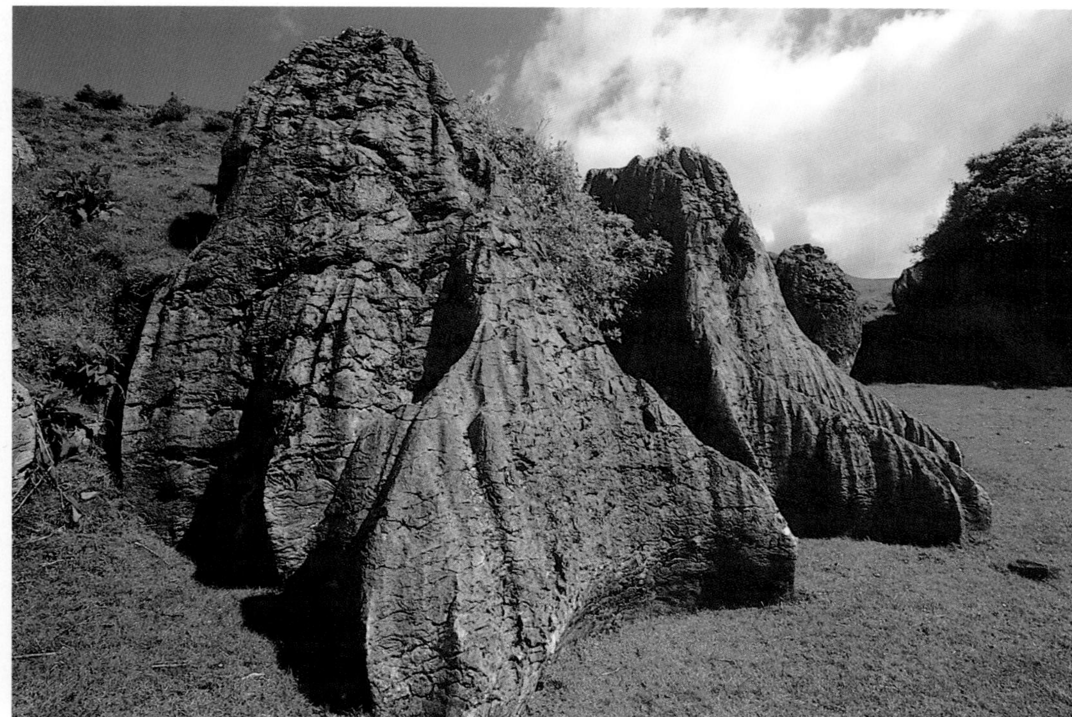

Rich in caves and odd limestone formations, the Waitomo area has many interesting walking tracks through some spectacular arches and gorges, and under great cliff faces

PLACES OF INTEREST

AWAKINO
Township on a wild, surf-lined shore at the mouth of the Awakino River and the entrance to (or exit from) the impressive Awakino Gorge with its dazzling limestone battlements and tall treeferns. A small but interesting museum and craft shop provides a picture of pioneer life on this robust, now thinly inhabited coast. There are minibus tours to **WAITOMO CAVES** through the rugged King Country landscape. Between Awakino and **MOKAU**, in a small Maori graveyard (signposted), is what is said to be the anchor stone of the *Tainui* canoe, which populated the King Country.

Also south, the Ocean View Aquarium (open daily) offers jet-boat excursions up the nearby Mokau River. Beginning at Awakino, a meandering coastal route leads north to Waitomo Caves and **KAWHIA**. Awakino means 'bad river', presumably because it was difficult to navigate far inland.

KAWHIA
On tidally wandering Kawhia Harbour, this lonely backwater township of 400 people was a bustling port in the 19th century. It served Maoris of the King Country and lower Waikato, who shipped produce to Australia and California, until the war of the 1860s, and finally the railway ended its usefulness as a port.

In Maori folklore, Kawhia is the place where the great migratory canoe *Tainui* finally came to rest and was buried. On sacred ground behind the marae at Maketu Pa on the Kawhia shore, large stones mark its prow and stern. The carvings of the meeting-house Te Auaukiterangi tell the *Tainui* story, as do the carved panels in the Kawhia Methodist Memorial Church on a small hill behind the town.

Enriched by royalties from the export of ironsand to Japan (from a site at Taharoa just to the south of Kawhia Harbour), Kawhia now has one of the most prosperous marae in New Zealand, as its large new dininghall demonstrates. Just above the marae a monument marks the site of a house of learning founded by Hoturoa, captain of the *Tainui* canoe. At nearby Karewa beach is the massive pohutukawa tree – also called Karewa – to which *Tainui* was moored.

Nineteenth-century Maori chief Te Rauparaha fought his way out of a trap on the south shore of Kawhia Harbour, and then battled south to ravage much of the lower North Island and South Island. Maori launch men provide sightseeing excursions. At Te Puia Hot Springs on the ocean beach (4 kilometres) hot water seeps from the sand at low tide. Bathers can scoop out a pool and enjoy a hot mineral bath. The road north to Raglan (see page 85) passes the lonely shore of Aotea Harbour and the spectacular Bridal Veil Falls.

Visitors may browse and buy local crafts at Ohaki Maori Village near Waitomo Caves

MAROKOPA
This small resort and fishing community at the mouth of the Marokopa River once thrived on timber felling and flax harvesting, with six stores and a shipping service. One of the King Country's few outlets to the open sea, Marokopa is at the end of a fascinating 48-kilometre drive from Waitomo Caves, which passes the magnificent Marokopa Falls.

Other signposted attractions are the Marokopa Natural Tunnel, and the Mangapohue Natural Bridge – the remains of a collapsed cave bridging a stream. A little farther, amateur cavers can explore the Piripiri Caves Scenic Reserve, where the limestone provides a fossilised record of ancient marine life. The Waitomo Caves Museum Society publishes an informative booklet entitled *A Trip Through Time*. South of Marokopa along the road to Kiritehere, there are panoramic views of the rugged King Country coast.

MOKAU
At the southern coastal limit of the King Country, this settlement is 88 kilometres north of Taranaki's New Plymouth, on the mouth of the Mokau River. It was once a port shipping out timber and coal from the King Country interior, but a flood in the early 20th century made the river unnavigable for large vessels. The river offers striking scenery to today's jet-boating or canoeing visitors. Upriver, huge but as yet unexploited coal deposits will do much to help provide for New Zealand's future energy needs.

A German mine washed ashore in World War II can be seen in the town. Five kilometres north is what is said to be the anchor stone of the *Tainui* canoe (see also **AWAKINO**). Driving south from Mokau along the coastal road there are impressive views of the North Taranaki Bight and Mt Taranaki.

OHURA
This small coal-mining hamlet, lately favoured by 'alternative lifestylers', is on Highway 40, the spectacular but rugged route from **TAUMARUNUI** through to the Taranaki coast. A scenic drive on Highway 43 via Whangamomona leads to central Taranaki. Ohura's museum (open on request) tells the story of coal-mining, farming and forestry in this largely forgotten pocket of the King Country. The frugality of pioneer life may be glimpsed in the Astbury Whare, built of totara and pine in 1914. Visitors can also see the entrance to the old Tatu mine, which was shut and finally sealed in 1970, and a King Country shop and a pioneer parlour. There is still a little open-cast mining in the vicinity.

OTOROHANGA
Market town of 2800 people on the Waipa River, which began as a trading post. Workers on the main trunk railway and timber men camped here in the late 19th century. The Kiwi House and

REWI MANIAPOTO

South of Te Awamutu lie Kihikihi and Orakau, two locations important to the story of Rewi Manga Maniapoto (c.1815–94)

At Orakau, a memorial stone on a small hill marks the site of the famous battle of that name. On March 31 1864, the first assaults on Orakau Pa began. Brigadier-General Carey was in command, with some eleven hundred troops, against Rewi Manga Maniapoto's three hundred besieged men and women. It was hoped that an outright victory would end both the Waikato War and Maori resistance.

Despite a shortage of water, food and ammunition, Rewi held out for three days. When General Cameron arrived with a further one thousand men, Rewi decided to attempt a daylight breakout. The defenders stormed the imperial lines and escaped. The war petered out, but Rewi's prestige rose amongst the *Pakeha*, for when Cameron had invited him to surrender, he had replied that he would never make peace – ever. Ahumai Te Paerata, the daughter of a west Taupo chief, added that if the men were to die, the women and children would die with them.

The irony of history is that Rewi's fame was not universal amongst his own people. The Orakau Pa site was badly chosen (though Rewi may have opposed it), the losses were heavy and any long-term strategic advantage was squandered. Rewi remained an important voice in the King Country, but he did not gain the popular support he had hoped for through his campaigns. The *Pakeha* took a different line: Rewi received a hero's welcome in Auckland in 1879, followed by a tribute in the form of a public monument erected at Kihikihi during his lifetime. He was also given a government pension.

Although he had been an advocate of war, it was Rewi who advised King Tawhiao against aiding Te Kooti. In later years, he supported a government survey of the King Country, the very thing he had fought so bitterly against for much of his life.

Rewi Maniapoto supervised the building of his own tomb in Kihikihi's main street

IN THRALL TO A MAGICAL PEAK

Tradition says Taranaki was populated by the people from three voyaging canoes. The *Tokomaru* arrived at either the Tongaporutu or Mohakatino Rivers. The voyagers and their descendants spread south beyond present-day New Plymouth, composing a number of subtribes within the powerful Ati Awa. Still farther south along the seaboard was the Taranaki tribe who were descended from voyagers on the *Kurahaupo* and took their name and mana from the mountain (Taranaki literally means 'bare peak'). A third vessel, *Aotea*, contributed its tribal settlers to southern Taranaki.

The first known European to sight Taranaki was the Dutchman Abel Tasman. In 1642 he named the extremity of the land round which he tacked Cape Pieter Boreels. Travelling along the coast from the north in 1770, James Cook saw Mount Taranaki through lightning, cloud and rain. It was, he said, 'of a prodigious height and its Top is covered with everlasting snow'. Cook's botanist, Joseph Banks, described it as 'certainly the noblest hill I have ever seen'. Cook named the peak and the cape it overlooked in honour of Earl Egmont, former First Lord of the British Admiralty. But for the Maori it remained (now with official concurrence) Mount Taranaki.

It was fifty years before any other Europeans arrived and then, just a few whalers; it was seventy years before Europeans began settling in number. Muskets came first. In the hands of the Waikato and Ngati Maniapoto tribes to the north, they depopulated the northern Taranaki for more than a decade. The Ati Awa fled and the seed of even more substantial conflict was sown.

In 1839, the New Zealand Company's vessel *Tory* arrived off the coast, near the site of present-day New Plymouth. Colonel William Wakefield purchased land from the few Maoris living there, unaware that the traditional owners were temporarily elsewhere. After climbing to the top of Mount Taranaki, the company's naturalist, Ernst Dieffenbach, reported that the surrounding land was 'the finest district in New Zealand'. And a young company draughtsman named Charles Heaphy became the first in a long line of distinguished artists to paint Mount Taranaki.

In England's Plymouth, a group of citizens purchased the land allegedly owned by the New Zealand Company. On March 31, 1841, the *William Bryan* arrived with seventy adults, sixty children and a few company officials. Three more ships loaded with colonists came the same year, followed by another three in 1842. In gentle and genteel New Plymouth society, it soon became desirable to claim at least one ancestor aboard one of the first four ships, just as the Maori claimed forefathers on the *Tokomaru*, *Kurahaupo* or *Aotea*.

SIMMERING LAND PROBLEMS

As New Plymouth grew from a few muddy tracks and huts to lanes with durable colonial cottages, the region's original Maori population and rightful owners drifted back. They were dismayed and aggrieved. It was only a matter of time before conflict came. In 1855 New Plymouth colonists, sensing menace, formed a militia.

In 1860 long-simmering land problems, brought to a boil by a disputed block of land at Waitara, became lethal. New Zealand's Governor, Gore Browne, clumsily sent in troops to end Maori muttering. Colonists had to abandon open country. Their farmhouses burned as they huddled behind the stockades and entrenchments of besieged New Plymouth. Women and children were shipped to Nelson. Within a year three thousand armed men guarded the settlement.

The conflict sputtered on through several battles at the beginning of the eighteen-sixties, and surfaced in the south where the Hauhau warriors began guerilla warfare. Maori of the Hauhau wished to hurl all Taranaki colonists back into the sea.

Armed tension persisted long after the bloody bush-fighting ended in 1869. In the eighteen-seventies, Hawera's colonists, dissatisfied with the protection given by the government, briefly declared themselves a republic. Similarly the Maori of Taranaki formed a commune at Parihaka, under Mount Taranaki's western slopes, peacefully dedicated to the preservation of Maori land and character. Under the guidance of the tenacious prophet Te Whiti O Rongomai (*c.* 1830–1907), the commune's inhabitants practised both agriculture and civil disobedience.

Finally, in 1881, some fifteen hundred of the colony's militia surrounded the unarmed and outnumbered dissidents of Parihaka. When the assault force moved in, they were met by a welcome party of two hundred dancing children. The village was nevertheless burnt to the ground, and Te Whiti and his lieutenant were imprisoned. The government, fearing that a jury might not convict Te Whiti, or that a judge might pass too lenient a sentence, introduced a law detaining him indefinitely without trial. Today the nonentities who tore Te Whiti from his people are forgotten. Te Whiti is celebrated in poems and songs, and his grave in the village of Parihaka is one of New Zealand's few shrines.

For most of a century thereafter, Taranaki's character was largely determined by its capacity to grow grass and sustain dairy cows. Towns like Inglewood, Stratford, Eltham and Hawera grew to serve farmers, and the port of New Plymouth to speed their produce round the world. The region knew less pioneer heartbreak than the neighbouring King Country and Waikato, although its photogenic character is a result of much backbreaking labour.

For more than a century after its founding, New Plymouth retained a wistful colonial character. Yet the potential for a very different city was there from the beginning – and suggested by the oil seeping from its shoreline.

In the eighteen-sixties, New Plymouth had the first functioning oil wells in the British Empire. The wells were never abundant and were shut down a century later. The revelation that Taranaki sat on a huge resource of energy came not at New Plymouth but to the south, where strikes of natural gas rather than oil occurred at inland Kapuni, and offshore in the Maui field. Productive oil wells have since begun working.

Yet it was New Plymouth, rather than rural Taranaki, that was to take most of the shock, as the city and port of the region. Oil-company employees and construction workers descended on the town. The old-world city shook off its crinolines and put on blue jeans.

Even so, the region's magic remains intact. Dairy cows still graze lush pastures, trout still rise to the fisherman's fly, and the mountain hasn't even rumbled a little to identify with the human puffing and panting below. The people are still in its shadow – here on Taranaki's terms.

Above: *The Gables, built as a colonial hospital in 1848, originally stood on the site of the present New Plymouth Girls High School. It was moved to Brooklands Park in 1904*

Right: *Te Henui Parsonage, two kilometres from St Mary's Church, was built by William Bolland, the deacon in charge of the parish. It now serves as an arts centre*

Top: *St Mary's Church, rich in the history of Taranaki, is also reputed to be the oldest stone church in New Zealand. Its graveyard holds the remains of many of the district's early settlers* **Above:** *Hurworth Cottage, New Plymouth, was once the home of the nineteenth-century premier Sir Harry Atkinson* **Right:** *The graceful Pukekura Park is considered one of New Zealand's most beautiful, with its fernery set in terraced glasshouses, rhododendron dell, lakes and waterfall*

The White Cliffs – Paraninihi to the Maori – form a serene stretch of the Taranaki coastline to the north of Pukearuhe. Sandstone cliffs, two hundred and forty-five metres high, thrust down to the sea; they hide sea-carved caverns in which early Maori drawings have been discovered

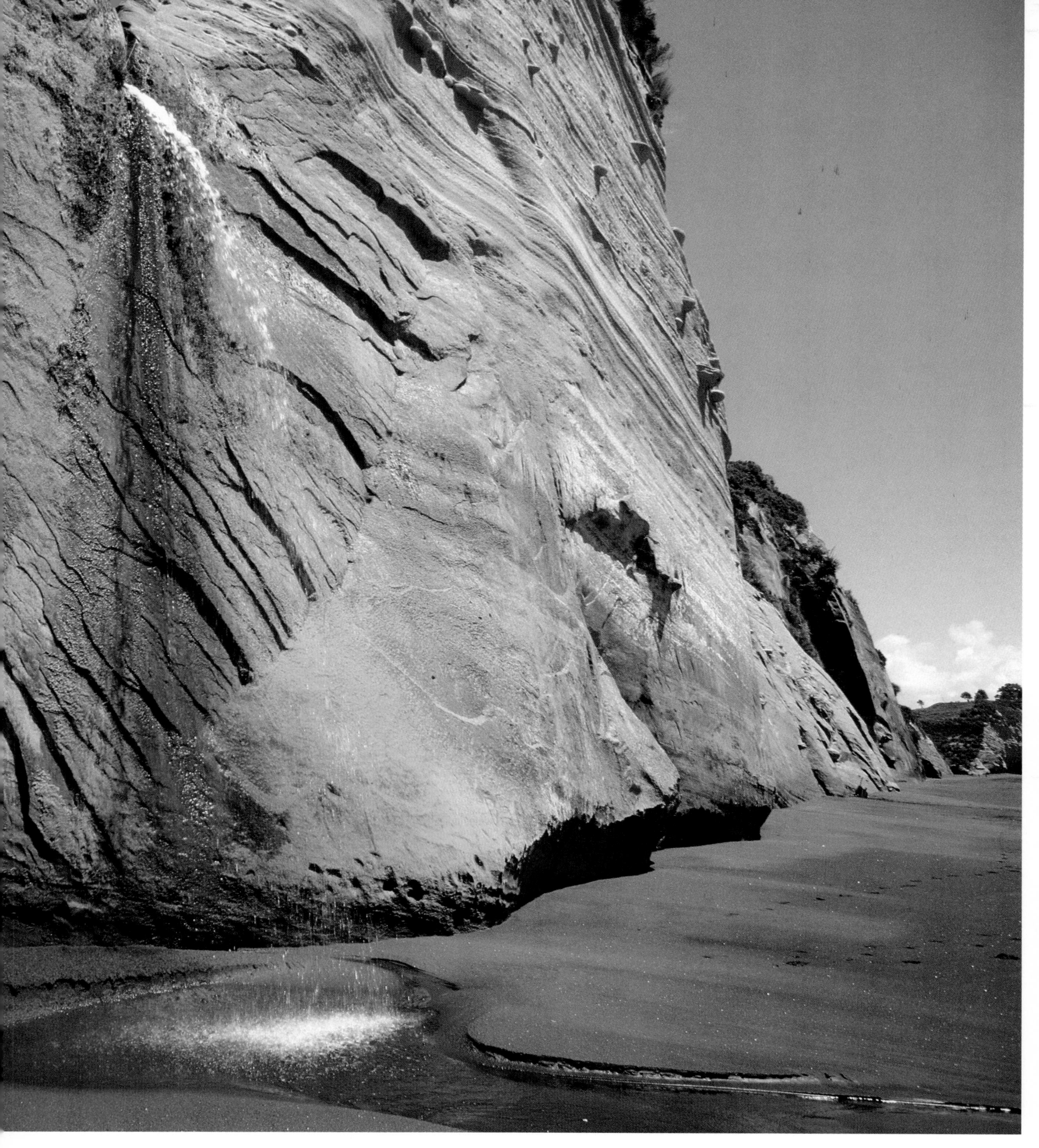

THE GRIEVING MOUNTAIN

According to the Maori, Taranaki's beginning is a tale of sex and violence – the mountain is too commanding to be explained by less

According to folklore, Taranaki dwelt at the centre of the North Island in a village of volcanoes. The lovely Mount Pihanga was the only female volcano. Although the others lusted after her, she was loyal to her handsome husband Tongariro.

When Tongariro was away however, Taranaki wooed and won Pihanga. Tongariro returned and surprised the pair in the transports of passion. The skies darkened and the earth shook in a blistering brawl. Uproar ensued, and one volcano after another exploded. Finally the adulterer was driven out. In his flight from fiery Tongariro, Taranaki carved out the bed of what is now known as the Wanganui River. In heartbreak and despair, he slept near the sea, where the Pouakai Range pushed out a spur and trapped him forever. It is said that when mist covers the mountain's summit, and rain lightly falls, Taranaki can be seen grieving for the love of his life.

Today the mountain is still trapped, but protectively so, within Egmont National Park. As early as 1881 it was decreed that all land within six miles (nine and a half kilometres) of the summit was to be spared from axe and plough. The national park as such came into existence in 1900. So Mount Taranaki, alias Egmont, rising from a green lake of forest, survives as an island set apart from the affairs of humanity, though skiers glide down its snowfields in winter and trampers walk its tracks in summer.

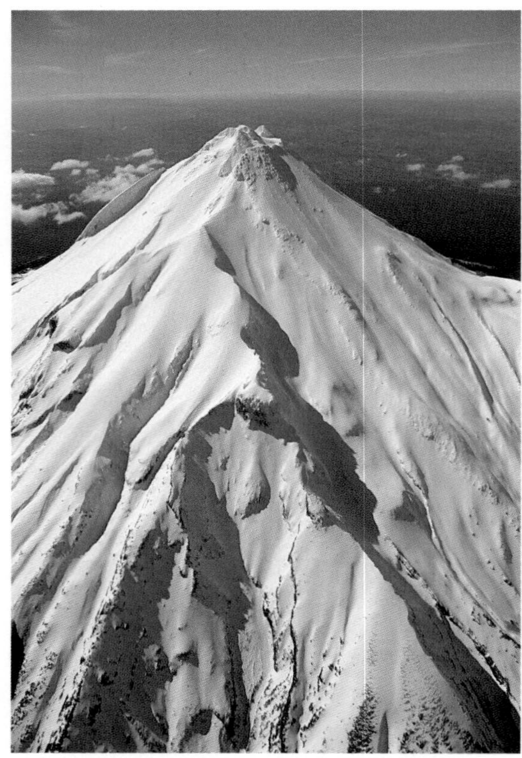

Above: *Mount Taranaki (Egmont) has distinctive furrows*
Below: *Storm clouds gather near Taranaki's cone at sunset*

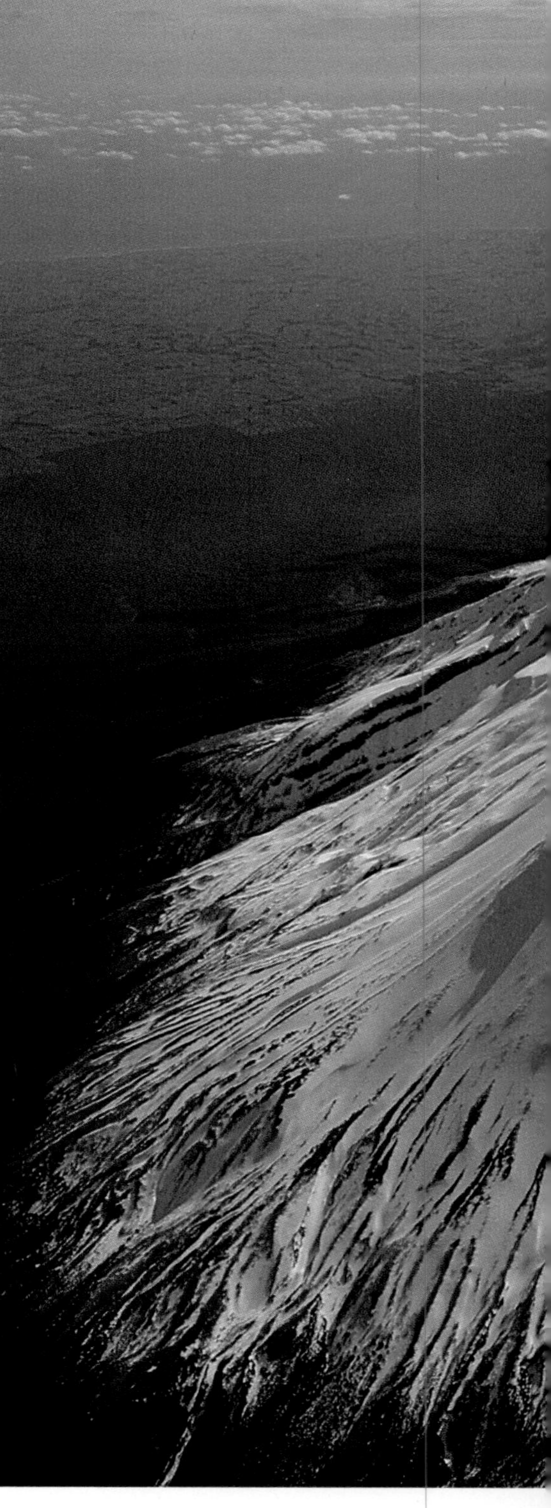

Below: *Water flows down through the deep crevices of volcanic rock to the Taranaki plains* **Left:** *Taranaki's snow-clad peak is relatively easy to climb during the summer* **Far left:** *Sunset dramatically colours the mountain*

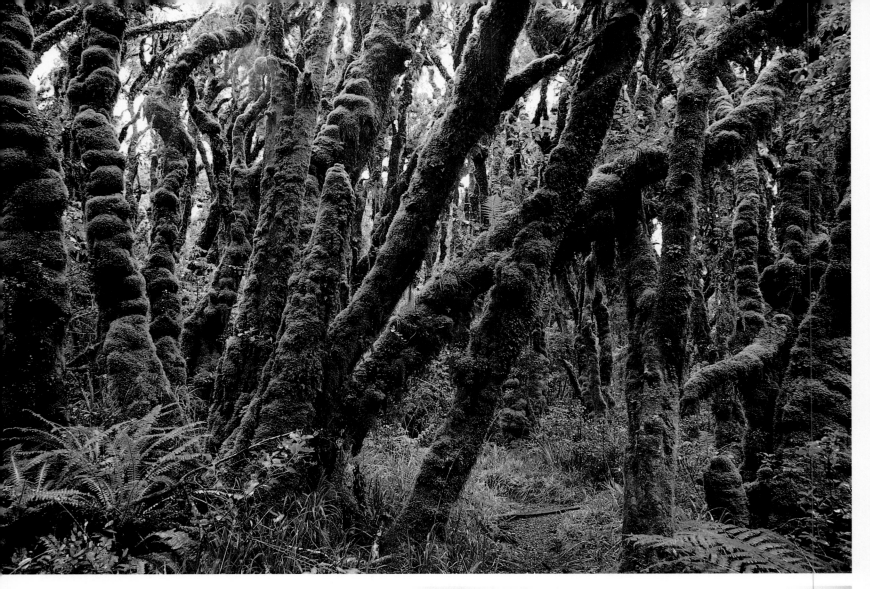

Topographically and ecologically, Mount Taranaki *is* an island. It was the last – and by far the largest – of the volcanoes that formed the Taranaki region. Its alpine area is distant from other alpine regions. With no near influences, evolution has been free to indulge itself in the creation of plants and insects unique to the mountain. Even migrant species have a character not found in the same species elsewhere.

Among the park's distinctive plants are the Egmont red tussock, the Egmont harebell and mountain daisies. A fern unique to Mount Taranaki, *Polystichum cystostegia*, graces rocky gullies up to fourteen hundred metres. Insects include rare moths and the indigenous wolf-spider, camouflaged high on bare scoria screes. The fat New Zealand wood pigeon, the kereru, can be seen and heard in squeaky flight for a thousand metres up the mountain. Tuis, bellbirds and fantails are commonly found up to thirteen hundred metres. The grey warbler nests in subalpine scrub as high as seventeen hundred metres. Beneath the tall rimu and rata of the lower forest zone and the kamahi and kaikawaka (or mountain cedar) of the upper slopes, the ground is lush with ferns, creepers and moss.

For the Maori, Taranaki was revered, feared and useful. They laboured up its lower slopes in search of red ochre for pigment. They deposited their distinguished dead in mountain caves. Densely vegetated ridges and valleys offered refuge – and temporary sites for settlement – after defeat in war. Its silent places allowed tribesmen to communicate with the whispers of dead ancestors. But the upper reaches of the mountain

were not to be trodden. They were the haunt of the *ngarara*, the mythical reptile of the Maori, whose chilling howl could be heard in high wind.

Today's visitors may feel they are in an enchanted domain too, but one with far easier access. From the three main centres – New Plymouth, Stratford and Hawera – it is a half-hour journey. Three good roads lead up to visitors' centres and signposted walking tracks. Mount Taranaki may be the most climbed mountain in New Zealand, but some experience and care is needed. The weather can change suddenly and mists can blow up. Less experienced climbers should take a guide, or a companion familiar with the mountain.

Egmont National Park is more than a winter playground. In summer it offers a leafy sanctuary from lowland heat. Its forest paths are among the most pleasant to walk in New Zealand. The rain-fed vegetation, mantled with shiny moss, is a lavish spectacle. Streams rattle between boulders, and roar over cliffs. The views – with the mountain above and much of the North Island below – are imposing. The tired traveller can find strength and delight returning in the sweet mountain air.

Mount Taranaki may still grieve for lost love, as Maori mythology tells. Indeed, until recently, Maori were reluctant to live along the path the mountain might take should it march off to do battle with Tongariro and reclaim Pihanga. Meanwhile Pihanga's loss is human gain.

Opposite, above: *Trees smothered in moss evoke mysterious images in the forest of the Enchanted Walk. This one-and-a-half hour tramp starts at the Mountain House, crosses the Patea River and ends at the flat land known as the Plateau*
Left: *Low bushes and varied undergrowth on the Potaema Track make for a most pleasant walk*

Above: *The Potaema Track, near the Pembroke Road, is full of dense foliage. The track leads to an elevated timber walkway over the Potaema swamp, from which can be seen fine views of the mountain and the surrounding rainforest*
Above right: *Symmetrical tiers of delightful alpine flowers blossom in Egmont National Park, close to Dawson Falls*

PLACES OF INTEREST

TWO TARANAKI FAMILIES

Near the centre of New Plymouth, on the corner of Ariki and St Aubyn Streets, a small stone cottage is a reminder of Taranaki's early colonial history

Stone-built Richmond Cottage (1853) is furnished in the period style

The cottage belonged to Christopher Richmond, MP for New Plymouth and later a notable judge. The Richmond family was one of the most powerful in Taranaki's formative years. They decided many of the directions to be taken by the colony.

With their friends the Atkinsons (Christopher Richmond married Harry Atkinson's sister Emily), the Richmonds emigrated to Taranaki during the eighteen-fifties. Their first priority was to become landowners, and both families supported the purchase of the Waitara Block which precipitated war in 1860.

Both families became active in politics, partly to promote Taranaki interests but also to accelerate the acquisition of land. Local politics led to national power. Harry Atkinson (1831–92) and Christopher Richmond (1821–95) both became cabinet ministers. Atkinson was later four times premier of the colony, while Richmond eventually became one of the colony's most respected judges.

In an era of aggressive expansion, the Atkinsons and Richmonds exemplified the virtues and faults of settlers. Although they were practical, capable and committed to progress, they were also land-hungry, impatient and as war-like as the Maori they feared. But they were never simple racists; nor were they motivated by selfishness or plain greed. They shared the common Victorian belief that they were the agents of a moral, civic and economic force which would bring the benefits of enlightenment and civilisation to the world.

As they grew older, Richmond the judge and Atkinson the politician softened in their views. Richmond became broader and more tolerant in his social and religious outlook. Atkinson changed from his earlier role as a representative of land interests and advocated radical ideas such as the introduction of national insurance to combat poverty, and leasehold reform to encourage a more democratic spread of ownership over farmlands.

EGMONT NATIONAL PARK
Taranaki's public heartland features 33 543 hectares of forest and alpine slopes, with the 2518 metre summit of Mt Taranaki at its centre. Perhaps the loveliest peak in New Zealand, Taranaki (also known as Egmont) has long been celebrated for its symmetry, and often compared with Japan's Fujiyama. A dormant volcano, its last eruptions occurred in about 1500, 1665 and 1755. The volcano's secondary cone – Fanthams Peak on the southern side – is named after Fanny Fantham, who became the first woman to climb this mountain in 1887 at the age of 19.

Mt Taranaki offers skiing in winter, spectacular tramping in summer along 300 kilometres of track, and trout fishing in the streams at its base. At Dawson Falls Lodge and Stratford Mountain House there is comfortable mountain accommodation. Hut accommodation is available through the visitors' centres.

ELTHAM
This inland Taranaki town of 2400 people, 53 kilometres south-east of **NEW PLYMOUTH**, is best known for its fine blue-vein cheese. Once a timber town on an old Maori trail, Eltham cradled the cooperative dairying movement in New Zealand. A Chinese merchant by the name of Chew Chong, who arrived in New Zealand in the wake of the gold rushes, determined the town's – and Taranaki's – future when he exported two kegs of Eltham butter to England in 1885. One of the town's most distinguished sons, Australian poet and playwright Douglas Stewart, celebrates early Eltham vividly in his lyrical autobiographies *The Seven Rivers* and *Springtime in Taranaki*. The former cinema at the town centre in Stannes Street is a masterpiece in corrugated iron.

Eleven kilometres to the east is 18-hectare Lake Rotokare. Fed by natural springs, and set in a pocket of Taranaki's original vegetation, this 200 hectare wildlife refuge has an attractive two-hour walkway along the lakeside and through forest. There is also a picnic area with a boat ramp.

HAWERA
South Taranaki's major market town, with a population of 11 400. New Zealand's only republic, declared here by dissident settlers in the 1870s,lasted a fortnight. More recently, the town was home to comic novelist Ronald Hugh Morrieson (1922–72), a literary hermit who seldom moved outside the town. Morrieson lived at 1 Regent Street. The town's most prominent feature, a 50 metre watertower (it figures in Morrieson's bawdy books), offers wide views of Taranaki's terrain. Entrance and information can be obtained at the Hawera Information Office.

Hawera began as a beleaguered settlement in Taranaki bush country during the 1860s. North-west of the town (23 kilometres) is the battlefield of Te Ngutu-o-te-manu where the bush-fighting Prussian-born Major von Tempsky (1828–68), succumbed to the firepower of warrior chief Titokowaru. The site is now a reserve and picnic place.

Within sight of the battlefield is the first of Taranaki's large energy projects, Kapuni Natural Gas Plant, which processes gas for industrial and domestic purposes. Near by, a petrochemical plant converts treated gas to produce 160 000 tonnes of urea fertiliser annually. (Visits can be made by asking at the plant's information office.)

Nearer town (2.5 kilometres to the north-east) are the magnificent earthworks of the Maori fortress Turuturu-mokai. One of the best preserved pre-European pa in New Zealand, it has huge ramparts, deep trenches and storage pits. There was even a tunnel running under the Tawhiti Stream to one of the five satellite forts in the vicinity. The defensive genius of its builders was eventually matched by crippling subterfuge on the part of attackers, and the ensuing massacre gave the place its name (*turuturu-mokai* means, roughly, 'dried heads on stakes'). The horror was such that no Maori set foot on the site for centuries after. The carved Maori post at the centre of the fort was set there in 1938 to ward off evil influences and to protect visitors.

A British redoubt built alongside the ancient fortress in the late 1860s was stormed by a Hauhau party helped by the part-Red Indian deserter from the British Army, Kimble Bent. A memorial to the dead marks the redoubt site.

King Edward Park at the centre of Hawera has a restful willow-pattern garden, a rose garden, and an azalea and rhododendron dell. In the park, there is a British naval cannon once used to instruct colonists in artillery warfare. The Tawhiti Museum on Ohangai Road, just out of town (hours of opening from Hawera Information Office), is dedicated to the colonial past, and it includes a full-size reconstruction of the Normanby redoubt and blockhouse of 1879. The town also has one of New Zealand's most unusual specialist museums, dedicated to the memory of American singer Elvis Presley (at 51 Argyle Street; visits can be arranged through the information office).

The nearest beach is at Ohawe (6 kilometres), where moa hunters once feasted and where early naturalists fossicked among the discarded bones. The fine beach of **OPUNAKE** is 43 kilometres to the north-west and Dawson Falls on the side of Mt Taranaki is 40 kilometres.

The impressively rugged Tangarakau Gorge

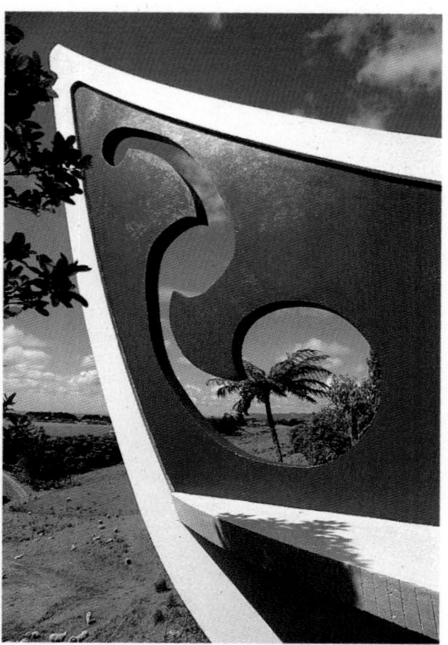

Politician and anthropologist Sir Peter Buck's grave is under a canoe prow at Urenui

MANAIA

Fifteen kilometres west of **HAWERA**, this township of 1000 has an elegant band rotunda (1921), flanked by memorials to those of the Armed Constabulary who died in the fighting of the 1860s, and to the district's World War I dead. On its golf course (just east of the town) stand two preserved militia blockhouses in a redoubt built on an old Maori fort to reinforce European grip on confiscated land. There is also a concrete replica of the wooden watchtower that stood here to warn of Maori incursion.

NEW PLYMOUTH

Between mountain and sea, Taranaki's one city still has a mellow colonial character at its centre, despite headlong expansion and population growth (to 47 000) in the wake of energy discoveries. It remains one of New Zealand's most charming provincial cities.

St Mary's Anglican Church (1845) survives as the heart and soul of the modern city. It was New Zealand's first stone church, initially designed by Frederick Thatcher, but largely the work of its builder, George Robinson, now buried beside it. Headstones shaded by oak and fir tell of New Plymouth's embattled beginnings. Troops once marched to the church with loaded muskets; and there was a powder magazine in the churchyard, with a 12-pound gun. In effect, it was a redoubt, and women and children were sometimes crowded inside for safety.

A walk up Marsland Hill to the rear of the church discloses the lonely grave of a close friend and confidant of poet John Keats, Charles Armitage Brown (1786–1842). He arrived when the settlement was founded, but died soon after. His son (also Charles) became prominent in colonial politics.

Other historic New Plymouth buildings often have religious character. The exquisite remnant of Te Henui Parsonage (1845) at the end of Courtenay Street has been restored by the NZ Historic Places Trust (open weekend 1–4).

Among surviving pioneer buildings open to the public, two are associated with prominent 19th-century families. Stone-built Richmond Cottage (1853) now sits at the centre of the city, next to the public library. Once known as Beach Cottage, and associated with both the Richmond and Atkinson families, it was moved here to save it from developers and furnished in period style (open Monday, Wednesday, Friday, 2–4; weekends and holidays 1–4).

Hurworth Cottage (1855) is just out of town at 548 Carrington Road (open Wednesday to Sunday, 10–12, 1–4). It was associated with the same families, particularly with Harry Atkinson (1831–92), four times premier of New Zealand. A typical austere wooden farmhouse of its time, and set in a beautiful garden, it is one of the NZ Historic Places Trust's most delightful examples of restoration and preservation. Hurworth was abandoned to rebel Maori during the warfare of the early 1860s, but miraculously never razed.

Also rich with original charm is The Gables (1848) in Brooklands Park, a cottage hospital designed by the notable colonial architect Frederick Thatcher (open weekends, public holidays and for a month after Christmas, 1–4; or by special arrangement). The Gables stands above the beautiful gardens of Pukekura Park, perhaps New Zealand's most ravishing, a medley of flora, water and mountain.

Another remarkable garden is Pukeiti, founded in 1951 by the Pukeiti Rhododendron Trust. The park's 360 hectares of exotic and native plants lie at the edge of **EGMONT NATIONAL PARK**, between the high Pouakai and Kaitake Ranges, 29 kilometres from the city (open all year dawn to dusk). Hurworth Cottage and Pouakai Wildlife Reserve (open daily) can be visited en route.

The Te Henui walkway offers a mix of rural, urban and forest views within the city's boundary. It includes the Te Henui Parsonage, the Pukewarangi Pa site and the Te Henui Cemetery where many early citizens of Taranaki are interred. (Start

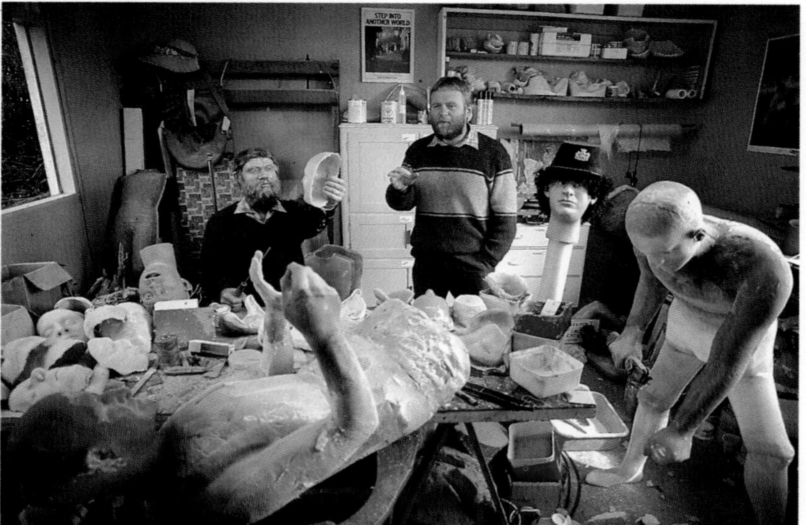

Life-size dummies are made in Tawhiti Museum's own workshops at Hawera

TITOKOWARU, LEADER AND WARRIOR

Halfway between Eltham and Hawera, the turn-off to Kapuni passes through the historic site of Te Ngutu-o-te-manu Pa, between the Kapuni and Inaha Streams

Death of von Tempsky at Te Ngutu-o-te-manu, *the incident as imagined by the artist Kennett Watkins. The lithograph hangs in the Taranaki Museum at New Plymouth*

Te Ngutu-o-te-manu was one of the pas of Titokowaru (*c.*1820–88), the Ngati Ruahine chief who was the finest Maori general in the war of the eighteen-sixties. Against forces up to twelve times larger than his own, he planned and manoeuvred his way to victory. His enemies paid him the highest compliment – they tried to play down his importance in the hope that he might be forgotten.

As well as being a brilliant strategist and a master of guerilla warfare, Titokowaru became a spiritual leader. Initially, he had preached peace, encouraging his people to accept the *Pakeha* acquisitions of land. But when land confiscations increased, he began to advocate passive resistance, encouraging his people to uproot survey pegs and drive stock away. Finally, in 1868, Titokowaru declared war.

His two victories over British troops at Te Ngutu-o-te-manu and Moturoa Pas left heavy casualties, including the death of the dashing Major von Tempsky. Titokowaru's strategy consisted of goading colonial troops into pursuing him into death-traps where his troops were waiting. When the soldiers retreated, they were pursued and harassed.

For a while, Titokowaru regained much of the lost land as settlers and soldiers withdrew. His name could cause near-panic. It was even feared (possibly correctly) that he would attack Wanganui.

Then mysteriously, Titokowaru ceased to pose any further threat. At his newest pa at Tauranga-ika (near Nukumaru, between Patea and Wanganui, just off Highway 3), possibly the most deadly trap he had devised, there was an argument over a woman and his supporters left him. It was felt that his *mana* had been lost and his prestige evaporated.

Although pursued across Taranaki, Titokowaru was never captured. His attitudes turned full-circle – again he advocated peace and passive resistance. Eventually, he became a supporter of Te Whiti at Parihaka (see page 140).

and finish at East End Reserve or Welbourne Terrace, time two hours; further information from New Plymouth Public Relations Office.)

New Plymouth's artificial harbour at the other end of town is overlooked by 154 metre Paritutu, which offers splendid views to the climber, and the 198 metre chimney of the New Plymouth thermal power station. Close to the port, in Centennial Drive, the Rangimarie Maori Arts and Crafts Centre has an impressive range of work on sale (open daily).

Taranaki Museum (corner Brougham and King Streets) holds an exceptional array of material from the Maori past, especially stone sculptures and pre-European carvings. There are many exhibits from the pioneer period (open Monday to Friday, 10.30–4.30; Saturday and Sunday 1–5). The Govett-Brewster Art Gallery in Queen Street houses visiting exhibitions and contemporary collections, including the celebrated kinetic work of the Taranaki-born North American sculptor, painter and animator Len Lye (open Monday to Friday 10.30–5 Saturday and Sunday, 1–5).

Close by, new St Joseph's Catholic Cathedral contains murals and stunning bas-relief stations of the cross by New Plymouth's best-known artist of this century, Michael Smither. The raw material for many of his paintings may be seen just beyond the port, at Back Beach. The city has several vast beaches: East End, Fitzroy and Strandon, and **OAKURA** 14 kilometres away.

PARIHAKA'S PEACEFUL RESISTANCE

Parihaka Pa, south of New Plymouth, off Highway 45, was the centre of a Christian-based, non-violent resistance to land encroachments by settlers

Te Whiti's grave, at Parihaka Pa, is a shrine visited by many Maoris

The leader of this movement was Te Whiti O Rongomai (also known as Eruiti Te Whiti), who lived from *c.*1830 to 1907. Having seen Maori lands confiscated, and his people's spirit crushed by war, Te Whiti felt there was nothing to be gained by more bloodshed. He evolved a new policy of organised, peaceful opposition to further land losses.

Te Whiti had set up a model community in Parihaka based on communal farming using modern agricultural techniques. When the government, spurred by the settlers' appetite for more land, sent in survey parties to subdivide this sector of west Taranaki, Te Whiti encouraged his people to pull out survey pegs, to erect fences across roads and to plough-in the crops on confiscated land.

Then, while the supposedly pro-Maori Governor Gordon was out of the country in 1881, his Native Minister, John Bryce, moved to stamp out this opposition. Te Whiti and his co-leader Tohu were arrested and held in the South Island for almost two years without trial. The model village was destroyed.

Te Whiti, a superb orator and a student of the Bible, was sometimes regarded as a prophet. But he was less interested in being a prophet than in achieving practical reforms. He was one of the first and greatest of the new-style Maori leaders; a man of hope and courage who offered the chance for Maori to reclaim their personal dignity while outwitting physical force with moral integrity.

Parihaka saw civil disobedience and obstruction turned into a new form of politics: passive confrontation instead of force of arms; good humour in place of bitterness; social cohesion in place of despair; and persistence in the face of intimidation.

OAKURA

One of Taranaki's best surf beaches, just south-west of **NEW PLYMOUTH** on the road round the mountain. Four kilometres behind the town (then a five-minute walk) is Koru Pa, a fascinating Maori fortress about 1000 years old. It has walls of stone instead of the earthworks that formed the base of most Maori fortresses. The fortress was abandoned after muskets were first used by Waikato warriors in the early 19th century. Just south of Oakura is Lucys Gully, a shady picnic spot near the entrance to **EGMONT NATIONAL PARK**. At the top of the gully is an impressive stand of giant redwood.

OPUNAKE

Southern Taranaki's best beach. The town of 1600 began in the 1860s as a British redoubt, part of a chain of fortified coastal positions extending towards **NEW PLYMOUTH**. Now it offers the best on-shore view (on clear days) of the Maui natural gas field with its giant 20 000 tonne production platform. Just north (8 kilometres) at Oaonui is the large processing and servicing plant for the gas field. The plant's information office has a huge scale model of the offshore platform.

PARIHAKA PA

Set in a faintly fairytale countryside of conical hills below Mt Taranaki's western slopes, this now tiny village was for four decades (from the 1860s to the early 1900s) the base from which the Maori prophet Te Whiti and his colleague and rival Tohu preached (see page 140). After the warfare of the 1860s, the village was the command post of a long, effectively mounted campaign dedicated to Maori self-sufficiency and passive resistance to things European. The climax came when 1500 men of the colonial militia descended on the defenceless community in 1881, razed its buildings, and led its leaders off to prison without trial. The tale is told dramatically in Dick Scott's *Ask that Mountain*. Te Whiti's grave in the village has become a shrine visited by many Maoris.

PATEA

Taranaki's southernmost centre. Once military settlement, once port, once freezing-works community, Patea is now none of these – with a thinning population of 1600 after the closing of its freezing works and the loss of hundreds of jobs in the early 1980s. The commanding feature of the main street (apart from Mt Taranaki, which seems to close off the northern end) is a 17 metre replica of the *Aotea* canoe, which brought the first Maori settlers to this part of Taranaki's coast. The celebrated commander of the canoe, Turi, sits inside it with his family. Near by, the Patea Historical Society has a comprehensive and fascinating collection of material in a still-expanding museum (open weekends, holidays and by request). It features murals of the New Zealand wars, painted in the 1950s by the Maori primitive artist Oriwa Haddon to grace the walls of Hawera's now-demolished Commercial Hotel.

At the mouth of the river are the remains of Patea's once busy port, with a good surf beach around the corner. Inland is Lake Rotorangi (formed for hydro purposes), now a centre for jet-boat tours, trout fishing and all water sports. A handsome walkway has been pushed through surrounding wilderness.

Hardship, poverty and basic living conditions were the lot of many pioneer settlers. At the Taranaki Pioneer Village, south of Stratford, buildings, models and original relics tell much of the story of the surrounding region. In addition to the old Okato house and Kaponga gaol, there is a comprehensive collection of historic electrical equipment

STRATFORD

Market town of central Taranaki, with a population of 5600, Stratford was named after Shakespeare's birthplace, and many of its street names are those of Shakespearean characters. At first a mill town in the 1870s, it is now the service centre for one of the world's most prosperous dairying regions.

Stratford is closer to the mountain than any other Taranaki town of substance. Its rural land, won by clearing the rainforest, is vividly described in the comic *Me and Gus* tales of Frank Anthony, written in the 1920s, when the author was a struggling settler. Two kilometres south of the town, the growing Taranaki Pioneer Village displays much of the region's past, including replicas of Okato house (1862), Kaponga gaol (1914), and Tariki railway station (1902) (open Monday to Friday and Sunday until 4).

Stratford Mountain House, with skifields and mountain walks near by, is 15 kilometres from the town, and Dawson Falls 26 kilometres. The drive from here to the King Country's Taumarunui (160 kilometres on Highway 43) passes through much of the North Island's rugged and forested interior.

Alternatively, a guided tour takes in the territory which includes the Mt Damper Falls, one of the North Island's largest, in the Tangarakau Gorge.

TONGAPORUTU

At Taranaki's northernmost limit, this small fishing and resort settlement lies at the mouth of one of the three large rivers that empty into the North Taranaki Bight (the Tongaporutu, Mokau and Awakino) and which were once intensively Maori-settled. At low tide, caverns in sandstone cliffs are uncovered, disclosing early Polynesian drawings (ask for directions locally). Farther south is the Drover's Tunnel, a 50 metre militia-built passage, once used to move livestock. The village is at one end of the scenic coastal Whitecliffs walkway, a 5-hour (9.5 kilometres) tramp to the former British garrison of Pukearuhe (the walkway is closed July to September); check times of high tides. A lonely cliffside cairn at Pukearuhe commemorates the missionary John Whiteley, who was killed here in 1869. There are extensive views of the North Taranaki Bight and Mt Taranaki.

URENUI

On the north Taranaki shore, this village is notable for the frankness of its naming, possibly after a chief of some distinction (*urenui* means 'large penis'). It is chiefly known as the birthplace of the internationally honoured Maori doctor, politician and anthropologist Sir Peter Buck (Te Rangi Hiroa) (*c.* 1877–1951), whose books *Vikings of the Sunrise* and *The Coming of the Maori* remain crucial to understanding of the Polynesian Pacific. After his death in Hawaii, his ashes were brought home to Urenui, where they are now entombed at Okoki Pa, 4 kilometres north-east of the town, under a striking memorial canoe prow on the site of a former Maori fortress.

CHEW CHONG, AN ENTERPRISING PIONEER

On Eltham's west side, near the bridge over the Waingongoro River, stood a butter factory that played an unlikely part in the early days of the New Zealand dairy industry

Chew Chong, the man who brought prosperity to pioneering Taranaki farmers

High production standards were ensured at his Jubilee Butter Factory

Chew Chong (*c.* 1830–1920), a Chinese toy-pedlar, scrap-metal dealer, one-time servant, goldminer and storekeeper, built his first dairy factory on this site in 1887 and began to produce butter for export.

Earlier, in 1885, Chew Chong had sent two barrels of Eltham salted butter to England. Although the quality of the initial shipment was poor, it signalled the beginnings of a butter trade that continues – at times precariously – to this day.

This commercial breakthrough came only after a bizarre discovery by Chew Chong. On his travels as a pedlar, he noticed a fungus growing on newly burnt trees during the clearance of Taranaki farmlands. The fungus resembled a prized Chinese delicacy. During the thirty years from 1872 to 1902, he exported thousands of tonnes of 'Taranaki wool' to China.

His curious trade meant that Chew Chong could provide Taranaki farmers with hard cash at a time when much of their butter was being traded for basic supplies. The only other source of cash to develop farms was occasional bush-felling or roadwork. Chew Chong invested the profits from the fungus trade in butter-making. The result was confidence and trust within the farming community. He also developed the first dairy refrigerating machine in 1889.

The advent of cooperative dairy factories spelt the end of Chew Chong's butter plant at Eltham and his creameries elsewhere. But he had helped bring higher standards of butter production and prosperity to Taranaki farmers. In 1910, settlers from all over the province presented Chew Chong with an illuminated address to honour his services.

WAITARA

This freezing-works town and former port, population 6500, is 16 kilometres north of **NEW PLYMOUTH**. It is now set in a landscape commanded by energy projects, particularly the large gas-to-gasoline plant at Motunui, which began producing in 1985, and the methanol-producing plant in the Waitara Valley. Also close is the McKee oil field, now a significant contributor to the nation's energy needs (visitors' centre at Motunui). The NZ Historic Places Trust and the Department of Lands and Survey have combined to produce an intriguing historic trail (19 kilometres or a half-day long) of the Waitara campaign, one of the first battles of the 1860s. Designed for motorists and cyclists, and linking a number of places over which Maori and Briton warred, the trail climaxes at the site of the long-contested Pukerangiora Pa, set dramatically above the Waitara River. Maps and directions are provided in a booklet, *Waitara Campaign Historic Trail*, published by the Department of Lands and Survey and obtainable locally. Set high above the town is Manukorihi Pa, with one of this century's most distinguished carved Maori meeting-houses, Te Ikaroa-a-Maui (1936). It is a memorial to the Maori leader Sir Maui Pomare, whose statue stands beside it above a crypt containing his ashes.

Wanganui–Manawatu–Horowhenua

The margin of this region is defined by a one hundred and sixty kilometre arc of North Island coast stretching from Patea in Taranaki to Paekakariki in Wellington, backed by mountains and forests. Three rivers, the Wanganui, the Rangitikei and the Manawatu, give the region its character. Unlike most of northern New Zealand, there are vast expanses of flat riverland and sandy coastal country. Highways often run hypnotically straight for dozens of kilometres through shimmering grasslands.

Grass thrives in this climate and, of the original lowland vegetation, only the tenacious flax survives on riversides and in swamps, often because it is harvested for its fibre. South of Levin, orchards and market gardens colour the warm coastal plain and subtropical fruits flourish. The beat of surf and roar of rivers in flood are all that is left of the landscape's old resonance.

The Maori, who knew the rivers intimately, believed the Wanganui was carved out by adulterous Mount Taranaki as he fled the wrath of cuckolded Mount Tongariro (see page 134). The mountain-piercing Manawatu was formed when a great totara tree growing in Hawke's Bay was given the power of motion by the gods. Furrowing through the landscape, it crashed through cliffs and across mountains, leaving the Manawatu Gorge in its wake, until it found rest in the Tasman's tides.

For the Maori, the rivers were much more than canoe routes to the interior. In the densely forested, often swampy lowland, they enjoyed tribal prosperity and security. They trapped birds and caught eels, cultivated kumara on the river flats and built many fortifications. One scholar has counted eighty-three riverside settlements along seventy-five kilometres of the Manawatu River. Even Lake Horowhenua, only three kilometres long and one and a half kilometres wide, had twenty-one named canoe-landings on its shores.

In 1843, the missionary Richard Taylor found a hundred canoes beached for a *hui*, or festival, in an obscure tributary of the Wanganui. On the river's two hundred and ten navigable kilometres beyond the tidal zone, there are two hundred and thirty-nine rapids, each of which has a Maori name. Groves of karaka trees, which were planted

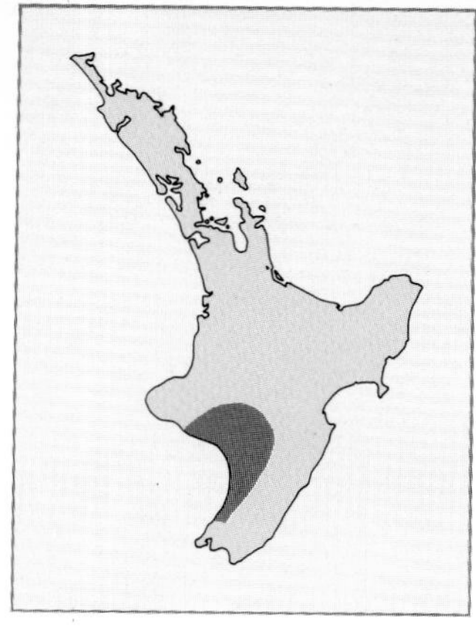

WHERE MIGHTY RIVERS FLOW

for their berries, now are the only evidence of the former density of the population, a last link with the first food-producers in an abundant region.

Maori folklore tells that the region was populated by migrants from two canoes, the *Kurahaupo* and the *Aotea*. It is said, however, that just one man was responsible for the naming of the waterways. Haunui-a-Nanaia of the Rangitane tribe was not allowed to join the voyaging canoes because of his unreliable character. Yet somehow he arrived on the east coast of New Zealand in time to welcome his tribe ashore. According to legends, either he shaped a cloud into a canoe, or he travelled steerage in a whale's belly. When his wife ran off with another man, Hau pursued them across the island. As he travelled down the west coast, towards the terrain his fellow tribesmen would soon call their own, he confronted one river after another.

The first was a remarkably wide torrent Hau named Whanganui, 'big water'. When he crossed the next river it is said that he had to bale out his canoe, or else that he splashed the water with his taiaha. He called it Whangaehu, 'to bale a canoe by splashing'. The third was close too, so near it seemed that a tree felled on the shores of the Whangaehu might reach it. This one he named Turakina, 'to be felled'. Tikei, 'to stretch the legs', seemed an appropriate name for the next river, now the Rangitikei, because it was a long walk from the Turakina. Then came a wild river that struck fear into Hau, so he called it Manawatu, 'apprehension'. Hokio, 'whistling wind', was named after the gale that was blowing when Hau reached it.

Feeling that he had earned the honour of naming a place after himself, he called another river Ohau, 'the place of Hau'. Finally, after bestowing a few more names on the region, he gave himself to domestic matters, ran his errant wife to ground and turned her into a rock pillar. Hau's epic journey was related in song at every Rangitane fireside.

The peaceful riverside life of the Rangitane and other tribes came to an end in the eighteen-twenties when Te Rauparaha and his tiny Ngati Toa tribe moved south with their muskets, after escaping Waikato tribes at Kawhia Harbour. With the aim of conquering most of southern New Zealand, which he almost did, Te Rauparaha based himself on rugged Kapiti Island and terrorised mainland tribesmen. In two decades of slaughter and cannibalism, he all but depopulated the coast. A few Europeans arrived – whalers and traders – and provided even more firearms in return for Te Rauparaha's protection. His rampages became more deadly, but they happened to serve European ends. Colonists often found landscapes empty of living Maori.

European settlement began in earnest at Wanganui. The New Zealand Company schooner, *Surprise*, arrived at the mouth of the Wanganui River in May 1840. Seven hundred Maori scrambled for a few heaps of clay pipes, mirrors, trinkets and blankets. They handed over sixteen thousand hectares of land without knowing what the transaction meant. Thinking the goods were gifts, they returned the favour with thirty pigs and ten tonnes of potatoes. By the end of 1841, two hundred colonists had arrived and established a rough bush township.

Friction with Maori who felt cheated by the original land deal, prompted the colonial government to garrison the town and build a stockade in the late eighteen-forties. There was even talk of abandoning the settlement. Six British and Maoris were killed and twenty wounded in a pitched battle. In 1848 the government negotiated a new deed of sale, paying an additional three pence an acre for the land already taken – and took still more. Wanganui chiefs surrendered eighty thousand acres (thirty-two thousand, four hundred hectares) for one thousand pounds (two thousand dollars) and were left no loophole. 'All the land within these boundaries', they later mourned, 'we have wept and sighed over, bidden farewell to, and delivered up for ever to the Europeans.'

Terrain to the south of Wanganui had fewer Maoris and fewer problems. Land purchases were mammoth. In 1849, the Rangitikei Block of one hundred and eighty-six thousand acres (seventy-five thousand, three hundred hectares) was sold off for twenty-five hundred pounds (five thousand dollars). In the Manawatu, one survey alone took in two hundred and fifty thousand acres (one hundred and two thousand hectares). Block by block, great reaches of forest fell to Europeans.

In the following decades, the southern North Island darkened with smoke as land was cleared. Scandinavians were brought in to help master hostile forest country. Ditlev Gothard Monrad, the deposed prime minister of Denmark and Bishop of Lolland and Falster, arrived in the Manawatu after the humiliation of his country's defeat by Prussia in 1864. Here, his enemy was nature. For three years he lived in a hut of rammed clay and straw in the dark, sodden heart of the Manawatu bush. This scholar-statesman inspired many Danes to follow and take up forty-acre (sixteen hectares) bush sections. Although Monrad returned to Danish parliamentary life in 1869, his two sons remained behind. One, Johannes, demonstrated a revolutionary cream separator to Manawatu farmers in 1883. Monrad and other Scandinavian names like Petersen, Andersen and Christiansen pepper Palmerston North telephone directories to this day.

PEACE AND PROSPERITY

Except near Wanganui, the region escaped the Maori-European conflicts of the eighteen-sixties. Most Wanganui Maori, whose own land grievances had been largely settled, took the British side. In 1864 they saved Wanganui from Hauhau invasion. In late 1868, the coast north of Kai Iwi was for a time virtually ceded to Taranaki's Titokowaru. Under the famous warrior Major Te Rangihiwinui Kepa (also known as Major Kemp), local tribesmen fought vigorously against both Titokowaru and Poverty Bay's Te Kooti. The spread of grass has done much to erase pioneer scars on the lowland. In the Tararua Forest Park and up the Wanganui River the original forest cover persists and prospers, spreading over land lacerated by pioneers. Elsewhere, only flooding rivers protest human dominion by disturbing the serenity of sheep and dairy pastures, orchards and gardens, and towns and cities. To discover the region as it once was, and perhaps find a Maori flint knife or pendant, a pioneer ruin or rusty shovel, visitors should take a leafy track high into the Tararuas, or follow the mighty Wanganui River into the silent heart.

A telling reminder of New Zealand's mistier past is preserved just outside Waverley, north off the highway. The Maori rock carvings at Kohi could be the oldest surviving Polynesian artwork in the North Island, and are certainly among the most important in the land

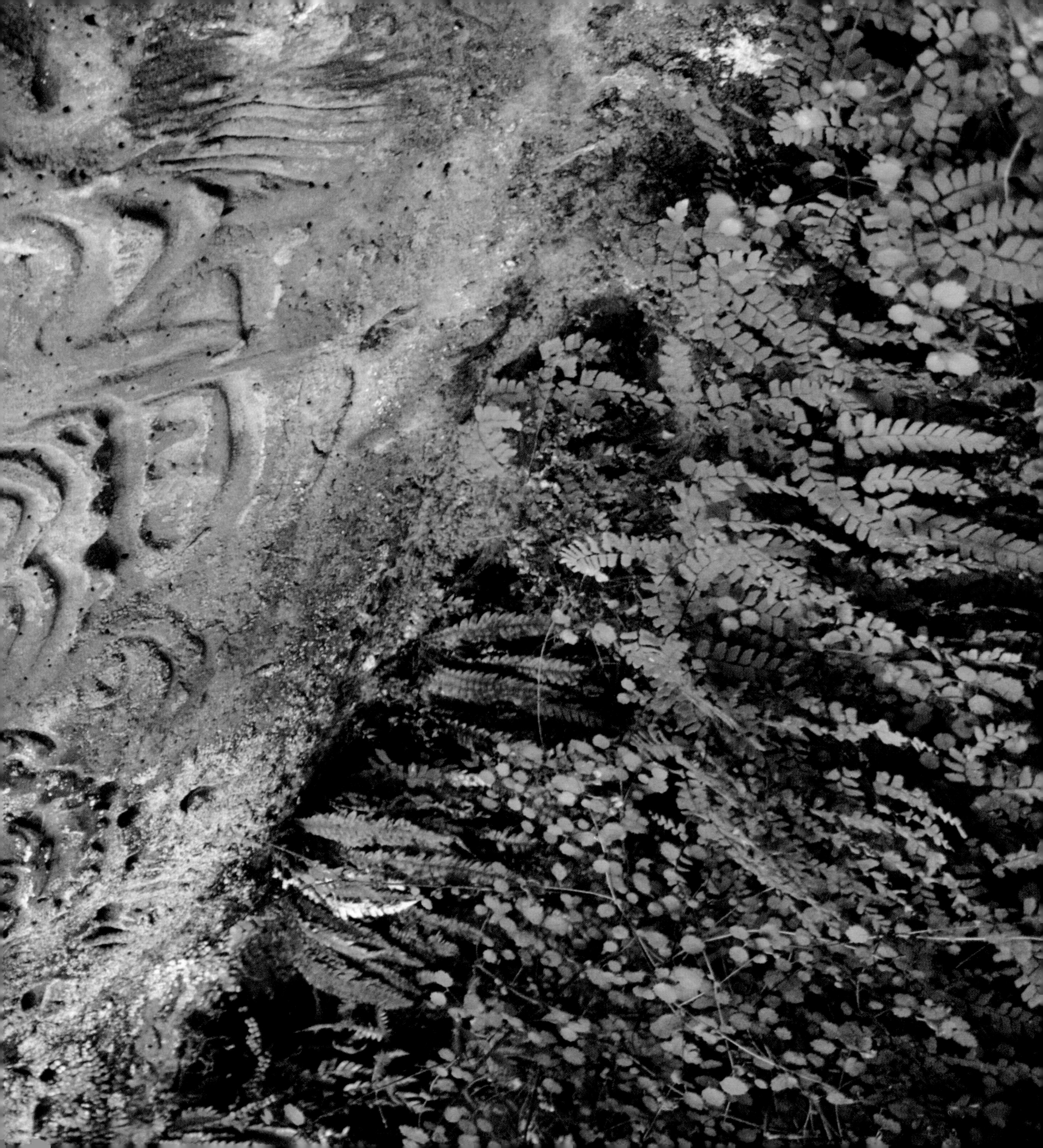

Left: *Raised in 1849, Otaki's Rangiatea Church, one of the nation's most distinguished Maori churches, is – with its powerful columns and decorated beams – dramatic testimony to early mission influence on this coast* **Top:** *Carving in the meeting-house Te Paku-o-te-Rangi which stands within the Putiki Pa on the banks of the Wanganui outside Wanganui City* **Above:** *Entrance to the Maori cemetery on the Wanganui River Road at Koriniti, a Maori settlement that boasts two meeting-houses, a church and an old mission house*

THE WITCHING WANGANUI

It may not be the longest of New Zealand's rivers, nor the largest, but the wild Wanganui is rich in legend, history and spectacular scenery

Its headwaters rise in the volcanic interior. Swelling with tributary after tributary, the Wanganui drains nearly seven and a half thousand square kilometres, taking two hundred and ninety kilometres to find its way between mountain and forest to the Tasman Sea. For the Maori and the first Europeans it was a route into the heartland of the country.

In Maori legend it was first a path of sorrow made by the lovesick Mount Taranaki in his flight from Mount Tongariro (see page 134). The great fissure left in the land filled with Taranaki's tears and formed the river. It became a landscape for mortals less than a thousand years ago.

The Wanganui River Road, opened in 1934 after thirty years in the building, winds for eighty kilometres above the river to Pipiriki, offering frequently changing views

The Polynesian explorer Kupe was the first human being to breach the river's silences. He travelled a score of kilometres upriver on the tide and then turned back. Centuries later, a tribe called the Te Ati Hau began drifting up the salty lower reaches of the river and settling its ferny banks. Kumara were planted on fertile riverside, and the surrounding forest provided birds, berries and fern roots. The river was rich in eels – the staple diet of the tribe – and lamprey and whitebait in season. Maori fishing weirs were elaborate and vast, some capable of catching up to eight thousand eels or lamprey in one night. They traded their harvests with downriver tribesmen for produce from the sea.

Built high on the river's steep cliffs, their fortified pa gave protection from intruders. Vine ladders were lowered to reach the river. Maori greatly respected the Wanganui River. The powerful *taniwha*, or water monsters, that tipped men from their canoes, or caused the Wanganui to flood, had to be placated regularly (and still are by the Maori who dwell here). In the valley's silences old folklore lingers. It has has been given a modern voice in the poetry of James K. Baxter, who lived his last years on the river's banks among tribesmen and was given a Maori burial.

The first known European contact with the great river was less serene. In 1831 a trader in dried heads named Joe Rowe tried to travel up the Wanganui. In an earlier encounter with Rowe, the local Maori had glimpsed the heads of two of their chiefs among his wares. They fell upon his party and killed all but one, an American black named Andrew Powers. Powers watched as his companions were turned into marketable commodities. He was then taken as a slave up the Wanganui River, the first non-Maori ever to see it, before being bartered off to a trader for eleven kilos of tobacco.

For centuries the mighty stretches of the Wanganui River were the inland 'highway' for Maori canoes travelling into central North Island. Today the European canoes (left) and jet boats (above and right) ply the same route, with tourists replacing the war and trading parties of long ago

Three years later a whaler known as 'Scotch Jock', whose safety may have been ensured by his Maori wife, paddled almost the entire negotiable length of the river. For twelve months he shared a life of high adventure with embattled tribesmen. Once he paddled his canoe, flying an old Union Jack, with a two-thousand-strong war party. Popular with the Maori, who pleaded with him to remain, he finally sailed downriver taking a hundred and eighty pigs with him.

The Wanganui's towering cliffs and deeply forested valleys, precipitous sides dressed in a huge variety of fern and tree-fern, make the river a favourite scenic route for the tourist

Holly Lodge Estate Winery's riverboat recaptures times when steamers plied the languid reaches of the Wanganui

Oyster Cliffs, near Parakino on the Wanganui River Road. The huge deposits of oysters are high in the cliffs above the road, four kilometres north of the settlement

In the early eighteen-forties the river was still virgin ground for missionaries. In 1843, the Reverend Richard Taylor journeyed upriver again and again, conducting baptisms and marriage services, establishing Anglican churches and missions and planting the poplars and weeping willows that still grace the lower Wanganui. Taylor estimated that five thousand Maoris lived along the river.

To mark their break with the pagan past, the Maori on the river asked Taylor to rename their tribal *kainga*, or villages. This he did, leaving a distinctive string of names such as Hiruharama (Jerusalem), Atene (Athens), Ranana (London) and Koriniti (Corinth). Catholic missions came soon after, but it was not until 1883 that Sister Mary Joseph Aubert, a remarkable and tenacious French nun, established a secure base for the faith at Jerusalem.

Christianity's most dramatic effect on the Wanganui was agricultural. Riverside Maori planted grain instead of kumara. By 1848 it was estimated that there were thirty thousand acres (twelve thousand hectares) of wheat along the river, and by the eighteen-fifties water-driven flour mills were working. The Kawana Mill, which survives in restored form at Matahiwi, produced flour for the rest of the century.

PEACE BRINGS RIVERBOAT TOURISM

In the eighteen-sixties the Hauhau rebellion spilled downriver from Taranaki. River-dwelling Maori were divided in their sympathies. The passage of the rebels towards the town of Wanganui was blocked by Maori of the lower Wanganui, more out of reverence for their sacred waterway than from loyalty to the British Crown. After a bitter battle on Moutoa Island in May 1864, there were at least a hundred dead and wounded, but the Hauhau were driven upriver again. Although there were clashes farther upriver at Pipiriki in 1865, and *niu* poles for Hauhau rites (see page 127) were erected until 1872, the *mana* of the river was never seriously menaced again.

One who died fighting them off was the Putiki chief Hoani Hipango, who had been to England and met Queen Victoria. Grateful Wanganui colonists mistakenly attributed his courage, and that of others who fell with him, to Christian virtue, and raised thirty-two pounds for a

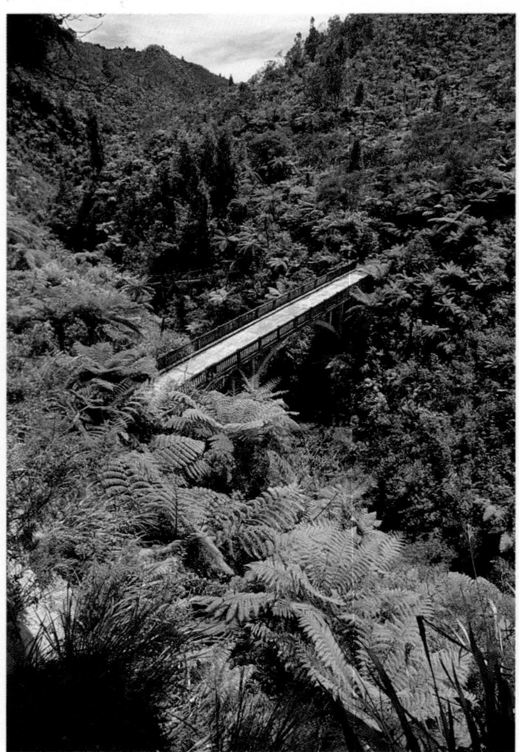

From Mangapurua a forty-minute walk through the bush leads to the 'Bridge to Nowhere', built in 1936 to open the valley at a time when farmers were already abandoning it

Top: *In its upper reaches the Wanganui River grows wilder, racing over rapids between its high rocky walls*
Above: *Wheelhouse of the* Ongarue, *a riverboat that worked the Wanganui more than fifty years. It now stands on dry land – a reminder of more leisurely travel in the past*

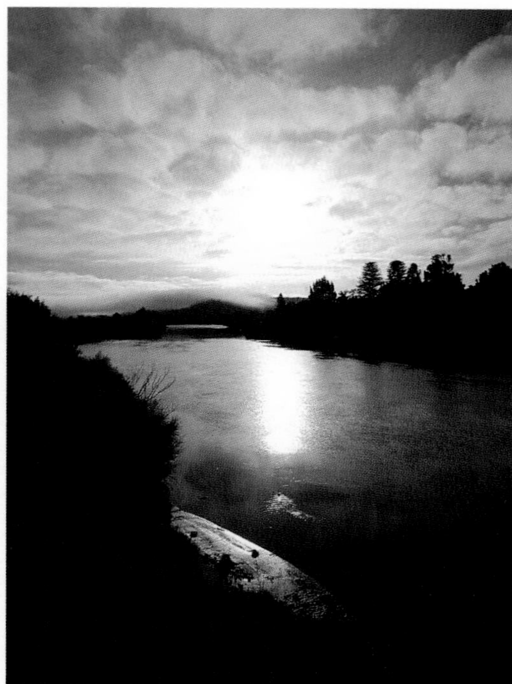

Sometimes calm, sometimes seething, the Wanganui River flows over a course of nearly three hundred kilometres

memorial banner. But Hipango and his fellow warriors had died for their god-like river.

As the North Island interior opened up to colonists in the eighteen-eighties, Europeans, like the Maori before them, recognised the Wanganui's value as a waterway. Navigable channels were opened, snags blasted and cables installed to winch boats over rapids. The steamer services that began in 1886 did more than link lonely settlers and settlements with the rest of New Zealand. The spectacle of the Wanganui's verdant upper reaches soon drew thousands of visitors. At the peak of the riverboat years, fifteen boats were ferrying travellers and tourists up and down the river. The largest of these was the thirty-two metre stern-wheeler *Manuwai*, which could carry four hundred passengers at a time.

Pipiriki once boasted some of the most splendid accommodation in the colony, although there is little evidence of it in the village today. A hotel called Pipiriki House held a hundred guests, and had a winter garden, billiard and smoking rooms, lounges, tennis courts and a croquet lawn. At the beginning of the twentieth century, it was accommodating twelve thousand guests a year. And the luxurious houseboat *Makere*, with space for thirty-six guests, had electric light, hot showers, silverware on the table, and chandeliers.

By the nineteen-twenties new roads and the railway had ended the Wanganui's importance as a highway. Tourists with motor vehicles found other diversions. By 1934 there was even a winding road up the Wanganui Valley to Raetihi, Taumarunui and places beyond. One riverboat service struggled on into the nineteen-fifties, but the heyday of high-living sightseers was past.

Gone too were most of the soldier-settlers, veterans of the First World War who had struggled in vain for two or three decades to make riverbank farms prosper. Maori abandoned their centuries-old waterside *kainga* for towns and cities, for education and jobs. Today hardly five hundred live where missionary Richard Taylor once tallied five thousand.

The rediscovery of the Wanganui began just as the last riverboat service was expiring. In 1957 South Island farmer-inventor Bill Hamilton demonstrated his prototype jet boat on the river (see page 270). Zipping across rapids, gobbling up long reaches in minutes rather than hours, the jet boat was a craft made for the river, and soon a tourist service was running. At about the same time, lovers of the New Zealand outdoors discovered that the Wanganui, with its deep gorges, wilderness and waterfalls, made spectacular canoe country. Conservationists campaigned for the conservation of the river's character. Tramping tracks along old Maori trails were opened up. The Wanganui was in business again. In 1987, the area was declared Whanganui National Park.

Downriver at the city of Wanganui, two restored riverboats carry today's sightseers up the tidal zone. Jet boats take them farther into the mountainous North Island past riverbanks rich in Maori legend. At Pipiriki and from the King Country's Taumarunui, other river tours start, both by jet boat and canoe.

Tourism has a distinctly different character now, perhaps best indicated by the fact that for almost the whole length of the great river – from Wanganui to Taumarunui – there is hardly any formal accommodation. The days of luxurious houseboats, croquet lawns and tennis courts are long gone. Much as that may be lamented, there is much to celebrate too. No elegant tinkle of silverware can substitute for the sound of birdsong. Canvas tents do greater justice to this terrain than cushioned lounges. This is a landscape with little to muffle the sounds of wilderness and water. Those who venture into it can experience old New Zealand's 'soft witchery' observed by colonial painter Charles Blomfield as he canoed here in the nineteenth century.

PLACES OF INTEREST

ATENE

See WANGANUI RIVER ROAD.

BULLS

This community of 1800 people is set on productive river flats at the junction of Highways 1 and 3 near the mouth of the Rangitikei River. Originally called Bull Town, it was named after its first settler, the noted English wood-carver James Bull. (He designed the panelling in London's House of Commons.)

The major defence installation of Ohakea Air Base is visible from the road. On the way to the river mouth and Moana Roa Beach is Flock House, where youths are trained for life on the land. Founded in 1924 as an expression of gratitude from New Zealand's sheep farmers, it was first intended to train the sons of British merchant seamen who had perished in World War I. Swimming, boating, fishing and picnic areas can be enjoyed at Dudding Lake Reserve (on Highway 3, towards the city of WANGANUI).

FEILDING

A prosperous town with a population of 12 000, Feilding grew from the dream of Lieutenant-Colonel William Feilding. Through the Emigrants' and Colonists' Aid Corporation, he endeavoured to make a new life here for the poor from England's Manchester and Liverpool. In 1874, 250 settlers arrived to occupy the bare town site. The town plan was based on the layout of Manchester, with two central squares. It was one of New Zealand's most successful planned settlements. Early wealth came from milling timber from the forest that covered the 42 000 hectare Manchester Block, and farming followed. England's landless poor often became affluent landowners. The arrival of the railway and the establishment of a freezing works confirmed Feilding's importance as a rural market town for the Manawatu.

The Waireka Estate museum, Wanganui

Despite the spillover of population from nearby (19 kilometres) PALMERSTON NORTH, Feilding has retained its original character. In Beattie and Goodbehere Streets there are two groups of late 19th-century workers' cottages. Other historical buildings of interest include St John's Anglican Church, and Victorian and Edwardian buildings at the town centre. Many native and exotic plants are laid out in fine private gardens at Mount Lees Reserve, a gift to the nation from Ormond Wilson (11 kilometres, in Ngaio Road, off the Mount Stewart–Halcombe road; open 9–6 daily).

FOXTON

Foxton was the first substantial European community in the Manawatu. It was founded in 1855 and renamed in 1877 after a local prominent settler, the former New Zealand premier Sir William Fox. Situated near the Manawatu River mouth, its importance as a port depended on a thriving flax industry and general trade with Maori and colonists.

When industry gradually subsided and then the railway bypassed the town, inland PALMERSTON NORTH began to command the region. Today Foxton's population numbers only 2700. The commercial area just off Highway 1 has a number of historic buildings, including a museum in the old courthouse (open Sunday, 2–4). Foxton's residential and resort area is 6 kilometres away on the coast at Foxton Beach. Just south, the North Island's longest bridge spans the Manawatu River. Nine kilometres to the north is the Himatangi radio transmitting station, a vital link in the country's communications.

JERUSALEM (HIRUHARAMA)

See WANGANUI RIVER ROAD.

KAI IWI

A township north-west of WANGANUI on Highway 3, with a reputation for fine cheeses. A fine sample of the region's original vegetation can be seen at 85-hectare Bushy Park Reserve (8 kilometres inland). A pioneer family's gift to the nation, the reserve is administered by the Royal Forest and Bird Protection Society. There are natural history displays in the elegant Frank Moore homestead (1905), which also provides modestly priced accommodation for society members and the public (signposted at Kai Iwi, open 10–5, Wednesday to Sunday).

KORINITI

See WANGANUI RIVER ROAD.

LEVIN

This busy rural centre, with a population of 18 000 in its vicinity, was founded as a railway town in 1889 on fertile land between the Tararua Range and the Tasman Sea. Bounding the residential area, 2 kilometres off Highway 1, is Lake Horowhenua, once commanded by artificial island fortresses built by local Maori. Little remains of these unique creations, which were desperately defended in the days of Te Rauparaha's reign of terror on this coast. At Lake Papaitonga (signposted off Muhunoa Road) where Maori warriors once duelled to the death, a walkway now passes through rare surviving wetland forest with abundant birdlife. Both lakes are popular picnic spots. Hokio Beach (10 kilometres) was once a Cobb & Co. coaching stop. At Waitarere (signposted 8 kilometres north), the wreck of the sailing ship *Hyderabad* thrown ashore here in 1878, can be seen. The beginning of the Ohau Track into the TARARUA FOREST PARK is signposted on Gladstone Road. Waiopehu Native Reserve, 4 kilometres from town has picnic areas.

MARTON

Originally called Tutaenui, 'big dung', the town was renamed in 1869, the centenary of Cook's landing in New Zealand, after the navigator's Yorkshire birthplace. The Captain Cook Pioneer Cottage (open Sunday, 2.30–4.30, or by arrangement) has no connection with Cook, but preserves much of the character of the North Island's colonial era. Marton has grown from a drovers' watering hole and early railway settlement to a rural market town with a population of 5000.

Ratana's twin-towered temple, home of a spiritual movement that helped rally Maori identity

Notable buildings include the Church of St Stephen (1871), built on the site of a military redoubt (Maunder St), and the late Victorian brick courthouse (1897) in the town centre. An historic precinct of old commercial buildings in Broadway, preserved by the NZ Historic Places Trust, includes the White Hart Tavern and the Bank of New Zealand.

Westoe (1874), the palatial and high-towered Italianate home of Sir William Fox (1812–93), the politician and painter who was four times premier of New Zealand, is still in private hands. The house and grounds can be viewed from Kakariki Road, just off Highway 1. Another stately homestead, Elizabethan-style Maungaraupi (1906), provides country-style refreshments, tours and overnight accommodation (off Highway 1 on the way to Hunterville). Lakeside picnics, swimming and trout fishing can be enjoyed at Dudding Lake Reserve (11 kilometres, the other side of Highway 3).

OTAKI

This historic township, with a population of 4500, is an hour's drive north of Wellington on Highway 1, in a farming and market gardening district. The missionary Octavius Hadfield (1814–1904), later Bishop of Wellington, set up here in 1839, when the region was still reeling from the shock of war chief Te Rauparaha's terrorism (see page 143). Hadfield persuaded his flock to till the earth rather than compound terror and to export produce to Wellington.

The magnificent Maori Church, Rangiatea (1849), is the greatest testimony to Hadfield's proselytising talent. Its plain weatherboard exterior is a shell for one of the finest Maori churches in New Zealand. The 24 metre totara ridgepole and its 12 metre tall supporting pillars were floated by river and sea to the site. An 18 metre high scaffolding was built to set them in place. *Rangiatea* means 'abode of the absolute'. Behind the church a stone marks the original resting place of Te Rauparaha. According to legend, his bones were later buried on Kapiti Island, his former stronghold.

In Te Rauparaha Street there is a small church dating from about 1857, and other buildings dating from about 1900. These are part of the Roman Catholic mission, originally founded here in 1844. Raukawa meeting-house in Mill Road (1936) celebrates local Maori tradition in

Te Paku-o-te-Rangi, carved meeting-house on the outskirts of Wanganui City

its carvings. The historic Bank of New Zealand building now houses a museum of Maori and European pioneer relics, and is open most afternoons. There is a fine beach 2 kilometres west of the town. To the east is the **TARARUA FOREST PARK** and Otaki Gorge (9 kilometres), a picnic place with swimming and walkways into the Tararua Range.

PALMERSTON NORTH

New Zealand's second largest inland city, Palmerston North has a population of 70 000. It was one of the last sites in the region to be settled. The terrain it now occupies was first viewed by Europeans in 1846 as a natural clearing in the Manawatu forest and was known to the Maori as *Papaioea*, 'how beautiful!' The local Rangitane tribe used such secret forest places for sanctuary when Te Rauparaha was on the rampage. They sold their land to the government in 1864, and the first permanent settlers arrived in 1866. Ruthless razing of the forest followed. The settlement was named Palmerston after the 19th-century British statesman and 'North' was added to distinguish it from the town of the same name in South Island.

Laid out to the town planning ideal of the period, the centre of Palmerston North consisted of four large spaces covering 7 hectares of gardens and trees. This central area was later split in two by the railway, but was restored and relandscaped in the 1960s when the railway was moved farther west. The entire city is laid out on level ground. Beside the Manawatu River, the Esplanade features 27 hectares of bushwalks and parkland. A cherry-tree drive draws thousands of visitors at blossom time in the early spring.

On the leafy south bank of the Manawatu River is Massey University, named after William Massey, the farmer who was prime minister from 1912 to 1925. Monro Lookout overlooking the university is dedicated to the memory of Charles Monro, who introduced Rugby to New Zealand in 1870. The university campus is open to the public weekdays (9–4.30), and conducted tours can be arranged at the information office.

Beside Manawatu Museum in Church Street (open 10–4, Tuesday to Friday; 2–4, weekend) are three historic buildings; Totaranui Pioneer Cottage (1875), Awahou South School (1920), and a reconstructed smithy and early general store. The Rugby Hall of Fame (at the corner of Grey and Carroll Streets) displays memorabilia associated with the history of the national sport (open daily, 1.30–4). The Manawatu Art Gallery in Main Street has a comprehensive collection of modern New Zealand works (open Tuesday to Friday, 10–4.30; weekend, 1–5). The Tokomaru Steam Engine Museum (18 kilometres on the road to Shannon) displays stationary steam engines, traction engines and a working steam railway (for working hours telephone Tokomaru 853).

At Pohangina Valley Domain (34 kilometres north-east) there are 344 hectares of bush reserve, featuring the tallest totara of the region, with bushwalks, swimming, picnic areas and an approach to the **RUAHINE FOREST PARK**. The massive Manawatu Gorge (16 kilometres towards Woodville) divides the Ruahine and Tararua Ranges. When a road was built through it in the 1870s, workmen were sometimes suspended by rope from the cliff tops. Mount Lees Reserve (see **FEILDING**) is a short drive, and the west-coast surf beaches of **FOXTON** and Himatangi are both less than an hour away.

The Lido swimming complex is near the Esplanade in the city. The Palmerston North Public Relations Organisation can advise on and arrange visits to several nearby farms and privately owned historic homesteads, including Pukemarama (at Tangimoana), Merchiston (Rangitikei Valley), and Maungaraupi (see **MARTON**).

PIPIRIKI

See **WANGANUI RIVER ROAD**.

RAETIHI

This township of 1300 at the gateway to the region from the King Country and the Volcanic Plateau was once a wagoners' stopover and sawmilling centre. From Raetihi there are two routes to **WANGANUI**, the spectacular **WANGANUI RIVER ROAD**, or the less adventurous Highway 4 via Parapara that passes the impressive Raukawa Falls (and through much stark pastoral country).

Until well into this century Raetihi's only link with the outside world was the Wanganui River. In 1918 the township was caught in one of New Zealand's largest-ever forest fires. Nine sawmills and 150 houses were burnt down, and miraculously only 3 lives were lost. In contrast to this traditional country township is the nearby stylish mountain town of Ohakune (see page 114).

RATANA

A tiny, virtually all-Maori township, 23 kilometres south-east of **WANGANUI**. The community of 500 owes its existence to a vision seen by the Maori farmer Tahupotiki Wiremu Ratana in 1918. He said an angel instructed him to unite the Maori people and turn them from tribal rivalry and old superstitions to Jehovah. The church he subsequently founded (the Ratana Church) has had considerable influence on Maori life and politics since the 1920s. Often all four Maori seats in Parliament have been filled by Ratana men and women. Today adherents of the Ratana Church in New Zealand still number more than 35 000.

The unique twin-towered temple (1927) here, usually open to the public, is the centrepiece of a complex that is a repository of a fascinating folk-art created by a people caught between cultures. Ratana's original homestead – and the veranda from which he had his vision – still stands. A museum contains walking sticks and crutches thrown away by the infirm after Ratana healed them (open by arrangement). Celebration of Ratana's birthday on January 25, with bright costumes and music, is the country's most colourful religious festival.

RUAHINE FOREST PARK

To the north of **PALMERSTON NORTH**, these 93 600 hectares of wilderness between the Hawke's Bay and Manawatu regions offer hunting, tramping, huts and picnicking at road-end sites. Above 1400 metres there is alpine grassland. Otherwise the vegetation consists of kaikawaka, mountain beech, pink pine and Hall's totara, together with small patches of exotic forest and kanuka and manuka scrubland. The wildlife includes most surviving North Island native birds, red and sika deer, goats, pigs and opossums. Access is from Pohangina Valley East Road, Table Flat Road and Mania Road. Further information from the Department of Conservation in Palmerston North or **WANGANUI**.

TAIHAPE

Scenically perched at the edge of the Volcanic Plateau, this commercial centre of 2500 people serves a district commanded by large-scale grazing properties. Some of the country's largest estates are located along the former coach road to Napier. The settlement started as a railway construction camp in dense bush. Canterbury colonists followed the railwaymen to make an egalitarian beginning, but soon went their separate ways.

THE POET OF JERUSALEM

The long loop from Highway 4 at Raetihi snakes along the side of the Wanganui River, taking in Pipiriki and Jerusalem (Hiruharama)

Jerusalem's most notable recent association is with the poet James K. Baxter (1926-72) whose work his fellow-poet Vincent O'Sullivan has described as: 'the most complete delineation yet of a New Zealand mind. The poetic record of its shaping is as original an act as anything we have.'

Born and raised in Dunedin, Baxter drifted north, first to Christchurch then to Wellington, where he acquired a university degree, married and worked as a postman among other occupations. He was an alcoholic and joined Alcoholics Anonymous. He converted to Roman Catholicism, and in 1969 left for the mainly Maori settlement of Jerusalem (Hiruharama) to establish a commune for those in need of help or in search of an alternative way of life.

These bare details of Baxter's life convey only the vaguest sense of the scope of his poetic genius, his generosity of heart and the enormity of his vision. Anecdotes of Baxter as poet, spiritual guide, drunk, dreamer, friend, talker, debunker and entertainer are endless, often contradictory, yet almost always seem quite likely.

In an interview Baxter once remarked that he was seeking an alternative to the 'chemical solutions' we give to our problems. His own answer was that 'the smashed myths had somehow to be replaced or reconstructed'. He then explained that this was why 'I have become a Christian guru, a barefoot and bearded eccentric, a bad smell in the noses of many good citizens.'

James Baxter . . . 1967 drawing by E. Noordhof

Though his attitudes and actions will always be matters for debate, there is no doubt that his larger memorial will be the huge and impressive *Collected Poems* (Oxford University Press). The little grave at Jerusalem is its final haunting footnote.

The Maori name was originally *Otaihape*, meaning 'the place of Tai the hunchback', presumably an early resident. The township has a small museum in Huia Street (open Sunday, 1–4; daily in school holidays, 10.30–3.30), and offers fishing, hunting, safaris and jet-boat excursions through the magnificent canyons of the upper Rangitikei. The Flat Hills Woolshed and Farmyard at Ohingaiti (34 kilometres south) features rural activities, country-style refreshments and crafts. Rafting or jet-boat tours can also be arranged. Similar tours are also available from the picturesque township of Mangaweka, 22 kilometres south of Taihape. The long, winding Taihape–Napier road (169 kilometres) was once the town's only link with the outside world. For today's visitor it makes an interesting approach to Hawke's Bay through extensive pastoral country.

Kawana Mill on Wanganui River Road

TARARUA FOREST PARK

This 116 000 hectare park extends some 100 kilometres along the Tararua Range, which divides the Wairarapa Valley from the Horowhenua region. Its two major peaks, Mitre and Hector, rise above 1500 metres. There are many walking tracks and approximately 60 public and private huts and bivouacs. The park provides for tramping, hunting, easy bushwalking, fishing and picknicking.

The vegetation ranges from alpine grassland or subalpine and low hardwood forest at higher levels to podocarp hardwood and beech forest on the lower slopes. Native birds are prolific, including kaka and kiwis. There are also pigs, deer, opossums and stoats. For the Maori, these mountains were a refuge in times of strife. The landscape was extensively logged by early settlers, but native forest is regenerating quickly.

Park headquarters are at Mount Holdsworth Lodge on the Wairarapa side (at the end of Norfolk Road, off Highway 2 south of Masterton). On the western (Horowhenua) side there are several points of access, though landowner permission may be required. Full information and hunting permits can be obtained from the Department of Conservation at **PALMERSTON NORTH**. Information is also available from public relations offices.

WANGANUI

This city of 40 000 was one of the first to be founded in New Zealand (1841). Its name, possibly a corruption of *Whanganui*, 'big water', derives from the great river that flows through it. For the European settlers, as for the Maori, it was the ideal settlement site, offering a natural highway to the interior.

Stockaded, but never besieged during the New Zealand wars, the people of Wanganui erected a monument that has left a sour taste for many, in memory of those 'who fell in defence of law and order against fanaticism and barbarism'. Although the Hauhau chief Titokowaru who menaced the settlement is now seen as a great Maori patriot and general, the defamatory monument still stands in the historic riverside reserve, the Moutoa Gardens, where the first land transactions took place. There is also a monument to the Maori warrior Major Kemp, who fought against Titokowaru.

The restored Tylee Cottage at the corner of Bell and Cameron Streets was built in 1853 for the head of the British commissariat in Wanganui and is now used by community groups. Among other historic buildings is the colonial-classical wooden Opera House (1899). The city's oldest public building, St Peter's Church (75 Koromiko Road, Gonville) was built in 1865 and moved to its present site in 1921. A watchtower in Cooks Gardens once warned firemen of 19th-century blazes.

The richly decorated interior of St Paul's Church (1937) at Putiki (the fifth on the site) is a magnificent blend of carving, painting and weaving. The carving was supervised by the great Pine Taiapa (see page 167). The breathtaking *kowhaiwhai* (painted rafters) were the work of another fine craftsman, Oliver Haddon, and Maori politician Sir Apirana Ngata directed the weaving of the *tukutuku* (wall panels). There are guided tours daily (9–10 and 2–3, Monday to Saturday; Sunday 11–12, 2–3) or by arrangement. Guided tours can also be taken to Putiki Marae, where the legends of the Wanganui River are told.

Wanganui Regional Museum in Queens Park contains a particularly rich collection of Maori artefacts, and reconstructions of river life in pre-European and pioneer days (open Monday to Friday, 9.30–4.30; Saturday and Sunday, 1–5). Among the many treasures, or *taonga*, is the 23 metre war canoe *Te Mata-o-Hoturoa*. Its hull is still embedded with bullets from the defence of the settlement in the 1860s. Also in Queens Park, the Sarjeant Art Gallery has a wealth of colonial paintings as well as contemporary New Zealand works (open Monday, 12–4.30; Tuesday to Friday, 10–4.30; Saturday and Sunday, 1–4.30).

A splendid view of the city (and Mt Taranaki on a fine day) can be obtained from the 32 metre memorial tower on top of 66 metre Durie Hill. Take the 205 metre tunnel that pierces the hill, and then the lift to the hill's summit. Two restored riverboats run trips upriver through the tidal zone to Hipango Park (26 kilometres) or the Holly Lodge Estate Winery, where there is a museum. Jet boats may also be hired.

At the Waireka Estate there are gardens, an historic homestead and an extensive private museum. Details of fast excursions to Pipiriki and beyond can be obtained from Wanganui Public Relations Office. Canoeing, camping and tramping expeditions are available.

An alternative is to take the **WANGANUI RIVER ROAD** to Pipiriki and hire a jet boat there. The Department of Lands and Survey runs a summer program of excursions through the Whanganui National Park between late December and late January (contact the senior ranger at Pipiriki). There are pleasant walks through the parks of Wanganui, especially Virginia Lake and St Johns Hill. The best-known beach is at Castlecliff (8 kilometres) near the mouth of the river. To the north is Mowhanau Beach (16 kilometres) and to the south, Turakina Beach (30 kilometres).

THE OLD SERPENT OF KAPITI ISLAND

Kapiti Island can be observed offshore from Paraparaumu, or from the many vantage points on Highway 1 as the road descends from the Wanganui–Manawatu region and starts on the approaches to Wellington

Kapiti Island, seen here from Raumati Beach, is now largely a bird sanctuary

The rectangular-shaped island, only ten kilometres long and two kilometres wide, with a highest point of 521 metres, is a remnant of the lost land bridge which connected the North and South Islands.

It was also the adopted home of Te Rauparaha (*c.*1768-1849), 'The Old Serpent', the Ngati Toa chief who occupied the island in the eighteen-twenties about the same time that Europeans were arriving in the area to hunt and trade whales.

Te Rauparaha was one of the last of the great chiefs in the days before organised European settlement. He spent his last years in constant confrontation with land-hungry immigrants. One of the great warriors in the tribal wars which raged from the Waikato to the middle of the South Island, he epitomised the old-time Maori virtues of bravery, cunning, treachery, cruelty, compassion, generosity, rage and gentleness – in about equal proportions – which together formed the code of *tika*, by which all actions were directed to the triumph and increased prestige of the tribe.

By the standards of his time Te Rauparaha was one of the great exponents of *tika*, and if he earned a reputation for deep villainy it was because he was so often more successful in the art of survival than many of his contemporaries.

It was Te Rauparaha who had dealings with the New Zealand Company when it claimed to have acquired huge areas of Wellington and Nelson. The details of this story are long and complex, but Te Rauparaha was little to be blamed for the bloodshed that inevitably followed the settlers' drive onto Maori land.

Governor Grey captured the elderly chief at Porirua in 1846 and held him without trial for eighteen months. The irony was that Te Rauparaha possibly regarded the cunning by which this was done as an example of *Pakeha tika* and therefore bore Grey no ill will. The New Zealand government acquired most of Kapiti Island in 1897. Te Rauparaha's old headquarters, and the scene of one of his greatest intertribal battles, is now a forest reserve and bird sanctuary.

WANGANUI RIVER ROAD

Although the Wanganui is best seen by boat, the slow, winding, 80 kilometre route from WANGANUI to Pipiriki allows the visitor to stop and enjoy the river environment. A canoe or a jet boat hired at Pipiriki or Taumarunui can complement the road journey, the most dramatic section of the river being beyond Pipiriki.

The road took 30 years to complete. When it was finally opened in 1934, it ended the dependence of riverside people on water transport. Little more than half of the road is sealed, there are no petrol stations, no accommodation and few places to buy food. The road passes many former Maori fortresses high above the river, villages boasting the names of the world's great cities (Athens, London), but largely abandoned, and many historic sites. *A Motorist's Guide to the Wanganui River Road*, published by the Whanganui Historical Society is a helpful companion.

Among the many places of interest along the first stage of the route to Raetihi are St Mary's Church (1875) at Upokongaro (12 kilometres); the Oyster Cliffs (28 kilometres) with oyster shell fossils; the Atene (Athens) meeting-house (1886), now extensively renovated (35 kilometres) and the spectacular Atene Skyline Walk (six hours or 18 kilometres return), or the more modest Atene Nature Walk (20 minutes) at the northern entry to the Skyline Walk. According to legend, a reach of the river beyond Atene was the haunt of fair-haired, fairy Maoris. Known as the 'Children of the Night', they fished the river by night and were never seen by day. At Koriniti (Corinth, 46 kilometres), Hikurangi Museum stands between the restored 19th-century meeting-houses, Te Waiherehere and Poutama. The mission church (the third on the site) was built in 1920.

Maungaraupi Homestead, near Marton

Beyond Koriniti the surface is no longer sealed and the road becomes even more tortuous. The meeting-house (1917) at Matahiwi Marae (54 kilometres) has carvings representing Maoris serving in World War I. The Kawana Mill (56 kilometres, built 1854) ceased functioning in 1913, but was reopened in 1980 after restoration by the NZ Historic Places Trust. Next to it stands a two-room miller's cottage. Ranana (London, 60 kilometres) was an early Roman Catholic mission station. A kilometre beyond Ranana, the road overlooks slender 900 metre long Moutoa Island where Maori of the lower Wanganui battled Hauhau intruders for the *mana* of the river in 1864.

Six kilometres farther on is Jerusalem (Hiruharama) where, at the Catholic mission (re-established 1883), a young French nun named Suzanne Aubert (later Mother Mary Joseph Aubert) became legendary for her compassionate care of orphaned and destitute children, and of the aged and the weak. She also respected the indigenous knowledge of the Maoris.

A later and more enigmatic legend was left by another Catholic, the poet James K. Baxter (see page 153). In 1969 he founded a commune in Jerusalem for young urban people who had been afflicted by drugs and drink. The controversial commune collapsed after his death, but lives on in his poems, especially the *Jerusalem Sonnets*. The centre of the commune was the house high on the hill to the right of the road, beside which a stone slab bears the simple inscription 'Hemi' (Maori for James, or Jim). Hundreds of young people, fellow writers, cultural figures and social workers gathered here for Baxter's *tangi*, or Maori wake, and interment in October 1972. The picturesque Catholic church dates from 1892.

Three kilometres past Jerusalem is the Ohoutahi Scenic Reserve. There is an accommodation hut for canoeists and hunters on the river bank at Te Puha (74 kilometres). The abandoned Te Poti Marae can also be glimpsed.

At Pipiriki (79 kilometres), the road leaves the river. Jet boats travel its spectacular upper reaches. From the late 19th century to the 1950s Pipiriki was a busy tourist resort. Only the steps of the grand accommodation house remain. The camping area is on the riverside where tourists once played tennis and croquet. Alternative accommodation is upriver by jet boat, at a renovated pioneer farmhouse, Ramanui Lodge. An elegant restored colonial house (*c.* 1885) refurbished by the NZ Historic Places Trust is a small museum and information centre on the Wanganui River Valley (open daily throughout the summer and on public holidays, otherwise by request at the ranger's house). The house was first the dwelling of Maori canoe crew, and later the home of a riverboat skipper. Opposite is a shelter with a fireplace, hot and cold water.

The reconstructed riverboat *Ongarue* can also be seen here. Pukehinau Walk (1 kilometre) has panoramic views of the river valley and leads to a summit fortified by Hauhau warriors who besieged a small colonial contingent at this spot. Upriver from Pipiriki other remnants of past human occupation include the forest-smothered 'Bridge to Nowhere', built too late (1936) to save ex-soldier riverside farmers from isolation and ruin. Still farther upriver are some Hauhau *niu* poles (see page 127).

MOTHER AUBERT

In 1883 Sister Mary Joseph Aubert was sent with several Sisters of St Joseph to open a mission at Jerusalem (Hiruharama) in the Wanganui region

Mother Aubert, founder of a nursing order

Sister Mary Joseph's arrival in the central Wanganui area was the curious realisation of a prophecy by the Curé of Ars in her native France. Against her parents' wishes, he encouraged the young woman to become a nun and described to her the place where she would one day be sent, though at the time neither he nor she knew the geography of New Zealand.

Her father had allowed her to train as a nurse in Paris – a background that was later to prove of immense benefit to her and the young colony. She was briefly a fellow-student with Florence Nightingale, and she had taken piano lessons from Franz Liszt.

When Bishop Pompallier sought recruits for New Zealand, she joined a group that left for Auckland in 1860. Here she became involved in the education of Maori girls in Ponsonby. Her efforts once involved her in a dangerous crossing of Hauhau lines. She became a student of Maori, and later compiled and published *A Manual of Maori Conversation*.

She continued charitable and nursing work throughout the province until in 1871 she joined the Hawke's Bay Mission. For twelve years she covered an immense area as a nurse and chemist, often dispensing medicines based on her knowledge of native plants and cures. Her success in Hawke's Bay led to her appointment to Jerusalem, where she devoted herself to the care of all who called on her for the following sixteen years. By now Mother Aubert, she founded the Daughters of Our Lady of Compassion.

Mother Aubert's next destination was Wellington, where she established a Home for Incurables, and the original Home of Compassion that was the first to adopt the new Plunket system of child care.

A visit to Italy before the First World War kept her away for seven years, but she returned at the age of eighty-five and again threw her energies into the care of the ill and needy. When she died in 1926 aged ninety-one, many of those at her huge funeral agreed she had become the greatest woman in New Zealand.

WAVERLEY

On the coast road to Taranaki 46 kilometres from WANGANUI, this quiet farming town of 1500 is known nationally for its race meetings, and particularly for breeding the Melbourne Cup-winning horse, Kiwi. From nearby Waipipi, ore-rich black ironsand is exported to Japan. The town grew on land ceded to the Hauhau by Europeans and was long a military outpost. Beneath the clock tower are the earthworks of an old British redoubt. At Moturoa, a few kilometres behind the town, in dramatically gorge-cut terrain, colonial forces suffered their most devastating defeat by the Maori rebel Titokowaru.

Carvings on a rock overhang at Kohi are possibly the oldest surviving Polynesian art in the North Island. Take Kohi Road to about 3 kilometres from the highway until you cross a bridge. Then follow a rough trail (usually signposted) up the left bank of the stream. The rock overhang is about 15 metres from the waterside and partially obscured by vegetation. The carvings incorporate the distinctive spirals of Classic Maori art as well as bird and lizard motifs possibly of an earlier Polynesian period. They may have been the work of a tribal *tohunga* who performed rites in this remote spot and wished to warn away the uninitiated with images of Whiro, the lizard-like God of Death.

WHANGANUI NATIONAL PARK

New Zealand's 11th national park was opened in a vice-regal ceremony at Pipiriki in February 1987. Centring on the Wanganui River, this park extends in 3 major sections from Te Maire 17 kilometres downstream from Taumarunui to its southernmost part just 35 kilometres outside WANGANUI.

East Coast–Urewera

Bulky ranges and thundering surf, shadowy forests and shimmering lakes – and a dramatic history – make up the East Coast-Urewera region. It takes its character from Maori tribesmen still tenaciously in place on their traditional land, from the terraced hilltop forts of their ancestors, and from newly carved meeting-houses that argue undiminished Maori pride.

From the north, its beginnings are distinct a few kilometres past the Bay of Plenty town of Opotiki. Whether you take the route to Gisborne through the rugged and often misty Waioeka Gorge, or the spectacular coastal road via Cape Runaway, population is sparse or almost non-existent – even more so if you approach through densely wooded Urewera country from the Volcanic Plateau. Only Poverty Bay, a well-groomed pocket of plenty at odds with its name, provides a picture of people in number.

Even where it meets the sea, most of the region is mountainous. The interior is dominated by two great ranges – Urewera's Huiarau and the Raukumara, striking up towards East Cape. Some peaks are higher than fifteen hundred metres. Hikurangi, the highest, is said to be the first part of the New Zealand mainland to catch the rays of the rising sun. From Opotiki to Cape Runaway, the mountains reach right down to the ocean. Even on the east-facing shore, from Hicks Bay to Gisborne, there is little lowland. Between summits and sea lies deeply dissected hill country, mostly grazed by sheep and often eroded after deforestation. The coastal climate is mild and relatively dry, but rainfall is high in the hilly interior. The Urewera highlands are notorious for sudden haze and heavy rain.

Moa-hunting Polynesians seem to have made little of the region's mixed character and to have found only Poverty Bay's sunny plain congenial. The later Classic Maori, however, have left their mark on scores of coastal heights remodelled as forts. According to tradition, three great voyaging canoes populated the region. To the north, those who arrived aboard the *Mataatua* seeded the Ngati Awa, Whakatohea and Whanau-a-Apanui tribes, spreading up the coast to Cape Runaway. Settlers from the *Horouta* landed between Cape Runaway and Poverty Bay, and founded the powerful Ngati Porou. The *Takitimu* populated Poverty Bay with the first of the Rongowhakaata tribe. In the early days of Maori settlement, there were rich fishing grounds, sands and rocks abundant with seafood, and forest stretching down to the shore, where pigeons were trapped and fern roots foraged. The silty river flats allowed the cultivation of kumara.

Only the inland Tuhoe tribe complicate a tidy pattern. Early European ethnologists discovered little of the origins of these people, the one Maori tribe living by choice in chilly highland terrain. The Tuhoe trace their ancestry back to the land's beginnings. They say mountain mated with mist maiden in the sunrise of the world, and begat a red-haired fairy people. Their daughters in turn bedded with sons of the *Mataatua* canoe, whose issue became the Tuhoe. Whatever their origin, the tall, fierce Tuhoe warriors were notorious among coastal tribes as women snatchers and consigners of men to the spirit world.

It was on the East Coast that James Cook landed on October 9, 1769, two days after a ship's boy on the *Endeavour* named Nicholas Young had sighted land – the first European to sight New Zealand in a dozen decades. The southern extremity of Poverty Bay has since been known as Young Nicks Head. When Cook rowed ashore with his botanist Joseph Banks and a party of men, their peaceful intentions were misunderstood and they were attacked by local Maori tribesmen, several of whom were killed. Cook finally sailed on, naming the place Poverty Bay 'because it afforded us no one thing we wanted'. At Tolaga Bay, to the north, he found 'A kind of second Paradise', as botanical artist Sydney Parkinson recorded.

Fifty years passed before the consequences of European contact became visible. Armed with European muskets, Hongi Hika and his fellow Ngapuhi tribesmen from the Bay of Islands brought terror to the region, much of which was left unexplored until well into the nineteenth century. Adventurous traders and whalers made their way slowly down the coast in the eighteen-twenties and thirties. Whaling flourished, persisting in some places well into the twentieth century. Missionaries arrived in the eighteen-thirties. A Catholic, Father Claude Baty, and an Anglican, William Colenso, reached the Urewera separately in 1841, and were two of the first Europeans to see Lake Waikaremoana. Meeting there by chance, they turned their backs on the view to argue the case for their respective beliefs before an audience of Tuhoe tribesmen. The baffled Tuhoe remained pagan.

The signing of the Treaty of Waitangi in 1840 made little impression here. Many chiefs neither signed nor acknowledged the treaty. Others never even knew anything of a document purporting to transfer sovereignty over their soil to Britain. By 1851 Poverty Bay, for example, had only forty-four Europeans and some half-castes. There was no systematic settlement; most Europeans were squatters on Maori sufferance. European-style agriculture, however, was made welcome. With seed from traders, the coastal Maori were growing maize in the eighteen-thirties and wheat in the forties. Ten years later they were shipping their harvests to Auckland and other colonial settlements and had even mastered European market-rigging, holding back produce until prices rose. With such self-sufficiency it was not surprising that the Treaty of Waitangi continued to mean little. The first governor of New Zealand to visit the East Coast – Gore Browne in 1860 – received a lacklustre welcome.

The warfare in Taranaki and the Waikato in the first half of the eighteen-sixties had little initial effect beyond intensifying Auckland's demand for food. A few dissenters departed to side with the embattled tribes, and later the Tuhoe, wishing to protect their highland home, marched to join Waikato tribesmen. The new Hauhau faith fluttered across the North Island from Taranaki. At Opotiki the missionary Carl Volkner was executed as a British spy. Before long, civil war spread through the region. Some *hapu* (subtribes) supported the Hauhau, while others were loyal to Queen Victoria. The Queen's Maori prevailed. Government confiscation of rebel land began, and a number of rebels were sent into exile in the Chatham Islands.

MAORI MOSES LEADS HIS PEOPLE

One of those exiled was a former schooner skipper and trader named Te Kooti. He had fought for the Queen, but many Maoris and Europeans of Poverty Bay conspired to be rid of this nouveau-riche Maori who both threatened traditional tribal life and undercut the local European trader.

Denounced as a Hauhau spy, he was exiled without trial to the distant Chatham Islands. In 1868, after two years of exile, he masterminded an astonishing escape, seeing himself as a Maori Moses destined to lead his people back to the promised land. With nearly two hundred armed men, and a hundred women and children, he

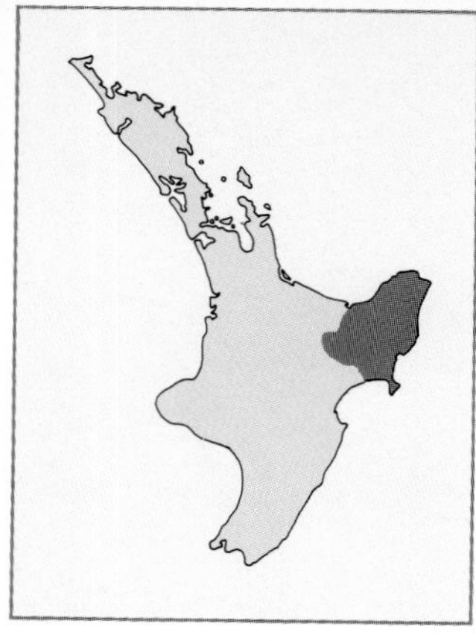

LAND OF PROUD WARRIORS

sailed to Poverty Bay. Although he protested that his intentions were peaceful, armed Europeans tried to check his progress into the Urewera. They were left counting their dead. The rebels then took terrible vengeance for their lost land. Te Kooti and his followers swooped down on Poverty Bay and in one night left thirty-three colonists and thirty-seven Maoris dead.

The Poverty Bay massacre was the most shocking incident in the years of strife between Maori and Europeans, and triggered the most ferocious fighting of the eighteen-sixties. Although successful in lightning strikes, Te Kooti was defeated in pitched battles against the combined strengths of East Coast tribesmen and colonial troops at Ngatapa behind Poverty Bay and later at Te Porere on the Volcanic Plateau. He escaped to the Maori-ruled King Country, where eventually he was granted an official pardon. While the names of most who hunted him have been forgotten, Te Kooti is still remembered, particularly among followers of the Ringatu faith, which he founded in his last years.

In the eighteen-seventies the town of Gisborne was established and became the gateway for hundreds of European settlers. In the back country of Poverty Bay and all the way north, forests were burned, grass was sown, and sheep and cattle were grazed. The reckless burning continued in some areas until the nineteen-twenties. It often led to erosion, only recently checked by a new planting program.

Only part of this back country is European-owned. Some is leased from Maori owners, and much territory north of Gisborne is still under tribal control. While elsewhere in the northern North Island Maori tribes were left demoralised by defeat, the East Coast's Ngati Porou retained both their tribal pride and most of their land. It was natural that from the eighteen-nineties the region should become a base for a determined Maori effort to retain racial and cultural identity.

The Ngati Porou have produced many leaders in peace and war. The most notable of these was Sir Apirana Ngata (1874-1950), the Maori politician who did much to prepare a place in the twentieth century for his people. Roughly two-thirds of the East Coast-Urewera region's rural population, and a third of the population of Gisborne, are Maori. The finely carved meeting-houses that can be seen every few kilometres along the region's roads attest to the nationwide Maori

Top: *Holidaymakers from all over the North Island enjoy the golden sands and good surfing and fishing at the beaches near Gisborne. Camping areas with cabins, caravan sites and picnic areas are available near most beaches. The crayfishing is especially good here* **Above:** *An ancient pohutukawa tree growing at Te Araroa. With its twenty-two trunks, it is said to be the biggest in New Zealand* **Right:** *Margaret Biddle, a Maori safari guide, leads week-long treks from Ruatahuna. The wide, Maori-farmed valley is the traditional stronghold of the Tuhoe people. Six meeting-houses in the area reflect the continuing spiritual strength of the tribe* **Far right:** *Wyn McFarlane is a well-known member of the Tuhoe community at Ruatahuna*

Left: *Paua (or abalone) shell shines from this Maori carving in the Memorial Hall at Ruatoria. The hall commemorates the gallantry of a local tribesman during World War II* **Top:** *A carving of impressive symmetry forms part of the Maori meeting-house at Mataatua, built for Te Kooti during the 1870s* **Above:** *The renovated Rongopai meeting-house at Waituhi is one of New Zealand's most remarkable*

renaissance which began here. Many of them were carved in the first half of the twentieth century, the most impressive by a pupil at Ngata's school, Pine Taiapa, who enshrined the traditions of his people in the wood of the totara tree.

The heartland of the Urewera, on the other hand, remained a mystery and the Tuhoe people proudly recalcitrant after their alliance with Te Kooti. Few Europeans travelled through the territory in the eighteen-eighties, and hostility to the building of a road in the eighteen-nineties brought two hundred troops into the district. Later, in the lonely settlement of Maungapohatu, the Maori prophet Rua Kenana (1869-1937) founded a self-contained one-thousand-strong community which wanted no part of the First World War. In 1916, a column of armed police rode into the Urewera to arrest Rua on the pretext that he had breached the country's liquor laws. After a brief battle in which one of Rua's sons and another Maori were killed, Rua was led off to imprisonment and trial. In return for his release he was later seen favouring the conscription of Maoris for the European war.

Government purchase of land for the conservation of forest began in the nineteen-twenties. Most of the Urewera is now a national park. Many of the dark, durable Tuhoe have moved to the timber-based communities of the Volcanic Plateau. Of those who remain, some are farmers, others hunters. Much of their land remains as it was when humans first arrived.

Elsewhere, everything has changed. Gisborne has grown into a busy port and provincial city of thirty-three thousand people, supported by market gardening, fishing and food processing in the fertile Poverty Bay area. Local grapes contribute to some of the country's best wines. But the cattle and sheep stations backing the coast, with their Maori cowboys, still give the region its character. In its small, largely Maori communities, memorials to the local dead of two world wars are as much a part of tribal tradition as ancestral fortresses. This is still a land of warriors.

Sturdily-buttressed against sea winds, the Catholic church at Raukokore has a whalebone arch outside its main door, a reminder of pioneering days. The tiny communities along the coast of this region often began as whaling settlements

WATERFALLS AND WILDERNESS

No reach of wilderness in New Zealand is more resonant with the human story than the Urewera National Park

The dense forest is lavishly laced with lakes, rivers and waterfalls and with the legends and tragic story of the Tuhoe people who made this high terrain their own. It is to the landscape itself that the Tuhoe trace their ancestry. Tuhoe folklore invested every tree, rock and river with meaning, and summits were linked genealogically with the most powerful chiefs. This was the realm of Tawhirimatea, the Maori god of storm whose winds cleansed the soul, and Tane, the Maori god of the forest, who was never more revered than here.

But the name of their domain has a more mortal origin. Maori warriors never slept with their women on the eve of battle. Without his wife for warmth, a chief named Mura Kareke slept too close to a campfire, suffered emasculating damage and died of shock and shame. His death is commemorated in the name *Urewera*, which means 'burnt genitals'.

Above: *Once a system of valleys, vast Lake Waikaremoana was created by a huge landslide over two thousand years ago*
Left: *The lake's name means a 'sea of rippling waters'*

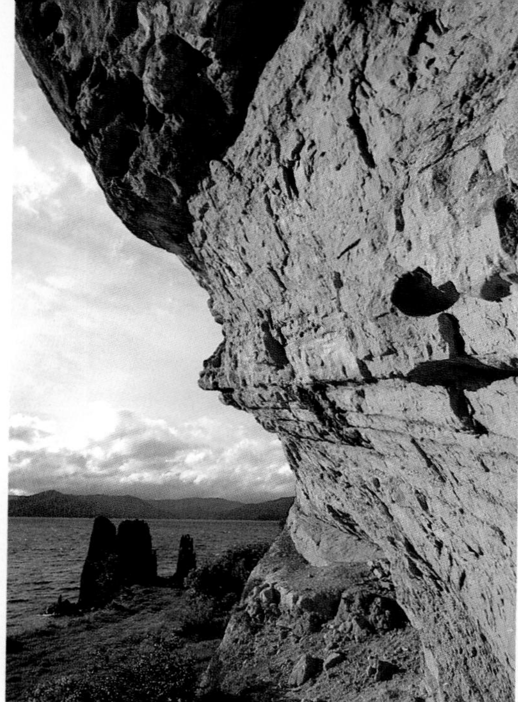

According to Maori legend the lake was created by a water monster, which is still concealed below its calm surface

They may have been fierce fighters, especially when defending their territory against revenge-seeking lowland tribesmen, but the Tuhoe must have expended just as much ferocity on their daily survival in so inhospitable a place. Their mountain waters were empty of eels and low in other fish. The kumara could not be cultivated. It was not until the potato was introduced that they had a staple crop. They lived off roots, berries and birds; and forest rats were a delicacy. Even flax for the weaving of protective clothing was not plentiful. 'Many of them have never seen the sea', Captain Gilbert Mair recorded of the Tuhoe, in 1871. '[They] are a wild, restless set with large shaggy heads of hair and clad in mats made from coarse fibres.' Another early observer wrote, 'Mountain and bush bred, they are as active as cats, and it is marvellous to see [one] with his swag and rifle run up and down hills covered with dense undergrowth through which Europeans would move at a snail's pace. . . their feet, as a rule, are very large'.

STRATEGY OF ISOLATION

When Europeans first arrived in New Zealand, they left the spartan Tuhoe alone. The tribe was too poor to interest traders, the land too rugged to tempt settlers. A missionary station that was set up in 1847 lasted only five years. It was another seventy years before missionaries successfully established a second station.

Meanwhile, Te Kooti (see page 169) used the mountains as a base for his campaign against British colonists and their Maori allies. The Tuhoe never hesitated to send their sons to their death for a cause in which they believed, and Te Kooti, though not of their tribe, provided such a cause. They gave him their loyalty and in return suffered huge losses. Their crops were destroyed, their animals slaughtered, and many of those who survived starved. Entire Tuhoe communities were extinguished. After the horror ended, Te Kooti was (and still is) revered as a prophet of divine inspiration. His Ringatu faith, based mainly on his reading of the Old Testament, still fills Tuhoe life with meaning.

Not until the end of the nineteenth century was Queen Victoria's writ said to run here. It was also said that 'the Tuhoe tribe have not very much use for Christianity'. Long after Maori rebels had compromised with the colonists elsewhere, the Tuhoe remained hostile to intruders. Pursuing a strategy of isolation, they made certain that tracks into the interior remained rough and confusing. Surveyors and road-builders were treated with suspicion and hostility. Tuhoe feeling against outsiders was reinforced in 1916 by the gunfire that ended Rua Kenana's commune of one thousand people at Maungapohatu (see page 168). Only in 1930 was a road finally completed through this isolated territory.

THE LAW OF THE NATURAL WORLD

Even now the outside world has not made much impression. If the isolation of the Tuhoe has ended, it is because many of them have gone out to work in the forest and timber towns of the Volcanic Plateau and in the larger New Zealand cities. Te Kooti and Rua Kenana remain their heroes, and the Ringatu faith is not easily discarded. They leave with the knowledge that they can, as the Tuhoe proverb prescribes, return to the mountains for a purifying of soul in the winds of the storm god Tawhirimatea. The law of the natural world still prevails. The tribesmen who remain are largely farmers, forestry workers, hunters of deer and trappers of opossum.

The wild hills of the Urewera country near Ruatahuna were once heavily populated by the Tuhoe people. Now many have left, although Ruatahuna is still the tribe's headquarters

Today's visitors will also find reason to rejoice in the Tuhoe wilderness. They may see it as the nineteenth-century ethnologist Elsdon Best did in his pioneer study *Children of the Mist*, 'a land driven by the great forces of nature in times long passed away, but now a fair land of many charms, forest clad [and] a land of myths'.

Geologically speaking, however, the Urewera is young country. It is still being sculpted by wind, water and earthquake. Starkly eroded heights, deep canyons and crashing rivers lend it distinction. Forests – of totara, kahikatea, rimu, northern rata, tawa on lower ground, and hard

Colourful lupin and sober pine fleck the approach to Urewera National Park. The park has extensive walking tracks

Above: *The spectacular cascading streams of Papakorito Falls are accessible from Lake Waikaremoana by gentle walking tracks* **Right:** *The massive rock formations at the edge of the lake are a remainder of the rockfall that created it*

red and silver beech, higher – cling to the steepest slopes and literally hold the land together. Above eleven hundred metres, dwarfed and wind-twisted silver beech predominates in rainforests where trees are interspersed with filmy ferns, dangling lichens and glowing mosses. New Zealand's native birds – tui, kaka, kokako, pigeon (kereru), shining and long-tailed cuckoo, morepork and kiwi – all inhabit the Urewera.

High above sea level, lonely Lake Waikaremoana is the park's most impressive feature – a shimmering fifty-four square kilometre expanse of water surrounded by abrupt forest-clad ranges. According to legend, a chief drowned his delinquent daughter here. In her death throes she became a *taniwha*, a water monster, which in its desperate but unsuccessful attempts to escape filled the valleys with water and created the lake. Her spirit is said to agitate the waters even on windless days. *Waikaremoana* means 'sea of rippling waters'. Geology says that Waikaremoana is a drowned valley system, created over two thousand years ago by a huge landslide. Visitors who explore the walking track that weaves round the lake will find themselves refreshed by wind and clouds, water and birds, mountains and trees in the world of the Tuhoe.

PLACES OF INTEREST

A flowering garden flanks the walls of Wyllie Cottage, Gisborne's oldest complete dwelling

CAPE RUNAWAY

See WHANGAPARAOA.

GISBORNE

This city of about 33 000 has developed on the site of the first clash between Maori and Britons in 1769, when James Cook landed on the coast of Poverty Bay bringing an end to New Zealand's oceanic isolation. A statue of Cook in admiral's uniform, which he never wore, stands on Kaiti Hill, and there is a model of the *Endeavour* in the main street. The promontory to the south of Poverty Bay, Young Nicks Head, is named after Nicholas Young, the ship's boy who first sighted land, and whose statue stands outside the city's Olympic Pool complex. Although Cook named this shore Poverty Bay because tribesmen prevented him from replenishing his ship's larder, Gisborne is now a thriving city, spreading to the east, north and west of the Turanganui River, in which Cook moored. The population is involved in food production and processing.

The best general view of Gisborne and its surroundings can be seen from Kaiti Hill lookout. Behind this city of many bridges lie Poverty Bay's fertile plain and upland sheep stations. Gisborne is the meeting place of the Waimata and Taruheru Rivers (together they form the Turanganui). From the 1820s onwards, it was also a meeting place of cultures (under its original Maori name of Turanga), and a logical site for a trading post. Matawhero, just west of the city, is the site of the Poverty Bay massacre, where former Turanga trader and schooner skipper Te Kooti killed Europeans and Maoris in the early hours of November 10, 1868 (see page 169).

The town was surveyed and in 1870 was renamed Gisborne (after the Colonial Secretary Sir William Gisborne) to avoid confusion with the Bay of Plenty's Tauranga. Today Gisborne is a pleasant resort, which also serves as a base for exploring the East Coast seaboard, and for ventures into the Urewera and Raukumara interior. Gisborne has a very warm climate, claiming (after Ruatoria) the North Island's second highest recorded temperature. With a large Maori population (one in three of its citizens), the city also serves as a market centre for many more Maoris living to the north. At the foot of Kaiti Hill, Poho-o-Rawiri meeting-house (1925) is the centre of Maori community life, incorporating much old carving. At Manutuke, south-west of the city, are the two remarkable 19th century meeting-houses, Te Mana-o-Turanga and Poho-o-Rukupo. Manutuke's church, Tokotoru Tapu (1913) also has a carved interior.

The Rongopai meeting-house (1888) at Waituhi was hastily built for Te Kooti's return to Poverty Bay, which never happened. Its interior is colourfully painted instead of carved, with panels reinterpreting Maori tradition and depicting scenes from colonial life. Maori art might well have developed along these lines, but disapproving tribal elders virtually closed the building (thus preserving the paintings). Meeting-houses may be visited with local Maori permission. It is customary to make a *koha*, donation, towards maintenance.

The Gisborne Museum and Arts Centre in Stout Street (open Tuesday to Friday, 10–4.30; weekends and holidays 2–4.30) tells the story of both races in Poverty Bay and on the East Coast, with photographs, relics (including a whaleboat), and a diorama reconstructing Cook's arrival. Nearby Wyllie Cottage (1872) is the oldest complete dwelling in Gisborne and the first of European construction to be built across the Taruheru River. Beside it can be seen one of the 'sledge homes' for which Poverty Bay was famous. Because local Maoris refused to sell land, prospective colonists dwelled in rough huts such as this. The runners under the hut allowed it to be bullock-drawn from one muddy site to another.

Today surfers from all over the North Island enjoy Gisborne's superb beaches. To the south, on the coastal route to Wairoa, are the Morere hot springs. In the hill country to the west are the impressive Rere Falls, set in a picnic reserve. A kilometre or two beyond this, the site of Te Kooti's old stronghold, Ngatapa Mountain, can be seen. To the north, a spectacular coastal highway leads via TE ARAROA and CAPE RUNAWAY to Opotiki. Alternatively, there is the equally dramatic inland road through the Waioeka Gorge with wonderful forest and river views.

HICKS BAY

Midway on the GISBORNE – Opotiki road, this spectacular cleft in the East Coast was named after one of Cook's officers. A wharf and derelict freezing works testify to the decline of sea transport on this coast. Maori pride is reflected in a distinctively decorated meeting-house called Tuwhakairiora. Famed for its crayfish, Hicks Bay is a popular summer campsite, especially for fishermen. There is a glow-worm grotto a short walk from the hillside motel above Horseshoe Bay.

LAKE WAIKAREMOANA

The largest gem in the Urewera's crown, this breathtaking 54 square kilometre lake is fed by waterfalls, and surrounded by forest-clad mountain ramparts (see also page 164). There is a spectacular 44 kilometre walking track round the lake with splendid fishing and swimming, and accommodation huts (information at park headquarters at Aniwaniwa). There are short and long walks and scenic launch excursions. Launches can also be hired to drop tramping parties at points on the lake's shore. Waikaremoana was the setting for sorties made by colonial troops and Maori allies against the rebel guerilla leader Te Kooti (see page 169). At Onepoto, at the south-eastern end, the lake outlet is used for hydro-electricity. Also at Onepoto are the remains of a military redoubt, and the graves of men who succumbed to Te Kooti or to the rough terrain. The climb up Panekiri Bluff to Pukenui trig is climaxed by a magnificent view of the lake in its lofty setting, some 600 metres above sea level.

MAUNGAPOHATU

A score of kilometres on a rough road east of RUATAHUNA, this remote settlement is at the heart of the Urewera country. The fortress-like and often mist-shrouded Maungapohatu Mountain rises 1366 metres beside it. With its cliffs, caves and crags, the mountain – a symbol of Tuhoe

APIRANA NGATA

Te Araroa, north-west of Tikitiki, was the birthplace of Apirana Ngata (1874–1950), one of the most accomplished and influential New Zealand leaders in this century

Ngata's influence was felt in all areas of national life. A fine scholar, he was the first Maori university graduate, and one of the few men of the time to hold a double degree. He was also a great politician, an incisive thinker, a successful farmer and a collector of hundreds of Maori songs and chants.

Among his most impressive accomplishments was a school of Maori arts and crafts at Rotorua, which inspired the creation throughout the country of many great meeting-houses that have since become community focal points. Ngata had tireless energy. In his youth he helped found the Young Maori Party which aimed at working through parliament to benefit the Maori people, especially by land reform and raised living standards. He was on the boards of museums, societies and institutions, and for many years he was a member of parliament and a cabinet minister.

His lasting memorial is less tangible than achievements such as meeting-houses, schools and forums. He helped his people to lift up their spirit and to share in the benefits of a changed world while retaining their culture, dignity and vision – the sense of identity we know as *Maoritanga*.

Sir Apirana Ngata, the great modern New Zealander, is still very widely respected

A gifted orator and a fine leader, Ngata was a great modern New Zealander. He was knighted, and received an honorary doctorate from the University of New Zealand.

identity – was once a burial ground. A meeting-house and derelict dwellings survive from the commune of 1000 people that the prophet Rua Kenana established here early in the 20th century. The commune was ended by European gunfire in 1916, but the land about is farmed by people who still revere Rua's memory, many of them his direct descendants. The meeting-house is still frequently used by Tuhoe Maori returning from the city in search of their Urewera roots. The dry-weather road into the settlement is often closed (ask locally). Walking tracks, notably Rua's Track – an impressive three-day wilderness trek – also lead into Maungapohatu.

RAUKUMARA FOREST PARK

Minimally developed for public use, with few tracks and huts, this mountainous 115 000 hectare park extends between the East Coast and the Bay of Plenty. There are small patches of exotic forest, but for the most part it is beech country interspersed with native conifers. Tawari, kaikawaka, pink pine, mountain toatoa and broadleaf are abundant. Most of New Zealand's surviving native birds can be seen, including parakeets, kaka and brown kiwis as well as the native bat – the country's only indigenous mammal. Red deer and wild pigs flourish in the Raukumara Range, providing meat for many small Maori communities. There are brown and rainbow trout in the rivers.

The mountains make an imposing backdrop to the East Coast, and on much of the Opotiki – CAPE RUNAWAY side reach right down to the Pacific. The highest are Hikurangi, emblem of the Ngati Porou tribe (1752 metres), and Raukumara (1413 metres). Two rivers cross the park: the Raukokore and the Motu, New Zealand's most famous rafting river. The rough, breathtaking journey takes five days. Access to the park is from Old Motu Road, 35 kilometres east of Opotiki, or up the Motu River by jet boat. Information is at forest service offices at GISBORNE, Opotiki, RUATORIA or Rotorua.

RUATAHUNA

This wide, grassy Maori-farmed valley on the upper reaches of the Whakatane River has a few scattered dwellings, a motel named after the guerilla leader Te Kooti, and a general store. The traditional headquarters of the Tuhoe tribe, it was ravaged and razed by colonial militia and their Maori allies in 1869 after Te Kooti's Poverty Bay massacre. In this tiny community, six meeting-houses in a radius of 4 kilometres bear witness to the spiritual survival of the Tuhoe people. The most impressive of these is Te Whai-a-te-Motu, at Mataatua, a 4 kilometre detour off the highway. Inspired by Te Kooti, it was built between 1870 and 1888. Its name, 'flight across the island', celebrates Te Kooti's escape from colonial vengeance. Inside, folk art blends with traditional Maori carving, and painted rafters tell of the life of the Tuhoe in the Urewera forest. The Tuhoe ancestor Toroa, the navigator of the *Mataatua* canoe, has been carved wearing European dress under a Maori cloak. Ask permission locally to enter, and leave a *koha*, donation, for the upkeep and care of the building.

On the way to Mataatua is a small cemetery with graves of troops killed in the campaign against Te Kooti and the Tuhoe. Maori hunters and trappers still live in this community. Some have also become safari guides, leading five- and seven-day treks from Ruatahuna (contact Te Rehuwai Safaris).

RUATORIA

This small rural community on the East Coast is the largest town north of GISBORNE (130 kilometres). It is the headquarters of the prosperous Ngati Porou, overlooked by their sacred tribal mountain of Hikurangi. Although mostly allied with the British in the 19th century, they have made very little concession, especially in land, to European New Zealand. In keeping with the past, however, the Ngati Porou contributed more dead to the battlefields of both world wars than any other tribe.

THE MASTER CARVER

The small town of Tikitiki, almost half way between Opotiki and Gisborne, was home to Pine Taiapa, New Zealand's greatest Maori carver

The carver Pine Taiapa, who rediscovered the art of using the chisel and the adze

St Mary's Anglican Church in Tikitiki, which was started in 1924 to commemorate Ngati Porou servicemen who died in the First World War, is a fine example of the richly decorated Maori churches of New Zealand. It is also notable as the first building worked on by Pine Taiapa (1901–72), the master carver of the modern period, who is buried in the marae graveyard just below the main church building.

It was at Tikitiki in about 1925 that the young Taiapa first picked up a chisel and began to carve. He soon proved his enormous gifts and dedication, and he went to Rotorua to study at the school of crafts founded by Apirana Ngata. Before long Taiapa the student had become Taiapa the teacher, but his realisation that modern carvers had become copiers rather than creators led him to find a way to breathe life back into a stilted and dying tradition.

The breakthrough came when, after a long search, on a remote farm he came across one of the few remaining Maoris who had been trained in the use of the adze, although he no longer practised it. Taiapa then relearned the creative rudiments of wood carving.

Taiapa was also thoroughly versed in Maori lore and legend. Few contemporaries could match his knowledge of genealogy. This deep understanding of his culture is reflected in all his buildings. From 1927 to 1940, he worked on sixty-four buildings.

In 1940 he completed his masterpiece, the great multi-tribal meeting-house at Waitangi. He then went to North Africa as a captain with the Maori Battalion. Wounded, he returned to take up his chisel and adze again, and worked on another thirty-nine buildings before his death.

Hikurangi, the highest peak in the Raukumara Range, is held in great awe by the Maori

In the town, the carvings of Whakarua Memorial Hall recall the gallantry of Second Lieutenant Moananui-a-Kiwa Ngarimu, who won the Victoria Cross posthumously in the 1943 Tunisian campaign. The carvings are by the great local carver, Pine Taiapa, whose work can be seen elsewhere on the East Coast, and throughout much of New Zealand, and who is buried at nearby TIKITIKI. Mangahanea Marae (3 kilometres) is the formal meeting place of the Ngati Porou tribe. The marae's meeting-house, Hinetapora, was built in 1896, and some of its carvings date from before its construction.

At Waiomatatini (14 kilometres) several heroes are buried. They include tribal heroes Major Ropata Wahawaha, who campaigned ruthlessly against the Hauhau and Te Kooti in the 1860s, and Sir Apirana Ngata, the politician and famous Maori leader. Ngata's former home, 'The Bungalow', can be seen here. Near by is the Porourangi meeting-house (1888), a masterpiece of Maori carving that took 16 years to complete and was intended to end rifts among the Ngati Porou (seek permission to visit from the Maori Affairs Department in Ruatoria).

TE ARAROA

This tiny settlement near East Cape is located on an extremely long white beach that was once a Maori highway. Its name means 'the long path'. The people of the village are both fishermen and hunters. The pub at Te Araroa is said to be the world's most easterly. Close by is a 600-year-old pohutukawa tree, *Te Waha-o-Rerekohu*, which has 22 trunks, a girth of 20 metres and a spread of 37 metres, and is reputed to be the largest pohutukawa in New Zealand. Behind the beach, Ngapuhi chief Hongi Hika is said to have slaughtered many Ngati Porou on one of his raids south from the Bay of Islands. From Te Araroa it is a 21 kilometre coastal drive to the East Cape lighthouse, the easternmost point of the New Zealand mainland. The 14 metre high lighthouse stands 140 metres above sea level.

TE KAHA

Until as late as the 1930s, the lovely cove of Te Kaha was a whaling base. The pub on the site of the whaling station features some interesting photographs. The fine carvings of the Maori meeting-house are the work of John Taiapa, the brother of the celebrated Pine, and they tell of old Maori battles with the mighty whale.

Torere Memorial Church (1956) is distinctly European outside yet its interior is unmistakably Maori. There are other delightful coves and bays to the north and south of Te Kaha, with particular interest for visitors, especially for fishermen and divers.

TE PUIA SPRINGS
A tiny lakeside village 100 kilometres north of **GISBORNE**. The hot springs after which it is named are located in camping grounds behind the hotel. Natural gas, never much exploited, bursts from nearby fissures. A deviation can be taken down to the coast to charming, though deserted Waipiro, once the largest European settlement on the East Coast. It was a port where livestock was ferried ashore in surfboats, and wool shipped out. Now bypassed by the main highway, it is declining slowly; the swimming and fishing are excellent.

TIKITIKI
On the north bank of the Waiapu River estuary, 150 kilometres north of **GISBORNE**. The magnificent little Maori memorial church, St Mary's, was built in 1924 in memory of the Ngati Porou warriors who died in World War I. Its interior is richly carved and decorated. Especially notable are its *tukutuku*, or woven wall panels, and *kowhaiwhai*, rafter patterns. The Ngati Porou call St Mary's 'our cathedral'. The great Maori carver Pine Taiapa (see page 167) lived near Tikitiki as a young man, and it was here that he began his monumental work. His supreme creation, an amalgam of all tribal carving styles, is to be found in the meeting-house in the Treaty House grounds at Waitangi in the Bay of Islands (see page 52). Pine Taiapa is buried in the little graveyard beyond the Tikitiki marae, on the other side of the highway. The marae's austere meeting-house is not graced by Taiapa's work.

TOKOMARU BAY
This township, 90 kilometres north of **GISBORNE**, was named after one of the ancestral Polynesian voyaging canoes. A wharf and an old freezing works testify to an optimistic past. Other buildings straggle along the shore of this once busy port. Te Mawhai, the point at the south end of the bay, was contested during the Hauhau insurgency of the 1860s, when local tribesmen were divided over the rights and wrongs of that rebel faith. Women, two warriors and three elderly European whalers miraculously held the point against the determined Hauhau assault from the north of the bay.

TOLAGA BAY
A mainly Maori community of only 500, 56 kilometres north of **GISBORNE**. James Cook had his first friendly dealings with New Zealand Maori here in October 1769. Cook's first amicable contact with the Maori was actually at Anaura Bay just to the north, but the locals directed him here for safer anchorage. The original name for the bay was Uawa, but the present name, recorded by Cook, is possibly a corruption of *Rtaraki*, meaning 'wind'. The township's streets are named after men of Cook's crew.

A 5 kilometre walk there and back, Cooks Cove Walkway leads from the south end of the bay (take Wharf Road turnoff, 2 kilometres south) to the amphitheatre-like cove where the *Endeavour* anchored for six days. The forest that once greened the cove has gone, but the 'most Noble Arch or Cavern' (popularly called the Hole in the Wall) that bewitched Joseph Banks (and was later painted by botanical artist Sydney Parkinson) is still here.

UREWERA NATIONAL PARK
These 212 670 hectares of the North Island's most rugged and striking wilderness are still invested with the folklore of the enigmatic Tuhoe tribe, who made their homes in these densely forested highlands and fought off intruders for centuries (see page 162). The two leaders and folk-heroes to whom the Tuhoe have given allegiance, Te Kooti and Rua Kenana, are celebrated in a large mural by artist Colin McCahon, at national park headquarters at Aniwaniwa,

MAUNGAPOHATU'S PROPHET

Maungapohatu, one of the most prominent peaks of the Huiarau Range of the Urewera country, is where Rua Kenana Hepetipa founded a charismatic Maori sect

This two-storey temple designed by Rua once stood near the present meeting-house

Rua Kenana Hepetipa (1869–1937), whose father was killed at Makaretu, fighting for Te Kooti, formed a sect which was just one of several that arose out of the Maori struggle for survival in the nineteenth century. Like most of these faiths, it was based largely on the Old Testament, identifying the tribulations of its followers with the sufferings of the Jews, and predicting an ultimate glorious triumph.

Rua felt himself to have been called as a prophet, fulfilling a prediction by Te Kooti. Gathering his followers, he led them to Maungapohatu, where they set about creating a new Jerusalem at the foot of the mountain.

The Tuhoe, unlike many other tribes, had held on to most of their land, for the Urewera was inaccessible to the new settlers. The Tuhoe also had a reputation as superb guerilla fighters. What Rua gave them, in addition, was the will and spirit to hew farms out of virgin bush; and a sense of destiny based on religious fervour. All the land at Maungapohatu was owned in common, the labours and produce shared.

Rua's followers knew a prosperity they had never experienced before. His community flourished, but the world outside always misinterpreted his intentions. He gave thousands of hectares of the Urewera to the rest of the country as a national park, expecting in return a liquor licence of great potential profit to his community. The argument over this issue led to confrontation.

The First World War had begun and Rua chose to forbid his followers to enlist. He was goaded into angry words against the war, the King and England. In 1916, sixty armed police were sent to arrest him for sedition. Shots were fired in what was said to be the last battle between Maori and *Pakeha*, and Rua was imprisoned.

Apirana Ngata is credited with securing his release after nine months, but by that time the spirit was gone from Rua's community. Much of it had fallen into disrepair and his huge, circular temple had been demolished.

However, Rua's *mana* was not diminished by imprisonment, and he and his followers subsequently moved to Matahi, a little to the north.

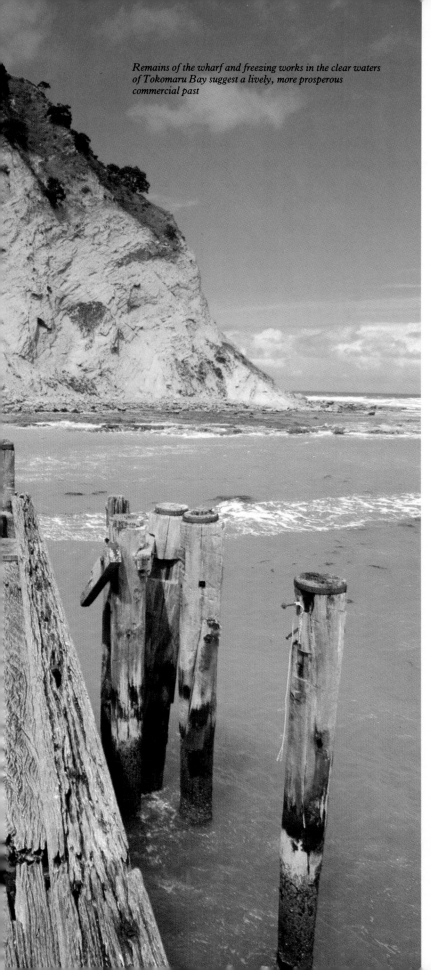

Remains of the wharf and freezing works in the clear waters of Tokomaru Bay suggest a lively, more prosperous commercial past

RIKIRANGI TE TURUKI–TE KOOTI

Lake Waikaremoana, on the southern boundary of the Urewera country, was the setting for the great manhunt for Te Kooti during the eighteen-sixties

Rikirangi Te Turuki (*c.*1830–93), known to history as Te Kooti, was supposedly on the *Pakeha* side during the battles of the eighteen-sixties. But he was accused of aiding Hauhau rebels and exiled to the Chatham Islands without trial. In 1868 he captured a ship and sailed back to the mainland just south of Gisborne. From then on, Te Kooti was pursued until he carried out his threat to attack, killing thirty-three Europeans and thirty-seven Maoris at Matawhero, Poverty Bay.

The true version of events leading up to and following the massacre has been obscured by prejudice and intertribal rivalry. What is beyond doubt is that Te Kooti was one of the most charismatic Maori leaders. He founded his own Ringatu faith, based on his vision of the Maori as being like the Jews, a chosen yet persecuted and dispossessed people.

Sketch of Te Kooti by T.H. Hill (1892)

Te Kooti had the personal magnetism of a great leader, and was a fighter of considerable brutality. But his own followers suffered worse atrocities than he ever perpetrated against his enemies – after the battle on Ngatapa Mountain in 1869, one hundred and twenty of his men were summarily executed. Although he was an object of terror to the settlers, he actually killed many more of his own people than Europeans. As a guerilla leader and master of escape in the wild country round Lake Waikaremoana, he had few equals, but his set-piece battles were disasters.

The four years Te Kooti spent on the run ended when he was given protection by King Tawhiao in the King Country. But it was not until 1883 that he received an amnesty, and in 1891 the government granted him land at Ohiwa, Bay of Plenty, where an accident led to his death.

near **LAKE WAIKAREMOANA**. Information about walking tracks, huts, hunting and fishing can be obtained from the headquarters. There is also material on the park's natural and human history. Ranger stations on the park's perimeters at Taneatua and Murupara also provide information.

From **RUATAHUNA** there are guided safari excursions through the park's remote interior. Many of the park's forest walkways follow ancient Tuhoe trails. The 44 kilometre walking track that skirts Lake Waikaremoana has accommodation huts along the way. Only one road crosses the park, from Murupara on the Volcanic Plateau to Wairoa in Hawke's Bay, but an approach may be made from the Bay of Plenty side. From the ranger station at Taneatua, where displays feature natural history and Tuhoe folklore, it is a 20 kilometre drive to the beginning of forest walkways.

WHANGAPARAOA

This Maori settlement is at the end of the magnificent marine drive from Opotiki. From here the road turns briefly inland towards **HICKS BAY** and **TE ARAROA**. *Whangaparaoa* means 'bay of whalers', and Europeans based here once raided the mammals as they passed. When the moki run in June and July, the settlement becomes a busy fishing town, with scores of Whanau-a-Apanui people returning from town and city to rejoice in the riches of their tribal shore. Cape Runaway, which encloses the bay, was named by Cook when Maori canoes fled at the sound of his cannon. Just south, on the pohutukawa-fringed shore, Waihau Bay is a big-game fishing base with a long-established guest house, a licensed restaurant and views of the coast up to Cape Runaway. A dozen kilometres south-west towards **TE KAHA**, an elegant church (1894) stands among Norfolk pines at Raukokore.

WHANGARA

This seaside settlement, 27 kilometres north of **GISBORNE**, is said to have been begun by Paikea, the founding father of the Ngati Porou people. A carving of Paikea mounted on his whale can be seen in the *tekoteko*, carved figure, that surmounts the meeting-house. The carving and the meeting-house (1939) are the work of the great Maori carver Pine Taiapa (see page 167). Ask locally for permission to view the building and do not forget a *koha*, donation.

Hawke's Bay -Wairarapa

For the traveller journeying from the north to the south of New Zealand, Hawke's Bay and the Wairarapa make a distinct transition zone. Here, rather than Cook Strait, is the divide between New Zealand north and New Zealand south. Untidily grown towns and dense settled dairyman's countryside characteristic of most of the North Island is left behind; Maori population is less conspicuous. Hawke's Bay was developed and given character by gentleman colonists: men who came with money and made even more. Both Hawke's Bay and the Wairarapa were shaken into their present shape largely by powerful landholders who saw the pastoral potential in empty hills and vacant valleys purchased from the Maori. So in this region New Zealand's great sheep stations at last become conspicuous – and landscapes which, according to Hawke's Bay's most vivid chronicler, naturalist-farmer H. Guthrie Smith, were 'stamped, jammed, hauled, murdered into grass'. Not that nature has been a passive bystander. Earthquake, flood and erosion have since had a say in the making of the region too.

Both Hawke's Bay and the Wairarapa are backed by the North Island's mountain spine – the Kaweka, Ruahine, Tararua and Rimutaka Ranges – and both are part of the North Island's eastern hill country. In both regions there is seldom more than sixty kilometres between summit and sea. The Heretaunga Plain, near Hastings, is the only large patch of lowland. The climate is mild and Mediterranean, with low rainfall and many hours of sunshine.

A NEW KIND OF GENTRY

Moa-hunting Maori began the firing of the forest along the coastal strip. Classic Maori folklore says that the region was first settled by Kahungunu, son of the navigator of the *Takitimu* canoe. The barbed promontory to the south of the blue bight of Hawke Bay (distinguished from the region Hawke's Bay by the lack of a possessive) was seen as being *Te Matau-a-Maui*, the 'fish-hook of Maui', still embedded in the trembling torso of the North Island, *Te Ika-a-Maui*, the mighty fish of the Polynesian folk-hero.

In 1769 Cook named Hawke Bay after Sir Edward Hawke, Britain's First Lord of the Admiralty. Ngati Kahungunu tribesmen sailed out to the *Endeavour* to barter dried fish for European cloth. When they attempted to snatch away a Tahitian boy who had accompanied Cook, the ship's guns opened fire. The boy escaped, but three Maoris were killed. Thereafter *Te Matau-a-Maui* was marked on mariners' maps as Cape Kidnappers. After searching unsuccessfully for a harbour farther down the coast, Cook sailed north again, and left a name even more significant for the headland at which he turned back: Cape Turnagain. It was here, after circumnavigating the North Island, that he later determined that New Zealand was not the limb of a continent.

Europeans settlers took fifty years or more to arrive, and then it was as whalers establishing bases at locations like Mahia and Wairoa. In 1840 there were perhaps a thousand Maoris and twenty Europeans living along the shores of Hawke's Bay. In the eighteen-forties William Colenso founded a mission station at Ahuriri. He introduced fruit and grains to the local Maori. Meanwhile, Wellington settlers began moving into the Wairarapa and negotiating with Maori landowners for the lease or purchase of land. By 1847 there were fifteen sheep or cattle stations; similar terrain to the north in Hawke's Bay was also eyed with interest.

In 1851 the colonial government began purchasing Maori land. Five years later over a million acres (nearly half a million hectares) were divided between more than thirty sheep stations, and new stations were established on leased Maori land. The human population was tiny compared with the livestock numbers: more than a hundred and thirty thousand sheep, three thousand cattle and four hundred horses. In isolated homesteads a new landowning gentry began to prosper.

To the south of Hawke's Bay, and the north of the Wairarapa lay the Seventy Mile Bush, a dark rainforest swarming with birds. After the success the former Danish prime minister Ditlev Monrad and his sons had found farming Manawatu, the colonial government of the eighteen-seventies began recruiting Scandinavians. As many as five thousand Norwegians and Danes finally arrived in New Zealand – most of them on assisted passages – to clear and farm the district. They were exploited and forced to pay far more for their tangled acres than British-born settlers ever paid for more amiable terrain.

Their tenacity founded townships like Norsewood and Dannevirke, 'Danes' work'. Dannevirke settlers split thousands of totara sleepers for the railway track that was to end their isolation. Later they mingled and intermarried with their British neighbours. Scandinavian names are still common in the region; wooden Scandinavian-style churches are another legacy.

An impressive episode in the Hawke's Bay–Wairarapa story was the reclamation of the alluvial Heretaunga Plain. Rivers were controlled and the land was drained and subdivided into smallholdings. Market gardening began to develop and Hastings expanded. By 1904 the district's first cannery was in business. Today the cultivation, canning and sale of fruit and vegetables provide employment for many.

NATURE'S BONUS

Napier also grew as a result of reclamation, thanks to nature rather than to human intervention. One morning in February 1931 an earthquake destroyed Napier and much of Hastings, taking more than two hundred and fifty lives. Though it was scant compensation, nature paid a dividend. More than three thousand hectares of new land were thrown up from the sea. As rebuilding began, cramped Napier expanded across the plain. The first buildings were low and designed to withstand earthquakes. Only later did they rise above two storeys. Much of the commercial area was built in the Art Deco style typical of the thirties. Recently Napier has become known as an Aladdin's Cave of Art Deco jewels.

In other respects too, Napier has made itself a resort against the odds. Its grovelly shore slopes shapely into wild surf. So man has laboured to make good nature's lack. A lavishly illuminated Marine Parade, with coloured lights strung among Norfolk pines and all the fun of the fair, has taken over the seafront. A distinctive medley of traditional bed-and-breakfast houses and modern motels, coffee shops and restaurants gives the city seafront something of the character of Britain's Blackpool or Brighton. With its mix of old and new, there is no city in New Zealand quite like it. Today, conservationists are fighting to preserve Napier's distinctive blend.

A few kilometres inland, rebuilt Hastings is a less raffish city at the heart of a thriving horticultural and agricultural district. Sheep and thoroughbred studs, extensive market gardens and orchards thrive on the fertile Heretaunga Plain. Not only do Hawke's Bay fruit and vegetables nourish New Zealanders – they are exported all over the world. In addition, the vineyards here contribute up to half of New Zealand's annual wine production.

The Wairarapa region, between the Tararua Range and the precipitous Pacific coast, is less populated than Hawke's Bay. A chain of settlements stretches along the lowland from

ROLLING SHEEP LANDS BEGIN

southern Hawke's Bay to the Rimutaka Range. Communities such as Pahiatua, Eketahuna, Masterton, Carterton, Greytown and Featherston are typical of rural New Zealand.

The upper Wairarapa was tamed in the last decades of the nineteenth century. Backbreaking labour cleared the heavily timbered Forty Mile Bush (the southern arm of the Seventy Mile Bush). Milling villages grew and then vanished again. Now cattle and sheep graze where giant trees were toppled and fires raged.

The lower Wairarapa was the first substantial segment of New Zealand settled by Europeans. They were mainly Wellington colonists seeking to escape the hilly prison of the New Zealand Company settlement after its founding in 1840. They founded great sheep runs on open land already cleared by old Maori fires. Later, modest smallholders arrived, led by men of democratic temper, battling for a place in the sun. Today, a rail tunnel through the Rimutaka Range and fast trains mean that the lower Wairarapa is still an accessible retreat from Wellington.

The wild Wairarapa coast has never been a tourist draw; it is merely magnificent. From the cleft in the coast called Akitio down to the mighty sweep of Palliser Bay, the sea shovels sand between steep limbs of rock. The surf soars off reefs, which have ripped open ships and left drowned seamen strewn ashore. Lighthouses flash from perilous headlands.

Only Castlepoint and Riversdale Beach resemble resorts. Palliser Bay is said to be the place where the Polynesian navigator Kupe shook the sea from his feet, and was named (like Castle Point headland) by James Cook. Its lonely beaches are divided by rivers and rocky headlands and backed by tussock-covered hills. Local people run sheep, gather seaweed and crayfish or surfcast, and there are farmhouses and a few wind-savaged holiday homes. For those who wish a whisper of the world as humans first found it, this barbarous coast is a bonanza.

Just inland from the mighty sweep of Palliser Bay, at the western foot of the Aorangi Mountains, rise the rocky forms of huge grey pillars backed by sheer fluted cliffs known as the Putangirua Pinnacles. They are reached from Te Kopi

THE DELIGHTS OF ART DECO

In the aftermath of one of New Zealand's greatest natural disasters, a remarkable architectural heritage was created

At mid-morning on February 3, 1931, an earthquake measuring 7.9 on the Richter scale surged through Hawke's Bay and the northern Wairarapa, demolishing the two major centres of Napier and Hastings. Buildings still standing were ravaged by fire, and survivors mourned two hundred and fifty-six dead.

Despite the Depression of the early nineteen-thirties, funds were quickly found for reconstruction. Elsewhere in New Zealand urban construction was at a standstill, but here two cities rose again in defiance of nature. In seaside Napier where death and destruction had been greater, the new townscape was inspired by and dedicated to that lively style known as Art Deco. It lent the new centre of Napier – and much of neighbouring Hastings too – a twentieth-century elegance and coherence without equal in New Zealand.

Whereas Art Nouveau had been a reaction *against* the age of the machine, registering its protest through its flowing lines and organic forms, Art Deco celebrated a new era of humanity. Its angular and jazzy forms owed nothing to nature. Its links were with cubism, futurism, functionalism and other movements that distinguished the early twentieth century.

Art Deco was formally recognised in 1925, at the *Exposition Internationale des Arts Décoratifs et Industriels Modernes* in Paris (from which the style took its name). In architecture, Art Deco found its most monumental embodiment in North American cities. Ebulliently decorative, it was the distinct style of the nineteen-twenties.

After the Wall Street crash of 1929 – and the accompanying disillusion and social misery – Art Deco architecture became more austere. Past decorative excesses were seen as out of keeping with the world's cooler, more menacing climate.

The nineteen-twenties style of New York's Empire State Building imbued the rebuilding of Napier after the earthquake of 1931. Architects chose Art Deco not just for its 'modern' look – it was a style that subordinated ornament to form and function, well suited to buildings that would withstand earthquakes. The geometric designs lent themselves to casting in reinforced concrete. From simple domestic architecture (left) to details on commercial structures – zig-zag or wavy friezes, stylized lettering and sunbursts, decorative panels – the style stamped itself on Napier

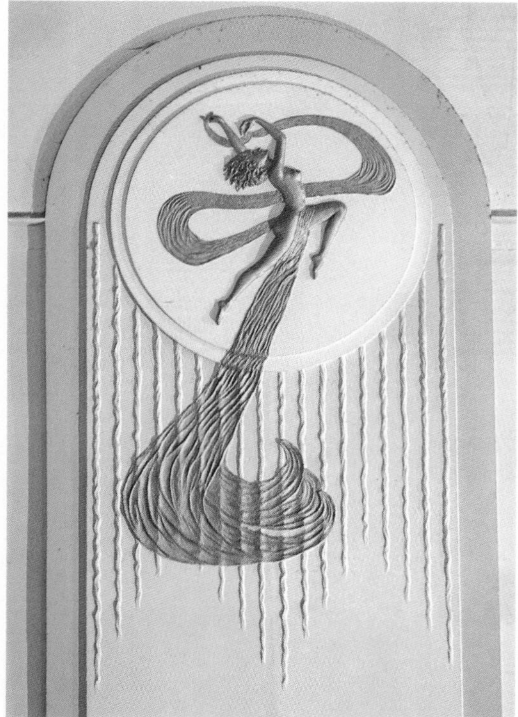

Detail from the facade of Kidson's Building shows architect H. Alfred Hill's favourite zig-zag motif

As they rose again, Napier and Hastings became nurseries for the favoured architectural styles of the nineteen-thirties: Spanish, purged classical, and above all Art Deco. Today Hawke's Bay is a showcase of that decade's architecture. Much of this legacy is due to the talented Napier architect Louis Hay (1881–1948). Although he had never been to North America or Europe, he was already familiar with the work of the American architect Henry Hobson Richardson. He was also influenced by the architects Frank Lloyd Wright and Louis Sullivan who had reshaped the city of Chicago at the end of the nineteenth century.

Napier's State Theatre. . . Art Deco accepted new materials and mass production as suitable for artistic expression

As the rebuilding of Napier began, the town's architects (including Hay) joined forces. They rejected the ornamented pseudo-classical style of former commercial building in New Zealand, favouring a simple geometric style, sparingly highlighted rather than overwhelmed by decorative motifs – Art Deco. In seaside Napier, the buildings they designed seem to soak up the sun and sea. Battling to keep pace with builders, architects and their staff laboured in shifts to complete working drawings for business premises and major public buildings. In a short time the most concentrated collection of Art Deco buildings in the world had arisen. Building continued even after the business areas of Napier and Hastings were functioning again.

The T. & G. Building on Marine Parade. . . strict classical lines, yet part of a remarkably homogeneous cityscape

During the following three or four decades the people of Hawke's Bay took this architectural bonanza for granted. Many had even begun to resent the rather dated character of the post-earthquake construction. It reminded them of death and destruction, rather than of a life-enhancing miracle of urban resurrection.

The Bank of New Zealand in Hastings Street is distinctive for its use of traditional Maori motifs in its decoration

In recent years the work of the designers and builders of Napier and Hastings has been rediscovered. Citizens have become proud of their remarkable heritage. 'Napier', said a visiting British scholar Dr Neil Cossens, 'represents the most complete and significant group of Art Deco buildings in the world, and is comparable with Bath as an example of a planned landscape in a cohesive style. Napier is without doubt unique.'

The cleaned and repainted Art Deco facades of Napier and Hastings now glow again, and the NZ Historic Places Trust is listing buildings. Already visitors detour to these cities to take in nineteen-thirties streets and buildings rarely to be seen other than in movie reconstructions. An extraordinary decade has been perfectly preserved.

The splendid entrance of the National Tobacco Company Building, now Rothmans, in Bridge Street, Ahuriri

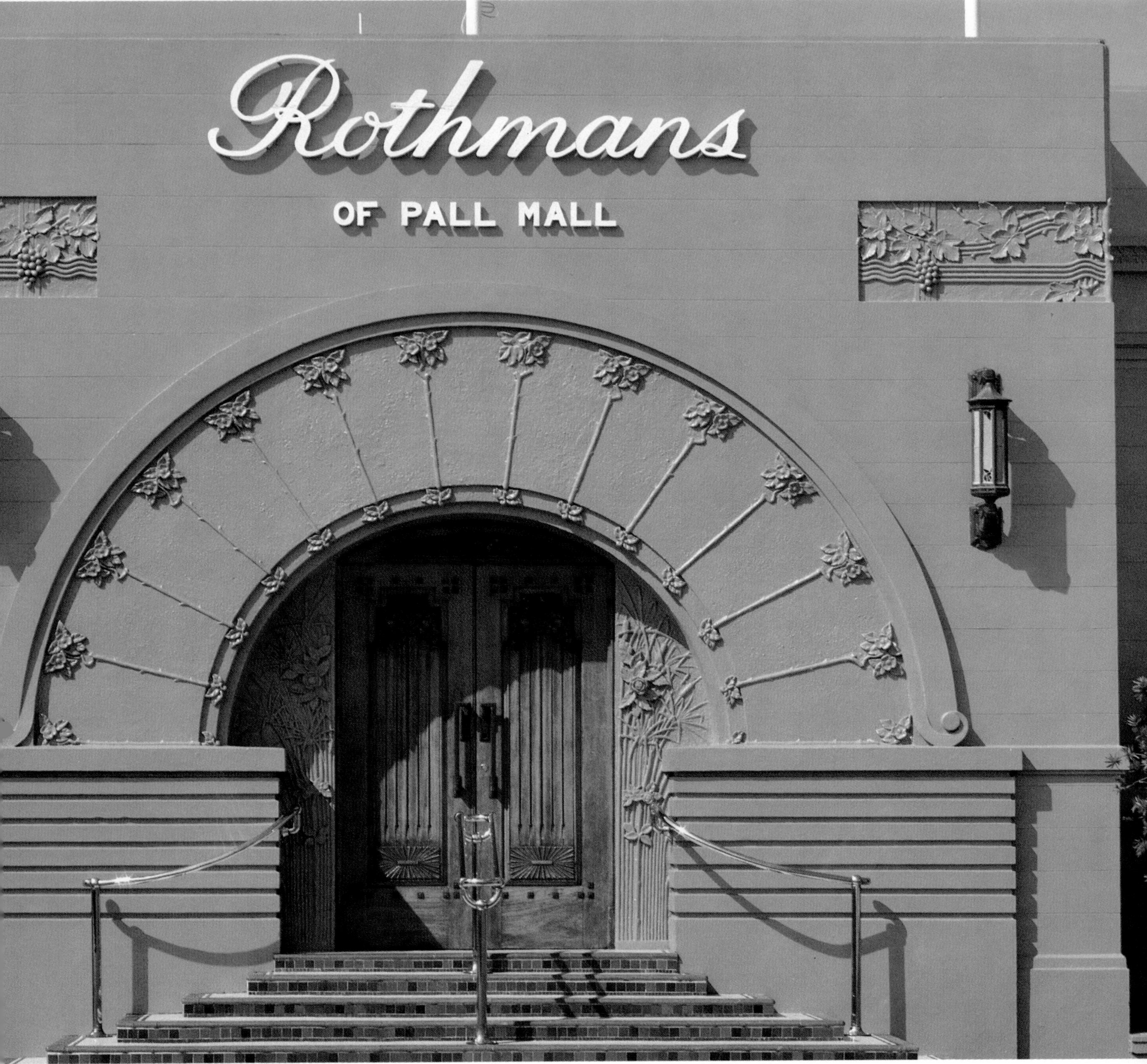
Rothmans
OF PALL MALL

PLACES OF INTEREST

CAPE KIDNAPPERS

The promontory named by James Cook after Maoris attempted to kidnap a young Tahitian boy sailing on the *Endeavour*. Its original name was *Te Matau-a-Maui*, meaning the fish-hook of Maui. Maui was the legendary Polynesian folk hero who fished up the North Island from the deep Pacific Ocean.

The Takitimu meeting-house at Wairoa has some of the finest examples of modern Maori carving

A century after Cook's visit, the New Zealand naturalist Henry Hill discovered a newly established colony of some 50 nesting gannets on the cape. By 1914 there were some 2300 pairs nesting on high headlands. Today's estimate is 4500 pairs. A bird sanctuary established in 1933 now covers 13 hectares. It is closed during the nest-building and hatching months from July to October. From November to February the plateau on the cape teems with birds and their downy chicks. Migration to Australia begins in late February, and by May the cape is deserted. Access to the colony is by an easy 8 kilometre (2-hour) beach hike from Clifton, 21 kilometres south of **NAPIER**, (depending on tides). There is a rest hut for visitors and fresh water is available. Four-wheel-drive and tractor-drawn trailer commercial excursions can also be arranged. A ranger is on duty from November to February. Consult Napier Visitors' Information Centre and check tide times.

CARTERTON

This Wairarapa town of 4000 is a service centre for the surrounding farming district. Beyond the fat-lamb and dairy farms and the market gardens around the town are the large sheep runs of the hill country. Known as Three Mile Bush in the 19th century, Carterton began as a community of road-builders who turned to milling and farming when government funds ran out. It was later named after the popular local politician Charles Rooking Carter. The imposing public library dates from 1881; and there is a splendid Victorian cast-iron band rotunda. Near by is the Tararua Forest Park (see page 154). On the fringe of the park is Mount Holdsworth Domain with many bushwalks and a track to the summit of 1470 metre Mt Holdsworth.

CASTLEPOINT

Cook named the headland, this 'remarkable hillock which stands close to the sea', Castle Point because of its resemblance to a castle fortress. It was also known as Deliverance Cove, after missionary William Colenso's storm-beaten schooner found shelter here. Now a 23 metre high lighthouse (1913) warns ships to stay clear. The locality of Castlepoint, a former port, is one of the Wairarapa's two seaside resorts. It has surf and sheltered lagoon swimming.

DANNEVIRKE

The town's name, meaning 'Danes' Work' was also the name of the great 9th-century stone wall built in Denmark to protect the country against Saxon invaders. In the 1870s Scandinavian migrants cleared the totara forest also known as the Seventy Mile Bush. They built homes in clearings and began farms, but few survived to see affluence arrive. Today Dannevirke, with 6000 inhabitants at the centre of a prosperous district, is a fine memorial to its pioneers. The domain in Christian Street has a dell with deer, and an aviary. Waihi Falls Reserve is 40 kilometres south-east.

EKETAHUNA

This picturesque Wairarapa riverside township of 600 was one of the settlements developed by Scandinavian migrants in the Forty Mile Bush, like **DANNEVIRKE**, **NORSEWOOD** and the nearby (8 kilometres) railway township of Mauriceville. Its original Scandinavian name, Mellemskov, was discarded in favour of the Maori Eketahuna, meaning 'to run aground on a shoal'.

At Mauriceville North is New Zealand's most magical rural church, Scandinavian-style, with a tapering spire. Eketahuna itself has St Cuthbert's Church (1898) and a cottage museum in Bengston Street. The Pot Pourri craft shop functions as an information office for the district. **MOUNT BRUCE NATIONAL WILDLIFE CENTRE** is 16 kilometres south, on Highway 2.

FEATHERSTON

Wairarapa town of 2500 at the foot of the Rimutaka Range serving as a commuter outpost for those who work in Wellington and Hutt Valley offices and factories. In World War II some 800 Japanese prisoners were held here. In 1943, faced with apparent mutiny, the New Zealand guards opened fire with machine guns and killed 48 prisoners. The facts of the affair have never been wholly disclosed, and a neutral Swiss finding on the events is under embargo until the 1990s.

In World War I tens of thousands of young New Zealanders were trained for French trenches at Featherston. Anzac Hall, at the corner of Bell and Birdwood Streets, was built for the entertainment of World War I troops.

A restored Fell engine in a museum near the town centre was once used on the rugged rail route that crossed the Rimutaka Range to Wellington. After the Rimutaka tunnel through to the Hutt Valley was opened in 1955, the original rail route became a popular walkway (with tunnels) used by visitors to the Rimutaka Forest Park. Nearby shallow Lake Wairarapa (8 kilometres) with its ducks and eels has long been a life-giving resource for the Ngati Kahungunu people. Water entering the lake is now controlled by floodgates, part of a massive conservation and flood control project. A road past the lake leads on to wild and wonderful **PALLISER BAY**, with its remarkable rock formation, the Putangirua Pinnacles.

GREYTOWN

The oldest Wairarapa settlement, between **FEATHERSTON** and **MASTERTON**, was founded in 1854. It was named after Sir George Grey, the governor who promoted the Small Farms Association Scheme which gave landless labourers a chance to prove themselves on smallholdings. Today Greytown with a population of 1800 is one of the most productive areas of the Wairarapa, with many orchards and market gardens.

Papawai Marae, to the south-east of Greytown, is the largest in the region and was the site of many meetings and negotiations between Maori and colonists. Carvings record the sale of Lake Wairarapa in 1896. The Cobblestones Museum is on the site of a Cobb & Co. coaching depot and has stables dating back to the 1850s. There is an 1858 woolshed and an 1862 cottage. Among many other historic buildings is the Borough Council Chambers (1892), a splendid example of Victorian colonial architecture. The foothills of Tararua Forest Park (see page 154) are near by, and Waiohine River Gorge, west of the town, is a popular swimming and picnicking spot.

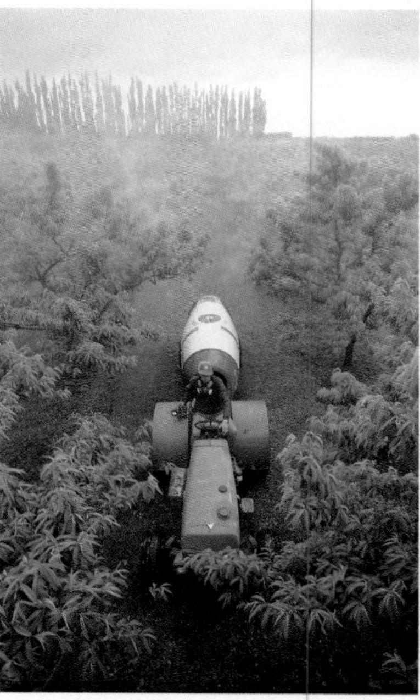

Spraying fruit trees in a Hastings orchard

HASTINGS

Named after the first governor-general of British-ruled India, Warren Hastings, **NAPIER**'s twin city narrowly escaped being called Hicksville, after Francis Hicks, the man who planned it. Although there are only 20 kilometres between them, Hastings and Napier are distinctly separate cities. Hastings is inland, on the rich and immensely productive Heretaunga Plain, and has a population of approximately 55 000. **HAVELOCK NORTH**, 5 kilometres south-east of Hastings and below the Te Mata peak, with a population of 9000, serves as a select residential suburb for both cities.

Hastings is at the centre of a fertile fruit- and wine-producing area often referred to as 'the fruit bowl of New Zealand'. Food-processing is a major industry and the city exports to dozens of countries round the globe. Visitors are welcomed at the district's many vineyards, including the Mission Vineyards at Greenmeadows, the country's oldest established winemaker. Information on the wine trail and on industrial tours can be obtained from information centres in either Hastings or

THE GANNETS' CAPE

Cape Kidnappers, the impressive landmass to the south-east of Napier, is famous for its huge colony of Australasian gannets

Gannets flock to nest at this rocky sanctuary on Cape Kidnappers

The Cape was named by James Cook after local Maoris tried to kidnap a Tahitian member of Cook's crew. Today it is known for its spectacular colony of Australasian gannets, *Morus serrator*. It is the only permanent mainland nesting site of gannets in the Southern Hemisphere.

More than fifteen thousand tourists and ornithologists visit the colony each summer. The country road that crosses the Tukituki River south of Napier ends just past Clifton, leaving an eight kilometre walk (at low tide only) as the alternative to a trip by four-wheel-drive vehicle. The breathtaking spectacle of the gannet's torpedo-like dive – sometimes from a height of thirty metres – makes it one of the most fascinating of sea birds. Gannets pair for life and thousands of pairs nesting just out of reach of each other provide intriguing viewing for bird-watchers and ornithologists.

The older male birds arrive at the colony from late July onwards to reclaim their old nesting sites. They are followed by the younger males who must first establish their own territory. After mating, the male collects the nest-building materials while the female guards their territory.

The female produces one large egg, which is incubated by both parents in turn. Both parents also feed the chick when it emerges after six weeks. The chick takes fifteen weeks to develop sufficient adult plumage to fly.

Most young gannets migrate as far as Australia. The survivors return to their natal colony within five years to breed. The average life span of a gannet is about twenty years, one of the longest for any species of sea bird.

Napier. Leopard Breweries provide a tour of their premises where there is a small replica of an English pub.

The 1931 earthquake killed 88 people in Hastings. Like Napier, Hastings has some fine examples of the Art Deco architectural style favoured at the time of post-earthquake reconstruction. The city has elegant parks, particularly Windsor Park (25 hectares) containing Fantasyland, a children's playground.

The Agricultural and Pastoral Show on Labour weekend in late October attracts thousands of visitors. The Highland Games at Easter are also popular. The Hastings City Cultural Centre houses a museum of Maori artefacts. The attractions of the surrounding area are much the same as those of Napier.

HAVELOCK NORTH

A residential area on Nob Hill above **HASTINGS**, Havelock North was named after Major-General Sir Henry Havelock, British hero of the Indian Mutiny (1857-58). The Indian connection is preserved in the name of Lucknow Lodge, a historic home that is now a gallery (open to the public daily). Two of New Zealand's best-known private schools, modelled on English public schools, are situated in Havelock North, and English-style fox hunts are a not unfamiliar sight. Of the 9000 residents of Havelock North, many are retired and some are from the great Hawke's Bay sheep runs. The distinctive contemporary church, Our Lady of Lourdes, was designed by the Maori architect John Scott.

The summit of Te Mata Peak (399 metres) is accessible by a gently climbing road (6 kilometres). There are spectacular views of Hawke's Bay and much of the eastern North Island. On fine and windy weekends, hang-glider enthusiasts leap from the peak to float far below on the air currents of the Tukituki River valley. In Te Mata Park (98 hectares), there are easy walkways, one of which is a Royal Forest and Bird Society nature trail.

KAWEKA FOREST PARK

This rugged wilderness playground comprises 66 970 hectares of western Hawke's Bay. Among its rock formations, imposing peaks and deep gorges there are a number of tracks. Twenty-nine huts are available for use by trampers, hunters and trout-fishermen. South and east there is scrub and tussock, with dense native forest in the valleys. The northern part comprises beech and podocarp forest. The prolific wildlife includes many species of native birds, blue duck, parakeets and kiwis, as well as introduced animals such as red and sika deer, pigs, opossums, hares and rabbits. There is provision for picnickers and casual campers. Most walks are easy, and there is rafting and fishing on the Mohaka River, and canoeing and jet boating on the Ngaruroro River. Information and permits can be obtained at park headquarters on the south-east boundary of the park (Napier–Taihape road), or otherwise at the district headquarters of NZ Forest Service at **NAPIER**.

LAKE TUTIRA

This willow-fringed lake 40 kilometres north of **NAPIER** is a bird sanctuary and place of pilgrimage for naturalists and lovers of literature. The original Tutira station (9700 hectares) was farmed by the naturalist and conservationist H. Guthrie-Smith, who meticulously documented its natural and human history in the classic *Tutira – The Story of a New Zealand Sheep Station*, first published in 1921 and reprinted several times. Once a food source for the Maori, Lake Tutira offers swimming, trout fishing (best at the northern end) and lakeside camping. There is also a 5-hour round-trip walkway through the landscape that inspired Guthrie-Smith.

MAHIA PENINSULA

At the northern extremity of the Hawke Bay bight, this striking peninsula with its splendid beaches and fine fishing was once a place of refuge for war-stricken Maori in the early 19th century. Later it was a base for eight whaling stations. In 1850 a Wellington newspaper called it 'the Alsatia of the Colony whither all the disorderly and desperate characters resort to be out of the reach of the law'. One would never guess it now. Lovers of serene Mahia return year after year.

MASTERTON

The Wairarapa's major commercial and market centre, with a population of 20 000, Masterton is known nationally for the Golden Shears contest which is held in March. The town was named after Joseph Masters (1802–74), who headed the Small Farms Association and successfully battled to give migrants of limited means the chance to own small lots of land. (A noticeboard on the bypass west of the town tells the small-farmer story.) In green and shady Queen Elizabeth Park there is a memorial dedicated to the long-standing friendship between Maori and Europeans in the Wairarapa. The Wairarapa Arts Centre in Bruce Street incorporates the Wesley Methodist Church (1878), and displays a small but fine collection of New Zealand work. The Vintage Aviation Museum at Hood Aerodrome is open by request.

The nearest beaches are at **CASTLEPOINT** (68 kilometres) and **RIVERSDALE BEACH** (56 kilometres). Inland, Tararua Forest Park (see page 154) is most easily approached through the Mount Holdsworth Domain (22 kilometres), from which there is a fairly easy day-return track to the summit of 1470 metre Mt Holdsworth. The **MOUNT BRUCE NATIONAL WILDLIFE CENTRE** is 30 kilometres north on Highway 2.

MORERE

This northern Hawke's Bay township 40 kilometres east of **WAIROA** is known for its hot springs set among native nikau palms in a 200 hectare bush reserve. The thermal springs have both public pools and private baths (open daily, 10–6).

MOUNT BRUCE NATIONAL WILDLIFE CENTRE

North of **MASTERTON** and south of **EKETAHUNA** on Highway 2, this fascinating wildlife reserve shelters many rare and endangered species of native birds, as well as the more common varieties. The reserve forms part of the great Forty Mile Bush which once stretched from Mauriceville to Woodville. After the rediscovery of the supposedly extinct takahe in Fiordland in 1948, a site was urgently required to care

The Mount Bruce National Wildlife Centre, between Masterton and Eketahuna, is home to many rare and endangered species of bird

WILLIAM COLENSO

Near the small settlement of Clive, between Napier and Hastings, a plaque commemorates the Waitangi mission station founded by William Colenso

William Colenso, photographed in 1862 when he was a member of parliament

The one-time 'ruler' of Hawke's Bay, William Colenso (1811-99) was born in Cornwall, England and came to New Zealand in 1834 as printer to the Church Missionary Society. He set up the country's first successful printing press in Paihia in the Bay of Islands.

By 1837 Colenso had hand-set and printed the first Maori New Testament. He felt a call to the church and was ordained at St John's at Waimate in 1844. Bishop Selwyn sent him to Hawke's Bay, where he dominated the political and social life of the district, advising on civil and spiritual matters.

But there was more to William Colenso: he was also the country's first great botanist. He collected hundreds of new plant specimens and in 1866 became New Zealand's first Fellow of the Royal Society. Following routes known previously only to Maori explorers, Colenso roamed extensively through the wild back country of Hawke's Bay. He made seven gruelling crossings of the Ruahine Range, each time bringing back remarkable botanic discoveries. One of his early walks was a zig-zag journey across the North Island that was greater in distance than the whole length of the island from north to south.

In 1852, following an affair with a Maori woman, Colenso was suspended from the Church. He was not readmitted until 1894. Despite this setback he continued to devote himself to science and – with less success – to Hawke's Bay politics.

Although he was a practical, brilliant man of a passionate nature, Colenso's great fault was his dogmatic and intolerant attitude towards others. He laboured hard as a missionary and devoted himself to his interests with tireless energy and intellect. In his day he was undoubtedly the leading authority on the Maori people and their language, in addition to being the country's finest botanist. It was probably his inability to concentrate on one field that prevented him from gaining greater stature.

for young takahe and ensure the survival of the species. The Mount Bruce centre was established with breeding and research as its priorities, rather than public display (open daily 10–4, except Christmas Day). The centre was expanded, adding walkways, ponds, a nocturnal house and a visitors' centre. It offers an intimacy with New Zealand's native fauna not duplicated, or even approached, elsewhere in the country. On Highway 2, 10 kilometres towards Masterton, there is the Mount Bruce Farm Museum (open first and third weekends of the month between October and April; daily from December 17 to January 12, 10–3.30).

NAPIER

Although a devastating earthquake levelled the city of Napier in 1931, it also uplifted more than 3000 hectares of seabed, across which the new city has spread. An anthology of architectural styles favoured in the 1930s, the commercial centre of Napier is seen as the most complete and concentrated collection of Art Deco buildings in the world (see page 174.) It is also a thriving commercial centre, port and resort with a population of 53 000.

The Marine Parade with its coloured lights, bed-and-breakfast houses, coffee shops and restaurants has a distinctly British flavour. Its attractions (many of them opened daily) include an aquarium, a marineland, a nocturnal wildlife centre, a Lilliputian village, a colonial museum complex and waxworks, a mini-golf course, a skating rink, a sound shell, the Christmas Mardi Gras, and a sculpture of the legendary Pania of the Reef. Pania was a mermaid who forsook her marine world for a human lover – but returned to the sea and was lost for ever (see page 181).

Napier's first European settler of account was the missionary and explorer William Colenso, who survived clerical disgrace to become an influential political figure and respected scholar. Colenso was followed by tides of sheep, and large run-holding families.

Napier was originally laid out by the politician and poet Alfred Domett, who left a literary flavour in street names, such as Tennyson, Shakespeare, Emerson, Browning and Dickens. Like **HASTINGS**, Napier was named after a British military hero, Sir Charles Napier. During the wars of the 1860s the settlement was disturbed only once – by a Hauhau incursion that was repelled by colonists at Omarunui. The Ngati Kahungunu of Hawke's Bay generally sided with the British – especially in the campaign against the guerilla leader Te Kooti.

Bluff Hill (signposted scenic road to the summit) is the best place for a general view of Napier. The Botanic Garden is an attractive public reserve on the slopes of Hospital Hill. Many of the country's pioneers are buried in the old cemetery beside it. They include William Colenso; Major-General Sir George Stoddart Whitmore, the frustrated hunter of Te Kooti; and Sir Donald McLean, the politician and land-purchaser who did most to open up Hawke's Bay for settlement. Members of the Williams missionary family rest here too. The Hawke's Bay Art Gallery and Museum has an effective audio-visual show about the 1931 earthquake and the reconstruction of the city. Books and pamphlets are available on Napier's world-famous Art Deco architecture (open Monday to Friday, 10.30–4.30; weekends and holidays, 2–4.30).

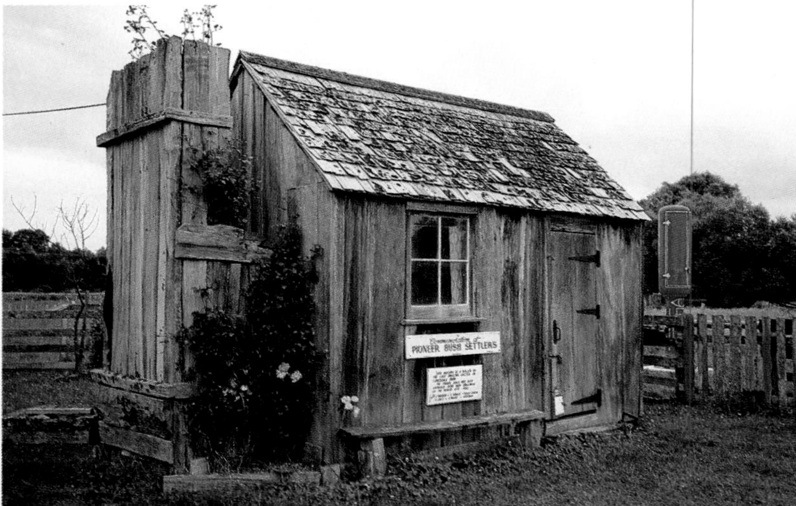

Replica of an early pioneer bush settler's hut at Ongaonga built from original materials

The Bank of New Zealand is a particularly indigenous and unique example of the Art Deco style, featuring Maori motifs and, inside, a remarkable ceiling. Tennyson, Emerson and Hastings Streets have the most concentrated collection of Art Deco buildings in the world. On Marine Parade the sound shell and the fountain are also Art Deco. Just outside the business area is the outstanding National Tobacco Company building at Bridge Street, Ahuriri, with its splendid entrance and foyer.

To the north and south of the city there are fine beaches. To the south (32 kilometres) is the gannet sanctuary at **CAPE KIDNAPPERS**. There is picnicking, swimming and a wildlife refuge at **LAKE TUTIRA** (40 kilometres north) on the estate developed by the philosopher and naturalist H. Guthrie-Smith. It is possible also to visit the celebrated vineyards in the area. Information may be obtained from the Napier Visitors' Information Centre on Marine Parade.

NORSEWOOD

This Scandinavian bush settlement of 300 people, north of **DANNEVIRKE**, has retained more ethnic character than its counterparts elsewhere in the region. At Christmas and on other festive occasions, costumed children still perform Norwegian folk-dances in the main street. The Nordic past is preserved in the Norsewood Pioneer Museum, a cottage built in 1888 for the Lutheran pastor of the then isolated village (open daily 9–4.30, except Christmas Day and Good Friday). Near by stands a fishing boat presented as a centennial gift by the government of Norway. The township's one industry, owned by a Norwegian firm, produces Scandinavian-style wear.

PALLISER BAY

Rich in Maori legend, this dramatic sweep of shore at the south tip of the North Island once had a large Maori population. Soon after European settlement, however, it was given over to sheep, and human population remains sparse to this day. Access to the bay is by way of Lake Ferry settlement, on the shore of Lake Onoke. The Lake Ferry pub used to hold its licence on condition that the publican ferried travellers across Onoke. Until recently that service was performed once annually to ensure renewal of the publican's licence. The lake swimming is safe and the nearby ocean beaches are superb for surfcasting.

At Te Kopi (a whaling station until an earthquake in 1855 lifted it high and dry) a 45-minute walk leads to the castle-like rock formation called the Putangirua Pinnacles, a spectacular freak of uneven erosion. Between Whatarangi and Te Humenga Point are Maori stone walls that once divided kumara plots.

The tapering spire of this church at Mauriceville North suggests its Scandinavian origins

Ngawihi, the largest settlement on the road to Cape Palliser, is a fishermen's base with excellent crayfish. Near the cape is the striking rock outcrop known as 'Kupe's sail'. It is said that Kupe, the Polynesian discoverer of New Zealand, had a sail-making contest with his comrade, Ngake. Kupe finished his sail first, and triumphantly hung it on the landscape for display, where it has remained ever since. Another rock, which has a passing resemblance to Queen Victoria, is named after the queen.

Since 1897 the lighthouse on the cape has warned ships to stay clear of the treacherous coast, which has claimed many wrecks and lives. Behind Palliser Bay is 19 380 hectare Haurangi Forest Park, which is popular with hunters and trampers. Huts are available, and there is easy family hiking. The resident ranger at Te Kopi will provide further information and advice.

RIVERSDALE BEACH

A sheltered resort not far from the only other resort on the formidable Wairarapa coast, CASTLEPOINT. There is a good sandy beach on an otherwise generally inaccessible stretch of coastline, which offers surfing, good fishing and bathing.

TAUMATAWHAKATANGIHANGA-KOAUAUOTAMATEAPOKAI-WHENUAKITANATAHU

The longest place name in New Zealand, and claimed as the longest in the world in its unofficial 85-letter version. It means the 'summit of the hill where Tamatea, the traveller with big knees and swallower of mountains, played his flute to his loved one'. A folk singer has managed to make a chorus of the name. Signposted south of WAIPUKURAU, this hill is on an unremarkable ridge 8 kilometres south-west of Porangahau, where Tamatea is said to have played.

WAIPUKURAU

Riverside farming centre of southern Hawke's Bay, with a population of 3700. Like neighbouring Waipawa, it owes its existence to the subdivision of some of the larger Hawke's Bay sheep runs – and the subsequent rise of small landowners. The Waipukurau Museum, in an early settlers' home, contains many relics of the community's beginnings. Nearby Ongaonga, a former sawmilling settlement under the Ruahine Range, has several historic buildings, including a one-roomed, kauri-shingled schoolhouse that has been preserved as a museum (key from hotel). To the south at Takapau, the imposing Italianate 1870s homestead Oruawharo testifies to the opulent heyday of Hawke's Bay sheep stations.

Te Aute College at Pukehou, 12 kilometres to the north, towards HASTINGS, was founded as an Anglican mission school for young Maori in 1854. Among its former pupils are many distinguished Maori leaders, including Sir Apirana Ngata, Sir Peter Buck and Sir Maui Pomare. With permission it is possible to visit the superbly carved hall (the work of Pine Taiapa in the 1930s).

WAIROA

The lighthouse at the heart of this northern Hawke's Bay riverside town of 5500 is illuminated nightly. From 1877 to 1958 the kauri-built structure stood on Portland Island and warned ships away from the rocks and reefs of MAHIA PENINSULA. When it was finally replaced, the original lighthouse was brought here to Wairoa (which means 'long water').

European flax traders appeared here in the 1820s, whalers in the 1830s and missionaries in the 1840s. The settlement was also a martial outpost in campaigns against the Hauhau and later, Te Kooti. The Maori population is still large. Sheep and cattle farms form the main economic base of the district, but deer and goat farms have also been developed.

The Takitimu meeting-house (1935), upriver on Waihirere Road, is a fine example of the work of the great Maori carver Pine Taiapa. Inquire at the Maori Affairs Department for admission and leave a *koha*, a gift, for the upkeep of the building. The museum (open daily 2–4; holidays, 10–4), sheds light on a district especially rich in history. It is a short drive to Lake Waikaremoana and the Urewera highlands, and to the Mahia Peninsula and MORERE hot springs.

At the wildlife haven of Whakaki Lagoon, 18 kilometres east of Wairoa, giant totara logs are said to have been intended for a 12-pillared temple that the Maori elder and Old-Testament-inspired prophet Te Matenga Tamati (Te Kooti's successor) planned to build in fulfilment of a vision. In 1895, 12 huge totara trees were felled at the headwaters of the Wairoa River and named after the 12 sons of Jacob. The logs were to find their own way to the sacred site. Eventually by 1904, 11 logs had drifted 8 kilometres north to the proposed site. The twelfth, Joseph, had to be fetched back from the Mahia Peninsula, and this was seen as a poor omen. The exhausted and ageing prophet proclaimed that the temple would not be built in his lifetime, but by a prophet inheriting his vision. Te Matenga died in 1914 and the totara pillars survive on Iwitea beach.

THE LEGEND OF PANIA

On Napier's Marine Parade, a statue of Pania, the Maori mermaid, is a reminder of the spiritual relationship between coastal communities and the sea

In Maori folklore, conflict and connections with the sea were always present. Although the sea was a source of food and provided easy travel, it also presented dangers. The Maori were in constant awe of the sea.

According to legend, Pania was a Maori mermaid who was attracted to life on land, although she belonged to the Sea People. Her curiosity led her to hide in tall flax by a spring, where she watched the activities of land-dwelling people. Each evening she would spy on them and each morning she would return to the sea.

One evening she was discovered by a man who took her to his home. Pania began to stay with him every night, but she would disappear to join her own people in the sea at dawn. When Pania gave birth to a boy, the man went to a *tohunga* to ask how he could keep Pania and the child with him all the time. The *tohunga* advised him to put cooked food on their bodies while they slept. This would make them *noa*, free from *tapu*.

When the man did this, Pania woke up and took her child back to the sea. Because the man had tried to violate her *tapu*, she could no longer return to him. Her child became a *taniwha*, living in the harbour at Napier. Pania died from a longing to return to her nightly home on the land, and became a reef below the Hukarere Cliff. At low tide the shape of the reef resembles Pania's outstretched arms reaching towards land and her hair has become the seaweed that streams from the rocks.

Like Andersen's Little Mermaid, Pania was fascinated by the land and its people

Wellington

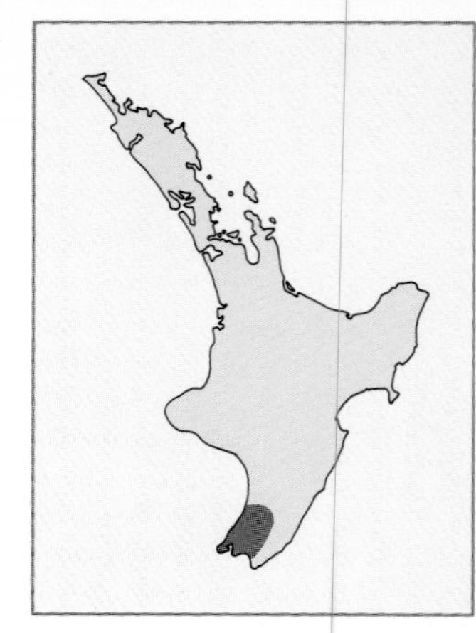

No New Zealand city is more cursed, none more celebrated. Outsiders may libel the capital's citizens, lament its wild weather, scorn its stark situation. Nevertheless, there is no New Zealand city more a metropolis, nor one with more fervent lovers. Painters, writers, and photographers have all found poetry in Wellington, from its harbour to its heights. The production of books about the city – and the people who purchase them – plainly keeps publishing houses in profit.

Wellington's hill-crowded and sea-bitten setting at the North Island's spiny southern tip makes New Zealand's capital unique. It made it compact, gave it a coherence and a centre it has never lost, snake away though it may up tight valleys and over the hills. The story of the city is largely of a battle between man and terrain, a war with seldom a truce. Some of the set-piece engagements have been unusually spirited – hills have been tumbled into the harbour to make an airport and provide level house-sites for hundreds; tunnels have been drilled and canyons carved through hills to allow road and rail access to the city centre.

It is no surprise that it was the Wellington Infantry Regiment which won the highest point ever held by allied forces in the bloody Gallipoli campaign of 1915. The precipitous slopes of Wellington's Kelburn and Mount Victoria were sufficient training for the summit of Turkey's Chunuk Bair. Roads grope up to houses improbably perched on 44-degree slopes; in the evening the highest glimmer like hovering fireflies above the harbour.

Wellington began with its harbour, and could conceivably end under it. A monument to human optimism, the city has grown on one of the major faults in the geologic structure of the North Island; it lives on the whim of our planet's grinding tectonic plates. Yet that, indirectly, is the very reason for the city's site. A buckling of the earth's crust through earthquake, a shift of mountain blocks in times prehistoric, left a huge depression which the sea thunderingly claimed through the narrow gap which is now the harbour's entrance. From most vantage points the harbour, almost landlocked, looks more a lake. Water and rock make a powerful medley, and hills backed by mountains soar sharply from the waterside; there is a gaunt alpine beauty.

Maori tradition holds that the Polynesian navigator Kupe located the harbour a thousand

EDEN BECOMES A METROPOLIS

years or more ago. But Wellington's founder and pioneer was Tara, son of the great voyager Whatonga of the *Kurahaupo* canoe, who made his way here from Hawke's Bay. The harbour was named *Te Whanganui-a-Tara*, the 'Great Harbour of Tara'; the first people to dwell on its shores were of the Ngati Tara tribe. Seafood was plentiful and kumara was cultivated. Heights were hewn into shape as fortresses to guard the tribe's territory, but for the most part the shore was left as it had always been, with forest and fern leaping from summits to the lapping sea.

Cook, like many a European voyager later, missed the entrance to the harbour when he first sailed past in 1770. He was too distracted by the gusty strait between the North Island and the South which bears his name. In 1773, voyaging in the *Resolution*, he discovered 'a new inlet which had all the appearance of a good Harbour'. Wind and tide finally turned him away. But in two hours at anchor his shipmate George Forster, at least observed 'blackish, barren mountains, of a great height'. Maori ventured out in canoes to inspect the freakish newcomers to their coast. Cook distributed medals and nails as mementoes.

That was the last innocent encounter the locals had with the artefacts of European civilisation. Those medals and nails heralded the hellish muskets of Te Rauparaha fifty years later; harbourside people were paralysed by the horror. Recalled a victor: 'So amazed were they at the effects of gunfire that they stood still and did nothing. Then they began to bawl and wail . . . We remained three weeks at that place, cutting up and devouring the best of the bodies. As to the others, we cut the flesh from the bones and laid it to dry in the sun; it was then packed in vessels and the fat of the bodies was melted and poured over it to preserve it.' Survivors of cannibal cuisine fled deep into the forest. The harbour was taken over by the Te Ati Awa of Taranaki, at first allies of Te Rauparaha, then equally fearful of the murderous maverick from the King Country; they were not averse to welcoming white men. They promised to be better company than Te Rauparaha.

Whalers, traders and missionaries drifted in and out for a time. A small band of prospective British colonists looked in briefly in 1826, aboard the *Rossana*, under Captain James Herd, but did not find the terrain inviting. Herd, who corrected Cook's first cryptic chart, was dazzled by the harbour's eight thousand hectares of deep water. 'The navies of all the nations of the world,' he wrote, 'could lie at anchor here.' He named the place Port Nicholson, a name sometimes still in use today, after his friend the Sydney harbourmaster. (It was abbreviated to 'Port Nick' early, and to 'Poneke' by the Maori. Wellington Maori, who now far outnumber the original inhabitants of the harbour, use the name 'Ngati Poneke', tribe of Port Nicholson, to cover people of many tribes who now dwell here.)

WAKEFIELD'S UNRULY EDEN

Modern Wellington began with the arrival of the *Tory* in 1839. Aboard were officers of the New Zealand Company looking out for land on which Edward Gibbon Wakefield's dream of a new and better Britain in the South Sea might might be tested. His brother, Colonel William Wakefield, was one of the arrivals; the expedition had the backing of the victor of Waterloo, the Duke of Wellington, for whom the future settlement would be named. William Wakefield judged the harbour the best offering for the scheme, and snapped up twenty million acres (some eight million hectares) – or thought he had – from those Maori visible on the shore. A hundred muskets, a hundred blankets and a mountain of trinkets were exchanged for what in effect was most of the lower North Island. Unversed in local matters, the Wakefields had next to no comprehension of the fact that Maori were a tribal people, that their land was communally owned. The tribesmen who took the muskets often had no right to sell.

Nevertheless, the *Tory* was the pebble heralding a landslide. The first ships carrying settlers followed hard behind – the *Aurora* in January 1840, and shortly afterwards four more. By the end of 1840 there were twenty-five hundred settlers.

The first arrivals were landed at the foot of the Hutt Valley, present-day Petone; and were distinctly not enamoured of their situation. The vegetation was dense and gloomy; it could take a day to hack out a humble tent site. Wind bit and rain lashed; the land was swampy, their tents often flooded. And they felt their first earthquake. Thinking the commotion a Maori raid, some men fired off muskets and pistols and accelerated the panic. The 'veritable Eden' promised by the New Zealand Company had, said one arrival, become 'wild and stern reality'.

They packed their bags and moved again, to the less sodden southern shore, where modern Wellington has now risen high. But local Maori denied having parted with that reach of Poneke. Some of the rival tribesmen involved in the original transaction fell to feuding among themselves, leaving dozens dead. It was the first of the bitter land problems, largely the result of the New Zealand Company's hasty purchasing, which were to afflict New Zealand for the next thirty years.

Clinging to the disputed southern shore, settlers were never short of grievances – about the Maori, the New Zealand Company, and newly constituted British authority in the north. New Zealand's future capital was a community embattled and entrenched on the lip of a hostile land. One observer noted that in a few short years the bold British colonists of Wellington had become 'bitter, abusive, disloyal, democratic, in short colonial' – in other words, New Zealanders. They were already a far cry from Edward Gibbon Wakefield's ideal citizens. Wakefield, who came late to the settlement, and died here a disappointed colonial politician, must have known the game was up when most of his 'gentleman colonists' – as distinct from 'emigrants', or steerage passengers, the great majority of settlers – fled Wellington for the devil they knew. Only eighty-five of the original four hundred and thirty-six men of means and manners remained in Wellington by 1848.

Wellington workmen certainly thought so. Led by a libertarian carpenter named Samuel Parnell, they promptly demanded and won an eight-hour day, something unthinkable in Britain and not altogether what the New Zealand Company had in mind. (Unsurprisingly, perhaps, Wellington has no monument to Wakefield, the man who fathered it, and just one of obscure nature to the midwife, his brother William.)

The obstinacy of the early settlers was rewarded in 1865; in that year Wellington became capital of the colony of New Zealand. It was the third and final choice after Russell (now Okiato) and Auckland had been discarded.

A COLLECTION OF CITY-DWELLERS

From that point Wellington's story is in large part New Zealand's. With government came politicians; with politicians came bureaucrats; with bureaucrats came banks, insurance companies, stock and station agencies, shipping companies, business houses and businessmen. This was the theatre in which New Zealand's national dramas were played, and have been for

Wellington's land-locked harbour, extensive enough for 'the navies of all nations', lies secure beyond this narrow entrance

six score years; where star-turns the like of Richard John Seddon, William Massey, Michael Joseph Savage, Peter Fraser, Keith Holyoake, Norman Kirk – and more recently Robert Muldoon and David Lange – have performed.

As the country has grown, and the needs of government, so has Wellington and its population. The Hutt Valley has been swallowed all the way back to the Rimutaka Range for industry and housing; settlement was marched over the high walls of the Hutt into communities like Wainuiomata and up the coast to Porirua. In the nineteen-sixties and seventies motorway builders blasted a path through nineteenth-century Wellington for the commuters from such outposts. In the central area, with level land precious, apartment houses and hotels and office blocks and embassies yearly grow taller. All told, the Wellington region is now home to a third of a million New Zealanders.

Human artifice has done little to dim the magnificence of Wellington's setting, or to tame its native idiosyncrasies. It is a city which survives in sufferance to earthquake and wind. Though the terrain has not been in major upheaval since 1855, its position on the fault line is often gently disclosed by creaking floors and swaying lights. But the wind funnelled from the Cook Strait never minces matters. It is either there or it is not. If it is, hang on. As long ago as 1850 it was said that a Wellingtonian could be identified by the way he clutched his hat. 'No one,' pronounced Bishop Selwyn, even earlier, 'can speak of the healthfulness of New Zealand until he has been ventilated by the breezes of Port Nicholson . . . enterprise [is] evidently favoured by the elastic tone and perpetual motion of the atmosphere.' The tactful Selwyn was the first in a distinguished regiment of writers – not the least of them Ireland's James Joyce, in his garrulous masterpiece *Ulysses* – who have saluted Wellington's most potent characteristic. 'It so shakes the frames of houses', said Jan Morris in awe, 'that you feel yourself to be actually at sea, in some stout old wooden-waller plugging down to Lyttelton'. It gusts over thirty knots for more than a hundred days of the average year. A terrible 107-knot gale in 1968 took fifty-one lives when it smashed the inter-island vessel *Wahine* into Barrett Reef at the mouth of the harbour while wind-bound Wellingtonians had to look on largely helpless.

A cable car winches its way up a one-in-five gradient to take passengers from downtown Wellington to hillside Kelburn

Downtown Lambton Quay: land reclamation transformed a seafront of small jetties into a commercial and shopping area

New Zealand has trekked a long way from that decently decorous British society envisaged by Edward Gibbon Wakefield and so has Wellington; it is here, in archives and architecture, that the trail is most perceptible. Yet from a distance – from the window of a plane, the deck of a ship – the city can still be seen clinging tenuously to an island's edge, under a tide of hills; much as that first Wakefield settlement of the eighteen-forties. Lieutenant-Colonel Mundy, bewitched by sight of the settlement in 1848, chronicled 'a crystal bay in its bronze frame of rugged hills, the ships lying calmly at their anchors. . . the long wood-built town curving round the horns of the haven, or creeping like ivy up the spurs of the mountains behind.' Colonel Mundy would still find Wellington familiar. Give or take its downtown towers, Wellington is still Wellington, and mostly more so.

Inner-city Newtown: a captivating blend of Victorian and Edwardian cottages that encapsulates the older Wellington

Dawn sets modern Wellington aglow: New Zealand's most spectacular man-made skyline in a superb natural setting. The air is also said to be cleaner than in other cities – because it never stays in one place long enough to get dirty!

IBM
AA
europa parking centre
dfc

A YOUNG COUNTRY'S HERITAGE

No parts of Wellington are more precious than those that survived the urban disembowelling committed in the name of the motor vehicle and modernity

Much of nineteenth-century Wellington disappeared as dignified buildings deemed earthquake risks began toppling and motorway builders bashed a dead end into the downtown area. Yet much persists of that colonial capital in which Katherine Mansfield – New Zealand's most renowned author – saw 'singular charm'. That community endures vividly in her short stories: *It's a small town, you know, planted at the edge of a fine deep harbour like a lake. Behind it, on either side, there are hills. The houses are built of light painted wood. They have iron roofs coloured red. And there are big dark plumy trees massed together, breaking up those light shapes, giving a depth – warmth – making a composition well worth looking at.*

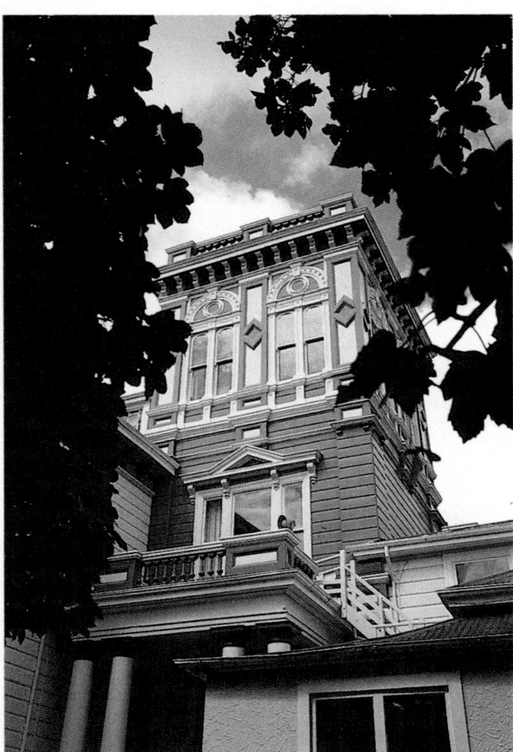

Above: *Queen Margaret College with its Florentine tower*
Right: *Narrow, tall houses in Tinakori Road back on to another road – where they appear comparatively small*

That was how she recalled her birthplace after long years of European exile. In search of serenity in the last years of her short life, she stitched her memories of Wellington and its surroundings into a tapestry of tales as luminous as any in the English language: *At the Bay*, *Prelude*, *The Garden Party*, among others. 'A young country,' she recorded, 'is a real heritage, though it takes one time to recognize it'. Harvesting that heritage on

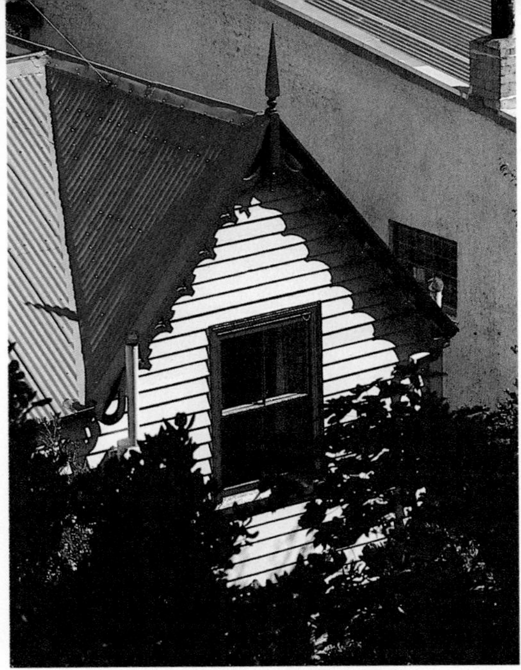

foot – walking her city 'of the wind and the sun and the mists' – is one of the capital's greatest pleasures today. Wellington still has warmth and depth; it is still a composition worth looking at.

Most conspicuously there is Mansfield's own Thorndon. She was born here (in a grand house built by her banker father Sir Harold Beauchamp) in 1888, and so was Wellington when settlers shifted here from the exposed Petone shore in 1840. Those who first looked over the site saw it as 'a second Italy, and a most picturesque spot'. Though disillusion set in soon, Thorndon's picturesque situation – under Tinakori Hill, which Mansfield saw as 'spread like a great wall behind the little town' – cannot be argued.

The first dwellings did not survive. Fire took some; earthquake took others. Roofs of split timber and raupo were a fire risk; buildings of clay and brick were hostage to the earth's upheavals. Wellington's oldest buildings date from the eighteen-fifties. They are of wood and corrugated iron, materials more suited to the shaky environment. Most of Thorndon's colonial buildings rose in the sixties and seventies, a period of high migration. The now toytown area of modest cottages bounded by Tinakori Road and Bowen

Left: *Detail of an old cottage in steep Glenbervie Terrace*
Below: *Sydney Street West, Thorndon. The cottage on the right was the home and studio of the artist Rita Angus*

Inner-city Thorndon, the core of Wellington's settlement

The Government Buildings. Although designed to give the appearance of stone, the building is actually made of wood

Above: *The Shamrock Hotel, an early Wellington pub, was moved to its present site to make way for a motorway*
Right: *The house known as The Wedge – only one room deep and with steeply climbing Glenbervie Terrace on three sides*
Below: *The Public Trust Office, with its distinctive copper dome – a vigorous blend of Renaissance and Baroque*

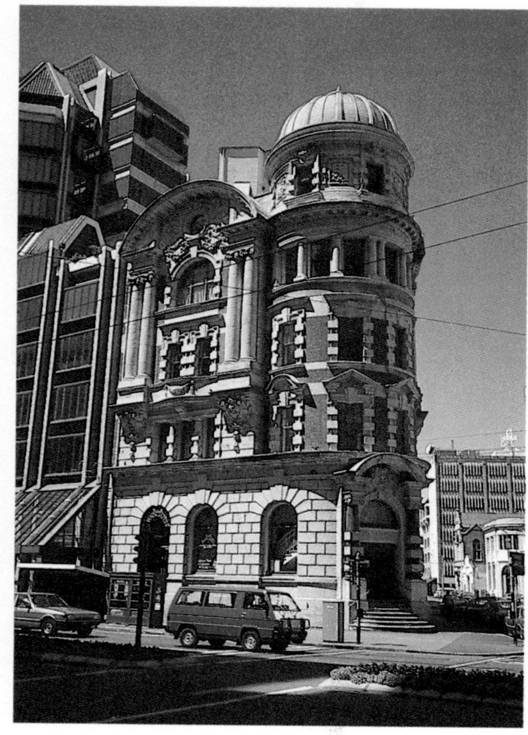

Street was largely a community of tradesmen and clerks squeezed on to sections averaging two hundred square metres, but often fewer.

Thanks to determined urban conservationists, who battled to see that the suburb survived as both an inner-city historical precinct and a multicultural community, Thorndon's nineteenth-century flavour is unique in New Zealand. Glenbervie Terrace and Ascot Street hold many marvels of high density colonial design, not least the strikingly lean building called The Wedge at number twenty Glenbervie Terrace.

Much of Tinakori Road, the location of the most famous garden party in English literature, is still more or less as it was in Mansfield's day: 'not fashionable...very mixed'. Workmen's Wellington, the 'little mean dwellings painted chocolate brown' of her best-known story, though now often repainted and renovated by young urban professionals, are still visible. The Shamrock

The solemn grey marble lines of Parliament House bridge the modern design of the Beehive (above) and the full Gothic detail of the General Assembly Library (right)

Hotel (1869, rebuilt 1893), one of Wellington's finest surviving last-century hostelries, and which once served Irish workmen with green beer on St Patrick's Day, has taken the cure and been relocated in Tinakori Road – after the remodelling of nearby Molesworth Street – and now holds shops, flats, a gallery and a restaurant. Still unrepentantly easing urban thirsts, however, is the tiny Thistle Inn (1866), New Zealand's second oldest, on the far side of the motorway which now splits Thorndon.

Also on the far side are many other distinguished survivals of the capital's past, if now a little lost and lonely in high-rising central Wellington. Old St Paul's Cathedral (1866) in Mulgrave Street was the work of Frederick Thatcher, who had left Auckland its most distinguished architectural legacy, and now set out to enrich the new capital of the colony. Making wood (exclusively New Zealand timbers: matai, rimu, totara and kauri) do the work of Europe's stone, he again wove a distinctive spell in Early English Gothic. Wellington's winds did their best to break the spell, the building soon had to be buttressed, but without imperilling its precious character.

About the secular centre of the nation's capital – Sir Basil Spence's buzzing Beehive (1981), perhaps the world's most monstrously faceless executive building, one which makes even the Kremlin look friendly – are three others eloquent of New Zealand's beginnings. The four-storey Italianate Government Buildings (1876) rose on a harbour reclamation after the 1855 earthquake warned Wellingtonians of the hazards of masonry. It is one of the world's most extraordinary wooden structures, and one of the largest. More than a million super feet of New Zealand's finest rimu, kauri and matai, along with some Tasmanian hardwood, were deployed to do the work of stone.

Parliament House (1922), on the hill above, retains its role as debating chamber for New Zealand's elected representatives. Unfinished, a symbolically uncertain proclamation of post-colonial intent, it was built of marble quarried in Takaka and ferried across the Cook Strait.

This reach of Wellington – Thorndon and thereabouts – by no means holds all Wellington's historic buildings. It doesn't include two of the

finest, Antrim House and Plimmer House, both in uptown Boulcott Street. What it does hold is an atmosphere denied other Wellington buildings because of overshadowing high-rise development. The survival of piquant fragments and flavours of the early-century 'little town' of Katherine Mansfield is no accident: these few historic hectares of the capital have been the arena for duel after duel between citizen and bureaucrat, conservationist and developer.

Nowhere is the atmosphere of the nineteenth-century capital richer than in the green and marble-studded pocket of Thorndon called Bolton Street Memorial Park, which is what survives of the cemetery set aside to serve the city in 1840, now bitten in two by the city's manic motorway. Edward Gibbon Wakefield is here; so is nation-shaking Richard John Seddon. And Samuel Parnell, the carpenter with a democratic dream. The headstones and memorials in New Zealand's most celebrated cemetery lend perspective to the quest for a young nation's heritage. Those who built Wellington were, after all, only human. So, flaws and all, is the city risen round them.

Left: *This 1902 home at 12 Boulcott Street, with its mansard roof, holds its own against its modern neighbours*

Above: *Eighteen-fifties merchant John Plimmer used the beached hull of a wrecked American barque as his store, but lived in this elegant cottage at 99 Boulcott Street*

Below: *A pavilion provides shade in the Botanic Gardens – twenty-six hectares of native bush and exotic flowers*

PLACES OF INTEREST

VANTAGE POINTS

KELBURN
A cable car ride to Kelburn is the most delightful way to take in Wellington's situation. The swift 610 metre journey from Lambton Quay, rising 122 metres on the way, has been operating since the early part of the century. In the 1970s the system was revamped for greater safety. The beloved old cable cars were discarded and replaced by sleek Swiss cars. The Kelburn terminus has walkways and balconies overlooking the city, a restaurant, and an information office serving the BOTANIC GARDENS.

Little more than half a kilometre away is the fashionable Kelburn shopping centre with boutiques, restaurants and another lookout providing glimpses of Kelburn's densely settled ridges and hillsides. From the terminus, visitors can descend through the gardens to the gates at Glenmore Street. The return to Lambton Quay includes Bolton Street Memorial Park where the city's founders and national leaders are buried.

MOUNT VICTORIA
A road leads to this 196 metre summit which gives a commanding Wellington panorama of the city and waterfront, the distant Hutt Valley, the 8000 hectare harbour and of seaside suburbs. Its Maori name was *Tangi-te-Keo*, meaning 'the sound of a screeching bird', after the *taniwha*, or dragon, which excavated Wellington Harbour and flew to the summit in the form of a bird. Certainly its sound seems echoed in the (often) screeching wind. The unrelated but bird-like structure on the skyline is a memorial to American polar explorer Richard E. Byrd who used New Zealand as a base.

TINAKORI HILL
With the most dramatic of city views, this 300 metre high hill looks down into what survives of early Wellington – Thorndon and environs – as well as the tall modern city. The radio masts crowning the summit serve New Zealand and South Pacific shipping. Access to Tinakori Hill is through Northland, first along the bus route, then a short walk.

MUSEUMS AND GALLERIES

ALEXANDER TURNBULL LIBRARY
Based upon the collections of New Zealand's most distinguished bibliophile (see page 194), the library has moved house twice in recent decades and is now in the National Library building in Molesworth Street. It has always featured displays of its precious Pacific and New Zealand material; and of its historic paintings. Prints are for sale. Inquire at Wellington Public Relations Office for opening hours. Originally, the library was the brick townhouse at the foot of

Queen Victoria surveys Courtenay Place

Bowen Street. It is now known as Turnbull House (1916) and designated an historic place.

CITY ART GALLERY
As distinct from the NATIONAL ART GALLERY, the City Art Gallery in Victoria Street is Wellington's own gallery. It has a distinguished exhibition program, and often shows art films and videos for city workers at lunchtime (10.45–6 daily).

DOWSE ART MUSEUM
By contrast with the conservative NATIONAL ART GALLERY, this is one of the liveliest galleries in the country. Its permanent collection is striking, and it has travelling exhibitions of contemporary New Zealand works. In Laings Road, Lower Hutt (open Tuesday to Friday 10–4.30; and weekend afternoons).

MARITIME MUSEUM
This museum saltily celebrates the city's magnificent harbour and its history. It features a large-scale model of the harbour. Harbour Board Office, Queens Wharf, Jervois Quay (open Monday to Friday 9–4; weekends 1–4.30).

NATIONAL ARCHIVES
It has regular exhibitions. Located at 129–141 Vivian Street (open to the public weekdays 9–5).

NATIONAL ART GALLERY
Off Buckle Street, overlooking central Wellington, the gallery shares its location with the NATIONAL MUSEUM and the War Memorial Carillon Tower. The gallery has an impressive collection of European art and of early New Zealand works. Although it languished for a long time in the wake of the Auckland Art Gallery in its holdings of contemporary New Zealand works, the gallery has become notably more adventurous in recent years. The work of most important New Zealand painters can be viewed here. Especially impressive are its watercolour collections, both English and 19th-century New Zealand (open daily, 10–4.45).

NATIONAL MUSEUM
Likewise off Buckle Street; its collections have been increased assiduously since the 1860s. There is a good collection of Maori material from the lower North Island, including the carved Maori meeting-house Te Hau-ki-Turanga (1843), shipped here from Manutuke in Poverty Bay in the 1860s. It is one of the oldest meeting-houses in the country, certainly one of the finest crafted. The figurehead from Cook's *Resolution* takes pride of place in the display of early European and pioneer artefacts (open daily 10–4.45).

SOUTHWARD CAR MUSEUM
At Paraparaumu, on Otaihanga Road off Highway 1, this museum has one of the world's finest and most comprehensive collection of vintage and veteran motor vehicles. Some 250 vehicles are on display in a 4400 square metre hall. There are also cycles, motor cycles, traction engines, stationary engines, and an engineering workshop is busy restoring more vehicles. The museum was established by collector and engineer Len Southward and today it is carried on by a trust (open daily 9–5, except Christmas Day and Good Friday).

TRAMWAY MUSEUM
Out of town at Queen Elizabeth Park (see KAPITI COAST), this museum rejoices in the remnants of Wellington's urban tram system. On weekends and public holidays the old trams clang along a kilometre-long track in a splendid seaside setting. At Paekakariki there is another museum, the Engine Shed (open Saturday 9–5) with carriages and working locomotives from the steam train era.

HISTORIC HOUSES

ANTRIM HOUSE
Now marooned among Wellington's rearing tower blocks, Antrim House (1904), at 63 Boulcott Street, was designed by Thomas Turnbull. The magnificent kauri mansion belonged to shoe manufacturer Robert Hannah. Today it is the headquarters of the NZ Historic Places Trust. Colonial paintings are on show and exhibitions feature the trust's concerns. Visitors are welcome Monday to Friday, 9–5.

12 BOULCOTT STREET
Once the townhouse of Dr Henry Pollen, this building was also designed by Turnbull and built in 1902. It provides a rich example of turn-of-the-century Wellington, suggesting the grand life style of early merchants and professionals.

CHEW'S COTTAGE
Built in 1865 on Ottawa Road, Ngaio, this was the residence of timber merchant John Chew. It is a magnificent example of a simple and elegant pioneer building.

GOLDIES BRAE
The conservatory-clad, curving concrete Wadestown home of Dr Alexander Johnston, one of New Zealand's most distinguished early men of medicine, was designed by Johnston himself (1876). He conceded that his contemporaries might think it 'very eccentric'. It is – and it is also an ingenious response to Wellington's climate and terrain.

68 NAIRN STREET
By contrast with Boulcott Street's merchants' residences, this is an artisan's cottage of the late 1850s. It has been lovingly restored and is now a museum of colonial Wellington (open Wednesday to Friday, 10–4; weekends 1–4.30).

PLIMMER HOUSE
At 99 Boulcott Street. Built in 1873, it was once the home of Wellington

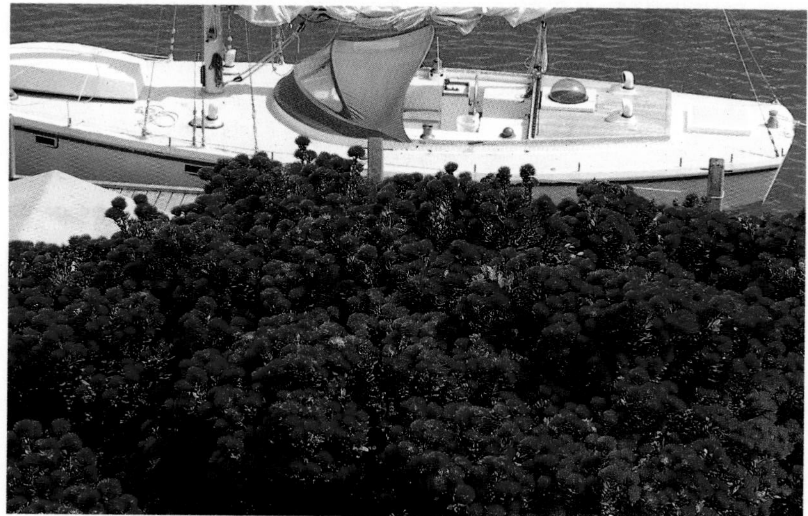
The pohutukawa, or New Zealand Christmas tree, blazes on Wellington's seafront. The tree is most at home on the cliffs, where it dangles its tortuous limbs almost into the sea

merchant John Plimmer, who moored his boat at the foot of Plimmer Steps near by. Now a restaurant, the house's gables and odd litle central tower make it perhaps the most elegant inner-city dwelling built in New Zealand.

SEXTON'S COTTAGE
Situated in Bolton Street Memorial Park, this cottage is of the same vintage (1857) as 68 NAIRN STREET – and as simple in design. It was built for the Anglican Church by soldiers of the 65th Regiment.

22 THE TERRACE
Now a gallery serving the NZ Craft Council, this house was built for Dr L.G. Boor in 1866 as a professional man's residence in what was then Wellington's grandest street. It is the city's oldest architect-designed building.

25 TINAKORI ROAD, THORNDON
This house was built in the year of Katherine Mansfield's birth (1888) for her banker father Sir Harold Beauchamp. He was leased the land on the condition that he build 'a good and substantial house to the value of £400 at least'. No one could argue that the money was not well-spent. The building is now being restored by the NZ Historic Places Trust.

296–306 TINAKORI ROAD, THORNDON
An especially dramatic response to Wellington's terrain, these workers' houses were built in 1903 on sections 200 metres square, one room wide and rearing up another three storeys behind.

WILTON FARMHOUSE
Built during the 1850s with additions in the 1880s, this house at 116 Wilton Road, was the home of farmer Job Wilton. He landed in Wellington as a seven-year-old in 1841, launched himself on the landscape beyond the city's hills, and became a citizen of importance. Perhaps the settlement's first conservationist of substance, he preserved 60 hectares of forest known first as Wilton's Bush, now the OTARI NATIVE PLANT MUSEUM.

HISTORIC BUILDINGS

BISHOPSCOURT
Once the sturdy totara home of bishops, notably the gentle Octavius Hadfield, defender of the faith and of the Maori people, this is an imposing piece of Victorian architecture (1879). It is located beside OLD ST PAUL'S.

CHRIST CHURCH
The Hutt Valley's oldest building (1854), at Taita, this gentle Gothic gem of pioneer pit-sawn totara once stood in a sombre setting of half-felled forest. It now dwells in suburbia as dense; its graveyard testifies to the Hutt Valley's stern beginnings.

GENERAL ASSEMBLY LIBRARY
Adjoining Parliament House, this jubilantly Gothic building (1898) suggests that New Zealand politicians once had more taste – even if Prime Minister Richard John Seddon did lop off the top storey to placate taxpayers. Look into the foyer – the interior is a museum of Victorian extravagance.

GOVERNMENT BUILDINGS
Facing the PARLIAMENT BUILDINGS, this is one of the world's largest wooden buildings (1876). With an area of nearly 10 000 square metres, it is a remarkable translation of 19th-century stone architecture. It was the last work of pioneer architect W.H. Clayton. Costs soared so frighteningly, the government of the day decided to do without an opening ceremony.

OLD ST PAUL'S
In Mulgrave Street, Thorndon, St Paul's (1866) once commanded the infant settlement of Wellington. Today its charm lies in its exquisite timber interior. In the 1960s the distinguished historian J.C. Beaglehole, campaigning against those who wished to demolish this masterwork of 'Selwyn' architect Frederick Thatcher, argued that simple wooden St Paul's embodied the mystery at the heart of all religious faith. Still consecrated, and much used, it is open to all 'who wish to ponder on its architectural glory, its historical associations, its hallowed memories, or simply to refresh themselves in its quietude', according to scholar Ormond Wilson of the NZ Historic Places Trust.

PARLIAMENT BUILDINGS
Parliament House (1922), and the Beehive extension (1981) by Sir Basil Spence, command the city. The first was quarried from native marble. The second, already an historical curiosity, from a distinguished international architect's after-dinner whim (from a design drawn on a napkin) and inspired, it is said, by the beehive symbol on a New Zealand matchbox. The politicians who embraced the whimsy seem never to have noted that the beehive is an authoritarian structure. Unless levelled by an earthquake, the building seems likely to bemuse New Zealanders and baffle outsiders for a century or two yet. Conducted tours of Parliament Buildings are available daily.

PORT BUILDINGS
A medley of fascinating seafront buildings on reclaimed land between city and harbour includes the rhythmical and Renaissance-roofed Harbour Board's Head Office and Bond Building (1891), which now houses the MARITIME MUSEUM the Star Boating Club building (1885); warehouses and surprisingly elegant wharf sheds built from the mid-1880s to 1920. The waterfront is open to the public. Among the many tourist itineraries available from Wellington Public Relations Office is a Wharves Walk.

PUBLIC TRUST OFFICE
Designed by John Campbell in a rich blend of architectural styles favoured in the Edwardian period, this building (1909) occupies a corner at Lambton Quay

QUEEN MARGARET COLLEGE
Originally the home of architect W.H. Clayton, this was the first (*c.* 1870) Wellington residence made of concrete (or, strictly speaking, of lime, coarse gravel, clay and shells from the Wellington waterside). Located in Hobson Street, Thorndon, the building was later (1878) sumptuously remodelled and enlarged by architect Charles Tringham and topped with a wooden Florentine tower.

SEAMEN'S INSTITUTE
At the corner of Whitmore and Stout Streets, this building (1903) is a crusty survivor of the contest between urban conservationists and city developers; it is distinctive for its odd and striking mix of Gothic and classical.

AN OUTSTANDING LITERARY LEGACY

At the City end of Bowen Street, the Victorian Tudor brick house of bibliophile Alexander Turnbull is one of Wellington's literary landmarks

Alexander Turnbull turned his house into a library which is now a national treasure

Until recently, Turnbull's (1868-1918) house contained the outstanding library he built up over his lifetime. When he died, Turnbull bequeathed the entire collection to the nation, an act that has been described as the most generous gift in the history of New Zealand.

The library's precious Pacific collection specialises in New Zealand material. It has become the national research library and is the central repository of New Zealand history.

Also rich in books specialising in English literature, it has one of the world's finest collections of works by and about John Milton. Other rarities include a section of books devoted to the art of typography.

Alexander Turnbull was a naturally curious person. The son of a Wellington merchant, he was sent to finish his schooling in England when he was fourteen. Ten years later he returned to New Zealand with an already well-developed interest in book-collecting. He led a busy social life, was a keen yachtsman and took out membership in several learned societies.

Since his death, the library has been added to several times. Though it continues to be one of the great libraries of the southern hemisphere, its core shall always be the fifty-five thousand volumes, manuscripts, pictures and maps collected tirelessly by its inspired founder.

The old house in Bowen Street is now a meeting place with a coffee shop. The collection has outgrown the building and has been moved to become part of the National Library.

Wellington's tribute to the car is the vast Southward Car Museum at Paraparaumu, which houses a world-class collection of vintage and veteran vehicles and all manner of engines

TAJ MAHAL

This pinkish concrete-and-plaster Baroque public lavatory at the end of Courtenay Place is the most celebrated loo in the land. One of Wellington's oddest distinctions for six or seven decades, it was marked for demolition during the 1960s. The roar of civic protest could be heard in Auckland and Invercargill. A bronze and beady Queen Victoria, who has kept the Taj company since it first rose, was distinctly not amused either. It was saved and has since been turned into a gallery and restaurant.

THISTLE INN

Built in the 1840s in Mulgrave Street, and rebuilt after fire in 1866, the Thistle Inn is typical of Wellington's vanished wooden inns. It holds the second oldest continuous licence in the country. Dinghies were once moored at its seafront door while seamen roistered within; the shade of poet Denis Glover presides here too. The Thistle's Thorndon cousin, the Shamrock, once the hideaway of tippling politicians, has fallen on temperate times, been moved to Tinakori Road and tarted up with shops and a restaurant.

UPPER HUTT BLOCKHOUSE

A memorial to the unease felt by Wellington's outlying settlers in the colony's early decades. In the 1840s, Te Rauparaha's Ngati Toa attempted to drive colonists from the Hutt Valley. This blockhouse was built at Wallaceville in 1861 and manned briefly, but Wellington was never menaced. Local Maori tended to side with colonists.

The blockhouse is now being restored.

WILLIS STREET

There are two extremely fine wooden churches in this street, St Peter's (1879) and St John's (1885), both designed by architect Thomas Turnbull as free adapations of the Gothic style popularised by Frederick Thatcher in colonial New Zealand. Turnbull was also responsible for the graceful Wesley Methodist Church (1880) in nearby Taranaki Street. Contrast the warmth of Turnbull's wooden forms with the rather cold concrete and brick St Mary's of the Angels (1922), the work of Frederick de J. Clere, near the meeting of Willis, Manners and Boulcott Streets.

ENVIRONS

HAURANGI FOREST PARK

A challenging environment for the city-dweller, this 19 380 hectare park (in the Wairarapa region) backs the mighty sweep of Palliser Bay (see page 180). Park headquarters is at the one-time whalers' base of Te Kopi on the Bay. The park's northern block is riven with gorges and commanded by limestone crags. The southern block was logged for rimu and later abandoned. It is now reverting to its original forest cover. Much of the park's flavour comes from its proximity to Palliser Bay, a popular retreat for citizens of Wellington who have forsaken the balmier but often crowded KAPITI COAST.

KAPITI COAST

Past PORIRUA and Pukerua Bay on Highway 1, there is a spectacular curve of coast with Kapiti Island commanding the horizon. Paekakariki is the first community to appear; next are Paraparaumu, Waikanae, and Otaki with its striking Rangiatea Church (see page 152). Four kilometres beyond Paekakariki is 638 hectare Queen Elizabeth Park. It has a delightful 3 kilometre sea frontage, a mix of native and exotic trees and space for picnickers and campers. At the northern end, the TRAMWAY MUSEUM runs vintage trams down to the coast on weekends and public holidays. There is also Whareroa, a government-owned working farm open to the public (daily 9–6).

The Blockhouse at Upper Hutt, constructed and garrisoned in 1861 as part of Wellington's defences, never came under fire

The memorial gates at McKays Crossing are one of the few visible reminders of the thousands of US Marines who lived and trained here before island-hopping up the Pacific in World War II. These soldiers had a notorious predecessor. The coast was once the realm of Te Rauparaha who had his base on Kapiti Island. Paraparaumu is commanded by a 14 metre high sculpture of the Virgin Mary, 'Our Lady of Lourdes' (1958).

Lindale Farm has shearing and sheepdog displays. The famed SOUTHWARD CAR MUSEUM is near by on Otaihanga Road off Highway 1, on the way to Waikanae. East of Waikanae, the delightful Hemi Matenga Memorial Park has one of the largest surviving kohekohe forests in the land. The Nga Manu Sanctuary, a reserve at the mouth of the Waikanae River, holds approximately 80 species of birds including the Siberia-bred godwit or kuaka (open 10–4.30 weekdays; 10–5.30 weekends). The Reikorangi Pottery has crafts, an animal park and a picnic area, and a museum and restaurant (open Tuesday to Sunday). Just before Otaki at Te Horo is the lively Hyde Park Craft Village and museum complex.

The climate is distinctly warmer on this vivid shore and the surf is friendly. In recent years the region has become densely settled. It is popular with city workers and retired people. Detours back to Wellington can take in the attractive Akatarawa Valley with the Staglands Wildlife Park and its deer, trout and aviaries (open seven days); and Pauatahanui Inlet.

MARINE DRIVE

The drive begins at Oriental Bay and ends 30 kilometres later at Owhiro Bay with a walk along RED ROCKS COASTAL PARK an optional extra.

The road hugs both harbour and open shore all the way and is remarkable for its contrasts. There is the Riviera-like atmosphere of Oriental Bay emphasised by the monastery of St Gerard (1905), and vast hill-clinging villas together with tall apartment buildings. At the other extreme, there is wild surf, fanged rocks and bleak headland – New Zealand untamed. An appropriately barren patch of earth, chosen for its likeness to the Gallipoli peninsula, is dedicated to both New Zealand and Turkish dead of the disastrous campaign in 1915. At the end of the drive the community of Island Bay has something of the colour and climate of Britain's Cornwall and a still largely Italian fishing fleet. The mountains of the South Island glimmer beyond the seething sea of the Cook Strait. Full information from Wellington Public Relations Office; otherwise follow signs.

PETONE SEAFRONT

On the seafront is a memorial (1940) marking the landing of Wellington's first European settlers in 1840. Until it was abandoned by suffering and sodden settlers, Petone might well have been New Zealand's capital. There is a small museum inside the memorial (open weekdays 12–4; weekends 11–4). A cross of Iona marks the first Presbyterian service in New Zealand. In nearby Te Puni Street is the grave of Te Puni, the Te Ati Awa chief who protected settlers against attack in the 1840s.

PORIRUA

Whalers and early farmers settled here over the city's hills before Wakefield's colonists decided on the harbourside location. Wool was shipped out before most of New Zealand had heard a sheep's bleat. And there was strife here between settlers and Maori in the 1840s following ill-negotiated land sales. History is most tangible at the head of Pauatahanui Inlet where delicate St Alban's Anglican Church (1895) stands on the remains of Maori entrenchments. Not far away is St

PARNELL'S EIGHT-HOUR DAY

Korokoro, a Wellington suburb on the northern side of Highway 2, is where the first eight-hour working day was negotiated by Samuel Parnell in 1840

Samuel Duncan Parnell (1810-90) was born in London where he became a carpenter. Influenced by the advanced theories of Welsh social reformer Robert Owen, the idealistic young tradesman emigrated with the New Zealand Company to Petone in 1840.

Parnell had organised himself well. He brought his own house out in sections to assemble as soon as he arrived. This so impressed a fellow-passenger named Hunter that he asked Parnell to build him a store at Korokoro. Parnell agreed on the condition he would work eight hours only each day. His theory was that if eight hours were given to work and eight to sleep, then the remaining eight hours was owing to all for private needs and recreation. With some reluctance, Hunter agreed. But the shop was never finished by Parnell as the two men eventually quarrelled.

Word of an eight-hour day spread fast through the colony. Others also began to demand it as a right. Ships coming from overseas were often met by men who would spread the word among the new arrivals that an eight-hours-a-day job was both desirable and attainable.

Parnell's innovation eventually became the standard working day, and on October 28, 1890, a ceremony was held in Wellington to honour the founder of a movement that was to sweep the Western world.

Samuel Parnell... his convictions became a cause for world labour movements

In 1899, Labour Day (it is still a statutory public holiday) was instituted to celebrate the eight-hour working day and the principle Parnell had established at the very foundation of the colony.

Joseph's Catholic Church (1878), the Wellington region's oldest surviving bastion of the Catholic faith. The Taylor Stace Historic Cottage (1847) round the inlet is now a craft shop (open 10.30–5 Tuesday to Sunday). Two historic buildings are the Gear Homestead (1882), a distinguished residence that was built above the town by butcher and meat-shipper James Gear, and now a cultural centre; and nearby Papakowhai, of the same vintage. At Titahi Bay there is a seaquarium (open weekdays 10–5; weekends 10–6).

RED ROCKS COASTAL PARK

West of Island Bay, beyond a car park on the far side of Owhiro Bay is a 4 kilometre walk along dramatic and sea-lashed Wellington coastline. Distinctively coloured rocks of red argillite are worth seeing, as is the seal colony at Sinclair Head. Along the way, rock pools hold an abundance of sea life and skindiving is popular. The mountains of the South Island loom in the distance on a fine day.

ROUND THE HARBOUR

This 50 kilometre return drive via the Hutt motorway and the **PETONE SEAFRONT** takes in Wellington's most resplendent residential suburbs and several attractive and safe beaches. At Petone, a memorial stands where baffled British migrants first confronted a raw and forbidding reality in 1840. Along the curve of the harbour are the exclusive suburbs Lowry Bay, York Bay and Mahina Bay. Days Bay is where

KATHERINE MANSFIELD

Katherine Mansfield's family home on Tinakori Road is a small but essential clue to the life of one of New Zealand's greatest expatriate writers

Katherine Mansfield (centre) with sister Jeanne and brother Leslie ('Chummie')

The Beauchamp family home where Katherine Mansfield was born in 1888

Kathleen Beauchamp (1888-1923), who wrote under the pseudonym Katherine Mansfield, was born at number eleven (now twenty-five), Tinakori Road, Wellington, only a short walk from parliament.

Her four grandparents had come to New Zealand from Australia but despite this old colonial family background, the young writer felt drawn to England. In 1908, at the age of nineteen, she set off for London with a one hundred pounds (two hundred dollars) annual allowance from her banker father.

Soon after her arrival, Mansfield plunged into a literary and Bohemian life. She married G.C. Bowden, a singing teacher, and left him the following day. She conceived a child (not by Bowden) which she miscarried in Germany, the setting for her first collection of short stories, *In a German Pension* (1911).

Shortly after this Mansfield met the editor John Middleton Murry with whom she was to share the rest of her brief life. They married in 1918, sometimes parting, then reuniting. She travelled, seeking a cure for her tuberculosis, and always writing – as though frantically racing against time.

The trauma that caused her to return in her imagination to the New Zealand of her childhood was the visit to London in 1915 of her beloved younger brother Leslie on his way to fight on the Western Front in France. Leslie was killed soon after. Mansfield emerged from her grief to write about her New Zealand background, as 'a debt of love'. These stories, published under the title *Bliss and Other Stories* (1920), form the basis of her reputation as a great short story writer.

The Wellington she had been so eager to leave at nineteen formed the reference point to her genius.

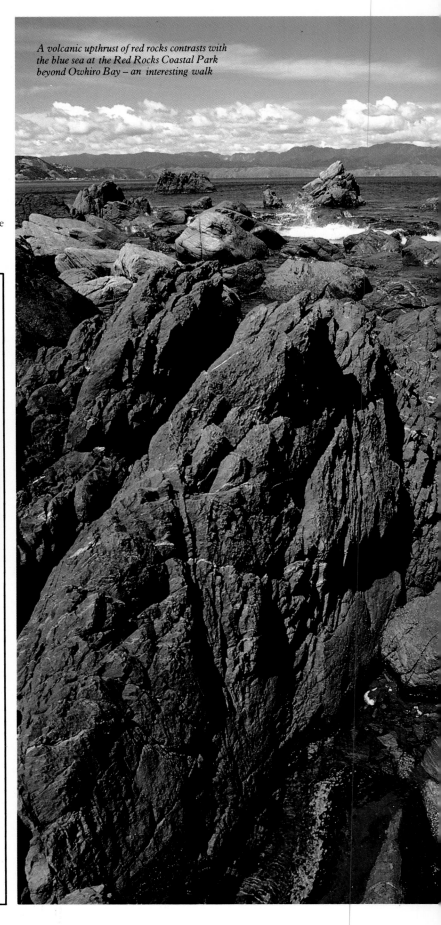

A volcanic upthrust of red rocks contrasts with the blue sea at the Red Rocks Coastal Park beyond Owhiro Bay – an interesting walk

Katherine Mansfield spent childhood summers, summers preserved forever in perhaps her finest story *At the Bay*. Beyond is trendy Eastbourne, a larger suburb with dwellings climbing hillsides to catch harbour views. Walks lead off to Pencarrow Lighthouse (now a designated historic place) and Butterfly Creek.

RIMUTAKA FOREST PARK

The park comprises 14 770 rugged hectares between the Hutt Valley and the Wairarapa. Its highest point is 941 metre Mt Matthews. The Rimutaka Range lends the harbour its alpine quality.

Uniquely, the ramparts of this forest park include the old and precariously placed Wellington–Wairarapa railway route, opened in 1878 and closed in 1955 when the Rimutaka tunnel was opened. Today the route is a rewarding walkway with a miracle of human engineering underfoot. Other tracks allow access to trampers, hunters and fishermen. The vegetation at higher levels is stunted scrub; at lower levels gorse, beech and podocarp thrive.

Wellington's pre-European Maori hunted the moa, trapped pigeon and hid from rampaging war parties here. The wildlife now includes red deer, goats, pigs, opossums and rabbits. There is camping and picnicking in the Catchpool Valley 9 kilometres south of Wainuiomata off the Coast Road; and also at the Waiorongomai River. Information is available at the park headquarters in the Catchpool Valley, and station headquarters in Upper Hutt.

THE EXTRAORDINARY WAKEFIELDS

Wellington has strong links with members of the Wakefield family, many of whom played important roles in the development of the colony

Edward Gibbon Wakefield, one of the founders of the New Zealand Company, was both an idealist and a ruthless man of action – engraving from an 1823 drawing by A. Wivell

The Bolton Street Memorial Park, through which the Wellington Urban Motorway passes as it enters the main administrative and commercial area of the capital, contains the grave of Edward Gibbon Wakefield (1796-1862). The most famous member of the extraordinary Wakefield family, his theories, actions and manipulations were to be one of the most important guiding forces in the colonisation of New Zealand. He helped found the New Zealand Association (later renamed the New Zealand Company) in the eighteen-thirties, but he himself did not come out until almost twenty years later.

One of Edward's four brothers, William (1803-48) led the first company colonists to Wellington in 1839. He was principal agent, and the man who most probably deserves the title, Father of Wellington.

Arthur (1799-1843) was also influential in New Zealand Company affairs. He had the misfortune to be killed in the land dispute with Te Rauparaha that became known as the Wairau Affray.

Daniel (1798-1858) became an important lawyer and judge in Wellington. For a while he was the attorney-general of the short-lived province of New Munster.

Felix (1807-75), the youngest of the brothers, became an engineer and South Island horticulturalist.

Edward Jerningham (1820-79) was Edward Gibbon's only son. He wrote *Adventure in New Zealand* (1845), an absorbing but fictionalised account of early life in the colony. He was an explorer who became a politician in Wellington and Christchurch.

Two of the sons of Felix, Oliver (1844-84) and Edward (1845-1924) also became prominent in New Zealand public life. Oliver was a government official and Edward was a journalist, editor and politician.

Along with their autocratic bluster, impulsiveness, ambition and powerful personalities, the Wakefields showed a remarkable understanding of New Zealand's future. Such attributes were often considered assets in the rough and tumble of early colonial life, an environment that probably magnified both their virtues and defects.

ENTERTAINMENTS

BOTANIC GARDENS

These 26 hectares of central Wellington are a marvellous medley of vegetation – sometimes native on rugged terrain, and elsewhere exotic, trimmed, tamed and tidied to the Victorian taste of Wellington's first British settlers. As a colonial garden, its character has been sensitively retained. The wrought-iron gate at the Glenmore Street entrance is an especially resplendent piece of Victoriana, as is the Custodian's Cottage, 1876.

Begun on 6 hectares in 1869 and later extended, the garden is a place of many pretty, quiet enclaves. Among its formal, less historical attractions are the Lady Norwood Rose Garden, featuring nearly 2000 varieties; the Begonia House, with a display of 5000 flowering plants; a lately established herb garden; and a peace garden dedicated to New Zealand's dead of two world wars and featuring trees and shrubs from the lands in which they perished. There is a tea house adjoining the Begonia House. The entrance is at Glenmore Street or from the KELBURN cable car terminus, where there is also an information office. Landmarks on the latter approach include the Carter Observatory, the Dominion Observatory, the Geophysics Building and the Meteorological Office. The visitor may also take in the adjoining Bolton Street Memorial Park, where the city's and many of the 19th-century colony's founders now rest; also the restored SEXTON'S COTTAGE (1857). The Botanic Gardens are open daily until dusk.

OTARI NATIVE PLANT MUSEUM

This sanctuary in suburbia, unique in the land, has 60 hectares dedicated solely to the aboriginal vegetation. Founded by the distinguished botanist, Dr Leonard Cockayne, this open-air museum is a scientific storehouse for plants that have become rare elsewhere. Well-marked walks wind among trees rich in birdlife (open daily.)

THEATRES

A small but adventurous theatre, Circa was formed by an actors' cooperative and occupies premises at 1 Harris Street. The longest established theatre, Downstage is in the Hannah Playhouse at the corner of Courtenay Place and Cambridge Terrace. Its program comprises a mixture of classic and contemporary drama. One of the city's few new buildings of genuine distinction, and adjoining Wellington's vintage neo-classical town hall, the Michael Fowler Centre (1983) is named after a former mayor of Wellington who did much to enliven the downtown area of the city. The architects Warren and Mahoney also designed Christchurch's splendid town hall. Wall hangings by the Wellington artist Gordon Crook symbolise the city's moods. Maori-carved pillars distinguish the foyer. (Tours are between 10.30 and 2.30, depending on bookings of the building.) In Alpha Street, Depot is a younger theatre group specialising in New Zealand drama.

WELLINGTON ZOO

The oldest in New Zealand, the Wellington zoo houses almost 1000 species of animals. It has had much success in breeding endangered species. The kiwi house is a feature (hours 10–4). Located at Newtown, the zoo is open daily 8.30–5.

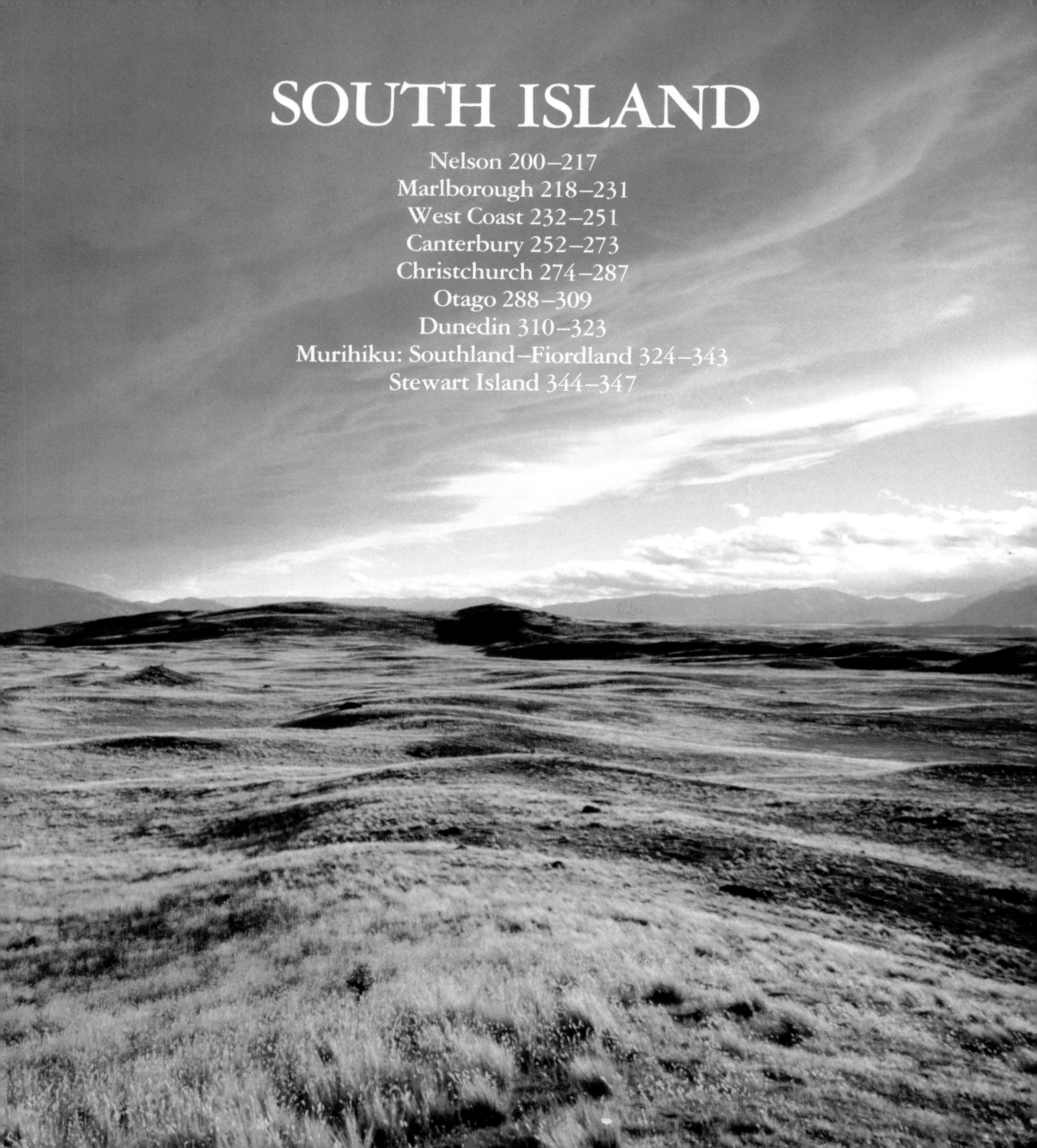

SOUTH ISLAND

Nelson

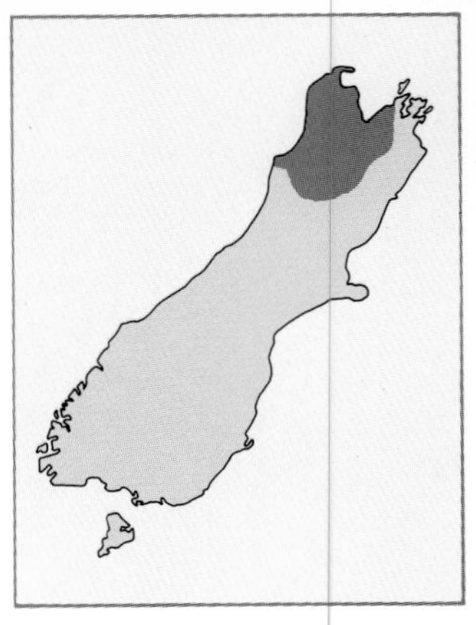

To know Nelson is to know New Zealand. Creation choreographed this northernmost reach of the South Island with most of the country's native ingredients, and then lit it lavishly with sun. The region's medley of mountain and sea mediates between the north and south of New Zealand. Its warm, sandy seaboard is typically North Island, but its mountains and rivers belong unmistakably to the South Island. Subtropical vegetation meets alpine species as most of the northern trees and ferns give way to the southern beech forest.

The human story echoes nature's. Northern and southern Maoris fought over this fertile and productive region. It changed hands often until armed northern tribes won. When Europeans began settling here, there were no Maoris left who could truthfully call Nelson their tribal earth.

Today the region's seventy thousand people, though distinctly of the South Island, look more to the North Island. High ranges behind Nelson make the remainder of the South Island seem remote, whereas the North Island is only two or three dozen kilometres away. The region's mild climate makes it a popular retirement place for people of both islands. In recent years, craft workers have come from all parts of New Zealand and from overseas. Newcomers have felt their freedom here and many have made the region a refuge from conventional livelihoods. The arts thrive; bookshops and galleries reflect a literate and creative community. Its environmentally sensitive citizens have preserved both the natural and the human character of the region.

On the same latitude as Wellington but without the capital's worrying winds, Nelson shares the country's sunniest location with neighbouring Marlborough. This bright and gently watered climate ripens grapes, apples and hops; and subtropical species such as kiwifruit, avocado, feijoa and tamarillo. The city of Nelson is one of New Zealand's oldest and most delightful townscapes. Dominated by its cathedral, it retains the air of a Victorian village. By contrast, this relatively small region also contains great tracts of wilderness, including two national parks and perhaps the country's most impressive forest park.

The first possessors of the region, according to Maori tradition, were the Waitaha and Rapuwai tribes, probably descendants of earlier moa-hunting Maoris. Archaeological evidence indicates that they may have lived in coastal settlements of two to five hundred people. They made fine stone-age tools from rich deposits of argillite. In the classic Maori era, interest shifted to a different mineral. *Pounamu* – South Island greenstone or New Zealand jade – was the equivalent of gold, diamonds and platinum to the stone-age Maoris. Because of its strategic location on coastal and overland tracks to the rivers and valleys of the west coast (where greenstone was most abundant), the Nelson region was savagely contested. The Ngati Mamoe from the north were the first to conquer it. The Waitaha and Rapuwai tribes vanished into the mists of Southland and Otago. Later, the Ngati Mamoe (later known as 'the lost tribe') suffered a similar fate at the hands of the Ngai Tahu and disappeared for ever in Fiordland's forests. In their turn the Ngai Tahu were driven south by the Rangitane and Ngati Apa of the lower North Island. Finally came Te Rauparaha's fierce Ngati Toa.

The Dutch navigator Abel Tasman was the first outsider to experience the ferocity of Nelson's inhabitants (see page 215). In 1642 his two tiny storm-battered ships *Heemskerck* and *Zeehaen* sailed into what is now Golden Bay. Tasman's small craft were met by Maori canoes and four Dutch sailors were slain. Dutch guns retaliated, powerfully expressing disillusion with the discovered land, and the distressed Tasman fled. The South Island had a new and melancholy name: Murderers' Bay.

Nearly one hundred and thirty years later, Captain James Cook found no Maori who knew about the incident. The tribe encountered by Tasman had become a small fugitive band in the South Island interior. When Te Rauparaha and his Taranaki allies raided Nelson's shores in the eighteen-twenties, slaughter, slavery and cannibal ovens left the region largely depopulated. Later when white faces became familiar in New Zealand's south, Te Rauparaha sold off land in Tasman Bay and Golden Bay to the New Zealand Company before officials had even inspected it. For the equivalent of less than one thousand pounds, paid in goods like blankets, axes, flour, tobacco, guns and gunpowder, more than eighty thousand hectares fell into European hands. Upon inspection, those lands were recognised as an ideal site for the first organised British settlement in the South Island.

In 1841 an advance party under Captain Arthur Wakefield arrived to survey for a town site and to reconcile the local Maoris, with more gifts, to Te Rauparaha's sale of choice land from under their feet. Beyond the thirteen-kilometre natural breakwater now called the Boulder Bank, Wakefield's party discovered a sheltered sheet of water that was perfect for a harbour. They named it Nelson Haven. On February 1, 1842, the first migrant vessel, the *Fifeshire*, hovered offshore, soon followed by the *Mary Ann* and later the *Lloyds* and *Lord Auckland*. The ships deposited five hundred settlers. The arrival of the *Lloyds*, however, was to blight Nelson's beginnings. It carried wives and children of the men of the advance party. Sixty-five children had perished during the voyage, and the women had been bedded by the captain, surgeon and crewmen. The official report styled it 'a floating bawdy house'. The word 'Lloyds' soon became a synonym for immorality. Later the citizens of Nelson were seldom to make much of their connection with the first four ships, unlike the descendants of the New Plymouth and Christchurch pioneers.

By mid-1842 there were about two thousand new settlers. Immigration barracks were the first substantial buildings. At first, religious services were held in the surveyors' messroom. In August, Bishop Selwyn pitched a tent on Church Hill that accommodated two hundred people and took services in Maori and English from dawn to dusk. By the end of 1842, however, the settlement seemed to be disintegrating. There were too few gentlemen with too little capital. Those who did have some money often had no knowledge of agriculture and ended up returning to Britain. Men who had been promised employment found no jobs. Much of the land surveyed by the New Zealand Company was held by speculators in England who had no intention of migrating. What remained was expensive and unpromising, and bankruptcies became common.

Expansion seemed an answer to the pioneers' problems. The ambitious Arthur Wakefield wanted to plant Nelson's flag on Marlborough's grassy Wairau plain, which Te Rauparaha had never sold. In a swift and lethal clash, twenty-two Nelson settlers were killed (see page 231), including Wakefield himself. Governor FitzRoy acknowledged the justice of the Maori response and Nelson's humiliated citizens were left licking their wounds.

By the middle of the eighteen-forties Nelson's edible produce consisted mainly of wild pork, pigeon and potatoes. Tempted by New Zealand Company promises, gritty German settlers arrived to take up land at Upper Moutere. The vineyards and orchards that they established soon demonstrated the horticultural value of Nelson's

WHERE NORTH MEETS SOUTH

hinterland. Pastoralists who could afford the 'sufficient price', fixed by the New Zealand Company to keep land in the hands of an antipodean gentry, acquired mountain acres. But wealth from wool did little to help Nelson's poor. Later the colony's government obliged the New Zealand Company to reduce its prices, and the settlement's impoverished labourers began to establish themselves on smallholdings. Thanks to the region's gentle climate, and a great deal of hard labour, Nelson began to prosper at last. In 1858 Queen Victoria decreed that 'the said Town of Nelson shall be a City'. The character of that city was to be determined more by emancipated labourers than by landed gentry.

Gold gave confidence too. In 1857 New Zealand's first significant gold strike was made at Golden Bay (as Murderers' Bay has been renamed). Coarse gold, sometimes in nuggets of two or three ounces, was located by pig hunters in the Aorere Valley, behind present-day Collingwood. Before long more than two thousand people were working on the goldfield. Collingwood, then called Gibbstown, boomed into life. Though it was never very rich and most of it was exhausted by 1860, Collingwood's deposits were sufficient to make many settlers masters of their own fate. Finds in neighbouring Marlborough – in the Wakamarina Valley, behind Havelock – enriched Nelson merchants.

With gold came greed and crime. In 1866 the most notorious nineteenth-century murders were committed by bushrangers Burgess, Levy, Kelly and Sullivan who preyed on travellers to and from the goldfields on the bridle path under Maungatapu Mountain (see page 216).

Today Nelson is a city with durable colonial charm. Much of the surrounding region is lushly planted. The first shipment of cold-storage apples was exported in 1911 to London; today Nelson apples, some forty per cent of New Zealand's total production, are exported all over the world. Kiwifruit are evident everywhere. All New Zealand's hops are grown here, and half the annual harvest is used for brewing German beer. Raspberries, boysenberries and strawberries flourish and distinctive wines are produced from Nelson's vineyards. The region's fruit juices are consumed throughout the country and overseas. Nelson's mountainous back country is productive too. Steep wasteland left behind by logging and burning has been reclothed in pine forest. By the end of the twentieth century, pine milling and processing may become Nelson's major industry.

Kiwifruit were first grown on a commercial scale in New Zealand; here they are being trimmed in a Nelson orchard

Sea produce from the nearby fishing grounds in Cook Strait is also abundant. Tasty Tasman Bay scallops are now outrivalled commercially by the green-lipped New Zealand mussel, or kiwiclam, which is exported to discerning restaurateurs and chefs in Europe and North America. Factories process locally caught fish, and salmon farms have been developed. The biggest and busiest fishing port in the country, Nelson is not only a base for New Zealand fishermen but also for foreign vessels fishing on licence in New Zealand waters. Russian, Japanese, Korean and Taiwanese boats lend cosmopolitan colour to the port.

Harvest time on one of the several hundred tobacco farms in New Zealand. Tobacco was one of the earliest crops

Soil and sun, forest and sea remain the ingredients of the good life for the people of the Nelson area today, just as they were for the first Polynesian arrivals. With less than three per cent of New Zealand's population, this is one of the least crowded and most relaxing regions for the traveller. When young Thomas Arnold, son of Dr Thomas Arnold of Rugby, set foot here as a prospective colonist in 1848, he wrote: 'To the stranger the climate has a sort of intoxicating effect; you feel as if the burden of life and human cares were suddenly thrown off, and as if you had nothing to do now but enjoy yourself.' He might have been writing of Nelson today.

Aotearoa, 'land of the long white cloud' – a mural at Wakefield Quay in Nelson provides a convincing illusion

AO TEA ROA

LUTHERAN CHURCH
NEW ZEALAND
St. Pauls
DIVINE SERVICE
SUNDAY SCHOOL

Left: *The Lutheran Church of St Paul (1905) in Upper Moutere replaced an earlier church; some headstones in the graveyard, inscribed in German, provide a link with the original settlers who established orchards and vineyards*

In a city remarkable for its abundance of well-preserved buildings from the eighteen-forties and eighteen-fifties still in use today, this quaint cottage in the main shopping area is an outstanding example

*Nelson's Nile and South Streets offer examples of the city's nineteenth-century buildings – like the simple workmen's cottages (***top***) and the Bishop's School (***above***), which has been restored as an educational museum*

*Painter Jane Evans (***top***) and jeweller Jens Hansen who works in paua (abalone) shell and silver (***above***), are among the new colonists of the Nelson area – a growing population of commercially successful artists* **Right***: Nelson is known for its long tradition and vigorous interest in the arts and crafts, and is home to a thriving creative community, including basket weaver Chris Flaherty* **Far right***: The clay found in and around Nelson is particularly good for pottery and there are more than seventy full-time potters doing a brisk trade in the city – among them is Steve Fullmer of Tasman*

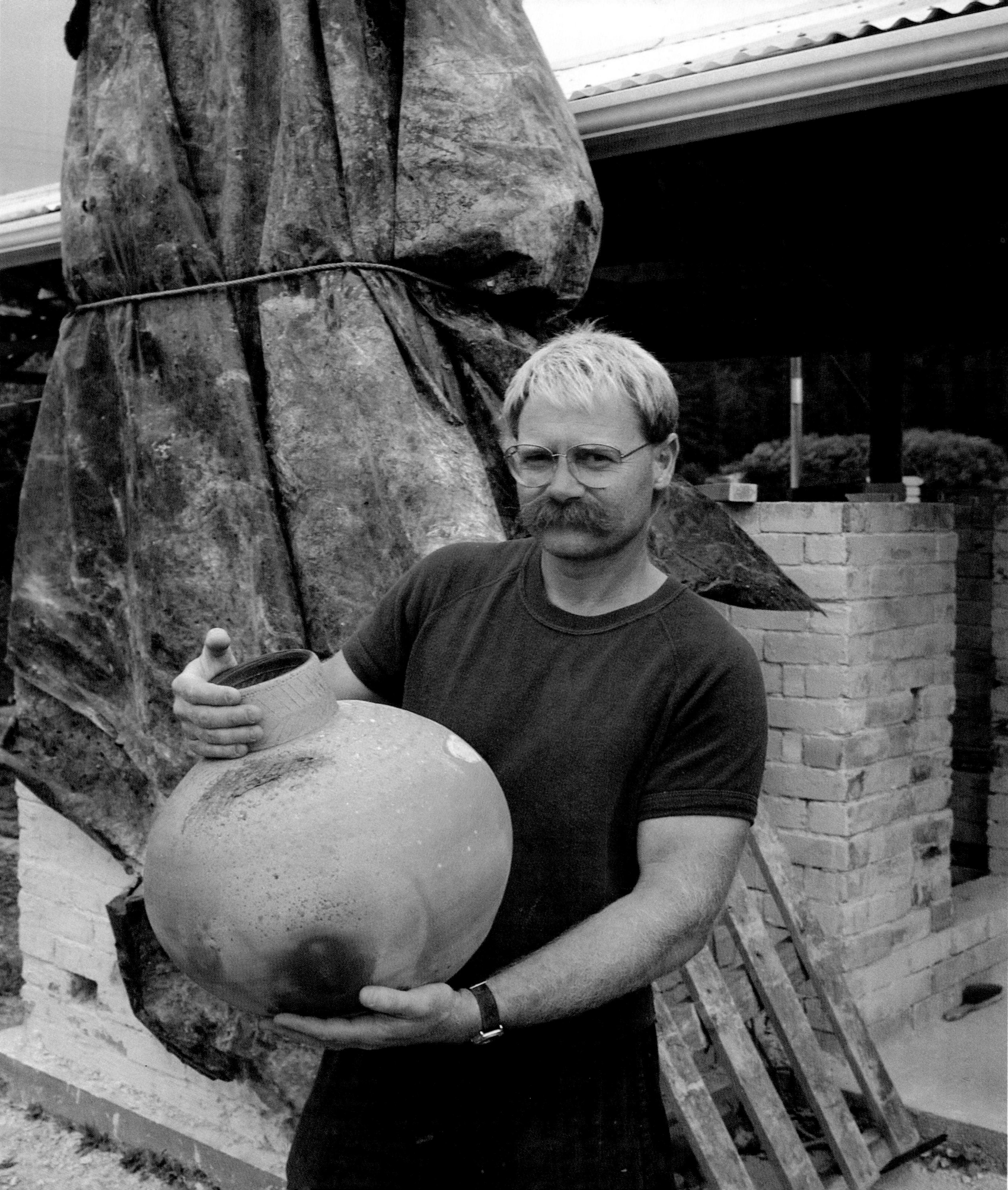

NELSON'S NATIVE WILDS

Native parks, stretching over two-thirds of a million hectares, contain a wealth of unspoiled wilderness

Most low-lying land near Nelson city is extensively cultivated and extravagantly fruitful. Native Nelson is to be found mainly within two national parks and two vast forest parks, one of which is the largest in New Zealand. Together these citadels of the natural world total hundreds of thousands of hectares. Furthermore, the wilderness here has never been packaged and marketed (unlike that of Mount Cook and Milford Sound); there are few hotels outside the city and tourist coaches are rare.

The wilderness begins just behind Golden Bay. A road twists over Takaka Hill and snakes down to the Takaka Valley. Human occupation is suddenly thin. Dairy farms in settings redolent of Swiss countryside appear beneath formidable mountains. At Takaka township the highway follows the curve of the coast towards Farewell Spit. To the right lies the Abel Tasman National Park, with its steep granite country and forests sweeping down to golden sands. On this coast of coves, headlands, caves and reefs, Europeans and

Mountain beeches form vast tracts of forest in the Nelson region; this open forest interior is near Cobb Reservoir

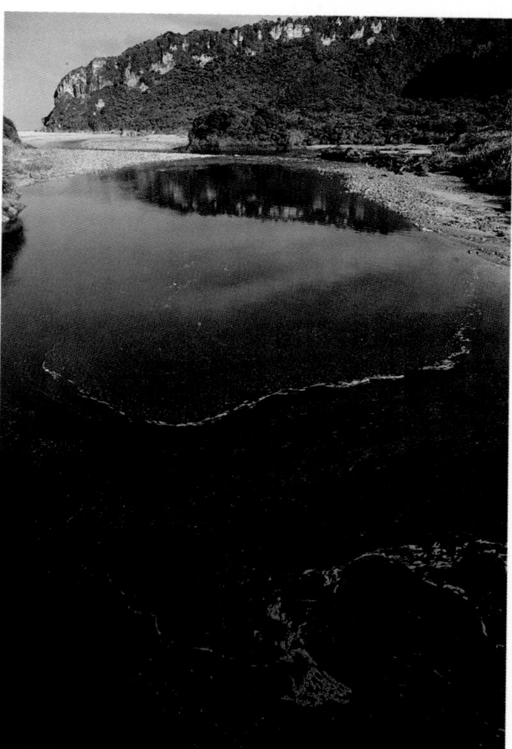

The reward after several days of walking on the Heaphy Track from Collingwood: the coast and spectacular vistas

Above: *Sculptured outcrops of fluted grey marble mark the top of Takaka Hill, also known as Marble Mountain. Beneath is a honeycomb of limestone caves, including Harwoods Hole* **Above left**: *A stand of impressive nikau palms on the Heaphy Track. The tree grows to a height of about ten metres* **Left**: *Manukas, or tea trees, near Cobb Reservoir. Manukas shed their bark in thin strips, and their oily aromatic leaves make the air heavy with a peppery smell*

Maoris had their first fatal meeting. That encounter is commemorated by a small reserve and in the name of the park itself, created in 1942 to mark the tricentennial of Tasman's visit.

Abel Tasman National Park is the smallest of New Zealand's national parks. Its beaches are Polynesian in character, but unlike most others in the populated Pacific, they remain untouched by developers and tourist promoters. Much can be seen only on foot. Colonial surveyor Frederic Carrington all but lost his bearings here in 1841 and became a beachcomber. It was, he reported, the part of New Zealand that most nearly approached his notion of the beautiful and romantic. 'I cannot adequately describe the beauty of the little nooks on the coast, every one with its beach of the most beautiful yellow sand, with an impenetrable mass of evergreen shrubs rising in the background, presenting to the eye every shade of the rainbow...if ever I settle in New Zealand [this] would be the spot I give preference to.'

Pioneer millers and farmers cleared much of this part of Nelson, but after more than four decades of recovery the protected coastal vegetation is almost as lush as it was when Tasman saw it. Human activity has made little impression on the mountainous kingdom of marble and schist to the west of the park. Interaction between acid water and marble has honeycombed Takaka Hill and left the extraordinary spectacle of Harwoods Hole diving hundreds of metres into its heart.

Beyond Takaka, Collingwood is the only community of any size. Born of New Zealand's first gold rush, it is the last flutter of civilisation before the Heaphy Track and Farewell Spit. Cars must be left behind when exploring Farewell Spit,

Flocks of oystercatchers, also called redbills or toreas, forage the Collingwood sands for limpets, mussels and chitons

Above: *A clouded sky and sandbanks at low tide near Collingwood, a quiet town on the lazy curve of Golden Bay*

Right: *Beech-fringed Lake Rotoiti in Nelson Lakes National Park, with mountain ranges rising on either hand*

the sandy arc that offers a glimpse of New Zealand still in the making. For thousands of years the sea has freighted sand, glacial silt and pebbles up the western coast of the South Island and finally jettisoned its cargo here. Farewell Spit grows by more than three million cubic metres of debris every year – widening rather than lengthening. Its swamps, mudflats, salt marshes and tidal pools are a sandy realm of seabirds.

The Maori once hunted along the spit, perhaps warred over it, but left little mythology behind. Whining winds and rustling sands – and its faintly menacing loneliness – have given it a reputation for being haunted. In the nineteen-twenties, wind and tide are said to have temporarily revealed a vast Maori graveyard. A woman once reported a vision of a fierce tribal battle raging among its dunes. Nineteenth-century Europeans turned fire and then cattle loose here. Since 1938 however, it has been a wildlife sanctuary with more than ninety species of birds.

Wharariki Beach and the sand dunes of Cape Farewell, the most northerly point of the South Island

Farewell Spit. . . a delight to tourists, a haven for birds

To the south of Collingwood are Bainham, the vast North West Nelson Forest Park, and the beginning of the Heaphy Track, one of New Zealand's best known walks. The Maori once used this rugged overland route to reach Westland's lodes of greenstone. It is named after Charles Heaphy, the nineteenth-century explorer, soldier and artist (see page 217). In 1846 Heaphy and his fellow explorer Thomas Brunner were the first Europeans to walk the track's coastal section. Government agent James Mackay was first to hike the full distance in 1860, after which it became a route for gold prospectors working between Westland and Golden Bay. Today, with huts for shelter at regular intervals, the track passes through tall stands of native forest and across tussock downland to the ferns and nikau palms and roaring surf of Westland.

MAGNIFICENT MOUNTAIN LAKELAND

Back over the Takaka Hill, south of Motueka towards Nelson city, is the mountainous Nelson Lakes National Park, part of the Southern Alps. It is named after the two long, narrow lakes – Rotoroa, 'long lake' and Rotoiti, 'small lake' – left behind by retreating glaciers. In the eighteen-forties, Europeans arrived to locate and explore land optimistically purchased in London. Instead of a neat, ordered terrain, they were greeted by a

Awaroa Bay, south of Totaranui, is an introduction to the fascinating coastline of Abel Tasman National Park

dense maze of rivers, ravines, forests and lakes that had never seen much human habitation except for the foraging Maori tribesmen who came seasonally from the coast in search of eels and freshwater mussels. Although pastoralists would later press into the area, and prospectors would

The sands of Wharariki Beach near Cape Farewell. Farther along the coast is the Pillar Light, then the slender sandbar of Farewell Spit, which is a constant hazard to shipping. There is another lighthouse at the eastern end of the spit

pick over the rivers and rocks in pursuit of gold, the region was not well regarded in the nineteenth century. In 1864 it was described by one surveyor as 'a land of forest, water, stone, a lovely desert pleasing to the eye, but spiritually and intellectually a gloomy waste'. In short, it was a place with no lucrative lure whatsoever.

For the German geologist Julius von Haast, however, the natural world here was pure joy. Employed to scout the area by the colonial government, he recorded his delight in the beauty of Lake Rotoiti in 1860, 'its deep blue waters reflected the high rocky mountain chains on its eastern and southern shores which, for a considerable height from the water's edge are clad with luxuriant primeval forest.' He marvelled at the thousands of birds and looked forward to a time when Nelson's mountain lakeland would become 'a favoured abode and resort to those whose means and leisure will permit them to admire picturesque and magnificent scenery'.

Above: *The Heaphy Track links Golden Bay with the West Coast over easy grades rising to nine hundred metres*
Right: *Experienced trampers recommend starting at Golden Bay so that the Tasman Sea is the climax of the walk*
Above right: *Pillar Light on Cape Farewell affords fine views in all directions, particularly of Farewell Spit*

Below: *Old jetty at Collingwood – relic of its golden days*

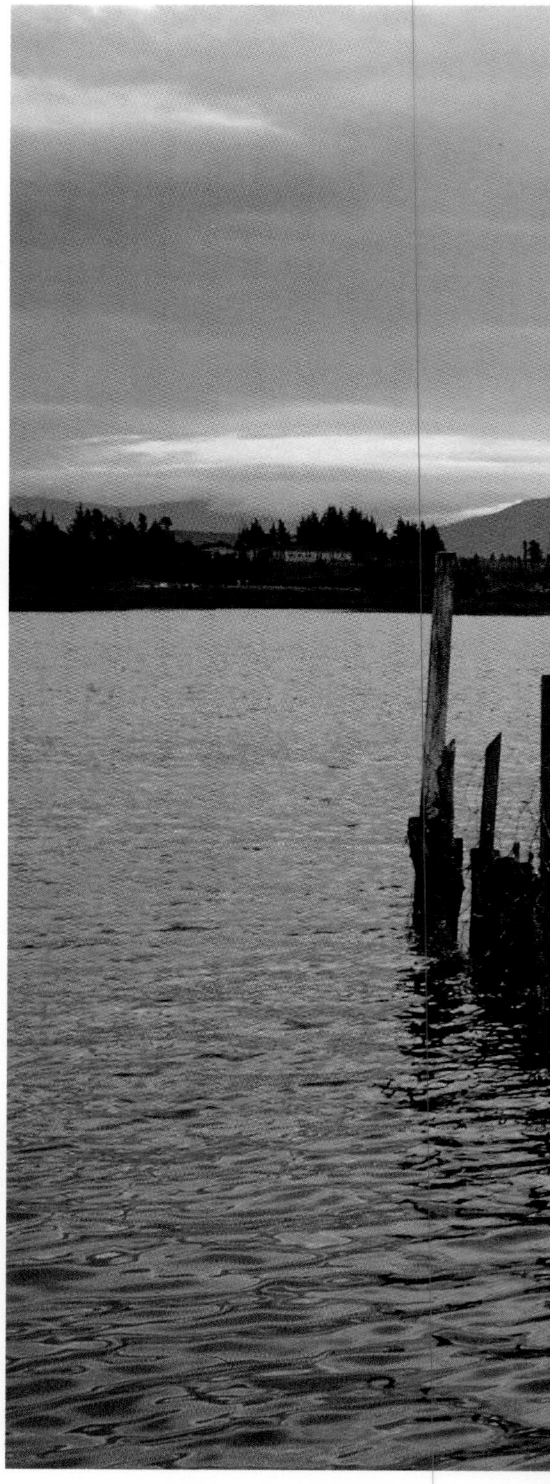

It took most of a century for that vision to be realised – not just for the affluent few, but for everyone. From the nineteen-thirties, motor vehicles and better roads brought hunters, fishermen, trampers, skiers and lovers of watersports. In 1956 the splendour of the natural riches of the region were at last recognised and Nelson's lakeland was made a national park.

To the south of Nelson city, and fingering east right into Marlborough, lies Mount Richmond Forest Park, backed by the South Island's great alpine fault. Much of its landscape was picked apart by pastoralists, burned off, grazed and then abandoned to erosion. Gold-seekers served their time here too. Today that human assault has left few relics. The Pelorus River swerves through gorges and rides between beech forests. The silver fern of the North Island surrenders to the tussock of the South. No less than two hundred and fifty kilometres of tracks traverse the park. More than thirty huts accommodate trampers, hunters, fishermen, amateur gold-panners, rock-hounds and bush browsers, and there are plenty of sites to pitch a tent.

All told, the Nelson region has over two-thirds of a million hectares in wilderness reserves – nearly ten hectares for each of its seventy thousand people. Small wonder that outsiders are envious, and that many find their way here to holiday, and often to settle. Although the first colonists saw little money-making potential in the region, their loss is the nation's gain.

PLACES OF INTEREST

ABEL TASMAN NATIONAL PARK
New Zealand's smallest national park (22 530 hectares), and historically the richest. The road from TAKAKA passes coves, limestone battlements, dramatic cliffs and tiny islands, all of which formed the setting for the first contact between Maoris and Europeans. Finally, it winds through forest to popular Totaranui beach, one of many strands of golden sand that braid the coastal perimeter of the park. The landscape has suffered at the hands of pioneer Europeans but is fast returning to its native state. There are superb walks along a shore that bewitched early European voyagers such as Frenchman Dumont d'Urville who, in 1827, left many names here. Other walkways climb into the forest above idyllic bays. Full details can be obtained at information offices at Takaka and Totaranui. There is a ranger at Marahau.

BRIGHTWATER
This largely anonymous settlement 19 kilometres south of NELSON was the birthplace of the renowned nuclear physicist Lord Rutherford. A roadside monument commemorates the region's most famous citizen. The attractive St Paul's Anglican Church was built in 1857. Newmans, the transport company, began modestly in Brightwater in 1879, when brothers Tom and Harry Newman made their historic journey by a horse-drawn coach south to the Murchison goldfield with the mail.

COLLINGWOOD
Tiny Collingwood is all a last outpost should be,with one wide, sleepy street and a scatter of wooden dwellings set at the mouth of the Aorere River, on Golden Bay's lonely shore. It was first called Gibbstown, after pioneer settler William Gibbs. Some 2000 diggers lived in or near the township during the 1857 gold rush. Later it was renamed after Admiral Collingwood, Lord Nelson's understudy at the Battle of Trafalgar. Only one hotel remains of the seven that once served thirsty diggers. In those early days, it was thought that Collingwood would grow larger than Nelson. Now it has less than 200 residents. Its interest to travellers is its proximity to FAREWELL SPIT. Four-wheel-drive excursions are available to the lighthouse at the spit's extremity (contact Collingwood Safari Tours). Otherwise vehicles are forbidden, and even walkers are restricted to an area 2.5 kilometres from the base of the spit.

St Cuthbert's Church (1873), built of pit-sawn timber, was designed by the great Nelson-Westland explorer, Thomas Brunner. The old courthouse functions as a tearoom, and the town's lock-up is a small museum. The Aorere Valley, where diggers laboured, holds much of interest. At Rockville (9 kilometres south) there are the Te Anaroa limestone caves, the curiously sculpted formations called the Devil's Boots and a small private museum. Farther on (16 kilometres) is the hamlet of Bainham at one end of the HEAPHY TRACK. Another road leads north from Collingwood to the tranquil harbour of Whanganui Inlet on the South Island's west coast.

FAREWELL SPIT
Named by Captain James Cook as he sailed for home after making his epic circumnavigation of New Zealand in 1769 and 1770. This furthermost point of the South Island was built of the debris dumped by Westland's stormy seas and is still growing. Virtually the whole spit is a wildlife reserve, with only organised excursions permitted from COLLINGWOOD. At the base of the spit, Puponga Farm Park has scenic, archaeological and botanical features of special interest, also views of the spit itself. Among the birds to be seen is the Siberia-breeding godwit, which makes a dramatic departure for the northern hemisphere in late March or early April. Other birds feeding and flourishing here include the black swan, oystercatcher, shag, heron, turnstone and pied stilt.

HEAPHY TRACK
Named after artist, explorer, soldier and Victoria Cross winner Charles Heaphy (see page 217), the track threads through 78 kilometres of magnificent South Island terrain – all within the vast NORTH WEST NELSON FOREST PARK – down to Karamea in Westland. Once used by Maoris to reach Westland's greenstone, and later by gold-diggers, the track has now been upgraded, with bridges over streams and huts for shelter and sleep at regular intervals (no more than four or five hours' walk apart). The diverse vegetation includes highland beech, lowland rimu and kahikatea, coastal nikau, and the alpine herb fields and flowers of the red-tussocked Gouland Downs. Maoris felt happier with the open and surf-lashed marine section of the track; they saw the downs as the abode of mountain demons who preyed on the unwary. The views are spectacular.

Visitors should allow 4 or 5 days; small aircraft will fly trampers back to base. Starting points are just north of Karamea in Westland, or Bainham, behind Collingwood in Nelson. Aficionados of the Heaphy recommend the latter, so that the coast is the climax of the walk. Few New Zealanders find the time and money to walk Fiordland's remote Milford Track, but the Heaphy is democratically within reach of all and equally

A tourist feeding eels at Anatoki, near the junction of the Anatoki and Takaka Rivers

THE FATHER OF NUCLEAR PHYSICS

A monument beside Highway 6, in the small township of Brightwater near Nelson, marks the birthplace of Baron Rutherford of Nelson, OM, FRS, the greatest physicist of his time

Ernest Rutherford (left) in 1925 with Thomas Easterfield, director of Cawthron Institute

Fellow-scientists have called Ernest Rutherford (1871-1937) 'the father of nuclear physics' and 'the greatest experimental physicist since Faraday'. Certainly he was one of the most influential scientists of our age. He was the man who first split the atom and thus gave the world a new source of energy – and the possibility of global destruction. After graduating at Canterbury University, Rutherford spent most of his working life in Canada and England. He returned to New Zealand to marry and for other brief visits. But the land of his birth remained important to him and he did much to help New Zealand scientists.

In 1895 Rutherford arrived at the Cavendish Laboratory at Cambridge in England, where he started work on the newly discovered X-rays. Three years later, at the age of twenty-eight, he was appointed Professor of Physics at McGill University, Montreal, where he undertook brilliant research into radio-activity. In 1903 he was elected Fellow of the Royal Society and in 1907 he was appointed Professor of Physics at Manchester University in England. With Hans Geiger, a German, and Ernest Marsden, a New Zealander, he advanced the theory of the nuclear atom.

In 1908 Rutherford was awarded the Nobel Prize – for chemistry, not physics. His work was interrupted by the First World War, during which he carried out vital research for the Admiralty on submarine detection. After the war he returned to Cambridge as Cavendish Professor of Experimental Physics and Director of the Cavendish Laboratory, posts he held until his death.

Rutherford made his most important contribution to the science that became nuclear physics when he produced in 1919 the first artificial disintegration or transmutation of an atom by nuclear bombardment. He bombarded nitrogen gas with alpha particles and found that protons (hydrogen nuclei) were ejected as the atoms of nitrogen were changed into atoms of oxygen.

Rutherford's genius was shown not only by his many scientific discoveries, but in his success wherever he went in attracting a team of brilliant colleagues to work with him.

impressive. For full information, contact the NZ Forest Service at **NELSON**, **MOTUEKA** or **COLLINGWOOD**; trampers should in any case notify their itinerary to the nearest NZ Forest Service ranger.

KAITERITERI

Beach and holiday resort 14 kilometres north of **MOTUEKA**. Originally considered as the site for the first colonial settlement, Kaiteriteri was rejected when the natural harbour of Nelson Haven was sighted. A low stone wall at the end of the beach surrounds the spring from which Nelson's founder, Arthur Wakefield, gathered water in 1841. Launch trips are available to the **ABEL TASMAN NATIONAL PARK**, and to pick up and deposit trampers.

Open-air art: an environmental sculpture by Campbell Ewing near the Cobb Reservoir

MOTUEKA

After **NELSON** city, this is the largest community in the region, with a population of 5000. It is set on Tasman Bay and backed by rich rural land. The flat main street exactly follows the clearing burned by the first European settlers from dense bush. In summer seasonal pickers, sorters and packers of berries, apples, hops, tobacco, and kiwifruit flock to the township. One of the South Island's few Maori churches, Te Ahurewa (1897) in Pah Street has a carved interior and houses an old canoe once used on the Motueka River. Inquire at the marae for access. **KAITERITERI** is the nearest, most attractive beach.

MOUNT RICHMOND FOREST PARK

These 188 000 rugged hectares rise abruptly between Marlborough's Wairau River and Nelson's Waimea Plains, the highest peaks reaching almost 1800 metres. The park has 250 kilometres of walking tracks. Its vegetation ranges from coastal scrub, podocarp and beech forest to alpine grassland, with some milled patches of exotic forest. Much of the forest is being regenerated on land once burned off by pastoralists and ravaged by erosion. Maori argillite quarries can be seen, and there are gold-rush relics near the Wakamarina field. The most extensive of many possible excursions is the Pelorus Track, a 3- or 4-day hike for experienced trampers and enthusiastic trout fishermen.

The more popular Hacket area of the park, accessible from **NELSON** city or **RICHMOND**, has easier tramping tracks (hours rather than days) and takes in a spectacular limestone waterfall and mineral-rich terrain once mined for chromite and copper. Between Maungatapu (on the Pelorus River) and Nelson's Maitai Valley lies the original overland route between Nelson and Blenheim, the setting for the Maungatapu murders (see page 216). Huts are available in the park. Inquire at NZ Forest Service offices at Nelson, Blenheim, Rai Valley or Renwick.

MOUTERE (UPPER AND LOWER)

Between **NELSON** and **MOTUEKA**, two communities are of particular human interest. German settlement began in the apple-producing lands of Upper Moutere, where St Paul's Lutheran Church (1905) confirms the community's central European character. A German-speaking viticulturist now produces distinguished wines where the vineyards of the firstcomers failed. The Riverside Community of Lower Moutere is New Zealand's longest-lived and most successful commune. It began as a Christian pacifist community in 1940. Membership is based on the renunciation of private property and profit, repudiation of war, teamwork and shared responsibility for the maintenance and administration of the community. A number of the buildings are of rammed or fortified (soil and cement) earth. Visitors are always welcome and the commune's choice farm produce is for sale.

MURCHISON

Mountain-trapped Murchison is 130 kilometres south-west of **NELSON** and 102 kilometres east of Westport, between the Nelson region and Westland. The settlement began during the gold rushes of the 1860s, largely as the creation of the legendary swashbuckler, prospector, publican and self-styled sheriff George Fairweather Moonlight (1832-84). It later sobered into a market town for heartland farmers. In 1929 it was reduced to rubble by New Zealand's most powerful earthquake since the beginning of European settlement. The topography of the area was completely altered; hillsides collapsed; bridges, roads and buildings were demolished; 17 people died. Scars on neighbouring landscape can still be seen. Now a township of 600, Murchison takes its name from nearby Mt Murchison (1469 metres), which was named by the geologist Julius von Haast after a famous Scottish geologist. Murchison's story is recorded in the town museum (open Monday to Friday, 2–4, in summer). Traces of oil and natural gas in the vicinity have been explored but a successful strike has still to be made. There is a spectacular drive from Murchison into Westland along Buller Gorge, with many attractive riverside picnic places.

DUTCH DISCOVERER OF NEW ZEALAND

Abel Tasman never set foot in New Zealand, but several major geographical features in the country bear his name

After confrontation with Maori warriors Tasman named his anchorage Murderers' Bay

Abel Janszoon Tasman (1603-59) first sighted the South Island on December 13, 1642. Soon afterwards, his two ships, *Heemskerck* and *Zeehaen*, sailed north and then east to find a safe anchorage, away from the dangerous West Coast surf. Rounding what is now called Cape Farewell, he came into Golden Bay and noticed the first signs of settlement: smoke rising from several points. It was not long before canoes approached, and Tasman made the mistake of firing a cannon, an act that was certainly interpreted as hostile by the Maori paddlers. The following day, seven canoes drew close, intercepted a ship's boat from the *Zeehaen* and rammed it. Three of Tasman's men were killed, another died later and three escaped by swimming back to safety. The first meeting between Maori and *Pakeha* had ended in bloodshed – at what Tasman chose to call 'Murderers' Bay'.

The two ships then made their way to the north, again attempting to go ashore at the Three Kings Islands to find fresh water. This time it was the heavy surf that frustrated Tasman's two attempts to land, and he sailed away, never to return.

It was the Dutch East India Company that had sent out Tasman's expedition, to seek trading opportunities in the rich lands believed to lie in the Pacific region. Those expected trade benefits did not materialise and the East India Company was not impressed by Tasman's descriptions of Staten Landt – the name it gave to New Zealand in the mistaken belief that it might be attached to the South American territory of the same name.

Little is known of Tasman's early life. Born in Lutjegast in the Netherlands, he sailed to the East Indies three times – ultimately never to return to his homeland. His journeys took him as far as Japan, Cambodia and Sumatra. Eventually, Tasman left the East India Company's service to become a private sea-trader.

NELSON

New Zealand's first-named city, by decree of Queen Victoria in 1858 (though a town of less than 3000 inhabitants at the time). Still small, with a population of 44 000, Nelson has retained much of its Victorian character. Before its site had even been seen, Nelson was planned in London by the New Zealand Company as a model settlement. Its Maori name – Wakatu, 'dump of broken canoes' – was quickly changed to that of the hero of Trafalgar. Other naval names were given to streets and parks, such as Nile, Trafalgar, Hardy, Collingwood, and the first ships *Fifeshire*, *Whitby*, *Arrow* (but not the disastrous *Lloyds* (see page 200).

After much early confusion and hardship, Nelson eventually became a haven for Britain's underprivileged. Evidence of its beginnings can be seen in both humble cottages and grand homes, the latter mainly those of self-made merchants. At the centre of the city near Church Hill are a number of modest 19th-century cottages in the historic precinct of South Street. Facing Nile Street, three distinctive buildings serve as showplaces for Nelson's craftspeople. By contrast, at outlying Stoke, there is the elegant two-storey Broadgreen, one of New Zealand's largest and finest cob dwellings. Built in 1855 for Nelson

MURDER AT MAUNGATAPU

Over a century ago, on a lonely bridle track over Maungatapu Mountain to Nelson, a gang of bushrangers committed multiple murder

Thomas Kelly . . . many convictions

Philip Levy . . . violent criminal history

Joseph Sullivan . . . turned in friends

Richard Burgess . . . hanged for murder

Murderers' Rock is the grisly name given to the spot where, on June 12, 1866, five men were killed in two hold-ups. A party of four, Felix Mathieu, James Dudley, John Kempthorne and James Pontius, was carrying gold (to the value of three hundred pounds) to Nelson when it was ambushed, and all four were murdered. Their bodies were concealed, together with that of James Battle, a farm labourer.

Four men who later cashed three hundred pounds worth of gold at Nelson were arrested. Their names were Joseph Sullivan, Richard Burgess, Philip Levy and Thomas Kelly – all notorious criminals in England, Australia, West Coast and Otago. One of them, Sullivan, testified against the others, ensuring their conviction. They were hanged in Nelson gaol on October 5, 1866 amid considerable public jubilation. Sullivan was rewarded with two hundred pounds and a free pardon.

However, the case was not over. Sullivan's pardon was only for the murders of the four gold prospectors. In revenge for Sullivan's treachery, the prisoner Burgess had implicated him in the murder of 'Old Jamie' Battle. Sullivan was tried for this crime, convicted and sentenced to hang. This was later commuted to life, followed by deportation.

The list of crimes committed by the gang was legendary. Some had possibly committed murder in Australia, and the death of a storekeeper and a surveyor on the West Coast can almost certainly be credited to them. It was also believed that Levy had murdered several gold prospectors near Arrowtown in Central Otago, disposing of their bodies in the Kawarau Gorge. After an earlier and violent incarceration in Dunedin gaol, Burgess and Kelly 'swore they'd take a life for every lash and indignity laid on them'. Maungatapu was the first of their planned days of reckoning.

merchant Edmond Buxton, it has been extensively restored and superbly furnished (open Wednesday and weekend, 2–4.30; more frequently in school holidays; closed June and July). Isel House (*c.* 1885), in Stoke's Isel Park, is a splendid timber and stone dwelling containing a large china collection, antiques, paintings and portraits (open weekend, 2–4; also Tuesday and Thursday in January). Behind Isel House, Nelson Provincial Museum has displays covering the region's history, including the death masks of the bushrangers Burgess, Kelly and Levy, who were hanged here in 1866 for the Maungatapu murders (open Tuesday to Friday, 10-4; weekend and public holidays, 2–4).

Graves of early Nelson settlers and the Maungatapu murder victims can be seen at St Barnabas Church (*c.* 1860, since remodelled), near the entrance to Isel Park. Other preserved public and private buildings in the city include Fairfield House (*c.* 1880) at the top of Trafalgar Street, a residence restored as a community centre (open daily, 10–6); Melrose, in Brougham Street, a palatial Italianate residence of the same vintage; Grove House (*c.* 1868), built by wealthy publican and hop-grower Charles Harley and now occupied by the Cawthron Institute, a soil and plant research centre; and the Californian Guest House (1893) at 29 Collingwood Street.

A walk anywhere along the banks of the Maitai River, which threads through the central city, discloses more interesting Victorian houses and cottages. The small but distinguished Suter Art Gallery houses a collection of 19th-century colonial artists, notably John Gully. Overlooking the city, Christ Church Cathedral (begun in the 1920s) is not itself historic, but it is the third church to rise on the site since 1842. The nave section is of solid Takaka marble (open daily, 8–4 and during services; guided tours at set times in summer).

Early ecclesiastical Nelson is best represented by Bishop's School (Nile Street East; 1881), Nelson's first church school, now restored by the NZ Historic Places Trust as an education museum (open Sunday, 2–5; more frequently in school holidays). The Chapel of the Holy Evangelists (Waimea Road, Bishopdale; 1877) was built for students for the ministry. As well as numerous Anglican churches, Nelson's other notable churches include Trinity Presbyterian Church (1891), St John's Methodist Church (1899) and St Mary's Catholic Church (1882) with its strong wooden shingled spire.

To the east of the city, Founders Park

displays salvaged and restored buildings of the region (open daily). The superb beach of Tahunanui is close to the city centre and many other beaches are easily accessible around Tasman Bay, especially at Rabbit Island and **KAITERITERI**. In the Maitai valley there is also freshwater swimming, with picnic places.

NELSON LAKES NATIONAL PARK

Over 96 000 glacier-gouged hectares of forest, mountain and lake. Through the park runs the great Alpine Fault and the western boundary of the Southern Alps. The high St Arnaud Range forms the park's eastern boundary. Snow-crowned for much of the year, some of the park's mountains rise above 2000 metres. Rainforest shares the terrain with subalpine growth.

The park's two long lakes – Rotoroa and Rotoiti – give it special character. Lake Rotoiti (610 metres above sea level) has the most open space and is the more popular of the two, particularly for swimming, boating and all water sports. At the northern end of Lake Rotoiti, St Arnaud village is a good base for excursions. Lake Rotoroa, less than 500 metres above sea level, is larger, deeper and lonelier, but is much loved by trout fishermen. The highlight for bird-watchers is the protected New Zealand scaup, a diving duck which can easily be seen here. There are many tramping tracks throughout the park. Water taxi services and sightseeing excursions are available on both lakes. Full details are available from park headquarters at St Arnaud, or from the ranger station at Lake Rotoroa.

Tahunanui beach, a sheltered stretch of sand that is Nelson's principal swimming spot

NORTH WEST NELSON STATE FOREST PARK

New Zealand's largest (376 500 hectares), richest and most rugged forest park. It is traversed by the **HEAPHY TRACK**, which takes the walker from Golden Bay's gentle shore into stark Westland. A spectacular road along the Cobb Reservoir (110 kilometres from **NELSON** city, 28 kilometres from the Upper Takaka turn-off) passes through terrain once grazed by pioneer sheep and cattle, but now drowned to generate hydro-electricity. The rocks are rich in fossils, the mountains covered in alpine flowers, and there are picknicking and camping spots. There is plentiful trout fishing, and hunting is possible (with a permit). Mt Arthur Tableland, with its dramatic landforms, is just an hour's drive from Nelson city up the Graham valley. There is a forest ranger in the valley and information can be obtained from the NZ Forest Service at Nelson or **MOTUEKA**.

RICHMOND

A Nelson suburb with a population of 7000. Set among orchards and gardens, the area is noted for its pottery, stoneware and craftwork. The Waimea Pottery is a large craft workers' collective with a pleasant restaurant. The impressive Holy Trinity Church (1872) is built in traditional Early English style.

RIWAKA

Last settlement before Takaka Hill. With a population of 1000, Riwaka sits among hop fields and tobacco plantations. Like neighbouring **MOTUEKA** (5 kilometres), it is populated by cosmopolitan seasonal workers for much of the year. At the foot of Takaka Hill is an attractive reserve at the source of the tree-fringed waters of the Riwaka River.

TAKAKA

Takaka Hill (or Marble Mountain) separates this township from the rest of the Nelson region. Takaka, with just 1000 people, is the village capital of one of New Zealand's loneliest and loveliest marine environments, almost everywhere starkly mountain-backed. To the right of the highway is the main entry point into **ABEL TASMAN NATIONAL PARK**. Ahead lie **COLLINGWOOD** and **FAREWELL SPIT**.

The district has been quarried for gold, coal, iron and marble. Takaka marble was one of the materials used in Wellington's Parliament Buildings. At Onekaka are the remains of a once productive ironworks. Just before the town is reached, tame eels can be fed by hand at the Anatoki River. About 6 kilometres north-west in a scenic reserve off Highway 60 are the famous Waikoropupu (or Pupu) Springs, formed by the bubbling outflow of a river long lost in mazes of subterranean marble. The springs are considered to be among the largest in the world, the flow of the main spring reaching 21 cubic metres a second. Gold-diggers' trenches and water-races can still be seen in the area.

The principal industry of Takaka is at the Golden Bay Cement Works, on the road to Abel Tasman National Park. Places of interest include the museum in the town's main street (open daily, 10–4); the Sacred Heart Catholic Church, and the Artisan Shop, a craft cooperative. The major attaction, however, is Takaka Hill itself, with its bizarre marble outcrops, the 371 metre deep Harwoods Hole, and the fluted and finned limestone sculptures of the Canaan plateau.

WAKEFIELD

This township of 900 people in the hop country of rural Nelson was named after Nelson's founder, Arthur Wakefield. St John's (1846) is the South Island's oldest church and New Zealand's second oldest, after Russell's Christ Church. The district was settled by New Zealand Company labourers, and the austere little church built by voluntary labour reflects its egalitarian beginnings. Here no pews were sold off to the wealthy, as was the custom elsewhere in Nelson. The church was embellished as the district became affluent. Its kauri lining is particularly fine. In the churchyard rest many pioneers, descendants of whom are still to be found working the surrounding farms.

NEW ZEALAND'S FIRST ARTIST

Charles Heaphy, the first non-regular soldier to be awarded the Victoria Cross and an important colonial artist, is commemorated by the famed Heaphy Track

The Heaphy Track, from nikau palms . . .

. . . to rocky coast, a magnificent, walk

The Heaphy Track begins at the end of the country road that follows the Aorere River valley south-west from Collingwood. It leaves the Aorere River to cross the North West Nelson Forest Park for some fifty kilometres, then follows the Heaphy River for another ten kilometres before turning south down the coast to meet the country road from Karamea.

Although Charles Heaphy (1820-81) was a volunteer soldier of outstanding courage, his major influence was not on the military stage. As a public official he occupied many powerful posts. As Auckland Provincial Surveyor, he planned the soldier settlements of the Waikato and drew a survey for the future town of Hamilton. At various times he was MP for Parnell, Government Insurance Commissioner, Land Claims Commissioner and Judge of the Native Court. He also farmed for some years in the Nelson district and took part in two epic West Coast journeys up the Buller River and south of the Arahura River.

But these activities still do not account fully for the man. Heaphy was an artist of outstanding merit, and can lay claim to being New Zealand's first great painter. It was as an artist and draughtsman for the New Zealand Company that he arrived on the *Tory* in 1840 at the age of nineteen. His task was to produce artistic impressions and surveys of lands for the Company's colonisation projects. He travelled through many uncharted areas of the young colony, compiling a record of mountains, rivers, settlements and events. Today these represent a valuable source of information of the period, surpassing written descriptions.

In 1881, Heaphy gave up public office on the grounds of ill-health, and sailed for Australia. He died of tuberculosis in Brisbane that same year.

Marlborough

Whatever route the traveller takes into Marlborough – overland by mountain pass or coastal highway, or by sea through the Marlborough Sounds – the journey is spectacular. But the northern approach is the most familiar to visitors. For many the submerged valleys of the sounds, their luminous waters lapping against the vessel as it glides towards Picton, is their first introduction to the South Island. But Marlborough is more than a gateway to the south; it is as rich and complex a region as any in the country. Its mountains, valleys and labyrinthine waterways give some northerners the feeling they need know no more of South Island than this, and year after year Marlborough is their journey's end.

Marlborough is often seen as being one with Nelson, sharing the top of the South Island. Both regions certainly share New Zealand's sunniest location, and Marlborough's first *Pakeha* were men of means who chafed at the confines of proletarian and impoverished Nelson. But pastoralism and politics led to divisions between the two regions early in the country's post-European history, and the rugged terrain between them has since confirmed the identity of each.

FIRST ARRIVALS

For the first Polynesian arrivals the bays, inlets and islands of Marlborough must have been a paradise, since the sea was central to their livelihood. Inland, the densely forested valleys were home to numerous species of birds. There were ducks in the wetlands, and great numbers of moa were hunted until they were no more. The region also had a climate well-suited to the cultivation of the Maoris' staple vegetable, the kumara. What more they made of their environment, what folktales they told, is largely lost. Ancient midden, moa bones and shells, and greenstone worked into weapons and ornaments, have survived, but the break with the pre-European past is otherwise almost total.

The terrain was always bitterly contested, and most of the local legend was extinguished when the muskets of Te Rauparaha's army sounded along the seaboard. He was the last in a line of northern raiders, and the most obliterating. Marlborough Maoris went the same way as the moa. What little we know of them, apart from the archaeological evidence, comes from the journals of Captain James Cook and his fellow explorers. It was here the great navigator found a haven in the stormy southern seas. On January 15, 1770, he reached the South Island, anchoring in a 'very snug cove' – today known as Ship Cove – which would become the base for his Pacific exploration. His first visit lasted three weeks.

Cook described the precipitous hills covered with growth as 'one intire forest'. More poetically, botanist Joseph Banks recorded: 'This morn I was awakd by the singing of the birds . . . their voices were certainly the most melodious wild musick I have ever heard, almost imitating small bells but with the most tuneable sound imaginable.' The local Maoris traded dried fish and wild celery for Cook's nails and English cloth. They amiably showed the newcomers human bones, the remains of a recent feast, 'and to shew us that they had eat the flesh they bit and naw'd the bone and draw'd it thro' their mouth and this in such a manner as plainly shew'd that the flesh was to them a dainty bit'.

To hoist the Union Jack, Cook climbed high and looked out for the first time on the gusty waters which today bear his name: Cook Strait. He claimed the South Island for King George III, named Queen Charlotte Sound, and toasted Her Majesty's health with wine – the empty bottle being promptly claimed as a receptacle by a Maori onlooker. Between 1770 and 1774 Cook spent a total of four months here resting and refreshing his men. He gave the Maori potato to plant and released pigs and goats so that the country would in time 'be stocked with these animals'. Marlborough was the part of New Zealand Cook knew best and loved most; his reports were so vivid that for decades literate English people thought of New Zealand in terms of Queen Charlotte Sound. Later explorers on the New Zealand coast, the Russian Bellingshausen, and the Frenchman Dumont d'Urville, would also find Marlborough's waters a haven.

So did the whalers. In 1827 English mariner John Guard, having wrenched his vessel clear of cliffs during a storm, found himself in these quiet waters observing whales close inshore. He founded the first substantial European settlements in the South Island (at Te Awaiti in Tory Channel, and later at Port Underwood). The whaling industry he began on Marlborough's coast thrived until the nineteen-sixties.

Other rough communities of whalers followed. Some pioneers took Maori wives, but they did not always escape the attentions of raiding Maori from north and south during the unruly eighteen-thirties. Marlborough's unwholesome reputation rivalled that of Kororareka in the Bay of Islands. The first missionary to arrive was not made especially welcome. He was told to keep his 'bloody Sundays' to himself. When Port Underwood, for a time the busiest whaling base in the Pacific, was finally tamed, and the lawless locals persuaded of the virtues of holy matrimony, the inventive man of the cloth used brass curtain rings at wedding ceremonies, at which he simultaneously baptised the many children of those unions.

Captain John Blenkinsopp, a whaler and a swindler with an eye to the future, 'acquired' some twenty-six thousand hectares of Marlborough hinterland by persuading Te Rauparaha to fix his mark on a deed of sale in exchange for a cannon. When Blenkinsopp died, his widow sold the deed to the New Zealand Company. The document ensured colonisation of the South Island began with a bang.

In 1843 the tiny New Zealand Company settlement at Nelson, hardly more than a year old, was in depression and desperate for useful land, since much of the best land thereabouts was owned by absentee London speculators. It seemed time to make use of Blenkinsopp's fraudulent acquisition. Surveyors pegged out the claimed land. The Maoris protested. Te Rauparaha rightly denied having parted with so much land for a mere cannon. Nelson mounted an armed party of fifty men to assert British authority. The upshot was massacre. Twenty-two European corpses, including that of the Nelson contingent's leader Captain Arthur Wakefield, testified as to who was master of Marlborough. No further land grab was attempted in Te Rauparaha's vicinity.

THE PASTORALISTS

Yet the region's open space – especially in the Wairau and Awatere valleys, all the way up to the snowline – remained choice. Within three or four years squatters, coming from Nelson and driving their sheep before them, were again tempting fate – and Te Rauparaha's warriors. Governor George Grey stepped in and paid three thousand pounds for a block of land that extended almost to present-day Christchurch. The way was open for occupation on a scale unseen in the South Island.

As Australia had already shown, wool-growing was an occupation fit for gentlemen. A stampede for lucrative runs followed. Dozens of ambitious Nelsonians took up leases ranging from three thousand to thirty-six thousand hectares. By 1853 about one hundred and thirty thousand sheep were grazing the region; by 1870 there were well

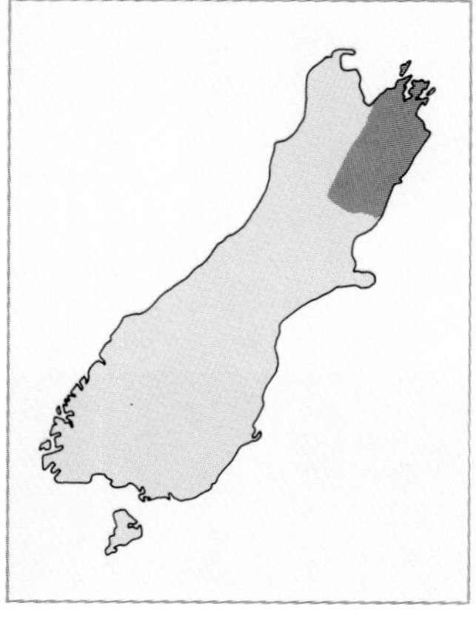

SILENT BAYS AND SETTLERS

over one million. Marlborough became the seedbed of southern pastoralism. The Wairau and Awatere valleys began supplying the South Island with breeding stock after the settlement of Canterbury, Otago and Southland. In the eighteen-fifties, up to twenty-four thousand sheep annually were being driven south across mountain passes. Marlborough was the foundation on which the vast estates of the South Island were built.

The pastoralists of Marlborough, technically still governed by the unkempt colonists of Nelson, now thought it time to call their own tune. They wanted growing homesteads and their wealth buttressed by political favours. In 1858 they pushed for and won independence from Nelson. With a population of barely one thousand and its own provincial legislature, the region was named Marlborough after the fighting Duke and victor of Blenheim, just as Nelson had been named after Britain's greatest naval hero.

Soon after the sheep barons established their realms, a settlement servicing their needs grew inland on the Opawa River. First known as The Beaver, it later became Blenheim. Further north on Queen Charlotte Sound, Waitohi, now Picton, was founded. Rivalry between the few dozen electors of these two aspirant towns was to bedevil the region for decades. Blenheim became capital of the province; Picton, after being boosted as a possible national capital, had to be content with being Marlborough's port. But content was a long time coming. The bitter struggle between so few settlers for a little extra privilege or prestige was the colony's scandal, and one which helped to bring about the demise of provincial government in New Zealand in 1876. Something of that early rivalry has continued to characterise Marlborough's local politics for more than a century. In the nineteen-eighties the affairs of the Marlborough Harbour Board were by far the nation's most fascinating; more so after the spectacular sinking in 1986 of the large Russian cruise liner *Mikhail Lermontov* in the sounds with a local pilot at the helm.

Today Marlborough has a quiet and conservative character, certainly by contrast with the often unconventional neighbouring Nelson. Much of Marlborough still depends on sheep, but its rural perspective is distinctly more democratic and a good deal more populous. Marginal hill country has been developed as forest, both public and private, with more than fifty per cent in the hands of small growers; the harvest promises hundreds of new jobs. Lowlands once part of

Quaint gabling lends the 1875 post office in the popular holiday resort of Havelock a distinctly ecclesiastical look

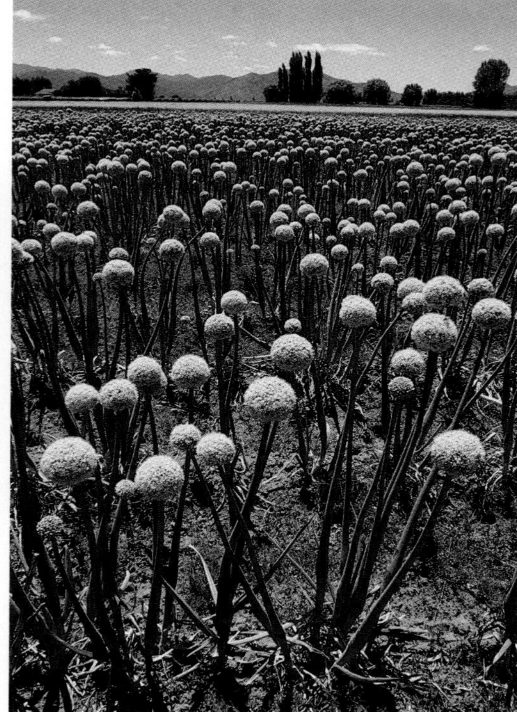

Blenheim's sunny climate brings out the best in the land – here the humble onion blossoms in the field

the great sheep runs of last century are now intensively farmed horticultural smallholdings. Marlborough cherries and berries are flown round the world. In the past two decades twelve hundred hectares of former sheep grazing have been converted into huge vineyards. Once this potential of Marlborough's climate and soil was recognised in the nineteen-seventies, no time was lost in the production of distinctive and highly exportable wines. The sea also provides an abundance, and today the quiet waters of the Marlborough Sounds are invaded by mussel farms; the green-lipped mussel, now marketed in North America and elsewhere as the kiwiclam, has become a significant export. Salmon farming is another growth industry. In contrast to most of the South Island, Marlborough, especially Blenheim, has prospered in the economically difficult nineteen-eighties.

Pioneer cob cottage at Robin Hood Bay, thought to be named after Robin Hood's Bay in Yorkshire, England

In the high country, the great sheep runs were often over-grazed. This, along with the damage caused by regiments of rabbits, turned alpine tussockland into crumbling desert. In the nineteen-thirties, in a move without precedent in rural New Zealand, the government stepped in to save the land and the livelihoods dependent upon it. By that time only the government could. Four large and near-derelict sheep stations formerly farmed under Crown lease were amalgamated. Sheep were removed and war was waged against rabbit, deer and goat. Cattle were introduced gradually. The now profitable Molesworth Station, by far the country's largest single holding, is an epic of rural enterprise; it is also New Zealand's greatest conservation success story. Because of its isolation – and perhaps too because of suspicion of state initiative – it is a success too little celebrated. But change is coming about cautiously, as the station is gradually being made available to the public.

For the most part, Marlborough remains the wild landscape of tussock and alpine herbfield, of rivers and soaring mountains that the first pastoralists knew. Outside Blenheim and Picton, the only centres of substance, it is one of New Zealand's least populated regions. Occupation of the intricate Marlborough coastline remains insignificant too. Holiday homes far outnumber permanent residences. Pleasure-craft are more evident than motor vehicles. In summer they seem to recall a prophecy made by Dumont d'Urville in 1827: 'These silent bays, traversed now by infrequent frail canoes, will be furrowed by ships of every size . . .' Yet the vast sea-filled valleys are still rich in silence: the silence of an older New Zealand, the land the Polynesians first knew. Our breakneck century is still just a whisper on these waters.

This cob cottage at Riverlands near Blenheim has served variously as a dwelling, school, stud-sheep shelter and hayshed. It has been refurbished and is now a museum

HISTORY'S MAGICAL SEASCAPE

The Marlborough Sounds have inspired centuries of legend, from the Polynesian arrival to modern times

Land and sea intertwine to give the sounds their character

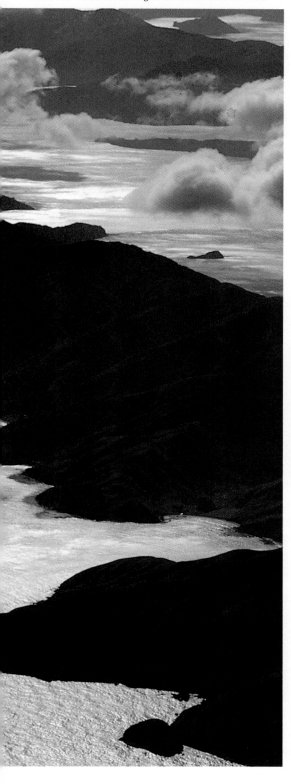

There are two creation stories about the tangle of waterways called the Marlborough Sounds. The first is from the Maori. It seems that before humans walked abroad on the earth a party of adventurous gods mounted a canoe excursion here from the heavens. But things went awry, and they eventually wrecked their canoe. The Marlborough Sounds are the carved fragments of the shattered prow.

The geological story isn't too dissimilar. It holds that the sounds are the shattered remains of mountain ranges that collided with what is now the North Island. The separation of the South Island, and later the rise of the world's waters after the last ice age, turned precipitous mountain spurs into islands; beating waves modelled smaller spurs into bony reefs; valleys became deep-water bays. Everywhere the remnant land rises sharply from the sea, displaying its alpine past; there is next to no lowland. The few human communities here have been established on sandy scraps of level shore.

A SNAKING NETWORK OF SEAS

Either way, as divine debris or as geological record, the result is magical. The first Polynesians must have thought so; Captain James Cook, when he dropped anchor here in 1770, certainly did. The birds seemed to sing more sweetly here than anywhere else in New Zealand; moreover the local Maoris were obliging. But even after five visits, Cook never guessed at the extent of the sounds.

A sailor's dream, scalloped with bays and coves . . .

Pelorus Sound and Queen Charlotte Sound – the two great flooded valleys – together command close to one thousand kilometres of twisting waterways. Cook found only one of the two entrances into Queen Charlotte Sound. He remained oblivious of Tory Channel, the narrow waterway later used by whalers and today travelled by the ferries that provide the road-rail link between North Island and South Island. Pelorus Sound, in fact, was not fully explored by the newcomers until 1838 when HM Brig *Pelorus* nosed its way through and skipper Philip Chetwode eventually found himself fifty-six kilometres from the open sea. It was an awe-inspiring journey. Here, as in Queen Charlotte Sound, islands are not easily distinguished from mainland; the sea, snaking away on all sides, adds further confusion with its wealth of reflections.

Left: *The South Island snakes long fingers into the sea to form the intricate fretwork of the Marlborough Sounds, a magical gateway from northern New Zealand*

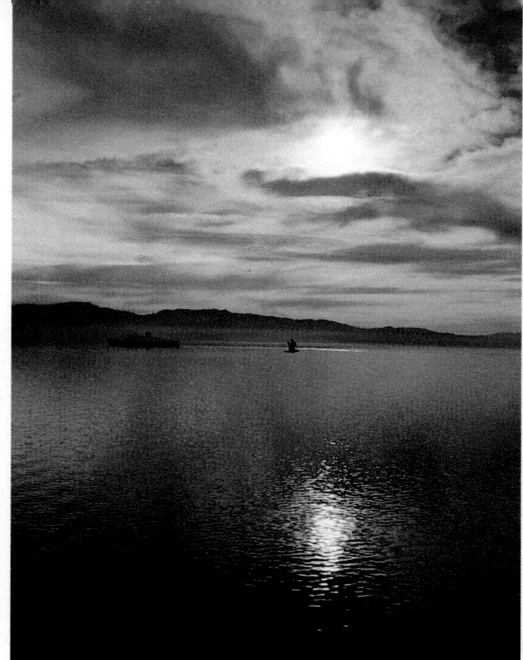

The Cook Strait inter-island ferry brings passengers through the wind-whipped waters that separate the North Island and the South Island into the peace of the Marlborough Sounds

Today's waterborne travellers find the perspectives of the sounds no less pleasing. They may come as boatmen, beachcombers, fishermen, sun-lovers or sightseers. The sounds provide many choices. Some forty-three thousand hectares are held in trust for the nation within the Marlborough Sounds Maritime Park. For many the jewel is still that 'snug cove', Ship Cove, beloved of Cook. Here, far from the tourist traffic of Picton, the seascape is still history's.

Visitors will almost certainly hear the story of Pelorus Jack, the most famous inhabitant of the sounds until his disappearance in 1912. He was first spotted in 1888 as ships between Nelson and Wellington travelled through French Pass. A dolphin, Pelorus Jack danced in the bow wave of vessels, sported around them, and otherwise intrigued visitors for almost a quarter of a century. In that time it became the world's best known dolphin since classical times (though its fame has dimmed beside that of a rival, Hokianga Harbour's Opo). Pelorus Jack was formally and solemnly given government protection in 1904

The idyll of Queen Charlotte Sound . . . little wonder that Captain Cook found here his ideal anchorage, where ships and seamen could recover from their harsh voyages

after an insensitive passenger on the SS *Penguin* had fired a rifle at the dolphin. Five years later the *Penguin* sank, taking seventy-five lives with it. This event was interpreted as springing from a Maori curse by those who believed Pelorus Jack

The port of Picton thrives with traffic from roll-on roll-off car-rail ferries to and from the North Island

was the dolphin from the Ruru legend. The story is of two men living in Pelorus Sound who were besotted by the same woman. When she finally chose one, the other, named Ruru, plotted the destruction of the lovers. He hurled them into the sea from a cliff with an incantation so vile that it killed a passing dolphin. A *tohunga*, or tribal priest, persuaded Ruru's spirit to enter the body of the dolphin, and ordered it to meet canoes approaching French Pass. The *tohunga* died and Ruru's task became eternal. When Pelorus Jack disappeared in 1912, it was surmised that the murderous Ruru's spirit at last knew peace.

Sawmillers, graziers and predatory animals have destroyed some of the forest cover at which the first Europeans in the sounds marvelled. Here and there, however, trees are growing sturdy again, and there are still places as undisturbed as when the Polynesians first arrived. Tennyson Inlet – named after the poet – was hardly molested, as native birds, tree-ferns and nikau palms testify.

Given the relative lack of human pressure throughout the Marlborough Sounds – a vast watery world that could serve three million New Zealanders comfortably as a vacation land – it is possible to feel, even at the height of summer, that one has this world to oneself.

*Whether it is the launches (**Above**) that ply the hidden reaches of the enchanting Marlborough Sounds, or the ferries (**Left**) that bring tourists in their thousands every year, bustling boats against a peaceful marine background give Picton's waterfront a special feel – relaxed yet alive*

LONELY HIGHWAY 1

North of Kaikoura, the lonely coastal road affords the motorist a rare and undisturbed grandeur

Beyond the Marlborough Sounds, beyond the fertile Wairau and Awatere plains, the rearing peaks of the South Island unfurl raggedly from the Pacific seaboard above the most dramatic marine highway in New Zealand. These are the Inland Kaikouras and the Seaward Kaikouras. For the traveller from the north, freshly landed at Picton, these mountains make a sturdy introduction to the South Island. Dwellings and farms gradually become fewer, level land diminishes and Highway 1 fast empties of traffic as the traveller rides between pounding surf and mountain heights.

Becalmed off the coast in 1770, Captain Cook named them the 'Snowey Mountains'. Maoris paddled out from the Kaikoura Peninsula to observe the *Endeavour* in awed silence, which caused Cook to name their peninsula the 'Lookers On' – a name a later navigator transferred, more aptly, to the Seaward Kaikouras. The highest peak in this range is Manakau, which rises to two thousand six hundred and ten metres. Giant of the Inland Kaikouras is Tapuaenuku at two thousand eight hundred and eighty-five metres.

A flight over this rugged terrain reveals a vast expanse of fiercely eroded mountain country split by three great parallel faults in the earth's crust. Alpine torrents course through the labyrinth of valleys. Snow-peaked in winter, both mountain ranges make a dazzling vista; in summer they

Mount Tapuaenuku in the Inland Kaikoura Range, a pressure fold ridge rising to nearly three thousand metres

rear barren and brown. Among these seemingly diminutive pastoral pockets is New Zealand's greatest farm, the eighteen hundred square kilometre Molesworth Station, but for the most part the vivid landscape remains undisturbed. A few seabirds flutter from swampy valley floors; where patches of native forest persist, or regenerate, a shy bellbird or two may be heard. Otherwise all is quiet, the more so in winter when the hills are muffled by snow two to five metres deep.

Under the mountain wall, the one hundred kilometres of sparsely settled coast, which the motorist passes from the Waima River to Oaro, is not especially hospitable either. Great rivers, often muddy with mountain storms, pour into the Pacific; surf soars from the rocks. Nowhere – apart from the North Island's Desert Road – is Highway 1 lonelier. Those who do make their homes in this region are a few dedicated fishermen who harvest crayfish. The name *Kaikoura*, in fact, means 'meal of crayfish', and roadside signs advertise New Zealand's greatest marine delicacy. A one-time whaling base, with a wealth of relics and set on the peninsula of the same name, the salty town of Kaikoura is where the crayfish are packed for the profitable export market. No town

Top: *The original homestead at Molesworth Station, which was to become the largest single holding in the country*

Above: *Aerial view of a holding in the Blenheim plains, an area of extensive and diverse agricultural production*

The second homestead at Molesworth, built twenty years after the first in 1885, was still fairly primitive

The Kaikoura Star *still shines, though the whaling industry on which the town thrived for many years has long ceased*

in New Zealand is more appropriately named.

Kaikoura Peninsula, once an island, is at base a limestone reef, the bonded debris of billions of tiny sea creatures. River silt and mountain rubble accumulated through thousands of years to link the reef to the mainland. Beneath the peninsula's lonely lighthouse lives one of New Zealand's most impressive seal colonies, prospering again after the pitiless slaughter by Sydney-based sealers in the early nineteenth century. The Kaikoura Peninsula gives the traveller a mariner's perspective on alpine Marlborough, its peaks rising from the Pacific surf, the same rugged vista Captain James Cook saw more than two centuries ago.

Pink-tinged Fyffe House near the Old Wharf in Kaikoura

Kaikoura's Garden of Memories, shaded by Norfolk pines, its paths arched with the rib bones of whales

The exterior of the later homestead at Molesworth – a simple building, but well-proportioned and unobtrusive

PLACES OF INTEREST

BLENHEIM
On the Wairau Plain at the once swampy junction of the Omaka and Opawa Rivers, Blenheim (now with a population of 19 000) originated in 1850 as a depot and store servicing the South Island's first significant pastoralists. Schooners and riverboats brought settlers and supplies to The Beaver, as it was originally named because of a flood that had left early surveyors stranded and saturated like beavers in mud. It was later renamed after the Duke of Marlborough's greatest victory. The great sheep runs from which the settlement grew are now found nearer to the high country, having been replaced by orchards, vineyards and other intensively worked horticultural enterprises. Blenheim, with Nelson, is in New Zealand's most consistently sunny area. A short distance from the town are New Zealand's most extensive vineyards.

In the centre of the town, in Market Place, is an elegant little band rotunda (1903) of the kind that distinguished many early New Zealand communities. In Seymour Square, designed as a memorial to Marlborough's war dead, sits what is said to be the cannon with which Blenkinsopp attempted to defraud chief Te Rauparaha of the Wairau Plain (see page 218). Later, in 1843, Blenkinsopp's fraudulence claimed 22 colonists' lives in a bloody affray at Tuamarina. The site of that disaster – the only significant armed clash between Maori and European in the South Island – is marked by a roadside memorial, 9 kilometres north towards **PICTON** on Highway 1. The oldest pioneer dwelling in Blenheim's vicinity is the Cob Cottage at Riverlands (1859, 4 kilometres east on Highway 1), now open to the public as a museum. The 6 hectares of Brayshaw Museum Park (open daily), on New Renwick Road, enshrine much of the region's robust rural history, including a reconstruction of The Beaver. Pollard Park (in Parker Street), which includes the Waterlea Gardens, makes a cool oasis in Blenheim's hot summers. Woodbourne Aerodrome, an RNZAF base 8 kilometres west on Highway 6, is the site from which Australian aviator Charles Kingsford Smith took off on the first east-west air crossing of the Tasman, which in 1928

MOLESWORTH'S MAGNIFICENT RECOVERY

The road up the Awatere valley, on the Dashwood turn-off from Highway 1, south of Blenheim, is well worth a day's hard driving

Molesworth Station is slowly opening up to trampers and horse-trekkers

The Inland Kaikoura Range forms the southern backdrop to the road. The mountains are white-capped all year round, with the majestic Tapuaenuku their highest point. Winding river flats, eroded hills, huge tussock lands, misshapen cabbage trees and shrubs, make this an unforgettable landscape.

Eventually, the road leads to Molesworth Station, which occupies the enormous horseshoe formed by the arc of the Clarence River, plus part of the upper Wairau River. The Awatere River runs from its centre. Molesworth, with an area of eighteen hundred square kilometres, is the largest farmholding in the country.

Heavy overgrazing and other disastrous practices by the original sheep-farmers, as well as invasions of rabbits and deer, almost turned the area into a desert. The hills, in particular, suffered extreme soil erosion and in the end many farmers simply walked off their properties. The area was close to becoming New Zealand's largest memorial to agricultural folly. Molesworth was saved by scientific agricultural management, systematic pest eradication and a change from sheep to cattle grazing.

Many of Molesworth's huge hills are now stony ruins, but the farm has gradually been returned to useful tussock. High-country farmland and some of the worst eroded areas have been repaired. The restoration was accomplished by government takeover in the nineteen-thirties, under the former Department of Lands and Survey, yet it has been achieved at very little cost to central government funds. The priorities were to eradicate rabbits by systematic poisoning and to prevent the original cause of destruction – fires. The early runholders used to burn off the tussock in spring, creating new growth for the sheep to eat. The outcome was twofold: the new growth provided the ideal environment for rabbits and continual firing left the land open to erosion by frost, wind and water.

The Lands and Survey department discouraged visitors to Molesworth in its early years of restoration, but it is now possible to visit on organised safari tours by four-wheel-drive vehicles from Blenheim. There are, however, several country roads which allow unrestricted access to parts of the property.

took 22 hours. On Highway 1, 35 kilometres south-east, is Lake Grassmere and New Zealand's only solar salt works, with its strange salt pyramids beside evaporating ponds; it produces 100 000 tonnes annually.

HAVELOCK

At the head of Pelorus Sound is yet another Marlborough location distinguised by the name of a British warrior, in this case Sir Henry Havelock of Indian Mutiny fame. A quiet township with a distinct period flavour, Havelock was founded on the site of a former Maori village as a port serving the short-lived Wakamarina goldfields and the busy millers of Marlborough Sounds timber. Today a stable population of about 400 processes and packs mussels, which are farmed near by, and scallops dredged from the seabed. Two world-famous scientists mastered their first sums in the surviving schoolhouse here: atom-splitter Ernest Rutherford and space rocketeer William Pickering. The schoolhouse is now a youth hostel.

Havelock is the base for exploring Pelorus Sound, with launch trips on offer to various destinations. The launches also serve farmers in remote reaches of the sounds with mail and supplies. The steep-gabled Havelock Post Office (1875), built soon after settlement began, is a fine example of a small-town wooden public building. A small but interesting museum, which commemorates scientists Rutherford and Pickering, is housed in the former Methodist Church; outside stands an old logging locomotive that once hauled timber from the hills. Near by, along Highway 6 towards Nelson, beside the Trout Hotel at the foot of the once populous Wakamarina goldfields, is a distinctive memorial, mounted with relics, to the many who sought their fortunes there. Up valley, beyond the site of Canvastown, some 3000 diggers toiled; the riverside still yields colour to patient panners. (Pans may be hired from the motor camp.) There is access here to Mount Richmond Forest Park (see page 215). Trout fishing is good in this vicinity, and sea fishing down the sounds is justly celebrated too.

The limestone of the dramatic but inhospitable Kaikoura Coast throws up many fascinating rock forms, some of them with knife-sharp edges

SOUTH ISLAND'S FIRST WHALER

Kakapo Bay can be reached by the mainly coastal loop road, north-east from Picton past Waikawa, or else east from Tuamarina then north past Rarangi

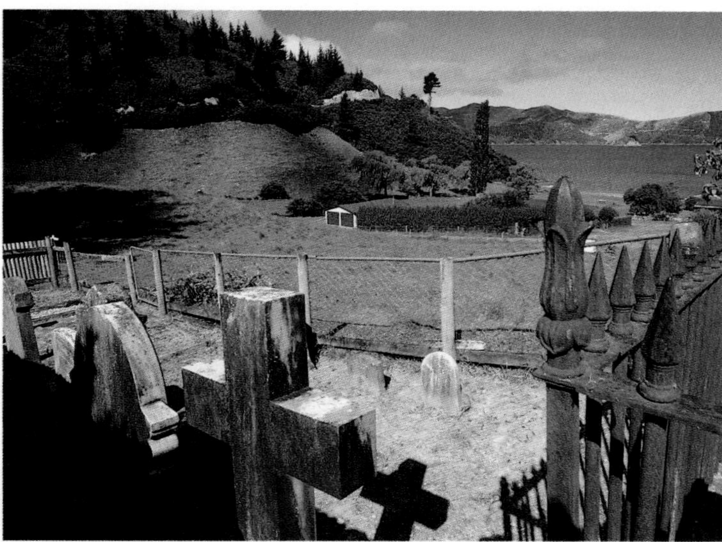

John Guard lies buried in this small cemetery opposite the family homestead

Kakapo Bay is the burial place of John Guard, South Island's first whaler, and his wife Elizabeth. The family homestead, built by their descendants in the eighteen-eighties, stands opposite the cemetery where they lie.

Guard shipped the first consignment of New Zealand whale oil to Sydney from Port Underwood on February 3, 1830, but his first whaling station was actually at Te Awaiti, further north on the Tory Channel. The Port Underwood station was founded the following year. Guard's wife, whom he married in Sydney, was the first white woman to live in the South Island. Their son and daughter, John and Louisa, were its first native-born white children.

Although Guard had a sharp eye for whales and was the first to notice the presence of large numbers of the baleen species in Cook Strait, he was dogged by ill-fortune and bizarre adventure. His first ship was wrecked, then subsequently pillaged and burnt, by Maoris at Waikanae Beach in 1833. He then acquired a share in another which was wrecked a year later off Cape Egmont. Guard, his wife, children and crew were captured. A dozen of the crew were killed and eaten, but Guard was set free to ransom the rest. Some months later, HMS *Alligator* was sent to the rescue from Sydney. When the hostages were released the ship's guns were turned in revenge on the hundred or so Maoris on the beach. Questions were asked in Parliament in London.

Guard thought he had bought title deed to a huge area of land from Te Rauparaha, but the claim was never recognised and eventually lapsed. He did some piloting in the Marlborough Sounds, including the historic voyage of HMS *Pelorus*, and some maritime surveys for Colonel William Wakefield of the New Zealand Company. He also whaled for some years from Waipapa Bay, thirty-two kilometres north of Kaikoura. In the eighteen-forties, he retired from the sea and farmed at Kakapo Bay, where there are Guard descendants to this day.

Guards Bay on one of the remote arms of the north Marlborough coast is named after him.

KAIKOURA

Kaikoura began as a Maori settlement famed for its succulent crayfish (its name means 'meal of crayfish'). Centuries on, this town of 2000 maintains its reputation. In the 19th century it served as a bridgehead for whalers in the Pacific's most profitable waters; from here, until the 1920s, they struck at passing schools. Today there is little to be seen of that brutal heyday of the town; just whalebone arches in the town's Garden of Memories, and a few buildings bearing testimony to the town's beginnings.

Fyffe House at 62 Avoca Street, built by a whaler in 1860, rose on piles of whale vertebrae, and takes its distinctive pink hue from the whale oil mixed with its first coat of lead paint. Today this expansive colonial dwelling, once at the centre of a substantial village, is the property of the NZ Historic Places Trust and is open to the public (hours vary). The nearby Old Wharf was built in 1882 to serve whaler and settler; the trypots, in which whale blubber was rendered down, are still there. Today Kaikoura's fishing fleet functions from the so-called New Wharf (1906). A substantial colony of seals may be seen on the peninsula. The Kaikoura Museum houses exhibits from both the Polynesian and European past of the peninsula (open weekends 2–4; other times by arrangement).

Walkways – or the drive to the tip of the peninsula – take the visitor through country rich in history, and with impressive vistas of the Seaward Kaikouras (see page 225). South on Highway 1 (3 kilometres) is the Maori Leap Cave, hollowed by subterranean streams through cliffs now studded with marine fossils. The cave takes its name from the unlikely story of a hunted Maori warrior who, preferring death to slavery, hurled himself from a 30 metre cliff and lived to tell the tale. Since 1978 the Kaikoura area has given rise to even stranger tales. The world's best documented sightings – including film – of UFOs occurred here.

ISLANDS OF THE SOUNDS

The best access to views of the offshore isles of the Marlborough Sounds is by boat – usually from Picton or Havelock

Last of the peaks to hold their heads above water are the islands of the sounds

Of these many beautiful islands a few have particular interest: the one that is most familiar to road-and-ferry visitors to the South Island is Arapawa, which the inter-island ferry seems almost to touch as it passes through Tory Channel to Queen Charlotte Sound and Picton. This, surely, is one of the most spectacular views from a regular ferry service.

Arapawa Island was where, on January 23, 1770, Captain James Cook climbed a ridge (Cook's Lookout) and first sighted the strait that was named after him. Before this the separate existence of a North and South Island was unknown to the Europeans. Here too John Guard established at the Te Awaiti whaling station the first European settlement in the South Island. Later in 1770, at *Motuara Island*, between Arapawa Island and Ship Cove, Cook landed to claim formally possession of the country in the name of George III.

The largest of the islands is *D'Urville*, which Cook believed to be part of the mainland. It was not until 1827 that the French explorer Dumont d'Urville discovered and sailed through what is now called French Pass, a navigable passage only one hundred and ten metres wide. Dumont d'Urville sailed his boat, the *Astrolabe* through this narrow waterway, scraping its sides and smashing its false keel. In later years it was used as a short-cut for ferries from Wellington to Nelson and became world famous for Pelorus Jack, the dolphin that for years met every ship and rode through the pass on its bow waves (see page 222).

On September 1, 1838, Lieutenant Chetwode in command of HMS *Pelorus* named a small group of islands at the head of Pelorus Sound after himself, and thus reserved for the *Chetwode Islands* a place among the illustrious names usually applied to new discoveries. The Chetwodes are now an important nature reserve.

Maud Island, appropriately off Tennyson Inlet, is the home of the rare Hamilton's frog (see page 96). *Stephens Island*, three kilometres north of D'Urville Island, is the home of another native frog. It is also the breeding ground for varieties of small petrels and boasts the largest colony of the 'living fossil', the tuatara.

Horahora-Kakahu, an islet in Port Underwood, is where Chief Nohuroa signed the Treaty of Waitangi on June 17, 1840 and the British flag was raised to a twenty-one-gun naval salute, thus proclaiming British sovereignty over the South Island.

PELORUS BRIDGE

On Highway 6, just before the hills that separate Marlborough and Nelson, is this attractive 1000 hectare reserve that includes a large picnic and camping area. The Pelorus River joins here with the Rai and feeds into Pelorus Sound. There are walks of varying distance beside the river and through beech forest. One of the longer walks carries on via the Mount Richmond Forest Park (see page 215) towards Nelson's Maitai Valley, along the infamous Maungatapu murder track. It was here the bushrangers Burgess, Levy, Kelly and Sullivan killed travellers from Wakamarina goldfields (see page 216).

PICTON

Despite the bustle of its port – which serves thousands of travellers and links North and South Island by road-rail ferries day and night – Picton's seafront has managed to retain its original character. An elegant Victorian and Edwardian watering place, Picton is enshrined in Katherine Mansfield's story *The Voyage* as the town with 'the landing stage and some little houses . . . clustered together, like shells on the lid of a box', and the Picton boat as 'all strung, all beaded with round golden lights . . . as if she was more ready to sail among stars than out into the cold sea'. Travellers to Picton, passing another ferry at night, will be familiar with that image. (Mansfield, as Kathleen Beauchamp, came often to stay in Marlborough's sounds, with her father's family at Anakiwa, where 'the shapes of the umbrella ferns showed, and those strange silvery withered trees like skeletons'.)

Consistent sunshine and drying winds combine to make New Zealand's only source of solar salt at Lake Grassmere, south of Blenheim

Sailing boats still find a safe haven where Captain Cook s ship lay at anchor in Queen Charlotte Sound some two hundred years ago

The town that once, with a few dozen inhabitants, aspired to be the capital of New Zealand has become instead its hub – in a very real sense. Here North and South Island meet, and rail and road traffic rumble non-stop close to what remains essentially a small resort town of 3700 people, its harbour brimming with pleasure-craft. Whaling, which began in the sounds with John Guard in Tory Channel, continued longer here than anywhere else in the country, coming to an end finally in the 1960s.

The Smith Memorial Museum on the seafront is full of mementoes of New Zealand's first large-scale industry (open daily, 9.30–3). Long a local landmark, the beached hulk of the migrant vessel *Edwin Fox* (Indian-built in 1853) was lifted from the water in 1986 for restoration. For those travellers wishing to spend time exploring Marlborough's marvellous drowned valleys, local firms provide a variety of excursions. The most popular take in Captain Cook's haven in Ship Cove, which his lengthy reports made the most familiar part of the South Pacific to literate Englishmen. It is also the place where Cook recorded hauling in '300 pounds weight of different sorts of fish', a feat that dedicated fishermen still try to emulate. In this still beautiful 1100 hectare reserve there is an extensive picnic area beside the stream from which Cook's men drew water, but there is no camping site. Picton has a large and useful information centre serving the whole region.

PORT UNDERWOOD

The eastern flank of the sounds, often neglected by travellers in favour of the more celebrated Queen Charlotte and Pelorus Sounds, is this magnificent stretch of water – 20 kilometres from Picton. A drive along its shore road is especially rewarding.

This was the territory of whaler John Guard and his family, the South Island's first serious European settlers; his descendants still live here. After founding a community in Tory Channel, Guard moved here because Port Underwood gave easier access to Cloudy Bay; slain whales could be towed into calm water more easily, beached and boiled down. Missionaries later found Port Underwood a heavy cross to bear, with the 'scum of every maritime nation'. They found Te Rauparaha's murderously talented 'cannibals and pagans' more desirable neighbours. What the Bay of Islands was to the north, Port Underwood was to the south; in this vicinity the South Island's first major colonial dramas took place. Southern Maori chiefs fixed their signatures to the Treaty of Waitangi on the island of Horahora-Kakahu, which can be seen from the road around the harbour (signposted). The South Island's second mission station was founded in Ngakuta Bay at the head of the eastern arm of the port in 1840 by the Reverend Samuel Ironside, who warned Nelson's colonists against trespassing on Te Rauparaha's territory, and was ignored. This led to the Wairau Affray in 1843 in which 22 of the land-grabbing colonists were killed.

There are several buildings of note along Port Underwood's shores. Robin Hood Bay has a cottage (of cob and rickers) which is possibly the South Island's oldest surviving dwelling. An 1880s homestead still occupied by descendants of the South Island's founding family, the Guards, stands on the site of the original whaling station at Kakapo Bay. The graves of the original Guards can be found in a small plot just up from the shore. The first telegraph cable joining North and South Islands came ashore on South Island at Whites Bay; the telegraph station (1867), which functioned until 1895, survives as a small museum beside an exceptionally pleasant surf beach. Now pylons and cables carrying South Island's hydro-electric power to the north, via the Cook Strait undersea cable, are more conspicuous in the vicinity. South of Whites Bay, the Wairau Bar may be viewed from on high. It is one of the richest archaeological sites in New Zealand, and one that has disclosed much about the area's moa-hunting Polynesians.

Cooked crayfish, sold on the roadside when in season, make a fine meal in the Kaikoura area

RAI VALLEY

The last Marlborough settlement on Highway 6 to Nelson, the secluded Rai Valley boasts a beautifully restored pioneer cottage – at Carluke, on the road to Tennyson Inlet. It was built in this once remote location (by Charles Turner) in 1881 of pit-sawn totara slabs. The roof is shingled and the fireplace made of river stones. Although not open to the public, the interior has been furnished to period by the NZ Historic Places Trust, and may be viewed through windows, giving some idea of the region's more spartan beginnings. The cottage is accessible all year. Rai Valley affords road access to the striking Tennyson Inlet and to other reaches of Marlborough's sounds.

RENWICK

On Highway 6, 12 kilometres beyond BLENHEIM, Renwick has a small museum celebrating Marlborough's past, and a reconstruction of an early tavern. In holiday periods, trips on pioneer wagons may be arranged. Outside the town is the large drive-through Marlborough Zoological Park (open daily).

SEDDON AND WARD

These settlements are on Highway 1, where the road leaves populated Marlborough for the lonely Kaikoura Coast. At the foot of the Awatere valley, the area was the setting for the South Island's first large-scale pastoral farming in the 1840s. What began here on land leased or bought from the Maoris transformed much of the South Island. Flaxbourne, the first of these patrician empires, was subdivided at the beginning of the 20th century – in the more democratic era of Richard John Seddon; the settlers named their community after him in gratitude. Similarly, Ward settlement was named after his colleague Sir Joseph Ward. At the alpine end of the Awatere, four great estates, humbled by the homely rabbit, fell into government hands in the 1930s and now comprise New Zealand's largest farm, Molesworth Station. The original cob homestead of Molesworth still stands. Inquiries must be directed to the Department of Lands and Survey at BLENHEIM or elsewhere for conditions of access to this 1800 square kilometre tract of territory.

Oxley's Hotel in Picton, built as the Bank Hotel by William Pugh in 1870 and rebuilt in 1902

HOW THE WAIRAU AFFRAY OCCURRED

At Tuamarina, on Highway 1, between Picton and Blenheim, a memorial cairn and old cemetery commemorate the Wairau Affray of June 17, 1843

Te Rauparaha . . . revenge after swindle

The spot on the riverbank where the killings occurred is marked. An old titoki tree, to which a canoe was moored as a makeshift bridge while the angry preliminaries were conducted, still stands there. Twenty-two settlers and workers from Nelson and about six Maoris were killed in a confrontation arising from the settlers' understandable need for land and the equally understandable refusal of the Maoris to part with it.

The problem of the ownership of the Wairau Plain began in 1839 when John Blenkinsopp, a sea captain, visited the area for timber and supplies. Noting the potential of the river flats, he tricked Te Rauparaha and Te Rangihaeata into signing them away in return for a small cannon. Blenkinsopp told them the document to which they fixed their marks was a receipt for the timber he had exchanged for the cannon. The document had no legal validity.

After John Blenkinsopp's death by drowning, his widow sold the spurious contract to Colonel William Wakefield, who instructed his brother, Captain Arthur Wakefield, to survey the plain for settlement.

Despite repeated warnings, surveyors moved in. The Maoris removed their pegs and escorted them off the land. Henry Thompson, the fiery and unstable Nelson police magistrate, organised a party to arrest Te Rauparaha on the feeble grounds that he had burnt down a raupo hut.

At Tuamarina, Thompson's small and ill-equipped band met a well-armed and deployed force of warriors. Thompson ordered his men to fix bayonets and arrest the Maori chief. Someone fired a shot and there were volleys from both sides. Thompson's force fell back and Wakefield finally ordered them to surrender, though some had by this time fled.

In the firing, one of Te Rangihaeata's wives had been killed. He demanded *utu*, 'revenge', and the prisoners, including Wakefield and Thompson, were executed. To the outrage of Colonel Wakefield and the New Zealand Company settlers, Governor FitzRoy decided in 1844 that the blame lay with Thompson's party who, in their wish to arrest Te Rauparaha on some pretext, 'had violated the rules of the law of England, the maxims of prudence, and the principles of justice'.

West Coast

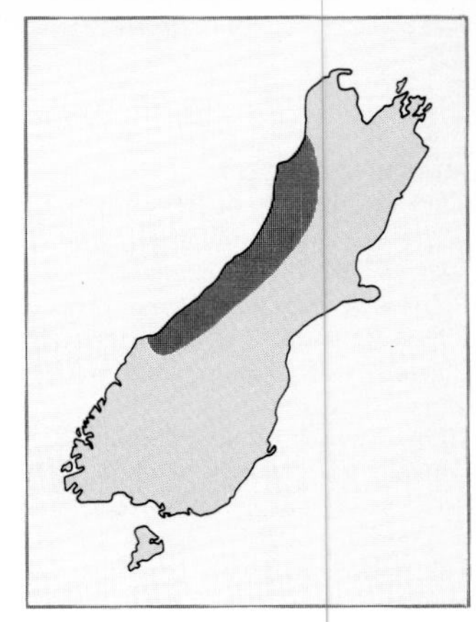

Geographers style it Westland, but for most New Zealanders it remains 'the West Coast', more often 'the Coast', as if no other coast rated a mention. Its people are simply 'Coasters'. Native New Zealanders are reared on the folklore of this lean western shore of the South Island, running five hundred kilometres from Jackson Bay in the south to Karamea in the north. Outsiders too may soon find themselves talking of the Coast and Coasters with good reason. Never more than fifty kilometres wide, the region has hardly any hinterland – and much of that is forest and peak. The region commands the affections not only of its thirty-three thousand inhabitants; 'the Coast' may belong to the South Island, but it has a claim on all New Zealanders. Many New Zealand families can name a Coaster or two as ancestor; a gold-digger or tree-feller who started out on the land. Some return here much as Irish Americans do to Ireland, looking for their beginnings.

PIONEER PAST KEPT ALIVE

The Coaster lives up to legend: gritty, resilient, enterprising, hospitable, a sardonic teller of tall tales, and never quite at ease with twentieth-century New Zealand. Wherever visitors move in Westland, they will find the land's pioneer past alive and still in business, not so much in the mocked-up facades of pioneer villages as in its people. For adult New Zealanders a visit to the Coast peels away the decades: its time warp takes them back to their childhood.

Yet in 1642, when Abel Tasman saw mountain ramparts rising above rainforest, he immediately turned north. In 1770 Captain James Cook passed it by too: 'No country on earth can appear with a more rugged and barren aspect than this doth from the sea . . .'he wrote. French voyager Jules de Blosseville in 1823 saw 'one long solitude, with a forbidding sky, frequent tempest, and impenetrable forests'. His countryman Dumont d'Urville used one word: 'Frightful'. When Europeans at last arrived, they remained unpersuaded of its virtue. Sealing parties from Sydney survived loneliness and hardship. At least one party was consigned to cannibal ovens.

The first European to travel the length of the coast – looking for potential pastoral land after the cramped community of Nelson had been established in 1842 – was Thomas Brunner. His epic five-hundred-and-fifty-day journey confirmed that the wilderness was as formidable as passing mariners had judged. 'For what reason the natives choose to live here I cannot imagine,' the explorer said in his journal. 'It is a place devoid of all value or interest.'Brunner's most telling journal entry was a howl of pain: 'Rain continuing, dietary shorter, strength decreasing, spirits failing, prospects fearful.' Without his diligent Maori guide Kehu, along with the kindness of other Maoris they met, and a diet of fern root, penguin, rat and his own dog, the ailing and often near-demented Brunner might never have seen civilisation again. Emaciated, barefoot and in rags, he had long been given up as lost when he staggered back to Nelson. He reported: 'There is nothing on the West Coast worth the expense of exploring, but I certainly think the natives there require something to be done for them.'

For more than a decade the region remained the lonely realm of the few Maoris who dwelled on its shore and along its rivers. Though Brunner had tallied fewer than one hundred living between Karamea and the latitude forty-four degrees south, it can be assumed that their numbers had once been much greater. For Maori the length of New Zealand, the West Coast's greenstone (nephrite or jade) had virtually been a currency and often a cause for conquest. The beds of two great Westland rivers, the Arahura and Taramakau, were rich in greenstone.

Those Maori found by Brunner were a mix of Ngai Tahu (who had come as conquerors from Canterbury and were now known as Poutini Ngai Tahu) and the survivors of the defeated Ngati Wairangi, who discovered the greenstone of Westland and kept it profitably under control between 1400 and 1700, trading it off to North Islanders. By the time Brunner blundered into their territory, steel was replacing greenstone as the material to make tools.

By the end of the eighteen-fifties, with increased European migration to New Zealand, Westland began to seem more promising for settlement and mineral exploitation. Traces of gold and deposits of coal were found. 'Instead of the wilderness,' predicted geologist Julius von Haast, 'we shall have the dwellings of men; instead of a few birds, now its only inhabitants, we shall have a busy population of miners enlivening the country; the shriek of the locomotive will resound through its valleys, and busy life and animation will everywhere be seen.'

Also found, and also destined to bring revenue in the twentieth century, were the great glaciers creeping almost to the sea in the south. For just three hundred pounds – about three pounds for each Maori inhabitant – the government bought seven and a half million acres (three and a quarter million hectares) from the Poutini Ngai Tahu, between Kahurangi Point in the north and Milford Sound in the south. Westland's Maoris, however, cannily retained considerable reserves.

On the other side of the South Island's alpine divide, in Canterbury, people were already pondering what wealth and wonders Westland might hold. One was the future Victorian writer, then a dusty young sheepman, Samuel Butler. He wrote (in 1860) of 'the West Coast, that yet unexplored region of forest which may contain sleeping princesses and gold in ton blocks, and all sorts of good things.'

Gold, yes. And if not in tonne blocks, at least in kilograms. The Buller area, in from Westport, was the first worked, though not particularly profitably. Diggers were soon drawn away by impressive finds in Marlborough and Otago. But in January 1864, two Maoris, Simon and Samuel, out looking for greenstone on the Hohonu Stream near Greymouth, levered up a block of the stone and revealed coarse gold beneath. Reporting to their chief Tarapuhi on the desirable block of greenstone, they mentioned the gold. More interested in the greenstone, Tarapuhi set off to get a heavy iron hammer and drills to split it into manageable pieces, and in passing mentioned the gold to a pair of prospecting Europeans.

Within months, as find after find was turned up, diggers were storming Westland by boat and across blizzard-prone alpine passes. By the end of the year there were nearly a thousand prospectors, and the future boom town of Hokitika had been founded among 'a vast pile of driftwood' at the Hokitika River mouth. The scene was set for one of the Pacific's great gold rushes.

In the first half of 1865, enthusiastic skippers wrecked twenty-seven vessels at the mouth of the Hokitika River. By the end of 1865 they had successfully landed fifteen thousand people, and before much longer, between thirty and forty thousand were on Westland's fields. The sodden terrain, with its heaving forest and glittering snowfields, was unlike any the seasoned miners from California, Victoria and Otago had worked. The vegetation suffocated and strangled, and flooding rivers could snatch the unwary away. Diggers were confined to shingly streams. But town after town rose and passing vessels observed lantern-lit settlements glowing and campfires blazing along nearly two hundred kilometres of recently uninhabited coast.

LIVES SHAPED BY A HEROIC LANDSCAPE

Hokitika typified Westland's wildest years. Until 1864 a mere name on a map, it was a town of eight to ten thousand people by 1866, with thousands more near by using it as a base. Auckland aside, it was the busiest port in New Zealand. In 1865-67 more than thirty-seven thousand people disembarked; in 1866 close to half New Zealand's new settlers were landed at Hokitika. It was the colony's sixth largest settlement and, claimed contemporary chroniclers, the fastest growing place on the planet. 'San Francisco did not rise so fast,' said the visiting English politician Charles Dilke. The town had a fourteen-hundred-seat opera house, one hundred and two hotels and too many wrecks to count – some threatened to sail up the main street on a high tide. Human wrecks, drunken and disappointed diggers, were conspicuous too. Said one sniffy Canterbury journalist of Hokitika: 'I would not wish my worst enemy there.'

Today the traveller might stand in sleepy Hokitika and wonder where the San Francisco of the South Sea went; the opera house, the hundred-odd hotels, the gambling tables, the bushrangers, the dancing girls? A memorial or two; rotting wharf timbers beside a river no ship now negotiates... Nearby communities, once hundreds, sometimes thousands strong, have even less to show; often an overgrown graveyard is all that remains.

Westland was losing its golden lustre by the end of the eighteen-seventies, and diggers were already moving on, leaving Chinese migrants to pick over their tailings. Before the century was over giant dredges too would grind over the ground. At Reefton and other inland areas, quartz reefs would be worked. But the rapture of the great rush was soon gone, and Westland's timber and coal began to seem more significant. A modest amount of farmland was hewn from the forest, and drained.

At its peak, Westland had close to fifteen per cent of New Zealand's population; now it supports just one per cent. Coasters, like the Maoris Brunner found here, have become something of a lost tribe too. But since the nineteen-sixties, their numbers have been slightly swelled by young refugees from city tower blocks. With its cheap houses, space, and slow rhythm, the Coast has become a haven for craft workers and others seeking peace. The rain – no inhabited region of New Zealand is wetter – soon sorts the dedicated latter-day colonists from mere dreamers; this is no Riviera.

Ferns in rich variety – tree-ferns and kidney ferns, climbing and clinging ferns, and these luxuriant ladder ferns on the road to Mitchells – make the greatest contribution to the character of the rainforests throughout Westland

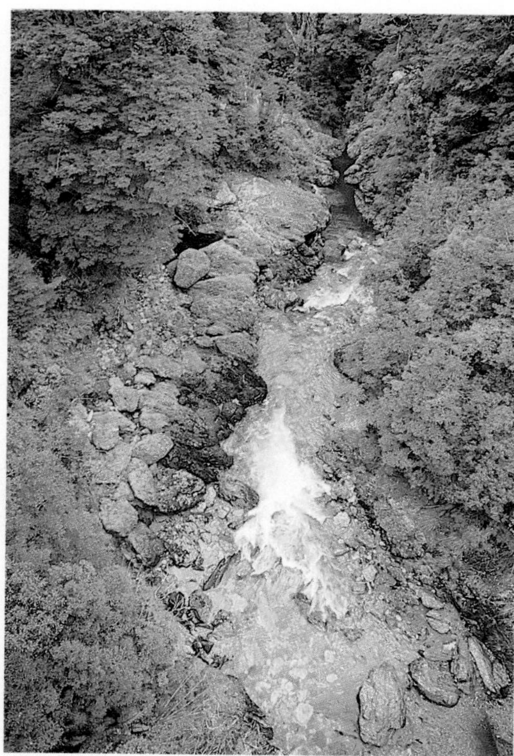

Fish River is just one of many rivers and streams that flow over stony moss-lined beds on the Haast Pass road

Coal in the north of the region – especially up the Grey River and near Westport – helped Westland keep up a head of steam until well into the twentieth century. It seeded dozens of settlements (Granity, Blackball, Denniston, Runanga) whose names are now legend in labour history. Politics began with a bang on the West Coast in sympathy with the martyred rebels of Ireland. At Hokitika and Addisons Flat in 1868, a prominent priest was gaoled, a thousand special constables patrolled the streets and troops were sent from Wellington. The Coast has never lacked outspoken liberals and radicals, the most commanding being the mighty-voiced Richard John Seddon (1845-1906), a goldfield storekeeper from Kumara, premier of New Zealand for more than a decade and founder of the welfare state. The dusty mines and weathered coal-towns of Westland were the proving ground for a generation of New Zealand's labour leaders. For a century the region had a political importance out of all proportion to its population.

Coal has now lost its significance, more due to the quirks of economic planners than to depletion of reserves. Though it is still there in quantity and mines are still worked – sometimes by collectives – many have been abandoned. Communities have diminished and died; deserted coal-towns have gone the way of gold-towns of the last century, with the bush taking over. Timber became the

A tree camouflaged by clinging vines, lichens and mosses on the banks of the Oparara River near Karamea. Farther up the Oparara Valley are two remarkable limestone arches spanning the river to form a massive tunnel, and also close by is Honeycomb Hill with its labyrinth of caves

salvation of Westland communities after the goldfields died, but now the abundance of that resource has likewise been reduced, first by the felling of precious native trees, then by the success of environmentalists in saving the lowland rainforest unique to the region. Plantations of exotic forest *(Pinus radiata)* have been established to keep mills working. Others are promised, though environmentalists oppose the pine forests. This has brought bitter resentment – Coasters have never taken kindly to urban New Zealanders telling them how to live their lives.

Fishing has become more crucial to the Coast's economy, along with deer – either farmed or hunted in the mountains. Tourism – especially since the opening of the Haast Pass to the south in 1965, Westland's long-awaited link with Otago – has eased the Coast's isolation. Craft workers have given fresh character to many faded communities: some carve the Coast's original commodity, greenstone, into souvenirs.

LAND OF SURVIVORS

Westland was always a place for the rest of New Zealand to plunder. First greenstone, then gold, finally coal and timber. With gold gone, timber and coal providing fewer livelihoods, little seems left for the traditional Coaster, the feller of forest, hewer of coal, panner of gold, hunter of wild pig and deer, and dab hand with a net when whitebait run up the rivers in spring. At least the dramatic territory remains intact – the booming shore, the breathtaking forests and lakes, the glittering glaciers and gleaming alps. Intact too, are the characteristics of the Coaster, not least their friendliness to outsiders.

Above left*: The curious rock formations of the Pancake Rocks, so called because of their astonishing resemblance to stacks of giant pancakes, are a spectacular sight*
Far left*: Otira Gorge provides New Zealand's most awesome alpine route, from the small railway settlement of Otira through beech-forested ravines to Arthur's Pass*
Left*: The cattle of Otira Gorge face a stony passage to reach their riverside grazing grounds. Sheep were once driven over this route to feed the hungry goldminers*

Above: *After rising in the Southern Alps, the Haast River travels rapidly northwards until joined by the much larger Landsborough. Here the Haast flows more gently through a wide, glaciated and gravel-floored valley flanked by beech and rimu forest and banks of swaying reeds*

The licensing laws of the Coast have always been inventive as the area has never taken much interest in legislation passed by parliamentarians in Wellington. Travellers will still find whitebait fritters on their breakfast plate. And with so many Coasters of Irish descent, St Patrick's Day continues to be celebrated more enthusiastically here than elsewhere in New Zealand.

This austerely lovely land has been granted a reprieve by 'progress' and by national concern for conservation. It now seems safe for all time. Beaches sprawl as long and forests rise as tall for today's traveller as they did for the heroic Brunner and his Maori guides. Conservationists could now consider the preservation of that unique and endangered species, the Coaster.

Above: *The rugged mountain sides of the Southern Alps on the road to Otira are snow-flecked even in mid-summer*

Left: *Surging sea round the Pancake Rocks, Punakaiki, reveals the power that shaped these limestone formations*

Above : *In glacier country the mists descend at about midday to obscure the surrounding peaks, clearing in late afternoon*

Below: *Lake Paringa, in the shadow of Fish Hill, provides an idyllic setting for fly-fishermen*

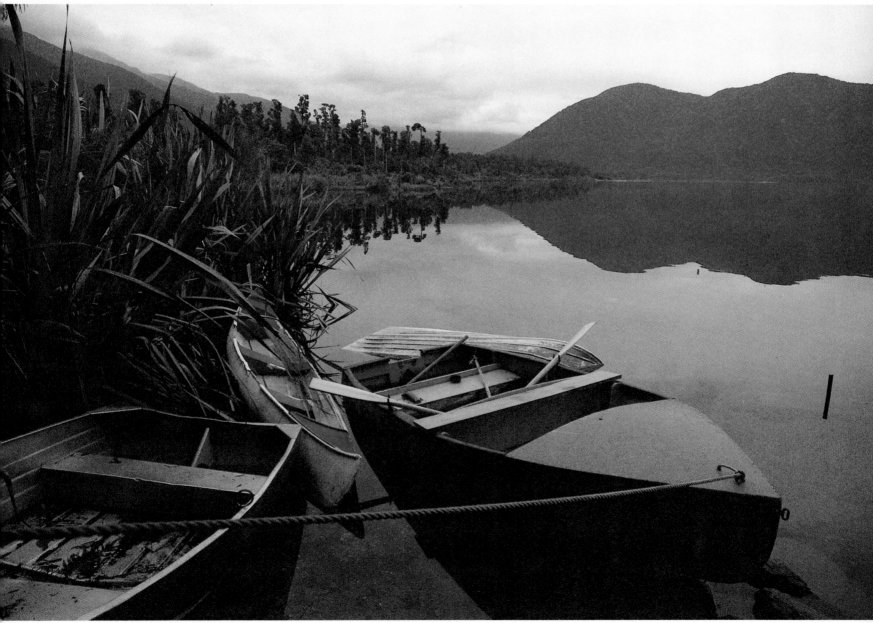

Left: *The Haast River rages under the Gates of Haast*

GREEN AND GOLD FORTUNES

Captain James Cook was the first European to note the treasured greenstone weapons and adornments of the Maori

Old neglected cottages like the one above are a reminder of Reefton's golden heyday in the eighteen-seventies

When he asked about greenstone, Cook heard 'a hundred fabulous stories'. The one that most impressed him was that greenstone had been a fish which, when hauled from the water, turned to stone.

So lovely and precious a material had to have legends. The most persuasive of these says that in the Polynesian homeland of Hawaiki there was a great navigator named Ngahue, who was pursued across empty sea by a green water monster called Poutini. The coast of New Zealand and the gleaming snows of Aorangi (Mount Cook) hove into view, and with the monster still roaring in pursuit, Ngahue beached his canoe at the mouth

A window from a gold buyer's office in Okarito is now on show in Hokitika's West Coast Historical Museum

of Westland's Arahura River and fled upstream. Poutini was killed in the river's rapids; as the creature perished it turned to stone. The grateful Ngahue chipped off pieces, carried them home and used greenstone tools to fashion great voyaging canoes that would later bring his people to New Zealand. So much for fable. The fact was that greenstone gave Maori tools a cutting edge unsurpassed by that of any other stone-age culture. Greenstone – nephrite to the geologist, jade to craftspeople, *pounamu* to the Maori – was a result of the South Island's molten making.

*In Reefton's gold- and coal-bearing prime, the School of Mines (**Top**) trained the miners, while the Oddfellows Lodge (**Above**) cared for them when lung disease took its toll*

The Maori considered the stone to be a gift of the gods. It brought material wealth and spiritual health. In a stone-age society, stone tools built houses and canoes, and tilled the soil. It also made efficient weapons. It could transform the timber of New Zealand into carvings to enshrine racial and tribal memory. The first colonisers of New Zealand, if they were to prosper, had to have reliable hard stone. In greenstone – when it was finally found, perhaps about AD 1400 – they had an ideal material. Moreover, when ornamentally worked, it gave up an extraordinary milky-green, transparent beauty.

Greenstone was all the more precious for being won from the most forbidding terrain in New Zealand. Overland trade routes – with slaves sweating under the burden of heavy blocks of

The Hilton Hotel in Blackball recalls a livelier time when the town was a bustling coal-mining community

A miner's cottage in Blackball. The little township still houses a few miners but none work in the town itself

pounamu, sometimes to be slain at the end for their pains – ran out from Westland to the rest of New Zealand. A material so laboriously and murderously gained attracted *mana*, 'prestige'. No other substance indigenous to New Zealand did more to determine the nature of Maori society. To many tribes the South Island was known as *Te Wai Pounamu*, 'the waters of greenstone'.

Ross, a former goldmining town south of Hokitika, now exploits its past for the tourists – as with this old cottage tranformed into a museum and information centre

Gold was the greenstone of the European, and likewise it did more than anything else to determine the social character of post-European New Zealand. Gold brought far more migrants than the New Zealand Company's planners ever did. In Canterbury, on the other side of the Southern Alps to Westland, there was an awareness, even before the first substantial strike had been made in the South Island, that the sedate little British colony might be rudely shaken. The *Lyttelton Times* warned that the gambling spirit engendered by gold rushes had demoralising consequences and did not inspire greatness of heart and character in a nation. The *Nelson Examiner* announced that it would have been 'as well pleased had gold never been discovered in New Zealand'. It was a stance that derived from a distaste for democracy. Gold – 'the great friend of the masses', in the diggers' song – gave many of modest means a stake in the country; it gave them enough capital to buy land, build homes, establish farms and businesses, and begin to prosper.

Westland was the end of the line for many veterans of the Californian, Victorian and Otago gold rushes. By and large, they were fit, active and imaginative settlers. Often too, they were more literate and better educated than colonists elsewhere in the young colony. The egalitarian comradeship of Westland's goldfields – along with a healthy irreverence for authority, and a pragmatic radicalism – would soon show itself powerfully in the country's political life. Westland's gold-rushes – unlike those of Nelson and Marlborough, Otago or Coromandel – left a distinctive and highly articulate community in its wake: that community is still visible today. The *Lyttelton Times* to the contrary, Westland's gold rushes did much for the heart and character of New Zealand; some might say that this is where the nation's heart and character really resides.

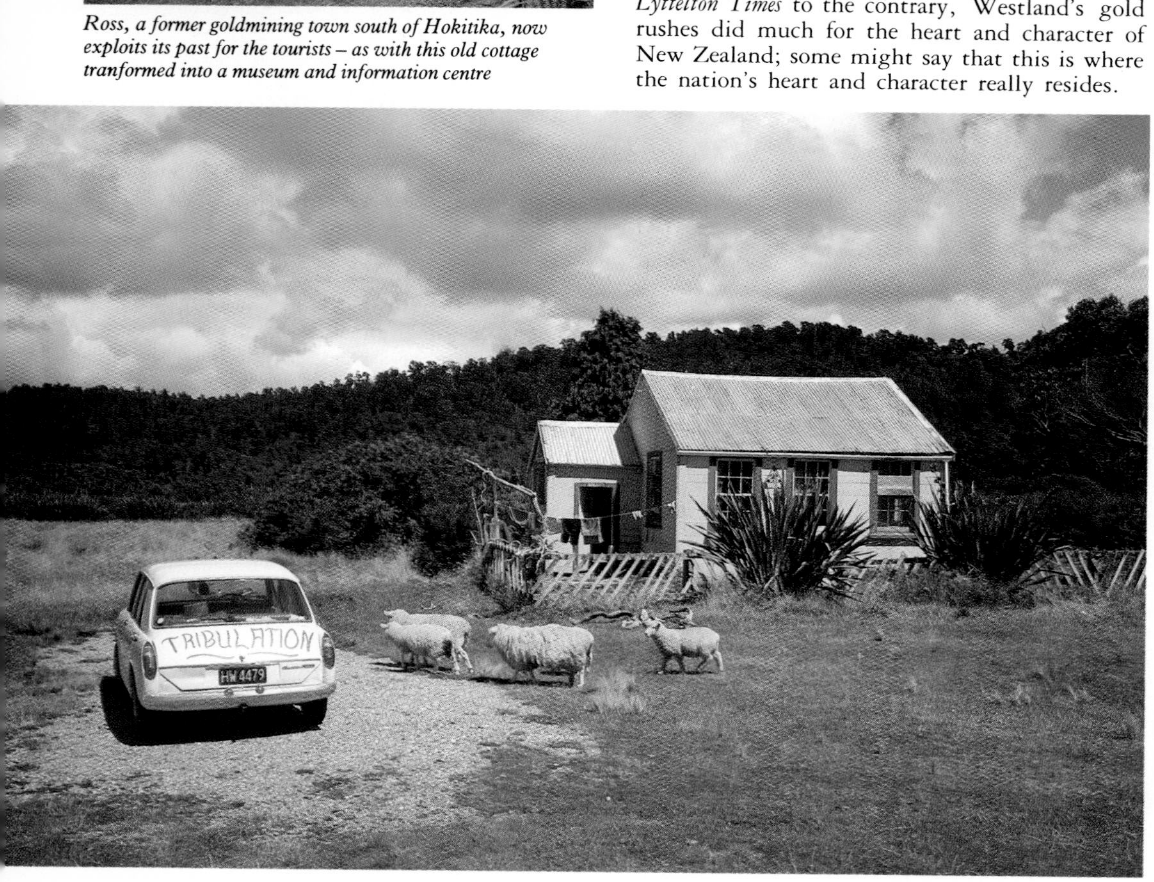

Housed in an 1876 timber church, the Blacks Point Museum near Reefton includes a working water-powered gold battery

Coal might not have the grace of greenstone, or the glamour of gold, but it has been, along with the region's timber, a more durable commodity. Westland's coal has fired industry, warmed lives and provided livelihoods for thousands for more than a century. As gold waned in importance, coal and timber gave the region a continuing economic role in the nation.

Miners lacked the mobility and independence of gold-diggers. There was no leaping from one lucky strike to the next; they were tied to their employment and their employers. They lived in close and sometimes sunless communities along the lower Grey valley, or on stark and windy hilltops beyond Westport, in something of a brotherhood: men dedicated to their occupation, fierce in defence of their rights, and united in adversity. (New Zealand's biggest mining tragedy at the Brunner Mine in 1896 took sixty-seven lives.) Here, New Zealand's infant trade unions survived their first stern tests. Here, socialist orators like Bob Semple and Paddy Webb, later cabinet ministers in the Labour government of 1935-49, began their political lives. That government could be seen in the making here from 1900; no communities did more than the diminutive coal-towns of Westland to determine the course and nature of New Zealand society.

For half a century, the three minerals of Westland – greenstone, gold and coal – have been central to life in this land. They continue to colour the human character of the country.

Left: *Okarito, which enjoyed a brief but boisterous boom in the eighteen-sixties, has few permanent residents today*
Right: *When gold flowed freely at Reefton, one well-heeled citizen adorned his garden with this remarkable fountain*

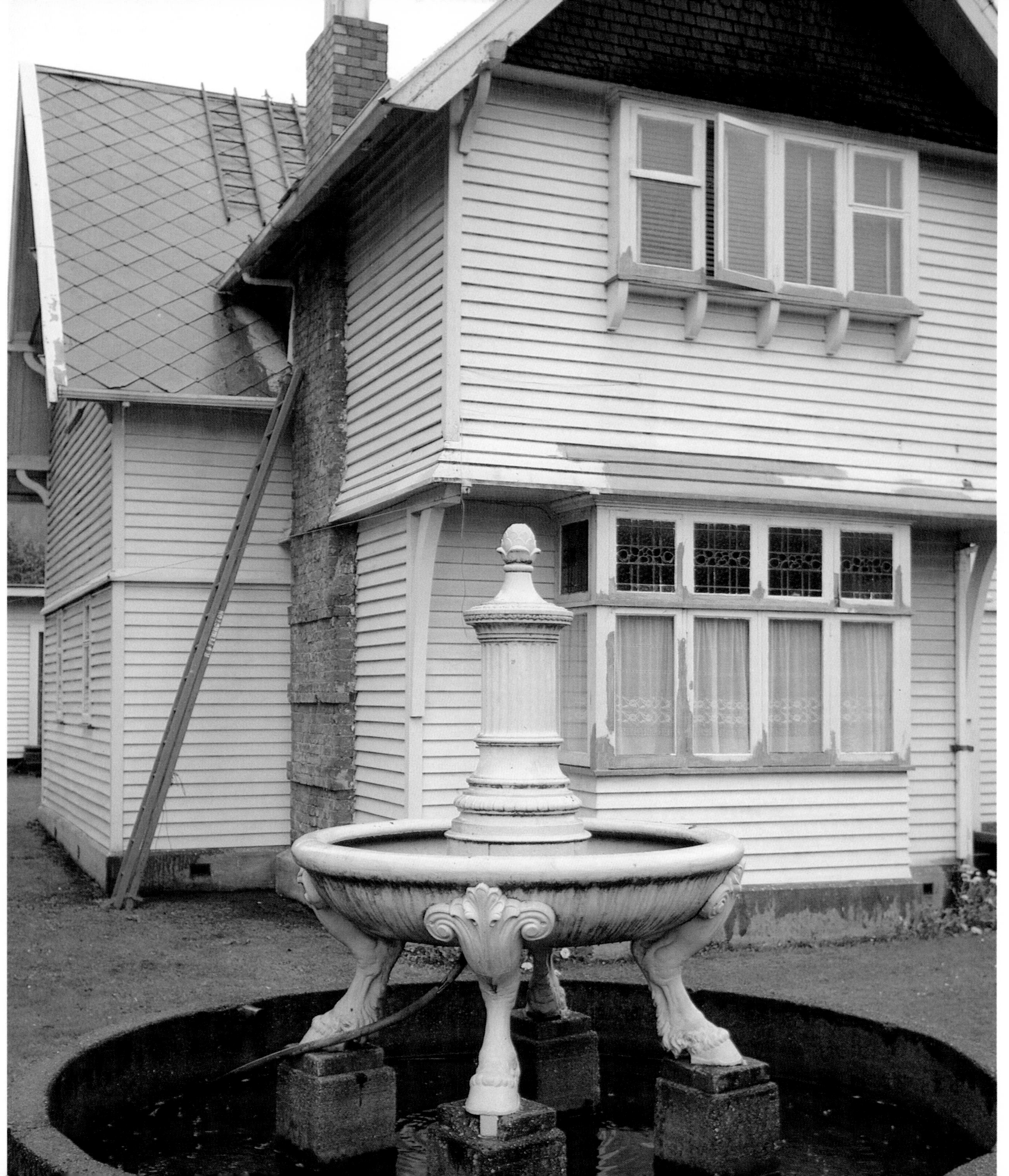

VALLEYS OF ICE

In the north of Westland, people have mined minerals, felled forest, drained swamps. In the south, human affairs are less obvious

The forest rises undiminished; the mountains close with the sea. Dusky lakes fill with alpine reflections, and two great glaciers spill spectacularly from the Southern Alps towards the Tasman. This is South Westland's world, still as rich, rugged and ice-rimmed as it was when it first rose theatrically into the view of early European voyagers. 'As far inland as the eye can reach,' wrote Captain James Cook as his ship *Endeavour* coasted by in 1770, 'nothing is to be seen but the summits of these Rocky mountains which seem to lay so near each other as not to admit any valleys between'.

Above: *Potters Creek, in glacier country, rattles over ice-cut rock on its way from Mount Downe to Lake Mapourika*
Right: *Framed by monoliths, Franz Josef Glacier's frozen fall descends to feed the Waiho River*

It is a measure of South Westland's remoteness that it was nearly a century before other voyagers disclosed South Westland's most surprising spectacle: its glaciers. Cook had been perplexed by valleys that seemed filled with snow; he knew nothing of glaciers. In 1859 two Canterbury men, Francis and Young, sailed round the South Island in search of grazing land. They saw little of promise in Westland, but their ship's log recorded: 'We saw what appeared to be a streak of mist running between two peaks. . . Abreast of Mount Cook, close inshore, we could see distinctly that it was an immense field of ice, entirely filling up the valley formed by the spurs of the twin peaks, and running far down into the low land. . . it appeared to be quite a mile in width.'

The Fox and Franz Josef Glaciers descend freakishly between beards of forest to three hundred metres above sea level. Tropically lush rainforest and tall fern frame their lower levels. They stand at only forty-four degrees south. In the northern hemisphere no glaciers reach so low an altitude until sixty-seven degrees north. Moreover, it was possible to walk on to the glaciers

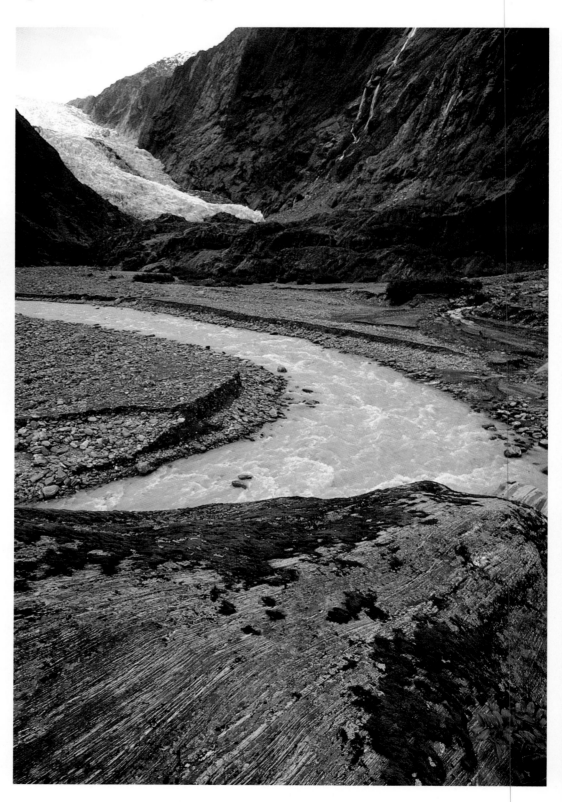

Below: *The terminal face of Franz Josef Glacier shows the deep crevasses caused by the stresses of uneven flow. The glacier moves more rapidly at the centre than at the sides*

Below: *The bush sometimes seems to enter right into Fox Glacier, the larger and longer of the twin glaciers*

with relative ease. One of the first to set foot on the frozen torrents was the German geologist Julius von Haast who recorded: 'If anything will give to geologists an insight into the power which glaciers have of destroying gigantic mountains and carrying their debris to lower regions, a journey to that part of the West Coast will easily effect this object.' More lyrically, he wrote of the glacier he named after the Emperor of the Austro-Hungarian empire: 'The white unsullied face of the ice [was] before us, broken up into a thousand turrets, needles and other fantastic forms, the terminal face of the glacier being still hidden by a foreground of pines, ratas, beeches, and arborescent ferns, giving to the whole picture a still stranger appearance.' Haast painted with words. Others were soon recording the glaciers in paint, among them premier William Fox, after whom the second great glacier was named.

Above: *With a pair of tough boots, a stout staff and a raincoat, the visitor is equipped to walk on Fox Glacier*

Prospectors who pushed into South Westland found gold in the black sand of the beaches, plucking it from the breakers in a brief, boisterous bonanza. In 1866 Okarito was suddenly a town of thirty-three stores, hotels, dance halls – even a brewery – and more than a thousand people, with two or three thousand more at work on the sands near by. Two years later it was over; Okarito reverted to being the unmenaced breeding ground of New Zealand's rare white heron, the magical kotuku. A few diggers would remain, some to farm. Dredges would work the district later in the century; sawmills would begin work; flax mills would ship out fibre so long as markets lasted, but never again would wildest Westland be so populous. For years it would be the lonely realm of trail-blazers and surveyors. Prominent among them was the dogged explorer Charles Douglas (1840-1916), who gave forty solitary years to this landscape; he haunts it still.

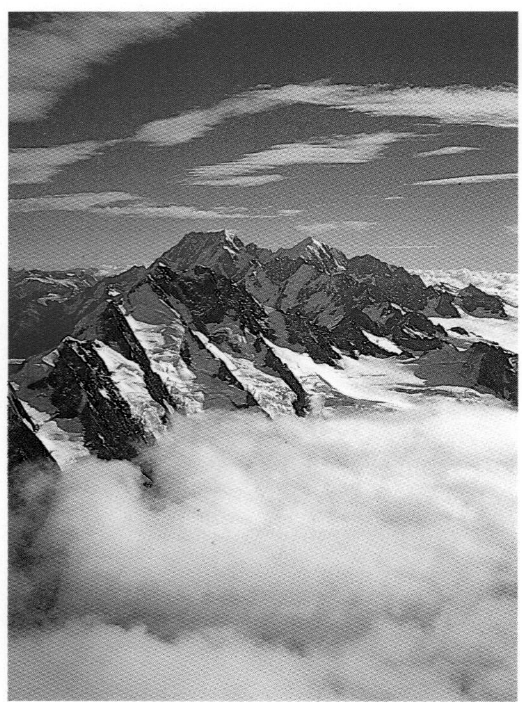

Far above the two thousand four hundred hectares of névé that feed the Franz Josef Glacier, the peaks of Mount Tasman and Mount Cook jut through the clouds. They are among seventeen mountains in the area that exceed three thousands metres and nurture permanent snowfields

It was Douglas's vocation to open up much of the region to the tourists he despised. 'It isn't,' he said censoriously, 'by trotting out of a hotel and back again the same day that Nature's true wonders can be seen.' The founding father and unofficial patron saint of the conservation movement in New Zealand, he was more at home with forests and birds than with his fellow humans. Douglas most feared the greedy mineral-seekers who might tear his beloved reaches of Westland apart – ruthless exploiters 'whose wealth goes direct home to shareholders who never saw the country and never intended to'.

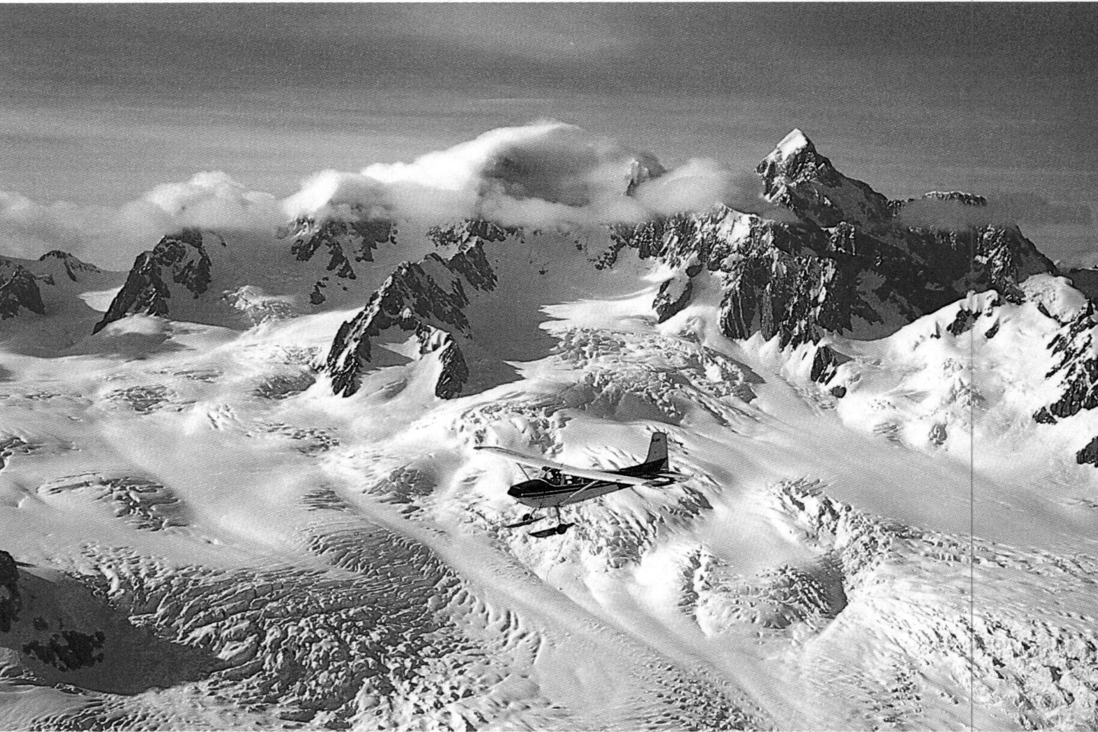

Ski planes take visitors over the Fox Glacier névé, the snowfields at the head of the glacier that will become ice. When conditions permit a ski landing is made

Douglas also foresaw South Westland's fate; he accurately sensed that to be most lucrative, exploitation depended on entire preservation. 'The mines they intend to develop are the silver and gold in the pockets of tourists,' he observed. 'No more roads for diggers but tracks to waterfalls and glaciers.' The first travellers into the region stayed in remote farmhouses. Guest houses followed, then hotels. Governors - general and premiers came to see the glaciers; hoteliers were provided with finance to build huts and develop tracks. Rivers were bridged and roads crept down the coast. Scenic reserves in the area were gazetted from 1910 onward. South Westlanders for a time opposed a national park; they saw potential mineral sources and profitable stands of timber being locked up. But the tide of tourist interest and conservationists' campaigns dictated otherwise. In 1960 the Westland National Park was formed. Meanwhile, to the chagrin of conservationists, milling of lowland forest continued on the perimeters of the park – endangering among other things, the breeding ground of the kotuku at Okarito, Finally in 1982, another thirty thousand hectares of forest were added to the park.

A PRICELESS POSSESSION

Essayist M.H. Holcroft, in his pioneering book on New Zealand's character, saw the vine-wrapped walls of Westland's towering forest as containing 'something that is not ours, something that has never belonged even to the Maori . . . some dream of life too strange for our minds to grasp'.

Dream or nightmare, botanists have devoted their lives to disentangling it. Botanist Leonard Cockayne found some thirty-eight plant families and three hundred and fifteen varieties along a sixteen-kilometre hike from Franz Josef to the sea in 1910. He judged Westland's forest 'a unique production of nature, found in no other land . . . a priceless possession'. Among better-known species, rimu and miro climb to six hundred metres; rata, kamahi, totara and pink pine to nine hundred metres; and ancient kaikawaka and scrub to twelve hundred. Vegetation thins and vanishes over sixteen hundred metres. The park's mountains rise over three thousand metres to join Mount Cook National Park. The glacial valleys, like the two low-dipping glaciers that give the park its distinction, date from the last ice age, which ended ten thousand years ago.

The opening of the Haast Pass road to Otago in 1965 accelerated the growth of hit-and-run tourism; it meant that Westland National Park, especially its glaciers, could be included comfortably in a round-the-island itinerary. Though scores of thousands of travellers pass through the park every year, human pressure remains slight, visible virtually only in the settlements at Fox Glacier and Franz Josef. Charles Douglas's caution still holds: nature's true wonders don't disclose themselves to day-trippers. It is a place to linger. Then a visitor exploring in this wilderness on foot may understand what the old explorer meant when he summed up his years in this lonely part: 'Men call me a fool for wasting my life in mountain solitudes, but if in doing so I have found nothing new in thought or worth giving to the world, I have at last gathered glimmerings of Truth as to how nature works, glimmerings which if they bear no fruit in this life, may in the next where darkness will be light.'

Right: *Alpine huts are maintained for the use of climbers attempting high ascents or transalpine climbs*

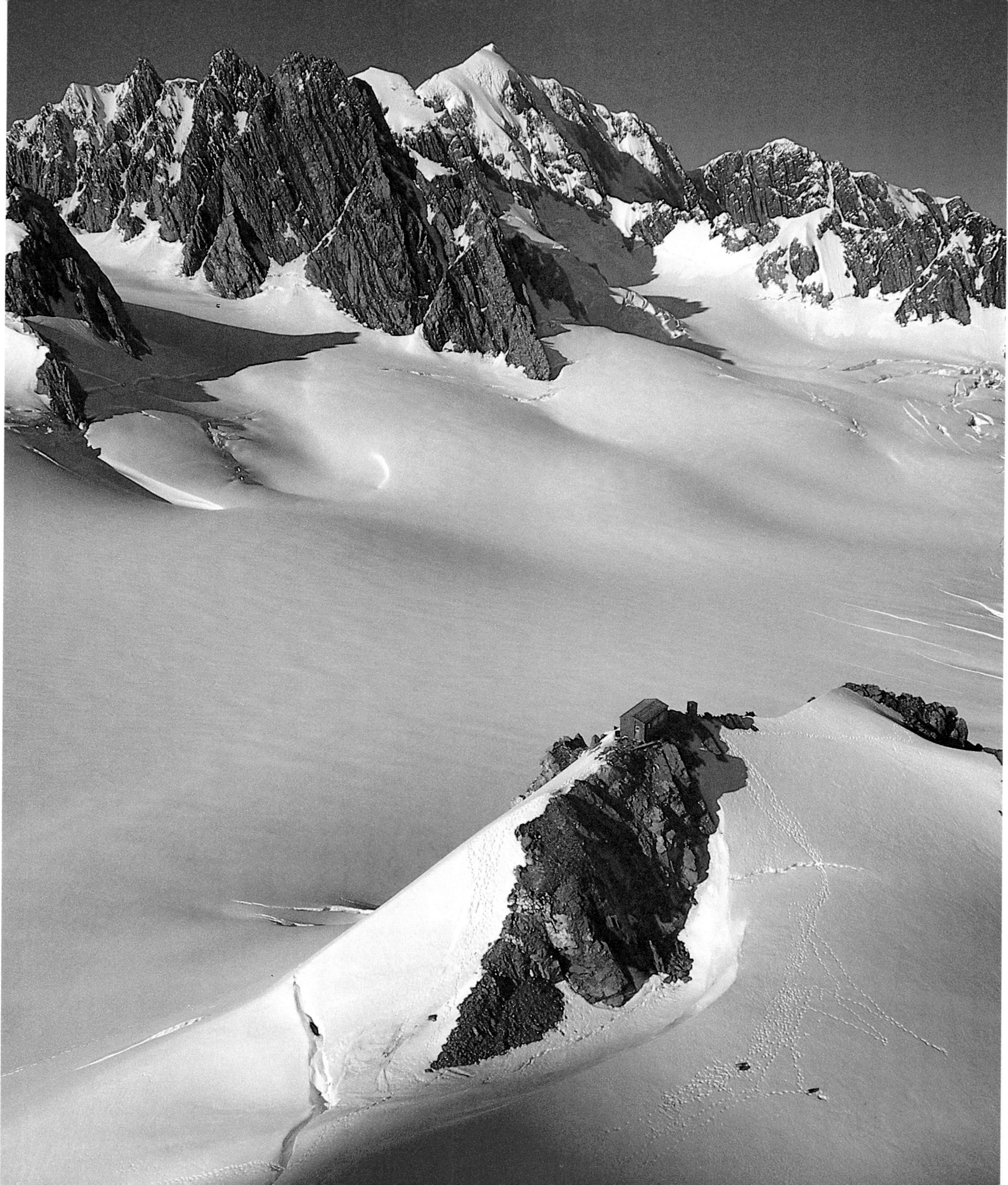

PLACES OF INTEREST

ARAHURA
Westland's one surviving Maori community (descended from the Coast's original owners) lives here on the Arahura River, north-east of HOKITIKA. The river was the richest source of fine greenstone in the pre-European period and is now owned by the Maori people. Permission to enter the riverbed and for mining rights must first be obtained from the Mawhera Incorporation.

BLACKBALL
This riverside Westland colliery township is just outside GREYMOUTH. A successful three-month miners' strike here (to win a half-hour lunch break) in 1908 did much to determine the direction and future leadership of the New Zealand labour movement. Now with a population of 400, it is the home of ex-miners, miners working elsewhere in the region and forestry workers. Cottages, a hotel and a mine manager's house (now a community centre and museum) recall Blackball's heyday. The remains of the old mine are just outside the township.

The stark remnants of Denniston's once thriving coal industry look out over the coastal lip of Westland

BRUCE BAY
A small settlement on the site of an old Maori village, Bruce Bay is between Fox Glacier township and Haast, 224 kilometres south of HOKITIKA, at the mouth of the Mahitahi River, on the richly interesting road to Westland's southern extremity. The area is exploited for timber and cattle and its river-running whitebait. A 'duffer rush' – a dead-end gold search – led to hundreds of diggers taking the Coast's shortest-lived boom town apart in 1866. The last tolerable beach on this wild route has rimu forest growing close to the water's edge. Further towards Haast (40 kilometres) is Knights Point with a vantage point and a memorial to HAAST PASS road-builders.

BRUNNER
Named after the explorer who first walked the length of Westland and reported a promising seam of coal here,Brunner is a collection of four faded coal-towns: Dobson, Wallsend, Stillwater and Taylorville, on both sides of the Grey River, upriver from GREYMOUTH. The district began producing coal in 1864. The Brunner Mine, site of the NZ Historic Places Trust's first large venture in industrial archaeology, was the 1896 setting for New Zealand's worst mine disaster, with 67 miners killed. A historic reserve, with walkways and information boards, has been created about the remains of the Brunner Mine. Among the more interesting relics are the brick beehive coke ovens. Access to the mine site is by footbridge across the Grey. There is also a roadside memorial to the explorer.

CHARLESTON
Named after a skipper (Charles Bonner) who braved ferocious seas to bring food and liquor to starving diggers here, Charleston, 26 kilometres south-west of WESTPORT, boomed between 1866 and 1869. It was said there were more pubs than houses, more publicans than sinners. Catholic patriots and Protestant loyalists warred here. Little is left beyond diggers' graves and the remains of their workings in the bush. At nearby Mitchells Gully is a reconstructed working goldmine. The present European Hotel is successor to one with ballroom and orchestra that ran night and day and turned on dancing girls at two shillings a time (drinks included). Now only historic photographs come with drinks in the bar.

DENNISTON
This ghost town, high in the mists above the Buller coast, produces coal still. Its steep and dramatic incline – an engineering marvel of its era – sent coal-wagons roaring 600 precipitous metres down to a coastal railhead for almost a century. Before the mine closed in 1967, 30 million tonnes of coal were shipped out from this bleak site on which some 2000 people managed to survive. It seems the end of the earth, especially when dank cloud swirls up from the valleys.

Early trade unionists met secretly on the bare tableland beyond the town, with lookouts posted and admission by whispered password. Old mine buildings and cottages survive, and there is a shelter with photographs and information at the head of the incline. A few people still live here, and a little coal is still recovered by a mining collective. Just 24 kilometres north from WESTPORT, via Waimangaroa, Denniston may prove the most moving human monument in a Westland itinerary. It can be complemented with a visit to Westport's Coaltown. Another largely abandoned coal-town in this vicinity is Stockton, with its 8 kilometre coal-carrying cableway. Open-cast mining continues today. A fire deep in an old mine has been smouldering here since the beginning of the century and its smoke sometimes mists the landscape.

Okarito Lagoon. This lonely outpost is New Zealand's breeding station of the white heron

FOX GLACIER
Set in WESTLAND NATIONAL PARK and named after William Fox, a former premier of New Zealand and distinguished colonial painter, the glacier falls 2600 metres on its 13-kilometre journey from the Southern Alps, making it longer than neighbouring FRANZ JOSEF GLACIER. Like its neighbour, it has retreated since the first European sighting, but it remains imposing. The terminal face is accessible on foot. The approach road crosses ancient moraine and gravel outwashes left by melting ice. The crumbling valley walls, no longer supported by the glacier, are slowly receding behind waterfalls.

The valley is built on a bed of ice more than 300 metres deep: rock bottom has never been sounded. On the floor of the valley small plants have seeded in the silt between boulders and rock fragments; larger species grow as humus slowly builds up, and finally more Westland forest. The glacier itself remains magnificent, a mighty ice river, its terminal face – partly patched with terminal moraine – creaking and arching over the cave from which the Fox River flows pale with powdered rock. Tracks across the ice demand no more than average fitness and a pair of tough shoes. Here as at Franz Josef a helicopter trip up the glacier – with optional touchdown – is unforgettable. Near Fox Glacier settlement is an undemanding nature walk to Lake Matheson, which mirrors the alps, especially Mt Cook and Mt Tasman. It is probably the most photographed part of New Zealand. Further information is available from WESTLAND NATIONAL PARK headquarters, at Franz Josef or visitors' centre at Fox Glacier township.

FRANZ JOSEF GLACIER
This 11 kilometre-long glacier, the land's best known, was named after the Emperor of the Austro-Hungarian empire by geologist Julius von Haast in 1863. Since then, it has ebbed and flowed down the valley, gradually losing ground like all the world's glaciers. But it can still take the breath away as it rises beyond the forested approach road. The gleam of its crumpled ice eerily colours the surrounding rocks and vegetation.

The Franz Josef is roughly 7000 years old. It originated from a larger glacier that swept all the way to the sea 14 000 years ago. The present terminal face is only 19 kilometres from the shore and 300 metres above sea level. Below the terminal face are heaps of moraine dumped by the glacier during extended halts – dating about 1600, 1750 and 1825 – on its withdrawal from a warming world. In the valley, vegetation has taken over hundreds of hectares once covered by ice. The glacier feeds the wild Waiho River, which carries away powdered rock and blocks of ice. Depending on the temperature, the glacier can advance a metre or more a day, and then retreat as fast. A long winter and heavy snow in the alps means glacial advance. Scenic flights (and helicopter excursions) show the glacier's size and reveal bizarre ice sculptures. Novices can make short unaccompanied trips on the glacier, but guides are recommended. A number of tracks lead to vantage points. The track to 1295 metre Alex Knob is a 4-hour climb, past keas (the New Zealand mountain parrot) and speargrass (taramea to the Maori, and made into perfume) to an alpine panorama. Visitors need solid shoes and wet-weather gear. Considering its isolation, the settlement at Franz Josef offers comfortable accommodation. Tiny Tudor-style St James Church has an alpine view . Lake Mapourika near by is one of the land's loveliest.

GILLESPIES BEACH
This reach of rocky coast, accessible from Fox Glacier township, was worked by gold prospectors. It had 650 diggers in its prime and 11 stores. Now there is a cemetery and the rusting remains of a gold-dredge that worked the foreshore. A 3-hour return walk takes the visitor to a lively seal colony. Sealing gangs from Sydney were dumped here, sometimes to starve, but sent tens of thousands of sealskins back to their employers. The seal population is slowly recovering.

GREYMOUTH
With 8000 people, this is the unchallenged capital of the Coast: it takes its name (Coasters mostly abbreviate it to 'Grey') from the Grey River, in turn named after twice New Zealand governor Sir George Grey. The port and town grew on the site of the largest Maori community in Westland and much of it is still Maori-owned. In the gold strikes of the 1860s, it was the depot for thousands of diggers. Coal, timber and hinterland agriculture later took over the town's economy. In the 1940s miners boycotted the public houses for six months to save the sixpenny beer; the publicans finally capitulated. The pubs of Greymouth make a warm refuge when the notorious wind named 'The Barber' funnels between the stark limestone walls of the Grey Gorge.

Some 13 kilometres south of Greymouth is the Coast's most popular tourist drawcard, Shanty Town, a flamboyant rather than faithful reconstruction of a Westland gold-rush town. Coasters teach the technique of gold-panning. Buggy and locomotive rides are available and there has been imaginative restoration of old buildings. There is a fine wildlife park near by at Paroa near Shanty Town. Up the Grey River a historic reserve, with well-documented display boards, has been established about the remains of the BRUNNER Mine. Inland, glacier-made and moraine-dammed LAKE BRUNNER offers swimming, boating and fishing.

HAAST PASS
The mightiest highway in New Zealand: peaks push skyward all around; snowfields glimmer among the clouds and the sound of distant avalanches echoes down green valleys. In a startlingly sudden transition at the highest point in the pass, the rivers and rainforests of Westland disappear and are replaced by the sunny, almost treeless grasslands of Central Otago (or vice versa). The route, which follows an old Maori war trail, was rediscovered by gold prospector Charles Cameron in 1863 (followed soon by geologist Julius von Haast, who promptly named it after himself). It was only a packhorse trail for the rest of the 19th century. Westland's long-awaited link with Otago was opened in 1965, after 30 years of road-building. The road is still hostage to the powerful terrain it invades, teetering alongside alpine torrents, ducking round waterfalls, pushing through beech forest. It can be the most exhilarating experience in a South Island journey, but the climate can also make it the most dampening.

The last known Maori excursion along the route was that of Te Puoho, a distant relation and ally of the murderous Te Rauparaha. In 1836, he crossed the mountains with a *taua*, 'war party', on a raid against the Ngai Tahu people of Otago and Southland. Tradition says that the journey took Te Puoho most of a year. He slew some Maoris on arrival in Otago, but news of his coming travelled and Te Puoho's epic journey ended in a bloody Southland ambush, which neither he nor most of his party survived. At its highest point (564 metres), Haast Pass is the lowest of the South Island's alpine passes, and is seldom under snow.

HOKITIKA
This seaside community of 3300 was the land's fifth largest when diggers followed the first Westland gold strikes in the 1860s. At times the population may have reached 10 000, with another 5000 on nearby fields. There were 102 hotels, casinos and theatres, even a 1400-seat opera house. The Hokitika River mouth proved a perilous port and gamblers bet on whether ships would survive its sand bar. The port now has a few rusting relics but no ships negotiate the river mouth.

Architecturally, Hokitika holds little of distinction, but St Mary's Catholic Church (1914), the largest in Westland, testifies to the faith that sustained the Irish diggers and their descendants. Hokitika's place in New Zealand history is recorded in the West Coast Historical Museum (open weekdays, 9.30–4.30; weekend and public holidays, 2–4).

Many locals still pan for gold, but commercial gold operations are still important. The Goliath Mining Group has eight operations in the Hokitika area. One of the three civic statues is of an anonymous digger (the others are of goldfield storekeeper Richard John Seddon who became premier, and, curiously, of poet Robert Burns). Just out of town is Hokitika's glow-worm dell, New Zealand's largest display of outdoor glow-worms, on banks 10 metres and more high, to be viewed after dark. North-east, towards GREYMOUTH, is Shanty Town, and 18 kilometres inland is Lake Kaniere, a wildlife haven set in 7000 hectares of forest and alpine reserve. The Shamrock Creek Reserve, established by the NZ Forest Service (via the Stafford-Dillmanstown road, 10 kilometres north-east), includes the site of the now vanished, once nine-hotel goldfield town of Goldsborough, with walks ranging from five minutes to all-day through intensively worked terrain.

The Hokitika Gorge Reserve near Kowhitirangi (26 kilometres south) is another local highlight. It has

BRUNNER'S EPIC JOURNEY

Thomas Brunner's long-term claim to fame will probably remain his discovery of 'black gold', but it is his heroic exploration of the West Coast that captures the imagination

Brunner Mine as it is now

Relics of a once productive coal mine

From its source at Lake Christabel, high in the Southern Alps near the Lewis Pass, the Grey River twists over one hundred and twenty-one kilometres through a complex watershed of mountains and tributaries to Greymouth, the administrative and mercantile centre of Westland. It was on the Grey, eleven kilometres upstream from Greymouth, that Thomas Brunner (1821-74) in January 1848 first saw a seam of the coal that was to become the West Coast's 'black gold'.

Posted as a survey assistant to the New Zealand Company in Nelson, Brunner undertook two arduous preliminary surveys to the south and west. The first, early in 1846, was with two artists, William Fox, who later became premier, and Charles Heaphy. Shortly after their return, Brunner left again with Heaphy, to explore the coast south of Cape Farewell to the mouth of the Buller River. They returned in August and the following December Brunner was on his way again, this time with four Maori companions – two men and their wives. This expedition to explore the sources of the Buller River and lands south was to be one of New Zealand's epic journeys.

The weather was appalling. As they made their way down the Buller and its valleys, the rain was ceaseless and the rivers swelled into torrents. There were constant delays to seek shelter. As the weeks then months dragged by their hardships increased. Wet bush, difficult river crossings, huge bluffs and broken and trackless terrain meant the party could travel only four to five kilometres a day. Food was scarce – an eel to eat became a luxury. At one stage they lived on rats.

After six months they reached a small pa, where Westport now stands, and rested to regain their strength. They then continued south, far below the Waiho River, which flows from the Franz Josef Glacier. Here the party turned and headed back to the site of modern Greymouth. A year after setting off from Nelson, they began the return journey by canoe up the Grey River. It was at this stage that Brunner noticed a large seam of coal exposed on the riverside.

Their route next took them to the large lake which now bears Brunner's name, then on a wide circuit to the Inangahua River and on to the Buller River. Here their troubles began again. Huge outcrops of rock, deep ravines, dense bush, bucketing rain and rivers in flood halted their progress. Then disaster struck: Brunner became paralysed down one side. Two of his companions deserted him, but the other couple stayed behind and for several weeks helped the crippled Brunner to drag himself onwards.

In June 1848 it began to snow, but fortunately they had by now left the Buller River system and reached the Nelson high country. On June 15, Brunner staggered into Fraser's Station – five hundred and fifty days after setting out from there, and long since given up for dead.

magnificent bush scenery, and a swing bridge spans the colourful waters of the Hokitika River. The hinterland community of Kowhitirangi was the scene of the stand by a demented farmer, Stanley Graham, who seemed to hold the country hostage in a bloody duel with authority in 1941. Seven men were slain before Graham himself was stalked and killed. *Hokitika* means 'direct return', which is exactly what many descendants of Westland's diggers do annually. It is the last community of substance – and a useful place to pause – before the glaciers and the demanding HAAST PASS, indeed before Otago's distant Wanaka on the far side of the alps. The district deserves at least a day, especially for those who want an insight into New Zealand's more robust past. ROSS, 30 kilometres south-west, is not be neglected either.

JACKSON BAY

South of Haast township, beyond the Arawata River, this was the site of a planned milling and fishing settlement (*c.* 1875) that foundered. Grazing land has reverted to bush; graves and a few relics remain. There is now a small transient population of hunters and fishermen, the latter especially in the whitebait season. A wharf was built here in 1937, too late for the isolated pioneers, to land machinery and material for the HAAST PASS road. This was the stamping ground of the legendary gold-seeker Arawata Bill.

KARAMEA

Westland's northernmost reach, 98 kilometres north-east of WESTPORT along a scenic road, Karamea is a community of 200 in a fertile setting. Unlike the rest of Westland, subtropical fruits flourish here in a mild, sunny micro-climate. Nelson North West Forest Park backs the settlement. Settlers from Nelson were dumped here on swampy, back-breaking land in the 1870s and virtually left to starve. Their descendants finally tamed the area though it suffered another blow when the Murchison earthquake demolished the tiny port in 1929.

Access since has been overland only. Hopes were that Karamea might be joined by highway to Collingwood in Nelson, roughly by way of the Heaphy Track (see page 214), but the route was never built and no longer seems likely to be; Karamea remains one of New Zealand's most isolated communities. A scattered settlement with no centre, it is now popular with vacationers, especially trampers, hunters and fishermen. The Heaphy Track to Nelson begins just up the coast. Those not wishing to brave the wilds for five days can still walk through some of the spectacular coastal section. Another, though more demanding track into Nelson, the Wangapeka, begins some 25 kilometres south (via Te Namu) along the Little Wanganui River; it should be tackled only by experienced trampers. Full information on both can be obtained from the NZ Forest Service in Karamea. The local highlight is the Oparara Valley, a landscape of limestone canyons, caves and arches backed by granite ranges – 9 kilometres north of Oparara township, then along a timber road. Ugly logging operations threatened the valley and were successfully opposed by conservationists. A scientific reserve has been established.

The Oparara Arch, at the end of a 20-minute riverside walk, is 43 metres high and 219 metres long. Much of the area is trackless and many caves remain unexplored. Caves at Honeycomb Hill were found to contain the bones of thousands of birds, some extinct, like the moa and the New Zealand eagle. The place is now virtually a museum of the land's past birdlife. Crevices, caves and holes functioned for thousands of years as a vast bird trap, locking wildlife into a lethal maze; other bird remains were washed into the caves. Some 52 species have been identified, 27 of them extinct and two of them previously unknown. The streams are the haunt of near-extinct native fish species like the kokopu and koaru. The NZ Forest Service at Karamea provides excursions and guides to the caves. *The Oparara Guidebook*, published by Friends of the Earth, is an introduction to this little-known pocket of Westland.

KUMARA

This depleted gold township, near the much-dredged Taramakau River, has a distinct place in New Zealand history. It was from here that storekeeper Richard John Seddon barnstormed into national politics and, as 'King Dick', became New Zealand's most celebrated leader (see page 251). A plaque marks the site of his home. With the resurgence of gold prices, alluvial claims are again being worked here. But an 80-hotel town of perhaps 4000 is now a 2-hotel town of fewer than 400. Just east of the town is Londonderry Rock, a 3000-tonne boulder dumped by an ancient glacier. It sits in a landscape devastated by gold-dredges.

LAKE BRUNNER

Inland from GREYMOUTH, this is Westland's largest lake, and like others has been formed by a retreating glacier. The shore offers picnic places, the waters boating, swimming and excellent trout fishing. There is a small lakeside settlement at Moana, and another at Mitchells. The Maori name for the lake was Moana Kotuku, 'sea of the kotuku'; the rare white heron (kotuku) may still be seen along its shores.

OKARITO

One of Westland's shorter-lived goldtowns, with sands once rich in minerals. It had its own brewery and three theatres. Okarito, off Highway 6 and 27 kilometres north of Franz Josef, has a memorial to Dutch explorer Abel Tasman. It was somewhere offshore in 1642 that Tasman glimpsed 'land uplifted high' – the first known European sighting of New Zealand. A walk to the nearby Okarito Trig is rewarded by one of the finest views across the Southern Alps. The Okarito Lagoon is the one breeding ground of the kotuku, the white heron, which Maori legend says is seen but once in a lifetime. In the 1980s the lonely settlement achieved prominence when one of its few permanent residents, novelist Keri Hulme, produced an international best-seller, *The Bone People*.

OTIRA

The gateway to the Coast from Canterbury, the railway settlement of Otira stands at the western end of the Otira Tunnel. Opened in 1923 it is one of the longest rail tunnels in the world (8.6 kilometres). Its builders survived blizzards and rockfalls to push a path under the Southern Alps and give Westland a reliable overland link. The road through and up the Otira Gorge to Arthur's Pass in Canterbury is New Zealand's most awesome alpine route. Dutch artist Petrus Van der Velden (1837-1913) painted the towering landforms and rushing torrents of Otira Gorge. His Otira paintings, now in major New Zealand galleries, mark him as a formidable colonial artist. Towards GREYMOUTH, at Jacksons (19 kilometres), a tavern dating from 1879 has been restored as an old coaching inn.

PUNAKAIKI

Locality on the coast road between WESTPORT and GREYMOUTH. Punakaiki is best known for the nearby Pancake Rocks and blowholes. This strangely stacked and sculpted collection of limestone columns spectacularly traps the surf and funnels it explosively; spray detonates high in the air. There is a small settlement and camping ground nearby; good swimming in the Pororari River or at Pororari beach (2 kilometres north).

REEFTON

The Inangahua district – of which Reefton, now with a population of 1200,

ARAWATA BILL

A solitary prospector of South Westland was named after the wild Arawata region

The worn face of William O'Leary

Arawata Bill with Dolly, his packhorse

The Arawata River runs into Jackson Bay in South Westland. The road that leads there from the north is the last route into this remote south-west corner of New Zealand. Adventurous motorists are advised to make the journey in good weather. After crossing the Haast Bridge, the main West Coast road (Highway 6) turns inland on its way to Lake Wanaka and Central Otago. But a small country road branches from the bridge in the opposite direction – towards the sea – then south-west forty four kilometres to Jackson Bay.

Twelve kilometres before the tiny Jackson Bay settlement the road crosses the Arawata River. It was in this rugged region that William O'Leary (1865-1947), better known as Arawata Bill, settled. Having once overheard a chance remark that there was gold in the area, he spent more than forty years in an effort to prove the truth of what was soon to become for him an obsession. Arawata Bill's father had prospected in the Gabriels Gully, Otago, gold-rush in the eighteen-sixties, so if it is possible to inherit a footloose and single-minded interest in a precious metal then Bill certainly had gold in his blood.

The Arawata basin and the river and mountain systems around it form some of the most broken, storm-battered river and mountain country on the West Coast. In this wilderness, Bill and his mare, Dolly, who was said to be forty years old when she died, became a familiar figure to the farmers, prospectors, climbers, hunters and trampers who began to wander in increasing numbers through the area.

Bill's gold fever included an obsessive search for the 'Frenchman's Gold' – a treasure supposed to have been buried in the area – and for the 'Lost Ruby Mine' which he claimed mysteriously to have located.

But his lasting memory lies in the powerful sequence of poems called *Arawata Bill* by Denis Glover, published in 1953.

The unspoiled bushland around Lake Brunner offers many attractive picnicking spots

is the main centre – proved to be one of the most highly mineralised in the land, so attention turned here as alluvial gold dwindled. Backed by forested hills above the Inangahua River, the town roared into existence when rich gold-quartz reefs were found above Blacks Point in 1870. Two years later Reefton had its own stock exchange, the only one on the Coast. In 1888 Reefton became the first town in New Zealand, perhaps the southern hemisphere, to be illuminated by electric power. Work on Inangahua reefs continued through the first half of the 20th century. Coal is still being mined from long-profitable seams.

More than any other town in Westland, Reefton retains its original goldfield character. A precinct of historical buildings is identified by plaques – including the Court House (1872), the town's first public building, where miners brought their claims; the old School of Mines (1886), which functioned until 1970, finally serving uranium prospectors, and today housing an extensive mineral collection; and two churches, Sacred Heart and St Stephens (both 1878). Lodges provided welfare for miners suffering from lung diseases, and two lodge buildings, the Oddfellows (1872), and the Masonic (1892) survive. The Blacks Point Museum, in an old pitsawn church (1876), has maps, models, mining equipment, and a rebuilt gold battery (open Wednesday and weekend, 1.30–3.30; longer in summer). At Crushington, 4 kilometres south-east on Highway 7, are the remains of the great Wealth of Nations Mine, and near by, across the river, is the huge Globe Battery. The **VICTORIA FOREST PARK** has recreational gold panning areas and tracks that once linked outlying goldfield communities. Among these is Waiuta, at the end of a turn-off signposted 21 kilometres towards **GREYMOUTH**, a mining township of 150 people until as recently as 1951, a ghost town still in the making, and rich in relics. The mine, the second richest in the land, closed not because the gold gave out, but because a ventilator shaft collapsed. A full day's hike south from Reefton or 5 hours north-east from Waiuta leads to the gold mine at Big River, where the poppet head, mine buildings and cyanide tanks remain. This too worked well into the 20th century.

ROSS

This village, 30 kilometres south of **HOKITIKA** on the road to Franz Josef, almost became a ghost town as the alluvial goldfields of Westland were exhausted, but it soldiered on with sawmills, limestone crushing and farming. With a population now fluctuating around the 400 mark – in contrast to 4000 in the 1860s – Ross parades its past for the visitor.

A reserve at its centre holds a restored miner's cottage, now an information centre and museum. The town's traditional firebell tower stands here too. The reserve is the starting point for two well-developed walkways into surrounding goldfields. The Water Race Walk includes the old Ross cemetery, where headstones record death by drowning and in digging disasters; a restored miner's hut provides shelter along the way. The Jones Flat Walk is more demanding; it takes in the district's heavily-sluiced diggings, and the site where Westland's largest nugget, the 99-ounce 'Honourable Roddy' (named after the then minister of mines, Roderick McKenzie) was discovered in 1909. It sold for a mere £400 and was presented to George V as a coronation gift.

Trampers may hire gold pans in the town and try their luck too. The City Hotel is the oldest on the Coast (1865), but has been substantially renovated. St Patrick's Catholic Church, floored with Baltic pine and with a totara-built altar, served Irish miners from 1866 on. The 900 hectare Lake Ianthe, fed by bush streams and surrounded by kahikatea and giant matai forest, is 30 kilometres south.

VICTORIA FOREST PARK

This covers 210 000 hectares of Westland's wild gold country, between the Inangahua valley and the South Island's alpine divide. The names of the mines – Wealth of Nations, El Dorado, Keep-It-Dark, and Nil Desperandum, among others – reflect the heady climate of the 1870s. Within the park the most eloquent remains are those of the Big River settlement, a day's excursion on foot from **REEFTON**. Mountain beech forest has begun taking over. The forest surrenders to scrub and tussock at higher levels. The peaks rise to 1900 metres. Areas are set aside for amateur goldpanners in the park. There are a number of developed tracks, along with overnight huts for more ambitious trampers. Full information is available from forest park headquarters in Reefton.

WESTLAND NATIONAL PARK

Its 117 547 hectares, from sea level to the 3498-metre summit of Mt Tasman, contain the two great glaciers **FRANZ JOSEF** and **FOX**, alpine grassland, dense rainforest rich in birdlife, surf-beaten shores, and rivers and lakes. National park headquarters is at Franz Josef, where full information on the park's walking tracks is available. There is also a visitors' centre at Fox Glacier township.

WESTPORT

With a population of 4600, this is Westland's second commercial centre and major port. Its lasting asset was (and is) the bituminous coal of the Paparoa Range which backs the town. The limestone quarries of Cape Foulwind, cement works fired by local coal, and timber from neighbouring forest have been important too. Westport's architecture has proved more durable than that of the goldtowns and it has retained its handsome period flavour. Among the most interesting buildings are the Bank of New South Wales, St John's Anglican Church and the Borough Council Chambers. An imaginative museum, Coaltown, housed in a 19th-century brewery building offers a trip through a simulated coal mine (open daily, 9–4.30, with a café). The town makes a base for visiting such old mining areas as **DENNISTON** or Stockton. The 33 kilometre drive to Cape Foulwind discloses New Zealand's largest cement works, a seal colony at Tauranga Bay, the Cape Foulwind Lighthouse, and the safe surf at Carters Beach.

KING DICK, THE UNCROWNED MONARCH

A dynamic, impetuous, fiery and bullying temperament made Richard Seddon a failure in commerce but contributed to his success as a political leader

Hokitika's stone memorial to 'King Dick'

Highway 73 is a scenic motoring treat; it leaves the West Coast at Kumara Junction, follows the Taramakau River past the township of Kumara to the Otira River and the Otira Gorge, crosses the Southern Alps at Arthur's Pass, continues down the Waimakariri River to Cass, then turns south to Lake Pearson and Porters Pass, descends to the Canterbury Plains and heads almost straight to Christchurch. The journey of more than two hundred and thirty kilometre takes in climatic, botanical and geological regions of bewildering contrast. It embraces also areas of great historical interest.

Kumara township is one such place. Situated twenty-five kilometres south of Greymouth, it was the centre of a gold-rush in the eighteen-seventies, when it became briefly one of the most prosperous settlements in the South Island. It boasted no less than eighty hotels, and still possesses one of the few remaining country race-tracks. Richard John Seddon (1845-1906), New Zealand's longest serving premier was the town's first mayor.

Lancashire-born Seddon set out for Australia when he was eighteen. After three unsuccessful years on the Victorian goldfields he was drawn to Hokitika and the West Coast workings. He again failed as a prospector and opened a store. The store prospered enough to gain a liquor licence, which he transferred to Kumara. Here he made a name as an athlete, a prize-fighter and as a lay advocate specialising in mining cases.

Seddon narrowly escaped bankruptcy in Kumara, but he turned to national politics, having acquired a taste for power in the law courts and the stormy arena of local politics. He seemed to epitomise the New Zealand character as the electorate pictured it – often contradictorily: masculine, extrovert, flamboyant, genial, aggressive, generous, jingoistic, nationalistic, yet liberal and idealistic in legislative outlook.

Many great reforms were accomplished under Seddon's administration, including the age pension and free secondary education. A fervent imperialist, Seddon sent New Zealand troops to the war in South Africa. He also actively sought the acquisition of New Zealand territories in the Pacific and the ousting of the French in Tahiti and New Caledonia, for which he was dubbed 'King Dick, Lord of the Isles' – the name by which he is still popularly remembered.

Canterbury

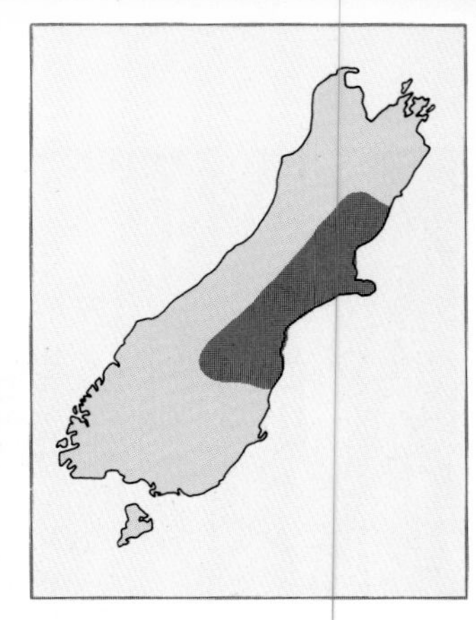

Everywhere immoderate, Canterbury seems more a corner of a continent than a region of an island. To the traveller it presents a pageant of great plains, great rivers and great peaks. It contains New Zealand's largest spread of level land and by far its bulkiest mountains. It takes in New Zealand's most intensive rural tapestry, as well as terrain that has never known so much as a mountaineer's sigh. A distinctive natural history and a piquant human one set it apart from the country's other regions. Just over three hundred kilometres long and about one hundred at its widest, Canterbury is bounded by oceans, alps and rivers. The Pacific lies to the east, with the Southern Alps to the west. To the north and south flow the alp-fed Conway and Waitaki Rivers. Within these limits live half a million people (including the population of Christchurch), or two out of every three South Islanders. Most dwell in communities close to the coast. Yet as it climbs inland, this most populous of South Island regions fast empties of people. Pockets of space become panoramas of mountain.

Canterbury often seems five times larger than its real size. A commanding sky works the illusion. At least twelve thousand square kilometres of Canterbury consists of plain; no other region of New Zealand parades less terra firma and more firmament. It is a sky worth watching. An arch of cumulus cloud over the mountains to the north-west heralds New Zealand's most infamous wind – the dry, dusty and hot Canterbury nor'wester, which frequently hoists temperatures suffocatingly high – more than thirty degrees Celsius in summer. A chill wet southerly often slams in its wake, with temperatures slumping ten or fifteen degrees. Small wonder that the weathered Cantabrian has a sensitive skyward squint.

The region's character was largely determined on the sea floor two hundred and fifty million years ago. Thousands of metres of coarse sand and thick pebbles were compressed to form great building blocks. These were capriciously crumpled until they burst above the Pacific to form a long, rudimentary mountain range, from which the Southern Alps were to be fashioned and Canterbury fathered. Water, wind and ice went to work. Erosion built the plain. Mountains became footed and frilled with lagoons and estuaries. The sea silently crept back and added clay, sand and limestone before its final retreat. As the last land rose from the sea, lava oozed from the earth's crust and built what is now Banks Peninsula, coastal Canterbury's most conspicuous quirk. It began as an island, but glacial and riverborne debris later linked it with the plain. Then flattening glaciers finished what the sea had modelled.

A FEATURLESS PLAIN

Nature never really had time to make up her mind how best to clothe Canterbury. After the retreat of the glaciers she was still experimenting with vegetation when human beings arrived. The Canterbury coast was highly populated in the early Polynesian era – that of the moa hunter. Fire was the easiest means of flushing the great birds from cover. Raging out of control, the flames destroyed the sluggish moa, all other bird life and all forest. In the nineteenth century, Europeans were met by a treeless and all but featureless plain, brutally bared to the wind. They were not slow to see the potential of such open, golden grass country for grazing animals.

The terrain had been cleared in an even more ruthless respect. In the late eighteen-twenties and early eighteen-thirties the Ngai Tahu tribe of Canterbury had been virtually wiped out by the Ngati Toa chief, Te Rauparaha. The few hundred survivors of his ferocious raids were ready to part with much of their birthright for a pittance, in the hope that European presence might at least bring peace. They were also wooed from other landholdings, which they believed they had retained.

The first beachhead for Europeans in Canterbury was Banks Peninsula, with the safe harbour of Akaroa and its pleasant bays and coves. Flax traders appeared in about 1810, and sealing gangs followed. In the eighteen-thirties whalers founded a settlement, and shorthorn cattle were set ashore in 1839. Runaway sailors and retired whalers found Maori wives and domestic comfort on the peninsula. In 1840, the year of the signing of the Treaty of Waitangi, French migrants landed at Akaroa, but the weary Gallic colonists made no attempt to contest British sovereignty and settled for life under the Union Jack.

A second and fervently British migration decided Canterbury's social climate. It was here that coloniser Edward Gibbon Wakefield and his New Zealand Company came closest to planting a lasting little Britain in the South Sea. Wakefield first contemplated an Anglican settlement in 1843 and, with Irish lawyer John Robert Godley, began winning clerical support for the scheme in 1847. The egalitarianism of other colonial communities was to have no place in Canterbury. In Wakefield's plan the price of land was to be set beyond the means of Britain's landless poor. This would ensure an adequate supply of labour for the gentleman colonists and aspirant capitalists whose realm Anglican Canterbury would be. Only 'respectable' working people with 'reputable' morals were encouraged to apply for assisted passages to the new settlement. As to the suitability of those who needed no assistance, *The Times* reported that the gentleman colonists were 'distinguished from the mass of emigrating colonists no less by high personal character, than by their social position at home'.

In 1850, four ships – the *Randolph*, *Charlotte Jane*, *Cressy* and *Sir George Seymour* – sailed to settle Canterbury. They carried a formidable cargo of gentry along with a useful selection of shepherds, agricultural labourers, servants and tradesmen. Canterbury was 'quality' from day one, or so native mythology would soon insist, unlike other provinces whose population was, according to Edward Jerningham Wakefield, 'nothing more nor less than a straggling, struggling mob'. As the race for good land began, those notionally above the herd nevertheless provided a stampede. It was not in coastal Canterbury that a colonial gentry was to prosper. Even though the grasses of the Canterbury Plains might sustain livestock better than English oats, the land was best suited to smallholders, crop-growers, men of little imagination. For visionary gentleman colonists, the sky was literally the limit, at the least the permanent snows of the alpine interior. Australian experience – and more recently that of Marlborough – argued that large-scale pastoralism was an occupation fit for antipodean gentlemen, that wool was the quick way to wealth. This was not how Wakefield had visualised the Canterbury scheme. He wanted something closer to English counties, with crop-growing landowners never more than a short ride from the village and the church.

TYRANNY OF THE WOOL-KINGS

Not for the first time, Wakefield was confounded by the character of New Zealand. Within two or three years of the founding of the Canterbury settlement, flocks were being pushed across the plain into the alpine foothills beyond. Estate after estate – ranging in size from fifteen to sixty thousand hectares – was established. Of the founders of these estates, social historian Oliver Duff observed, 'they had no sooner performed miracles of enterprise and endurance than they

A PAGEANT OF PLAINS AND PEAKS

forgot they were the creators of a brave new world and sent back to England for their top hats'. According to historian Stevan Eldred Grigg, a descendant of one of Canterbury's first large pastoralists, it was less a brave new world than the greedy old one underwritten with wool: 'By the end of the decade [the eighteen-fifties] the golden fleece was making fortunes . . . South Island landowners collected their cheques and began to think about mansions.' Before long the wool-kings of Canterbury would be denounced as a menace to democracy in New Zealand. Sir George Grey declared that Canterbury had been founded on the principle of injustice. He saw the wool-kings as 'a tyranny' denying 'the entrance of the poor into what they came to seek'.

In later, more democratic times, Canterbury's humble did gain access to the kitchen, if seldom the sitting-room, of the colonial dream. Many, living frugal lives, finally won modest landholdings. Yet Canterbury is the one region in New Zealand where a residual patrician class remains conspicuous, where descent from arrivals on the first migrant ships means something. Rurally, however, it is now dominated by farmers rather than large landowners. Canterbury towns, like the crop-patched plain on which most are placed, have more in common with America's Mid-West than with leafy English villages. Outside the centre of Christchurch, the suburbs, townships and people of Canterbury are indistinguishable from those of the North Island.

IN THE RECESSES OF THE ALPS

It is not surprising that colonial Canterbury shaped New Zealand's first European folk-hero, the Scottish sheep stealer James McKenzie. This shepherd wooed flocks from the wealthy with his magical dog Friday and secreted them by the thousand (at least in legend) in his alpine hideaway – the then undiscovered Mackenzie Plain (see page 260). McKenzie may well have inspired Samuel Butler's famous fantasy, *Erewhon*, in which the narrator blunders into a secret civilisation in the Southern Alps. In 1860 Butler followed thousands of his fellow Englishmen to the Canterbury settlement. He explored mountains and rivers in the recesses of the alps, and proved a more than adequate

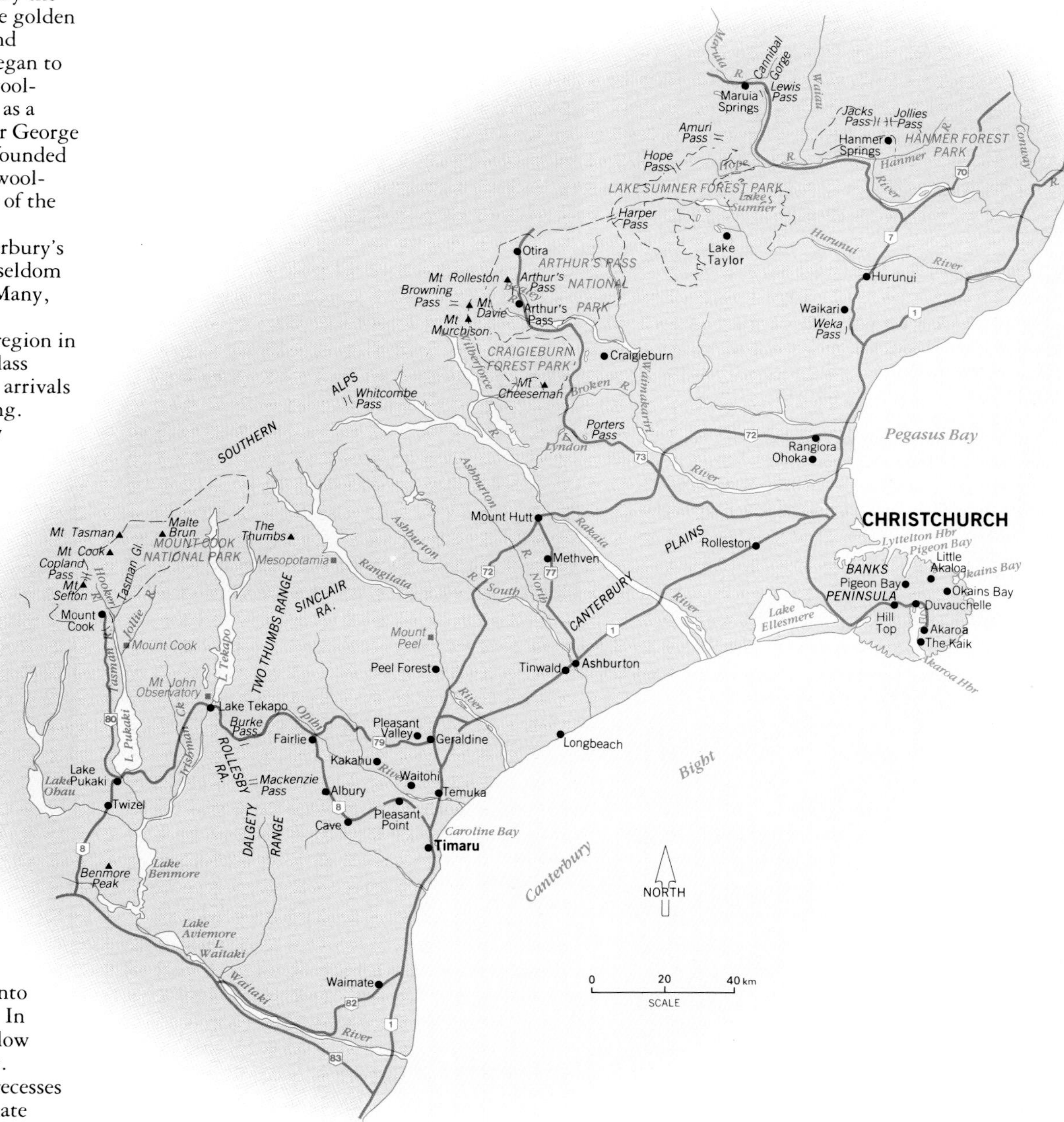

Potts River and the Rangitata valley, with the Arrowsmith Range in the background: good salmon and trout country

A friendly discussion at a sheep sale in Sheffield, a settlement near the intersection of Highways 72 and 73

sheepman. For four formative years, the Southern Alps massed marvellously in his eye and mind. 'Never,' he was to write, 'will I forget the utter loneliness of the prospect – only the little faraway homestead giving sign of human handiwork: the vastness of mountain and plain, river and sky . . . Higher, I would look down on a sea of whiteness through which would be thrust innumerable mountain-tops that looked like island.' Little has changed. More than a century later travellers still see the high country much as Butler did.

For many New Zealanders, Canterbury's immense plain, and even its formidable back country, are mere appendages to the Southern Alps. The upland journey remains as imposing for today's motorist as it was for Samuel Butler when he led his packhorses through high passes into a vast land of lakes, rivers, shingle-slide, peaks and plateaux. The road to The Hermitage, towards mighty Mount Cook, is a voyage into the very heart of the Southern Alps, a road so single-minded that it has no exit. At its end – quite suddenly, it seems – peaks rise around in shimmering bulk. Beside these mountains, Canterbury – with its crops, towns, cities, and grazing sheep – seems quaintly remote. Though only a few steps away from warm and comfortable accommodation, the visitor is hostage to a huge and chilling world heaved thousands of metres skyward from the floor of ancient seas.

Ohoka homestead out-buildings: Canterbury's prosperity was reflected in the buildings and homesteads erected at the time

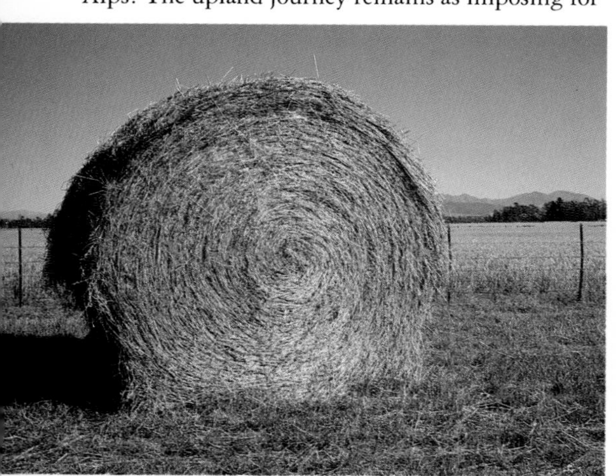

Temuka lies in a prosperous agricultural area and bales such as this are a feature of the countryside at harvest time

High-country sheep station at Double Hill in the Rakaia valley, just south of the junction with the Mathias River. Agriculture forms the primary basis of Canterbury's wealth

Long shadows in a moonscape! The skiers are among the icefalls of the Hochstetter Dome, a peak on the main divide of the Southern Alps at the head of the Tasman Glacier

PENINSULA PANORAMA

A strange outcrop on the Canterbury coast, Banks Peninsula is set apart from the rest of the region by its climate, history and terrain

Akaroa has traces of its origins in its early architecture, and some of the street names are still in French

When Captain James Cook mapped the South Island in 1770, he made two mistakes. He thought Stewart Island a peninsula, and Banks Peninsula an island. It was forty years before an alarmed mariner found land looming ahead where Cook's chart showed sea. The name Cook gave the notional island – to honour his botanist Joseph Banks – has survived correction. The great British navigator was deceived by the striking profile of the peninsula, out of kilter with the low-lying Canterbury coast. The peninsula was shaped from two vast volcanoes, which had grown up to fourteen hundred metres high – half as high again as the peninsula's tallest point today – before cooling and eroding to a less commanding size. The craters of the volcanoes filled with sea to form the dramatic harbours of Lyttelton and Akaroa.

Langlois-Eteveneaux House, the home of an early French settler, has had a modern museum added at the rear

In fact, Banks Peninsula *was* an island until relatively recent times. When the first European settlers arrived, they found a fifteen kilometre fringe of swamp and reedy waterways separating it from the rest of the South Island. At that time, the alpine debris on which Canterbury is built was still washing down to complete the bridge between the island and the mainland. Climatically as well as physically Banks Peninsula is an anomaly. In sheltered places, citrus and other subtropical fruits – which would never survive the frosts of the rest of Canterbury – find sufficient sun and warmth to ripen.

Banks Peninsula has an equally quirky history. Maori tribesmen from the north seem to have found it more congenial than the Canterbury Plain. This was the southern outpost of the kumara, the vegetables staple of the Maori diet. The first Polynesians to arrive dwelled in dry, comfortable all-weather caves. Later, villages rose among cultivation. The podocarp forest – including totara and matai – sheltered birds in abundance. The coast yielded fish and shellfish.

With the shelter its fractured coast afforded, Banks Peninsula was favoured by the first Europeans too. Sealers, whalers and seekers of timber and flax found a haven for their transactions in the south. At the beginning of the eighteen-thirties they were well established when Te Rauparaha's musket-armed Ngati Toa raided the peninsula, helped by an unscrupulous British skipper. Hundreds were slain, eaten, and enslaved. Surplus flesh was taken back to the North Island in baskets. The peninsula's Maori population never recovered. Villages occupied for centuries disappeared in a decade.

Akaroa, Maori for 'long harbour', was appropriately named

By the end of the eighteen-thirties the scene was set for a tableau which was to give the peninsula its greatest historic distinction. An ambitious

Some Victorian period buildings show classical influence

The stillness and lush greenery of a herb garden surround a typical colonial cottage in an Akaroa street

French whaling skipper named Jean Langlois negotiated the purchase of Banks Peninsula – for the equivalent in trade goods of a hundred and fifty francs – from a few Maori survivors of Te Rauparaha's raids. He urged France to annex the rest of the South Island. Having failed to make much impression, he was instrumental in the founding of the Nanto-Bordelaise Company in 1839 – a company designed to establish a new French colony at Akaroa.

In 1840 some sixty French settlers arrived in the harbour aboard the *Comte de Paris*, escorted by the corvette *L'Aube*. They found a Union Jack fluttering ashore. Under the Treaty of Waitangi, signed while the French vessels were on their way to New Zealand, Britain's title to the South Island was now more convincing, certainly far more so than the Langlois claim to Banks Peninsula. Once ashore, the French settlers had to make the most of modest five-acre blocks, planting walnut and chestnut trees, grapevines and herb gardens. Their first dwellings were humble and makeshift, but Akaroa's later, more durable buildings were to be an antipodean salad – British colonial with a *soupçon* of French.

By 1844 Akaroa was a European village of two hundred and fifty people, Canterbury's first. There were fifty British settlers, a score of Germans, and perhaps a hundred Maoris, but the five dozen French colonists were to give Akaroa its lasting character. It was not until the founding of the Canterbury settlement by New Zealand Company migrants in 1850 that the French found themselves unmistakably marooned in a British tide. Pioneering Britons began laying siege to the forest of Banks Peninsula to supply treeless Christchurch with timber. Farms grew around the peninsula's bays. There were soon eighteen dairies – later compressed to five factories – producing cheese and butter. Self-sufficient communities of two or three hundred people grew in the bays. Farms were not large, at least not by Canterbury measure; most covered no more than two hundred hectares. Contact with the outer world was by sea. It was an intimate and more egalitarian society than that of greater Canterbury.

Today Banks Peninsula, though largely depopulated, holds many vestiges of its pioneer past – exotic trees, homesteads and cottages. There are also steep, winding and laboriously built roads linking community to community. Akaroa, the first community, is the only substantial survivor. Its population is not much larger than in the township's nineteenth-century heyday. The difference is that the French have finally, if belatedly, triumphed. Street names are French. The garage sells *essence*. Restaurants have French menus. Architecturally, the colonial salad now has an even stronger French dressing. Akaroa has been busy cultivating and promoting its French connection for decades. Yet it isn't altogether tourist make-believe. The telephone directory lists many French names. There is a French cemetery above the town. Two of the town's oldest buildings – St Patrick's Church (1864) and Langlois-Eteveneaux House (*c.*1845) – are distinctly French in style. But there is more to Banks Peninsula than Akaroa. The visitor should take the spectacular Summit Road behind Akaroa Harbour, and sample the lovely and long-settled little bays far below. The tide-washed landscapes of the peninsula have drawn writers, painters and craft workers as new settlers. The peace of the peninsula survives too. Captain Cook's instinct was right. It *should* have been an island.

The post office sign at Duvauchelle, on Akaroa Harbour

The Gallic flavour of Akaroa spreads even to its hoardings – but a French-English dictionary is not really needed!

THE POWER OF A LEGEND

In the austere, mountain-girt Mackenzie Country, the gripping tale of a 'Scots' folk-hero still haunts the imagination

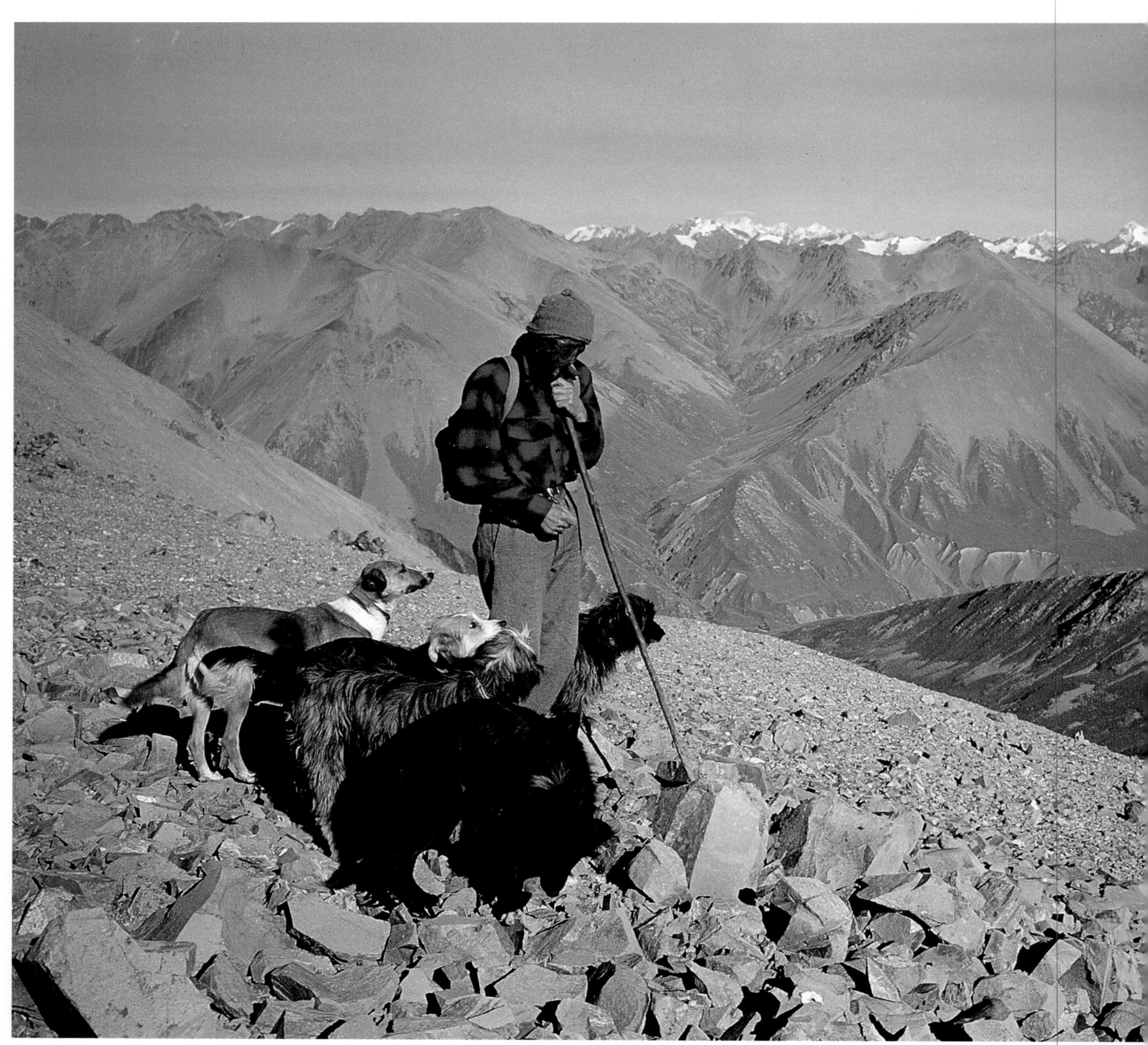

Below: *Sheep musterer and his dogs in Canterbury high country, typical of the landscape of James McKenzie's hidden world* **Right**: *The monument on Mackenzie Pass at the probable spot where the romantic figure of McKenzie was caught* **Far right**: *Memorial to the sheepdogs of the Mackenzie Country at Tekapo. Such is the power of the James McKenzie legend that this bronze sculpture is often confused with McKenzie's own dog which, in the more colourful versions of the tale, was hanged or shot as a witch*

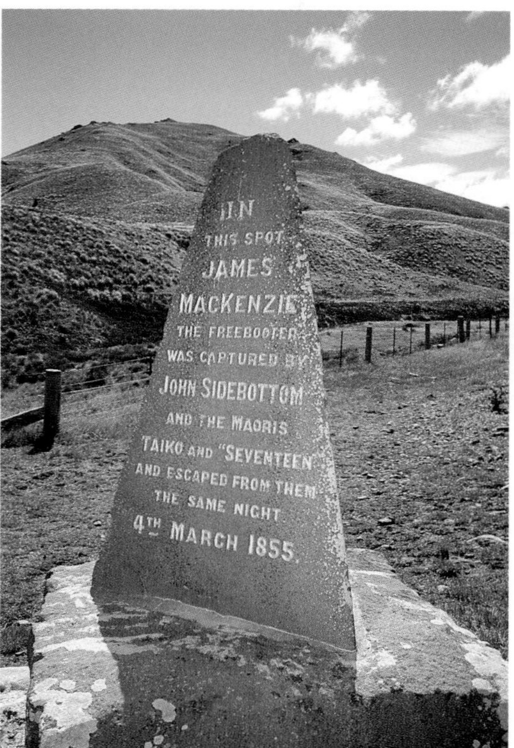

IN
THIS SPOT
JAMES
MACKENZIE
THE FREEBOOTER
WAS CAPTURED BY
JOHN SIDEBOTTOM
AND THE MAORIS
TAIKO AND "SEVENTEEN"
AND ESCAPED FROM THEM
THE SAME NIGHT
4TH MARCH 1855.

Legend said he could eat a brace of birds for breakfast. Legend said he could fell a bullock with his fist and outrun any horse in the land over a measured mile. Legend said his wily dog was hung as a witch. Legend said most things, and then a few more, about the Scotsman named James McKenzie. His name – even if mispelled – seems certain to reside for ever on a half million mountain-ringed hectares of highland Canterbury, now called the Mackenzie Country.

Top: *Sheep muster in Canterbury high country, with a view of snow-covered alps* **Above**: *A sheep sale at Lake Tekapo*

No legend was launched on less. The facts are that he was a hundred and eighty centimetres in height, that his hair was light-coloured, his eyes grey, his face long and thin. He was 'excitable', one observer said, and 'sensitive', with a nervous habit of cracking his fingers. He affected to understand no English; Gaelic was his tongue. Other than this, we know only that he was thirty-five years old when apprehended in the company of a thousand stolen sheep in March 1855. With his dog Friday, he was caught in the act of pushing them through an obscure mountain pass into the then unsettled territory that today bears his name. He was taken to Christchurch, charged with sheep stealing, found guilty and sentenced to five years in prison. He protested innocence and underlined it by attempting to escape three times – twice successfully.

SUPERHUMAN DIMENSION

For Canterbury's humble, McKenzie became a folk-hero. The region's wool-kings wanted him hanged, but (in the most apocryphal version of events) had to make do with his dog. He was certainly suspected of stealing many more sheep than his charge-sheet said. It was soon argued that no prison built could contain the man. It was also said that without his magical dog Friday he was an antipodean Samson shorn of his hair. The law was soon in two minds. He served less than a year of his sentence. Pardoned, he disappeared in the direction of Australia and was never heard of again. Legend was left with the business of making him plausible. Some say his ghost, with the faithful dog Friday, still drives spectral flocks across the Mackenzie Country.

Alas for legend, some recent research suggests that McKenzie may not, after all, have been a sheep stealer. He may have been as innocent as he protested, and just the dupe of common criminals. No one is likely to put the record straight now. Anyway, the tale is too good not to be told again and again: the tale of the mysterious, simple Highland shepherd whom none saw come, none saw go, but who filched his flocks from Canterbury's tyrannical wealthy pastoralists and led them off to graze in a lost mountain world. There was some remarkable quality in the marriage of James McKenzie with the time and place that gripped the human imagination and continues to haunt it. There is no other New World folk-hero of anything like his superhuman dimension.

Lake Pukaki, the second of the Mackenzie Country's great lakes, is only marginally smaller than Lake Tekapo

The legend resists other recent libels. It is now even said that the Mackenzie Country is his only in name and that the Maori had known it, and his secret pass, for centuries. One or two early European explorers are said to have come upon the plain before McKenzie and merely failed to recognise its pastoral potential. Nevertheless documents argue that McKenzie had a remarkable knowledge not only of highland Canterbury, but also of Otago and Southland, where he was thought to have driven and sold off his stolen flocks. A sober contemporary source, the *Lyttelton Times*, announced on May 10, 1856, under the heading 'Discovery of Additional Sheep Country':

Haldon, a cattle station in Canterbury high country near Lake Benmore, the largest man-made lake in New Zealand

'At the time Mackenzie was captured, a report was current that an extensive plain existed beyond the gorge of the snowy mountains through which Mckenzie was travelling when taken...We understand that further search has confirmed the truth of this report and that a plain of immense extent has been discovered...' By whom? By James McKenzie. Let legend rest its case. The Mackenzie Country it remains.

MAGICAL BUT HARSH

From Canterbury there are two ways into the Mackenzie Country. The best known is via Burke Pass, between the Two Thumb and Rollesby Ranges. A conventional sealed highway gobbles up distance and leads into a marvellously level landscape of tussock and lake with mountains brimming around. Those with decent respect for legend – and history, for that matter – will take the alternative and more adventurous route from Timaru to journey into McKenzie's kingdom, via the Mackenzie Pass, much as he must have done. It is still no more than a rough rural road. Foothills surge suddenly into the solid mountains Canterbury sheepmen first saw as an impenetrable barrier. Leaving the willows and poplars that grace Canterbury's lower landscape, the road twists between cool heights tawny with tussock and flecked with thorny native matagouri bush. It is not difficult to imagine McKenzie pushing his bleating band through this country, with dog Friday at heel, and his pursuers toiling behind. Finally, the mountains part to reveal a sudden V-shaped view of a huge plain with peaks in the distance. On a fine day, particularly towards sunset, the first sight of this territory can be as magical as the McKenzie story itself. At the foot of the pass a cairn marks the presumed place where 'James McKenzie the freebooter was captured by John Sidebottom and the Maoris Taiko and "Seventeen"...' The inscription is in English, Gaelic and Maori, representing the three races involved in the episode.

A faintly shimmering light – the combined effect of lake, clouds and white peaks – seems to distinguish the Mackenzie Country from the rest of Canterbury. Despite a hundred and thirty years of settlement, there is still a real sense of arrival in a hidden and legendary land. It is largely treeless terrain, with boulders and bluffs, snow-fed rivers and lakes, tussock and thorn. Its roads come to a dead-end among the mountains. The English colonists of Canterbury faltered in the forbidding climate here, and mostly failed. Scottish settlers restocked abandoned sheep-stations and began to pit their lives against the harsh land, burrowing through the big snows of the nineteenth century. Headstones in the graveyard at Burke Pass tell of death by avalanche, drowning, frostbite and falls from horseback. The climate has not grown more kindly, with frosts most of the year. Of New Zealand's settled districts, its severity is equalled only

The waters of Lake Pukaki are milky blue because of the 'rock flour' milled from the mountains by the glaciers.

The snow-covered Southern Alps, main divide of the Soutn Island, rise majestically beyond Canterbury high country

in pockets of Central Otago. Homesteads are still often snowbound in winter; sheep must sometimes be raked from the snow after a blizzard. Today's Mackenzie sheepmen now call in helicopters to drop hay to starving sheep.

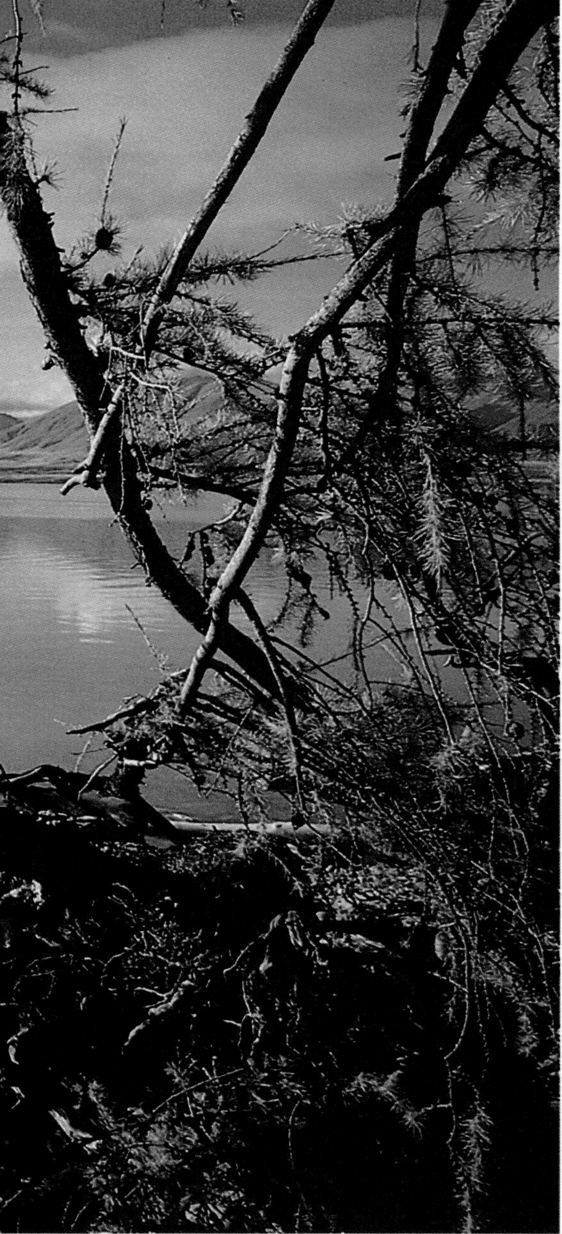

The Mackenzie Country is still stunningly empty. Often in summer, with sheep grazing the higher levels, there are only telephone wires and a rough road to tell of human occupancy. Tree-sheltered homesteads spin past to become faint dots between plain and peaks. The great glacier-fed lakes – Tekapo, Pukaki and Ohau – have a distinctive, delicate turquoise colour, which derives from the 'rock flour' ground from the mountains by glaciers. All three lakes fill glaciated valleys dammed by moraine more than fifteen thousand years ago. Their waters have been reined further by hydro-electric schemes to raise their levels and father a spectacular chain of storage lakes down the Waitaki Valley. In the process the Mackenzie Country's only community of substance, Twizel, was created. Half-abandoned, it looks less like a town than a suburb that has lost its moorings.

The village of Lake Tekapo remains the Mackenzie's spiritual capital. Here a simple stone chapel, the Church of the Good Shepherd, commemorates the hardy early runholders who proved the territory habitable. A short walk away is the sculpture of a sheepdog in bronze. The work of a Mackenzie Country farmer's wife, it is a tribute to the dour dogs which followed man into the mountains – creatures 'without the help of which', says the inscription beneath, 'the grazing of this mountain country would be impossible'. It was meant to represent all sheepdogs. But such is the power of the James McKenzie story that within months of the sculpture's unveiling, in the nineteen-sixties, it was identified as the old rustler's dog, Friday.

The storm clouds gather over Lake Pukaki, an often magical ingredient in the approach to Mount Cook National Park

For most visitors, the Mackenzie Country is an austere frame wrapped around Mount Cook, which is glimpsed for the first time beyond lake waters. It is worth lingering a little, and letting the imagination work. The sight of a lone musterer and his dogs working a mob of sheep evokes quite the most arresting legend left on a New Zealand landscape by Europeans.

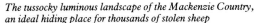

The tussocky luminous landscape of the Mackenzie Country, an ideal hiding place for thousands of stolen sheep

VAST ARENA OF GIANTS

At the heart of one of the world's most rugged mountain regions, Mount Cook National Park contains New Zealand's highest peaks

Above: *A carpet of flowers with Mount Cook in background*
Below: *Saddle Hut at the northern end of the Tasman Glacier. Again Mount Cook manages to get into the picture*

The extent of New Zealand's Southern Alps has never been defined precisely. The traveller first encounters them in Nelson and finally sees them disappear into the sea in Fiordland. Along the way they grab hundreds of kilometres of South Island horizon. Nowhere, however, are they seen to better advantage than in Mount Cook National Park. Elsewhere they fringe landscape and seascape, but here they tower centre stage. Seventeen mountains rise above three thousand metres, and scores soar higher than two and half thousand. Another one hundred and fifty peaks reach over two thousand metres. Through the park rides the country's longest glacier, the Tasman. The marvel is that this alpine concentration is so accessible.

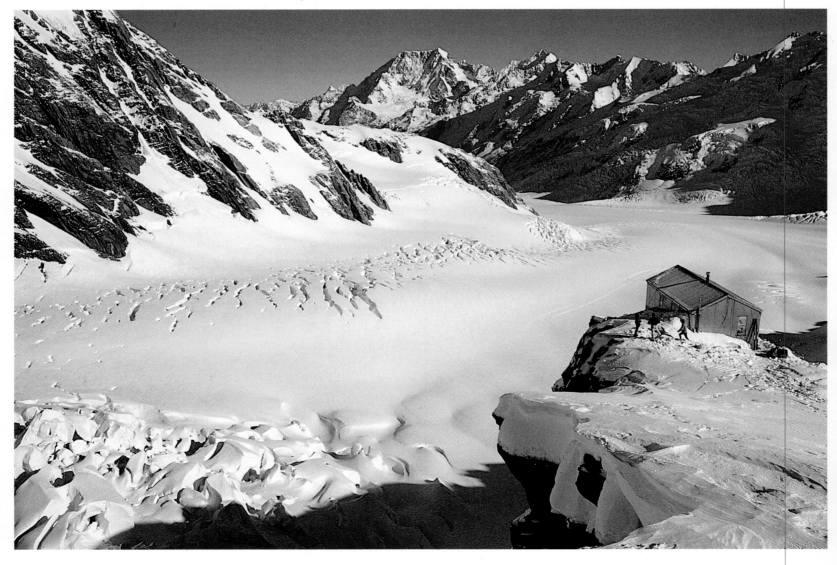

Mount Cook is certainly regal, but the robust personalities of its neighbours dazzle too, and have done so since the first humans beached in New Zealand. Immense Mount Sefton, although distinctly junior to Cook, is more obviously alive with avalanches and tapestried with waterfalls. It was known to the Maori as *Maunga Atua*, 'mountain of the gods'. Its sullen roar – of gods, or tumbling tonnes of rock and ice – can be heard for kilometres down valley. New Zealand's second highest peak, Mount Tasman, has never been short of suitors. 'Of all the mountains I have ever seen, in reality or even in dream, Tasman is the most faultlessly beautiful', wrote one English climber. To Malte Brun belongs one durable mountain legend – that of the young Timaru plumber, Tom Fyfe, who scaled the mountain alone in 1893. Seeing an avalanche getting into gear above him, he used his ice axe as support and glissaded down the snow at terrifying speed, just reaching safe ground as rocks crashed behind him. If ever there was a man destined to conquer the summit of Mount Cook, it was Tom Fyfe, as he finally did with two companions in the first successful ascent just one year later.

The scene-stealer in the park is not a peak, but the great avenue of ice heaved from the heart of the alps called the Tasman Glacier. If these mountains are home to gods, the Tasman is surely their highway. At one time it was fifty kilometres longer, reaching all the way into the Mackenzie Country. Its present twenty-nine kilometres – three kilometres wide in places – are arresting enough. Like all the world's glaciers, it is in steady retreat. A century ago, explorers had to climb a rampart of moraine ten metres high to get on to the ice. Today, at the same site, the ice is a hundred metres downhill. Nevertheless, the Tasman is still one of the world's greatest glaciers outside the polar zones.

Smooth ice at the top of Tasman Glacier provides New Zealand's most exciting ski-run. For years the problem was reaching the top to begin the run. In the nineteen-fifties, an inventive aviator named Harold Wigley came up with the answer – the world's first ski-plane, which would drop skiers wherever they wished. With his invention, Wigley opened up the glacier for mere pedestrians as well. Today's visitor experiences a giddying intimacy with the chaos of the earth's creation: smooth snowfields and jagged icefalls, deep crevasses and vast chasms, towering peaks and plunging ridges. Small aircraft now set down thousands of sightseers annually in the dazzling world of the upper Tasman Glacier, and buzz them safely back to the comforts of Mount Cook village. As peaks float past the wingtips of the plane , even the most world-weary tourist is likely to regain a numb wonder in his native planet.

For those who wish to experience the alps closer to terra firma, the park's many walking tracks are a delight. The Hooker Valley is the beginning of the three to four-day hike to Westland over the Copland Pass. The track begins at the memorial to the first mountaineers that Mount Cook claimed in 1914. It then winds through hillocks of glacial moraine, and past riverside meadows where the Mount Cook lily, the world's largest *Ranunculus*, masses its white flowers. Most of the sixty or so species of the sturdy native *Celmisia*, or mountain daisy, flourish along the way too. Everywhere there are flowering heads of hebe which, with more than a hundred species, is the largest plant genus in New Zealand. There are banks of snowberries, gentians, golden spaniards and the New Zealand edelweiss. During the short alpine summer the festive mosaic of vegetation at the foot of Mount Cook and its cousins encompasses more than four hundred species of fern, moss, tree, shrub, herb and grass.

Impressive Mount Sefton is one of the seventeen peaks in the Mount Cook area that rise more than three thousand metres. Avalanches are frequent down its steep slopes

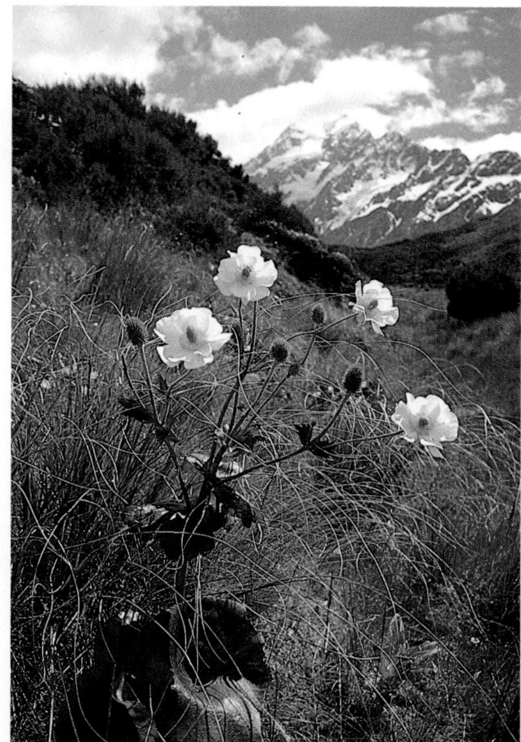

The Mount Cook lily, or giant mountain buttercup, is not a true lily but a member of the Ranunculus *family. Its white flowers can be seen all through spring and summer*

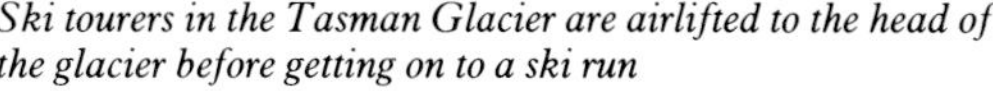

Ski tourers in the Tasman Glacier are airlifted to the head of the glacier before getting on to a ski run

A WORLD IN THE SKY

New Zealand's highest mountain, magnificent Mount Cook, is unforgettable for all those who have seen or climbed it

In 1851 the survey ship HMS *Acheron* was mapping New Zealand for mariners, correcting Captain James Cook's errors and omissions. As it sailed up the west coast of the South Island, 'a stupendous mountain' rose clear above the rest in the stunning alpine panorama to starboard. There was only one name possible for so mighty a peak. The captain of the *Acheron*, John Stokes, named it after his distinguished predecessor, the greatest European navigator the Pacific had known. He called New Zealand's tallest peak Mount Cook. A neighbouring height – Mount Tasman – was later named after the Dutch voyager Abel Tasman, who first disclosed New Zealand's existence to Europe. No navigators in history have finer memorials.

The men of the *Acheron* were not, of course, the first to see and name Mount Cook. Centuries earlier, Polynesians fresh from the tropical Pacific must have risked frostbite and lethal mountain rivers to make their way into upland Canterbury and look upon the mountain with awe, and perhaps reverence. Snow was so new to them they didn't even have a word for it. They called it *huka*, 'foam'. Never were they to see snow to greater effect than on Mount Cook. They too gave it what seemed the only name possible, *Aorangi*, 'clouds (or world) in the sky'.

Mount Cook seen from the highway that skirts Lake Pukaki

Everything ever said or written about Mount Cook is poor preparation for the real thing. The first glimpse of it, especially across the Mackenzie Country's turquoise-blue Lake Pukaki, is probably the one that will last the visitor a lifetime. Even New Zealanders, over-familiar with its profile on postage stamps and tourist posters, find themselves electrified. It isn't just the mountain's

Mount Cook, seen from the rushing waters of the Hooker River, appears as an almost perfect triangular peak

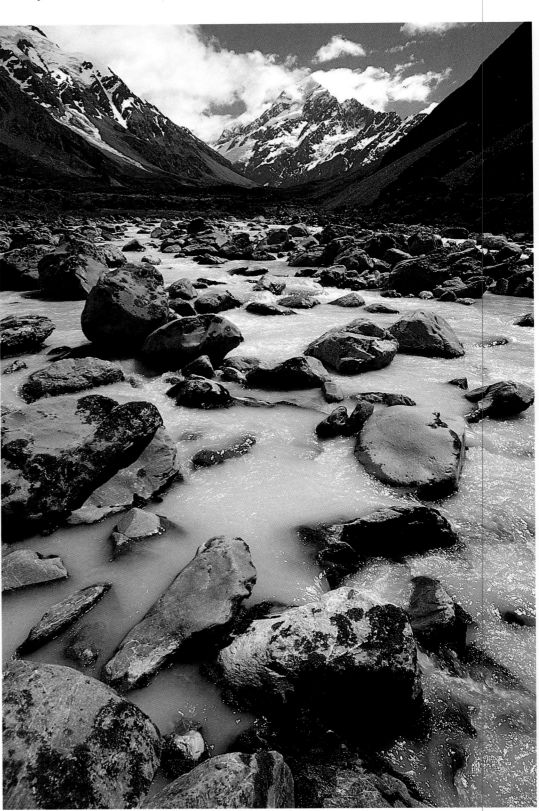

enormous size. As a giant among giants – surrounded by virtually all New Zealand's three-thousand-metre peaks – it remains strongly aloof and alone. Though its lofty neighbours compete for attention, Cook's vividly triangular form makes the spectacle no contest. Its base, which parts company with the main divide of the Southern Alps, is vast. Its summit ridge is more than one and a half kilometres long.

FERVENT PUBLICIST

Geologist Julius von Haast, in 1862, was one of the earliest Europeans to venture on foot into Mount Cook's kingdom. Of the mountain that towered above all others, he reported: 'As far as the eye could reach everywhere snow and ice and rock appeared around us and in such gigantic proportions that I sometimes thought I was dreaming, and instead of being in New Zealand, I found myself in the Arctic or Antarctic mountain regions.' Haast was looking for gold. Instead he found 'extreme delight, never to be forgotten'.

Another to succumb to Cook in the early eighteen-sixties was the English writer Samuel Butler, who can be seen as its first fervent publicist. He recorded that he was 'struck almost breathless by the wonderful mountain that burst upon my sight', and went on, 'If a person *thinks* he has seen Mount Cook, you may be quite sure he has not seen it . . . There is no possibility of a mistake.' Butler was so awed by the mountain that he thought it unconquerable. Within two decades, however, mountaineers were pitting themselves against the peak, and triumphed within three.

The eastern face seen from the head of the Tasman Glacier

Reports such as Haast's and Butler's were soon drawing sightseers, despite the hardships of the long journey from the Canterbury coast. One of the first, in 1873, was the Governor of New Zealand, Sir George Bowen, who recognised the tourist potential of the region. He promised assistance to members of the English Alpine Club wishing to make an attempt on the mountain.

Mounts Cook and Tasman from the Okarito trig in Westland

The western face, seen almost due north from The Hermitage Hotel – one of the most magnificent views in New Zealand

An Irish cleric, William Spotswood Green, was the first to pick up the gauntlet. He read Haast with care, studied photographs and concluded that Mount Cook would be a climb 'well worth the trouble of a long travel'. Green engaged two Swiss alpinists and embarked for New Zealand. The trio tangled with the mountain three times early in 1882. The third and herculean attempt – lasting sixty-two hours in ferocious winds – was almost successful. It was also almost fatal. With the approach of darkness, the three climbers had to abandon the summit when it seemed within reach, descend to a ledge where they secured themselves with pick-axes, and perch upright until dawn. Had they tempted fate further, Green concluded, 'our chances of returning to the haunts of men would be but slight'.

It was heady stuff in the haunts of adventurous young antipodeans. Mountaineering was then in its nursery stage in New Zealand. Surely a New Zealander should be the first to climb Mount Cook? With next to no experience, and little more in the way of equipment, Christchurch banker George Mannering and his companions made five attempts between 1886 and 1891. The last was abandoned fifteen metres short of the summit. All the same, Mannering rejoiced in something Europeans could never have, 'exploring and opening out virgin fields, learning to be our own guides – and porters – from that best of masters – hard experience'.

News that an English climber and a distinguished Swiss mountain guide were about to arrive in the country and claim Mount Cook spurred the next daring New Zealand attempt. On Christmas Day, 1894, three young New Zealanders, Tom Fyfe, George Graham and Jack Clarke romped the last metres to the summit. Despite the patriotic drama of their climb, they had no New Zealand flag to hoist. An old sugar bag had to suffice. The view seemed worth every inch climbed. Fyfe looked into 'the very heart of the Southern Alps . . . peak after peak in wild confusion, which impressed one with an almost overpowering sense of desolation and solitude'.

Another view from The Hermitage – with showers at dawn

Before long hundreds of climbers would be enjoying the same view. By 1910 the first climb had been made by a woman. Since then Cook and its companion peaks – the most concentrated climbing area in the world – have been a highway to the Himalayas and the Andes. This was where Everest conqueror Edmund Hillary, like hundreds of other New Zealanders, began testing himself against the tallest peaks on the planet.

For others, however, the Mount Cook region has been the end of the mountaineering road. A dozen deaths a year are not uncommon. New Zealand's mountain monarch remains an untamed tyrant. Human triumphs over the peak, for close to a century now, have left no lasting trace on the rock, ice and snow of its summit. It is still a world in itself, a world in the sky.

THE LEGACY OF A PASS

When the highway over Arthur's Pass was finally won, it left in its wake a charming alpine village and a spectacular national park

Other roads over South Island mountain passes pussyfoot, compromise, seek an easy way through. The road across Arthur's Pass, linking Canterbury with Westland, never leaves that impression. It tackles the Southern Alps head-on. Rising to more than nine hundred metres above sea level, it is New Zealand's highest alpine highway.

When gold was discovered in Westland in 1863, Canterbury colonists needed a reliable overland route to the goldfields. Mountains blocked their way at every turn. The first route through to Westland was Harper Pass, a path long familiar to Canterbury Maoris in quest of Westland greenstone. Hundreds of fortune-hunters and packhorses barrelled along the crumbling bridle track, once trodden only by small, slow parties of tribesmen. The Harper route was soon a ruin. Frantic to tap Westland's treasure, Canterbury authorities sought another way over the mountains. In 1864, surveyor Arthur Dudley Dobson and his brother Edward rode their horses up the Waimakariri and Mingha Rivers into boulder-strewn terrain at the head of the long Bealey Valley. They found an eastern approach into the mountains, and finally a modest break in the main divide of the Southern Alps.

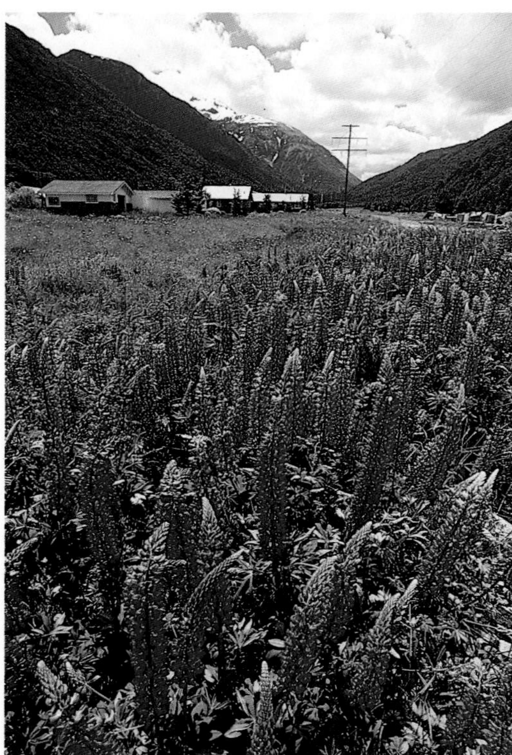

Arthur's Pass township, a convenient centre for visitors, is one of the few true mountain villages in New Zealand

Mountain beech trees, small-leaved and graceful, dominate the forests on the eastern side of the main divide

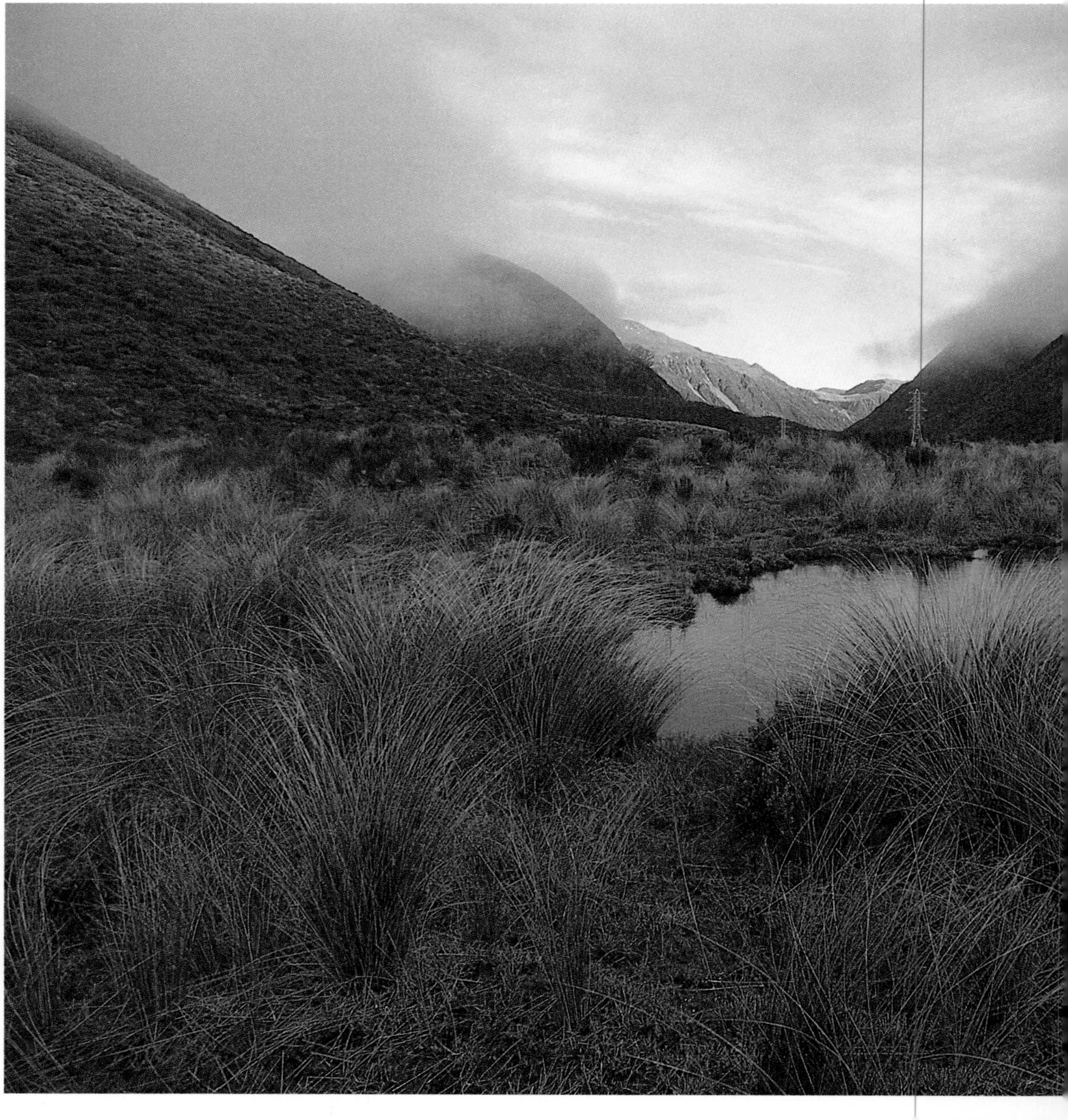

Dobson's first reaction was to marvel at the spectacular scene before him. 'The view was very beautiful looking up the forest-covered hillsides to the snow-capped mountains . . . The rata was in full bloom and its red blossoms made a brilliant contrast to the dark foliage of the birch trees.' Beautiful, perhaps, but this western side was also baffling. The land fell precipitously away to the green valleys of Westland. There might be just enough room to cut a zig-zagging and narrow bridle track – but a coach road? Arthur Dobson didn't even try to persuade his horses down; he had difficulty enough with a dog. At one point he had to build and descend a crude ladder, and the dog was then lowered on a flax rope. Later he pronounced the route difficult at best, perhaps impossible. Today's visitor, standing where the land leaps sheer to the Otira Gorge, and marvelling at the road dizzily weaving towards Westland, can still see why. Further search in the eighteen-sixties disclosed no less perilous way westward. It was Arthur's Pass or worse.

A thousand men with picks and shovels, labouring through bitter mountain weather, managed to hew this mad mountain highway in less than a year, a difficult feat even with modern earth-moving machinery. The initial cost was a mere one hundred and forty-five thousand pounds, soon to be exceeded by the cost of maintaining the road. In March 1866, a coach service linked Christchurch and Hokitika in a bruising, breathtaking journey of thirty-seven hours. Especially sturdy coaches had to be built to survive river crossings and axle-breaking boulders. The road failed to win Westland's gold for Christchurch. Only one gold-escort trip was ever made. Westlanders, who had never wanted the road

The wild scenery of Arthur's Pass – seen here at the main divide, boundary between Canterbury and Westland regions

anyway, and who were infuriated by its cost, stubbornly continued to ship bullion out by sea and to press for secession from Canterbury. The road did, however, prove to be a useful stock route; livestock to be slaughtered for hungry diggers were driven through Arthur's Pass.

The road's lasting virtue was its spectacle. Despite its discomfort and heart-stopping hazards, it almost immediately became a sightseeing route. For the first time, the colonists of Christchurch could show off their alps to visiting English cousins. Others, like pioneering New Zealand botanist Leonard Cockayne, also one of the world's first ecologists, came with a more serious intention. Cockayne pressed for the botanically precious area around the pass to be made a national park. By 1901 some one hundred and seventy thousand acres (seventy thousand hectares) had been protected. Formally created in 1929 and added to later, Arthur's Pass National Park is now New Zealand's fourth largest, covering nearly a hundred thousand hectares.

By the nineteen-twenties, the arrival of the railway and the building of the Otira Tunnel into Westland had established a modest community at Arthur's Pass. When the tunnellers left, it remained as a recreational centre. Arthur's Pass was now only an easy day trip from Christchurch. Mountaineers and trampers arrived, and in 1927 the first skiers. The settlement at Arthur's Pass slowly evolved from a shanty town into New Zealand's most elegant alpine village, including buildings of local stone.

With sixteen named peaks over two thousand metres and New Zealand's most northern glaciers, Arthur's Pass National Park is coloured everywhere by water and ice. It can be seen as a workshop of creation, for it is in these highlands that lowland Canterbury had its beginnings. The workshop is still noisily in business. Avalanches roar, and rains rip into alpine flanks. Debris – gravel, rock, silt – booms downriver as mountains erode and watercourses flood. Riverbed shingle near the Bealey has been estimated to be three hundred metres deep. When the Waimakariri floods, rubble to the depth of a metre or more lifts and moves towards the sea. Thus were the Canterbury Plains created. Here, among these spectacular mountains of the Southern Alps, there is a glimpse of New Zealand – and much of the planet – in the making.

Arthur Dobson rediscovered the Maori route across the main divide; a memorial dedicated to him stands at the pass itself

A spectacular waterfall plunges into the Devil's Punchbowl

Two-thirds of the park lies on the Canterbury side of the divide, the rest in Westland. The park shares the climate, vegetation and character of both regions. No other national park provides so accessible a cross-section of the Southern Alps. From the east, it is approached through high-country sheep stations and lacy beech forest.

The mountain daisy, or Celmisia, *is found in alpine scrub and grasslands, and flowers in the month of December*

Closer to the pass, subalpine growth becomes more evident. In the short mountain summer there are shimmering shoals of flowers, gentians, violets, hebes, foxgloves, daisies, and the Mount Cook lily, queen of them all. Across the pass, however, Westland's dense rainforest dourly wraps the land and another world begins. In summer the southern rata, which cannot be seen at all on the Canterbury side, rises densely to fleck danker Westland with scarlet blossom.

Dobson, looking to win a way to Westland's gold and enrich Canterbury's colonists, aspired only to leave a reliable road behind him. The legacy of his alpine labour was a highway which finally emptied more pockets than it filled, but one which fathered a priceless national park.

PLACES OF INTEREST

AKAROA

Nineteenth-century Canterbury can still be discovered in this village, 82 kilometres from Christchurch, on **BANKS PENINSULA**. Set beside the striking harbour from which it takes it name (meaning 'long harbour'), it was the region's first substantial European settlement. In 1840, French settlers arrived here to found a colony for France, only to discover British sovereignty over the South Island already established (see page 258). The village showpiece is the handsome Langlois-Eteveneaux House (74 Rue Lavaud). Built between 1841 and 1845 in Louis Philippe style, it has been immaculately restored, with a museum to its rear (open daily, 1.30–4; 10.30–5 in January). Another distinctive Gallic survival is the Roman Catholic Church of St Patrick (1864) also in Rue Lavaud. The less obvious Anglican presence in Akaroa is represented by the elegantly Gothic landmark of St Peter's in Rue Balguerie. A small but fine Maori church, Onuku (1878) at The Kaik, is virtually all that is left of the once vivid Polynesian settlement on Banks Peninsula. Most peninsula Maoris lost their lives during Te Rauparaha's raids.

What remains of pioneer architecture is mostly British colonial; few of the first French dwellings have survived. That hasn't deterred Akaroa's 800 inhabitants from making the most of the French connection. Some cottages have sprouted shutters in recent decades, and the garage sells *essence*. In the French cemetery on L'Aube Hill, the village's founding fathers rest under willows that began as slips taken from Napoleon's graveside on the island of St Helena. Walnut trees, Normandy poplars, roses and vines are another French legacy, as are the French names of Akaroa's streets and in its telephone listings.

Colonial buildings of interest include the pit-sawn, sod-lined Custom House (1852); the Old Criterion Hotel (1863), now a general store, and the Coronation Library (1875). There is also a variety of modest colonial cottages (*c.*1850-1870). A local trust ensures that new buildings remain in character. The old wooden Akaroa lighthouse (1880), which flashed at the harbour entrance for more than a century, now presides over the little fishing port and resort.

ARTHUR'S PASS

New Zealand's highest alpine pass (924 metres). Linking Canterbury and Westland, 100 kilometres from Greymouth, 154 kilometres from Christchurch, it was discovered in 1864 by surveyor Arthur Dudley Dobson, after whom it is named. A highway was hastily built over the pass so that Canterbury's colonists could reach Westland's goldfields. Westlanders, however, continued to trust their bullion to the high sea. The community that has grown 5 kilometres short of the pass among mountains and glittering beech forest, is perhaps New Zealand's one true alpine village. It developed during the building of the 8.6 kilometre Otira Rail Tunnel (1908-1923). The village now serves skiers, mountaineers and browsers in **ARTHUR'S PASS NATIONAL PARK** (see also page 268). The information centre for the park is located here. A museum details the story of the pass and the park, and features one of the Cobb & Co coaches used to make the heart-stopping journey between Christchurch and Hokitika. There is a memorial to Arthur Dobson at the pass itself. Near by a splendid one-hour nature walk winds through alpine growth. Within the national park there are many signposted tracks. From the pass the road dives down into Westland, via the Otira Gorge (see page 250).

Grain Processing Company Building in Ashburton, a fine example of industrial construction

The Bealey River and its valley are at the heart of Arthur's Pass National Park

ARTHUR'S PASS NATIONAL PARK

New Zealand's fourth largest national park, covering 99 270 hectares (see also page 268). Shared by Canterbury and Westland, the park takes in the east and west faces of the Southern Alps. There are at least 16 peaks higher than 2000 metres. Glacier-shawled Mt Rolleston (2271 metres) is the most conspicuous, but is not as high as Murchison, Davie and Wakeman. The park also contains the most northern of the South Island glaciers. The vegetation varies from the graceful beech forest of the Canterbury highlands to the dour rainforest of Westland. In between are many varieties of often colourful alpine flora. The road and the park thus provide a fascinating cross-section of the South Island. Many of New Zealand's native birds can be seen on both sides of the Main Divide, especially the kea, New Zealand's mountain parrot (see page 271). Full information on the many paths can be obtained from park headquarters at Arthur's Pass village.

ASHBURTON

This is the plains town of Canterbury, 87 kilometres south-west of Christchurch. It has grown from a lone accommodation house beside the Ashburton River to its present population of 14 000. The district is celebrated as New Zealand's granary, but the Southern Alps in the distance insist that this is not America's Mid-West. Early Europeans saw the treeless and tussock-tufted terrain as desert, but human enterprise fast changed it beyond recognition. As early as 1883 there were 100 000 Canterbury hectares in wheat alone. Small farmers worked the plains productively as large estates expired. Longbeach, one of the most imposing of the latter, survives to the south of the town as a reminder of Canterbury's pastoral beginnings. It is a working memorial to agricultural innovator, Cornishman John Grigg (1828-1901), whose statue is in Baring Square. The property, in private hands, can be viewed from the roadside. The homestead is recent (1937), but the farm buildings date from the 1860s and 1870s. Pioneer relics and buildings can be seen at the Plains Village at Tinwald (4.5 kilometres south-west). It features a railway with a K Class 2-4-2 locomotive of 1877 vintage, which pulled the first train between Christchurch and Dunedin. Also at Tinwald is the impressive Ashburton Vintage Car Club Museum.

BANKS PENINSULA

This stark volcanic peninsula with its deeply indented coastline is a prominent feature of Canterbury's coast (see also page 258). Thinly populated, the peninsula's largest community is **AKAROA**. Remains of early Polynesian settlement can be seen at the old fortress-site of Onawe Peninsula, which projects into Akaroa Harbour. Early European presence – especially French – still presides in Akaroa, and in the bays of the peninsula, which are worth the steep descent from the Summit Road. At Okains Bay a considerable private museum (open daily, 10–5) is dedicated to the peninsula's Polynesian and European past. The old store (1881) and nearby homesteads at Pigeon Bay are showpieces, while St Luke's Anglican church (1906) at Little Akaloa is carved in Maori style.

CAVE

A unique feature of this hamlet, located on Highway 8 into the **MACKENZIE COUNTRY** from **TIMARU**, is St David's Presbyterian Pioneer Memorial Church (1930). Built of uncut glacial boulders, with a Norman tower, it is a memorial to Andrew and Catherine Burnett. In 1856 the Burnetts established Mount Cook station in the wild Mackenzie Country, soon after the pursuit of sheep-stealer James McKenzie disclosed its existence (see page 260). The church is built on the outlying acres of the old Levels run, from which McKenzie was said to have stolen his flock. The pulpit is made of hearthstones from the first Burnett homestead, and the font is a Scottish mortar once used for grinding grain, resting on the hub of an old bullock dray. The woodwork is of rough-adzed mountain beech and carefully crafted totara. The church won architect Herbert Hall a gold medal from the NZ Institute of Architects in 1934.

CRAIGIEBURN FOREST PARK

One hundred kilometres north-west of Christchurch, between the **WAIMAKARIRI** and Wilberforce Rivers, this alp-backed 36 000 hectare forest park adjoins **ARTHUR'S PASS NATIONAL PARK**. The park's vegetation is a mix of mountain beech (on its lower slopes), subalpine

A RAUCOUS AND INQUISITIVE PERSONALITY

The kea or mountain parrot is found only in the South Island, usually in open mountain country, often in groups of a dozen or more by roadsides and carparks

Highway 73, between Porters Pass and Arthur's Pass, is quite likely to have one or two gangs of kea (*Nestor notabilis*) performing stunts to the delight of passing motorists. Unpredictable, exuberant, comical and rowdy, the kea has a feeding radius of fifteen to twenty kilometres and may turn up anywhere within this area. According to observers, keas are seen with increasing regularity along Highway 73. They are scavengers, and lunch scraps thrown from cars have become a sort of performance fee.

It is best to remain inside your car. Keas have been known to pursue and 'attack' people on foot, and the experience can be unsettling. One of the birds seems to set an example of inventive mischief, which the others often copy. Keas can be quite destructive; they have been known to tear tents, packs, hats and other items of clothing. One of their favourite comic routines consists of sliding down hut roofs, accompanied by diabolical screams of 'keeaaa'. The din, though entertaining at first, soon palls.

The reputation of keas as killers has been greatly exaggerated. For eighty years they were blamed for attacks on sheep, and a bounty was paid for their beaks. Only recently have they been reprieved from sentence of death.

Kea, the entertainer, up to his tricks

Keas live off insects, grubs, berries and other plants. They do scavenge on dead sheep, but eye-witness accounts of actual harassment of live sheep are rare. The birds nest in burrows or cavities in tree roots or beneath stones. Those seen by the roadside are usually young males which, until they reach maturity, are full of mischief, practical jokes, sport and noise.

scrub and tussock grassland (in highway parts). Runholders' fires, overstocking with sheep and hungry deer once devastated the area. Now this unstable and always eroding landscape is carefully monitored and protected. In winter it provides attractive skifields; in summer visitors can enjoy forest browsing, picnicking, tramping and an easy intimacy with the alps. There is a visitors' centre in the park, off Highway 73.

FAIRLIE

Service town of the **MACKENZIE COUNTRY**, with a population of 880. Fairlie is set in rolling country which contrasts with the stark, mountain-locked Mackenzie Basin, 26 kilometres to the west, beyond Burke Pass. A museum in a 19th-century cottage is dedicated to the district's past (open weekdays, 12–2; weekend, 2–4). In the Christmas – New Year period Fairlie celebrates its past with a spectacular country and western carnival. The interdenominational church at Burke Pass dates from 1872.

GERALDINE

This tree-shaded township of 2150 people is tucked between plain and hill country, on Highway 79. Geraldine began with a runholders' bark hut in 1854 and is now the service centre for a prospering farm district. The local historical society's museum is situated in an elegant bluestone building (1885) in Cox Street, and there is a vintage car and machinery museum in Talbot Street. Pioneer cottages survive in back roads. At Pleasant Valley (5 kilometres north-west), St Anne's is South Canterbury's oldest surviving church (1863), built of pitsawn timber and cob. Near Kakahu (18 kilometres south-west) stands the marble-and-limestone Norman tower of the Kakahu lime kiln (1881). Geraldine is the elderberry wine capital of the country. Introduced by colonists, elderberry later became a rampant weed in Canterbury. Barker's Wines, 8 kilometres outside town, provide tours and wine tastings daily, except Sunday. At Peel Forest Park (23 kilometres north), 600 hectares of Canterbury's original forest cover can be enjoyed, with picnic places among ferns, waterfalls and woodland. A short distance beyond stands the historic Mount Peel homestead (1865-66), built on a site where an English-style rural community was once planned. Closer to the alps, the road ends at Mesopotamia (69 kilometres), a station once owned by English novelist Samuel Butler (see page 273).

HANMER SPRINGS

A spa town, 135 kilometres from Christchurch, Hanmer Springs is set in woodland 370 metres above sea level, in North Canterbury. The warm springs, known to Maoris as a place to ease the aches of overland travel, were located in 1859 by William Jones, the manager of a sheeprun. Hanmer began as a rough dressing shed in tussock wilderness. It is now a resort with a population of 1000 and a considerable thermal pool complex. Queen Mary Hospital (1916) was established for the convalescent wounded of World War I and was later devoted to nervous disorders; it is now a major treatment centre for alcoholics. Except for the post office (1901), few buildings recall the township's more frivolous days when only Canterbury's fashionable society could afford to take the cure here.

Hanmer Forest Park was begun with plantings by convict labour on once treeless terrain at the beginning of the century. Its 17 000 hectares now boast the largest range of exotic trees in the country and provide pleasant woodland walks. There is an information centre within the park. Other local activities include horseback trail-riding, four-wheel drive tours in North Canterbury's back country, safari trips into Marlborough's immense Molesworth Station (see page 228), trout fishing and skiing. The old cob Acheron Accommodation House (1864) once served horseback travellers between Nelson and Canterbury, and has now been restored by the NZ Historic Places Trust (27 kilometres over Jacks Pass).

LAKE OHAU

This is the smallest (60 square kilometres) of the three great lakes formed by the retreat of glaciers in the basin of the **MACKENZIE COUNTRY**. Lake Ohau is popular with trout fishermen. Comfortable accommodation is available for trampers and travellers in summer, and for skiers in winter.

The courthouse in Temuka, now a museum

LAKE PUKAKI

Second of the **MACKENZIE COUNTRY**'s great lakes, Lake Pukaki is 500 metres above sea level and covers 81 square kilometres. It forms a frequently misty and often magical approach to **MOUNT COOK NATIONAL PARK** with Mt Cook itself as a splendid backdrop. Fed by the melting ice of the Tasman Glacier, the 'rock flour' of which gives the lake a distinctive turquoise-blue colour, Pukaki's waters lap the large sheep stations founded here after the discovery of the Mackenzie Country.

LAKE SUMNER FOREST PARK

This distinctive forest park, 100 kilometres north-west of Christchurch, takes in the eastern flank of the Southern Alps and covers a little-known and mountainous corner of Canterbury. Its 102 296 hectares encompass the beech forest of the Hope and Hurunui Valleys, and Lake Sumner on its southern boundary. Maoris once passed this way, up the Hurunui Valley and across Harper Pass, to reach the greenstone of Westland; gold seekers and drovers also used it until the **ARTHUR'S PASS** route was established. Vehicle access to the park is limited; there is one of several approaches on Highway 7 and another on Lake Taylor road. There are developed tracks and huts, good fishing, and canoeing on the Hurunui. The park information centre is the Hanmer Forest Park Headquarters at **HANMER SPRINGS**.

LAKE TEKAPO

Framed by tall alp and tussock highland, Tekapo's 88 square kilometres of milky blue water make it the greatest of the **MACKENZIE COUNTRY**'s large lakes. Its colour comes from the 'rock flour' ground from the mountains by glaciers. Beside the lake are Lake Tekapo village, with 400 inhabitants, and two distinctive memorials. The lovely boulder-built Church of the Good Shepherd (1935), with its altar-rail view of the alps, is a tribute to the men and women who braved the blizzards of the Mackenzie in the 19th century. Near by is a unique memorial to the sheepdogs of the Mackenzie who made it possible to pioneer this mountain basin. High above the lake is Mt John Observatory, which can be visited only by special arrangement. Tekapo is well stocked with brown and rainbow trout, and its skifield is popular in winter. At nearby Irishman Creek station (named after wild Irishman, the thorny native matagouri bush) back country farmer-inventor Bill (later Sir William) Hamilton (1899-1978) designed the world's first wholly functional jet boat to explore and fish the South Island's more inaccessible rivers (see page 272).

LEWIS PASS

The least taxing, though not the lowest (at 864 metres) of the passes across the South Island's main divide. Lewis Pass is 191 kilometres north of Christchurch and 66 kilometres from Westland's Reefton, and also provides access to the Nelson region. In pre-European days, it was a

INVENTOR OF THE JET BOAT

Irishman Creek sheep station, in the heart of the Mackenzie Country, was for a time a strange, busy and hugely creative oasis of industrial civilization

William Hamilton – an inventive genius

Irishman Creek station, which takes its name from the prickly wild Irishman plant, was the home, high-country farm, factory and experimental centre of Sir Charles William Feilden Hamilton (1899-1978), more commonly remembered as plain Bill Hamilton, father of the jet boat.

At school Hamilton's natural mechanical ability went unrecognised, and when his elder brother was killed in the First World War, he left Christ's College in Christchurch to return to the family farm. Five years later he seized the opportunity to buy the Irishman Creek station. Passionately interested in the sport of motor racing, he built racing cars in his own workshop and won several important events at home and overseas.

The need for a dam on the station led him to invent a mechanical scoop, which became a financial godsend in the Depression years. In 1936, the workshop was converted into a small factory, with Hamilton's own farmhands as workers. He next designed a shingle loader, a travelling water sprinkler and an air conditioner. By the outbreak of the Second World War in 1939, Hamilton was building large-scale earth-moving machinery. He switched to munitions, and soon his factory in the wilderness was employing seventeen ex-farmhands.

At the end of the war in 1945, Hamilton took a decisive step and opened a large engineering works in Christchurch. But he kept on the farm, with its old workshop and factory, and was soon once again spending much of his time there, inventing and designing. Increasingly his thoughts turned to marine propulsion and the possibility of a boat that would brave the power and surge of the Canterbury rivers and their rapids. He concentrated on developing and perfecting the principle of water-jet propulsion, and eventually came up with the jet boat, a revolutionary and versatile craft that has a very shallow draught but extraordinary manoeuvrability and power.

Today the jet boat has opened up the waterways of the world for sport and travel, even in the most turbulent waters and in previously inaccessible places. But many of Bill Hamilton's favourite waterways have vanished, for Irishman Creek is almost at the centre of the huge hydro-electric development in Canterbury between Lakes Pukaki and Tekapo.

well-worn Maori path to Westland's greenstone. Near the summit, at Cannibal Gorge, Westland slaves used to carry the greenstone were slaughtered to replenish the food supplies of the Canterbury-mounted expeditions. Rock drawings in limestone shelters near Weka Pass are gentler reminders of the Maori greenstone route. At the Timpendean Rock Shelter, in a historic reserve near Waikari (inquire locally), some of New Zealand's most famous, if faded, examples of early Polynesian art can be seen. Lewis Pass was long neglected by Europeans and it was not until the 1930s that a road was built. Travellers on the Canterbury side of the divide can delight in the immaculately restored Hurunui Hotel (1870), which still operates under an accommodation house licence granted in 1860. The splendid limestone building has been saved and restored by locals with help from the NZ Historic Places Trust. The thermal springs at **HANMER SPRINGS** (a slight detour) and Maruia Springs are also on the Lewis Pass road. At the Lewis Pass Scenic Reserve there are spectacular mountain views and magnificent beech forest.

MACKENZIE COUNTRY

This highland plain surrounded by rugged mountains is named after the Scottish drover James McKenzie. Accompanied by his supernatural dog Friday, he is said to have stolen thousands of sheep from Canterbury's tyrannical and wealthy wool-kings in the 1850s, and to have grazed them in this hidden world (see page 260). The tawny tussock country of the Mackenzie Basin is distinguished by three large lakes – **OHAU**, **PUKAKI** and **TEKAPO**. Together with the man-made lakes of the **WAITAKI VALLEY**, these lakes are now incorporated in the recreational Mackenzie Hydro Park. Full information can be obtained from park headquarters in **TWIZEL**. Ill defined, the Mackenzie Country covers about half a million hectares and has some three dozen sheep stations – ranging in size from a modest 1000 hectares to a huge 42 000, though much sheepland has now been submerged by hydro-electric power development.

MOUNT COOK NATIONAL PARK

Covering 70 000 hectares, this alpine heartland contains all but one of New Zealand's peaks over 3000 metres, including the monarch of them all, Mt Cook (3764 metres). Three more are Mt Tasman (3498 metres), Mt Sefton (3157 metres) and Malte Brun (3155) metres; in addition some 200 mountains rise higher than 2500 metres. The spectacular panorama is unrivalled elsewhere in the country. The park is traversed by the 29 kilometre Tasman Glacier, the longest in New Zealand and one of the five major glaciers in the area. A reliable road leads to the foot of Mt Cook Range, and the comfortable alpine accommodation and other services at Mount Cook village. There are many pleasant alpine walks, especially up the Hooker Valley, the first stage of the Copland Track which takes the keen tramper through even more mountain panoramas to South Westland. A dazzling ski-plane flight takes visitors to the top of the Tasman Glacier. The cradle of New Zealand mountaineering, the region has also been the nursery for many of the nation's great climbers, notably Edmund Hillary, who conquered Mt Everest in 1953. Mt Cook was named after the great British navigator, Captain James Cook, who never saw the mountain that would be his most resplendent memorial. Neither did Dutch explorer Abel Tasman see the park's second highest peak, which was named after him. The Maori name for Mt Cook was Aorangi, possibly after Tahiti's distinguished but much smaller Mt Aora'i (same name with dialect difference). Full information on the park can be obtained from park headquarters at Mount Cook village (see also page 264).

MOUNT HUTT

Canterbury's most recently developed skifield, near Methven in central Canterbury, usually enjoys a long season from May to October. It is a fast and easy drive from Christchurch or **TIMARU**.

PORTERS PASS

This 945-metre pass, 88 kilometres from Christchurch, is actually the highest point on the route to Westland via **ARTHUR'S PASS**, being some 20 metres higher than Arthur's Pass on the Main Divide. In the 19th century, hundreds of diggers tramped this way to reach Westland's goldfields. Today it is a popular tobogganing site in winter, with skating on nearby Lake Lyndon. There are also several skifields in the vicinity (Porters Heights, Craigieburn, Broken River and Mt Cheeseman).

RANGIORA

Not quite embraced by the city of Christchurch but within easy commuting distance (33 kilometres north), Rangiora is a rural market town of 6700 set in sheep and dairy country. Among its interesting older buildings are the Red Lion Hotel (1874) and the Church of St John the Baptist (1859-60). The Rangiora and Districts Historical Museum (open Sunday, and Wednesday during school holidays, 2–4.30) features an 1869 cob cottage, furnished to period, and accessible at all times. Ohoka, a brick building more than 100 years old, is one of the district's grander dwellings (7 kilometres south, Jacksons Road, Ohoka; open to visitors).

TEMUKA

This town of 3800, 146 kilometres south-west of Christchurch and 18 kilometres north of **TIMARU**, is noted for its ceramics. Pipe and tile production began in the 1860s, and Temuka now has both craft potters and large-scale industry. On the Main Waitohi Road (13 kilometres) a memorial marks the spot where an inventive farmer named Richard Pearse made what was possibly the first powered flight in a heavier-than-air machine in 1903 or 1904, and finished up in a hedge (see page 69). Temuka's older commercial and public buildings and shops – especially the 1904 Courthouse and 1902 Post Office – retain the character of Pearse's heroic, Edwardian decade. The sea-run trout and salmon of the Opihi River draw fishermen to Temuka from hundreds of kilometres away. A local and railway museum at Pleasant Point's abandoned railway station (14 kilometres west) features a 1922 steam locomotive and an 1895 birdcage carriage along with other relics of the heyday of the *Fairlie Flyer*, which for most of a century took travellers to and from **FAIRLIE**. The old buildings of Pleasant Point are in keeping with the museum (open daily, 1.30–4.30; extended hours during summer and school holidays). A short drive away, the 500 hectare Pioneer Park commemorates South Canterbury's pastoral beginnings.

TIMARU

Canterbury's second city, with a population of 28 000. For the Maori, Timaru was actually *Te Maru*, 'the place of shelter'. It provided a rough and ready haven for canoes travelling the South Island's eastern coast. With an artificial harbour, it is now a prosperous port serving industry and agriculture in South Canterbury and North Otago. The sand shifted inshore by the construction of the harbour formed the sweep of beach called Caroline Bay. This is the focal point for resort attractions, the best known of which is the three-week Christmas carnival, which pulls in thousands of holidaymakers. The city is thus an amiable mix of casual holiday town and busy market centre.

Timaru began when 120 British migrants landed from the *Strathallan* in 1859. Their story is told in the Pioneer

Hall Museum (open daily, 1.30–4.30, except Monday and Saturday). At the corner of Sophia and Church Streets is St Mary's Anglican Church (1880), shaped of local bluestone, with its distinctive crenellated stone tower. The striking twin-towered and copper-domed Basilica of the Sacred Heart (1910-11) in Craigie Avenue is one of architect F.W. Petre's most notable designs; look for the influence of Art Nouveau. The former Customs House (1902), on the corner of Cains Terrace and Strathallan Street, is a solid example of classic revival and Timaruvian commercial aspiration. The bluestone Board of Works Building (1874) in Stafford Street speaks of Timaru's early existence as an independent region. Another distinctive bluestone survival is the old Landing Service building (late 1860s) in George Street, located on Timaru's original shoreline. The six-storey Timaru Milling Company building (1882) in Mill Street is a monument to early Timaru commercial enterprise and a durable landmark in the history of New Zealand flourmilling. Also of interest are the old wooden Timaru lighthouse (1878), now stranded in Maori Park, and the Aigantighe Art Gallery (open daily, 2–4.30, except Monday and Friday), in an elegant 1905 brick and stone house, has a lively permanent collection and takes in touring exhibitions.

Timaru boasts an impressive quota of world champions, including world heavyweight champion Bob Fitzsimmons, feller of Gentleman Jim Corbett in 1897; Phar Lap, Australia's most famous horse; Jack Lovelock, winner of the 1500 metres at the 1936 Berlin Olympic Games; and longtime world billiard champion Clark McConachy. Inland from Timaru, via **CAVE**, lie the dramatic **MACKENZIE COUNTRY**, the Mackenzie and Burke Passes, and finally the Southern Alps. To the north is Pleasant Point, with its celebrated railway museum that stages journeys into nostalgia (see **TEMUKA**).

TWIZEL

At the margin of the **MACKENZIE COUNTRY**, Twizel developed rapidly during the construction of the hydro-electric power scheme that raised the level of the Mackenzie lakes and left artificial lakes the length of the **WAITAKI VALLEY**. Population reached over 5000 during the development, but now only 1700 remain. The information office for the Mackenzie Hydro Park – a huge recreational complex – is located here. The old Pukaki Inn, a former ferryhouse, was rescued from rising lake waters and relocated in Twizel. A sanitised painting of James McKenzie and his infamous dog still hangs outside.

WAIMAKARIRI RIVER

The most temperamental of Canterbury's theatrical rivers, the many-channelled Waimakariri ('cold water'), rides 161 kilometres from the alps near **ARTHUR'S PASS**, and disgorges into Pegasus Bay. Shifting and spreading shingle and silt along the way, it still effectively demonstrates how Canterbury's great plain was built from alpine debris. Jet-boat excursions are available upriver, and its lower reaches are popular with salmon fishermen. The Waimakariri's boisterous flow is largely controlled, but still far from tamed. In flood it discharges up to 50 000 cubic feet of water per second.

WAIMATE

This community of 3300 began as a sawmilling town, but was later established more permanently by pastoralists and horticulturalists. A representation of a Clydesdale horse, picked out in stones on a hillside, pays tribute to the four-footed helper of Waimate's pioneers. The Studholme family, one of the country's most notable pastoral dynasties, began on Te Waimate station. The family's first homestead, The Cuddy (1854) – a well-preserved totara slab cottage with thatched roof – survives in a private historic reserve, which may be visited with permission. The nearby woolshed and yards (*c.* 1855) are also in near original condition, and are classed as a historical treasure. Among the town's older buildings are the imposing county council chambers (1878); the wooden St Augustine's Anglican Church (1872) in John Street, designed by Benjamin Mountfort, who was also the architect of St Mary's (1880) in Ryan's Road, Esk Valley (turnoff on road to Timaru, 30 kilometres); and the most elegant Waimate Courthouse (1879) in Shearman Street, which now houses the local museum and serves as an information centre (open Monday–Friday, 1–5; Sunday, 2–4).

WAITAKI VALLEY

This valley and the Waitaki River form the boundary between Canterbury and Otago. Hydro-electric schemes have left artificial lakes fed by the controlled alpine waters of the Mackenzie Country. Lake Benmore is the most extensive artificial lake in New Zealand, covering nearly 8000 hectares – more than the area of Wellington Harbour. A recreational asset, the lakes are stocked with brown and rainbow trout, and are the habitat of landlocked salmon. The mouth of the river, near Oamaru, is noted for its river-running quinnat salmon, ocean-dwelling fish that ascend the river in autumn to spawn, when they are fished by anglers. Moa hunters and later hunters of the classic Maori era used the Waitaki Valley as their route to the interior. The Mackenzie Hydro Park is New Zealand's most remarkable aquatic playground (information office at **TWIZEL**); it incorporates the Mackenzie's natural lakes (**OHAU**, **PUKAKI** and **TEKAPO**) with those of human design (Benmore, Aviemore and Waitaki), together with canals linking the lakes.

Classical revival in Timaru: the former Customs House, now converted into a restaurant

THE AUTHOR AND PHILOSOPHER OF MESOPOTAMIA

At the end of the road system on the Upper Rangitata River lies Mesopotamia, the station developed by Samuel Butler

Self-portrait by Samuel Butler (1873)

Trained for the church but increasingly at odds with orthodox beliefs (and a domineering father), Samuel Butler (1835-1902) left England, aged twenty-four, and landed in Lyttelton. His aim was to set himself up as a man of independent means. He found that all easily accessible land had already been taken up in large runholdings, so he searched the upper river valleys. Finally he was rewarded with the discovery of an unclaimed run of about 2000 hectares between the Two Thumb and Sinclair Ranges. This he named Mesopotamia.

With two companions, Butler braved a winter on this land – only to discover that it was unsuitable for winter grazing. He promptly leased two more strips of easier supplementary land. On one of these sites, he planned to build a homestead, but found that a hut already existed there. Both Butler and the hut owner realised that the only solution was to buy the freehold, and the two men raced on horseback to Christchurch to be the first to sign the deeds. In *A First Year in Canterbury Settlement* (1863), Butler describes this thrilling race which, by good luck, he won.

Books, pictures, furniture and a grand piano were imported to Mesopotamia to create a remote outpost of comfort and civilisation below the Southern Alps. By leaving the running of the station largely to managing partners, he was able to devote himself to exploration and searching Canterbury for more land. With a companion, he discovered and crossed the Whitcombe Pass.

In 1864 Butler sold Mesopotamia, delighted that he had so soon doubled his initial capital. With his friend Charles Paine Pauli, whom he had met in Christchurch and who was to remain a financial drain on him in the years to come, Butler set off on a journey that was eventually to bring him back to London and the literary life – his true vocation.

Although he later wrote of the 'uncongenial' and 'monotonous' life of his four and a half years in New Zealand, the experience strengthened Butler as a man and a writer, and provided the invaluable source material for his novel *Erewhon* (1873), begun as a series of articles in the Christchurch *Press*. The work contains superb descriptions of his exploration of the Canterbury areas that will for ever be associated with his genius.

Christchurch

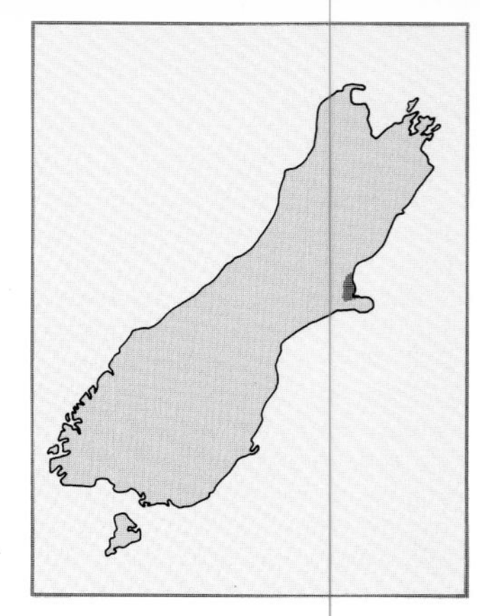

The first citizens of Christchurch, looking down from the Port Hills, viewed a swampy town site flecked with reeds and tufted with tussock. It could not have been more desolate, damp and daunting. The uninspiring location of their new settlement was backed by treeless, featureless, flat terrain all the way to the distantly glimmering alps. After twenty thousand kilometres of travel – with seasickness, dysentery, foul food, filth, and burials at sea – the pioneers seemed literally at the end of the earth.

Yet never did a New Zealand settlement rise more in tune with the melodic vision of those who fathered it. They cleared and cropped, dug and drained, and hammered up rough homes and churches. Those pioneers in whiskers, bowyangs and bonnets – certainly those who could not pay their own passage – had been certified as of 'sober, industrious and honest' character by their local vicars. They were meant to compose a creditable, upright cross-section of English society. By 1850 New Zealand had been settled haphazardly for twenty years by British migrants, and formally colonised for ten. Other planned settlements soon had a democratic character, but Christchurch – a Church of England enterprise in partnership with Edward Gibbon Wakefield's New Zealand Company – was to be different. This was to be more than another rough colonial community in the South Seas. Its founders foresaw a better Britain, decorous and devout, distinctly Anglican and presided over by landowning gentry.

NO ONE AT HOME

The first step was to ensure that empty land didn't turn humble heads. Hundreds of thousands of hectares of level, mostly fertile land were free for settlement on the eastern seaboard of the South Island. Little settled by the Maori, whose local population had recently been thinned still further by the raids of northern tribes, the area had been sold off cheaply to the English. But the planners of the Canterbury settlement fixed its resale price far beyond the reach of artisans and labourers. The land was reserved for those of social standing. Artisans and labourers were to be confined to that which they knew best: the provision of menial skills and muscle, rather than take up the profitable production of wheat and wool. In late 1850, some seven hundred and eighty migrants left England in the first four ships; five hundred and fifty of them were cruelly crowded in steerage, while the rest enjoyed comfortable cabins. Sir George Grey, Governor of New Zealand and later premier was to see the Anglican scheme as seeding 'great and future evil. . . from the very first moment of its colonization'. The ills of England were planted here too.

The migrants were dumped ashore in the port of Lyttelton with little ceremony. Lyttelton had come into existence of its own accord, and then had sixty houses and a couple of grog-shops. There were immigration barracks for the steerage passengers, but few roofs under which their social superiors could respectably shelter. Then all were obliged to toil up the rough bridle path over the Port Hills and down to the site surveyed for their town. The plan showed buildings already in existence, but even the keenest visionary could not detect them. There was just one rough riverside house, a heap of sawn timber, a beached dinghy, and no one at home.

'A FAVOURED RACE'

Within just a year, one Charlotte Godley, wife of John Robert Godley, the self-confessed despot of the fledgling community (see page 286), recorded delight at 'how very civilized' Christchurch had become. Others saw an exposed, dusty, ugly settlement as characterless as a whistle-stop on the American prairie. The dream survived cynics. As early as 1856, Christchurch had as many churches as hotels, something unique in any colonial outpost. By 1864 the foundations of its future cathedral had been laid.

With the best will in the world, Christchurch was never to be seen as an exclusively Anglican preserve. There were the obstinately Catholic Irish, Presbyterian Scots and Lutheran Germans. When the English novelist Samuel Butler arrived, the first man he met was a Methodist preacher. Then there were the Australian arrivals, whose religion was largely wool and wealth, and who joined the gentry in the race for land.

Today a fleece features prominently in the city's coat of arms. No urban society in the world was more firmly built on wool. Vast tracts of grazing land were seized by early arrivals and gave migrant gentry, Christchurch's aspirant elite, the economic base they lacked elsewhere in New Zealand. Here, according to the *Lyttelton Times* of 1876, land laws had allowed the gentry to become 'a favoured race. . . elevated into a position of boundless wealth and disgraceful monopoly'. Even Edward Jerningham Wakefield, of the colonising family which had done so much to settle southern New Zealand, finally denounced the landowners of Canterbury as 'degenerate'.

Often as not, the new rich of Canterbury left managers looking after their estates, and resided comfortably in Christchurch mansions. These wool-kings, in alliance with merchant-princes, were the movers and shakers of nineteenth-century Christchurch. The leafy appearance of the city – its shady squares and avenues, its riverside daffodils and sheep-grazing parkland – suggested its rural base. Willows trailed along the waters of the Avon River, near which Christ's College had risen to educate landowners' sons. Fashionable shops boasted of past services to aristocracy in competing for the custom of wool-kings and their wives. The wealth of the region soon materialised in civic architecture. Hand in hand with the planting of oak and elm, sycamore and poplar, substantial Gothic and neoclassical buildings began to appear. Soot soon darkened towers, turrets and facades. Christchurch was slowly ringed with industry and industrial suburbs, as wool-kings put their capital to work in their social headquarters. Christchurch was no longer an unkempt outpost of Empire, but a prosperous bastion of virtue, or so its leaders saw it.

Others saw vice, and not of the kind the colonial town's thirty brothels provided. They saw snobbery and social climbing as rampant as the gorse introduced from England for tidy hedgerows and now a satanic weed. The first families of Christchurch were accused of having a shameless appetite for titles. Nothing gladdened nineteenth-century civic leaders more than the observation that their community was 'comfortable and thoroughly English' – as novelist Anthony Trollope obliged them by saying in 1872, beginning a tactful tradition. 'More English than England,' remains the most acceptable compliment.

Now no more than a moderately arduous tourist excursion, the first pilgrim bridle path still climbs over the Port Hills from Lyttelton Harbour. Under the climber's feet, rail and road tunnels hum with subterranean traffic between the city and the port. Annually, on the nearest Sunday to December 16, hundreds of citizens re-enact the journey the city's founders made, up the tussock slopes to the point where, tight-lipped, they looked out on their promised paradise. The splendid coast, curving away to the north, is still there. So are the white alps floating one hundred kilometres beyond the Canterbury Plains. But the bleak, reedy swampland they saw has vanished. Under the vast Canterbury sky there is a sprawling city of nearly three hundred thousand

HISTORY AND HORTICULTURE

people. Factory chimneys compete with spires. Densely settled suburbs spill into crop-patched farmland. It might be any New Zealand city.

A walk through the centre of Christchurch, however, reveals a city less haphazardly grown than any other in New Zealand. It is far more than an antipodean facsimile of an English market town. No English city was ever quite so coherent – or contrived – in character. No English city was ever quite so manicured. Certainly no English city ever had streets, in one poet's phrase, 'closed with shining alps'. For all its affectations, Christchurch is still a frontier city raised by colonists – the colonists Samuel Butler saw as already un-English in the eighteen-sixties, 'shaggy, clear-complexioned, brown and healthy-looking [who] wear exceedingly rowdy hats'. They built as best they remembered, or as best they dreamed, and built durably. They wanted Christchurch to be more than a tradesman's entrance to Canterbury.

It was a garden – perhaps *the* garden, where Adam walked with Eve – that the pioneers most wanted. A garden was made. The city seems to be in bloom most of the year, with over three thousand hectares of parks and reserves.

Even factories pride themselves in immaculate floral settings. Such factories emphasise that Christchurch has long moved beyond dependence on wheat and wool. More than a third of the work force is employed in manufacturing, in more than a thousand factories. The most spectacular example of Christchurch's industrial enterprise is the Hamilton jet boat, which has revolutionised water travel around the world.

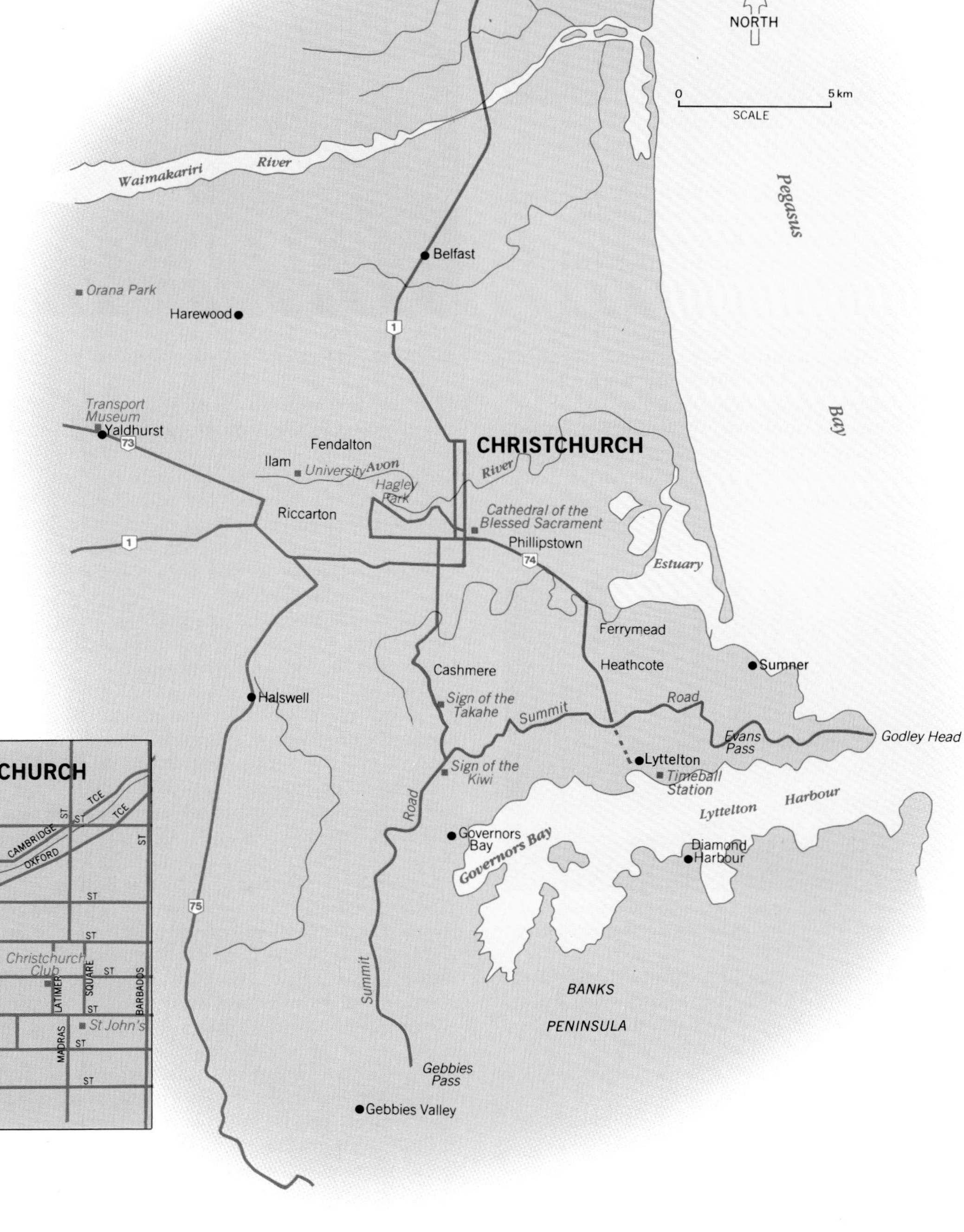

In spring Christchurch echoes and honours the homeland of its pioneer fathers with a blaze of daffodils in its parks

The conventional picture of Christchurch takes no account of its industry, nor of much else besides. The conventional picture is of a conservative city, but the truth is that it is a city with a long, strong radical tradition. The conventional picture suggests a transplanted culture. But two Christchurch groups did far more to establish a native New Zealand accent in the arts than those of any other city: a school of poets based on the city's Caxton Press in the nineteen-thirties, and another of painters, known as 'The Group', in the nineteen-forties and later. Christchurch architects have been the most innovative in shaping a New Zealand vernacular. The city's two contrasting cultural complexes – the elegant new riverside town hall, and the century-old, turreted, spired and cloistered Arts Centre – have no equal in the country. The conventional picture is of a sedate city. One look at lunch-hour Cathedral Square – with its official 'wizard' weaving his spells and its collection of orators – leaves that picture awry.

There are some three thousand hectares of parkland and reserves; Hagley Park alone contains almost two hundred

Finally, the conventional picture, highlighting the city's old-world connections, fails to take in its far more distinctive link with the new world of Antarctica. For more than a quarter of a century, Christchurch has been a busy rear base for Antarctic exploration and research, and headquarters for US Operation Deepfreeze. At Christchurch airport, where jumbo jets bring in visitors seeking the city's quainter qualities, there are also air freighters thundering south to deposit men, material and machines on a continent of ice. Christchurch is the service town of the world's most formidable frontier.

Exotic plants from all continents are represented in the parks; this magnificent magnolia in bloom is from Asia

But the conventional picture pays. History and horticulture have conspired to make the city's heart, quite suddenly, a most saleable commodity. Tens of thousands of North American and Japanese tourists annually saunter through Christchurch, persuaded that for the price of an air-ticket to New Zealand they can take in a bit of England too. No complaints are heard. Here is an England without the touts of Piccadilly, the ticket-scalpers of Stratford-on-Avon, without terrorist bomb scares. Here is England as it cosily ought to be. Hundreds of Japanese visitors are honeymooners; here they can have a second, English-style wedding with bells and bouquets, white gowns and gloves, tails and tuxedos, in a little Gothic church, with a video recording of their idyllic Christchurch nuptials. A fairytale is what they want. A frontier fairytale is what they have – one created by a tiny trickle of footsore men and women, labouring over the Port Hills and down to the desolate plain, burdened by their worldly goods and a vision of a better Britain. A century from now, the Anglophile oasis they planted on the Canterbury Plains may seem more extraordinary still.

The gardens of the Provincial Government Buildings contain flowering fruit trees and lawns that run down to the river. The Englishness of Christchurch may be a matter for dispute but its reputation as a garden city certainly is not

PILGRIM GOTHIC

With his lyrical interpretation of an architectural style, Benjamin Mountfort set a distinctive tone for the city's buildings

'I see nothing in the dream to regret or be ashamed of,' said Christchurch city father John Robert Godley (see page 286), when he departed from the tiny settlement in 1852, two years after its founding. 'I am quite sure that without the enthusiasm, the poetry, the unreality if you will, with which our scheme was overlaid, it would never have been accomplished.'

Above and right: *No Christchurch building is more interesting than the Provincial Government Buildings, designed by Benjamin Mountfort. The gold leaf and colour work in the lofty ceiling of the stone council chamber, the floor tiling, the colonnaded windows and arches are achievements in taste and balance that are a revelation to the visitor*

The Arcadian enthusiasm – or Utopian unreality – of the city's founders would determine the character of Christchurch. It would find vivid expression in the city's golden gardens and leafy parks. The dream of the Canterbury pilgrims was that of an instant, Anglican civilisation in the South Pacific. They fathered a community that largely defied and denied the land in which it was set. New Zealander's anarchic native vegetation would be kept at bay. The streets would be straight. The reedy river wandering through the town would be spruced up, named the Avon, and told where to travel. The poetry in the pilgrim soul was to reside in its buildings.

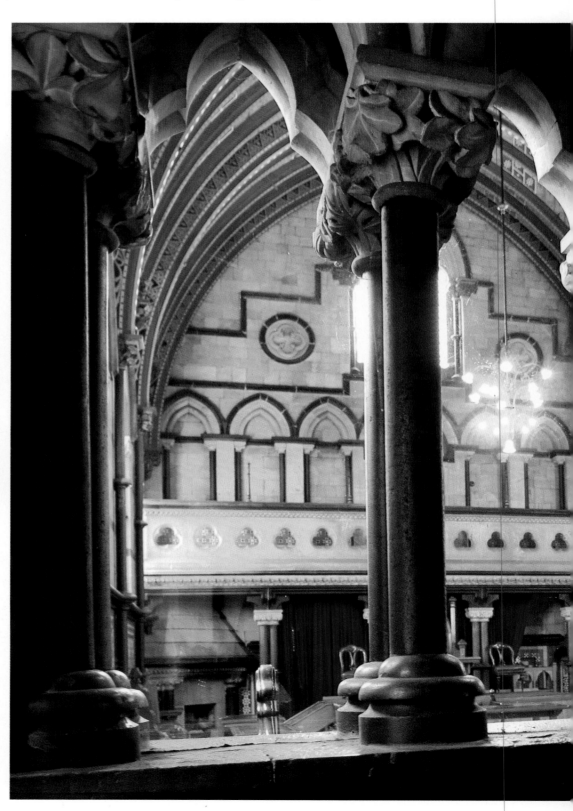

In the early Victorian period, when the city was founded, Gothic was the favoured style for Anglican architecture. Gothic colours both the ecclesiastical and the secular buildings of Christchurch. The first communion staged for the arriving pilgrims was in the loft of a Lyttelton warehouse. Seating was made from planks placed across barrels. When the pilgrims crossed the Port Hills to the Canterbury Plains, with no less than seven clergymen among them, or one for every hundred colonists, places of worship were a secondary consideration. The priority was to provide families with shelter from the sun, the rain, and the beating nor'westers. On a visit from Auckland, Bishop Selwyn denounced the new arrivals. 'Here,' he grumbled, 'I find neither church nor school nor parsonage. Money enough has been spent [but] not one sixpence of expenditure in any form for the glory of God.' Nor was he the only one to find early Christchurch a poor advertisement for Anglican renewal.

Nevertheless, embarrassed and harassed Anglicans *were* building. As crude and simple as their earliest dwellings, their first churches were little more than wooden huts, in which congregations huddled. In the mid eighteen-fifties more substantial buildings rose, but these churches were to be almost as temporary as the huts that preceded them. They lasted only a decade or two before being remodelled or completely replaced by more lasting structures. But if Christchurch was to be taken seriously as an Anglican enterprise, a cathedral must be built at its heart. And therein lies a small colonial and cultural saga.

Top: *Cathedral Church of Christ, the embodiment of Anglican ideals of the city's founders expressed in Gothic*
Above: *The various buildings that make up Christ's College form a microcosm of Christchurch's architectural history*

Planning for a cathedral began in 1858, soon after the arrival of the first Bishop of Christchurch, Henry Harper (the first candidate having collapsed and fled). The community had a bishop at last but no setting worthy of one. A site had been reserved for a cathedral, and George Gilbert Scott, one of the most celebrated Victorian architects, was commissioned to prepare a plan. Scott came up with an austere design in thirteenth-century English Gothic. There were no frills – surprising from the architect who later ran riot with London's Albert Memorial – and few fancies. It was a rather spiritless conception, tailored functionally for a distant colony.

In the early eighteen-sixties money was available for work to begin. Benjamin Mountfort, a talented young colonial architect who should in

Top*: Aggressively Gothic in style, the State Trinity Centre was designed by Benjamin Mountfort as a church*
Above*: The Press Building – reinforced concrete structure and Oamaru stone facing blend into Perpendicular Gothic*

justice have been commissioned to design the cathedral in the first instance, was also available to supervise. One of Canterbury's original pilgrims, he had arrived in New Zealand on the *Charlotte Jane* in 1850, as an idealistic and devout twenty-six-year-old with a creditable architectural background. One of his earliest projects was a Lyttelton church. Working with unfamiliar and unseasoned New Zealand timber, he soon had a disaster on his hands. The timber warped and bricks toppled. The church swayed in the Canterbury nor'westers and was finally demolished. It seemed as though his career as an architect was ended. He became a professional photographer, ran a stationer's shop and taught drawing. But by the eighteen-sixties he had won his way back into his profession. Although other local architects argued that Mountfort was the man to supervise the building of the cathedral, Bishop Harper refused to employ him. It wasn't just the matter of the collapsed Lyttelton church. Harper's fear was that Mountfort might blemish Scott's plan with 'work of his own devising'. So far as Harper was concerned, the grand English architect's design was sacrosanct and not to be impertinently tampered with by a colonial. A safe nonentity was brought in from England to carry the cathedral through. In 1864, with rain lashing down, Bishop Harper laid the cornerstone. By the end of 1865 the foundations were in place, but funds were depleted. The colony was in depression and Christchurch was suffering too. Grass grew over the cathedral site.

Novelist Anthony Trollope, passing through Christchurch in 1872, noted the abandoned foundations and recorded, 'I could not but be melancholy as I learned that the honest high-toned idea of the honest high-toned founders of the colony would probably not be carried out, but perhaps on that spot a set of public offices will be better . . .' Trollope was greatly impressed, however, with the Canterbury Provincial Government Buildings that had risen to serve the affairs of the region. 'Spacious and very handsome . . . [It]

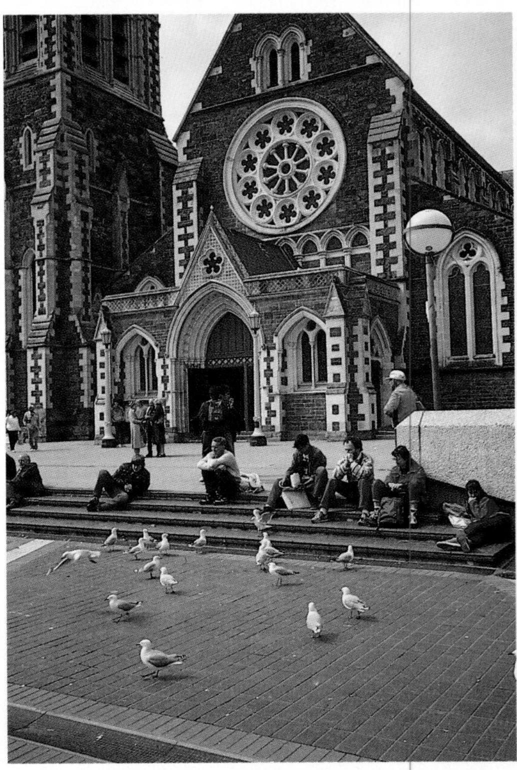

The Cathedral Church of Christ rises in Cathedral Square; at ground level the square is a meeting place for all

pleased me very much. It is partly of stone, partly of wood, but is Gothic throughout, the woodwork being as graceful and true to the design of the whole as the stone.' The designer of that Christchurch gem – and such it remains – was the same Benjamin Mountfort who had not been thought sufficiently trustworthy to work on the cathedral. While out of favour with Anglicans, Mountfort had been found reliable by Roman Catholics. He had given them St Mary's pro-Cathedral (1864), delightful St Patrick's at Akaroa (1864) and St Joseph's at Lyttelton (1865).

A GIANT AMONG ARCHITECTS

In 1873, when building of the cathedral resumed, Mountfort was engaged at last as supervising architect. Just as the good Bishop Harper had supposed, Mountfort boldly made free with Scott's bland design and substituted 'work of his own devising'. There were suddenly pinnacles and balconies embellishing the building. Decoration enriched it inside and out. Mountfort laboured on and off for the rest of his life, giving Anglican Christchurch a cathedral worthy of its pilgrim founders. It was not until 1904, four decades after the cornerstone had been laid and six years after Mountfort's death, that the transepts and chancel were finally completed.

Today, it is impossible to imagine Christchurch without Mountfort's work. The great cathedral he saved from mediocrity would soon be backed by the Gothic style of the Press Building (1907), and the Government Buildings (1911), designed by later architects to highlight the city's distinctive heart. Never to be wooed from the Gothic style, Mountfort set the city's tone. The Canterbury Museum (1870) is another imposing Mountfort creation, as are the Clock Tower Building (1877) and the Great Hall (1882) of the present Arts Centre, once Canterbury University. Among his other works are the brick Church of the Good Shepherd (1884), the 'New' classrooms of Christ's College (1886), and the stone State Trinity Centre (1874). Mountfort left churches not only in Christchurch, but the length of New Zealand, including Auckland's magnificent wooden St Mary's. But the exquisite Canterbury Provincial Government Buildings complex remains his most lyrical work. English architectural historian Nikolaus Pevsner pronounced its interior one of the finest High Victorian Gothic spaces outside Europe. Had Mountfort remained in England, he might well have known fame. Instead he threw in his lot with a new land and, in his own lifetime, received no more than modest recognition. He was not even so much as knighted for his contribution to Christchurch.

Exterior of the stone council chamber in the Provincial Government Buildings (see illustration pages 276-277)

A miniature spire on the south side of the cathedral was one of Benjamin Mountfort's additions to the original design

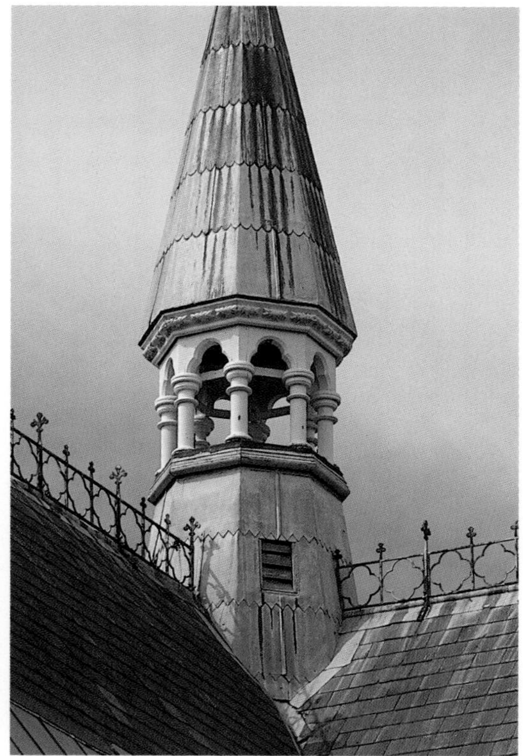

The Arts Centre, housed in the former university buildings, is full of interesting architectural details above eye level

The Great Hall is the dominant building of the Arts Centre

Other New Zealand architects – using wood here, stone there – also worked Gothic marvels in the nineteenth century. But there was a dedicated giant among them, using whatever the colony provided, working to glorify God and celebrate man. No one would ever weave anything quite to match Benjamin Mountfort's pilgrim spells.

PIONEER PORT

A tightly formed harbourside town in a dramatic setting, Lyttelton retains much of its nineteenth-century working-class character

It was at Lyttelton that thousands of aspiring nineteenth-century colonists first set foot on New Zealand soil. Until recently, when inter-island ferry services from Wellington ceased, Lyttelton was also the introduction to the South Island for travellers from the north. Its dramatic setting – the great, green volcanic crater of Lyttelton Harbour – often exceeded the most optimistic expectation. 'The land we passed,' recorded one arrival in 1850, 'was most beautifully situated – high and wooded, with glades of grass running up through the forest. We were all enchanted.'

Steep steps lead up to St Joseph's Catholic Church; although built in 1865, the church was not completed until 1941

The tiny port town of Lyttelton, however – as functional then as it is today – tended to terminate excitement. It was a rough, proletarian port in a still rough and ready colony. The devout Canterbury pilgrims, having sailed halfway round the world, found no friendly spire – 'no church, no schoolroom, no place in which we could hold a service'. Christchurch, on the other side of the Port Hills, began rising in elegant Gothic style. Although Lyttelton was New Zealand's busiest port for a time, it never changed much. Its population of three thousand is smaller than it was a century ago. In 1868 Lord Lyttelton, whose family name was given to the town, likened it to a small English seaport, 'a small and rather poor place. . . cramped in between shore and hills'.

Topography dictated that little would change. Lyttelton retains its tight harbourside townscape. It also retains its robust working-class quality. It was never a place for the fashionable of Canterbury to linger, merely a town to pass through, a graceless gauntlet to run. 'Scattered wooden boxes of houses', said Samuel Butler dismissively in 1860. Many of those nineteenth-century dwellings remain today. Lyttelton has survived with piquant period character, especially in its domestic architecture. The homes of Canterbury's humble contrast strikingly with the pastoralists' mansions of Christchurch proper.

From top to bottom: *Lyttelton, sea-door to Canterbury cramped between shore and hills; the harbour office; one of the town's many timber cottages with a veranda at the front; London Street, with a background of foggy hills*

Above: *Church of the Most Holy Trinity; the original church on this site led to Benjamin Mountfort's early disfavour*
Left: *This wooden cottage, opposite Lyttelton's gaol, served for many years as the chief warden's quarters*

Lyttelton's public buildings were equally modest. Regional institutions soon moved their headquarters into Christchurch, and only the prison was left to Lyttelton. Now remembered as the prison that failed to hold the legendary sheep-rustler James McKenzie for long, it has largely been demolished – with remnant walls and cells evoking the past. Convict-hewn stone still walls the steep Lyttelton streets. Another survival of the port's penal era is the large warder's house near by, with its high gables and long veranda.

The most arresting legacy of convict labour is the 1876 Timeball Station above the port. Unique in New Zealand, it was designed to give mariners the precise time so that they could fix longitude at sea. The NZ Historic Places Trust and the Lyttelton Maritime Association have combined to get the station in working order again. Another nautical survival is the graving dock, opened in 1883 and still in use.

Three stone churches in Winchester Street, all dating from Lyttelton's last-century heyday, reinforce the town's rather wistful character. The Anglican Church of the Most Holy Trinity (1859), built of volcanic rock, was the first. Then followed the stone and clay St John's Presbyterian Church (1864), with its distinctive spire, and the grey stone St Joseph's Catholic Church (1865), with its steep-stepped frontage.

Lyttelton's appeal, however, is less in individual buildings than in its salty townscape. 'We shot past a little point of land,' recorded one nineteenth-century traveller, 'and the town of Lyttelton burst upon our view – like a little village – but nothing more than a village – in snugness, neatness and pretty situation.' Few now pass through Lyttelton to see it as generations of seaborne travellers once saw it. The steam tug *Lyttelton*, built in Glasgow in 1907, now provides weekend harbour excursions and a marine perspective on the port for visitors. Durable Lyttelton seems destined to persist as a place of small and surprising visual pleasures.

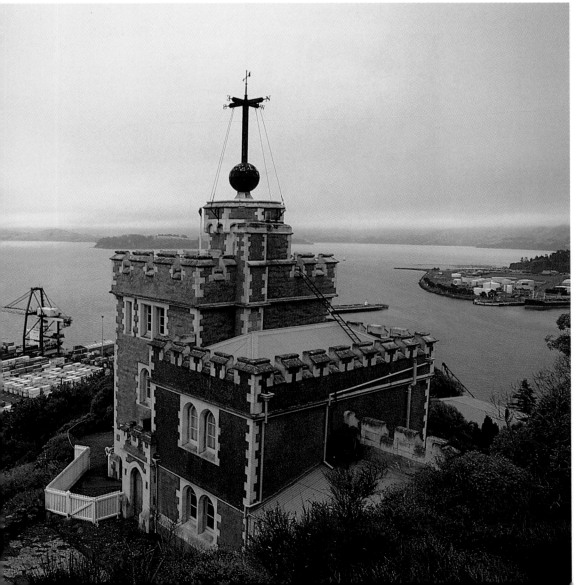

The Timeball Station is unique in New Zealand; the ball was hoisted each day and dropped at one pm precisely so that ships' captains in port could adjust their chronometers

PLACES OF INTEREST

VANTAGE POINTS

CATHEDRAL SQUARE
The inner city's only vantage point is the top of the Anglican cathedral's 30 metre tower, reached by a 133-step climb At ground level the square presents a far livelier human scene, with its lunch-hour orators, particularly the city 'wizard', lecturing on the shortcomings of *Homo sapiens* and Christchurch itself. A statue of city founder John Robert Godley contemplates the square. The first public statue in New Zealand (erected in 1867), it is the work of sculptor Thomas Woolner, founder member (with Dante Gabriel Rossetti and others) in 1848 of the Pre-Raphaelite Brotherhood.

PORT HILLS
The best place to view the largely level city, and grasp its extent, is where the historic Bridle Path crosses the Port Hills (see page 287) and where the Canterbury pilgrims had their first glimpse of their unpromising promised land. In the distance, the Canterbury coast, plains and alps present a bold backdrop. Behind is steep-walled Lyttelton Harbour, an old and extinct volcanic crater filled with sea, and the cramped port town (see page 282). The pilgrims' trek is commemorated by a small stone shelter.

MUSEUMS AND GALLERIES

BROOKE GIFFORD GALLERY
This is one of New Zealand's leading dealer galleries, with frequently changing exhibitions of painting and sculpture by New Zealand artists, and a strong South Island emphasis (112 Manchester Street; open Monday to Friday, 10.30–5).

CANTERBURY MUSEUM
The museum is housed in one of the city's most distinguished buildings (1870), designed by Gothic architect Benjamin Mountfort. With its powerful stonework and distinctive tower, the museum has long been a city landmark. It was first directed and developed by the enthusiastic geologist and explorer Julius von Haast (1822-1887), who bartered coveted moa bones with institutions around the world to build up an extensive collection. His successors have also done considerable fieldwork. Among other exhibits, the museum contains a reconstructed colonial Christchurch street and a replica of the cabin on the *Charlotte Jane* occupied by the first city superintendent, James Edward FitzGerald. The unique feature of the museum, however, is the window it provides on Antarctica, with which Christchurch has been closely associated since the beginning of the 20th century. British explorer Robert Falcon Scott used Christchurch as a launch pad to the southern continent, as do the aircraft of US Operation Deepfreeze today. The Hall of Antarctic Discovery highlights the heartbreak and heroism of early polar exploration, and there are films and changing exhibitions of Antarctic material (Rolleston Avenue; open daily, 10–4.30, except Good Friday and Christmas Day).

CANTERBURY SOCIETY OF ARTS
Works are for sale as well as on exhibition (66 Gloucester Street; open Monday to Friday, 10–4.30; weekend, 2–4.30).

CHRISTCHURCH ARTS CENTRE
Located in former buildings of the University of Canterbury (now at Ilam), this cluster of stone buildings dates from the 1870s and 1880s, and incorporates some splendid examples of the Christchurch Gothic style. The Great Hall and the Clock Tower Building are the work of the noted colonial architect Benjamin Mountfort (see page 278). Grouped around quadrangles (one cloistered), the old university buildings have been converted into an impressive cultural centre. They are mostly open to the public and include restaurants, galleries, a specialist cinema, craft shops and craft workers on site. The Court Theatre, New Zealand's most successful professional theatre, is also housed in the centre. Off the north quadrangle is the room where Ernest Rutherford, father of nuclear physics, began his career (see page 214) (Rolleston Avenue; hours vary).

LYTTELTON HISTORICAL MUSEUM
This small museum has a strong nautical flavour. There are also mementoes of Robert Falcon Scott's Antarctic expedition (Gladstone Quay; open weekend 2–4; also Tuesday and Thursday in summer; other times by arrangement).

McDOUGALL ART GALLERY
Beside the city's **BOTANIC GARDENS**, this impressive gallery has an extensive permanent collection of New Zealand work, from colonial to contemporary, and hosts travelling exhibitions. Notable in the colonial collection is the work of Petrus Van der Velden, now seen as New Zealand's most significant 19th-century painter. Among European works the gallery features two Rodins (Rolleston Avenue, entrance from Botanic Gardens; open Monday to Saturday, 10–4.30; Sunday, 2–4.30).

YALDHURST TRANSPORT MUSEUM
Located in the grounds of an early Canterbury homestead (1876), this museum features a fine collection of horse-drawn vehicles (the earliest about 1820), as well as vintage vehicles, motorcycles, aircraft, racing cars and steam engines (Main West Road, opposite Yaldhurst Hotel, 12 kilometres from city; open daily, 10–5).

A NATURAL LEADER

James FitzGerald was a witty, flamboyant and popular man who became one of Christchurch's leading personalities – a natural leader in all his fields of interest

The rise of James Edward FitzGerald (1818-96) from obscurity was fast and unpredictable. As an undersecretary at the British Museum, he seemed set for a career as a competent minor administrator. But the formation of the Canterbury Association released the curbed energies that were to reveal the true man. He had for some time interested himself in colonial affairs, and his commitment to Edward Wakefield's plans, though marred by mutual dislike, led him to emigrate in 1850 on the *Charlotte Jane*.

Within a few weeks of arrival, FitzGerald found his true vocation as publicist, politician, pamphleteer and polemicist with the foundation of the *Lyttelton Times*, whose first editor he became. Newspapers led him directly into politics and in 1853 he became superintendent of Canterbury province. He reduced the price of land by a third, pushed ahead with the Sumner to Lyttelton road (though later opposed a railway tunnel – a concept he had once favoured) and helped found Christ's College. He was elected member for Lyttelton in New Zealand's first parliament.

At the end of his term he went to England, but he quickly made his way back again to Christchurch where he founded and edited *The Press*, which remains one of the country's leading newspapers. He was re-elected to parliament but retired from politics in 1867 to become controller general (the official auditor) – a curious appointment for a man who had found it impossible to balance his own books. He held the post for thirty years, all the time offering advice on all manner of subjects, either in speeches or in print.

FitzGerald – man of parts and of taste

FitzGerald had always longed for large estates and riches but, apart from an eventual grant of land, the nearest he came to earn these from his own efforts was a dairy farm near Lake Ellesmere. A man of high though inconsistent ideals, he is one of the more endearing characters of New Zealand's colonial past. His interest in education and his lonely arguments against the Maori Wars and for a fairer deal over Maori land and Maori political advancement, mark him as a thinker far in advance of his time.

HISTORIC HOUSES

COB COTTAGE
This humble, restored colonists' cottage, just over the Ferrymead Bridge on the main road to **SUMNER**, is a typical early Canterbury cob dwelling.

DEANS COTTAGE
This is the oldest surviving dwelling on the Canterbury Plains (1843) (see **RICCARTON BUSH**).

HOLLY LEA (McLEAN'S MANSION)
Possibly the largest wooden dwelling in New Zealand, this domed, rambling building at 377 Manchester Street was the dream house of wool-king Allan McLean, built in 1902 after he finally sold off his sheep. After his death it served as a sanctuary for women in reduced circumstances. Today, like many Christchurch mansions, it testifies to the wealth won from the land by early Canterbury pastoralists.

NGAIO MARSH HOUSE
Author Ngaio Marsh spent most of her life in Christchurch, yet made an international reputation with crime thrillers set in London. In Christchurch itself she was better known as a theatrical impresario (a theatre is named after her), and for her Shakespearean productions (see page 285). Her house (1907) at 37 Valley Road, Cashmere, is now listed by the NZ Historic Places Trust.

TIPTREE COTTAGE
At Savills Road, Harewood, near the airport, Tiptree Cottage (1864) is a fine example of the cob houses of many early South Island small farmers. More ambitious in form than most similar dwellings, it has three storeys, the third of which is a small attic. Restored and refurbished, it is now a private museum open on occasional Sundays; the exterior alone, however, is worth the visit.

Rolleston . . . outside the Canterbury Museum

HISTORIC BUILDINGS

CANTERBURY PROVINCIAL GOVERNMENT BUILDINGS
The masterpiece of architect Benjamin Mountfort (see page 278), this medley of stone and wood is perhaps New Zealand's most precious complex of Gothic buildings. It was built between 1858 and 1865 in the days of provincial government (which ended in 1876). Aside from Southland's modest Kelvin Chambers at Invercargill, this complex is the only visible survival of that political era. With its solid exterior and richly decorated interior, it remains a monument to the prosperity and ambition of early Canterbury, and to early New Zealand pastoralism. The High Victorian stone council chamber is a Gothic triumph (open weekdays, 9–4; guided tours, Sunday afternoon).

CHIEF POST OFFICE
Standing on CATHEDRAL SQUARE, this finely proportioned Italianate and towered post office (1879) is still is use. Its secular liveliness tempers the more austere Gothic of the cathedral.

CHRISTCHURCH CLUB
This imposing wooden building (1861) at 154 Worcester Street, the Italianate work of Benjamin Mountfort and his partner Isaac Luck, was the headquarters of the wool-kings, a bastion of power and privilege in the early days of Canterbury settlement. When not musing in a sod hut on his Mesopotamia run, novelist Samuel Butler hob-nobbed with his lessers here in the 1860s, and complained that the talk was all gold and sheep.

CHRISTCHURCH TOWN HALL
Not strictly a historic building as it was opened in 1972, the city's riverside town hall is the most striking public building – and cultural complex – erected in New Zealand in recent decades. The work of architects Warren and Mahoney, it announces that Christchurch's architectural vision did not end with the 19th century. The main entrance is in Kilmore Street (guided tours half-hourly; afternoon only at weekend).

CHRIST'S COLLEGE
New Zealand's closest equivalent to an English public school, Christ's College was founded in the city's first decade and began on its present site in Rolleston Avenue in 1857. It aspired to be a school that would rival 'one of the great grammar schools of England'. By the end of the 19th century, Canterbury pastoralists ceased sending their children home to England to be educated and settled for Christ's College, where their sons could be most respectably reared in the faith of their fathers in a climate that was congenially and convincingly English. Until recently, college uniform included a boater. By its 'massive strength, stability and simplicity' the architecture of the college was intended to give a lesson to its pupils. The mosaic is Gothic and medieval, with a touch of Tudor. A number of architects contributed to the complex, among them the untrained James Edward FitzGerald, the Canterbury settlement's first superintendent (Big School, 1863), Benjamin Mountfort ('New' classrooms, 1886) and Cecil Wood (Hare Memorial Library, 1915; medieval dining hall, 1925).

A LIFE OF CRIME

The Christchurch home of Ngaio Marsh, internationally known writer of detective fiction and producer of Shakespeare plays, is listed by the NZ Historic Places Trust

Ngaio Marsh – a successful double career

Black Beech and Honeydew, the autobiography of Ngaio Marsh (1899-1982), describes her Christchurch childhood and upbringing with nostalgic charm. An only child of enthusiastic amateur actors, she seemed to be guided almost magically towards the theatre – which remained her first love and chief preoccupation.

Educated at the Canterbury University School of Art, it seemed at the time that she might become an artist. Then, at the age of twenty-one, a touring theatre company rekindled her early infatuation with the stage. She became an actress for some years, and also coached in a small Christchurch drama school, before leaving for England. It was there, in 1932, that she embarked on her life of crime, writing her first detective novel *A Man Lay Dead*, with the gentle and intelligent Roderick Alleyn as the hero; he was to be the central character in many of her later books and much loved by her readers.

Back in New Zealand, during and after the Second World War, Ngaio Marsh turned her talents to theatrical production, specialising in Shakespeare. Her productions of *Hamlet* and *Othello* are particularly memorable. The actors were students, yet they played to packed houses throughout New Zealand and Australia, and received rave reviews.

In 1950, she travelled again to England to find that her crime novels had made her a celebrity. But although Ngaio Marsh was outstandingly successful as a writer, her novels were always a means to an end, enabling her to indulge her passion for the stage. She established a touring theatrical company made up of Commonwealth actors, several of whom have since achieved considerable fame. A permanent memorial to her contribution to New Zealand theatre and dedication to young people is the Ngaio Marsh Theatre on the campus of the University of Canterbury.

Cathedral of the Blessed Sacrament; its dome can be seen from most parts of the city

LYTTELTON TIMEBALL STATION
Convict-built in 1876, this stone castle above the port of LYTTELTON was designed to help mariners fix their chronometers (when the timeball descended at precisely 1 pm). It functioned until the 1930s, and is now one of the few such buildings left in the world. It has been restored by the NZ Historic Places Trust and the Lyttelton Maritime Association, and is in working order again (open daily, except Good Friday and Christmas Day, 1.30–12, 1–4.30).

PRESS BUILDING
Built in 1907 on CATHEDRAL SQUARE, this building is as much a Christchurch institution as the Canterbury daily newspaper published within. It is perhaps the most fluent of New Zealand's Gothic commercial buildings. Designed by city architects Collins and Harman, it reinforces the character of Cathedral Square, especially with its corner tower.

SHAND'S EMPORIUM
At 88 Hereford Street, this simple wooden store, built in the late 1850s, is the oldest surviving commercial building in the city.

STATE TRINITY CENTRE
Benjamin Mountfort's unusual ability to find every melody in the Gothic score is seen in this building, dating from 1874, at 124 Worcester Street. Rubble walls and Oamaru stone make a striking contrast and the saddleback tower is also distinctive. Originally the Trinity Congregational Church, it is now in the hands of the State Insurance Company and used as a cultural centre.

VICTORIA CLOCK TOWER
One of the city's best-known landmarks, this imaginatively proportioned tower of stone and wrought iron in Victoria Street was erected on the opposite side of the city in 1897 to mark Queen Victoria's Diamond Jubilee and moved in 1930.

Deans Cottage (1844) at Riccarton Bush – faithfully restored and preserved as a museum

CHURCHES

CATHEDRAL CHURCH OF CHRIST

After Benjamin Mountfort had regained his spurs as an architect with the **CANTERBURY PROVINCIAL GOVERNMENT BUILDINGS**, he was employed to supervise the construction of the Anglican cathedral, and freely improvised on Gilbert Scott's rather undistinguished design (see page 278). The cornerstone of the cathedral was laid in 1864, but work was soon abandoned. Building resumed under Mountfort's supervision in 1873, but it was to be another three decades before the cathedral was finished, six years after Mountfort's death (open daily, 8–5; guided tours, Sunday after morning service; steps to tower, open daily, 9–4).

CATHEDRAL OF THE BLESSED SACRAMENT

The impressive Roman Catholic cathedral in Barbadoes Street was designed by architect F.W. Petre in 1899. Its construction proceeded far more rapidly than that of **CATHEDRAL CHURCH OF CHRIST**, and was completed in half a decade. Rising grandly on the city skyline, it is based on Neo-Renaissance forms, with a French flavour in the facade and parapet. In 1934, George Bernard Shaw offended the Anglican establishment of Christchurch by ignoring their cathedral and admiring Petre's work.

CHURCH OF THE GOOD SHEPHERD

Created by Benjamin Mountfort in 1884, this unusually rhythmic brick church in Phillipstown was also his place of worship, and thus perhaps meant most of all to him. After his death in 1898, the belfry at the west end of the church was built as his memorial. The building is now a Maori mission church.

DURHAM STREET METHODIST CHURCH

The first church built of durable materials in the city (1864), this sturdy Neo-Gothic structure, designed by a Melbourne firm of architects, defiantly flew the nonconformist flag in emphatically Anglican Christchurch. Essayist Oliver Duff, arguing that the true Christchurch story is 'as un-English as flax and cabbage trees', stressed the conflict that existed 'between a minority, predominantly Church of England, who had land and some education, and a majority, largely Methodist, who followed trade and said "baa" to the wool kings . . .' This building can be seen as their most notable 'baa'.

ST JOHN THE BAPTIST CHURCH

In an attractive leafy setting at the corner of Hereford and Madras Streets, in Latimer Square, St John's was the first stone-built Anglican church on the Plains, dating from 1864. It was the work of architect Maxwell Bury in collaboration with Benjamin Mountfort. At the time Mountfort was not thought reliable enough (by the Christchurch Anglican establishment) to supervise the building of the cathedral (see page 278). The Gothic building, with its three shades of stone, is an impressive vindication of his talent.

ST MICHAEL AND ALL ANGELS ANGLICAN CHURCH

This delightful wooden example of the Anglican Gothic style, on the corner of Oxford Terrace and Lichfield Street, dates from 1872. The detailed interior is especially impressive. Designed by W.F. Crisp, it replaced a still earlier pilgrim church, of which Benjamin Mountfort's free-standing belfry (1861) survives.

ENVIRONS

KAIAPOI

Once a river port separate from Christchurch, Kaiapoi (20 kilometres north) is now virtually a city suburb with 5000 people. Paddle-steamers once plied upriver to serve pioneer settlers in Canterbury. Today the old coastal trader MV *Tuhoe* runs tourist excursions along inland waters. Jet-boat excursions up the mighty Waimakariri River provide a more modern thrill. The delightful timber St Bartholomew's Anglican Church is the oldest surviving church in Canterbury; the nave dates from 1855 and architect Benjamin Mountfort added the sanctuary and transepts in 1862. Kaiapoi Museum is housed in the old courthouse (1890) on Williams Street (open Thursday and Sunday, 2–4).

LYTTELTON

The port beside deep and lovely Lyttelton Harbour – a vast extinct volcanic crater – was the first colonial foothold on greater Canterbury (not including Banks Peninsula). Lyttelton was already a community when Canterbury pilgrims arrived in 1850 to climb the hills above it and view the mire that was their town site. Shut off from Christchurch by the **PORT HILLS**, it is now linked to the city by rail and road tunnels. Lyttelton (population 3100) is noted for its 19th-century buildings – particularly the stone **LYTTELTON TIMEBALL STATION** (1876) and the stone churches of the Most Holy Trinity (1859), St John (1864) and St Joseph (1865), all in Winchester Street. In Oxford Street are the remains of the old Lyttelton prison; another prison was built on the same site (1861). The maritime gallery and the Antarctic gallery in the **LYTTELTON HISTORICAL MUSEUM** nearer the town centre are worth a visit. Harbour cruises are available on the 1907 steam tug *Lyttelton* on Sunday afternoons from November to April.

SUMMIT ROAD

The wild, windy and tussock-covered **PORT HILLS** were once the rim of the vast volcanic crater that became Lyttelton Harbour, and constitute the city's only prominent natural feature. The scenic Summit Road traverses the hills and provides access to walkways. Allow at least half a day for an excursion. To the north is Christchurch, the sweep of

A BRIEF BUT SIGNIFICANT STAY IN CANTERBURY

John Godley (1814-61) is deservedly remembered as the founding father of Canterbury; his statue stands triumphantly in Cathedral Square, Christchurch

Woolner's statue of administrator Godley

John Robert Godley's involvement in New Zealand affairs was brief: he arrived in the country in March 1850 and was gone again in December 1852, never to return. And yet he exerted more influence on the beginnings of Canterbury than any other man; for those few years he ruled the young settlement almost single-handedly. In his own day many considered him less a father than a despot.

Educated at Harrow and Oxford, a High Anglican and a Tory, Godley's Irishness is often overlooked. He was born in Dublin, the son of an Irish landowner, spent his childhood in Ireland, was called to the Irish bar and was deeply concerned in Irish affairs – a concern that led to an interest in colonial resettlement of surplus population, the theories of Edward Gibbon Wakefield and the cause of an Anglican settlement in Canterbury.

Godley's commitment to the Canterbury project was further motivated by his fears concerning the decline of church influence in everyday life, and the growing political ambitions of the lower classes. The Canterbury Association, formed in 1848 with Godley as virtual leader, shared these fears. He wished to see the creation of an industrious self-reliant colony led by its bishop and its gentry – democracy and the ownership of land by labourers had no part in his plans.

Ill-health led Godley to follow Wakefield's suggestion that he should travel to New Zealand in advance of the first four ships of Association colonists. The experience seemed to give him renewed vitality. He plunged into colonial politics and became the autocrat of Christchurch. It was Godley's decisive act in over-riding the plans of the London backers of the Association that opened Canterbury to large sheep runs.

After his return to England, Godley maintained his interest in the Canterbury settlement, and there is no doubt that his later career would have been highly distinguished but for deteriorating health. His wife Charlotte achieved posthumous fame as an author. Her letters, published privately in 1936 and in a public edition in 1950, as *Letters from Early New Zealand*, offer a starchy though absorbing account of contemporary social life.

Pegasus Bay and sometimes the Seaward Kaikouras. The Southern Alps stand white beyond the Canterbury Plains. To the east lies Banks Peninsula – also volcanic – and a gull's eye view of Lyttelton Harbour and the port town. The drive can take in leafy Governors Bay on Lyttelton Harbour. The Summit Road is best approached from **SUMNER** via Evans Pass Road. There are light refreshments available at the Sign of the Kiwi and more substantial meals at the **SIGN OF THE TAKAHE**.

SUMNER

A seaside suburb with a population of 3000, cool, sandy, salty Sumner (12 kilometres) provides quick relief for the citizens of landlocked Christchurch during the hot Canterbury summers.

ENTERTAINMENT

BOTANIC GARDENS

Set in a bend of the meandering Avon River, these 30 hectares of lawn, woodland and garden at the heart of the city reflect the Arcadian vision of the city's founding fathers. The first English oak was planted in 1863, before even the cornerstone of the city's cathedral was laid. The gardens have probably the finest collection of indigenous and exotic plants in New Zealand, with emphasis on the latter. Access to the **MCDOUGALL ART GALLERY** is through the gardens, and there is also a tea kiosk. Boats and canoes can be hired from the Antigua Boatsheds (1882) at 2 Cambridge Terrace to glide past the gardens and adjoining **HAGLEY PARK** (gardens and boatsheds open daily; boatsheds, 10–4).

FERRYMEAD HISTORIC PARK

These 44 hectares of land are devoted to an extensive museum of transport and technology, with operational vintage locomotives and tramcars. Collection includes 43 fire engines and 20 locomotives, as well as aircraft, vehicles, bicycles, gigs and wagons, and agricultural equipment and machinery. There is also a reconstructed early Canterbury township and an old-style bakery that functions at weekends. It was at Ferrymead that New Zealand's first steam train ran in 1863 (269 Bridle Path Road, Heathcote; open daily, 10–4.30).

HAGLEY PARK

As Hyde Park is to London, wooded and grassy, so is Hagley Park, 180 hectares of open space, to Christchurch. The first tree was planted in 1859 amid bracken and tussock on a featureless, flat site. Native New Zealand growth was vigorously weeded out to make a pocket of old England. With the daffodils in spring or the click of bat on ball in summer, the illusion is total. The park's attractions include sportsfields, shady corners, gardens and riverside walks.

MONA VALE

More than 4 hectares of wooded parkland on the banks of the Avon form the setting for an Elizabethan-style homestead (1905), long known as one of the city's most gracious homes and now a reception centre. The grounds and homestead provide a picture of how Canterbury's wool-kings lived at the beginning of the century (entry from Fendalton Road; grounds open daily, 8–6.30, October to March; 8.30–5.30 the rest of the year).

ORANA PARK WILDLIFE RESERVE

This large drive-through wildlife reserve was developed by a trust on 26 hectares just outside the city. It has more than 400 species of animals and birds, and features the South Island's only kiwi house (open daily except Christmas Day, 10–5).

PRIVATE GARDENS

With the help of the Canterbury Information Centre, the prize-winning garden streets of the city can be seen. This is a highly recommended activity for visitors to a city so dedicated to horticulture and history. The information centre is at 75 Worcester Street (open daily except Christmas Day, Monday to Friday, 8.30–5; weekend 9–4).

RICCARTON BUSH

Constrasting with the **BOTANIC GARDENS** and **HAGLEY PARK**, a little of pre-Adamite Christchurch remains intact here, in a fragment of the kahikatea forest that once fringed the bare city site. William and John Deans were the earliest Europeans to settle on the Canterbury Plains, preceding the first four ships by almost a decade. Their first cottage (1844) survives as a small museum. Near it stands Riccarton House (started in 1856), their second, more substantial dwelling (entrance in Kauri Road; grounds open daily).

SIGN OF THE TAKAHE

This rather extraordinary Gothic building in Hackthorne Road, above the city, dates not from the city's colonial beginnings, but from 1949. It was the dream of Harry Ell, a politician who fought to preserve the **PORT HILLS** from further development, and hoped to set them off with a series of distinctive roadhouses. Ell, who had never seen England nor a genuine medieval building, began building his folly in 1918 in the image of a fantasised motherland. It was still unfinished on his death in 1934. The Christchurch City Council eventually completed it. Today it serves as an elegant restaurant, with views of the city, of the plains beyond and of the Southern Alps in the distance.

BACKDROP TO A CITY

The Port Hills provide a dramatic frame to the city of Christchurch, a vantage point and playground for its citizens, and a boundary between Christchurch and Lyttelton

The volcanic Port Hills, once rugged in outline, now have contours softened by erosion

The Summit Road traverses the high wall of the Port Hills, from Godley Head (at the northern entrance of Lyttelton Harbour) to Gebbies Pass. It is now possible to cross the hills at several points, but the first Canterbury Association settlers to arrive in the flooded volcano crater which is now Lyttelton Harbour, found their way to the plains barred by the ancient rim of the volcano. This ridge we now know as the Port Hills, and the only route over it was by the Bridle Path, a precipitous track one settler appropriately named the 'Emigrant's Treadmill'. The Evans Pass route from Sumner, opened in 1857, was the first road to ease matters, although its notorious zig-zags were to remain unimproved until 1914. In 1867, the railway tunnel from Heathcote to Lyttelton was built, giving Christchurch easy access to a sea port for the first time. The Port Hills seldom rise over five hundred metres, but the tangled ridges and gullies make for busy driving along the Summit Road, and energetic walking along the many tracks. One compensation is the breathtaking views of city, sea, harbour and plain, and the distant panorama of the Southern Alps. Several species of native ferns and flowers, some quite rare, can be identified in the area, while there is archaeological evidence of Maori occupation.

For the preservation of the Port Hills, a debt of gratitude is owed to Harry Ell (1863-1934). As a member of parliament, Ell introduced the Scenery Preservation Bill of 1908, and by a combination of persuasion, argument, bullying, financial risk and frequent bending of rules, he saved the hills. He inspired the scenic Summit Road, the reserves, walking tracks and the rest houses that provide access and amenities for the citizens of Christchurch and other visitors.

The Sign of the Takahe in Cashmere has fine views of the plains and Southern Alps. Another roadhouse planned by Harry Ell, the more modest Sign of the Kiwi, is on the Summit Road

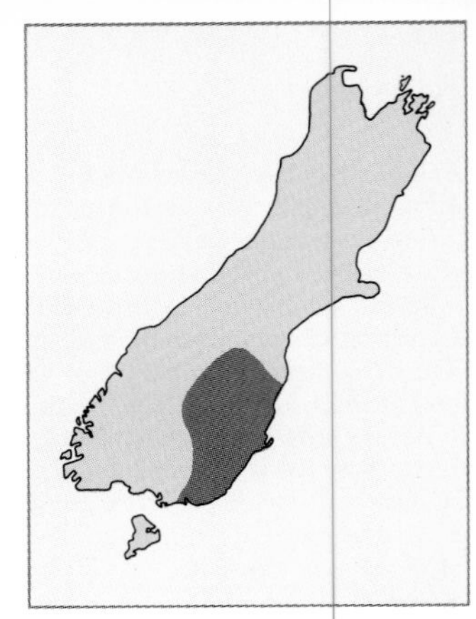

Robust Otago, roughly the size of Switzerland and seldom less spectacular, can be considered as two regions. Coastal Otago is moist, green, often misty, and its population is seeded evenly along its shores. Inland Otago is sunny, dry, brown and sparsely populated. For the southbound traveller following the coast, Otago begins at the broad Waitaki River and ends in the forested enclave called the Catlins. The large towns of Oamaru and Balclutha anchor the region's coastal corners, with the city of Dunedin set symmetrically between them. To the west Otago takes in high alps and long lakes. Most of the region is dominated by the great fragmented schist plateau of Central Otago, rising six hundred metres and more above the coast, in places sometimes only a few kilometres from the sea. Cutting deep gorges through almost the entire width of the plateau is the tumultuous Clutha, New Zealand's largest river in volume.

MOUNTAINS, LAKES AND GLACIERS

Although volcanic activity in Tertiary times shaped the Otago Peninsula, and sedimentary rock risen from the Pacific seabed constitutes the greater part of the coast, most of Otago was formed during the ice ages. The mica schist of its vast heart is a metamorphosed rock that erodes into fine clay particles and thin plates. Grinding glaciers have given hills a smooth, round appearance. Mantled thinly with tussock, their elemental character is powerfully depicted in the paintings of Otago-bred artist Colin McCahon, often as a backdrop to Biblical scenes. Bulldozing ice and morainic debris dumped in its wake have formed the three long, deep and narrow lakes of Hawea, Wanaka and Wakatipu, under mountains similarly sculpted by glaciers. Mount Aspiring and Mount Earnslaw are Otago's highest peaks, but its most striking range is Queenstown's The Remarkables, rising to nearly two and half thousand metres.

The climates of the two regions contrast sharply. Coastal Otago can be mild and is often moist, like many New Zealand maritime districts, but to the north droughts have been long and devastating. Inland, summer temperatures are the highest in New Zealand, but winters are among the country's frostiest. Sheltering mountains result in low rainfall.

Moa-hunting Polynesians, Otago's first inhabitants, have left little to tell us of their lives and beliefs: midden, bones, fish hooks, stone tools, and a few cave paintings whose religious meaning has been lost. A fragment or two of folklore survive in classic Maori tradition. One such myth tells of a tribe of demonic giants called the Kahui Tipua, who controlled the interior, disguising themselves as rocks and mountains.

We do know, however, what nourished Otago's original colonists, for archaeologists have located more than a hundred of their moa butcheries. With no apparent thought of conservation, thousands of hectares of forest were set aflame to smoke out the giant birds. In the process, lasting damage may have been done to congenial coastal microclimates where the kumara once flourished. Fires raged inland, up river valleys and into the alps. Hills were eroded and rivers flooded. Other plundered birds such as the swan became rare and finally extinct, too. Human beings, however, plainly prospered for a time. Evidence suggests that after AD 1100 the Otago coast was more densely settled than any other part of New Zealand. At its peak, the population may have been as high as eight thousand. At some point – certainly after the extinction of the moa and possibly as a result of general cooling of the Otago climate, which made the kumara difficult to cultivate – there seems to have been a drift north from the depleted region. Fish, seals and the roots of the cabbage tree sustained those who remained. When the first Europeans arrived, the Maori population was thin.

Oral tradition names a tribe called the Waitaha – presumably the original moa-hunters – as Otago's first inhabitants, who were overcome by the Ngati Mamoe from the north, perhaps towards the end of the fifteenth century. The motive for conquest was probably greenstone – *pounamu* or jade – which had been discovered in Otago's interior near Lake Wakatipu. This coveted treasure certainly sparked off the last and even more lethal thrust from the north, that of the Ngai Tahu tribe. Large, permanent villages dedicated to the winning and working of greenstone grew on the Otago coast. Heroic expeditions hauled it three hundred kilometres from the mountains. Craftsmen fashioned it into tribal requirements, and there was a vigorous trade with the north. Another resource was the muttonbird, or sooty shearwater, which had become a salty substitute for the extinct moa.

Cook made no contact with Otago Maori on his pioneering voyages into the South Pacific. Passing in 1770, he observed 'green and woody' land, but no inhabitants. Sydney-based sealers and roving whalers were the first to put ashore in the early nineteenth century. By the eighteen-thirties there were fourteen whaling stations along the coasts of Otago and neighbouring Southland. Some whalers grew wheat and potatoes for their own use, and for the Sydney market. Otago Maori, on the whole, welcomed the rough and often brutal visitors. For one thing, they brought the muskets which the Ngai Tahu needed to repel the raids of Te Rauparaha from the north. The Ngai Tahu, however, were ambushed by a more insidious enemy: measles. Some communities virtually vanished. Then whalers' rum took a toll of the survivors. It was an enfeebled tribe which began selling off land to European arrivals.

Otago's first notable European citizen was Johnny Jones, who took over a whaling station in 1838 on the Waikouaiti estuary near present-day Karitane. He persuaded Otago Maori to accept him as a chief and claimed two million acres of their land. Jones brought in settlers, including a missionary and a doctor, raised grain to sell to Sydney, and turned cattle and sheep loose on his coastal acres. In March 1848 he found a market nearer to hand, when some three hundred Scots colonists arrived at the head of Otago Harbour. The settlement of Dunedin was founded.

THE INTERIOR YIELDS ITS WEALTH

The potential of the fertile alluvial Taieri Plain, just to the south-west of Dunedin, was soon recognised. Draining and reclaiming began, and farms grew. In the eighteen-fifties, Dunedin's founders pushed further inland to look for grazing land. On the great plateau of the interior they found terrain with few comforts, but were undeterred. By 1860 most of the useful land to the east of the South Island's mountain spine had been taken, and Otago was grazing nearly three hundred thousand sheep on a hundred and twelve runs. Those flocks, hired or bought from Johnny Jones, or driven across mountain passes from Nelson and Marlborough to the north, brought

GOLDEN LAND OF GRANDEUR

quick fortunes and were the forerunners of more than nine million sheep roaming Otago today.

A year later Otago's interior began to surrender even larger fortunes. On May 23, 1861, Gabriel Read saw gold shimmer in his pan while prospecting along the Tuapeka River, just outside present-day Lawrence (see page 307). Within weeks the rush to the wintry Tuapeka fields had begun. Dunedin's civic leaders despaired as they witnessed the disappearance of their labour force and widespread disrespect for the sabbath. In July, gold was discovered at nearby Waitahuna, and by September there were six thousand men digging. Eight ships brought veterans of Australia's Victorian fields. Braving either blizzards or blistering sun, they pushed further inland and made even richer strikes. Wagons, bullock trains, bar girls, bushrangers and merchants followed. A find at the confluence of the Kawarau and Clutha Rivers in the winter of 1862 led to the disembarkation of some three thousand Australian miners at Dunedin within two days. In March 1863 there were no less than fourteen thousand arrivals.

TOWNS APPEAR OVERNIGHT

About forty tonnes of gold were taken from Otago in two years. The region's initial population of twelve thousand tripled and quadrupled, finally soaring past fifty thousand. Otago's despised desert-like terrain had suddenly made the region the richest in the country. In 1863 the increasingly affluent runholders of Otago slew a hundred and thirty-five thousand sheep for meat to keep diggers alive. Towns of cob, sod and canvas appeared almost overnight, with saloons, concert halls, brothels and banks. Drunken riots and bloodshed were frequent, but most crime went undetected, unless bodies were dragged from rivers. Others perished in floods, suffocated under avalanches or froze to death on lonely hillsides. Finally the great Otago gold rush spent itself on the shores of Lake Wakatipu, where barren mountains loomed on the horizon. Thereafter, although some claims remained profitable and quartz mines were opened, it was mostly a matter of picking over the leavings. Ambitious diggers departed for Westland's fresh fields on the far side of the alps and left migrant Chinese to rework abandoned claims.

Lake Wakatipu, despite tourist incursion, remains the jewel in the crown of Central Otago. Walter Peak rises majestically in the distance

Lindis Pass, the northern gateway to Central Otago, is bare, lonely country, far from settlements. Erosion-scarred mountains and tussocky valleys are the essence of the pass

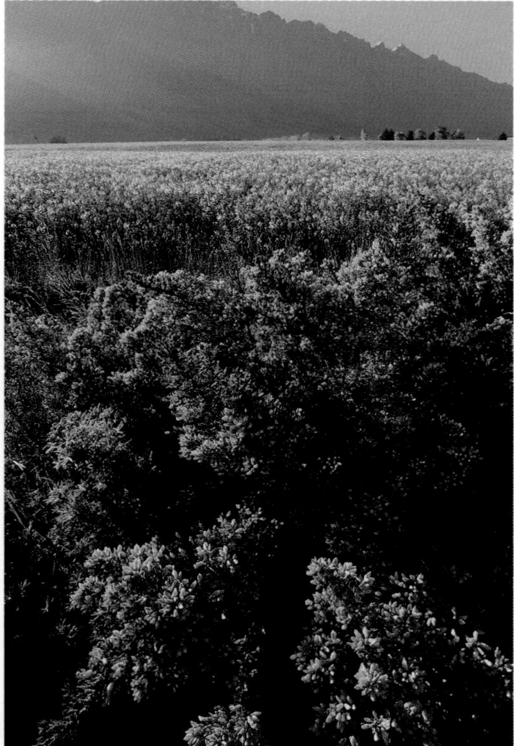

Flowers in bloom under the Remarkables. Much of harsh Central Otago has been softened by exotic plants

By 1871 Otago had some seventy thousand people, close to a quarter of the white population of New Zealand, including three thousand persistent miners. British novelist Anthony Trollope recorded the growth of Otago's towns when he journeyed through the goldfields in 1872. Despite being struck by winter sleet and snow, he shrewdly predicted that it would not be long before the Otago interior would be famed for its magnificent scenery.

OTAGO'S SOUTH SEA BUBBLE

Gold had a gleaming postscript in the last decade of the nineteenth century. Dredging Otago's rivers at first produced an impressive harvest. By 1900, at the height of this second rush, a hundred and eighty-seven immense dredges were working riverbeds and three hundred companies had been floated. When most of these sank soon afterwards, enriched confidence men caught the next boat out and impoverished investors lamented 'Otago's South Sea Bubble'. The last of the dredges ground on until the nineteen-sixties. Riverbanks were left scarred by the ramparts of sterile tailings that still characterise the region's interior. Other goldfield towns became firmly established, with hospitals, schools, lodges and modest churches. Diggers' water-races were converted into irrigation systems. Orchards and gardens began to green the barren valleys.

The Totara Estate Centennial Park – an evocative rural complex, now restored, that commemorates the founding of the frozen meat trade with Britain in the eighteen-eighties

A typical landscape in North Otago – thinly populated and often empty of all but scattered flocks of sheep

Fertile coastal Otago had fewer shifts of fortune than Central. Such communities as Oamaru, Palmerston, Milton and Balclutha grew fast to supply food to the goldfields of Otago and Westland, and to the expanding and flourishing city of Dunedin. As their flocks increased, pastoralists became as much concerned with the price of wool as the value of mutton. When New Zealand's frozen meat trade with Britain was inaugurated in the eighteen-eighties, they had another bonanza. But by then an unforeseen enemy, the rabbit, brought bankruptcy to some. Others, feeling a cold political wind, subdivided their properties or sold out to the government. Orchards and gardens run by small farmers, often former farmhands, became more numerous.

Today's Otago is still largely the tapestry stitched in the decade following Gabriel Read's discovery of gold in 1861. Inland, hydro-electric schemes have given the landscape new shape. Fast roads follow the old wagon trails into the mountains. For the most part, history has sweetened rather than soured the land. In autumn, poplar and willow trees colour formerly treeless terrain. Many tiny old goldfield towns retain a wistful period atmosphere. Queenstown, once a lazy lakeside village under tall peaks, is now a cosmopolitan tourist resort. In winter its snowfields draw tens of thousands of skiers, many from overseas. Its serene alpine situation brings just as many sightseers when the weather warms. The high-rise hotels on its shore, the motels, chalets and restaurants fail to diminish its magnificent setting. Dunedin may have dwindled in its importance to the nation's economy, but Queenstown now wins more revenue from Otago than the gold-diggers ever knew. Everywhere, from smoky surf to icy summit, Otago is a region in the grand manner. Once known, even on casual aquaintance, it remains indelible in the memory.

GOLD TOWNS GALORE

The towns in the interior of Otago grew rapidly in one impetuous decade, as the pitiless landscape surrendered its treasure

When pious Presbyterians first settled on Otago Harbour and founded Dunedin, they felt at home among hills as gentle, green and misty as the Scottish Highlands. They saw no virtue in hurtling inland. In summer, the centre of Otago was as dry and hot as an African desert; in winter as white as Siberian valleys. Moulded by mighty glaciers, with canyons cut by thawed ice, this stark plateau covering nearly twenty-five thousand square kilometres was not for faint-hearted pioneers. Surveyors who brushed with it returned in exhaustion to the comforts of the coast.

Yet the Biblical desolation of Otago's great fragmented schist plateau, rising six hundred metres and more above sea level and finally rearing towards mountains of two to three thousand metres, gripped the European imagination. Vincent Pyke, the early Otago explorer and author, was awed by 'its huge unshapely masses of rock – weather-beaten . . . blackened and seamed and scarred by I know not how many centuries of conflict with the elements'. A century later, J.B. Priestley marvelled at a landscape that 'makes the American South-West seem like tuppence' and at 'those sinister Central Otago mountains'. It was between those menacing mountains that aspirant pastoralists, inspired by the wealth of Marlborough wool-growers, squeezed their hungry flocks during the eighteen-fifties, finally to turn them loose on the tussock of the interior.

Stories of gold-rush riches from California and then Australia led to belief that Central Otago held similar potential. Dunedin's civic leaders did

Above: *A stark view of the Lindis Pass – mountains eroded by snow, wind and rain, and with very little vegetation*
Below: *There are numerous historic sites, memorials and relics of the goldmining era along the Shotover valley*

their utmost to dampen speculation. Gabriel Read's discovery of gold on the Tuapeka River in May 1861 had an electrifying effect on the still tiny coastal communities of Otago and especially on the then almost unpopulated interior. Towns emptied and the hinterland filled. In one impetuous decade Central Otago was transformed utterly. Today, still colourful towns – with facades faded here, recently refreshed there – remain where the gold rush once stormed through. Elsewhere sheep graze and orchards rustle around graveyards, roofless ruins, old water-races and mountains of rubble.

Read's find – and soon others near by – established Lawrence, the first goldtown, on untypically soft terrain at the entrance to Gabriels Gully, where the pastures of coastal Otago now finger inland. In this district the gold used to come in so fast that a bank once had to print its own money. A shepherd's wife, digging with no more than a kitchen knife, established a family fortune. For the early residents of Lawrence, calico, canvas, packing cases, sods and saplings served to keep out the weather. Solid buildings were erected only after alluvial hysteria had travelled on into the hard schist heart of Otago. As people settled down to the more demanding task of quarrying quartz reefs, two-storey banks and commercial buildings rose. Today the town is still much as it was then, with churches, villas, cottages and impressively large government buildings from the nineteenth century.

Lawrence was the gateway to greater riches. Glaciers, grinding down mother lodes in the high country, had seeded the bright metal throughout Otago's interior. A year after Read's strike, American Horatio Hartley and Irishman Christopher Reilly, who were following the Clutha River, pushed ahead of their fellow prospectors into harsh territory, which none but surveyor and sheepman had seen. With bare hands – their goldpan lost – and a broken shovel, they took over thirty kilograms of gold from riverbank beaches in bitter winter weather.

Thousands of optimistic diggers stormed the interior. One goldfield after another was located, but few of the newcomers were fitted out for their fearful task. To get at Otago's gold, they had to gamble their lives against a pitiless landscape. There was little fuel to warm them, no food to sustain them. Supplies were slow following. The territory was trackless and the climate murderous. Summer heat maddened as frosty valleys became furnaces. Winter cold drove some to suicide. In the heavy snows of 1863, up the Old Man Range, starving diggers tried to tramp from their claims towards food and warmth. Their bones and relics are still sometimes found on the heights. No one could number those who perished. Today a roadside memorial marks the common grave of the men whose remains were recovered.

Deserted goldtowns have a compelling period atmosphere **Left:** *Crumbled walls near Bendigo, where miners worked the quartz reefs* **Above, top:** *Ruined interior of the old bakehouse at Matakanui, originally named Tinkers* **Above:** *Skippers, site of a vanished Shotover settlement*

At the height of the goldrush period there was quite a fleet of boats on Lake Wakatipu; today only the stately Earnslaw *steams in and out of Queenstown with tourists*

At Horseshoe Bend there is another equally poignant memorial. In 1865 digger William Rigney discovered a shivering dog beside the body of a handsome young stranger who had succumbed to the cold. When he buried the unknown man, Rigney burned these words on a black pine slab: 'Somebody's Darling Lies Buried Here'. It became an eloquent memorial to all those unsung lives lost in the Otago interior. When Rigney himself died half a century later, he was interred at his own request next to the young man's grave. His headstone is engraved: 'Here lies the body of William Rigney, the man who buried "Somebody's Darling" '

DURABLE CLYDE AND LOST CROMWELL

Clyde was the next major settlement to rise on the diggers' route to the interior of Otago. It was a township with more gold than timber. Wood was so scarce at first that the theft of a privy door set off a manhunt. A baby's cradle changed hands for as much as five pounds, and was next seen as a miner's cradle in use on the riverside. As the administrative centre for the Dunstan goldfield, Clyde grew durably from stone, with a courthouse and school, cottages, stables, a town hall, inns and an athenaeum. When alluvial wealth waned, dredging of the Clutha River waxed, and Clyde remained a substantial community. Today, with next to no embellishment, no spurious grooming for tourist traffic, it remains one of Otago's most evocative small towns.

The next town to grow was Cromwell, beyond the great gorge where Hartley and Reilly made their strike. It was named after the ruthless conqueror of Ireland to hex Irish Catholic diggers, or so it was said. Cromwell has survived twelve decades on its picturesque site above the Clutha River but its central business area has been demolished and has been drowned by a vast hydro-electric scheme in 1989. A new and characterless community has developed to house and serve the new exploiters of Central Otago. But the quiet old Cromwell cemetery remains eloquent, with headstones of hexed Irishmen, and desperate diggers from Denmark to China.

Rock outcrop near Alexandra, early gold prospecting country

In late 1862, a veteran of the Californian and Victorian rushes named William Fox was furtively working a field up an obscure gorge on the Arrow River. Suspicious diggers tracked him down and were followed by hundreds more. A boisterous canvastown billowed suddenly and became Arrowtown. Soon clad in stone and wood, it was the roughest and toughest of old Otago's goldtowns, with billiard halls, brothels, grog-shops and gambling dens. The buccaneering Bully Hayes – notorious throughout the South Pacific – rode high here for a time. Law and order, first appearing as a revolver in a mounted policeman's fist, soon prevailed. Arrowtown became another goldfield administrative centre – with a sturdy prison. Under gaunt and often snow-whitened peaks, lapped by icy water, Arrowtown is the quintessential alpine goldtown. Upriver at Macetown, a few ruins are left of the homes in which quartz miners lived until well into the twentieth century. Snowbound much of the winter, they had a long and hazardous trip down to Arrowtown when the thaw came.

At one time gold dominated the activities of the Roxburgh district; today it is sheepfarming, coalmining, hydro-electric power and, especially, the cultivation of fruit

Others survived even more soul-chilling sites, such as those up in the infamous Skippers Gorge at Maori Point where, at the end of 1862, two Maori prospectors named Dan Erihana and Hakaraia Haeroa spied flecks of riverside gold. They dug out eleven kilos in a day. A small army of men followed them soon afterwards. The Maoris' alluvial find had been a fluke. Most of the gold was mother lode, trapped in mountain quartz, which was difficult to mine. Townships of sod and canvas grew, complete with butchers, bakers and banks. Today the terrifying old wagon road into the canyon swivels around precipices and peaks and past the ruins of those forgotten communities. As always in Otago, gravestones record the past most eloquently, with inscriptions telling of death by rock-fall, cave-in and drowning.

The White Horse Hotel (1864) at Becks, now in disrepair

As diggers pushed further inland and worked claims on the Shotover River in the early eighteen-sixties, Queenstown grew from the simple headquarters of a sheep run to become a depot serving the new goldfields. Its superb alpine setting on the shore of Lake Wakatipu ensured that it would outlast the gold rushes. The visitor now has to hunt long and hard for Queenstown's beginnings. Today, tourist vessels, jet boats and launches ply the lake, and a gondola takes visitors high above the town along an aerial cableway. Luxury hotels, restaurants and boutiques have largely banished the last of the brawny, bawdy nineteenth-century town. But the mountains soaring from the lakeside are the same, and it was in their shadow that the flame of the Otago gold rushes began to flicker low. Disappointed diggers turned elsewhere in Otago. In 1863 strikes were made at such sites as Naseby, Ophir and St Bathans. All three communities, set in a sun-bleached landscape, have gently outlasted the lust for gold that brought them into being.

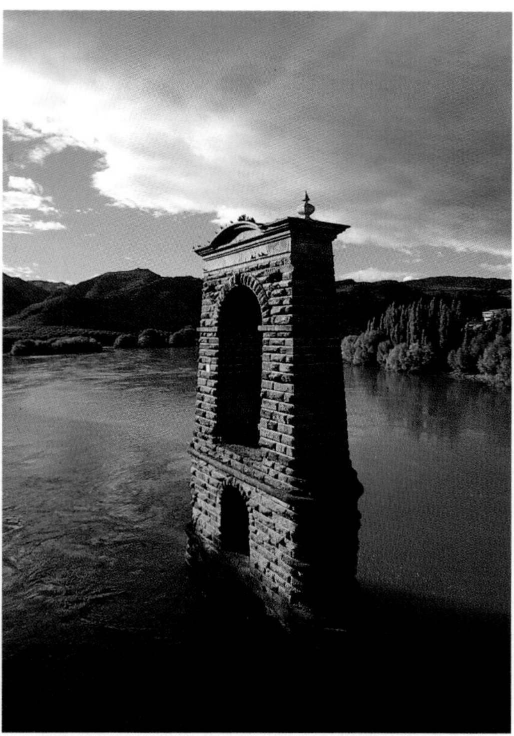

The substantial stone piers are all that remain of the 1882 suspension bridge that crossed the Clutha at Alexandra

By the middle of the eighteen-sixties, the winning of gold had become daily grind for those who had not moved on to Westland. The romance was gone, and with it the breathtaking riches. Many communities, after a decade or two more, expired quietly. Among them is a trio of lonely but once busy townships that are now merely marked Bendigo on the map. Based on the mining of quartz reefs, Bendigo, Logantown and Welshtown are set on successive levels above the Clutha River and on the slopes of the Dunstan Mountains. The surrounding terrain is laced with mine shafts. A few sad fruit trees and a pine or poplar or two suggest lives looking for permanence among Otago's bleak tussock. In the distance the snowfields of Mount Aspiring glimmer. The ruins, with just a few last stone cottage walls left standing, now melt into the debris discarded by the ice-age glaciers which gave Central its powerful character and stocked it with wealth. Here, as nowhere else in Otago, the region's human and natural history seem one.

The Vulcan Hotel, St Bathans, at one time one of thirteen

OLD OAMARU

A rare collection of fine colonial buildings fashioned from white limestone has turned this small township into a national treasure

Much of the North Otago town of Oamaru was built during a brief, rurally based bonanza that promised more than it delivered. In expectation of further affluence, the townsfolk of the mid-nineteenth century turned adventurous architects loose on the distinctive creamy limestone of their district, the building material now nationally known as Oamaru stone. The result was, and is, a townscape that towers over a modest community with a present-day population of fewer than fifteen thousand. One chronicler observed that the ambitious citizens of Oamaru would 'move Heaven and Earth to make Thames Street the modern Athens of the South'. Early Oamaru may have lacked philosophers and playwrights, but its huge banks gleamed like Greek temples.

In its heyday, Oamaru elegantly married pioneer optimism and capitalist enterprise in a neoclassical and Gothic Revival. The old mercantile heart of the town, in and around Tyne Street, may well make the visitor 'shiver with a sense of yesterdays', as it does the well-known Oamaru-raised novelist, Janet Frame. The unpopularity of its wreck-strewn port and the arrival of lean years left Oamaru, so it was said, 'the best built and most mortgaged town in Australasia'. It also left a precious precinct of colonial New Zealand intact for the twentieth century. Although some are abandoned and neglected, few of Oamaru's fine buildings have been levelled by developers. Harbour Street, once the principal thoroughfare, has the character of an empty film set waiting for costumed actors to appear and a director to call for action. In fact, in recent years, it has more than once been favoured by film-makers looking for authentic period flavour. No less than Dunedin, old Oamaru can now be seen as a national treasure.

St Patrick's Basilica was designed by F.W. Petre ('Lord Concrete'); the twin cupolas echo the sanctuary dome behind

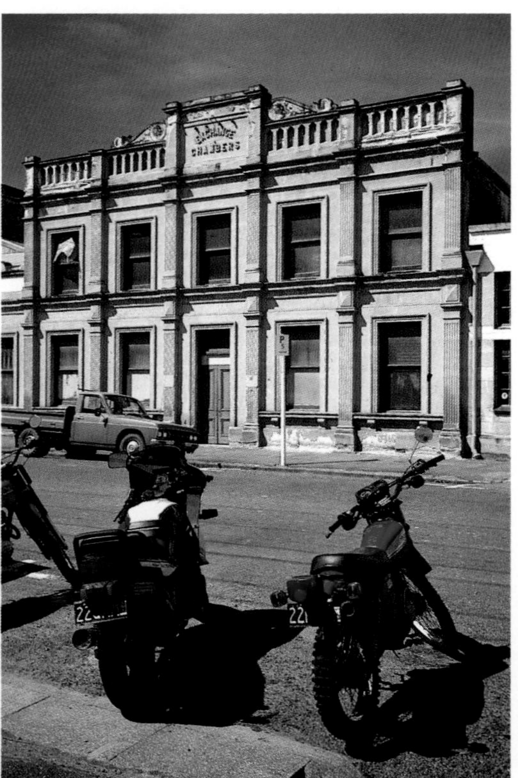

Tyne Street, once the mercantile centre – dubbed 'Wall Street' in good times and 'Mortgage Alley' during slumps

The buildings along Harbour Street, once Oamaru's main thoroughfare, are now used principally as warehouses

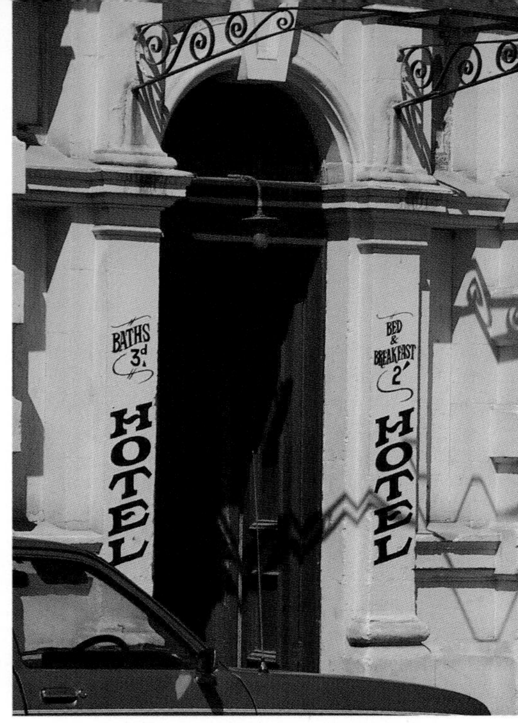

Architectural details **Far left***: Entrance to the now disused Criterion Hotel* **Left***: Warehouse window in Harbour Street*

Example of classical architecture in Thames Street: the 1882 Athenaeum, which now houses the North Otago Museum

Oamaru began humbly, in 1853, with a run-holder's hut of flax stalks and clay. As runs were taken up and more colonists arrived, limestone was used only for the chimneys of wooden dwellings. But the white stone was cheap, easily worked with a carpenter's saw and so plentiful that the area was at first called Whiterock. More and more quarries were opened. As the need for public buildings and large business houses arose, Dunedin architects were brought north. One notable trio of buildings was straightforwardly classical in inspiration: the National Bank (1870) and the adjoining Bank of New South Wales (1884), both designed by Robert Lawson; and the splendid courthouse (1883), designed by Thomas Forrester, a Scottish artisan turned architect who at one time was Lawson's employee. Elsewhere the Gothic style was lavishly adopted. Merchants vied for attention with Italianate facades festooned with urns, scrolls and wreaths, and arched windows hinted of Venice.

The former Bank of New South Wales in Thames Street, next to the equally fine National Bank, is now an art gallery

The most impressive of the classical buildings in Thames Street – and Oamaru's pride – is the Courthouse (1883)

Nowhere else in New Zealand was a local building material so comprehensively and liberally used. Visiting in 1878, New Zealand Premier Sir George Grey saw a town 'rising in stone of the utmost brilliance, of a kind I have never seen before'. Indeed, that brilliance was rarely to be seen elsewhere. Although Oamaru stone was widely used in New Zealand, even in Australia, it seldom travelled well. In the atmospheric conditions of large modern cities, it has lost its lustre, and its porous nature has also made it a poor bet for posterity in more moist climates. But on its warm, dry native terrain, in Oamaru's unpolluted atmosphere, the limestone of North Otago still shimmers in a remarkable assembly of majestic colonial buildings.

THE QUIET OF THE CATLINS

This wooded, wild coastal corner of Otago is the most unsung of South Island regions

The Catlins region fails to conform to conventional expectations of southern scenery. There are no tall alps, no deep fiords, nor are there any ruins left by gold-seekers or elegant homesteads built by sheepmen. The contrast between this moist, leafy hill country and Otago's dry, flinty interior is immense. Waves beat up deserted beaches of golden sand and batter dramatic headlands. Its population is now virtually non-existent, and there are no resorts. Much of it is as wild as it was when the first Maori saw it, and the rest is for the most part reverting to wilderness. In history and character the region seems to belong more to New Zealand's north than to the south. Even its name, permanently misspelled on the map, suggests a certain indifference to the area, and something of its recent neglect. A whaling captain named Edward Cattlin left most of his surname on this peaceful pocket of Otago in 1840, when he sailed cautiously upriver and saw potentially lucrative and easily accessible forest. He promptly tried to purchase all of it – about two hundred and fifty thousand hectares – for cash and muskets to the value of one hundred pounds. (At that time local Maori were disposed to sell off land cheaply to act as a buffer between themselves and the raiding tribes from the north.) The colony's new government determined that it was far from a fair deal. In 1873, seventeen years after Cattlin's death, his descendants were awarded less than one hundred hectares by way of consolation.

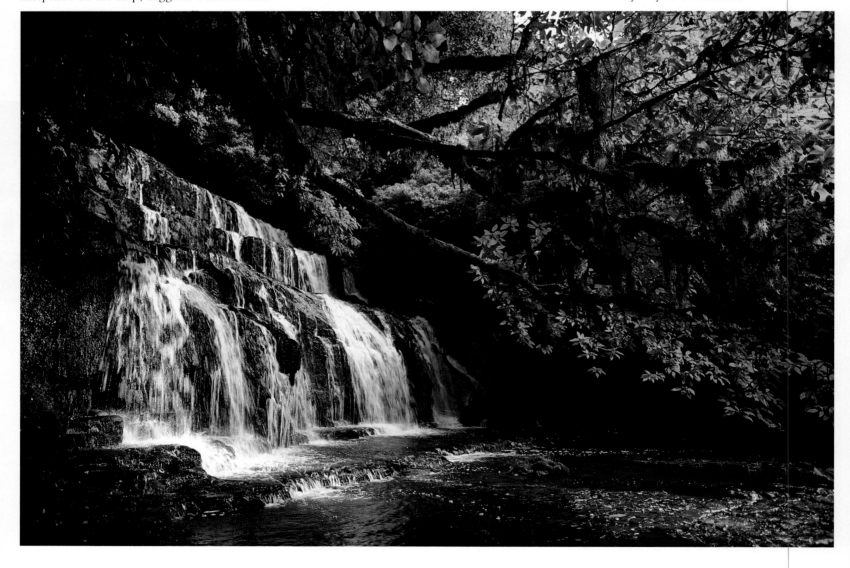

Above: *Seascape at Kaka Point, a popular holiday resort*
Below: *The Purakaunui Falls, surrounded by a canopy of beech trees, cascade over a series of broad terraces*

For two decades after Cattlin's reconnaissance the territory remained unexplored. A German geologist who ventured into its forests in the eighteen-fifties was never seen again. The region proved more rewarding for those who came later. It had the most abundant forest on the east coast of the South Island. After observing timber through his telescope, a runholder established the first sawmill here in the eighteen-sixties. Soon there were up to thirty workers and a shipyard. Ships took aboard timber at Hinahina, where the Catlins River broadens into a salty lake. The South Island's busiest timber port, it was also the stormiest – six vessels or more were lost at sea. A railway inched into the Catlins to carry out the harvest. Catlins rimu went into the homes of fast-growing Dunedin, where native wood was scarce.

As forest fell, settlers moved into the valleys and established small farms. Based on blocks of a hundred acres (forty hectares), their primitive settlements – where landowners also laboured on roads and railways – failed to prosper. Today a few surviving daffodils and blossoming fruit trees sweeten the bleak sites of their struggle with the bush and the poor soil. Most sawmillers and settlers left, and the railway was closed in 1971.

Catlins Lake, at the estuary of the Catlins River, is tidal; it is a popular venue for swimming and yachting

Owaka, with only four hundred people, is the only remaining community of any size, retaining a remote frontier character. The town now stands at the entrance to the serene, surf-washed Catlins Forest Park, which provides some of New Zealand's finest forest walking, especially among the mossy, fern-filmed trees crowding the banks of the Catlins River. A great forest of southern rata and kaikawaka crowns the hills. The rata trees often spill down to sea level and, in the short but vivid Catlins summer, light the shore with scarlet blossom, much like the northern pohutukawa. Waterfalls splash and crash and native birds sing in this primeval pocket of New Zealand.

Some think the Maori may have stalked the last moa in the Catlins. Their shellfish middens tell of mostly temporary settlements. Tribesmen camped here to fell totara trees and hollow out canoes. They needed all their guile as navigators to master the Catlins coast. The sea here has always been merciless to mediocre mariners, as the wrecks of later European vessels testify. The name Cannibal Bay is a reminder of the marauding Te Rauparaha's raid furthest south in the eighteen-thirties.

Although a rare species, the yellow-eyed penguin can be seen all year round near the mouth of the Catlins River

The Catlins region remains richer in natural history than human. The protected yellow-eyed penguin breeds in the bush behind the shore. Since the nineteen-fifties, it has extended its range beyond the Catlins northwards towards Banks Peninsula. Seals are recolonising headlands from which hit-and-run sealers once hunted them.

People are few along this coast of coves, caves, cliffs and crescents of sand – even in summer. New Zealand has no more beautiful backwater. Lovers of the calm Catlins mostly wish the unique region to remain unknown and unpopulated.

MOUNT ASPIRING'S VAST PARK

Sometimes called 'the Matterhorn of New Zealand', this majestic mountain towers above the rugged national park that shares its name

Approaching Mount Aspiring National Park by road from the east, Lake Wanaka beyond Glendhu Bay mirrors the mountainous landscape; thrilling glimpses of Mount Aspiring can occasionally be caught in the distance

Mount Aspiring, Otago's mighty north-west cornerstone, is where the region is closest to the sky, rising more than three thousand metres above sea level. The rushing waters of the rugged park surrounding it fill two of Otago's resplendent trio of lakes – Wanaka and Wakatipu – and finally feed the rumbling Kawarau and Clutha Rivers. To the north, the park's resident forest flows into the valleys of Westland; to the south the park trickles richly towards the arid Otago interior, greening the head of Lake Wakatipu.

Mount Aspiring National Park contains a variety of landforms left by the last ice age, with hanging valleys, moraines, lake basins, and some one hundred glaciers of varying sizes. The wildest parts are virtually impenetrable. A three-man prospecting party that launched recklessly into its more remote reaches in the eighteen-sixties was condemned to a diet of rats and fern roots, battered by blizzards and baffled by 'mountains of snow as far as we could see'. Westland explorer Charles Douglas, who later located four mountain passes, dismissed them as fit for none but 'an Alpine Explorer or other Lunatic'.

Shapely Mount Aspiring, on the other hand, has never been short of suitors. The Maori called the peak *Tititea*, 'the upright glistening one', which suggests respect. So does its English name, bestowed by the gifted Otago surveyor, John Turnbull Thomson, when he first saw it from

Stormy view from Falls Hut on the Routeburn Track, which traverses Mount Aspiring and Fiordland National Parks

Above: *Driving sheep on a station between Lake Wanaka and the eastern boundary of Mount Aspiring National Park*
Below: *Typical vegetation in the area is broom, which in spring covers vast tracts with its golden-yellow flowers*

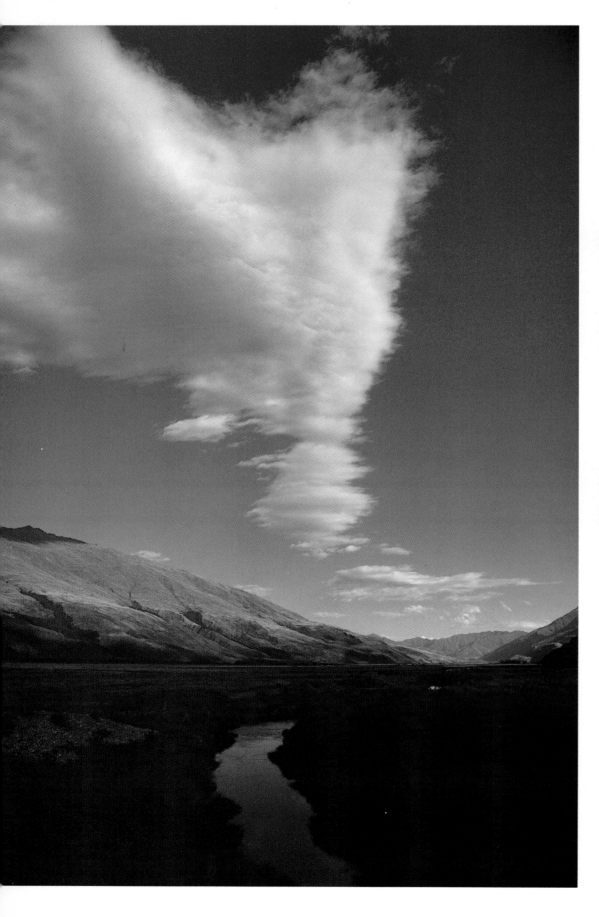

a distance in 1857. 'A glorious pyramid of ice and snow', he recorded. Map-maker James McKerrow, following Thomson in 1862, was even more overcome: 'Glacier Dome and Mount Aspiring, enthroned in perpetual ice, bid defiance to the sun and forbid the approach of the beholder, who is spellbound, impressed with awe and veneration at the stupendous forces of nature.'

Climbers from the beginning of the twentieth century have been less spellbound by Aspiring's scenic qualities than by the challenge of its steep ridges. The pioneering ascent was made in 1909.

Top: *Southern approach to the park along Dart River valley*
Above: *Mount Aspiring and nearby peaks from the south*

Sometimes called 'New Zealand's Matterhorn', the mountain has seen many failures and fatalities. Although Aspiring is the park's most majestic peak, many other notable mountains cluster about its summit including Castor, Alba, Pollux and Pickelhaube.

For those who wish simply to enjoy the park's powerful character rather than tackle its peaks, the Matukituki Valley is an enriching experience. The approach around the shores of Lake Wanaka is a visual feast in itself, with Aspiring beginning to gleam on the horizon, framed by the water-lapped willows of Glendhu Bay. Soon jagged ridges, bluffs and icefields loom above, and the Matukituki – the river Maori saw as 'the white destroyer' – rushes through the subalpine vegetation of the valley. When the winding road from Wanaka finally comes to an end, tracks continue up both branches of the river. Huts and grassy campsites are here for those who wish to linger and discover more of the Matukituki.

The easiest and most convenient access to the eastern boundary of the park is to follow the Matukituki Valley

PLACES OF INTEREST

ALEXANDRA
This is Central Otago's largest community, with 4700 people. Set under skeletal mountain ranges with distinctive names – the Old Man, the Old Woman and the Raggedy – its once barren landscape is now greened by orchards and irrigated gardens. Born of the 1860s gold rush, the town was named after Princess Alexandra of Denmark who in 1863 married Britain's Prince of Wales. Alexandra long played second fiddle to upriver **CLYDE**, and by the late 1860s it was a crumbling and emptying husk. But in the 1890s gold dredging repopulated the town. To feed the large labour force, imaginative settlers exploited the horticultural potential of the arid area, until then grazed sparsely by sheep. Miners' water rights were taken up by aspirant orchardists and Alexandra was soon blossoming.

Although Alexandra itself has retained little period atmosphere, it makes a comfortable base from which to visit many historic former goldtowns, such as Clyde, **MATAKANUI**, **OPHIR** and **ST BATHANS**. Surviving from the town's pioneer years are the piers of the suspension bridge that from 1882 served horse-drawn coaches travelling into Otago's interior. The Sir William Bodkin Museum (in Thomson Street) has interesting exhibits, particularly the relics of Chinese gold-diggers (open Monday to Friday, 2–4; other times by arrangement). In the Fruitlands area to the south, there are crumbling stone and earth cottages, hotels and stables. One of the stone buildings, meticulously restored, is Mitchells Cottage (1 kilometre up Symes Road), built by a Shetland Island family (open daily during summer).

WAKATIPU'S LEGEND

A Maori myth provides an explanation of a strange natural phenomenon

Lake Wakatipu's serene waters have a distinct rise and fall

Formed by a natural moraine dam in a glacial valley, Lake Wakatipu's curious, zig-zag shape gave rise to one of the South Island's most imaginative explanations of landforms. The Maori likened it to a resting body, with its head to the north, its knees bent at present-day Queenstown, and its feet to the south.

According to the legend, a giant-demon named Matau stole the daughter of a southern chief. The abduction was hindered by one of the powerful north-west winds that sweep down the Canterbury Plains and through Central Otago. Lying down to rest, Matau was discovered by the girl's tribe, who then set fire to him. Matau's body was consumed by the flames and a huge cavity was burned into the ground. Only his heart remained, still beating as the waters of nearby rivers began to pour into his outline and fill it.

Lake Wakatipu, like several large lakes, does in fact have something like a heartbeat. At five-minute intervals the level of the water rises and falls ten to twelve centimetres. The explanation of this phenomenon is not as romantic as the legend. Known as a seiche, it is the result of such influences as changes in atmospheric pressure caused by hot or cold air movements. The oscillations that result resemble a 'pulse', so that Matau's heart still seems to beat in Lake Wakatipu to this day.

ARROWTOWN
With a population of 700, this tiny former goldtown is now a popular, if commercialised, tourist centre. Old miners' cottages, the village gaol and other 19th-century buildings set amid aged sycamore trees are evocative of the district's past, which is also well presented in the town's museum. Under tall peaks and washed by the frosty waters of the Arrow River, Arrowtown began as the depot and rowdy rest station for 1500 miners after William Fox struck gold there in 1862. The bones of as many as 100, who were drowned in a torrential flood in 1863, now rest under the river's silt. Buccaneer and blackbirder Bully Hayes, like many other brawlers, roosted in Arrowtown in its riotous beginnings. With hired goldpans, visitors can still test William Fox's upriver claim – now marked by a cairn – for colour. There is a commercial excursion (or a day's hike) to the ruins of **MACETOWN**, quartz-mining township. The Lakes District Centennial Memorial Museum (open daily, 9–5; 10–4 in winter), partly housed in an old Bank of New Zealand building (1875), arranges access to the Arrowtown Gaol (1875). One of the row of privately-owned miners' cottages in Buckingham Street has been restored and refurnished in its original style (open to the public). Another cottage functions as a tearoom.

BALCLUTHA
Near the mouth of the Clutha River, 80 kilometres from Dunedin, this is Otago's southernmost town, with 4400 people. Land taken up here by Otago's colonists was fast dedicated to sheep farming, which still predominates in the area. A drive to Kaka Point and Nugget Point (known locally as 'the Nuggets') takes in Port Molyneux cemetery (19 kilometres), where there is a panoramic view of the Clutha River. Once a port, Port Molyneux was left high and dry when the Clutha changed its course after heavy flooding in 1878. The Nuggets are a striking collection of jagged islets where seals slumber and birds breed, among them gannets, shags and terns. The Catlins can be reached from Balclutha via **OWAKA**. On Highway 1, 12 kilometres towards Dunedin, is the Lovells Flat Sod Cottage, a pioneer dwelling restored and furnished to period (open daily).

BENDIGO
A rather spectral collection of gold-rush ruins, Bendigo is really three ghost towns: Bendigo, Logantown and Welshtown. Built on successive levels on the slopes of the Dunstan Mountains, they were for decades the location of one of Otago's few productive quartz-mining operations. Bendigo can be reached from **CROMWELL** via the **LINDIS PASS** road and Bendigo loop road (18 kilometres). The final uphill drive is difficult but rewarding. There are many mine shafts, some as deep as 170 metres.

Sun and shadow in the trees at Lake Hayes

CATLINS FOREST PARK
This lovely but little-known south-east coastal corner of the South Island, covers about 60 000 hectares. Although mostly trackless and relatively undeveloped, the park provides picnic places, campsites, nature trails and trout fishing. Instead of the drama of high mountains and fiords, this splendid stretch of wilderness offers the leafy, lonely serenity of its almost unpopulated coast, with golden sands, coves and caves. To the south of the park are the fossil-filled walls of Curio Bay. Access to the park is from Highway 1 or Highway 92. Full information can be obtained from the park headquarters and the museum established by the NZ Forest Service at **OWAKA**, or from the Southland end through the NZ Forest Service at Wyndham or Invercargill.

CLYDE
At the entrance to Cromwell Gorge, due to be inundated by a hydro-electric scheme in 1989, Clyde began soon after Horatio Hartley and Christopher Reilly struck gold on the banks of the nearby Clutha River in 1862. It became the administrative centre for the Dunstan fields, with banks, dance halls, and hundreds of diggers. Towards the end of the decade Frenchman Jean Feraud gave up the search for nuggets to demonstrate that with irrigation the landscape held more durable treasure. From his Monte Cristo farm he was soon selling grapes, peaches and apricots, and supplying distant Dunedin. With a present-day population of under 800, Clyde has retained its early character and should not be missed. The 1864 courthouse is now the Vincent County and Dunstan Goldfields Museum (open Tuesday to Sunday, 2–4). An old coaching inn, Dunstan House, still stands in the main street. The Athenaeum dates from 1874,

Sluicing diggers created a tortured landscape near Bannockburn; their huts are now in ruins

the town hall from 1868-69, and St Michael's Anglican Church from 1877. Olivers Courtyard and Restaurant is an imaginative and award-winning complex that makes the most of Clyde's 19th-century character. The Hartley Arms Hotel (*c.* 1865) is named after the American digger whose strike led to the growth of the township. Other historic buildings include a number of old stone cottages, and stone stables at the end of Naylor Street.

CORONET PEAK

New Zealand's premier skifield, attracting skiers from all around the Pacific basin. About 15 kilometres from QUEENSTOWN, with facilities and chairlift 1200 metres above sea level, Coronet Peak (1651 metres) is extraordinary for its year-round vistas of the treeless mountains and stark valleys of the Otago interior.

CROMWELL

Long the delight of photographers and postcard publishers, Cromwell's precarious cliffside commercial area was inundated in 1990 when the Clutha River was dammed, as part of a hydro-electric scheme, to form a 24 square kilometre lake. Cromwell's old-timers (fewer than 1000) were outnumbered when the town's population tripled during construction of the dam. Several of Cromwell's more distinguished old buildings have been relocated in a historic reserve in the new town, which is destined to be a tourist resort. The Old Cemetery tells of short, desperate lives lived in this landscape. And the desperate things that were done to the landscape are best seen at Bannockburn (9 kilometres from the town centre via Barry Avenue) where for 50 years sluicing diggers slashed a bizarre moonscape from Otago's terrain. Now part of the Otago Goldfields Park, the Bannockburn diggings are open to the public (closed between August 20 and October 20). A leaflet available at the car park has details of a historic walk through the area.

GLENORCHY–PARADISE

At the lonely head of LAKE WAKATIPU, these communities can be reached by a long lakeside road that sometimes climbs into the mountains, or by a more relaxing boat excursion from QUEENSTOWN. Surrounded by mountains, Glenorchy was once a scheelite miners' centre. A ranger is stationed here to advise on MOUNT ASPIRING NATIONAL PARK. A few kilometres further, Paradise, with just a homestead or two, has a dramatic view across river flats and tangled waterways. There is some dispute whether the place is named after the paradise ducks or the beauty of the area.

HAAST PASS

Alpine pass between Otago and Westland in MOUNT ASPIRING NATIONAL PARK. It marks a striking transition between the two regions as the arid, treeless heights of Otago give way to Westland's rainforest. Even in wet or misty weather, the pass can be impressive, with waterfalls lashing the roadside, and peaks and snowfields glimmering amongst the clouds. The highway, which follows an old Maori war trail, took a century to complete. The trail was rediscovered by gold prospector Charles Cameron in 1863, but named by geologist Julius von Haast, who followed soon after. A packhorse trail for the rest of the 19th century, Westland's long-awaited road link with Otago was finally opened in 1965, after three difficult decades of construction. Haast Pass (563 metres) is the lowest of the South Island's alpine passes and seldom under snow.

LAKE HAWEA

The smallest of Otago's trio of alpine lakes, Lake Hawea is nevertheless 31 kilometres long, and 141 square kilometres in area. The road through HAAST PASS to Westland skirts the lake for part of the way. A Maori community where Lake Hawea settlement now stands was destroyed by northerner Te Puoho when he marched through the pass and into Otago in 1836. The lake level was raised by up to 20 metres after the Clutha River was dammed to control its flow to hydro-electric plants downriver. While this devastated the lake's beaches, it does not detract from Hawea's spectacular beauty. Its waters are also generously stocked with brown and rainbow trout, and land-locked salmon.

LAKE WAKATIPU

The name of the lake is possibly a corruption of the Maori *Wakatipua*, 'trough of the monster', but Wakatipu was also known to the Maori as the waters of greenstone – *Te Wai pounamu*. Long (77.2 kilometres), deep (up to 378 metres), lean (4.8 kilometres at its widest) and large (293 square kilometres), this is New Zealand's most magical lake, with mountains rising sharply from its shore. Legend says the lake was formed by the body of a great monster that perished by fire but whose surviving heart still beats in the depths. Maoris see evidence of this in the rhythmic rise and fall of the lake's waters, up to 12 centimetres or more every five minutes, and in the spasmodic storms that tell of the monster's spirit seeking flesh (see page 305). Launches, yachts, jet boats and the elegant veteran steamer *Earnslaw* now ply where greenstone-loaded Maori rafts once travelled. The lake was first glimpsed by Europeans in 1853, but not explored thoroughly until Donald Hay paddled around it by raft in 1859. Soon after gold-diggers crunched along the shore, QUEENSTOWN was established. Although gold fever expired here, Queenstown survived as a tourist resort, from which many excursions on and around the lake are available. To the south of the lake is the small community of Kingston, and its historic steam train *Kingston Flyer*.

LAKE WANAKA

Below mountains moulded smooth by glaciers, Wanaka is the most benignly set of the South Island lakes. It is 45 kilometres long and covers 193 square kilometres. The Maori lived here as greenstone-seekers and traders, but the area was depopulated by northern raider Te Puoho when he marched into the region over HAAST PASS in 1836. The sheepmen of the 1860s found empty

A MEDICAL REFORMER

The innovative methods of this great New Zealand paediatrician motivated reforms throughout the world

Truby King started a revolution that has affected the lives of all New Zealanders

Karitane, a small coastal settlement to the north-east of Dunedin, is famous through its association with the work of Sir Frederic Truby King (1858-1938). It was at Karitane that he first tried his new paediatric methods, and his homestead still stands there.

Truby King's innovations in the care of mothers and infants now seem common sense, but just after the turn of the century they were quite revolutionary. He achieved worldwide acclaim for his work and succeeded in reducing child mortality in New Zealand by two-thirds.

The movement that Truby King founded in 1907 was officially called the Royal New Zealand Society for the Health of Women and Children. It was more popularly known as the 'Plunket Society' after the governor-general of the time who, with his wife, gave enthusiastic support to the reforms. The nurses trained in the new skills and methods were usually called the 'Karitane nurses'.

Following his father's wishes, Truby King's early career was in banking. After a few years he suddenly switched to medicine, training in Edinburgh and becoming the top student of his year. After qualifying, he returned first to Wellington then to Otago to become Superintendent of the Seacliff Mental Hospital.

While in Otago, he began to advocate the treatment of the whole patient rather than the particular, localised symptoms of an ailment. He concentrated on the care of children and the entire environment into which they were born, recommending a reliance on natural nutrition (especially breast-feeding), plenty of fresh air and exercise, regular routines for food and sleep, and the warmth, care and shelter provided by informed mothers. Ignorance and prejudice were always his greatest enemies.

Besides being a remarkable paediatrician, Truby King's talents were involved in many other fields, including psychiatry, alcoholism, plant and animal nutrition, conservation and agricultural acclimatisation.

The old post office at Lawrence, now in a state of disrepair, was originally a courthouse

tussock country. Wanaka receives the waters of the Matukituki and Makarora Rivers, and from it flows the great Clutha. Gold-seekers worked up the Clutha River almost to Wanaka, but the pickings were poor here. Today, excursions on the lake (from kayak to hovercraft) are available from WANAKA. As in all of Central Otago, the most spectacular season here is autumn, when poplars, willows and sycamores richly colour the landscape. Glendhu Bay (14 kilometres west of Wanaka town) is noted for its splendid lake views, with distant Mt Aspiring glimmering above the water.

LAWRENCE

Otago's first gold-rush town, originally named Tuapeka, later renamed after the British hero who defended Lucknow during the 1857 Indian Mutiny. At the height of gold fever, its population was 11 500, double that of Dunedin, making it one of the largest communities in the country. Today it has only 600 inhabitants. Lawrence stands at the entrance to Gabriels Gully, where in May 1861 Gabriel Read made his famous strike that sparked off a frantic and unprecedented gold rush (see page 308). There is a small memorial and museum at the scene of Read's strike. Travellers trying their luck with a gold pan are warned that the original terrain lies under tailings up to 25 metres deep, already well picked over by Chinese diggers after the initial fervour had passed. Having managed to resist commercialisation, Lawrence retains an especially rich 19th-century atmosphere. Among its more prominent historic buildings are the post office, originally a courthouse (1867); and the new courthouse (1876), now a community centre. The town is characterised by Victorian architecture. Ruins of a brewery at nearby Wetherston (3 kilometres) reflect the district's heyday as gateway to Otago's goldfields. Blue Spur township (5 kilometres) in the hills is another vestige of a once substantial community.

LINDIS PASS

This mountain pass, 970 metres above sea level, links the alpine Mackenzie Country (see page 258) with the stark and arid heights of Central Otago in a dramatic contrast of landscapes. Once a Maori route through the mountains, John Turnbull Thomson rediscovered the pass in 1857. Soon after, it was the setting for the short and unrewarding gold rush preceding Gabriel Read's strike at Tuapeka (now LAWRENCE). Among other 19th-century farm buildings in the Lindis River valley stands the vast stone woolshed of the Morven Hills sheep run. It was built in about 1873 to trim 135 000 sheep annually, from a run that extended more than 200 000 hectares.

MACETOWN

This now deserted settlement, some 15 kilometres up the Arrow Gorge from ARROWTOWN along an old bridle track with 22 fords, was first known to diggers as Twelve Mile. Quartz mining kept the community functioning until the 1920s. Snowbound much of the winter, its remoteness and the hardships endured here are legend. The remains of the village are now part of the Otago Goldfields Park. The poplars, sycamores and cottonwoods, planted by miners to soften their harsh environment, remain as pleasant little woodland. A four-wheel-drive excursion leaves for Macetown from Arrowtown or QUEENSTOWN. Those who prefer to walk to Macetown up the steep gorge should plan an overnight camp on the site to allow more time for browsing.

MATAKANUI

Site of an old goldtown, originally known as Tinkers, under the Dunstan Mountains. Its cluster of surviving buildings are noted for their adobe (sun-dried brick) construction, a material dictated by Otago's lack of timber but also tempering the region's extremes of climate. The old store still functions in a former diggers' dance hall. Stables, a bakery, the husk of the original hotel and some dwellings are also still standing.

MILTON

One of Otago's few substantial towns, with 2200 people, 55 kilometres south-west of Dunedin. There is some doubt about the origin of the name: it may simply be a contraction of Mill Town; on the other hand surveyor Robert Gillies claimed in 1886 to have named it after the English poet. Milton was settled early as Scots colonists pushed south, but emptied fast after the first Otago gold strike at nearby LAWRENCE. The town's economy was based on wool-growing and textile manufacture. Three distinguished churches grace the town: the stone Tokomairiro Presbyterian Church (1889), the work of the celebrated Dunedin architect R.A. Lawson; the small St John's Anglican Church (1866); and F.W. Petre's Catholic Church of the Immaculate Conception (1892). Timber predecessors of both the Presbyterian and Catholic churches stand beside them, dating from 1863 and 1869 respectively. On the Taieri Plain between Milton and Dunedin many early farm buildings can be seen.

MOERAKI

A tiny fishing community, with Maori flavour, 78 kilometres north of Dunedin. According to Maori legend, the remarkable spherical boulders lying on a nearby beach are petrified calabashes from the wreck of the *Arai-te-Uru* canoe. These geological curiosities each weigh several tonnes. Early whalers, working from Moeraki, marvelled at them and called them The Ninepins. The little Kotahitanga Maori church on the way into the village has stained glass windows from Rome and dates from 1862.

MOUNT ASPIRING NATIONAL PARK

New Zealand's second largest national park, encompassing 289 505 hectares of striking alpine scenery. With Mt Aspiring rising pyramidally 3027 metres at its centre, the park takes in the HAAST PASS to the north and feeds the waters of LAKE WAKATIPU to the south. The many peaks over 2000 metres give the park its rugged – and often close to impenetrable – character. Vegetation is diverse, especially in the 1000 metres of alpine growth between the treeline and snowline, where a wide range of alpine flora can be found, more than 90 per cent of which are unique to New Zealand. Throughout the park, silver beech forest predominates, interspersed with red beech and mountain beech more to the south. Birds are abundant, especially the kea, the New Zealand mountain parrot whose native terrain is here. Apart from the dramatic Haast Pass Highway, the easiest access to the park is through the ravishing Matukituki Valley, following the river upland from WANAKA. Full information is available from national park headquarters at Wanaka.

NASEBY

The tiny township of Naseby is located among shady trees at the head of the sun-bleached Maniototo Plain. It is the most charming of Otago's gold-rush settlements, with a wealth of surviving architecture, constructed mainly of adobe (sun-dried brick). Up to 5000 diggers once toiled on its fields. By contrast, its present-day population is no more than 200. The Early Settlers' Museum, housed in the old Maniototo Country Council chambers built in 1878, has a fine collection of early photographs, curling trophies and early gold-working implements (open 2–4 daily; extended hours during school holidays). Other buildings of interest include the Ancient Briton Hotel (1863) whose billiard room once served as a makeshift surgery for miners, the corrugated iron Athenaeum (1865), St George's Anglican Church (1875), and a watchmaker's shop in Leven Street (1868). The dam above the township provides summer swimming and an arena for curling (Naseby is national capital for the sport) and ice-skating in winter. From Naseby, a dramatic mountain drive (to be taken with care) follows the old diggers' trail through Danseys Pass, via the scoured and moon-crated landscape of Kyeburn Diggings. The Dansey Pass Hotel was built in 1870 by a distinguished and drunken stonemason named Happy Billy.

William Strong opened his shop in Naseby in 1868; it is still open for business today

OAMARU

Largest Otago community after Dunedin, with a population of fewer than 13 000. Much of Oamaru's old commercial quarter was built during boom decades of the mid-19th century, based on prosperous rural hinterland. The town is distinguished by its elegant buildings of creamy white limestone, known as Oamaru stone (see page 298). Architectural tours are conducted in summer from the splendid Forrester Gallery, dedicated to the Oamaru heritage, which is housed in R.A. Lawson's large, classical Bank of New South Wales (1884). (Tours depart Thursday and Sunday at 2; gallery itself open Monday to Thursday, 10–4.30; Friday, 10–8.30; Sunday, 1–4.30.) Note the superb plastered ceiling inside the old

OTAGO GOLD

A lucky strike by an enigmatic Tasmanian prospector brought sudden riches to Otago

Gabriels Gully: a memorial marks the site where Gabriel Read struck gold in May 1861

Gabriels Gully, near Lawrence, is a fold in the rolling hill country that forms the headwaters of the Tuapeka River, a tributary of the Clutha River. The name marks the site where on May 23, 1861, a Tasmanian gold prospector named Gabriel Read (1824-94), struck his shovel into a thin layer of gravel, 'arrived at a beautiful soft slate' and found gold 'shining like the stars of Orion on a dark frosty night'. A stone cairn, on which are set a prospector's pick and shovel, now commemorates the event – an event that changed the whole economy of Otago.

Read was one of the most altruistic of early New Zealand discoverers – and he was certainly the most generous of the gold-mad thousands who quickly joined the Otago rush. There is no doubt that he could have reaped a fortune by keeping his discovery secret for as long as possible, but he immediately announced the find in the newspapers for the benefit of all. Within two months of Read's discovery, the population of Gabriels Gully, at more than eleven thousand, was double that of Dunedin.

Read remains something of an enigma. A man of property in Australia, he sailed his own schooner to the Californian goldfields, then returned to join the Victoria rush before continuing to New Zealand. He was appalled at the immorality of the goldfields and soon tired of his profitable workings in Central Otago. The Otago Provincial Council rewarded Read with a grant of a thousand pounds for this discovery and encouraged him to continue searching. However, a wanderlust seems to have gripped him more powerfully than the attraction of gold. He drifted around the South Island for a while, then made an extensive journey through the North Island, before returning to Tasmania. He revisited New Zealand several times, but never with pick and shovel.

banking chamber. The more conventional North Otago Museum is located in the classical Athenaeum and Mechanic's Institute (1882) in Thames Street (open Monday to Friday, 1–4.30). In the Brydone Hotel (corner of Thames and Wear Streets), which was once vaunted as the best in the colony, some upstairs public rooms have been restored. The **TOTARA ESTATE** Centennial Park (8 kilometres south) is an evocative rural complex, restored and managed by the NZ Historic Places Trust.

OPHIR

Now with only a few dozen inhabitants, Ophir leapt to life with a population of thousands after a nearby gold strike in 1863. Sitting between the Manuherikia River and the Raggedy Range, it was soon a substantial town with four hotels, four stores, two banks, a courthouse and a hospital. The little schist-built post office (1886) with its handsome facings is now the property of the NZ Historic Places Trust (open weekdays, 9–12).

OWAKA

This village capital of the lonely Catlins (with only 400 inhabitants) was a frontier town that failed to flourish. The NZ Forest Service runs a small museum here and an information centre that deals with the **CATLINS FOREST PARK**; there is also a village museum. Owaka means 'place of canoes'; Maori tribesmen once travelled to Owaka to fell totara trees and hollow out their vessels.

PALMERSTON

A community of 900 in the lower valley of the Shag River in Coastal Otago, Palmerston developed at the start of 'The Pigroot', a trail leading to the booming goldfields and goldtowns of Central Otago. Prominent above the township is Puketapu, 'sacred hill' (343 metres). According to Maori legend, it is the petrified spouse of Chief Pukehiwitahi, whose canoe *Arai-te-Uru* was wrecked at **MOERAKI**. Today the hill is capped by a memorial to Sir John McKenzie (1838-1901), a local runholder who was minister of lands in Richard John Seddon's reforming Liberal government. Palmerston is named after the 19th-century British prime minister. A short drive off Highway 1 to the north of the town, leads to Shag Point and the Shag River mouth on the rugged Otago coast. Inland (32 kilometres) lies the old goldtown of Macraes Flat, where the legendary alehouse Stanley's Hotel still functions, today owned and operated by its rural regulars with help from the NZ Historic Places Trust. Golden Point Battery and several miners' huts can be seen (5 kilometres, turnoff signposted 1 kilometre towards Dunback). The gold battery, the last authentic one in Otago, can sometimes be seen working.

QUEENSTOWN

So named because it grew on a site 'fit for Queen Victoria', this lovely year-round mountain resort is regally set on the shore of **LAKE WAKATIPU**, among dramatic ranges, and is particularly striking in autumn. Visitors from all over the Pacific are attracted by its skifields in winter, and its scenic beauty in all seasons. With a population of 3600, Queenstown is still as cosmopolitan as it was when it served thousands of diggers in Central Otago. Yet commercial exploitation – still modest by international standards – has not marred its special character. Within easy distance of the town are the bare mountain ranges and rocky canyons where diggers sought riches in the 19th century. Skippers Road (served by commercial transport) threads precariously through the most dramatic of these locations. A less taxing excursion by way of the Crown Range road (not negotiable in wet weather, and closed in winter) leads via the Cardrona Valley and the old Cardrona Hotel (1870; now a restaurant) to the resort town of **WANAKA** and **LAKE WANAKA**. Other attractions include the famous goldtown of **ARROWTOWN** and other sites of former gold diggings; jet boating and rafting on the Shotover River; the *Earnslaw*, a veteran twin-screw steamer (1912) that makes leisurely trips around Lake Wakatipu; and the famous old steam locomotive, *Kingston Flyer*, which makes 75-minute excursions into Southland (with Devonshire teas) from Kingston at the southern end of the lake. For panoramic views, there are gondolas that take visitors 446 metres up Bobs Peak to a mountain-top restaurant, the **CORONET PEAK** chairlift and scenic flights.

Of the town's few remaining historical buildings, the old stone library and courthouse (both 1876), and part of Eichardt's waterfront tavern (1871) are of interest. By far the most elegant survival of old Queenstown is the Government Tourist Department Gardens, which have the atmosphere of a Victorian resort. The gardens were originally a gift to the community from pioneer merchant Bendix Hallenstein, who made his fortune on Otago's goldfields. Towards Frankton (3 kilometres) is the Goldfields Town Museum Park, which is part reconstruction, part salvage, of an 1860s goldfield town (open daily from 9). An effective audio-visual display at the Colonial Sound Museum also recreates the gold-rush era. The Motor Museum has an impressive collection of vintage vehicles (open daily), and at the Cattledrome (7 kilometres), beef and dairy cattle are on parade (twice daily, September to May; once daily, June to August). The walks in the area include those up Queenstown Hill (902 metres) and Ben Lomond (1748 metres). Details can be obtained at the town information office.

RANFURLY

Service town on the Maniototo Plain, to the north of the Central Otago Plateau, with a rail link to Dunedin. The remaining buildings (1861) of the old Hamiltons run are 15 kilometres south-east, possibly the first cob structures in Central Otago. Later, much of the surrounding sheepland was shifted by sluicing diggers.

ROUTEBURN VALLEY

Excursions into this green region leave from **QUEENSTOWN** around the head of **LAKE WAKATIPU**. Rich in red beech forest and river views, it contrasts strikingly with most of the Otago interior. There is, for the more adventurous, a four-day guided trek over the Routeburn Track to Fiordland. The track can also be walked unguided. Huts are available at reasonable intervals; they cannot be booked in advance and may be used for no

The post office and war memorial at Oamaru

more than two successive nights, except in bad weather (see also page 343). Further information is available from Queenstown Public Relations Office.

ROXBURGH
Approaching Central Otago from the south via LAWRENCE, the first parched landscapes of the interior are encountered in the Roxburgh district, where irrigated river flats now produce much of the country's harvest of apricots and peaches. At the time of its completion in 1962, the Roxburgh dam was the greatest in New Zealand. The township (population 750) still holds some period flavour, especially in its stone churches – St James's Anglican Church (1872), Teviot Union Church (1880) and the Methodist Church (1872), which served Welsh gold-diggers and now houses a museum. Signposted at Millers Flat (26 kilometres towards Dunedin) are Central Otago's most famous graves: those of the anonymous digger buried as 'Somebody's Darling' and William Rigney 'the man who buried "Somebody's Darling" ' (see page 294). Towards ALEXANDRA there is a roadside memorial to the many ill-equipped fortune-seekers who perished in the great Otago snows of 1863.

Sluice workings at St Bathans – now a lake

ST BATHANS
Beneath the Hawkdun Range and the Dunstan Mountains, and beside Blue Lake (a lake of kaleidoscopic colour left by sluicing and channelling gold-diggers), this community has a strikingly picturesque collection of adobe (sun-dried brick) colonial buildings, notably the old Vulcan Hotel (1869), sole survivor of 13 hotels. The population, hardly more than a score now, numbered 2000 for two decades. St Bathans's popular lake, now used for winter ice-skating and curling, was a 120 metre high hill until diggers began working; it is now a 69 metre hole. The hamlet's old cottages are now mostly weekend dwellings. The Anglican Church of St Alban the Martyr dates from 1882, St Patrick's from 1892.

SKIPPERS
New Zealand's most infamous road, leads to Skippers, 28 kilometres north of QUEENSTOWN; it plunges dizzily and unwinds terrifyingly through the bleakest and richest Otago terrain worked by diggers in the 1860s. With cruel mountains looming above and the Shotover River rumbling near by, the diggers gambled against blizzards and floods and often took final residence in the graveyard at the head of the gorge. All that remains of their townships of canvas, sod and schist are poignant collections of rubble. The least nerve-wracking access to the great canyon is by minibus excursions, which also provide goldpanning and diggers' black billy tea.

TOTARA ESTATE
The first shipment of frozen meat exported from New Zealand on February 15, 1882, was prepared at Totara Estate, and shipped form Dunedin's Port Chalmers. Exactly 100 years later the estate, 8 kilometres south of OAMARU, was opened to the public, imaginatively restored by the NZ Historic Places Trust. The farm buildings of Oamaru stone date from 1868; they contain interesting displays, including the slaughterhouse, carcass shed and the poignantly spartan men's quarters. Like the buildings of nearby Oamaru, Totara Estate should not be missed by visitors to Otago (open public holidays, 10–4; school holidays and Sunday, 1–4; picnic area). Just south at Maheno is splendidly restored Clark's Mill, built for the owners of Totara Estate in 1866 (open to the public). Associated with it are two Oamaru-stone millers' homes of the same vintage, one still in its original cottage form.

WAIKOUAITI
Otago's oldest European community, 42 kilometres north of Dunedin, Waikouaiti was established by whaler Johnny Jones in the 1830s. Having claimed 800 000 hectares of the South Island, Jones brought in respectable settlers, including a doctor and a cleric. Later Dunedin, supplied profitably by Jones, soon outdistanced his settlement in dimension. With a population of 850, today's Waikouaiti has several old buildings of interest: St John's Anglican Church (1858), built of pitsawn timber; the Waikouaiti Presbyterian Church (1863), now a Sunday school; and St Anne's Catholic Church (1871). There is also an Early Settlers' Museum on the main road (open weekdays 2–4). Near by (4 kilometres) on the coast, to the north of Matanaka beach, stands a remarkable cliffside complex of lonely farm buildings, dating from the early 1840s. Preserved and protected by the NZ Historic Places Trust, the buildings include a storehouse, granary, schoolhouse, stables, cottage and a three-hole privy. The homestead is still in private hands.

WAITAKI VALLEY
The valley of the wide Waitaki River forms the boundary between Canterbury and Otago. Hydro-electric construction has left a legacy of lovely lakes, fed by the alpine waters of Canterbury's McKenzie Country. The largest of these is Benmore, New Zealand's most extensive artificial lake which covers nearly 8000 hectares – about the same as Wellington Harbour. The lakes are stocked with brown and rainbow trout and are the habitat of land-locked salmon. The mouth of the river, 26 kilometres north-east of OAMARU, is famed for its river-running quinnat salmon. Moa-hunters and later hunters of the classic Maori era used the Waitaki Valley as their route to the interior. At Takiroa near Duntroon (2 kilometres west on Highway 83), early Polynesian cave drawings are accessible from the roadside. This region is rich in such remains.

WANAKA
Central Otago resort town of 1400 people, on the southern shore of LAKE WANAKA. At this point, the great schist plateau of Central Otago surrenders to the ice-fed waters and the steep, wooded slopes and snowfields of MOUNT ASPIRING NATIONAL PARK, whose headquarters, with a museum, are at Wanaka. There are many water excursions on Lake Wanaka, in different types of craft, but the 90 kilometre return journey up the Matukituki Valley is the local highlight. Trout fishing here and in nearby LAKE HAWEA is excellent. Leafy Glendhu Bay (14 kilometres) offers the best view of Mount Aspiring. Another interesting and scenic route is the drive to ARROWTOWN and QUEENSTOWN (closed in winter) over the Crown Range road via the Cardrona Valley. The road passes Cardrona Hotel (1870), once a rowdy rendezvous for gold-diggers and now restored as restaurant. Wanaka is the last all-comforts stop before the HAAST PASS into Westland, or the first on arrival in Central Otago. Like all Central, it is seen at its best when its exotic lakeside trees are incandescent with autumn colours.

THE MOERAKI BOULDERS

These geological curiosities lie about the beach like some forgotten giant game of marbles

The Moeraki Boulders, like many other features of landscape, are explained in legend

On the beach between the seaside villages of Moeraki and Hampden just off Highway 1, huge boulders lie strewn on the sands, some measuring over three metres in circumference and weighing several tonnes. The extraordinary feature of these stones is their rounded symmetry.

The boulders were formed by concretion – that is, they have accumulated around small cores. Lime salts gathered in the mudstone that formed on the ocean floor of the early Tertiary period (about sixty million years ago). The mudstone-calcite combination hardened into balls, which increased in size as the process continued. The boulders have crystalline centres, and the ribbing which gives them a net-like surface is an extrusion of yellow calcite.

As the mudstone in which they originated became 'dry land', the sea began to erode the cliffs, exposing the buried boulders. Some can still be seen jutting from the cliffs, still in the process of being uncovered, by wave action. An unknown number of boulders were removed from the beach in earlier times as scientific curios.

Maori legend connects the origin of the boulders to the wreck of the *Arai-te-uru* canoe during the migration from the ancestral homeland. The canoe is said to have formed the long reef jutting out into the sea at Shag Point, fifteen kilometres south. A prominent rock is the navigator of this craft and the nearby hills are its crew. The boulders are explained as the food baskets, eel-traps and gourds that fell overboard and were turned to stone.

Dunedin

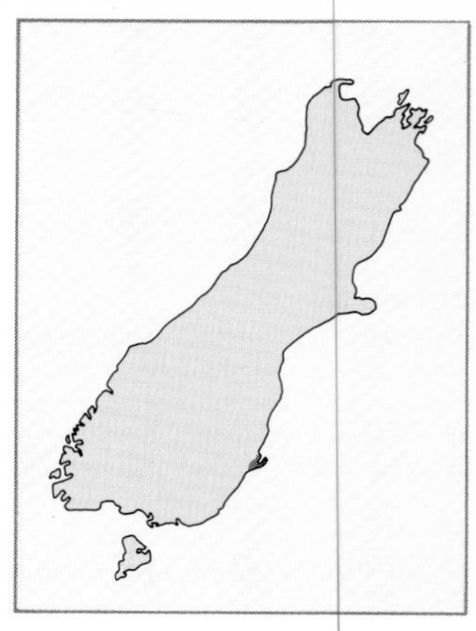

There is no New Zealand city of more durable distinction. As a Victorian enclave in the South Pacific, Dunedin grows more vivid and more precious by the year. High-rise and sprawl have given other New Zealand cities much in common: Auckland's glass towers might be mistaken for those of Wellington, Hamilton's suburbs for those of Christchurch. Dunedin is solidly itself, its brick and stone public buildings meant to last.

Already history-haunted, Dunedin has the character of a city with four or five centuries of existence, rather than a mere one hundred and forty years. Much of that character has been determined by the stern faith of its Scottish founding fathers, a climate in keeping, and a hinterland with gold enough to give colonial capitalism a heady start here; Dunedin was the base upon which many New Zealand business houses – and much of New Zealand's economy – was built. Today's gentle and civilised Dunedin, now that the clamour has gone, more and more of its people, and most capital too, is a monument to nineteenth century enterprise.

Novelist, playwright and critic J.B. Priestley, visiting the city in the early nineteen-seventies, was impressed by its robust urban facade but perplexed by the size of its population, which by the late nineteen-eighties barely exceeded one hundred thousand and was still falling. Priestley felt that a city of such distinguished dimension should have treble the number. Dismayed local politicians feel that way too: they dislike the notion of being mere museum caretakers. For the visitor, however, the city's venerable and magisterially weathered condition is a windfall.

AN ORNAMENTAL AND COMMODIOUS SITE

Dunedin's rugged and striking setting – under severe hills at the head of a long, twisting harbour – was shaped in part by volcanic outpour cooling to basalt and andesite. The risen sea, after the ice ages, did the rest. The moa-hunting Polynesian was familiar with these fiord-like waters, and the later Ngai Tahu people had 'greenstone factories' here where jade borne three hundred kilometres overland from Central Otago's Lake Wakatipu was fashioned into marketable form. Cook missed the entrance to the harbour, and a haven in which to rest his crew, when his *Endeavour* sailed past in 1770. He noted only the long white beaches of St Clair and St Kilda.

Early in the nineteenth century, sealers and whalers began using the harbour mouth. In 1817 a notoriously ruthless sealer named Kelly, of the brig *Sophia*, clashed with local Maori. In retaliation for the killing of three of his party, one of whom had been recognised as a dealer in preserved Maori heads, Kelly left seventy dead and the village of Otakou ashes before resuming the slaughter of seals with as much gusto.

Whalers wintering over on the South Island coast were the first to arrive, planting potatoes in their off-season before resuming the hunt. A permanent base was established at the rebuilt *kainga* of Otakou in 1831. Whalers corrupted the name of the place to 'Otago', a corruption preserved both in the name of the harbour and the region. The record argues that no European visitor set foot at the head of the harbour – the future city's site – until 1826. Prospective settlers were at first deterred by hills heavy with dank forest. Missionaries arrived, preached sermons, and left the landscape as forbidding as before and local Maori much confused. New Zealand Company surveyor Frederick Tuckett, searching out land for another colonising venture after Nelson had been established, thought the harbour and hills, however, offered a most 'ornamental and commodious site for a town'. That judgement reached Scotland and seeded Dunedin in the minds of men long before Tuckett's site was seen.

Though New Zealand Company coloniser Edward Gibbon Wakefield was never noted for religious enthusiasm, he had successfully managed to interest Scottish churchmen in the notion of a denominational colony in distant New Zealand. In 1843 there was theological dispute and disruption within the Presbyterian Church. The spiritual potential of a New Zealand colony was seen afresh by two members of the schismatic Free Kirk, Captain William Cargill, a veteran of the Peninsular War, then in his early sixties, and the Reverend Thomas Burns, an austere nephew of Scotland's roistering poet Robert. They wanted a community where 'piety, rectitude and industry would prevail' – and where, more dauntingly, the inhabitants would act as 'a vigilant moral police'.

It was towards that steely prospect the founders of Dunedin sailed in November 1847. Awaiting them were some one hundred and forty-four thousand acres of land (fifty-eight thousand hectares) purchased from Ngai Tahu Maori for twenty-four hundred pounds and subdivided already into hundreds of properties priced at two pounds an acre. Conditions were appalling for steerage passengers and they had the promise of another struggle for survival at journey's end.

In March and April 1848, the ships *John Wickliffe* and *Philip Laing* carrying three hundred settlers, dropped anchor in Otago Harbour. Cargill pronounced that 'the eyes of the British Empire, and may I say of Europe and America, are upon us'. God's colony was launched. 'Very splendid country and very healthy', was one verdict. The local Maori seemed 'quiet, peaceful harmless creatures'.

The first trials were of man's making, not the Almighty's. The supplies landed were insufficient and fast exhausted. Had it not been for the kindness of nearby Maoris and whaler Johnny Jones (with his rough, tough and well-established community at Waikouaiti to the north) many might have starved. Though the town had been meticulously planned nineteen thousand kilometres away with dour disregard for native contours, no roads, streets or boundaries yet existed. Winter rains sank settlers deep in mud. Romantic streams became roaring torrents. First choice of name for their community was 'New Edinburgh'; this was surrendered for Dunedin (Edin on the Hill), Edinburgh's ancient name.

FREEDOM AMID HARDSHIP

In eighteen months, by October 1849, the population of the settlement had risen to four hundred and forty-four; there were another forty at Port Chalmers towards the mouth of the harbour, and two hundred in nearby countryside. Though free of the disputes with Maori landowners which afflicted northern colonists, Dunedin's settlers had problems enough in a climate often less than kindly. Yet few cracked and fled as was often the case elsewhere. Historian William Pember Reeves argued that faith armoured them against the worst pioneering woes. Recalling the psalms chanted by the devout colonists on the voyage out, he observed: 'Settlers made of such stuff were not likely to fail in the hard fight with Nature at the far end of the earth; and they did not fail'.

Poorer men and women soon felt the freedom inherent in their lonely situation. There was genuine joy in cultivating and civilising the land. For a time, at least, they seemed masters rather than servants. In one small community – at Halfway Bush – each man ebulliently gave himself an aristocratic title. Says Otago historian Erik Olssen: 'They undoubtedly felt like Lords. They could hunt birds and wild pigs when and where they pleased; there were no game laws. It was as though they had stepped out of human

CITY OF LASTING SPLENDOUR

history and entered John Locke's state of nature where each man mixed his sweat with the land, owned his own tools, and the fruits of his labour'.

All the same, not everything went to plan. Labourers' leader Samuel Shaw, an English cuckoo in a Scottish nest, though at first enthusiastic about the egalitarian prospects of the colony, soon clashed fiercely with the authoritarian visionary Cargill on the issue of an eight-hour day. Ten was Scottish custom. Some rebellious labourers turned their backs on Cargill and Burns and went to live with Maoris who saw no sin in eight. By the eighteen-fifties the eight-hour day prevailed.

There were other cracks in the social facade. Though it was said that 'the principles on which selection of Emigrants is conducted preclude the possibility of Whiskey being in large demand', pioneer Dunedin had a rather awesome reputation for insobriety.

Along with a flame of faith and their equally inflammatory national drink, the settlers brought their traditional love of knowledge. Schools were an almost immediate concern and Dunedin had its first primitive circulating library within two years of the first tree being felled. Dunedin also gave New Zealand its first European poet of quality, the fiercely democratic John Barr.

GROWTH IN THE WAKE OF GOLD

Dunedin's isolation was not to last, nor its pious Scottish character. As gold talk grew, Burns and Cargill rightly feared the worst. An invading army of drunken, womanless diggers – worse still, of Irish Catholics – might well demolish New Edinburgh. When Gabriel Read located gold in 1861, and Dunedin became port for the diggings, the settlement was swamped. 'It is no use fighting against fate,' the *Otago Witness* devoutly sighed, 'Greatness is forced upon us'. Otago's population stampeded to sixty thousand. Dunedin was soon the largest and most prosperous town in the colony – no longer to be dismissed, as one newspaper had, as capital of a region ruled by 'Lords of Wastes and Princes of Deserts'.

It was a town noisy with the clink of money, of gambling dens, saloons, billiard rooms and brothels. The old identities of the New Edinburgh found solace in the booming marketplace of the South Sea Sodom. Burghers could at last look down on the north, then smoky with war. What price the Princes of Deserts now?

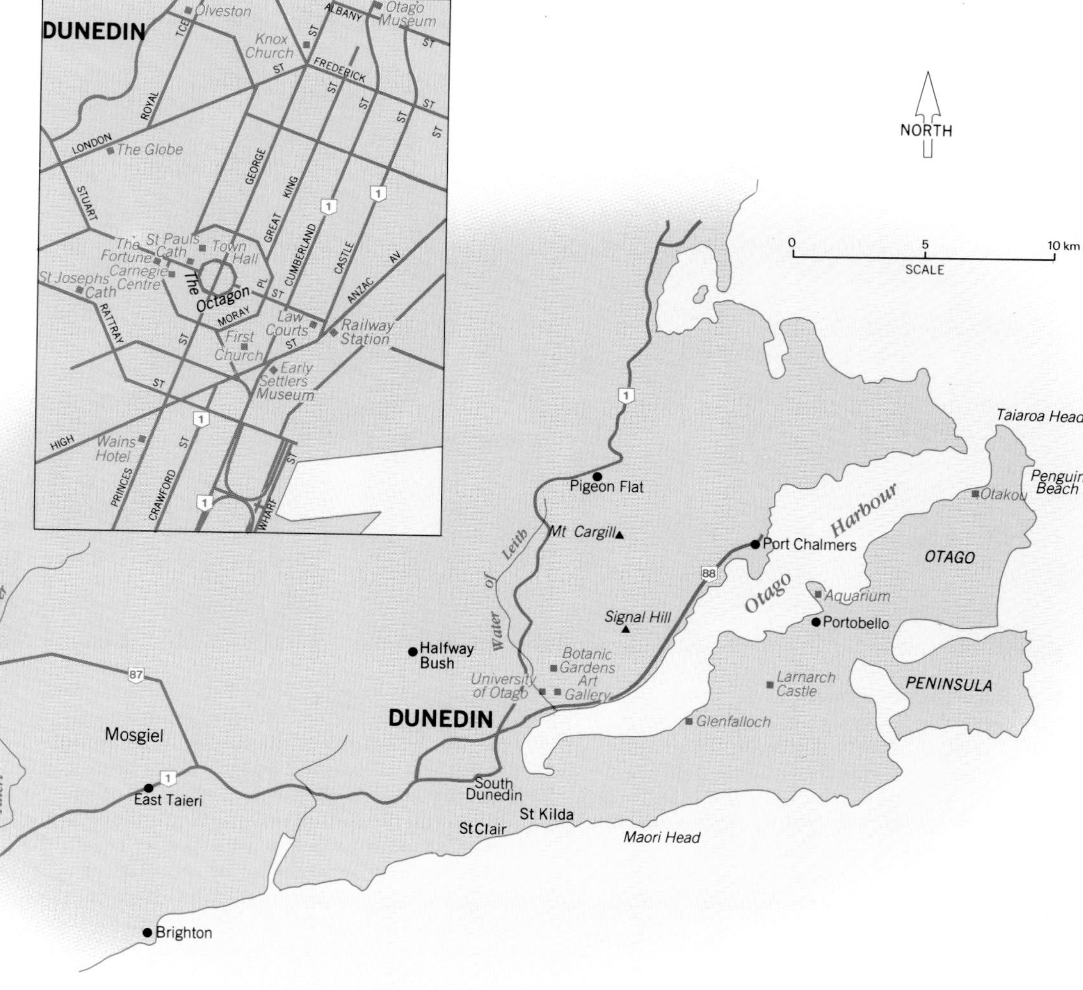

Mercantile princes there were. A decade after the discovery of gold, Otago had a population of seventy thousand, mostly centred on Dunedin. Unlike the restless and easy-spending diggers, Dunedin's merchants had let little gold slip through their fingers. Pastoralists had become entrepreneurs; shopkeepers had become manufacturers. Men of modest beginnings were suddenly building mansions, and taking part in political life. Indeed then and for much of the century, Dunedin tended to dominate New Zealand. In 1871 Dunedin had more factory workers than Auckland; it was the major *entrepot* port for much of New Zealand. The colony's first university was founded here. Tall churches grew too. By the standards of the struggling colony, Dunedin's prosperity was stunning. The muddy village of 1860 vanished under acres of brick and stonework with an almost instant patina of age.

It certainly surprised visiting English novelist Anthony Trollope when he viewed it in 1872. 'A remarkably handsome town,' he pronounced, 'and, when its age is considered, a town which may be said to be remarkable in every way. The main street has no look of newness about it. The houses are well built, and the public buildings, banks and churches are large, commodious and ornamental'. Trollope's Dunedin, expanded and embellished in the remaining three decades of Queen Victoria's reign, is still distinct for today's visitor. Something of its original Scottish character survives too. This is the one place in New Zealand with a manufacturer of kilts, a distiller of whisky, and with Burns nights of undiminished devotion to the national fluid. Some forty per cent of the population still professes Presbyterianism.

Dunedin's affluence was to leave a lasting mark on New Zealand. Business houses founded here became national names. The country's first woollen mills opened at Mosgiel in 1871; in 1882 the ship *Dunedin* set sail from Port Chalmers to

Left: *Dunedin's Early Settlers Museum gives a fascinating glimpse into what life was like for the city's founders. Here a gallery of portraits shows those stalwart Scots who built the city on religious fervour and a love of learning*

The First Church, a massive Gothic church faced with Oamaru stone, is visible from most parts of the inner city

establish the frozen meat trade with Britain. The city was bright with street lighting as early as 1863 and in 1900, with a population of fifty thousand, Dunedin had the land's first electric tram cars. The darker side of industrialism – slums, social misery, crime and prostitution – was soon evident too. The new-world slums of Dunedin were to produce New Zealand's most effective chronicler of poverty, John A. Lee, whose largely autobiographical novel *Children of the Poor* shocked the country shortly before its author became prominent in the first Labour government of 1935. ('This,' the dramatic opening lines read, 'is the story of how I became a thief, and in time very much of an outlaw . . . and of the circumstances which made my sister a daughter of the streets'.)

Dunedin's city fathers were a long time forgiving Lee for having blown the whistle on their ostensibly virtuous city. Yet even in the period in which Lee set his story (the eighteen-nineties, nineteen-hundreds) Dunedin was again setting the pace in social advance. The Plunket system of child care, begun in Dunedin under Truby King in 1907, soon made the country's infant mortality rate the world's lowest.

Dunedin railway station (1904) has a reputation among architectural students and railway enthusiasts alike

Dunedin's decline, relative to other New Zealand centres of population, began with the twentieth century. In 1900, its energy already

Scottish roots show again in this stone memorial to Robert Burns in The Octagon. The famous Scottish poet's nephew, Thomas Burns, was religious leader to the early settlers

Above: *Dunedin rests on the upper reaches of Otago Harbour, a narrow inlet first charted by Dumont d'Urville*
Right: *The harbour is enclosed by the Otago Peninsula, once a volcanic island but now attached to the mainland*

waning, its population was on a par with waxing Auckland's. In 1987, with Auckland marching towards a million souls, Dunedin was struggling to retain six figures. In a sense Dunedin had been the architect of its own diminution. Dunedin's abundant capital flowed north; it was only a matter of time before its people followed.

The quiet tramp of young feet northwards has been audible for most decades of this century. As determined to prosper as the city's first Presbyterian colonists, Dunedin-born have seldom been at a commercial loss in the north. The most dedicated Aucklander or Wellingtonian may well have a bearded ancestor among the portraits in Dunedin's Early Settlers Museum.

Meanwhile the city endured. Colonial mansions and modest workmen's cottages share inner-city streets. Central Dunedin's architectural medley, presided over by uncommonly sober poet Robert Burns in the Octagon, can be positively magical; its public buildings, originally an expression of parochial pride, have become a nation's glory. No one could ever mistake Dunedin for Sydney or San Francisco; it cannot even be confused with the Edinburgh for which it was first named. Mercifully, the silly and saddening phrase 'Edinburgh of the South' is heard less and less now. Dunedin is not some derivative Scots town with pretensions; it is an elegant and most diverting antipodean variation on a new-world theme and must be seen as such.

Old dry stone walls are a common sight on the Otago Peninsula where farms are small by New Zealand standards

Above*: The rural serenity of Portobello, on the southern shore of Otago Harbour, offers shelter to a variety of birds*
Left*: Seals bask on a bed of seaweed on the Otago Peninsula, a refuge for many animal species*

More and more talented migrants from the untidy north have taken refuge here, often drawn initially by the fellowships established for writers, painters and musicians at the University of Otago. No New Zealand city is coloured more by its university. In the academic year, students and staff constitute close to a tenth of the population. For more than a century, and until the nineteen-sixties, the university had New Zealand's only medical school; it has the only schools of dentistry, home science and physical education. The Hocken Library, with its rich collection of early New Zealand manuscripts and paintings, draws scholars from the length of the land.

For the rest, Dunedin's riches reside in its environment. This small, slow community is still hostage to its long harbour and dramatic hills. Central Otago provides the most potent hinterland of any New Zealand city. In just minutes, a Dunedin citizen can be quit of the city and travelling among mountains or along wild coast. This exhilarating freedom makes it unique among the nation's cities.

New Zealanders will find their country's beginnings here, a colourful colonial tapestry. The outsider, much as Anthony Trollope in 1872, may marvel at the enterprise and optimism which made Dunedin rise so durably. Dunedin may lack population; it will never lack lovers.

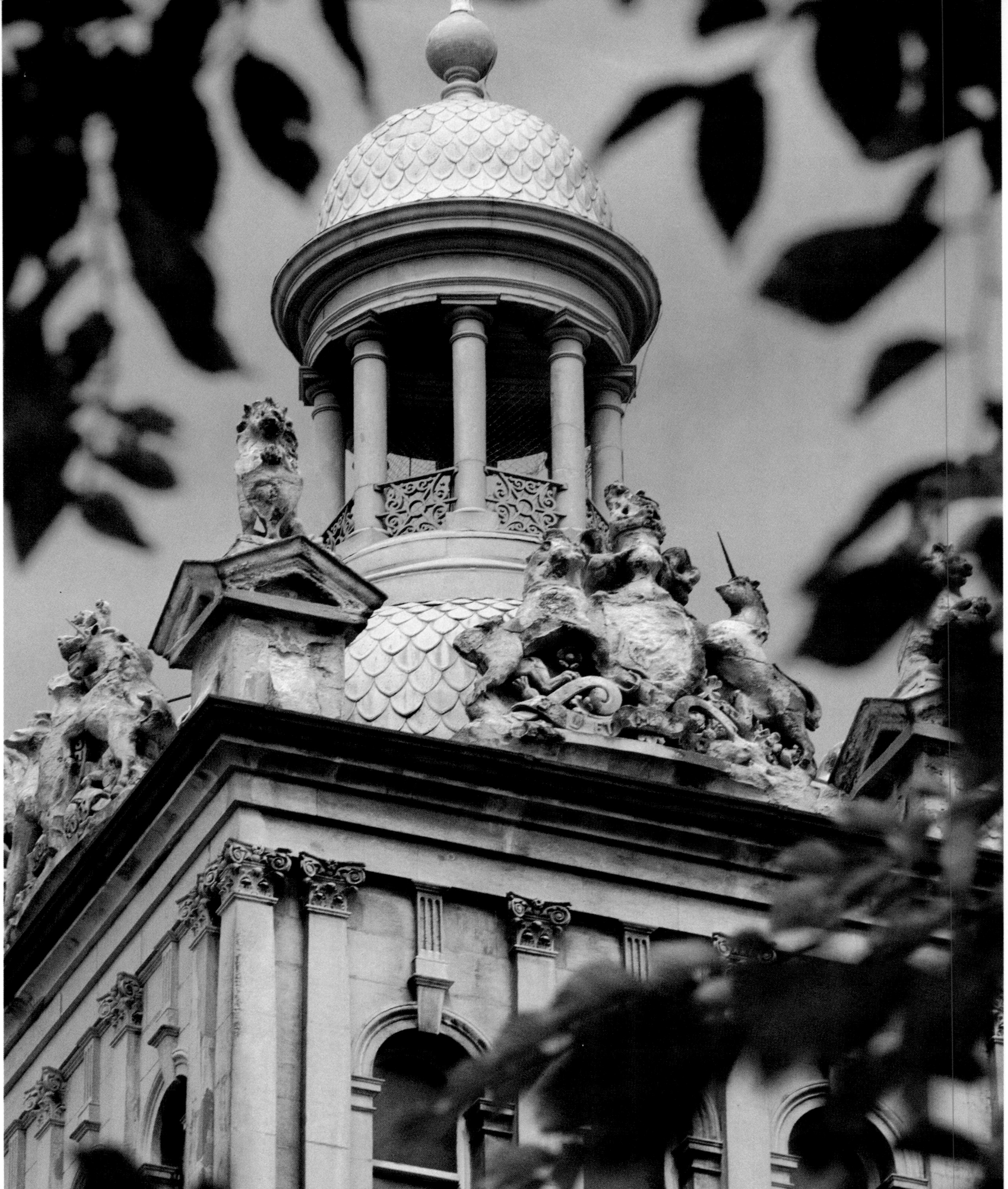

A VICTORIAN ENCLAVE

Its architecture is a mosaic of the forces which made Dunedin New Zealand's largest and most influential city in the nineteenth century

Dunedin has been called the world's most perfectly preserved Victorian city. Perfect? History is never perfect; the slings and arrows of outrageous economics have protected much of Dunedin and its immediate environment from profit-chasing property developers. Given sufficient population, and movers and shakers with more wealth, Dunedin might well have gone the way of many another nineteenth-century city. Any change has always been in the direction of visual impoverishment, recently in the face of opposition from citizens increasingly protective of their heritage.

Entrance facade of St Joseph's Roman Catholic Cathedral

But Dunedin manages to remain distinct, eloquently testifying both to the vision of its founders and its short and bewitching prosperity. The vision of its founders survives and soars in its church spires. Most commanding is that of magnificently Gothic First Church, set among lawn and tree at Dunedin's centre. By 1856, eight years after the settlement's founding, with horses and wagons still churning through muddy streets, spiritual leader Reverend Thomas Burns and fellow Presbyterians were planning a church which 'in point of style and architecture should do no discredit to the capital of the Colony'. The design of Melbourne architect R.A. Lawson was approved six years later, with Otago's gold rush rumbling inland and enriching local merchants. The talented Lawson did not miss the chance for a masterpiece, but Burns did not live to see it opened in 1873. Dunedin's Presbyterians kept Lawson wholesomely employed. Almost as notable is his Knox Church, opened in 1876 in the main street. This church would in itself have been sufficient to grace any colonial community.

Early Dunedin was as much a bonanza for architects as the nearby Otago goldfields were for fortune-hunters. Another to prosper and reflect the changing character of the community was F.W. Petre. His Roman Catholic churches were as distinctive a contribution to New Zealand architecture as Frederick Thatcher's Anglican churches in the north. Where Thatcher was modest, Petre was monumental. His first venture into Dunedin Gothic – and a revolutionary one – was St Dominic's Priory. Eschewing Oamaru stone in favour of concrete, then an unfamiliar material, Petre set up an austere and striking architectural rhythm in his use of pointed arches. It presented 'nothing that would recall a building fitted up for worldly purposes', judged *The Tablet*. 'An air of earnestness pervades it.'

Imposing St Joseph's Cathedral in Rattray Street followed in 1886. It might have been Petre's masterpiece, his answer to Lawson's First Church, but unlike its Presbyterians the city's Catholics lacked revenue. Never more than half finished, St Joseph's remains a meticulously crafted and vivid sample of Petre's talent. He turned to more austerely classical form with St Patrick's Basilica in South Dunedin (1894) before taking his imagination north.

Otago Boys' High School, a familiar landmark

Secular Dunedin was never short on the monumental either. By 1873 it was recognised that 'The class of building in Dunedin gives the city a character unique in the colony'. In short, unlike the largely wooden encampments of Auckland, Wellington and Christchurch, Dunedin was designed to last. Within three decades of its founding the community had more buildings of stone and brick than its rivals could tally in total. Useful quarries nearby and sturdy Oamaru stone were good reasons why; the mortar was gold.

Standing austerely alongside St Joseph's, the walls of St Dominic's Priory rise sharply from the edge of the street

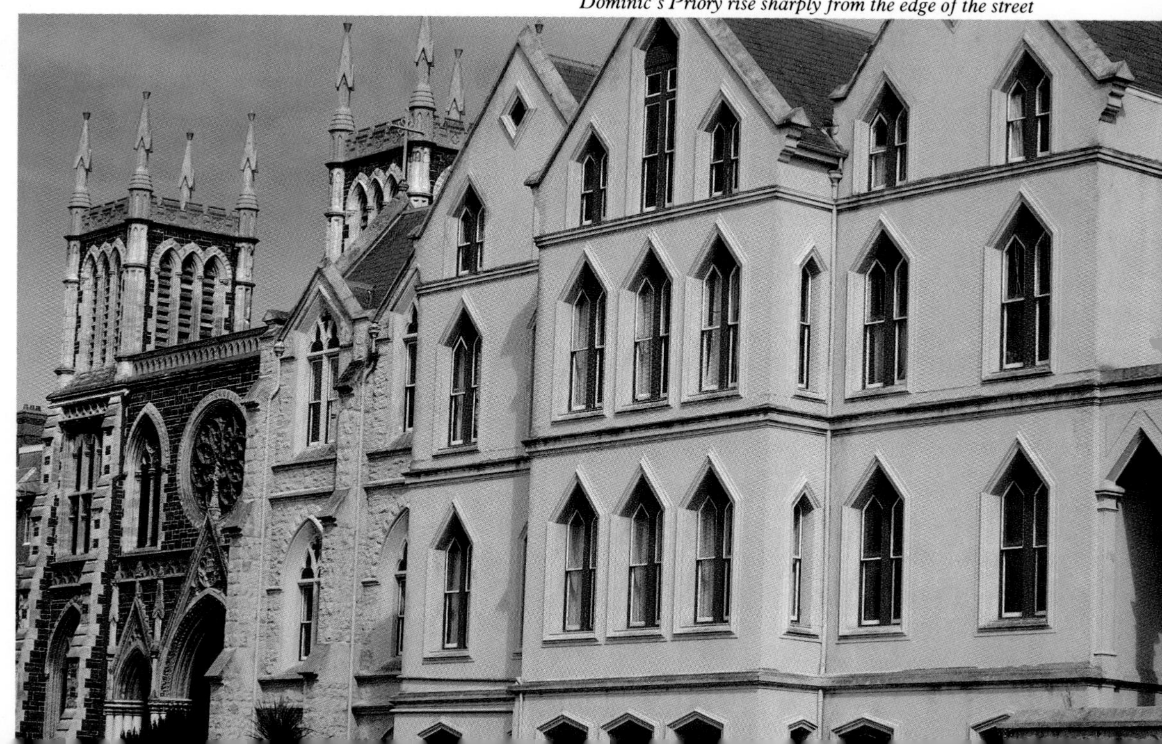

Left*: Dunedin's flamboyant railway station is dominated by a massive copper-capped tower cornered with heraldic lions*

Lawson, the designer of First Church, went on to pay Mammon due in such durable work as the Union Bank Building (now the ANZ), finished in 1874, a graceful example of Greek Revival. Lawson also translated civic pride in the sculpted stonework of the municipal chambers building (1880) with its elegant Italianate frontage. In an unusual episode of civic vandalism, Lawson's tower was lopped in 1962. It was restored in 1989. Even with its proportions awry, the building still dignifies the Octagon.

Fern Tree Lodge at Halfway Bush, built of tree-fern in about 1850, is probably Dunedin's earliest surviving house

Hostelries were a conspicuous if lamented feature of gold-rush days. There were more than eighty tending to thirsty citizens in the eighteen-eighties. One especially handsome survival is Wains Hotel (1878), with its four-storey Italianate facade in Princes Street which, though now encrusted with fire escapes, still whispers of Dunedin's heyday. It was famed through both New Zealand and Australia.

Olveston, a Jacobean home built in 1904-06, is now owned by the city; it reflects faithfully Dunedin's early prosperity

The beauty and authenticity of 521 George Street, built in 1881, are meticulously maintained both inside and out

Ornate decorations such as this stained-glass dome have made the restoration of Larnach Castle a major undertaking

Dunedin's two most spectacular examples of Victorian optimism, the law courts and the railway station, came at the beginning of the twentieth century, in the Edwardian era, capping four decades of civic expansion. Government architect John Campbell was responsible for the first: an imaginative Gothic original replete with details, sitting in an especially rich Dunedin townscape and facing the elaborately Flemish Renaissance railway station, the work of George Troup (who won himself a knighthood with it). As a celebration of rail travel it has no peer in New Zealand, and few in the world. Its ravishing mosaic floor (of more than seven hundred thousand porcelain squares) alone makes it unique. Its colonnades and balustrades serve its fairytale character. Troup was mocked as 'Gingerbread George' by rival architects as his capricious castle grew. Some have argued it is not the building – never altogether functional – that is inadequate to the needs of the twentieth century; it is the twentieth century that has been inadequate to the building. Gingerbread George's vision has long outlasted his detractors.

No community was more dedicated to education – free and universal – than Dunedin. Founders of the settlement saw it becoming 'the centre of civilization in the Southern Hemisphere'. Gold-rush revenue spurred the building of schools and then the establishment of New Zealand's first university, a mere twenty-one years after Scots colonists first ventured among dank vegetation at the head of Otago Harbour. A site to do so major an institution justice was found on the banks of the Leith in the eighteen-seventies and architect Maxwell Bury's proposed design – for 'a University with some architectural style' – prevailed over others submitted. Bury's buildings had an air of venerability even as they rose. A celebration of local stone on dramatic scale, the original clock-tower block and lecture rooms now serve the university administration. Within, the main entrance hall, staircase, upper landing and council chambers retain the grandeur of Bury's original design. Four professorial houses he also designed stand in St David Street.

Larnach Castle, the grandiose residence built by William Larnach who came to Dunedin in the wake of the gold rush

Dunedin's domestic architecture – from modest to manic – is rewarding too. When Scottish settlers established themselves on the harbour, they first lived in foreshore huts of split logs, clay and reeds. As commerce grew and horses and wagons became intrusive, they moved up slopes on to the hills. Homes became more solid, of cob and wattle, roofed with reeds. Another popular

material was *ponga*, or tree-fern logs. The oldest surviving dwelling from this still humble era is Fern Tree Lodge at Halfway Bush. The cottage dates from the early eighteen-fifties, a few years after Dunedin's founding.

Gold as much as architects dictated Dunedin's style. Wealth had to be seen, and was. Wealth had to be used, and was. Industry grew, and industrial housing. Terrace housing, unusual in New Zealand, began to rise. Dundas and Stuart Streets hold fine examples from the city's era as a prospering outpost of European capitalism. The surviving homes of the humble speak as forcefully of Dunedin's beginnings as any grand mansion. Small stone cottages, the work of masons brought in to bridge the streams of Dunedin, still distinguish several streets. Stone was also favoured by the affluent. Among the city's more resplendent dwellings is that at five hundred and twenty-one George Street which echoes the architecture of New Orleans with its use of decorative cast iron. Durable brick – covered with Moeraki pebbles and facings of Oamaru stone – was used in the making of the thirty-five-room Jacobean mansion of the Theomin family, Olveston, at forty-two Royal Terrace. Fifteen of those rooms are now open to the public on guided tours.

By far Dunedin's most bizarre building, high on peninsula hills above harbour and open sea, Larnach's Castle (1876) too is open to the public. This boisterously baronial dwelling was built for financier, merchant and politician William Larnach, who modestly called it The Camp – all four thousand square metres of floor space (including a ballroom) topped with a tower. It cannot fairly be called a folly; Larnach actually lived there. Its distinction lies in the work of the many craftsmen Larnach employed to embellish his elephantine residence. The stonework and woodwork are extraordinary. After Larnach's suicide in 1898 the property, which changed hands several times, once for as little as £1000, nudged owners towards madness with the problems of maintenance. (At one point sheep were kept in the ballroom.) Since the nineteen-sixties the castle, with much restoration, has a more tranquil character. It now seems likely to last as long as the remarkable Victorian city which engendered it.

PLACES OF INTEREST

VANTAGE POINTS

BRACKEN'S LOOKOUT
This intimate view of the city from the edge of Northern Cemetery is named after the colonial poet, journalist and politician who wrote New Zealand's national song (*God Defend New Zealand*). Thomas Bracken (1843-98), one of Dunedin's fervid admirers, is buried in Northern Cemetery along with other Dunedin celebrities including William Larnach of LARNACH'S CASTLE, whose remains rest in an extravagant mausoleum modelled on the FIRST CHURCH.

MOUNT CARGILL LOOKOUT
Close to 700 metres above the city and 8 kilometres from its centre, the lookout presents a striking panorama. The view takes in the long harbour, the hilly Otago Peninsula and New Zealand's most distinguished city. The mountain was named after the settlement founder Captain William Cargill.

SIGNAL HILL
At the top of this 393 metre hill (via Opoho) is a memorial to mark the centennial (in 1940) of British sovereignty. A piece of rock from the promontory on which Edinburgh Castle stands is incorporated in the memorial.

MUSEUMS AND GALLERIES

CARNEGIE CENTRE
This distinguished building (1908) at 110 Moray Place has galleries featuring the work of local artists and craft workers. Summer entertainment is provided by musicians and drama groups. The building was a gift to the city by the steel magnate Andrew Carnegie. Originally it was the city's public library.

DUNEDIN PUBLIC ART GALLERY
Founded in 1884, the gallery is the oldest in New Zealand and one of the land's most distinguished, due to Dunedin pride and wealthy benefactors. The extensive New Zealand collection includes work by Dunedin's two great artists, Frances Hodgkins and Colin McCahon. The foreign collection is just as impressive. An outstanding recent benefaction was from the de Beer family. The paintings include Claude Monet's *La Débacle*, the only major impressionist painting in New Zealand collections. At Logan Park, open Monday to Friday, 10–4.30; Saturday and Sunday 2–5.

EARLY SETTLERS MUSEUM
No other institution has an atmosphere to match. Patriarchs, matriarchs and their progeny from Dunedin's first two founding decades gaze down sternly from the walls of the gallery. The museum is crammed with tribal memories, mementoes and civic artefacts. No traveller has seen into Dunedin's soul without an hour or two spent here (open Monday to Friday, 8.30–4.30; Saturday, 10.30–4.30; Sunday, 1.30–4.30). Then step into the neighbouring Victorian RAILWAY STATION and view its glories.

Knox Church (1876) has a worthy spire; inside there is a splendid encircling gallery

OLVESTON
This is a historic house of the Edwardian era and also a museum. Of its 35 rooms, 15 are open to the public. Built for the Theomin family, it gives the visitor a view of the elegance and affluence of early Dunedin's prosperous citizens. While this house was being built (1904-06), only a few hundred metres away the young John A. Lee was living the dark and impoverished life described in his book, *Children of the Poor*.

Here antiques glow and silver shines. The Anglophilia of the era is noticeable too. An English architect designed the house in Jacobean style. The oak staircase and balustraded balcony were prefabricated in England. New Zealand figures in a fine collection of colonial paintings. At 42 Royal Terrace above the city centre, the house is open to the public with one-hour guided tours Monday to Saturday at 9.30 and 10.45, 1.30, 2.45 and 4; Sunday 1.30, 2.45 and 4; bookings are essential.

OTAGO MUSEUM
Early Dunedin's wealth is reflected in the stately building and its rich collections. Much is devoted to the founding and growth of Dunedin. Among the extensive Polynesian collection are rock drawings made by the earliest inhabitants of Murihiku (the southern South Island); and the disputed Mataatua meeting-house (1870s), carved at Whakatane and once presented to Queen Victoria, which North Island Maori have begun to reclaim. There is also a large classical collection built with the generosity of Dunedin donors (open Monday to Friday, 10–5; Saturday, 1–5; Sunday, 2–5). Once associated with the museum, now situated nearby on the university campus, is the Hocken Library, rich legacy of bibliophile and benefactor Thomas Hocken, with documents, books and paintings which tell New Zealand's story.

HISTORIC BUILDINGS

CARGILL MEMORIAL
This memorial (1863) all but qualifies as a building. Derived from Edinburgh's memorial to Sir Walter Scott, it has been a Dunedin landmark for more than a century. It commemorates the founder Captain William Cargill.

FERN TREE LODGE
At Halfway Bush, this dwelling reminds the city of its humble origins. It is the only pioneer dwelling of its kind – built of *ponga* or tree-fern – left standing in New Zealand. Open to the public.

DUNEDIN'S FOUNDERS

The city of Dunedin owes much of its character to the vision of its founding fathers, William Cargill and Thomas Burns

William Cargill, a modern-day Moses

Arch-Presbyterian, Rev Thomas Burns

William Cargill (1784-1860), Otago Agent for the New Zealand Company, was a regular soldier who was wounded in the Peninsular War against Napoleon. When he retired from the regular army in 1820, he first set himself up as a wine merchant, then joined a bank. He became the father of seventeen children, but still found enough time to take an active interest in religious matters and he found his attitudes firming towards those of the Free Church in its split from the established church.

A Scots nationalist, Cargill hoped to create a 'New Edinburgh' in the southern hemisphere founded on the strict principles of the breakaway church. Though small of stature, Cargill was a great, enthusiastic leader and a good organiser. From the founding of Dunedin he was recognised as its leading citizen and political advocate in its dealings with government. If some critics likened the argumentative and fiery Cargill to Moses leading the children of Israel, there was some point to the jibe. His dogmatic, dictatorial, pugnacious and inflexible character probably helped the early settlement survive, though as the years went by these same qualities became political defects.

The Reverend Thomas Burns (1796-1871), a nephew of the poet Robert Burns, was selected to be minister to the Scots settlement almost from the beginning of the scheme and he worked closely with Cargill to give Dunedin its Free Church accent.

Burns was often accused of strictness and lack of tolerance in matters of morals and religion, but he was a practical man, a good farmer, an amateur meteorologist and an accurate appraiser of land and minerals. He was also deeply concerned with the welfare of his fellow citizens, a believer in the eight-hour working day and a keen proponent of universal education.

He was awarded an honourary degree in divinity from Edinburgh University, helped found New Zealand's first university in Dunedin in 1869 and was appointed its first chancellor.

FIRST CHURCH
In Moray Place, the First Church (1873) remains a stone bastion of the faith that launched the first settlers on Otago's shore. A glory of antipodean Gothic, it was the dream of Thomas Burns (he wanted a 'monument to Presbyterianism') and the design of R.A. Lawson, who left buildings everywhere in early Dunedin.

GLENFALLOCH
Like LARNACH CASTLE, this homestead is on the OTAGO PENINSULA. Constructed in kauri, the substantial building has stood since 1871.

KNOX CHURCH
In George Street (1876), this modest understudy for the First Church confirmed that the Presbyterian grip on

THE MAN WHO 'BOUGHT' THE SOUTH ISLAND

John Jones was a wheeler-dealer who became feudal ruler of his own bailiwick: yet he saved Dunedin's moralistic colonists from starvation

Dunedin's impressive Fernhill Club was once the private home of Johnny Jones (1809-69), the whaler, pioneer farmer, land speculator, sea-trader, general merchant and dealer who claimed to have bought the whole of the South Island.

Jones was born in Sydney, probably the son of a convict. His early life, judged by the little he said of it, was brutal and deprived. Yet by the time he was twenty, he was an experienced coastal sailor with shares in three ships whaling in New Zealand waters. By 1839 his whaling ventures had so prospered that he owned six ships, with seven whaling stations employing two hundred and eighty men. Though whale-oil prices slumped soon afterwards, Jones was already speculating in land bought from local Maori in Otago and Southland.

As a member of a group of Sydney speculators, Jones claimed that in February 1840 he had bought eight hundred thousand hectares of the South Island from a party of Maori chiefs. After the Treaty of Waitangi, Jones applied for authentication of his claim. It was turned down by the Land Claims commissioners, though he was allowed nearly four and a half thousand hectares.

Jones had begun to break in and cultivate land in Waikouaiti as early as 1838 and, in 1840, he recruited a dozen families to farm the area. He brought his own family to Waikouaiti in 1843 and became not so much its squire as its feudal ruler. Luckily for the first Free Church settlers in Dunedin, Jones was able to supply them with produce at reasonable prices to save them from starvation.

John Jones, always a law unto himself

By 1854, Jones's business commitments had become centred on Dunedin and he moved there, eventually building the stone house which, as the Fernhill Club, remains a city landmark. A controlling investment in a small fleet of vessels plying New Zealand coastal waters and the route to Sydney maintained Jones's connection with the sea. After his death these interests developed into the Union Steam Ship Company.

Jones was a contradiction: he was a hard man, something of a tyrant in his businesses and outrageous in his speculations, yet his dealings with the early Dunedin settlers show him also to have had a developed sense of fairness. Unusually for a self-made city businessman of the time, he had no ambition for politics.

Dunedin was not to be prised loose easily. It was also Lawson's design and even more exquisite than the First Church.

LARNACH CASTLE

In its high and sometimes mysteriously misty setting on OTAGO PENINSULA, this building remains Dunedin's baronial *pièce de résistance*. Built in 1876 by banker, merchant and politician William Larnach (1833-98) for a surmised cost of £150 000 – an awesome figure in those days – it includes Italian marble, Aberdeen stone, Venetian glass, Marseilles cobbles and New Zealand kauri. The entrance foyer comprises mahogany, teak, oak, ebony and kauri. Three people spent more than six years carving the ceiling. There is a spellbinding view from the top of the castle's tower.

After Larnach's resignation from politics (by way of a self-inflicted gunshot wound), following the collapse of the Colonial Bank in 1898, the surrounding farmland was sold off. Later the building served as a mental hospital and cabaret theatre. Restoration by private owners since the 1960s has kept the castle, if not financially afloat, at least intact. There is a small restaurant.

LAW COURTS

The busy and richly Gothic facade of this building parades a distinctive Dunedin mix of breccia and limestone. It was claimed to be the cheapest building of its kind ever built in New Zealand (for £20 000 in 1902). It never for a moment looks cheap – the city got its money's worth and the law a handsome arena. The interior is quite as rewarding as the exterior. Next to it is the police station (1896), with something of the form of London's New Scotland Yard.

MUNICIPAL CHAMBERS

Another design by R.A. Lawson, and built on the Octagon in 1880. Though its tower has been mutilated, its Italianate frontage is still impressive.

MUTUAL FUND BUILDING

Formerly the NZ Express Building, in Bond Street, this was Dunedin's first venture into 20th-century architecture. This skyscraper, or so it seemed in 1910, has 7 storeys.

OTAGO BOYS' HIGH SCHOOL

The school's original tower block (1885), the work of R.A. Lawson, sits on a superb site in Arthur Street.

RAILWAY STATION

Though strictly Edwardian (1907), this building is the crowning glory of the half-century of Victorian energy that transformed the muddy town site at the head of Otago Harbour. Dunedin – and indeed New Zealand – would never see its like again. Nor would its creator 'Gingerbread George' (George A. Troup), who was later knighted. This Flemish Renaissance palace is almost as resplendent as ever it was. The mosaic floor has been handsomely restored.

ST JOSEPH'S CATHEDRAL

Situated in Rattray Street, like neighbouring St Dominic's Priory (1877), it was the Gothic work (1886) of talented Catholic architect Francis Petre. More austere St Dominic's was remarkable for its use of unreinforced concrete, and for the striking rhythm of its pointed arches. Petre's ambition was to be a sculptor rather than an architect and his distinctive work shows it.

ST PAUL'S CATHEDRAL

Anglicans were outnumbered by four to one in Dunedin's first decade and have never made up the leeway. St Paul's was started in 1915, on a site that had been waiting for half a century. Strictly speaking it wasn't finished until 1971.

UNIVERSITY OF OTAGO

The clock tower block (1878) beside the Water of Leith stands as a powerful witness to the Scottish love of knowledge.

Notable works of art as well as a collection of Maori artefacts are housed in Otago Museum, one of Dunedin's finest buildings

Indeed, the University of Otago was New Zealand's first university. Architect Maxwell Bury's sturdy design, a celebration of local stone, was transparently derived from the then newly built University of Glasgow. Walk among the buildings for full effect; contemplate also the four professorial residences built by Bury in St David Street.

WAINS HOTEL

Italianate-fronted Wains (1878) was once the city's grandest hotel. The grotesque figures festooning its frontage were the work of master carver Philip Godfrey, who was brought to New Zealand to embellish LARNACH CASTLE.

The colony of royal albatrosses at Taiaroa Head on Otago Peninsula is world-renowned

ENVIRONS

BRIGHTON

The wild coast from Brighton to the mouth of the Taieri River is especially theatrical and rich in literary associations. The poet James K. Baxter grew up here and the seascape lavishly coloured his work until the end of his short life.

OTAGO PENINSULA

The city's setting on the peninsula is striking. It boasts both human creations – LARNACH CASTLE, GLENFALLOCH Woodland Gardens – and a wealth of wildlife including royal albatrosses, penguins and seals. A 64 kilometre drive takes in most of the peninsula, but you must put aside a day. European settlement began at the Maori village of Otakou (from which the harbour and the region take their name), where a whaling station was established in 1831. Today a small Maori church and meeting-house stand on the site. To the rear of the church is a small museum (access by request). The graveyard behind holds the remains of Otago warrior chiefs who fought off Te Rauparaha and sold off their land to Presbyterians.

The peninsula was quarried and farmed by Dunedin pioneers. Taiaroa Head, once a sturdy Ngai Tahu fortress, is now topped by an equally sturdy lighthouse (1865). Hard by is the peninsula's world-famous colony of royal albatrosses, the only known mainland breeding colony of this giant bird. Nesting began in 1938, and the site is protected, with limited public access (inquire at Dunedin's information office). Breeding is from September to December and the fledglings fly off as far as Tahiti a year later. They return to reproduce up to a decade later. The oldest known albatross here was over 50 years old. On the eastern side of the peninsula at Penguin Beach is a penguin colony and seals.

The original Glenfalloch homestead still stands amidst the famous woodland gardens

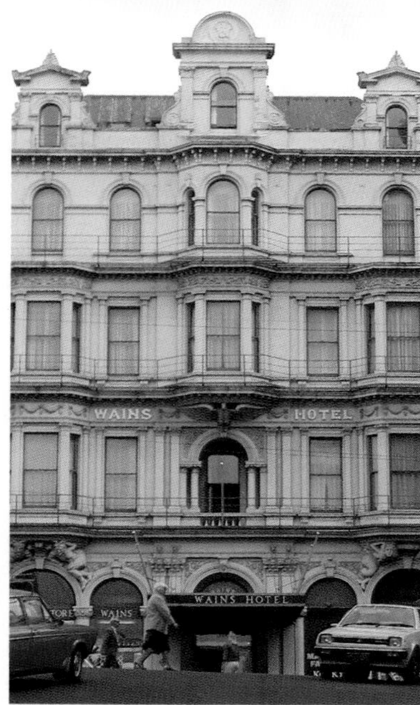

The ornamental four-storey stone facade of Wains Hotel has a series of carved figures supporting the first-floor balconies

For most travellers on the peninsula the highlights are Larnach Castle and the Glenfalloch Woodland Gardens. Glenfalloch was established as a commercial nursery in the 1870s but since has been gently developed as an old-world garden. Between world wars the gardens were styled 'a horticultural League of Nations'. Peacocks strut and doves flutter, and tea may be taken in the serene grounds (open daily, 9–5). The gardens are now the property of the Otago Peninsula Trust. Portobello Marine Laboratory and Aquarium is run by Otago University. It provides a rich glimpse of Dunedin's undersea environment, parading more than 100 forms of marine life (open daily, 9–5).

PORT CHALMERS

The deep-water port and fishing base for Otago, 12 kilometres from Dunedin on the northern arm of the harbour, Port Chalmers was acclaimed in 1882 when the first frozen meat was exported from here. It was also the last port of call for the polar explorer Robert Falcon Scott before he launched himself on the Antarctic. A 1914 memorial to Scott stands above the town.

Bluestone Chicks Hotel dates at least from 1864. There are three especially notable 19th century churches: Holy Trinity (1876), St Mary's Star of the Sea (1878) and Iona Presbyterian Church (1883). A precinct of historic 19th century buildings comprises two banks, the Provincial Hotel, the Town Hall and Municipal Offices.

ST CLAIR AND ST KILDA BEACHES

Both have adjacent reserve areas and are Dunedin's best ocean beaches. They are situated along the sand bar that joins OTAGO PENINSULA to the mainland.

WRITER AND RADICAL

John A. Lee was a borstal boy whose novels revealing the ugly face of New Zealand life did not endear him to the authorities – though he won recognition eventually

John A. Lee as a young man

Albany Street is near the centre of Dunedin. The name is associated forever with the bitter childhood of Albany Porcello, hero of the autobiographical novel *Children of the Poor* written by John Alfred Alexander Lee, DCM (1891-1982), better known as John A Lee. Lee, writer, politician and probably New Zealand's most famous juvenile delinquent, was once a pupil at the Albany Street School.

Lee, the son of a gypsy circus entertainer who abandoned his wife and three children, grew up in poverty. The boy stole to give money to his mother, but proved an innocent at the game and was caught twice in one month for minor crimes which netted him the equivalent of twenty-five cents. He was sent at the age of fourteen to Burnham Industrial School on the Canterbury Plains, south-west of Christchurch. The discipline was harsh, floggings commonplace and ferocious, and the recapture and beating of boys who tried to escape was almost a local sport. Lee was sentenced to this horrific institution for seven years without remission. One boy was doing twelve years for playing truant from school.

After almost three years of incarceration and many attempted escapes, Lee became one of the few to make a successful getaway. He took to the swag, worked at odd jobs and lived in terror of being recaptured. When the law eventually caught up with him he considered himself lucky to be sent to Mount Eden prison instead of Burnham. A year's sentence meant he spent his twenty-first birthday behind bars, but he became a free man at last.

As a soldier in the First World War the official records praised him for 'fearless gallantry'. He was awarded the DCM, though many who fought with him felt it should have been the Victoria Cross. He lost his left arm in a grenade attack.

Lee joined the Labour Party and after the first Labour government came to power in 1935 many expected his immense popular following would eventually sweep him to the premiership. But inside the party he became increasingly isolated in bitter arguments with fellow MPs and he was expelled in 1940.

However, Lee's lasting fame lies in the books he wrote to expose the conditions of the poor and to describe the lives and adventures of the ordinary soldier, the outsider and the hunted. He was New Zealand's first great native-born novelist.

In 1967 the University of Otago invited him back to his native city, where he had been sentenced to borstal for his twenty-five-cent crimes, this time to become an honorary Doctor of Laws.

TAIERI PLAIN

From Mosgiel to Milton, south of Dunedin, this fertile plain grew grain to feed tens of thousands of Otago gold-seekers. Farmers prospered more than the diggers. Today this lush landscape holds many historic cottages and churches.

ENTERTAINMENTS

BOTANIC GARDENS

In Great King Street and close to the city centre, the gardens (open daylight hours) provide a restful oasis for the footsore. They contain exotic and native flowers and trees, and an aviary. Occasionally a band plays in the rotunda on Sunday, a Victorian tradition long vanished elsewhere in New Zealand.

THEATRES

Dunedin's one professional theatre, the Fortune, has a lively program, often premiering New Zealand drama. It is located in the old Trinity Methodist Church (1869) in Moray Place. An unusually intimate urban theatre, at 104 London Street, the Globe is an extension of a private residence. It was created by the post-war theatrical pioneers Rosalie and Patric Carey. James K. Baxter's plays were first produced here, and many later professional actors began their careers on this tiny stage. It still supports a regular amateur program, with actors mainly from the university and the professions.

Murihiku: Southland – Fiordland

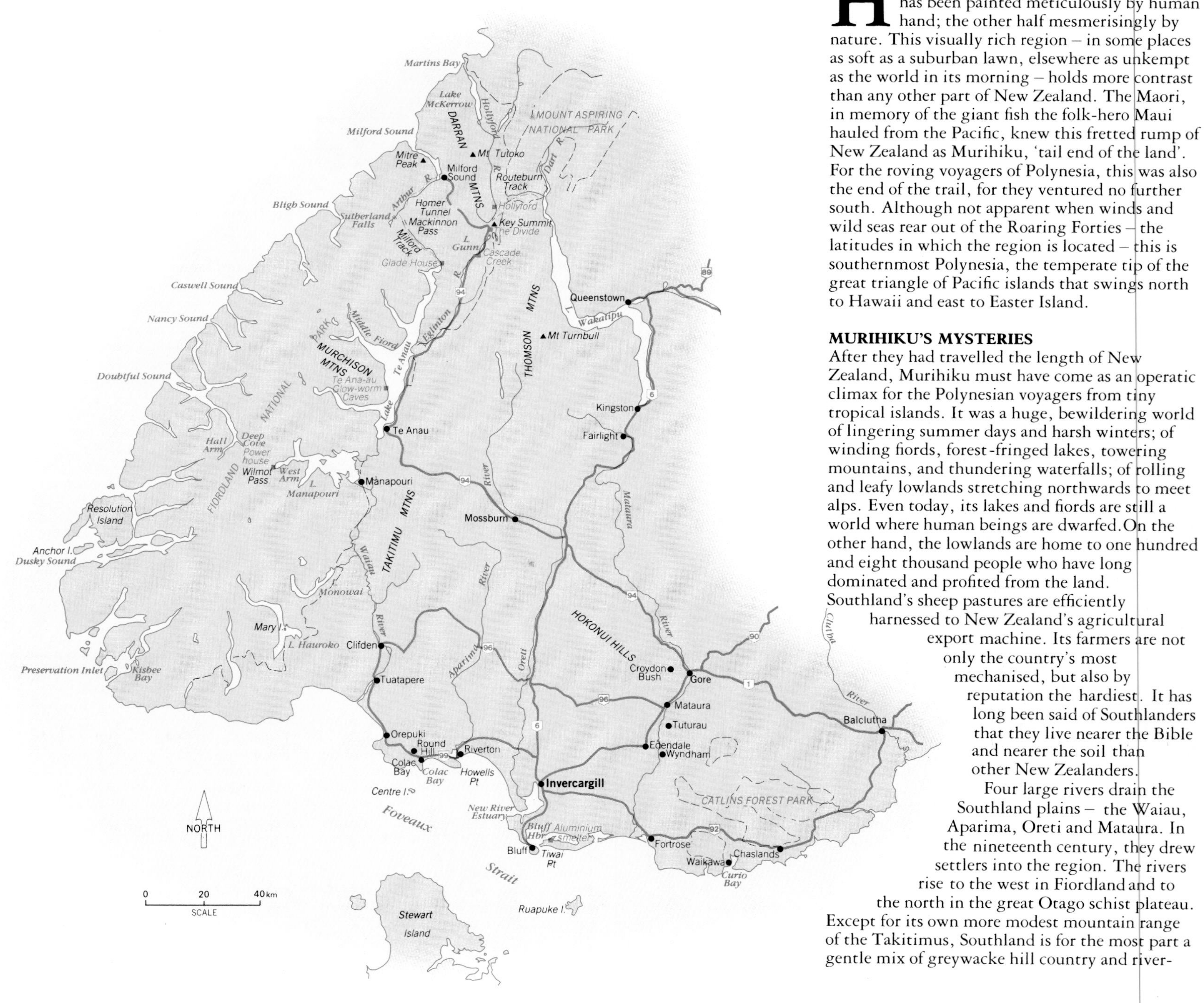

Half the Southland–Fiordland panorama has been painted meticulously by human hand; the other half mesmerisingly by nature. This visually rich region – in some places as soft as a suburban lawn, elsewhere as unkempt as the world in its morning – holds more contrast than any other part of New Zealand. The Maori, in memory of the giant fish the folk-hero Maui hauled from the Pacific, knew this fretted rump of New Zealand as Murihiku, 'tail end of the land'. For the roving voyagers of Polynesia, this was also the end of the trail, for they ventured no further south. Although not apparent when winds and wild seas rear out of the Roaring Forties – the latitudes in which the region is located – this is southernmost Polynesia, the temperate tip of the great triangle of Pacific islands that swings north to Hawaii and east to Easter Island.

MURIHIKU'S MYSTERIES

After they had travelled the length of New Zealand, Murihiku must have come as an operatic climax for the Polynesian voyagers from tiny tropical islands. It was a huge, bewildering world of lingering summer days and harsh winters; of winding fiords, forest-fringed lakes, towering mountains, and thundering waterfalls; of rolling and leafy lowlands stretching northwards to meet alps. Even today, its lakes and fiords are still a world where human beings are dwarfed. On the other hand, the lowlands are home to one hundred and eight thousand people who have long dominated and profited from the land. Southland's sheep pastures are efficiently harnessed to New Zealand's agricultural export machine. Its farmers are not only the country's most mechanised, but also by reputation the hardiest. It has long been said of Southlanders that they live nearer the Bible and nearer the soil than other New Zealanders.

Four large rivers drain the Southland plains – the Waiau, Aparima, Oreti and Mataura. In the nineteenth century, they drew settlers into the region. The rivers rise to the west in Fiordland and to the north in the great Otago schist plateau. Except for its own more modest mountain range of the Takitimus, Southland is for the most part a gentle mix of greywacke hill country and river-

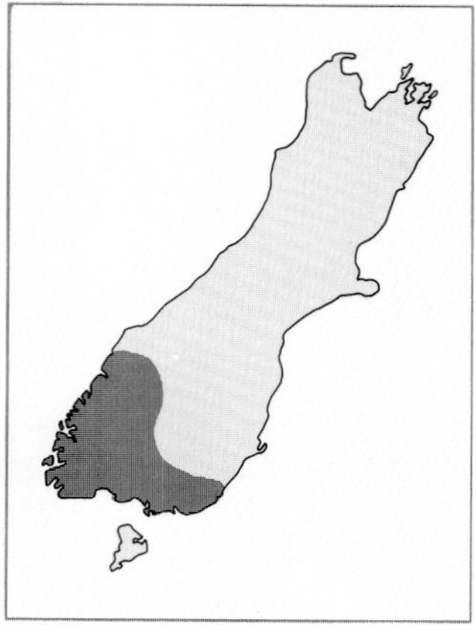

LAND OF CONTRASTS

sliced lowland. By contrast, Fiordland is New Zealand's most unmanageable medley of land forms. It is a great block of hard metamorphosed rocks, or gneisses, of the early Palaeozoic age. Deeply dissected by ice, it was invaded by the sea after the retreat of the glaciers to form the long, deep fiords which characterise Murihiku. On the eastern side of the Fiordland massif, glacier-scooped valleys, dammed with morainic debris, have filled with fresh water to form large lakes – Te Anau, Manapouri, Monowai and Hauroko.

A LOST TRIBE

The first people to settle in Murihiku fished the sea and hunted the moa, the muttonbird and the seal. Tribe after tribe, dispossessed and on the move south in the wake of war, tussled for possession of the land. The Waitaha, probably the original moa hunters, were destroyed by the Ngati Mamoe, who in turn gave way to the Ngai Tahu. By the end of the eighteenth century, the Ngai Tahu were in firm possession of the territory. The Ngati Mamoe, remembered in folklore as 'the lost tribe', made a final stand at Te Anau, and after a bloody defeat vanished into Fiordland's forests. When Captain James Cook camped for more than a month in Fiordland's vast Dusky Sound during his second visit to New Zealand in 1773, he encountered shy and possibly fugitive Maoris. These seem to have been the last of the Ngati Mamoe. For another century, Europeans in Fiordland reported mysterious 'wild natives' – inexplicable footprints, cooling campfires – and even well into the twentieth century rumours of the lost tribe have lingered.

Another Fiordland riddle is that of the moa, a creature long believed to have been hunted into extinction by the Maori centuries before the arrival of Europeans. A pioneer memoir reports a sighting in northern Fiordland in the eighteen-eighties, and an itinerant Danish gold prospector named Jules Berg claimed two sightings in the twentieth century. A moa skeleton was discovered bearing marks that may have been made by a metallic blade, which suggests at least one post-European killing of the creature. In 1948 the takahe, or notornis, another flightless bird also thought to be extinct, turned up near Te Anau. Might there still be surviving moas in Murihiku's sketchily explored wilds? An expedition mounted into Fiordland in the nineteen-seventies by a Japanese film crew failed to rendezvous with the last, lost moa.

LURE OF THE SEA'S HARVEST

Cook's crewmen killed seals while in Dusky Sound, and used the skins for rigging, the fat for oil to burn in the ship's lamps and the flesh to feed themselves.Less than two decades later, in 1792, the first European seal-hunters arrived in Murihiku from the newly founded Australian penal settlement of Sydney. Captain Raven of the *Britannia* set a party of sealers ashore, thus establishing the first European settlement – though of temporary nature – in New Zealand. In the following ten months Raven's shore party harvested four and a half thousand sealskins. They also built New Zealand's first European dwelling and the country's first European vessel. This thrust inspired others in Sydney, but a two-ship expedition in 1795 was less fortunate. One of the vessels foundered and sank in Dusky Sound. For a time – in a decade when there were no other permanent white residents in New Zealand – Fiordland had a castaway community of more than two hundred Europeans. Misfortunes were no deterrent. For Sydney's tea-drinking colonists seal skins were worth all the tea in China.

Skippers were soon dumping party after party of men on the shores of Murihiku, many of them freed or runaway convicts. Europe was suddenly storming ashore establishing beachheads. The men of such communities were abandoned to the menacing land for months, sometimes years. On occasion, their skippers failed altogether to return. When they did return they sometimes found that shore parties had vanished, swallowed up by the land, or possibly by cannibal Maoris. One young sealer who lost his companions became a tattooed Maori chief of rank and 'quite as open a cannibal as any'. Other sealers were enslaved. But the war on the seals of the south lost nothing in fervour. In 1806 an American captain sailed for Sydney with sixty thousand skins. In 1810, in one week alone, Murihiku skins to the value of a hundred thousand pounds were landed in Australia. This brutal bonanza made the region an annexe of Australia's frontier. The seals, beginning with the pups, were first stunned with a club, after which knives were used 'to cut and rip them . . . from the under jaw to the tail, giving a stab in the chest that will kill them'. It was the violent trade of mostly violent men; Maoris who impeded them were sometimes slain as efficiently. One observer, John Boultbee, found cause to consider the Maoris more edifying company than his fellow Europeans.

By the eighteen-thirties the fur seals of Murihiku were almost exterminated. It was the turn of the whalers to seek an equally profitable harvest from the sea. They founded Murihiku's first durable European settlements, located among Maoris who were by then largely resigned to white people picking Polynesia's world apart. Such a settlement was Jacobs River, now known as Riverton, established by Captain John Howell in 1836. There were other rough communities at Bluff and Preservation Inlet. As whale stocks in turn were depleted, the hunters looked inland at last, and saw potentially rich pastoral country. Howell of Riverton was the first to amass land. He accrued thousands of hectares as a dowry when he married the daughter of a Maori chief.

Whaler communities were well established in Southland by the time British colonisation of New Zealand began in earnest. The arrival of Scots colonists in Otago in 1848 brought nearly sixty years of haphazard settlement to an end. In 1854 the colonial government formally purchased the Murihiku block, comprising the greater part of Southland, for two thousand six hundred pounds. Early contenders for the territory – such as whaler Johnny Jones of Otago – had their claims dismissed or much reduced. There was to be no lawless squatting. From Dunedin a Scottish trek began into the badlands of Murihiku. It was country well suited to the hardy shepherds from the Scottish Highlands. Aspirant pastoralists, with thousands of acres in mind, moved in too.

INDUSTRIOUS SOUTHLANDERS

In 1856 a level site for a new southern settlement, the future city of Invercargill, was chosen and named after one of Dunedin's founders, William Cargill. As elsewhere in the South Island, surveyor J.T. Thomson left his mark here in his sensitive planning of the new community. By 1859 Invercargill had two hundred dwellings and close to one thousand people, with banks, churches and a school. While pioneers sweated it out in the hinterland, political wrangling soured the fast-growing town. Southland sought separate status from Otago province, won it, then lost it again. After 1876, with the abolition of provincial government, the issue no longer much mattered. Yet Southland retained its separate character, particularly in its speech. In a country with a largely classless accent, Southland speech has long had a distinct regional colour, the soft and pleasant 'Southland burr'.

Left: *Typical sheep farming country in Southland – the wide, flat plain at Mossburn extends to the mountains*
Above: *Another view of the landscape near Mossburn*

That burr has a rural Scottish base. As they cleared forest and drained swamp, the region's first farmers planted oats, and pastured sheep and dairy cows. At first dairying was the most attractive proposition. Southland once ranked with the Waikato and Taranaki in the production of cheese and butter, with something like forty factories. The Romney sheep was found to be the best suited to this territory. It is a measure of Southland's agricultural success that with fewer than four per cent of New Zealand's people it produces close to twenty per cent of the country's primary exports, and this with the shortest grass-growing season in the country. Nothing was ever easy here. Alluvial soil which at first looked promising to the pioneers was in fact leached and acid, and had to be rebuilt with lime and cobaltised superphosphate. It now seems the most remarkably green of New Zealand regions, more so when seen in its setting of dark blue sea. It is also a region that has never lost its first head of steam. There are few laments here about a population drift to the north. Unlike other South Island towns and cities, Invercargill – now with fifty-four thousand people – maintains modest growth. Intensive mechanisation on the land is backed by the busy export port of Bluff, with its thirty-two hectare artificial harbour and its monster meat loaders, the dinosaurs of waterfront technology. In the second half of the twentieth century Southland embraced industry too, in the form of the aluminium smelter at Tiwai Point, powered by Fiordland's harnessed waters.

The Manapouri hydro-electric power project, curbed in dimension by conservationists, remains the only major human breach of Fiordland's fortress-like wilderness. Just one major road – from Te Anau up the Eglinton Valley and through the Homer Tunnel to Milford – labours

Riverton is one of the oldest European settlements in New Zealand. This imposing brick house in Palmerston Street contrasts strangely with the typical nineteenth-century workmen's cottages in the same street. Riverton Museum and the Custom House are also in this street

A barley field near Wairio township. Southland farmers have always cultivated the land and pastured sheep and cattle

Above: *Riverton has an interesting collection of old cottages, among them is this one in Havelock Street*
Below: *The splendidly Victorian Railway Hotel at Invercargill recalls the days of more leisurely travel*

through this tall and little inhabited territory. Otherwise, a few Maori middens and lonely European memorials tell of a long-relinquished grip on its extremities. After the sealers and whalers had had their day, even the cries of seasonal Maori hunters ceased to sound faintly across the fiords and lakes. On the inland side, settlers pushed sheep and cattle as far as Lake Te Anau – and in one or two instances still further – but for the most part they found the region impenetrable. On the seaward side, a settlement on difficult terrain at Martins Bay soon foundered.

Through this rugged labyrinth lapped the ocean, not to speak of small freshwater seas locked up by mountain and moraine. And there was no sound save that of water, wind and birds until disappointed gold prospectors and solitary adventurers began their intrusion. One such intruder was former Garibaldi redshirt Donald Sutherland, whose name is preserved in the falls, now one of Fiordland's most famous attractions. He took up residence in Milford in 1878, building three huts and naming them 'The City of Milford'. He explored the fiord and fossicked for *tangiwai*, the pale tear-like greenstone treasured by the Maori. His hermit years ended in 1888 when explorer Quintin Mackinnon located a pass between Te Anau and Milford. Sutherland then married a Dunedin woman and established Milford's first accommodation house. A pioneer of Fiordland tourism, Sutherland welcomed visitors and the first trampers off the Milford Track when the route was opened in the eighteen-nineties. The large government hotel risen on the site of Sutherland's venture is still New Zealand's most isolated tourist accommodation.

Yet even in Milford Sound, the most visited part of Fiordland, human presence is wispy in a maze of mountain and water. A passing tourist launch may rumble there; a lonely plane may buzz there. Then silence speaks more potently.

Elsewhere a few steps off the beaten track lead into an unruly landscape older than pagan, where even Maori lore seems never to have taken deep root, and the European imagination has seldom moved more than feebly. Nowhere in the country have human beings left less of themselves. Nowhere in the country does the natural world give more. Fiordland is New Zealand at its mightiest, Murihiku at its most lavish.

NATURE'S FORTRESS

Almost exclusively made of mountain and water, Fiordland is by far the wildest, wettest and loneliest part of New Zealand

In this rugged terrain, fingers of the ocean reach far inland to flood alpine valleys, form harbours of dazzling dimensions and leave peaks wandering over the waves. The storms of the Roaring Forties beat at Fiordland's stony and precipitous bulk. This is one of the wettest places in the world, with Milford Sound registering on average a remarkable six thousand millimetres or more a year. What most travellers might consider catastrophic cloudbursts are a commonplace of the climate. Although rain may often mist the familiar picture-postcard panoramas of Fiordland, it produces a spectacle of a more powerful and less photogenic kind as valleys reverberate with rockfalls and avalanches, rivers begin to roar and waterfalls by the score seethe from heights and hanging valleys and slam down steep slopes to the sea. The rain also nourishes rich beech forest which, where it can find a footing, glitters up to a thousand metres above sea level. In the forest's highest reaches, as trees grow more stunted, nature compensates grossly with long lichen. When the mist curls through this landscape, it becomes goblin territory.

The permanent snows of rugged Fiordland in close-up: the photograph was taken in the Mackinnon Pass area

The eastern frontier of Fiordland, where the forest gives way to drier and pastoral Southland, is defined by large lakes. On the western boundary lies the convoluted Tasman coast. To the north the icefalls and white summits of the Darran Mountains are the highest part of Fiordland, dominated by Mount Tutoko at two thousand seven hundred and fifty six metres. The Fiordland massif began as sediment on the ocean floor four hundred million years ago. Pressure and the heat of the earth's core compacted the debris and

Fiordland's highest peak, Mount Tutoko, seen from an aircraft – the easiest way to approach it. Mountaineers claim that it is one of the most difficult peaks to scale

processed it into the metamorphic rock which characterises most of the region. Planetary convulsion hoisted it high above sea level, and then submerged it again to cake it lightly with more sedimentary rock. Finally – something like two million years ago – Fiordland again rose from the seabed. The ice ages completed its shaping. Up to fifteen thousand years ago, glaciers were still hewing great highways with perpendicular walls. Then, as the ice retreated, thawed waters filled inland basins and, on the west coast, the rising sea raced in to gulp up the valleys left by the glaciers. Vegetation clambered into the space left vacant between the mountains and the sea.

Many more millenniums passed before human beings – perhaps Polynesians paddling a canoe – made their entrance into this towering theatre. But even the boldest of intruders failed to play more than a bit-part here. It was mapped, but then for the most part left well alone. Fiordland National Park – more than the total area of all New Zealand's other national parks – includes over a million and a quarter hectares of the world's most arresting wilderness.

FRESHWATER FRONTIER

The two large lakes of Te Anau and Manapouri are still filled with the same awesome silence that met the first Polynesian explorers

Below: *Lake Te Anau, the second largest lake in New Zealand, sprawls at the feet of rugged mountains, with finger-like fiords penetrating into the mountain ranges*
Right: *The vast, cathedral-like, underground powerhouse of Manapouri power station. It is now in full operation, but when the scheme was first announced it was the cause of violent controversy, and the plans had to be modified*

Standing at the northern edge of Fiordland, these lakes also mark the last significant human intervention into the region. Beyond their waters the horizon climbs abruptly, and a green throng of mountains meets the sky. Both lakes have lyrical Maori names recorded by European cartographers, though later disputed. Both are rich in lonely and unblemished reaches. One thousand years of human settlement in New Zealand have left few obvious marks along Fiordland's leafy and winding waterways.

Lake Te Anau, the largest body of fresh water in the South Island, covers three hundred and forty square kilometres and has some five hundred kilometres of mostly uninhabited shore. The tourist resort of Te Anau – Fiordland's only substantial community – camps on the waterside, and still has a rather haphazard frontier atmosphere. From here, the traveller can drive up the Eglinton Valley towards Milford Sound or take a scenic flight into Fiordland's heart.

The lake's Maori name was once thought to derive from that of the grand-daughter of the man who discovered it, but some Europeans interpreted it as a contraction of *Te Ana-au*, 'the cave of rushing water'. To complicate matters further, Maori tradition also hinted at 'the cave of phosphorescence', *Te Ana hinatore*. But where? In May 1948 the cave was finally discovered with its incandescent roof of glow-worms. High in the Murchison Mountains beyond the lake, another discovery, also in 1948, confirmed that Fiordland could still hold secrets. The takahe, a New Zealand flightless bird long thought extinct, was located in a snow-grass valley. While the Te Anau Glow-worm Caves are now the lake's most popular tourist attraction, the terrain of the rare and declining takahe is off limits to visitors.

Lake Manapouri, deep and dotted with islands, has always seemed worthy of a marvellous legend. The map-maker who gave it its present name evidently thought so: *Manapouri* means roughly 'sorrowing heart'. The name was in fact stolen from another and less distinguished lake. Manapouri's original name – Moturau, 'a hundred islands' – perhaps seemed too literal for so haunted a location. Its forested islands, thirty-five of them strewn across one hundred and forty-two square kilometres, together with its intricate shoreline, give the lake its special character. During the nineteen-sixties and seventies, Manapouri was the setting for a long-running conservationist saga. A hydro-electric scheme was planned to power Bluff's projected aluminium smelter. The waters of Lake Manapouri were to be fed ten kilometres via turbines and a tailrace down a drop of two hundred metres to Doubtful Sound. This would have entailed raising the level of the lake, effectively leaving its verdant shores a desert of drowned trees. Fiordland already had one lake, Monowai, spoilt by such a scheme in the nineteen-twenties. Ripples of local protest reached the furthest points of New Zealand and rivers of support rolled back. For most of a decade politicians and civil servants, misjudging the situation, refused to take opposition to the plan seriously. In 1972 the saving of Manapouri became an election issue. Surprising shifts of votes argued that the conservation movement was at last to be reckoned with. New Zealanders, mourning the destruction of much of the environment since European settlement, were using Manapouri as a battle cry. Finally, a revised hydro-electric scheme went ahead, one that did not raise the level of Manapouri. The new government appointed local protesters as guardians of the lake. They have done their job well: the shores of Manapouri still shimmer. And the lake now has a legend undeniably its own. It begins, 'Once there was a lake so magical that it sank a government . . .'

The still waters of Lake Manapouri surrounded by mountains

Boat trips are a popular tourist attraction on the lake

WEST TO THE WILDERNESS

From Te Anau maritime Fiordland is approached by two overland routes of breathtaking beauty, both of them culminating at magnificent Milford Sound

The three- or four-day walk, or three- or four-hour drive are both visual feasts. New Zealand has long sold the Milford Track to tourists as 'the finest walk in the world', and even hard-nosed travel writers have never begged to differ. The track winds through some of the world's most vivid and least trampled wilderness. On the other hand many see the road into Milford as arguably the world's most stunning mountain drive. For the traveller with time, tramping in and riding out can put both claims to the test.

Maori legend say that Fiordland is a mighty sculpture, the loving labour of the god Tu, who was at pains to adze out a landscape that would live for ever. Hine-nui-te-po, the underworld goddess of darkness and death, found that Tu's masterpiece was too good for mortals. In a place of such beauty they might also wish to live for ever, and leave her with no clientele. So she deposited the sandfly – the *namu* – in Fiordland, to remind human beings of the fragility of the flesh and discourage them from lingering too long there. Captain Cook confirmed that Hine-nui-te-po's prescription had been effective, describing the insects as 'small black flies, which are very numerous, and so troublesome that they exceed everything of the kind I have ever met with'.

After years of searching, explorer Quintin Mackinnon, a Scottish ex-soldier who also answered to the name Rob Roy, found an overland route into Milford in 1888. He became the first guide on the Milford Track as the trickle of curious visitors became a modest rush. Mackinnon did not live

Moss-covered trees in the breathtaking Cleddau Valley, at the western exit of the Homer Tunnel on Highway 94

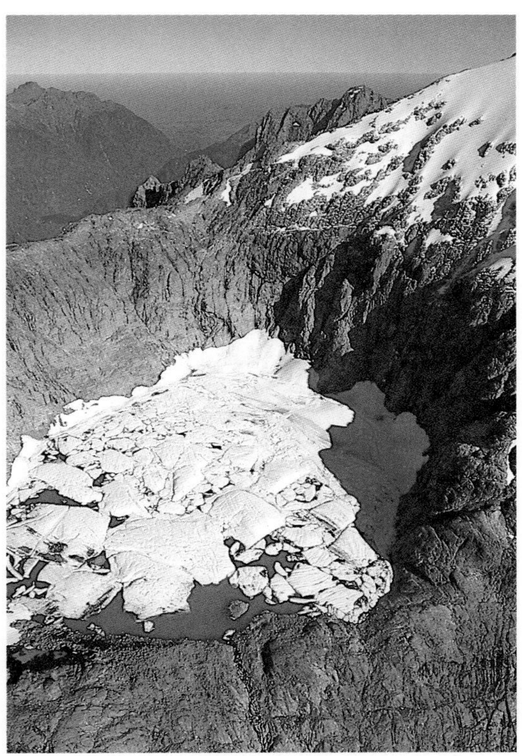
High alpine lake near Mackinnon Pass seen from an aircraft

long enough to see the bridges, rest benches and huts that further domesticated the rough trail he blazed through forest and mountains. He drowned in Lake Te Anau in 1892, and a stone memorial now stands on the pass he discovered. By 1913 the New Zealand government, recognising a considerable tourist asset, had taken the track over, but it was open only to guided parties.

In the second half of the twentieth century, this exclusive use of the track was successfully contested by 'freedom walkers', who wished to explore Fiordland at their own pace. Today thousands of walkers – some with guides and using congenial tourist accommodation, others without and using simple national park huts – take the relatively easy fifty-four kilometre walk into Milford annually. For four days spectacle upon spectacle is heaped to every horizon, and waterfalls, wildlife, canyons and summits enthral the tramper. There may or may not be a finer walk in the world. What can be said with confidence is that there is no hike in the world with a climax more ravishing than Milford Sound.

NO FINER DRIVE

The same can be said of the alpine drive up the Eglinton Valley. The relatively unsung road into the much celebrated Milford Sound is a scene-stealing revelation, and not to be rushed. Leaving Lake Te Anau, the highway soon reveals here rivers, lakes and tussock flats, elsewhere beech forests and everywhere precipitous mountains. Roadside picnic places and campsites ask to be occupied. As the road labours into a more rugged landscape, the sound of water becomes more pronounced, especially after rain, when it turns to a roar. The mountains are suddenly more demonic than decorative. Trees take on tortured shapes in a heath littered with rockfall. Snowfields disappear into the mountain mist, and waterfalls thread down a hundred barren rock faces.

The parking area at the entrance to the rough-hewn Homer Tunnel is a place to pause and consider the road-builders who made this dramatic route possible. The first picks and shovels went to work in 1929. In the Depression of the nineteen-thirties formerly unemployed men toiled in this often menacing location. Three were killed and others injured in avalanches that roared down on their campsites. Work on the twelve hundred and forty metre tunnel began in 1935, and the first private car travelled through it in 1954. Beginning at nine hundred and twenty-one metres above sea level, the tunnel drops one hundred and twenty-nine metres before daylight is glimpsed ahead and the green of the Cleddau Valley can be seen. Then it is suddenly all downhill to Milford Sound. No one would deny Milford its spell, but the highway wrested from Fiordland's wilds is bewitching too.

A cairn has been erected near the summit of Mackinnon Pass to commemorate its discoverer's first crossing in 1888

Lake Gunn with mirror-like reflections of nearby mountains

A watercourse among vegetation and rocks near Falls Creek

Eglinton Valley, on the motorist's scenic route to Milford

THE SOUND OF SORROW

Although much painted and photographed, magical Milford Sound still stuns visitors with its dramatic splendour

The Maori name for Milford Sound suggests that it has long been acknowledged as an enchanted place. They called it *Piopio-tahi*, 'a single thrush'. This bird was once the companion of the mighty Polynesian folk-hero Maui. When Maui courageously sought immortality for the human race within the womb of the sleeping Hine-nui-te-po, the goddess of darkness and death, the bird burst into loud song. Hine woke in a rage and crushed Maui between her vast thighs. The sorrowing bird, having extinguished humanity's last hope of immortality, flew to Milford Sound to live in solitude and repentance. Its tears turned into that precious local form of greenstone known as *tangiwai*, 'grieving tears' – more translucent and softer than its Westland counterpart, a bowenite rather than a nephrite, and prized for its ornamental character. Almost all we know of Milford's pre-European history is that Maori came here to gather *tangiwai* at least once in a tribal generation. What more the Maori made of Milford was lost with Fiordland's last 'wild native' at least a century ago.

Mitre Peak, the trademark of Milford Sound, at close range

The coming of the sealers, at the beginning of the nineteenth century, ended Milford's centuries-long seclusion. It is said that some Maoris collecting *tangiwai* innocently welcomed ashore the first sealers from Sydney, and were ruthlessly gunned down. The dead were heaped into a canoe, which was towed out to sea and then set alight. A charred canoe with human remains found washed ashore in the eighteen-seventies confirmed the poignant story.

Welshman John Grono, a sealer who worked this coast in the eighteen-twenties, named the sound after Milford Haven in South Wales. The first European to regard the magical location as more than a killing ground was Captain Stokes of the survey ship *Acheron* in 1851. Stokes marvelled at the 'towering cliffs which dwindled the *Acheron*'s masts into nothing'. The waterfalls leaping into the sound were just as aweing, especially the Bowen (named after Sir George Bowen who later became governor of New Zealand), near which the ship anchored. It seemed to Stokes 'to burst from a large reservoir and fall with incessant roar into the sound below'. A ship's artist produced the first known painting of Milford, thereby blazing a trail for tens of thousands of artists and others since. Stokes named Mitre Peak, now the sound's best-known feature, and pronounced Milford Sound 'the most remarkable Harbour yet visited by the *Acheron* in New Zealand'.

MONARCH OF MILFORD SOUND

Milford's first settler was ex-seaman and ex-soldier Donald Sutherland. Sailing into the sound in the eighteen-sixties he predicted, 'If ever I come to anchor, it will be here'. It was over a decade before he did so, taking up a hermit-like residence at the head of the sound in 1878, living off the land, hunting for gold and greenstone, and killing and stuffing native birds to sell as souvenirs to passing travellers. With a mineral-hunting companion he discovered the falls that now bear his name. He estimated the height of the falls to be between three and four thousand feet, perhaps even five thousand, which would have meant they were the highest in the world. Although their height was later established at a mere nineteen hundred and four feet (five hundred and eighty metres) by a surveyor, the Sutherland Falls remain the world's fifth highest and, with their three large leaps, perhaps the loveliest.

When Quintin Mackinnon (sometimes spelt Quinton McKinnon) found an overland route into Milford in 1888, pioneering the Milford Track, Sutherland was distinctly unimpressed. With his reign in Milford Sound coming to an end, and exhibiting a show of sour grapes, he pointed out that he could have disclosed the existence of Mackinnon's mountain pass any time he wished. As the number of visitors to the sound increased, Sutherland made the most of the situation. He married and established a twelve-room accommodation house, which operated at the head of the sound for nearly three decades. When Sutherland died in 1919, his wife became known as 'the Mother of Milford Sound'. After her death in 1923, the government took the Sutherland hostel over, extending and refurbishing it as the tourist hotel that stands on the site today. Yet seen from a distance – from the sea or by air – the hotel remains as trivial an intrusion on Fiordland as Sutherland's first campsite must have been.

Striking Milford Sound, the most accessible of the fiords

The two-tier Bowen Falls erupt from a hanging valley; after heavy rainfall there may be just one gigantic plunge

The wilderness that Sutherland and Maori *tangiwai*-gatherers had to themselves is a short walk away. Today's visitors share it only with a colourful cluster of crayfishing vessels that work the Fiordland coast. A meal of Fiordland crayfish is as much a highlight of a visit to Milford as a scenic flight to the secluded Sutherland Falls. But it is from sea level that Milford best discloses its magnificence, with torrents tumbling from hanging valleys and Mitre Peak glistening high above. The launch trip to the head of the sound is unforgettable. In the end even the most confirmed New Zealand sceptic, sated with the Milford so long flaunted by tourist posters, is reduced to silence by its primeval splendour .

The jetty and crayfish boats at Milford Sound, the local centre for all tourist activities at the head of the sound

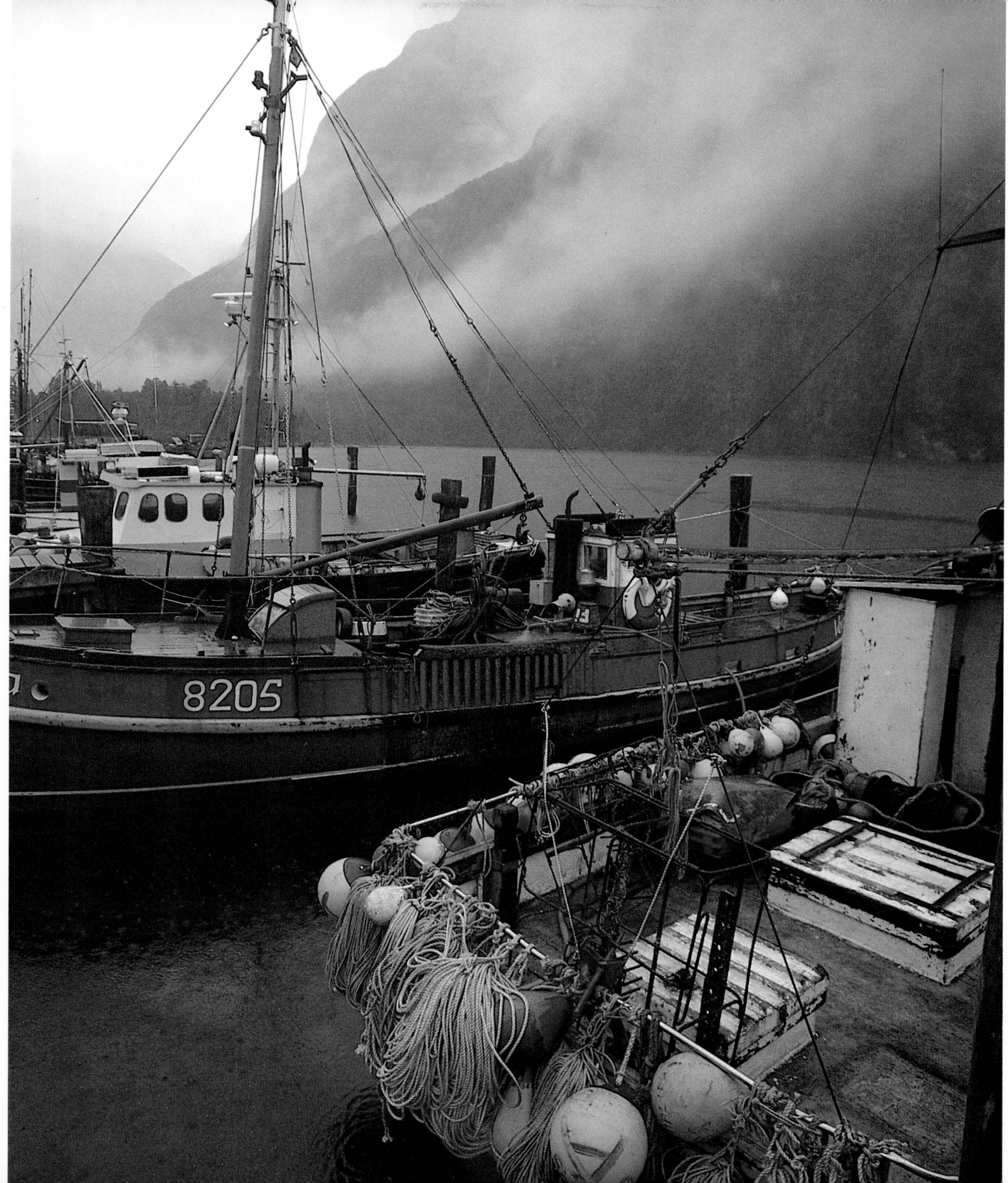
8205

THE SILENT SOUNDS

South of Milford Sound, the rocky coast is broken by a dozen other fiords, some larger and even more intricate

Scenic flights and boat excursions now make it possible to see two of these fiords, Doubtful and Dusky Sounds. Others, such as Caswell, Nancy, Bligh and Preservation Inlet are likely to remain the empty haunts of a few hardy trampers and hunters, and the crayfish boats working the Fiordland coast.

One by-product of the largest human intrusion into Fiordland – the Manapouri hydro-electric power scheme – has been to make Doubtful Sound more accessible; until a decade or two ago it was seldom seen or visited. This does not mean it is now possible to drive there. Unless a sightseeing flight is taken, it can be reached only by conducted tour. The first leg of the journey is by tourist boat across island-studded Lake Manapouri. The next, from Manapouri's West Arm, is by coach. A winding tunnel descends steeply through the ancient gneisses of the Fiordland massif to the humming heart of the power project. Seven great turbines are housed in an immense and chilly cavern, quarried more than two hundred metres below the level of Lake Manapouri. Here, as nowhere else in Fiordland, human accomplishment matches nature's; even the most fervent conservationist cannot fail to be impressed by this marvel of human enterprise, one which claimed fifteen lives in its making.

Surfacing again, the coach travels across the six hundred-and-seventy-metre high Wilmot Pass, with Doubtful Sound at last in sight. Then New Zealand's steepest road, the most costly in the country's history (at roughly two dollars a centimetre), descends seven kilometres to the shore of the fiord at Deep Cove through luxuriant rainforest. The stunning rainfall of the region – averaging over six thousand millimetres annually – nourishes the fantastically dense and diverse roadside vegetation, conspicuously tall ferns and festooning mosses. From Deep Cove, a boat excursion along the sound's Hall Arm idles around islands and cruises under awesome heights, while water crashes down hundreds of metres from hanging valleys.

A LOST WORLD

The twenty-kilometre long Doubtful Sound was given its name in 1770 by Captain Cook, who thought it imprudent to risk the narrow entrance and called it 'Doubtfull Harbour'. On his 1773 voyage he was less hesitant about entering the mightiest of all the fiords, the place he had already named 'Dusky Bay' when he first approached it at dusk one evening in 1770. All of forty-four kilometres long, Dusky's maze of wooded islands and wandering waterways can be appreciated as a whole only from the air. Even for New Zealanders who consider themselves familiar with the contours and colours of their native land, Dusky Sound comes as a numbing surprise. For those fortunate enough to find their way there, it seems more a lost world than a mere fiord.

Little has changed since Cook and his crew refreshed themselves in Dusky Sound, and repaired the *Resolution*, more than two centuries ago. The few Maoris Cook befriended in his six-and-a-half week stay (and whom his artist William Hodges painted in classical pose) have long since gone, leaving virtually no trace of their tenancy of caves and rock overhangs. There are now no permanent human inhabitants. Dusky Sound is populated by penguins and sooty shearwaters, and fur seals are slowly returning to bays and headlands where their ancestors once teemed. The stumps of the trees Cook's crewmen felled can still be seen, rather miraculously preserved. A boardwalk – one of the few recent human marks in this territory – loops around the clearing those same men created on Astronomers Point in Pickersgill Harbour. Once, there was a forge, tents for sailmakers, a workshop for coopers, and a small brewery producing a scurvy-beating ale from rimu and manuka. It was here that navigator William Wales finally established New Zealand's longitude by means of the sun and stars. Much of Europe's knowledge of New Zealand was derived from Dusky Sound. Naturalist Johann Forster and his son George meticulously chronicled and sketched birdlife. Botanical specimens were collected and catalogued. Crewmen detailed to fish hauled in large catches.

Dusky Sound is still as remote, lonely and lovely today as when Captain Cook and his crew sojourned there in 1773

This remote and still relatively little known enclave of the South Island saw Europe's beginnings in New Zealand. In that respect it has a greater claim on history than the Bay of Islands. Two decades after Cook's brief sojourn, the rough, ephemeral townships of sealing gangs began to appear. The first gang of sealers to be set ashore, in 1792, survived in Luncheon Cove on Anchor Island for ten months in the country's first European dwelling, measuring only twelve by five and half metres. They also built a sixteen metre boat, the first of European construction in New Zealand, in case they might have to find their own way home to Sydney. When their mother ship did return, they had harvested four and a half thousand sealskins and founded the country's earliest export trade. Soon afterwards, two hundred and forty-four people were stranded in Dusky (at that time there were no other European settlers in New Zealand) and some of them survived there for two years before being shipped out. Before long a permanent sealing settlement was established at Luncheon Cove and lasted about thirty years, until the virtual extinction of the Fiordland fur seal. Little is known about the human dramas played here. The ruins of a hut or two can still be found in dense vegetation, all that is left of the lonely lives lived by Fiordland Maoris and sealers.

Rugged Preservation Inlet, where the sea pushes thirty-six kilometres into the mountainous south, has more recent relics of human occupation. This southernmost fiord was near the great whaling grounds of Foveaux Strait and became a whalers' haven when sealers had finished with Fiordland. Later, when that slaughter too was done, Preservation Inlet was abandoned in its turn. At the end of the nineteenth century sawmillers operated there and gold-seekers worked its rivers and reefs, with modest success. A small community persisted until well into the first half of the twentieth century, but now old dwellings are rotting back into the forest. Crayfishermen still breathe a little human life into the place when they moor here. Float planes drop in hunters, and a few trampers battle overland, through largely trackless forest, to camp here a day or two. Otherwise the bays, beaches and islands of Preservation Inlet have retreated into a silence as deep as that of Dusky Sound.

PLACES OF INTEREST

BLUFF
New Zealand's southernmost town and export port of 2600 people is 27 kilometres from **INVERCARGILL**, on a peninsula extending into stormy Foveaux Strait. Named after the hill that overlooks the harbour, Bluff grew as a sheltered base for sealers, whalers, flax merchants and rum traders. Today it is a community of fishermen, oystermen, muttonbirders, crayfishermen and slaughtermen, many of Maori blood. Here Highway 1 ends at the Pacific. The only remaining part of New Zealand is Stewart Island, which may be reached from Bluff by sea excursion. The town's immense artificial island harbour sends frozen lamb carcasses by the million to the world's meat markets. Across the water, the Tiwai Point aluminium smelter produces some 240 000 tonnes of aluminium annually, using hydro-electricity from **LAKE MANAPOURI**. The Bluff oyster is dredged here from the Foveaux Strait; its condition and price when the harvest begins is always national news. And for good reason: the succulent Bluff oyster has no peer (see page 341). From the top of The Bluff (265 metres), Stewart Island can be seen on the horizon. Otherwise the ocean is empty all the way to the Antarctic.

CATLINS FOREST PARK
This little-known south-east coastal corner of the South Island called the Catlins lies between Southland and Otago (see page 300). Information on the Southland side of the park can be obtained from the NZ Forest Service at Wyndham or **INVERCARGILL**. Commercial day-long tours in the Catlins are organised by a firm based at Edendale.

THE INVERCARGILL SURVEYOR

The layout of Invercargill is the lasting memorial to the talents of John Turnbull Thomson, explorer, civil engineer and New Zealand's first surveyor-general

John Turnbull Thomson (1821-84) was born in England, where he trained as an engineer. At the age of seventeen he went to the Malay Straits and, three years later was appointed government surveyor in Singapore. His achievements in engineering and his skilful surveys of Singapore and the Malay coast were prodigious for one so young. At the age of thirty-two he returned to England, but four years later decided to emigrate to New Zealand where he became Otago's chief surveyor.

In the first busy year of his appointment, Thomson's industry and foresight were staggering. One of his first duties was to select the site for Invercargill and to lay out the town. The farming community was already spreading haphazardly and Thomson insisted on a regular pattern of well-designed streets with – unusual at the time – a belt of reserve land around the town and a garden area at its heart. The character of modern Invercargill owes much to Thomson's long-sightedness and wisdom.

In the same year (1857) he also explored the Waiau, Aparima, Oreti and Mataura Rivers to their sources, traced the Clutha River to Lakes Wanaka and Hawea and discovered the Lindis Pass – thus opening up three million hectares of farmland.

Among the long list of Thomson's other achievements is a bridge over the Mataura River, Dunedin's first metalled road, trunk roads across Otago, a survey of goldfields, precise astronomical observations to ascertain exact longitudes and – as the first surveyor-general of New Zealand – a complete overhaul of provincial survey departments and their reform into a national system.

John Thomson – innovative and inventive

Thomson was renowned for his cold personality and lack of humour. But he was also known for his sense of fairness, his integrity and his refusal to become involved in political bargaining or favours. Invercargill is the testament to his intellect, but his name is preserved in the Thomson Mountains – the range that runs from northern Southland to Lake Wakatipu. And should there be any doubt as to which Thomson the range is named after, it has a Mount Turnbull – his middle name.

CURIO BAY
A detour from Highway 92, 72 kilometres east of **INVERCARGILL**, leads to this bay, where a 160-million-year-old petrified forest lies exposed. At low tide, walk out on the rock platform, veering to the right, to see fallen trunks up to 30 metres long and stony stumps of subtropical species, sculpted by the sea. Along the coast either side of Curio Bay are the former whaling stations of the 1830s, such as Fortrose and Waikawa.

DOUBTFUL SOUND
In 1770 Captain James Cook named this many-limbed Fiordland sound 'Doubtfull Harbour' because of its suspect entrance. The 20 kilometre extent of the sound was not known until 1793, when Spanish navigator Malaspina, after whom the central arm of the sound is named, travelled up the inlet. Claimed to be the most beautiful of Murihiku's many fiords, it can now be reached by boat and coach tours from Manapouri. The road across Wilmot Pass and down to Doubtful Sound is a by-product of the hydro-electric project that divided the nation bitterly in the 1960s (see page 332). A tunnel leads to a subterranean powerhouse.

DUSKY SOUND
The largest fiord in New Zealand, Dusky is 44 kilometres long and has many islands. Captain James Cook named it 'Dusky Bay' in 1770 as he bypassed it towards nightfall. In 1773 he sheltered here several weeks to repair his ship *Resolution* and to rest his crew. The sound is still as lonely and lovely as it was when Cook and his men camped in Pickersgill Harbour and cleared Astronomers Point. Only the shy Maoris, whom Cook befriended and his artist William Hodges painted, have gone. From 1792, sealers worked here establishing New Zealand's first European settlements and first export enterprise. Float planes – and scenic flights – are the best way to reach the sound. There are also cruises from **DOUBTFUL SOUND**. Track information is available from **FIORDLAND NATIONAL PARK** headquarters in **TE ANAU**.

FIORDLAND NATIONAL PARK
Covering 1.25 million hectares, this is New Zealander's largest national park (more than the combined total of all the others) and one of the largest in the world. It is noted for its magnificent scenery, with towering mountain peaks, cascading waterfalls, vast beech forests, a dozen dazzling fiords (from **MILFORD SOUND** down to **PRESERVATION INLET**) and lakes such as **MANAPOURI** and Te Anau. The park includes the **HOLLYFORD VALLEY** and Martins Bay to the north. The Maori knew Fiordland as *Te Rua-o-te-moko*, 'the pit of the tattooing', possibly because glaciers had chiselled the land much as tattooers once worked on a face. Park headquarters are at **TE ANAU**.

GORE
With a population of 9200, this is Southland's second town. As the country and western 'capital' of New Zealand, it hosts the annual Golden Guitar Awards (on Queen's Birthday weekend in June). Gore is also the service centre for Southland's richest farmlands. The region's opulence can be attributed to the hard work of its pioneers, who turned thousands of hectares of swampy lowland and tussocky hills into productive pastoral country. The town takes its name from a 19th-century governor, Thomas Gore Browne. The nearby Hokonui Hills were once famous throughout New Zealand for the country's most potent moonshine liquor, now no more than folklore. Starting from the pleasant Dolamore Park, the 90-minute Croydon Bush Walkway takes in Whisky Creek and Whisky Falls, names bestowed in the bootlegging era. (A confiscated still can be seen in the Southland Centennial Museum at **INVERCARGILL**.) There is a deer park near the centre of town (signposted in Main Street), and some 40 trout streams in the vicinity.

Tourist vessel on Doubtful Sound

HOLLYFORD VALLEY
Just before the Homer Tunnel, on the **MILFORD ROAD**, a signposted road takes the visitor 17 kilometres into the Hollyford Valley, one of Fiordland's many wonders and part of the **FIORDLAND NATIONAL PARK**. At Hollyford (8 kilometres), there is a motor camp established by Murray Gunn, son of legendary trailblazer and cattleman Davy Gunn. At the end of the road there is a 4 to 5-day trek to Lake McKerrow and lonely Martins Bay, with national park huts along the route. There is also a guided tramp that provides comfortable lodges, jet boats to speed the journey and float planes to fly visitors out. In 1870 Martins Bay was the setting for the most

ambitious attempt to colonise Fiordland, but the settlement, known as Jamestown, was virtually abandoned after a few years. One family, the McKenzies, persisted into the 20th century, when Davy Gunn took over their leases and ran cattle until he was drowned in 1955.

INVERCARGILL

Civilization's last citadel in the South Pacific. Invercargill has a population of 54 000, half Murihiku's inhabitants. Named after one of the founders of Dunedin, Captain William Cargill, and meticulously laid out by pioneer surveyor John Turnbull Thomson, it rose on a level site occupied solely until 1856 by Irish ex-sealer James Kelly and his wife. Thomson named the settlement's principal streets after Scottish rivers – Dee, Tay, Esk, Yarrow and Forth – and made lavish provision for parkland. Invercargill still boasts more square metres of park per person than any other New Zealand city and the widest streets. Sailing ships and steamers once sailed up the New (Oreti) River virtually to the town centre, but the development of Invercargill as a port was soon abandoned. **BLUFF** became and remained Southland's port. Rich grassland and freezing works that process Southland lamb have contributed to Invercargill's pastoral affluence, recently reinforced by the Tiwai Point aluminium smelter. Southland's pastures are acclaimed in a polished steel sculpture, *Blade of Grass*, outside the civic buildings in Esk Street.

The Southland Centennial Museum and Art Gallery (Gala Street, by the main entrance to Queens Park) contains relics from wrecks and an abundance of other material from Murihiku's wild past. One of the many fascinating exhibits is an illicit still confiscated from the Hokonui Hills. A sample of fossilised forest from **CURIO BAY** stands outside the museum (open Monday to Friday, 10–4.30; Saturday, 1–5; Sunday and holidays, 2–5). The City Art Gallery, on the city's outskirts in 24 hectares of parkland, is housed in an elegant Georgian-style homestead, and holds an impressive collection of contemporary New Zealand painting. A carved Maori meeting-house stands in the grounds of the gallery (at Anderson Park, signposted 7 kilometres north via Dee Street; open, with tearooms, 2–4.30 daily except Monday and Friday, unless also a public holiday).

Lennel House, a Victorian creeper-covered residence in a lovely garden, was built in 1880 by the city's planner John Turnbull Thomson. The house is still inhabited by his descendants (at 102 Albert Street, limited public access through the NZ Historic Places Trust regional committee). The robust old Railway Hotel (1896) in Leven Street has survived the temperance movement that kept Southland dry for decades. The city's most historic building is modest Kelvin Chambers (1864) where local legislators once deliberated during Southland's brief era as a self-governing province. Except for the Canterbury Provincial Government Buildings in Christchurch, this is the sole survivor of provincial legislative chambers. It has been purchased and restored by the NZ Historic Places Trust.

Attractive Early English Gothic St Paul's Presbyterian Church (1876) served Southland's first Scottish settlers, followed by the larger First Church (1915) in Tay Street. The copper-domed Roman Catholic St Mary's Basilica in Tyne Street (1905) is a distinctive landmark and was designed by F.W. Petre, the architect of many fine Catholic churches in the South Island. St John's Anglican Church, in Tay Street, dates from 1887.

Another feature of Invercargill's skyline is the 32 metre water tower (1889), which was robbed of its cupola in the 1930s and is due to be restored. Contrasting early inner-city Invercargill dwellings can be seen on a 2-hour walk recommended by the NZ Historic Places Trust (Southland branch). Among these are cottages at 160 Yarrow Street, and 133 and 135 Leet Street; villas at 157 Yarrow Street and the north-east corner of Leet and Deveron Streets.

The cottage at 157 Yarrow Street, Invercargill – note the pleasing, simple symmetrical lines

OYSTERS – A MUCH LOVED DELICACY

Bluff is the terminal point of Highway 1, to the south of Invercargill. Mention its name almost anywhere in New Zealand and the likely response will be 'oysters'

Fishing Bluff oysters in Foveaux Strait

The Bluff oyster (*Ostrea lutaria*) – sometimes called the Stewart Island oyster – is claimed by New Zealand gourmets to be one of the finest in the world. It is in fact not exclusive to the Bluff-Stewart Island area but exists unattached (when it has reached an adult state) in colonies on mud and sand shelves in harbours and inlets throughout the country. However, the most productive beds are in Foveaux Strait, in depths of twenty-five to fifty metres.

The depth of the beds means that fishing boats have to be specially adapted for dredging. These boats have lent colour and character to Bluff Harbour, the oyster capital of New Zealand, for more than a century. The local fishermen must be licensed, and work to an annual quota to prevent depletion of the beds. In a good year the oyster trade in New Zealand is worth many millions of dollars.

The harvest season varies from year to year, depending on local conditions, such as the occasional devastations caused by disease or predators. However, dredging is largely a winter activity, commencing in late summer. At this time the oysters produce less shell and become plump as they build up their sexual condition. Bluff oysters are mature and ready for harvesting when they reach a minimum size of seventy millimetres, usually after four or five years of growth. The season ends in spring when spawning commences.

All oysters can change sex or become hermaphroditic, but the Bluff variety has one further unusual characteristic. It incubates its larvae for a far longer time than most other species, so that when the larvae eventually emerge from the parental shell, they already have a swimming organ and a 'foot'; they can immediately crawl to a suitable location to which they attach themselves. Later they will separate from this anchor.

Oysters have many predators, including starfish, crabs and snails, which exact a terrible toll on their population. But none of these enemies can compare with human beings, who have always regarded this succulent shellfish with relish.

KINGSTON

Waterside hamlet of a few dozen people at the southern end of Central Otago's Lake Wakatipu. The most famous of New Zealand's restored vintage steam engines, the 70-year-old *Kingston Flyer*, steams along the scenic line with elegant first-class coaches from Kingston to Fairlight (a 75-minute return journey) three or four times daily between October 1 and May 18. The line is a remnant of one that served Central Otago's gold-diggings in the 1870s.

LAKE MANAPOURI

Often claimed to be New Zealand's most beautiful lake, Manapouri covers 142 square kilometres and contains 35 wooded islands. It has certainly been the most embattled of the country's lakes in consequence of plans to raise the level of the lake for hydro-electric power generation in the 1960s (see page 332). Commercial excursions to **DOUBTFUL SOUND** via the West Arm power project start at the Tourist Centre (see page 338).

MATAURA

With 2300 people, this town is one of Murihiku's few centres of substance. A small industrial oasis in pastoral Southland (it has a freezing works and a paper mill), Mataura is set beside the river of the same name, famed for its fishing. It was at nearby Tuturau (8 kilometres south) that an attempt by Te Puoho to take over the entire South Island foundered in 1836 (see page 249). Te Puoho marched from Nelson, via dense Westland forest and over the icy Haast Pass, in the hope of surprising Murihiku's Ngai Tahu Maoris from the rear. A memorial on the road to Wyndham stands on the site of the *kainga*, 'unfortified village', where Te Puoho's raiders, after feasting on local Maoris, were themselves surprised and massacred by the Ngai Tahu under chiefs Tuhawaiki (best known to Europeans as 'Bloody Jack') and Taiaroa. Te Puoho himself was killed and his head became a Ngai Tahu tribal treasure.

THE HERMIT OF THE SOUND

Donald Sutherland was the discoverer of New Zealand's highest waterfall – Sutherland Falls

Sutherland regarded the whole of the Fiordland region with a proprietorial air

The huge five hundred and eighty-metre drop of Sutherland Falls – one of the features of the Milford Track – is broken into three spectacular leaps and forms the source of the Arthur River. The falls were named after Donald Sutherland (1839-1919), 'the hermit of Milford Sound', and were for many years thought to be the highest in the world. Over the past forty years, as other falls have been discovered, they have been relegated to a probable fifth place.

Sutherland was born in Scotland, served as a soldier for a year under Garibaldi in Italy, worked as a fisherman, then sailed for New Zealand in 1861. He joined the Armed Constabulary and fought in the Maori-European wars. But gradually he turned his back on human company: gold prospecting in the remote reaches of the West Coast and Fiordland attracted him for a while, and on occasions he worked at sealing, labouring or farming to supplement his income. His twin obsessions had by now become gold and isolation, and he would disappear for weeks.

Nearing the age of 40, Sutherland sailed a six-metre open whaling boat from Dunedin to Milford Sound – a feat of considerable seamanship. After a short trip further north, he returned once more, never to leave the Milford area again. The Arthur Valley became one of his favourite haunts and on his explorations there with John Mackay, another prospector, he discovered the falls that now bear his name.

In 1890 Sutherland married Elizabeth Samuel, a widow with a similar liking for isolation, and he became less of a dedicated hermit. They settled at Milford Sound and together they built a twelve-rooms accommodation house. Here they received the growing number of visitors to Milford and its increasingly famous Track – but guests were not always welcome.

In this new role, Sutherland soon regarded himself as the lord and master of the region. In his old age he was notorious as an authority (never to be doubted or contradicted) on the wildlife, botany, geography, tracks and passes of his huge domain.

MILFORD ROAD

The 120 kilometres of road threading through the Fiordland massif between **TE ANAU** and **MILFORD SOUND** has fair claim to being the world's most regal alpine avenue. Diversions include the Mirror Lakes at 56 kilometres, with the stretch known as the 'avenue of the disappearing mountain' (an intriguing trick of perspective) soon after, and Lake Gunn at 76 kilometres. The last facilities for travellers are at Cascade Creek, adjoining Lake Gunn, beyond which point caravans and trailers are not permitted. Starting near the camping ground, the 45-minute Lake Gunn Nature Walk through red beech forest gives an intimate view of birdlife, and ferns and mosses typical of the Fiordland forest. There are other signposted walks along the road to Milford – such as those to Lake Howden and Key Summit. A detour can be made to Hollyford Camp (at 85 kilometres to the right for 8 kilometres), where there is an interesting Murray Gunn museum. Beyond the camp (further 9 kilometres) there is a 30-minute return walk to the Humboldt Falls. Those not up to the 4-5 day trek through to Lake McKerrow and Martins Bay can at least see something of the **HOLLYFORD VALLEY** here. The approach to the Homer Tunnel (98 kilometres) is truly and barrenly alpine. Competing with the kea for the camera's attention are waterfalls – in hurtling scores after heavy rain. The road into Milford does nothing to diminish Fiordland's character (see page 334).

MILFORD SOUND

Reached by reliable road via the Eglinton Valley and the Homer Tunnel for eight months of the year, this is the most accessible of Fiordland's famous sights, and so the best known. A haunting mosaic of mountain and water, Milford is best seen at dawn, with its waters just taking colour and mist surrounding the 1692 metre Mitre Peak. A glacier some 1.5 kilometres deep once made its way to the sea here. Now waterfalls whisper and thunder from hanging valleys, with spray glossing the rainforest that greens the steep walls of the sound. Once every generation, voyaging Maori tribesmen of Westland and Murihiku braved wild seas to gather precious *tangiwai*, or Milford greenstone, at Anita Bay near the mouth of the sound. Launch excursions with crayfish lunches take the visitor down the sound towards the open sea. Although Milford is best seen from sea level, a scenic flight that takes in the great Sutherland Falls is dramatic too. Accommodation, whether in luxury hotel or humble hostel, should be booked in advance. The sound, which the Maoris knew as *Piopio-tahi*, 'a single thrush' (see page 336), was renamed by sealer John Grono after Milford Haven in Wales.

MILFORD TRACK

The best way to approach **MILFORD SOUND**, this spectacular 54 kilometre track (4 to 5 days) for guided parties and 'freedom walkers' begins at Glade House at the northern tip of Lake Te Anau and winds into and over the Fiordland massif. Milford Track first travels along the Clinton River, then through rainforest, followed by open alpine country – the Mackinnon Pass and Clinton Canyon – culminating with the thundering 580 metre Sutherland Falls. The route then leads down the Arthur Valley to Milford Sound, skirting Lake Ada. At Sandfly Point, Hine-nui-te-po, the Maori goddess of darkness and death, is said to have given life to the *namu*, the humble but troublesome sandfly found all over Fiordland. Comfortable accommodation is available along the route; 'freedom walkers' should approach Fiordland National Park headquarters in **TE ANAU** for permission to use the huts. The guided walk must be booked through travel agencies.

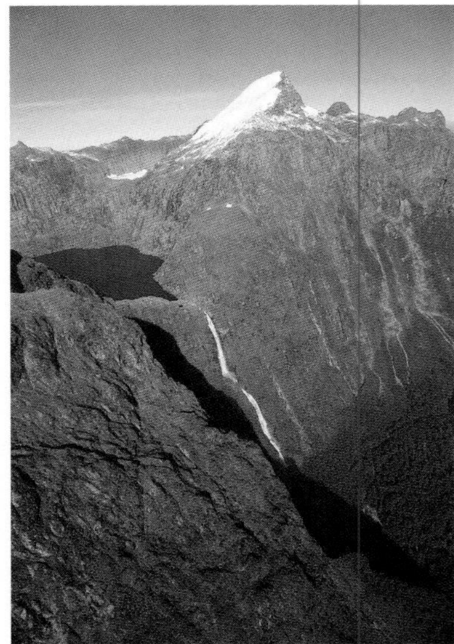

Sutherland Falls with Lake Quill behind

OREPUKI

Once a swarming community of 3000, Orepuki now has only 180 inhabitants and an atmosphere of a ghost town. Gold brought the district to life in the 1860s, at first discovered under coastal sand and then by sluicing on higher ground.

Approaching Homer Tunnel on the way to Milford Haven, the road crosses Monkey Creek

Although never as celebrated as Otago's riches, Orepuki's ore proved profitable longer than most gold strikes. At one time there were 600 Chinese working in the vicinity of Round Hill (13 kilometres to the east). Later in the century, shale and coal deposits looked promising, but works were abandoned in 1902. Local folklore maintains there is still colour for the persistent goldpanner. Nevertheless, the coast between Orepuki and **RIVERTON** has colour enough, with the intensely green Southland pasture stretching down to the deep blue Foveaux Strait.

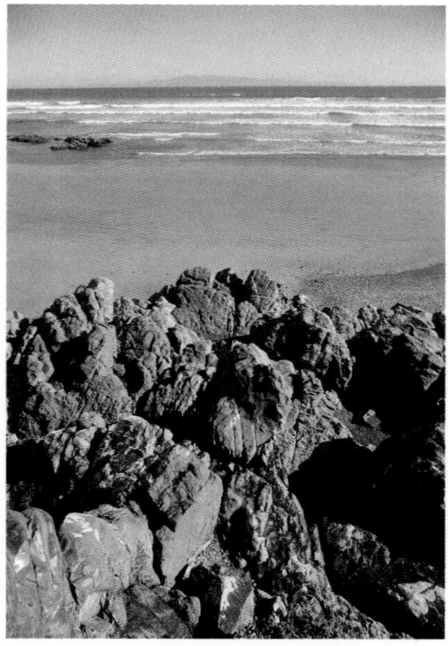

A rocky beach near Oraka Point, Colac Bay

PRESERVATION INLET

This southernmost fiord, 36 kilometres long, was the most extensively populated in its heyday, but is now one of the least visited. Sealers and whalers used it as they did all Murihiku, for whalers its advantage being its proximity to the whaling grounds of the Foveaux Strait. At the end of the 19th century the discovery of gold led to the development on Kisbee Bay of a town of 1000 people, with a school, a pub and a store. Some laboured on or prospected for further riches until the 1930s. Now only the hardiest find their way to Preservation Inlet overland. Fishing boats and float planes with hunters sometimes call, but otherwise its solitude is unshattered.

RIVERTON

Attractively set on the estuary of the Aparima River, Riverton, with 1500 people, is the oldest European community in Southland, as well as one of the oldest in New Zealand. Sealers sheltered here in the first decades of the 19th century, but the town was founded by whaler John Howell, who arrived here in the mid-1830s. Both settlement and river were first known as Jacobs River; the estuary is still known today as Jacobs River Estuary. After his marriage to a Maori woman, Howell raised nine children and established a riverside estate of 45 000 hectares, on which he ran sheep and cattle. Riverton seemed destined to become Southland's port, which it still is for hundreds of pleasure-craft, but **BLUFF** was better suited for large ships. The port's old Custom House survives beside the Riverton Museum in Palmerston Street (open daily 2–4). Amongst the many cottages and larger dwellings remaining from Riverton's colonial heyday, the most notable are Theophilus Daniel's house at 85 Palmerston Street, a cottage restored by the NZ Historic Places Trust at 86 Palmerston Street (opposite), and one at 114 Havelock Street. At the mouth of the river there is a memorial to town founder Howell.

Riverton is Southland's most popular marine resort, with beaches by the open sea along the peninsula that shelters the mouth of the Aparima River. The resort area, known as Riverton Rocks, extends some 9 kilometres to Howells Point. To the west is dramatically sweeping Colac Bay. At its nearer end (11 kilometres from Riverton) is an ancient Maori argillite quarry, where stone tools and ornaments were fashioned. Flakes and uncompleted adzes may still be found.

ROUTEBURN TRACK

Once a Maori route between Fiordland and Otago, this track is now followed by nearly 10 000 trampers annually. The 40-kilometre hike (3 to 4 days) takes in some of the country's most spectacular mountain scenery. Guided tours are available from Queenstown, and there are national park huts for the use of those wishing to walk it at their own pace. Like the neighbouring Dart River, the Route Burn was an important source of greenstone, which Maoris were still taking from here until as late as the 1850s. The track's departure point is from The Divide on the **MILFORD ROAD**. Many hardy trampers combine it with the **MILFORD TRACK**; they hike into **MILFORD SOUND**, then out to Otago's Mount Aspiring National Park (see page 307) by the Routeburn. Information on the track can be obtained either from **FIORDLAND NATIONAL PARK** headquarters in **TE ANAU** or from Mount Aspiring National Park headquarters at Wanaka in Otago.

RUAPUKE ISLAND

Once a stronghold of the Murihiku Maori, this low-lying 1400-hectare island, 20 kilometres south-east of **BLUFF**, is still owned and farmed by Maoris. Chief Tuhawaiki ('Bloody Jack') ruled the island during the difficult years for the southern Maoris when the sealers, whalers and settlers arrived. It was from Ruapuke that Tuhawaiki set out to terminate the advance into Murihiku of Te Puoho, near **MATAURA**. Gentler history began in 1844 when the missionary Reverend Johann Wohlers founded a Lutheran mission here. Since then the island has been virtually abandoned, except for grazing sheep.

TE ANAU

This township of 2800 on the shore of the South Island's largest lake (344 square kilometres) has seen rapid but haphazard growth in the last three decades as a major Fiordland tourist resort. **MILFORD SOUND** is a comfortable day excursion by car along **MILFORD ROAD**. There are scenic flights over the vast Fiordland coast and lake excursions to the 'inland fiords'. The vintage steamship *Tawera* (1899), now diesel driven, takes trampers up the lake to the starting point of the **MILFORD TRACK**. Excursions to **DOUBTFUL SOUND** via the subterranean West Arm hydro-electric power project can also be arranged from Te Anau, but leave from nearby **LAKE MANAPOURI**. Among local highlights is the water excursion to the Te Ana-au Glow-worm Caves which, lost for generations, were finally relocated in 1948 (see page 332).

TUATAPERE

Once better known as 'The Hole in the Bush', this farming and sawmilling community of 900 enjoys a pastoral setting on the banks of the Waiau River. Its frontier past is celebrated with an annual axeman's carnival on New Year's Day. The town is one of the main access points to the **FIORDLAND NATIONAL PARK**. Demanding treks to **PRESERVATION INLET** and **DUSKY SOUND** begin in this vicinity. Information can be obtained from the national park information office in Clifden (13 kilometres north), where an old road suspension bridge (1899) has been preserved by the NZ Historic Places Trust. Also reached from Tuatapere are Lakes Hauroko and Monowai. The shores of the latter were devastated when the water level was raised in 1925 for a hydro-electric power project. In 1967 a partially mummified Maori woman, propped upright in a burial cloak, was discovered in a dry cave on Lake Hauroko's Mary Island, to give Fiordland another legend – that of a 'Maori princess' of Fiordland's lost tribe. Alas for legend, the remains seem something like four centuries old. She has been left where she was found, now behind a steel grille cemented in by national park rangers to prevent desecration.

THE BIRDMAN OF DUSKY SOUND

Resolution Island, at the head of Dusky Sound, became a haven for threatened native birds, guarded by a solitary but remarkable observer

The origins of Richard Henry (1845-1929) are buried in time. He was born in Australia, and from boyhood was interested in natural history. It is known too that for a time he settled in Marlborough where he had a station running twenty thousand sheep – all lost to the rabbit infestations.

Henry can next be traced to Otago in 1877. Then, six years later he turned up at Lake Te Anau, where he built a house and acquired a five metre boat which he named *Putangi*. From this base near the Middle Fiord he began his famous explorations. He was successful in finding a route to the western coast of Fiordland – a route that turned out to be so difficult to traverse that it could not compete with the Milford Track as a commercial tourist venture, although it rivalled it in scenic beauty.

Henry had all this time been making another equally dramatic discovery: careful observations of the local flora and fauna convinced him that native birdlife was declining rapidly with the swelling population of rats and wild cats. Weasels, stoats and ferrets, introduced to control the plague of rabbits, made matters worse – especially for the kiwi, kakapo and other flightless birds. In 1891, in the face of the onslaught of these predators, Resolution Island at the head of Dusky Sound, was set aside as New Zealand's first bird sanctuary. Three years later, aged almost fifty, Henry was appointed curator and caretaker at Resolution Island, a job to which he was able to apply his unrivalled knowledge of local birdlife.

Richard Henry – a naturalist by nature

Henry brought his boat with him – demonstrating skill and bravery as he plied between shore and island to fetch threatened birds to breed in the sanctuary. But the seaways, which had seemed to him to provide an impassable barrier for predators, were eventually crossed by stoats.

Henry did not despair. He knew that his experience and meticulous records were an invaluable source of information for the sanctuaries that would follow. In 1909, the many years he had spent as the 'Birdman of Dusky Sound', came to an end. He transferred to Kapiti Island for a short period, then retired to Helensville, fifty kilometres north of Auckland.

Stewart Island

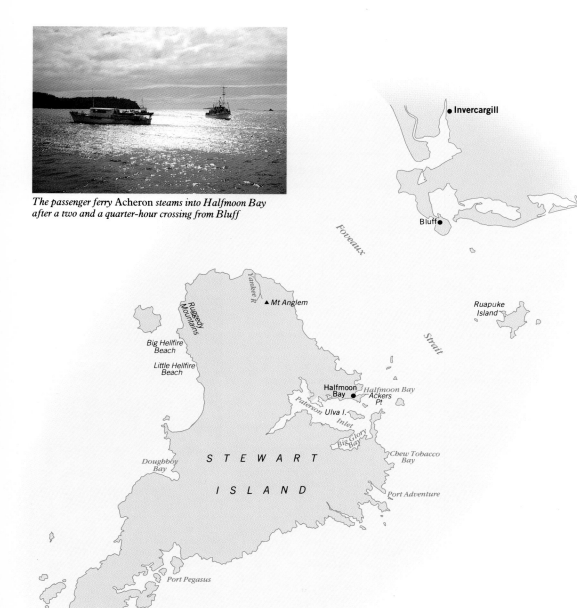

The passenger ferry Acheron *steams into Halfmoon Bay after a two and a quarter-hour crossing from Bluff*

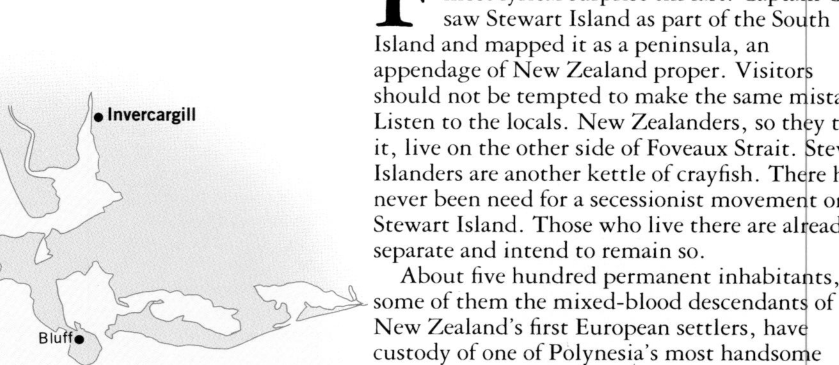

For the traveller, New Zealand saves its most lyrical surprise till last. Captain Cook saw Stewart Island as part of the South Island and mapped it as a peninsula, an appendage of New Zealand proper. Visitors should not be tempted to make the same mistake. Listen to the locals. New Zealanders, so they tell it, live on the other side of Foveaux Strait. Stewart Islanders are another kettle of crayfish. There has never been need for a secessionist movement on Stewart Island. Those who live there are already separate and intend to remain so.

About five hundred permanent inhabitants, some of them the mixed-blood descendants of New Zealand's first European settlers, have custody of one of Polynesia's most handsome islands. Even Tahiti's celebrated silhouette is not more striking from the sea. Among the world's more romantic islands, Stewart Island has one increasingly rare distinction. Its 174 600 hectares of woodland, headlands and heights are not overrun. Its 1600 kilometres of harbours, bays and beaches are mostly empty. No jet planes freight thousands of tourists in and out daily. Admittedly, it rains – after all, the island is 47 degrees south, well down in the infamous 'Roaring Forties' – but Stewart Island enthusiasts argue that one fine day here is worth six anywhere else in the world. Considering its location – with Patagonia as its only companion in this southern latitude – it is remarkably mild all year. There is warmth here when Southland is shivering.

Mostly hilly and heavily wooded, Stewart Island is a tattered triangle in shape. The igneous rocks of its north make it a cousin to Fiordland. Yet it is starkly individual in the lower granite shapes of its south, which have been modelled more by submarine convulsion and beating waves than by ice-age glaciers. Creation lifted Stewart Island no more than necessary. Its highest point is Mount Anglem (980 metres), a mere hill by South Island measure. Virtually all the island is mantled by native vegetation. Forests of rimu, rata and totara lie to the north and east. Subalpine and coastal scrubland of leatherwood and muttonbird scrub are found to the south and west. Most of New Zealand's more common native birds prosper here, and some of the rarer species, too. It is a proof of Stewart Island's isolation that the kakapo – by weight, the largest of all parrots – was discovered here in 1977. This flightless and nocturnal native bird is extinct in the North Island, and almost so in the South, but may yet survive on Stewart Island.

A WELL-KEPT SECRET

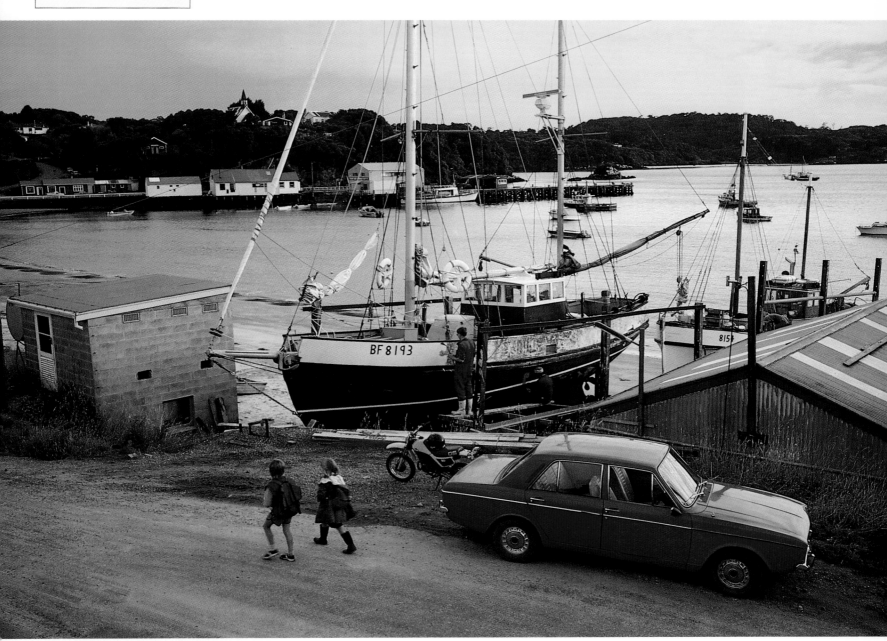

Although Halfmoon Bay is the principal social and tourist centre on Stewart Island, the pace of life is unhurried. The only cars on the island belong to local residents; visitors must leave their cars on the mainland either at Bluff (if travelling by sea) or at Invercargill (if travelling by air)

Stewart Island's oldest house, built by Lewis Acker of Charleston, USA, is a survivor from early whaling days. Now in a delapidated state, it is marked for preservation

Gravestones in the overgrown cemetery outside Halfmoon Bay are reminders of the Norwegians who worked on the island

The Maoris called Stewart Island *Rakiura*, or 'glowing sky', a name that surely derives from the long days and lingering sunsets of summer, perhaps also from the auroras of winter. There was an older name , *Te Puka-o-te-waka-a-Maui*, meaning the anchor stone of the canoe from which the mythological Polynesian folk hero Maui fished up the North Island. Maoris never lived here in great numbers. They valued Stewart Island most for its titi – the muttonbird or sooty shearwater – found especially on the small offshore islands.

When Ngai Tahu tribesmen parted with Stewart Island for six thousand pounds in 1864, twice the sum they accepted for most of Southland, they reserved their rights to the muttonbird. In autumn, before migration to the North Pacific begins, the titi are still harvested by the descendants of those original tribesmen, many of them dwelling across the water in Bluff and some much farther afield. By late May, between sunset and sunrise, the muttonbird has gone. Its departure is heralded by the spectral call of a mysterious bird called the *haki-wai*, named after the sound it makes in the night and never seen by human eyes. This may be a figment of folklore, but veteran muttonbirders swear by it and begin packing their bags.

In 1804, an American mariner named Owen F.Smith discovered a turbulent sea where Cook's chart indicated land. For a time the waters were called Smiths Strait, but were later renamed Foveaux after the then lieutenant-governor of Norfolk Island. On a sealing run, Smith was riding the boom that made Stewart Island part of Australia's frontier, along with the Otago, Southland and Fiordland coasts. Among the early arrivals was William Stewart, first officer of the *Pegasus*, a ship that deposited a sealing gang here. Stewart's name was also left on the island, and

Observation Rock offers panoramic views of Paterson Inlet

that of his vessel on its southernmost harbour. Although Stewart drew a chart or two, the naming of the entire island in his honour seems extravagant. The mystery is that the island has never reclaimed its evocative Maori name.

No one can quibble with the colourful names others bestowed on Stewart Island's features. Reading a map of the island suggests surreal verse of sorts: Chew Tobacco Bay, Yankee River, Big and Little Hellfire Beaches, Big Glory Bay, Port Adventure, Abrahams Bosom, Ruggedy Mountains, Murderers River, Dead Man Beach, Doughboy Bay, and Faith, Hope and Charity Islands. Most of these names derive from the days when seal slaughter reddened the rocks, and blubber spilling from whalers' trypots soiled the golden sands.

A HISTORY OF DISAPPOINTMENT

Whalers, rather than sealers, were responsible for permanent European settlement on the island. When the harvest of fur seals diminished, Sydney-based trading skippers began augmenting their cargo with flax, timber and especially whale oil. To meet market demand, whalers – unlike kill-and-run sealers – established more or less permanent residences and primitive communities. The whaling season was from May to October. When it was over, the whale-hunters would come ashore to their Maori wives, plant potatoes and perhaps run a few cattle and sheep. Such a man was American-born Lewis Acker , who first arrived in New Zealand waters in the eighteen-thirties. About 1834 he settled on the southern head of Halfmoon Bay, towards Ackers Point where his primitive house of stone, clay and crushed shells still stands. One of New Zealand's oldest European dwellings, it has been marked for preservation by the NZ Historic Places Trust. With his Maori wife, Mary Pui, Acker raised nine children. Later he gave up whaling to become a coastal trader and pioneer boat-builder. When the New Zealand government bought Stewart Island in 1864, Acker was dispossessed as a squatter and began wandering again.

Acker's was not the only disappointment here. Stewart Island, for most of its recorded history, has been more familiar with bust than boom. The seals went, and the whales. Then came the timber men, but accessible trees were not to last many decades. Since the last was toppled early this century, most of the island has been made a reserve for flora and fauna. Pastoral enterprise mostly failed. Foveaux Strait oysters (now better known as Bluff oysters) promised wealth, but finally were better harvested by mainland-based trawlers. Mineral prospectors found tin and gold. Legend says that goldminers found mostly tin, and tinminers mostly gold. Fishing – especially crayfishing – has been the islanders' only lasting enterprise. Most Stewart Islanders owe their living to the sea. The wharf at Halfmoon Bay (Oban), is the island's main social centre. Salmon farms have been established to augment catches of blue cod, tarakihi and groper shipped off to the mainland and to Australia. Crayfish, sold as rock lobster, is exported to the USA. Although tourism makes only a small impression on the islanders' traditional lifestyle, it contributes significantly to their income. As more travel writers discover Stewart Island, it may soon cease to be the South Pacific's best-kept secret.

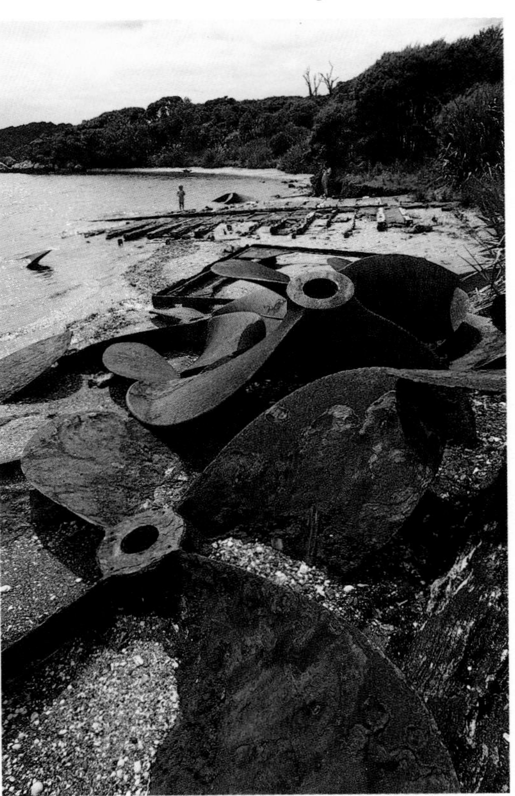

Whalers Base in Prices Inlet was the site of a shipyard and a Norwegian whaling station; relics can still be seen

Visitors to Stewart Island leave their cars at Bluff or Invercargill airport. There are only twenty kilometres of road on the island, and walking is the best way to explore. Halfmoon Bay (Oban) is now the only village, with a couple of shops, a hotel, a motel or two, a museum, and a NZ Forest Service information centre. The first sightseers arrived on Stewart Island in the eighteen-seventies and the locals have been doing their gentle best to show off their island to advantage ever since. There is a minibus tour designed to suit the day-tripper.

Colourful floats outside a house, or 'crib'. Most houses belong to commercial fishermen or to people living in retirement

For those who linger, there are water excursions to Port Adventure and up Paterson Inlet. This main feature of the inlet is the now uninhabited Ulva Island, a protected paradise for plants and birds. This description fits much of Stewart Island. In places the birdsong can be deafening. Kakas clatter in the tall trees. Wekas snuffle in the scub. Even the kiwis are noisy, and not just at night. Parakeets flash out by the score. Kererus, New Zealand's large native wood pigeons, rise in squeaky flocks. Shags work the shore, penguins potter, albatrosses lift on the wind, and mollyhawks wing over the waves. The walker wins a sense of what mainland New Zealand must have been when European voyagers first dropped anchor in its harbours. For those who wish to explore on foot, Stewart Island has some of New Zealand's finest marine and woodland walks, with haunting relics of past human occupation along the way. No more than three per cent of the island remains in private hands. The rest is protected wilderness. Tracks range from well-established to rough, from easy to risky, and advice should be taken. The NZ Forest Service has an extensive high-summer program of guided tramps and cruises. Longer expeditions may also be undertaken using Forest Service huts. Any route may lead visitors to rejoice, with early New Zealand naturalist H. Guthrie-Smith, in 'blown sands, clean seas, Heavens's vault above, and space illimitable . . .' They may also be grateful for that twenty-five kilometres of water Captain Cook failed to detect between the South Island and Stewart. The guardian waves of Foveaux Strait have done their work well. More so than most of the world's island paradises, Stewart Island remains a reverberant poem of a place.

INDEX

Page numbers in bold type indicate entries on Places of Interest pages or in boxes. Page numbers in *italics* refer to illustrations

U

V

W

Y

ACKNOWLEDGMENTS

Box stories for all regions were contributed by Kevin Ireland; boxes on pages 12–27 by David Underhill
Maps by Graham Keane, Max Peatman; illustration pages 12–13 by Montage Advertising
Contributing editors: Carol Natsis, Jane Richardson, Catherine Baker. Contributing artist: Jim Paton; paste-up artist: David Marlowe

Photographs in this book are by Brian Brake, with the following exceptions (t = top, c = centre, b = bottom, l = left, r = right): **Endpapers:** Brian Enting **14–15**: Warren Jacobs Photography **15**: t, Warren Jacobs Photography **16**: tc, Michael J. Meads; tr, John Kendrick; bl, Geoff Moon/Auscape International; br, Warren Jacobs Photography **17**: t, Joan Robb; bl, R. Morris/Department of Conservation; br, C.R. Veitch/Department of Conservation **18**: t, Brian Enting; cr, Warren Jacobs Photography; bl, Jean-Paul Ferrero/Auscape International; br, NZ Forest Service **23**: Roger Walker Ltd **24–25**: all objects in the collection of the Auckland Institute and Museum except **24**: tl, National Museum, Wellington; **25**: bc, Hawke's Bay Art Gallery and Museum, Napier **26**: tc, Robin White, *Mangaweka*, Auckland City Art Gallery; cl, Augustus Earle, 'The Village of Parkuni' in *Sketches of New Zealand*, Rex Nan Kivell Collection, National Library of Australia; bl, James Nairn, *Wellington Harbour* (1902), National Art Gallery, New Zealand; br, John Weeks, *Limestone Gorge, King Country* (1943), Auckland City Art Gallery **26–27**: Michael Smither, *Rocks with Mountain* (1968), Auckland City Art Gallery **27**: William Fox, *Akaroa*, Hocken Library, Dunedin **49**: Alexander Turnbull Library **50**: Auckland Institute and Museum **52**: Hocken Library, Dunedin **53**: t, House of Memories, Waipu, **86**: t, Auckland Institute and Museum **96**: tl, Joan Robb **116**: t, John Johns/NZ Forest Service **141**: tc, Chew Chong family; tr, Taranaki Museum **153**: r, drawing by E. Noordhof, Hocken Library, Dunedin **155**: r, Our Lady's Home of Compassion, Island Bay **166**: b, Alexander Turnbull Library **167**: t, NZ Herald **168**: Auckland Public Library **169**: Hawke's Bay Art Gallery and Museum, Napier **180**: tl, Hawke's Bay Art Gallery and Museum, Napier **194**: Alexander Turnbull Library **195**: b, Alexander Turnbull Library **196**: l, Alexander Turnbull Library **197**: Alexander Turnbull Library **214**: t, Alexander Turnbull Library **216**: (all) Nelson Provincial Museum **231**: c, Bett Collection, Alexander Turnbull Library **250**: (both) Alexander Turnbull Library **271**: t, Warren Jacobs Photography **272**: The Star Christchurch Ltd **273**: t, The Robert McDougall Art Gallery, Christchurch **284**: Alexander Turnbull Library **285**: tr, The Star Christchurch Ltd **286**: r, Warren Jacobs Photography **306**: Royal New Zealand Plunket Society **321**: Alexander Turnbull Library **322**: tl and tc, Alexander Turnbull Library **323**: tr, Otago Early Settlers' Museum, Dunedin **340**: l, Hocken Library, Dunedin **341**: t, Warren Jacobs Photography **342**: tl, Alexander Turnbull Library **343**: r, A.C. Begg

The following writers and books have been given particular mention in this book:
Antony Alpers *A Book of Dolphins* Boston, Houghton Mifflin, 1961; James K. Baxter *Collected Poems*, 1979; Elsdon Best *Tuhoe, the Children of the Mist* Wellington, Reed, 1972; Peter Buck *The Coming of the Maori* Christchurch, Whitcoulls, 1982; Peter Buck *Vikings of the Sunrise* Westport, Conn., Greenwood Press, 1985; Samuel Butler *Erewhon* Auckland, Golden Press, 1973; Samuel Butler *A First Year in Canterbury Settlement* Auckland, Blackwood & Janet Paul, 1964; John Logan Campbell *Poenamo – Sketches of the Early Days of New Zealand* Avondale, Golden Press, 1973; Denis Glover *Arawata Bill* Christchurch, Pegasus Press, 1953; Charlotte Godley *Letters from Early New Zealand* Christchurch, Whitcomb & Tombs, 1951; W.H. Guthrie-Smith *Tutira – the Story of a New Zealand Sheep Station* Wellington, Reed, 1969; John A. Lee *Children of the Poor* Christchurch, Whitcomb & Tombs, 1973; Jane Mander *The Story of a New Zealand River* New York, Lane, 1920; Frederick Maning *Old New Zealand* and *A History of the War in the North* Auckland, Golden Press, 1973; Katherine Mansfield *The Collected Stories of Katherine Mansfield* Penguin, 1981; Alan Mulgan *The Making of a New Zealander* Wellington, Reed, 1958; William Satchell *The Land of the Lost* Auckland, University Press, 1971; Andrew Sharp *Ancient Voyagers in Polynesia* London, Angus & Robertson, 1964; Douglas Stewart *The Seven Rivers* Sydney, Angus & Robertson, 1966; Anthony Trollope *Australia and New Zealand* London, Dawsons, 1968; Edward Jerningham Wakefield *Adventures in New Zealand* Auckland, Golden Press, 1975;

The publishers gratefully acknowledge the help given by Air New Zealand; NZ Historic Places Trust; National Parks and Reserves Authority; Department of Conservation; information centres and museums throughout New Zealand; Dame Te Ata-I-Rangi kaahu, Turangawaewae, Ngaruawahia; Witi Ihimaera, Ministry of Foreign Affairs; Maori Affairs Department; New Zealand Helicopter Line; William Main, Wellington; Arne and Sicilia Midtgard, Cape Reinga; Esther and Ron Crabtree, Ahipara, Kaitaia; David Horton, Auckland Aero Club; Andrew Neilson, Gannet Safari, Cape Kidnappers; Russell and Pat Tulloch, Ruatahuna; Maurice Takarangi, Wanganui; Peter Rule, Wellington; Marlborough Aero Club, and Department of Lands and Survey, Molesworth Station; Paddy Gillooly, Collingwood Safari Tours; Airfoto, Christchurch; Ben and Libby Hutchinson, Double Hill, Canterbury; Otago Peninsula Trust and Mrs Webb/Albatross Colony; Dr John Hall-Jones, Invercargill; Fiordland Travel, Queenstown; Margaret and Colin Hopkins, Stewart Island; Lau Wai Man, Auckland

**Typesetting by Best-Set Typesetter Ltd, Hong Kong
Reproduction by Curman Lithographics, Sydney
Printed and bound by Dai Nippon Printing Co. (H.K.) Ltd, Hong Kong**